HORROR STORIES

HORROR STORIES grew and developed across the nineteenth century and remain perennially popular, with the power to freeze the blood, revolt our senses, and keep us up at night. They offer up a distorted mirror to reflect our fears and anxieties, but also our fantasies and hidden desires. Horror stories frighten and shock, but they also thrill and delight.

As well as established horror classics from M. R. James, Arthur Machen, Bram Stoker, and Charlotte Perkins Gilman, the genre attracted some of the biggest writers of the century—Hoffmann, Poe, Balzac, Dickens, Hawthorne, Melville, and Zola—who are all included here. The twenty-nine stories collected in this anthology are some of the greatest of the period, and embrace categories as diverse as ghost stories, the supernatural and psychological horror, medical and scientific horror, colonial horror, and tales of the uncanny and precognition.

Darryl Jones's introduction and notes explore horror's literary evolution and its articulation of cultural preoccupations and anxieties. The horror story is a genre which can be perverse, exploitative, and ghoulish, but which also addresses serious questions about issues ranging from the nature of identity to the survival of the human personality after death and the moral mission of colonialism.

DARRYL JONES is Professor in English at Trinity College Dublin, where he has taught since 1994. His publications include *Horror: A Thematic History in Fiction and Film* (2002) and *Jane Austen* (2004). He has edited M. R. James's *Collected Ghost Stories* (2013), Arthur Conan Doyle's *Gothic Tales* (2016), and H. G. Wells' *The War of the Worlds* and *The Island of Doctor Moreau* (2017) for Oxford World's Classics. His latest book is *Sleeping With the Lights On: The Uneasy Story of Horror* (2018).

T0066457

OXFORD WORLD'S CLASSICS

*For over 100 years Oxford World's Classics have brought
readers closer to the world's great literature. Now with over 700
titles—from the 4,000-year-old myths of Mesopotamia to the
twentieth century's greatest novels—the series makes available
lesser-known as well as celebrated writing.*

*The pocket-sized hardbacks of the early years contained
introductions by Virginia Woolf, T. S. Eliot, Graham Greene,
and other literary figures which enriched the experience of reading.
Today the series is recognized for its fine scholarship and
reliability in texts that span world literature, drama and poetry,
religion, philosophy and politics. Each edition includes perceptive
commentary and essential background information to meet the
changing needs of readers.*

OXFORD WORLD'S CLASSICS

Horror Stories
Classic Tales from Hoffmann to Hodgson

Edited with an Introduction and Notes by
DARRYL JONES

OXFORD
UNIVERSITY PRESS

OXFORD

UNIVERSITY PRESS

Great Clarendon Street, Oxford, OX2 6DP,
United Kingdom

Oxford University Press is a department of the University of Oxford.
It furthers the University's objective of excellence in research, scholarship,
and education by publishing worldwide. Oxford is a registered trade mark of
Oxford University Press in the UK and in certain other countries

First published 2014
First published as an Oxford World's Classics paperback 2018

Impression: 7

Published in the United States of America by Oxford University Press
198 Madison Avenue, New York, NY 10016, United States of America

British Library Cataloguing in Publication Data

Data available

Library of Congress Control Number: 2018950678

ISBN 978-0-19-968544-8

Printed and bound in Great Britain by
Clays Ltd, Elcograf S.p.A.

ACKNOWLEDGEMENTS

I WOULD like to start by thanking Judith Luna, my editor at OUP, for her initial and continued enthusiasm for this book, for curbing most of my worst excesses, for insisting that I remove all references to David Bowie (except this one), and for her patience with my perpetual requests for Just a Little More Time.

This book is the fruit of many years of teaching, research, and reading, and of conversations with very many people, including Ailise Bulfin, Steve Cadman, Sarah Crofton, Nick Curwin, Nick Daly, Ruth Doherty, Daragh Downes, John Exshaw, Christine Ferguson, Trish Ferguson, Christopher Frayling, Kate Hebblethwaite, Paul Jackson, Zoe Jellicoe, Triona Kirby, Miles Link, Corinna Salvedori Lonergan, Xand Lourenco, Jenny McDonnell, Ruth McLaughlin, Michael Marsh, Stephen Matterson, John Nash, Sorcha Ní Fhlaínn, Helen O'Connell, Ed O'Hare, David O'Shaughnessy, Muireann O'Sullivan, Maria Parsons, Eve Patten, Terry Pratchett, Conor Reid, Brian J. Showers, Brenda Silver, Kevin Smith, and Neil Sutcliffe. As ever, my students at Trinity College Dublin taught me more than I ever taught them. Horror puts you in contact with the nicest people.

Mihai Zdrenghea and Dorin Chira generously invited me to give a series of graduate seminars at Babes-Bolyai University, Cluj, Transylvania, in May 2013 and Tang Weijie invited me to do likewise in Tongji University, Shanghai, in September 2013. Some of the ideas in the Introduction were formulated in discussion with students in these classes. Where better to think about horror than Transylvania?

Especial thanks to my dear friends and colleagues Dara Downey, Jarlath Killeen, Elizabeth McCarthy, and Bernice Murphy, who always know so much more than I do. They will recognize their fingerprints all over this book. Thanks, too, to Helen Conrad O'Briain for always being on hand to correct my very faulty Latin, and to John Connolly for generously feeding both my mind and my stomach, and for being living proof that there are still writers out there for whom the horror story is a real, continuing tradition. And to Nerys Brown, for inviting me to talk to a class of 9-year-olds, in Welsh, about horror stories.

My last and deepest thanks, as always, are to my wife Margaret and my daughter Morgan, who have to put up with my worst excesses on a daily basis. I dedicate this book to them, with love.

CONTENTS

INTRODUCTION

Readers who are unfamiliar with the stories may prefer to treat the Introduction as an Afterword.

IN Fitz-James O'Brien's 'What Was It?' (1859), the narrator, Harry, a writer of supernatural fiction very much like O'Brien himself, regularly smokes opium with his friend Dr Hammond in their boarding house, which has a reputation for being haunted. Generally, the pair's opium visions take a luxurious, orientalist turn: 'We flung ourselves on the shores of the East, and talked of its gay bazaars, of the splendors of the time of Haroun, of harems and golden palaces' (p. 131). But on the evening of the tenth of July—the evening in which Harry is later to have a terrifying encounter with an invisible, paranormal creature—the pair 'drifted into an unusually metaphysical mood'. This leads inexorably to a bad trip, in which the lush Baghdad of their imaginations is transformed into a city of 'afreets, ghouls and enchanters': 'Insensibly we yielded to the occult force that swayed us, and indulged in gloomy speculation.' It is at this point that Hammond asks the troubling question which may be what draws the entity to Harry later, as he lies in his bed reading Goudon's *History of Monsters*: 'What do you consider to be the greatest element of terror?' (p. 131).

This was a question which preoccupied the nineteenth century, and to which, like O'Brien's narrator, it came up with a variety of answers. Harry's speculations lead him in search of 'one great and ruling embodiment of fear,—a King of Terrors to which all others must succumb' (p. 132), but, as the contents of this anthology demonstrate, it is the very plurality of its terrors that characterizes the nineteenth century.

Horror is a *phobic* cultural form, both in the sense that it is designed to produce a specific reaction—fear and loathing—but also in the way that it is produced by and directly reflects cultural preoccupations, fears, and anxieties at any given moment, which it renders obliquely, in displaced and often highly metaphorical guises, as monsters, madmen, ghosts. A very clear example of this can be seen in the rise of colonial horror in the later nineteenth century. As the British Empire and the other empires of nineteenth-century Europe reached their zeniths, so appeared the 'reverse-colonization' narrative, a paranoid cultural form in which conquered or oppressed colonial subjects return to the West (or to Western officials in the colonies) to wreak terrifying revenge.[1] London, the great imperial metropolis, and immeasurably the largest city the world had ever seen, was fictionally attacked many times around the *fin de siècle*, by Irish Fenians, 'Yellow Peril' Chinese, Transylvanian vampires, or colonizing Martians. In this anthology alone (a tiny sample), the cuckolding surgeon in 'The Case of Lady Sannox' is sent to his fate by what seems to be an Ottoman emissary; in 'The Mark of the Beast' and 'The Wendigo', British administrators and explorers encounter malevolent supernature in India and Canada; 'The Monkey's Paw' itself is a horrifying souvenir picked up in India by an army sergeant-major; and in 'The Squaw' an American adventurer meets a gruesome end at the hands of a cat which may be possessed by the spirit of a Native American woman he has killed.

Horror is also a highly aesthetic, pleasurable form. As the many devotees of horror—from Catherine Morland in Jane Austen's *Northanger Abbey* (1818) to the most blood-spattered contemporary gorehound—will testify, an appreciation of horror can require often complex and sophisticated responses. But horror is, unquestionably, an extreme art form, potentially confronting readers at every point with the limits of their own tolerance, with issues of taboo, with violent and transgressive images. Like all extreme or avant-garde art, it may be that the function of horror is to shock us out of our complacency—*épater la bourgeoisie* (to shock the middle classes), as French *fin-de-siècle* poets put it. By definition, such art is not to everyone's taste, as it deliberately sets out to antagonize large parts of the population, and one response to this is to brand anyone with a taste for horror as a sicko, or even to attempt to ban extreme horror in the name of public decency. Does enjoying violent or transgressive art tend to make you a violent or transgressive person? These are debates which have accompanied horror in all its modern forms, at least since the publication (and immediate bowdlerization) of Matthew Lewis's Gothic shocker *The Monk* in the 1790s, and which resurface in every generation; 'video nasties' and graphic horror films have become

---

[1] For reverse colonization, see, for example, Patrick Brantlinger, *Rule of Darkness: British Literature and Imperialism 1830–1900* (Ithaca, NY, 1988); Stephen J. Arata, *Fictions of Loss in the Victorian Fin-de-Siècle: Identity and Empire* (Cambridge, 1996).

the locus for contemporary concerns about the potentially malign cultural affect of horror.[2]

But good art is rarely simple, and never a univocal medium for the transmission of any one ideology. And so, far from being a radical and transgressive form, horror can sometimes be understood as a comforting, conservative form, one which reassures readers in their assumptions about the state of the world. Some horror seems to police behaviour with extraordinary rigour, offering up condign punishments for any transgression. And so, in this volume, we have, for example, Lady Sannox's appalling punishment for adultery in Arthur Conan Doyle's story, or Fleete, cursed with lycanthropy for desecrating a Hindu altar (and, on a more secular level, violating the Indian Penal Code) in Kipling's 'The Mark of the Beast', or the Maculligan brothers' strange, interlinked fates in Ronald Ross's 'The Vivisector Vivisected'. On a rather more abstruse level, the myth of Pandora's Box and the punishment for forbidden knowledge seems to underlie certain types of horror: simple intellectual curiosity, for example, proves Mr Wraxall's undoing in M. R. James's 'Count Magnus'. This is perhaps classically demonstrated in one of the greatest of all horror stories, W. W. Jacobs's 'The Monkey's Paw', in which the titular fetish offers its possessors a chance to tamper with the natural order (in this case, for reasons with which readers are bound to sympathize, as grieving parents wish for their son to return to life)—at horrifying cost.

But this conservatism can take other forms as well, often written into the very settings of the stories, or the occasions for reading them. Very many of them take place in, or are framed by, the comfortable, establishmentarian settings of gentlemen's clubs or country houses. Ghost stories, in particular, can have about them an air of reassuring comfort, due in no small part to their deep connections, firmly established across the nineteenth century, with Christmas. Although, as Owen Davies argues in *The Haunted: A Social History of Ghosts*, the English, in particular, had believed since the Middle Ages that Christmastime was particularly ripe for hauntings, one could, in fact, argue that *modern*

---

[2] Much has been written on the ethics and censorship of horror. See e.g. André Parreaux, *The Publication of 'The Monk': A Literary Event 1796–1798* (Paris, 1960); Stanley Cohen, *Folk Devils and Moral Panics* (St Alban's, 1973); Martin Barker, *The Video Nasties: Freedom and Censorship in the Media* (London, 1984); David Kerekes and David Slater, *See No Evil: Banned Films and Video Controversies* (Manchester, 2000); Martin Barker and Julian Petley (eds.), *Ill-Effects: The Media / Violence Debate* (London, 2001).

Christmas celebrations and ghost stories developed together across the first half of the nineteenth century, with Charles Dickens as a major figure in the development of both: 'A Christmas Carol' (1843) is easily the best-known Christmas story of them all, and easily the best-known ghost story.[3] The success of 'A Christmas Carol' inaugurated a tradition of Dickensian ghost stories for Christmas, not all of which were overtly festive in subject matter. The best of them, 'The Signal Man', was published in the Christmas 1866 edition of Dickens's periodical *All the Year Round*, and is included in this volume. M. R. James, the greatest ghost-story specialist in English, was a distinguished Cambridge academic, many of whose stories were first told to colleagues and students huddled round the fire at the Provost's Lodge of King's College late at night on Christmas Eve.

Horror stories, then, are simultaneously radical and conservative, shocking and comfortable. Horror, in other words, is a *capacious* form, capable of accommodating contradictions, and capable also of a great diversity of styles and subjects. Cumulatively, across the stories collected in this anthology, we can see the form developing through the nineteenth century. There were no fixed generic rules or codes for horror at the time, and consequently no fixed boundaries. Thus, the horror story was a form which could contain a variety of very different subgenres. Any reader of nineteenth-century horror will soon encounter ghost stories, stories of vampires and the undead, stories of mad doctors and scientists, psychological horrors, colonial horrors, and tales of precognition, as well as many stories falling into more than one category, or into none. To understand why and how the genre took off when it did, we need to travel back briefly to the eighteenth century, to the Enlightenment and its dark shadow, the Gothic.

Between 1797 and 1799, the Spanish artist Francisco Goya produced a series of illustrations which he entitled *Los Caprichos* (*The Caprices*), the most celebrated of which, plate 43 (of 80), shows an artist (perhaps Goya himself), hunched sleeping over his work, assailed by night terrors: owls, bats, a wide-eyed lynx. The etching's famous epigraph, written on the artist's desk, is 'El sueño de la razón produce monstruos' (The sleep of reason produces monsters). (The lynx, according to Robert Hughes, was believed to be able to 'see through darkness

---

[3] Owen Davies, *The Haunted: A Social History of Ghosts* (London, 2007), 15.

and immediately tell truth from error'.[4]) It is tempting, especially in the light of Goya's famous illustration, to understand modern horror as the Enlightenment's *unconscious*, shadowing the Enlightenment virtues of secularism, modernity, rationalism, and progressivism with supernaturalism and superstition, the past, madness and extreme psychological states, chaos. For some of the French Enlightenment *philosophes*, in fact, the existence of the supernatural provided a test case for the whole Enlightenment project: Diderot, Voltaire, and Rousseau were all, in their different ways, particularly exercised by the existence of vampires, which had been enshrined as a fact in European law following the investigation into the Serbian vampire Arnod Paole in 1727. Paole, a soldier who had died after returning from Turkish campaigns, apparently returned from the dead and terrorized his home village. An investigation of jurists, doctors, and high-ranking military officers concluded that vampirism was indeed to blame for the villagers' deaths. Rousseau, musing on the Paole case, concluded that 'No evidence is lacking—depositions, certificates of notables, surgeons, priests and magistrates. The proof *in law* is utterly complete. . . . Yet with all this, who actually *believes* in vampires?'[5]

Enlightenment thinkers may not actually have believed in vampires, yet many of them were willing to contend that there were aspects of human experience about which rationalism had nothing to say. In 1757, the Irish politician and philosopher Edmund Burke published what was to become one of the key intellectual documents of Romanticism, and one of the most important works of aesthetics of its time, *A Philosophical Enquiry into the Origin of Our Ideas of the Sublime and Beautiful*. The sublime, Burke argued, was a fundamentally metaphysical, or even numinous, category, short-circuiting reason completely in its presentation of images and spectacles so vast, so overwhelming, that they produced an effect of reverent awe, and even terror, in those who experienced them. Pain, Burke wrote, is 'an emissary of the king of terrors'—Death—and thus:

Whatever is fitted in any sort to excite the ideas of pain, and danger, that is to say, whatever is in any sort terrible, or is conversant about terrible

---

[4] Robert Hughes, *Goya* (London, 2004), 171.

[5] Christopher Frayling (ed.), *Vampyres: Lord Byron to Count Dracula* (London, 1992), 31. For an account of the Arnod Paole case, which reproduces the official report, *Visum et Repertum* (*Seen and Destroyed*), in full, see Paul Barber, *Vampires, Burial and Death: Folklore and Reality* (New Haven, 1988), 15–20.

objects, or operates in a manner analogous to terror, is a source of the *sublime*; that is, it is productive of the strongest emotion which the mind is capable of feeling.[6]

The Burkean sublime was to become a central concept for understanding the Gothic. In 1826 Ann Radcliffe, the most celebrated Gothic novelist of her generation, and one of the pioneering figures in modern horror, outlined what was to become an important distinction for many theorists of the form, between 'terror' (numinous, metaphysical dread) and 'horror' (shocking, often disgusting revelation):

Terror and horror are so far opposite, that the first expands the soul, and awakens the faculties to a high degree of life; the other contracts, freezes, and nearly annihilates them. I apprehend, that neither Shakspeare [*sic*] nor Milton by their fictions, nor Mr Burke by his reasoning, anywhere looked to positive horror as a source of the sublime, though they all agree that terror is a very high one; and where lies the great difference between horror and terror, but in the uncertainty and obscurity, that accompany the first, respecting the dreaded evil?[7]

Though not all commentators accept it, the distinction between terror and horror has proved lasting and influential. For example, Stephen King, by far the most prominent living horror writer, makes it one of the cornerstones of his analysis of the genre in his important study, *Danse Macabre* (1981): 'So: terror on top, horror below it, and lowest of all, the gag reflex of revulsion. . . . I recognize terror as the finest emotion . . . and so I will try to terrorize the reader. But if I find I cannot terrify him/her, I will try to horrify; and if I find I cannot horrify, I'll go for the gross-out. I'm not proud.'[8] King himself cites 'The Monkey's Paw' as his 'quintessential' example of the tale of terror:

It's what the mind sees . . . It is the unpleasant speculation called to mind when the knocking on the door begins . . . and the grief stricken old woman rushes to answer it. Nothing is there but the wind when she finally throws

---

[6] Edmund Burke, *A Philosophical Enquiry into the Origin of Our Ideas of the Sublime and Beautiful*, ed. and introd. Adam Phillips (Oxford, 1990), 36.

[7] Ann Radcliffe, 'On the Supernatural in Poetry', *New Monthly Magazine*, 16/1 (Jan. 1826), 145–52, repr. in E. J. Clery and Robert Miles (eds.), *Gothic Documents: A Sourcebook 1700–1820* (Manchester, 2000), 168.

[8] Stephen King, *Danse Macabre* (London, 1982), 39–40.

the door open . . . but what, the mind wonders, *might* have been there if her husband had been a little slower on the draw with the third wish?[9]

What indeed? Similarly, in Algernon Blackwood's 'The Wendigo', it is the uncertainty as to what precisely it is that Défago encounters in the unutterably vast, remote, and silent Canadian wilderness that gives the story its power. For 'The Monkey's Paw' or 'The Wendigo' to reveal more would be to spoil their carefully calibrated atmospheres of terror. As M. R. James asserted when writing about his own chosen form, the ghost story: 'On the whole, then, I say you must have horror and also malevolence. Not less necessary, however, is reticence.'[10] That said, 'the gross-out' certainly has its place in horror fiction, as King recognizes, and readers in search of the schlockier end of the form could do worse than turn to Bram Stoker's tale of torture and feline vengeance, 'The Squaw'. It was with good reason that Herbert Van Thal, when in 1959 he edited the first of what was to become thirty volumes of the pulp horror series, *The Pan Books of Horror Stories*, chose 'The Squaw' as its shocking finale.[11]

The terror/horror binary may have become an important one, but Ann Radcliffe, it is fair to say, was no intellectual, and her reasoning (or phrasing) when distinguishing terror from horror seems confused, as elsewhere it is the 'uncertainty and obscurity' of the 'dreaded evil' that is the source of terror, not horror (which she later glosses as being produced from 'confusion'). But this may just point to the degree of definitional imprecision (confusion) inherent in the Gothic itself. 'Gothic', as Nick Groom has demonstrated, is a term with a bewildering variety of referents, taking in ethnography, architecture, fiction, music, youth subculture, and much else besides.[12] Furthermore, it has settled into a *very* imprecise usage in contemporary literary criticism, made to stand in for almost all forms of non-realist fiction.[13] To lapse into its own language (and the language of its critics), there is something *spectral* about the Gothic, something

---

[9] King, *Danse Macabre*, 36.

[10] M. R. James, 'Ghosts—Treat Them Gently!', in *Collected Ghost Stories*, ed. Darryl Jones (Oxford, 2011), 418.

[11] Herbert Van Thal (ed.), *The Pan Book of Horror Stories* (London, 1959).

[12] Nick Groom, *The Gothic: A Very Short Introduction* (Oxford, 2012).

[13] For an excellent account of nineteenth-century Gothic fiction and its criticism, see Jarlath Killeen, *Gothic Literature, 1825–1914* (Cardiff, 2009), 1–26, 166–86.

which can be detected, perceived, even understood, but not with any real formal rigour defined.

That said, the spectre of the Gothic does haunt nineteenth-century culture, and is a crucial element of most of the century's horror literature. Its *locus classicus*, the Gothic Castle or Abbey of Horace Walpole or Ann Radcliffe, repository of the past and its secrets, was domesticated across the nineteenth century into the Old Dark House, haunted by ghosts or malevolent spirits (Benson's 'The Room in the Tower' is a startling late example of this), or by memories of violent and disruptive events. Balzac's 'La Grande Bretêche', published in the 1830s but set a generation earlier, in the immediate aftermath of the Napoleonic Wars, is one of the greatest of all Old Dark House stories, and probably the finest example of full-blooded Gothic in this anthology:

The roof of this house is dreadfully dilapidated; the outside shutters are always closed; the balconies are hung with swallows' nests; the doors are for ever shut. Straggling grasses have outlined the flagstones of the steps with green; the ironwork is rusty. Moon and sun, winter, summer, and snow have eaten into the wood, warped the boards, peeled off the paint. The dreary silence is broken only by birds and cats, polecats, rats, and mice, free to scamper round, and fight, and eat each other. An invisible hand has written over it all: 'Mystery.' (p. 50)

The crumbling mansion, to which entrance is forbidden, slowly reveals its history to the narrator through multiple overlapping narratives told by a provincial lawyer, landlady, and servant. It is a history simultaneously political and psychosexual: the dread consequences of an affair between the lady of the house and a Spanish prisoner of war.

In the same vein, though more characteristically modern, in Charlotte Perkins Gilman's 'The Yellow Wall Paper' it is *domesticity itself* that is monstrous. The patterned wallpaper, behind which the narrator sees the form of a woman struggling to get out, becomes a symbol of the domestic entrapment of women, confined in marriage and by childbirth to their homes. Adopting a classic Gothic trope from Balzac and Poe ('The Cask of Amontillado'), Gilman's narrator is symbolically walled up in her own home.

As Gothic fiction grew into a distinctive genre by the early years of the nineteenth century, a new generation of literary journals started to emerge and proliferate. They became instrumental in the dissemination of fiction to a wide audience. More than this, they became the major source for the publication of genre fiction in all its forms across the nineteenth century. And the first of them made horror its own.

Blackwood's Edinburgh Magazine was founded in 1817, and became a roaring success.[14] This success was in part based on its notoriety, as *Blackwood's* had from the beginning a scabrous ultra-Tory outlook characterized by a propensity for vicious ad hominem attacks which led to a number of court cases and one fatal duel, in which John Scott, the editor of the rival *London Magazine*, was shot and killed. Barely a year after its first appearance, the pamphleteer Macvey Napier criticized *Blackwood's*' 'unmixed love of evil', denouncing it as 'the vilest production that ever disfigured and soiled the annals of literature'.[15] He was talking about the journal's politics and morality, but he could as easily have been talking about its horrifying contents.

Fiction was crucial to *Blackwood's*' success from the very beginning, and deeply interlinked with its fondness for sensation. *Blackwood's* actually ran until as late as 1980, and became, in John Wain's words, 'the cradle of Victorian fiction',[16] publishing a number of works by leading writers such as Edward Bulwer-Lytton, Anthony Trollope, George Eliot, Margaret Oliphant, and Joseph Conrad (both *Heart of Darkness* and *Lord Jim* first appeared in *Blackwood's*), while sustaining what John Sutherland has called the 'indignant moral tone' of its literary criticism, launching attacks 'against "low" novelists such as Dickens in the 1840s, or Hardy and the "anti-marriage" league of modern novelists in the 1890s'.[17]

While the presence of Trollope, Eliot, or Conrad later in the century might suggest a creeping canonical respectability, it was for its horror fiction that *Blackwood's* was initially best known. In this, it was to set the pattern for the periodical publication of horror stories across the nineteenth century and beyond. William Maginn's 'The

[14] For information on the history and contents of *Blackwood's* in this section, I draw on Robert Morrison and Chris Baldick, 'Introduction', in Morrison and Baldick (eds.), *Tales of Terror from Blackwood's Magazine* (Oxford, 1995), pp. vii–xviii.

[15] Christopher J. Scalia, 'Transcendental Buffoonery: Jacob Dousterswivel and the Romantic Irony of *Blackwood's*', *Studies in Romanticism*, 51/3 (Fall 2012), 375.

[16] Morrison and Baldick, 'Introduction', p. xi.

[17] John Sutherland, *The Longman Companion to Victorian Fiction*, 2nd edn. (Harlow, 2009), 66.

Man in the Bell' and James Hogg's 'George Dobson's Expedition to
Hell' both first appeared in *Blackwood's*. Both these authors had close
connections with the magazine, and Maginn, much given to scurrilous journalism, was particularly in tune with its sensibilities—he
was damned by his fellow countryman, the Irish nationalist leader
Daniel O'Connell, as a 'hoary-headed libeller'. In 1836, Maginn
fought a duel with Grantley Berkeley, MP, over a savage review he
had written in *Fraser's Magazine* of Berkeley's novel *Berkeley Castle*.
Neither party was injured.[18] (The early nineteenth-century periodical trade was clearly a pretty roister-doistering scene, and not for the
faint of heart.)

As a forum for the publication of fiction (and particularly sensational genre fiction), *Blackwood's* was enormously significant. In its
wake, and with material that veered dramatically across the entire
cultural spectrum, there followed, amongst many others, *Fraser's
Magazine* (from 1830, founded and edited by Maginn, and publishing Hogg, Thackeray, Carlyle, and John Stuart Mill), Dickens's two
great periodicals, *Household Words* (1850: Dickens, Wilkie Collins,
Elizabeth Gaskell) and *All the Year Round* (1859: Dickens, Collins,
Trollope, Bulwer-Lytton, Le Fanu), *Harper's* (published in New York
from 1850: Melville, Hawthorne, Mark Twain, Henry James, Jack
London), *The Strand* (1891: Conan Doyle, Kipling, Jacobs, H. G.
Wells), *The Idler* (1892: Jerome K. Jerome, Wells, Rider Haggard,
Hodgson, Mary Elizabeth Braddon), *The Windsor* (1895: Kipling,
Wells, London, Haggard, Edith Nesbit), and *Pearson's* (1896: Wells,
George Griffith, George Bernard Shaw). Over two-thirds of the stor-
ies included in this anthology first saw light in various magazines,
periodicals, and newspapers.

Horror fiction, as its best practitioners (such as Poe and James)
have asserted, is particularly (perhaps uniquely) suited to the short
form, best enabling it to provide a unity of setting and action (and
reading-experience: it can be consumed in one sitting), and to create a sustained, intensely realized atmosphere.[19] Poe, who did more

[18] 'William Maginn', *Oxford Dictionary of National Biography*, online at <http://
www.oxforddnb.com/view/printable/17784>.

[19] For Poe on the importance of unity of effect, and of keeping 'the *dénouement* constantly in view', see his essay 'The Philosophy of Composition', in *The Selected Writings of
Edgar Allan Poe*, ed. G. R. Thompson (New York, 2004), 675–84. James asserted that the
'two ingredients most valuable in the concocting of a ghost story are, to me, the atmosphere and the nicely-managed crescendo': James, *Collected Ghost Stories*, 407.

than any one figure to establish the horror story, was heavily indebted to what he read in *Blackwood's* (and most particularly to Maginn's 'The Man in the Bell', the traces of which can be seen across his work, from 'The Pit and the Pendulum' to his poem 'The Bells'). 'The Folio Club', a literary society whose meetings Poe originally intended to use as a framing device for his stories, contains among its members 'Mr Blackwood Blackwood, who had written certain articles for foreign Magazines'.[20] Aspiring author Miss Psyche Zenobia (aka Suky Snobbs), the narrator of Poe's 'How to Write a Blackwood Article', even goes so far as to consult William Blackwood himself for advice, and is told that 'The first thing requisite is to get yourself into such a scrape as no one ever got into before'—trapped in an 'oven or big bell . . . tumbl[ing] out of a balloon . . . swallowed up in an earthquake, or . . . stuck fast in a chimney'.[21] In 'A Predicament', the extraordinary *Blackwood's* pastiche that follows, Zenobia is trapped inside a giant cathedral clock, and narrates her own decapitation: as the hands of the clock reach 5.25, they sever her head, which 'rolled down the side of the steeple, and then lodged, for a few seconds, in the gutter, and then made its way with a plunge, into the middle of the street'.[22]

The large reading public for Victorian periodical fiction was made possible by dramatic societal shifts across the Industrial Revolution, leading to the creation of cities in their modern form—as Asa Briggs has argued, it may well be its cities (London, Birmingham, Manchester, Leeds, and others) that are the most characteristic feature of Victorian society, and its lasting legacy.[23] London, in particular, grew exponentially across the century to become by far the largest city the world had ever seen, half as big again by 1900 as its nearest international rival, New York.[24] This urbanization led in turn to two other characteristic nineteenth-century phenomena: the suburb and its inhabitant, the commuter—and as the century progressed, this commuter (stereotypically a white-collar city worker) was to become the target audience and implied reader of periodical fiction.

---

[20] Poe, 'The Folio Club', in *The Collected Works of Edgar Allan Poe*, ii. *Tales and Sketches*, ed. Thomas Ollive Mabbott (Cambridge, Mass., 1978), 205.

[21] Poe, 'How to Write a Blackwood Article', in *Selected Writings*, 177.

[22] Poe, 'How to Write a Blackwood Article', 189.

[23] Asa Briggs, *Victorian Cities* (London, 1963).

[24] See Jerry White, *London in the Nineteenth Century: 'A Human Awful Wonder of God'* (London, 2007).

Mass-market horror, therefore, can be understood as one indirect product of a culture which was urban, industrial, mercantile, technological, and scientific. At the same time, and for some of the same reasons, this culture was becoming increasingly secularized, a process which, broadly speaking, began with the Enlightenment. The publication of Darwin's *On the Origin of Species* in 1859 is often understood as the high-water mark of nineteenth-century scientific materialism, dealing Victorian religion a damaging blow, and one from which it never fully recovered.[25] But just as the Enlightenment gave birth to its own dark double, the Gothic, so too did nineteenth-century scientific materialism produce its own form of irrational monster, spiritualism. Spiritualism (along with its quasi-scientific twin, psychical research) was, as the historian Janet Oppenheim has noted, *the* major Victorian response to scientific materialism in general, and to Darwinian evolution in particular.[26] As with the relationship between the Enlightenment and the Gothic, Victorian spiritualism grew out of a profound sense that whole areas of human experience lay outside the remit of a materialist philosophy; as the novelist Catherine Crowe wrote in her best-selling compendium of the supernatural, *The Night Side of Nature* (1848):

To minds which can admit nothing but what can be explained and demonstrated, an investigation of this sort must appear perfectly idle . . . The pharisaical scepticism which denies without investigation, is quite as perilous, and much more contemptible, than the blind credulity which accepts all that is caught without enquiry; it is, indeed, but another form of ignorance assuming to be knowledge.[27]

For spiritualists, the 'two worlds' of spirit and matter were coexistent and often interpenetrating, though generally capable of being apprehended only through the intercession of a medium (who *mediated* between the two worlds), or at a seance, enabling participants to see reality for what it was, with new eyes. In Arthur Machen's

[25] For accounts of the Victorian 'crisis of faith', see e.g. Elisabeth Jay, *Faith and Doubt in Victorian Britain* (London and Basingstoke, 1986); Richard J. Helmstadter and Bernard V. Lightman (eds.), *Victorian Faith and Crisis: Essays on Continuity and Change in Nineteenth-Century Religous Belief* (Palo Alto, Calif., 1991).

[26] Janet Oppenheim, *The Other World: Spiritualism and Psychical Research in England, 1850–1914* (Cambridge, 1985).

[27] Catherine Crowe, *The Night Side of Nature; or, Ghosts and Ghost Seers* (London, 1848), i. 3–5.

occult classic *The Great God Pan* (1894), the unethical vivisector Dr Raymond is simultaneously a scientist and a spiritualist, who conducts his experiments as a means of contacting the other world:

'I say that all these are but dreams and shadows, the shadows that hide the real world from our eyes. There is a real world, but it is beyond this glamour and this vision . . . beyond them all as beyond a veil. I do not know whether any human being has ever lifted that veil; but I do know, Clarke, that you and I shall see it lifted this very night from before another's eyes.'[28]

It is these new eyes through which Ebenezer Scrooge, the archetypal nineteenth-century utilitarian, comes to see following his own encounter with the spirit world. With the intercession of the shade of Jacob Marley, he learns to see mercantile London for what it really is, a city of ghosts: 'The air was filled with phantoms, wandering hither and thither in restless haste, and moaning as they went.'[29]

Spiritualism pervaded virtually all corners of Victorian life in Britain (and was also very widespread in America). Far from being, as we might imagine, the province of a small number of fringe ideologues, cranks, and zealots, or a retreat for the socially marginalized and politically disenfranchised, spiritualism and psychical research attracted some of the most prominent scientific, cultural, and intellectual figures of the time: the Society for Psychical Research (SPR) was founded in Trinity College, Cambridge, in 1882, and included amongst its early presidents Henry Sidgwick, Arthur Balfour, William James, and Henri Bergson—a very formidable bunch indeed. As Oppenheim argues, spiritualism needs to be placed 'squarely amidst the cultural, intellectual and economic moods of the era'.[30]

It is no wonder, then, that the long nineteenth century was the great age of the ghost story, with Charles Dickens and his close contemporary Sheridan Le Fanu the most important mid-century exponents of the form, and M. R. James (heavily influenced by both Dickens and Le Fanu) becoming its greatest practitioner around the *fin de siècle*. Like the Gothic, to which it is closely allied, the ghost story represents a significant breach in the Victorian narrative of progressivism and modernity, an irruption into the present of a vengeful and undeniable

---

[28] Arthur Machen, *The Great God Pan*, in *The Caerleon Edition of the Works of Arthur Machen*, 8 vols. (London, 1928), i. 4.

[29] Charles Dickens, *A Christmas Carol* (1843), stave I.

[30] Oppenheim, *The Other World*, 4.

past, with terrifying implications and consequences. Between these
figures, and beyond James, as late as the mid-twentieth century, the
ghost story attracted innumerable writers.[31] Like Dickens before him,
James understood the ghost story primarily as a form of entertainment. In his case, it was a diversion from his serious scholarly work,
and yet it was also a by-product and continuation by other means
of his serious investigations into the meaning and materiality of the
past (he was by academic profession a manuscript scholar, well used
to rooting around in the physical stuff of history). James, again like
Dickens, was a kind of reflexive Anglican, fairly orthodox in his belief
but not much given to religious or spiritual questioning. While he
was a student and teacher at King's College, Cambridge, the SPR was
conducting its investigations from next-door Trinity. It might seem
strange that the foremost ghost-story writer should have given little
thought to the most high-profile organization of ghost-hunters, based
just a couple of minutes' walk from his rooms, but James was careful
to distinguish between 'the literary ghost story', of the kind which
he wrote, and 'the story that claims to be "veridical" (in the language
of the Society of Psychical Research)'. His story 'The Mezzotint'
casts the SPR in a highly unfavourable light as 'the Phasmatological
Society', a collection of busybodies shining their unwelcome beams
on the reticent mystery of ghosts.[32]

However, there was one important way in which even James's
remote, scholarly, highly aesthetic ghost stories were influenced by
their times. Prior to the rise of spiritualism and psychical research,
ghosts had generally been understood as *purposeful* actors in a teleo-
logical narrative, appearing in order to right wrongs and correct
injustices (often legal injustices), or to wreak specific supernatural
vengeance (the family curse), or to warn against impending calamity. But in 1894, in his study of psychical research, *Cock Lane and
Common Sense*, the influential folklorist Andrew Lang concluded
that the contemporary ghost was 'a purposeless creature', appearing
'nobody knows why; he has no message to deliver, no secret crime to
reveal, no appointment to keep, no treasure to disclose, no commis-
sions to be executed, and, as an almost invariable rule, he does not

---

[31] For an influential argument as to why the ghost story did not survive much beyond
the Second World War, other than as pastiche and exercises in deliberate nostalgia, see
Julia Briggs, *Night Visitors: The Rise and Fall of the English Ghost Story* (London, 1977).

[32] James, *Collected Ghost Stories*, 416, 31.

speak, even if you speak to him'.[33] In his analysis of Lang's observation, Owen Davies notes that the 'purposeless' ghost was largely a middle-class phenomenon, 'but an examination of other sources, particularly newspapers and folklore, confirms the continued significance of purposeful ghosts in popular culture'.[34]

But if the investigators of the SPR were middle-class intellectuals who tended to shy away from the cosmic credulity of folk beliefs, the same was true of the great majority of ghost-story writers. Rather against the tenor of its times, Richard Marsh's 'Lady Wishaw's Hand' contains an unambiguously purposeful ghost; this is a classic Family Curse narrative, albeit one that is undercut by its own self-conscious playfulness, as in the scene where the disembodied Hand runs amok in the dining room of a gentleman's club. By far the most celebrated Family Curse narrative of the *fin de siècle* is Conan Doyle's *The Hound of the Baskervilles* (1902), in which Sherlock Holmes, playing the role of psychical investigator, comprehensively debunks and secularizes the Great Grimpen Mire's demon hound. When M. R. James was asked (as must have happened often), 'Do I believe in ghosts?' his answer was one which would have gratified the SPR: 'I am prepared to consider evidence and accept it if it satisfies me.'[35] Unquestionably, though, James's *stories* accept the veracity of the supernatural, though they do so in a way which reflects the late Victorian culture of spiritualism and psychical research, in that his ghosts are rarely purposeful in the old style. 'Count Magnus's' Mr Wraxall, like the majority of James's protagonists, has no personal connection with the cause of his story—in his case, the Swedish De La Gardie family whose malevolent revenant pursues him to his death.[36] James's ghosts, like those of the SPR, simply *are*.

If the supernatural tale, as exemplified by the ghost story, set itself in explicit opposition to the prevailing Victorian materialism, then there is another strain of horror which is deeply embedded within this materialism. The mad scientist, or mad doctor, is a recurring figure in modern horror, from the publication of Mary Shelley's *Frankenstein*

[33] Davies, *The Haunted*, 8.
[34] Ibid. 9.
[35] James, *Collected Ghost Stories*, 418.
[36] There are exceptions: stories such as 'The Ash Tree', 'Lost Hearts', 'A Neighbour's Landmark', or 'Martin's Close' contain purposeful, vengeful ghosts and family curses—but these are all historical tales, set in seventeenth-century England.

in 1818 onwards. As the sociologist Andrew Tudor writes, 'The belief that science is dangerous is as central to . . . horror . . . as is a belief in the malevolent inclinations of ghosts, ghouls, vampires and zombies.'[37] Popular cultural Mad Science has developed its own immediately recognizable semiotics and rhetoric: the white-coated, wild-haired scientist, laughing maniacally; *'They call me crazy! Well, we'll see who's crazy!' 'And you call yourself a scientist?'* The mad scientist often claims to be pursuing 'disinterested' scientific research 'for its own ends', completely divorced from any ethical consideration. The implications of this cultural discourse of Mad Science have been understandably troubling to many practising scientists: as the astronomer Carl Sagan wrote, 'we can't simply conclude that science puts too much power into the hands of morally feeble technologists or corrupt, power-crazed politicians and so decide to get rid of it'.[38]

In part, *Frankenstein* and its successors are modern, industrial developments of the Faust legend—the scientist who sells his soul for forbidden knowledge. However, the anxieties surrounding science are also a product of its ever-increasing specialization, which took its concerns and its very language far from those of non-scientists. When the Royal Society was founded in 1660, part of its initial remit was the formalization of a specialized scientific *language* in which to report its discoveries, and although these linguistic strictures took a long time to be accepted absolutely, by the close of the nineteenth century they certainly were. In 1791, the natural philosopher Erasmus Darwin published *The Botanic Garden*, perhaps the last major scientific treatise to be written in verse. When in 1859, his grandson Charles published *On the Origin of Species*, probably the single most revolutionary book of the nineteenth century, he made sure that it was written in a style that was accessible to the educated lay reader. *On the Origin of Species* was in its turn heavily influenced by the formulation of geological deep time in Charles Lyell's *Principles of Geology* (1833), a work which was something of a best-seller. But works such as these stand out against the tenor of their times, which saw scientific theory become increasingly distant from the concerns, and even the comprehension, of most Victorians. Few, if any, non-scientists could hope to understand the

---

[37] Andrew Tudor, *Monsters and Mad Scientists: A Cultural History of the Horror Movie* (Oxford, 1989), 133.

[38] Carl Sagan, *The Demon-Haunted World: Science as a Candle in the Dark* (London, 1997), 14.

intricacies of the great late-century physicist James Clerk Maxwell, for example, let alone the work of Albert Einstein, who has settled in the public imagination as the archetypal remote, abstract scientific genius.

It is too simplistic, however, to view Mad Science purely as the product of an anti-scientific animus across the nineteenth century. Just because horror's many mad doctors perform unspeakable acts does not mean that their creators hated science. This is demonstrably not the case, for example, with Ronald Ross, winner of the Nobel Prize for Medicine in 1902 for his pioneering research into malaria. And yet, in the person of Dr Maculligan, Ross's 'The Vivisector Vivisected' presents the single most barking scientist in this book. Rather than being an abstruse scientific specialist or bloodless technocrat, Nathaniel Hawthorne's Aylmer, in 'The Birth-Mark', is very much an old-school Renaissance Man (based in part on the seventeenth-century polymath Kenelm Digby, one of the founders of the Royal Society), simultaneously a surgeon, a geologist, an alchemist, and a black magician. In fact, the implications of many Victorian scientific endeavours were all too comprehensible to the popular imagination. The cultural anxieties stemming from vivisection (experimentation on living subjects, a hotly contested political issue in the last decades of the century), or the 'pseudosciences' (an inadequate term, delivered with hindsight: better to call them 'outmoded sciences') of criminal physiognomy, eugenics, or racial theorizing were ripe for rendition in horror stories.

The paranoid colonial narrative and the supernatural tale both situate the locus of horror as radically Other, completely external to the story's sensibilities, its narrative, and its implied readership: *they are out to get you*. Another, and perhaps more distinctively modern, strain of the form looks within the tangled human psyche to find horror lurking there, potentially inside us all. Though his aims may on occasion be laudable, the mad scientist is *mad* because he lacks human empathy, unable to see human beings other than as *corpora vilia*—expendable experimental subjects. But beyond even this figure, horror writers have specialized in creating madmen who are completely enclosed within their own minds, and whose motivations are therefore simply incomprehensible to the reader. This, we shall see, has implications for the very act of reading tales of madness.

In the development of psychological horror, as in so much else, Edgar Allan Poe is a pioneering figure. 'The Conqueror Worm', the interpolated verse in his story 'Ligeia', contains what might almost be a manifesto for Poe's writing: 'And much of Madness and more of Sin, | And horror the soul of the plot.'[39] Poe's stories tend to be unsettlingly monologic: that is, they often have no external referent, and are thus wholly dependent on the veracity of narrators who are frequently highly unreliable, not least because they are frequently highly mad. This unreliability tends further to destabilize the already highly unstable world of his writing. When, for example, in 'The Fall of the House of Usher', probably Poe's most famous story, Roderick hears his sister Madeleine rising from her tomb, he exclaims to his friend the narrator: '*Madman! I tell you that she now stands without the door!*'[40] Who is the 'madman' here? Is it the solipsistic Roderick, addressing himself as he cannot see beyond himself, or is it the narrator? If the narrator, what effect might this have on our reading of the story? Like 'Ligeia', 'Usher', and a number of others, 'Berenice' manages to combine in compressed form Poe's three favourite subjects: narcolepsy and premature burial, madness, and the death of a beautiful woman. At the close of the story, in a passage which Poe later had to retract on grounds of taste (but which is restored in the version published here), the narrator Egæus breaks into his beloved Berenice's tomb, where she may have been placed alive, and removes her teeth. What, if anything, are our grounds for accepting the veracity of any of this narrative?

One of the pleasures and challenges of reading Robert W. Chambers's 'The Repairer of Reputations' lies in trying to establish what on earth is going on. The tale closes with what appears to be a documentary medical statement, an objective gloss taken from outside the story itself: '[EDITOR'S NOTE.—Mr Castaigne died yesterday in the Asylum for Criminal Insane.]' (p. 293). Has the entire story been narrated from within a madhouse? Is Mr Wilde, the deformed dwarf who seemingly controls New York, really the omniscient 'Repairer of Reputations', or a fellow inmate, or a figment of Hildred Castaigne's imagination? Has the American government really erected a lethal gas chamber in Washington Square, or is this the entrance to one of the many subway stations being built in New York around this time (the subway was proposed in 1863, and its first line opened in 1904), or is it something else altogether? The story begins in the manner of a characteristic *fin-de-siècle* literary subgenre,

---

[39] Poe, *Selected Writings*, 165.   [40] Ibid. 215.

the sociological future fiction: set in the 1920s, over a quarter of a century after the story was written, the opening paragraphs chart the rise of an all-conquering militaristic American Empire. But has any of this happened at all? The reader has simply no grounds upon which to answer any of these questions.

W. F. Harvey's chilling vignette 'Autumn Heat' is equally puzzling. The story closes with the narrator waiting in a room with the man who may turn out to be his murderer. Is 'Autumn Heat' really a tale of supernatural precognition, in which the narrator foresees his own murder? Is the seemingly blameless family man Chs. Atkinson, Monumental Mason, going to kill him when the clock strikes midnight? Is the narrator deluded, or insane? Or is the whole thing just a nasty coincidence? As the narrator himself acknowledges in the story's closing words, 'It is enough to send a man mad' (p. 426).

The Gothic is a psychological landscape as much as it is an architectural and geographical one. Its classic imagery—ruins, castles, dungeons, Old Dark Houses—offers a system of signs with which to represent the workings of the unconscious mind. The symbolism is important, as writers of the Gothic from Radcliffe to Poe to Stoker simply had no agreed technical vocabulary or scientific discipline at their disposal with which to describe and interpret the unconscious. The long and prolific career of Sigmund Freud was to change all that, beginning with *Studies on Hysteria*, his 1895 collaboration with Josef Breuer, and, most particularly, *The Interpretation of Dreams* (1899). The beginnings of Freud's career as a writer and theorist coincide precisely with the great flourishing of the horror story around the *fin de siècle*, and with good reason.

Like so many psychological horror stories, the lessons of Freudian psychoanalysis are that we are all ultimately unknowable to ourselves, and that the necessary condition of human existence in civilization is repression and consequently neurosis. (It is perhaps little wonder that, for many years, the dominant critical methodology for approaching horror was a Freudian one.[41]) Freud is one of the last and greatest

---

[41] See, amongst many examples, Ernest Jones, *On the Nightmare* (London, 1940); Marie Bonaparte, *The Life and Works of Edgar Allan Poe: A Psycho-Analytic Interpretation*, foreword by Sigmund Freud, trans. John Rodker (London, 1949); David Punter, *The Literature of Terror* (London, 1999); Steven Hay Schneider (ed.), *Horror Film and Psychoanalysis: Freud's Worst Nightmare* (Cambridge, 2004).

of the nineteenth century's Gothic writers, offering an imaginative world of contorted and disfigured sexual relations, in which the past (infancy) looms over the present (adulthood), exercising a monstrous, inescapable influence on individuals who are necessarily driven beyond the limits of sanity by the unbearable burden of repressing dark secrets and forbidden desires. Horror, for Freud, really was the soul of the plot.

When Freud came to formulate his theory of horror in his land-mark 1919 essay, 'The "Uncanny"', like any Victorian Gothicist Old Dark Houses were on his mind, as the German for 'uncanny', *Unheimlich*, literally translates as 'unhomely'. For Freud, that which characterizes the uncanny is indeterminacy, or uncertainty: it is this which produces horror and dread. Like our minds, our very homes, those places we thought most safe and secure, are alien and threatening to us. *All* our houses are Old Dark Houses, concealing more than they welcome, hiding terrible secrets, those things which, like forbidden lovers, protesting wives, or the corpses of ancestors and relatives, must, in the world of the Gothic, remain locked up at home: 'everything is *Unheimlich* that ought to have remained secret and hidden but has come to light'.[42]

Concealed within 'The "Uncanny"' is a sustained and virtuoso piece of literary criticism. When Freud looked around him for the most characteristically uncanny of all works of art, the work which, for him, answered Fitz-James O'Brien's question, 'What do you consider to be the greatest element of terror?', he returned to the beginning of the nineteenth century, to E. T. A. Hoffmann's 'The Sandman'. Fittingly, it is with Hoffmann that this anthology begins.

---

[42] Sigmund Freud, 'The "Uncanny"', in *The Standard Edition of the Complete Psychological Works of Sigmund Freud*, xvii. *(1917–1919): An Infantile Neurosis and Other Works*, trans. James Strachey (London, 1955), 225.

NOTE ON THE TEXT

THERE are thousands of nineteenth-century horror stories, and any one selection can only provide the tiniest of samples. In selecting the tales for inclusion in the anthology, I have been mindful of balancing the most important and influential writers and stories, without which an anthology such as this could not hope to be representative, with some rarer and more unusual stories. Sometimes, the anthology does both things: thus, Sheridan Le Fanu, unquestionably a major figure in the tradition, is here represented by 'Schalken the Painter', a rarely reprinted story (which also happens, I think, to be his best).

Wherever possible (which is in the great majority of cases), I have taken the texts of the stories from their first publication either in periodical or book form—more usually in book form, as these texts tend to be more reliable. In two cases (the stories by Poe and Le Fanu), there are very significant variations between different published versions—see the headnotes to the Explanatory Notes for details on these, and any other, smaller variations in the stories. The headnotes also give the initial publication details for all stories. My thanks to the librarians at Trinity College Dublin and the British Library for their assistance in sourcing some of these texts.

Acknowledgements

The following stories are reprinted by permission of the copyright holders:

Algernon Blackwood, 'The Wendigo', by permission of A. P. Watt *at* United Artists on behalf of Susan Reeves-Jones.

E. T. A. Hoffmann, 'The Sandman', from *The Golden Pot and Other Tales* (Oxford University Press, 1992), reprinted by permission of Oxford University Press.

Arthur Machen, 'Novel of the White Powder', copyright © Arthur Machen, reprinted by permission of A. M. Heath & Co. Ltd.

Despite every effort, it has not been possible to trace the copyright holder for the translation of Balzac's 'La Grande Bretêche' by Elizabeth McNally.

SELECT BIBLIOGRAPHY

General Studies

Baldick, Chris, *In Frankenstein's Shadow: Myth, Monstrosity and Nineteenth-Century Writing* (Oxford, 1987).

Carroll, Noël, *The Philosophy of Horror, or Paradoxes of the Heart* (London, 1990).

Cohen, Stanley, *Folk Devils and Moral Panics* (St Alban's, 1973).

Creed, Barbara, *The Monstrous-Feminine: Film, Feminism, Psychoanalysis* (London, 1992).

Daly, Nicholas, *Modernism, Romance and the Fin de Siècle: Popular Fiction and British Culture, 1880–1914* (Cambridge, 1999).

Frayling, Christopher, *Nightmare: The Birth of Horror* (London, 1996).

Gelder, Ken (ed.), *The Horror Reader* (London, 2000).

Halberstam, Judith, *Skin Shows: Gothic Horror and the Technology of Monsters* (Durham, NC, 1995).

Hills, Matt, *The Pleasures of Horror* (London, 2005).

Hurley, Kelly, *The Gothic Body: Sexuality, Materialism and Degeneration at the Fin de Siècle* (Cambridge, 1996).

Jones, Darryl, *Horror: A Thematic History in Fiction and Film* (London, 2002).

King, Stephen, *Danse Macabre* (London, 1982).

Morrison, Robert, and Baldick, Chris (eds.), *Tales of Terror from Blackwood's Magazine* (Oxford, 1995).

Punter, David, *The Literature of Terror* (London, 1999).

Skal, David J., *The Monster Show: A Cultural History of Horror* (London, 1994).

Tudor, Andrew, *Monsters and Mad Scientists: A Cultural History of the Horror Movie* (Oxford, 1989).

Tymn, Marshall, *Horror Literature: A Core Collection and Reference Guide* (New York, 1981).

The Gothic

Bloom, Clive (ed.), *Gothic Horror* (London, 1998).

Botting, Fred, *Gothic* (London, 1996).

Clery, E. J., and Miles, Robert (eds.), *Gothic Documents: A Sourcebook, 1700–1820* (Manchester, 2000).

Crow, Charles L., *American Gothic* (Cardiff, 2009).

Killeen, Jarlath, *Gothic Literature, 1825–1914* (Cardiff, 2009).

Punter, David, and Byron, Glennis, *The Gothic* (London, 2003).

Colonial Horror

Arata, Stephen J., *Fictions of Loss in the Victorian Fin de Siècle: Identity and Empire* (Cambridge, 1996).

Brantlinger, Patrick, *Rule of Darkness: British Literature and Imperialism 1830–1900* (Ithaca, NY, 1988).

Wynne, Catherine, *The Colonial Conan Doyle: British Imperialism, Irish Nationalism and the Gothic* (Westport, Conn., 2002).

The Supernatural

Barber, Paul, *Vampires, Burial and Death: Folklore and Reality* (New Haven, 1988).

Briggs, Julia, *Night Visitors: The Rise and Fall of the English Ghost Story* (London, 1977).

Davies, Owen, *The Haunted: A Social History of Ghosts* (London, 2007).

Frayling, Christopher, *Vampyres: Lord Byron to Count Dracula* (London, 1992).

O'Briain, Helen Conrad, and Stevens, Julie Anne (eds.). *The Ghost Story from the Middle Ages to the Twentieth Century* (Dublin, 2010).

Oppenheim, Janet, *The Other World: Spiritualism and Psychical Research in England, 1850–1914* (Cambridge, 1985).

Science

Beer, Gillian, *Open Fields: Science in Cultural Encounter* (Oxford, 1999).

Ferguson, Trish (ed.), *Victorian Time: Technologies, Standardizations, Catastrophes* (London, 2013).

Levine, George, *Dying to Know: Scientific Epistemology and Narrative in Victorian England* (Chicago, 2002).

Otis, Laura (ed.), *Literature and Science in the Nineteenth Century: An Anthology* (Oxford, 2009).

Pick, Daniel, *Faces of Degeneration: A European Disorder, c.1848–c.1918* (Cambridge, 1989).

Skal, David J., *Screams of Reason: Mad Science and Modern Culture* (New York, 1998).

CHRONOLOGY

	Horror Writers	*Cultural and Historical Background*
1770	James Hogg born in Ettrick, Scotland.	William Wordsworth, G. W. F. Hegel, and Ludwig van Beethoven born.
1776	E. T. A. Hoffmann born in Königsburg, Prussia (now Kaliningrad, Russia).	American Revolution and Declaration of Independence (4 July).
1794	William Maginn born in Cork, Ireland.	French Revolutionary Terror: execution of Danton, Lavoisier, and Robespierre.
1799	Honoré de Balzac born in Tours, France.	Alexander Pushkin born; death of George Washington.
1804	Nathaniel Hawthorne born in Salem, Massachusetts.	Napoleon crowned emperor of the French.
1809	Edgar Allan Poe born in Boston.	Abraham Lincoln and Charles Darwin born.
1812	Charles Dickens born in Portsmouth.	British Prime Minister Spencer Perceval assassinated; British–US War of 1812; Napoleon invades Russia; Byron, *Childe Harold's Pilgrimage*; Jacob and Wilhelm Grimm, *Fairy Tales*.
1814	Sheridan Le Fanu born in Dublin.	Napoleon abdicates as emperor of the French; Treaty of Ghent brings War of 1812 to a close; Jane Austen, *Mansfield Park*; Walter Scott, *Waverley*.
1815	Hoffmann, *Devil's Elixir*.	Battle of Waterloo ends Napoleonic Wars; restoration of French monarchy; Austen, *Emma*.
1816	Hoffmann, 'The Sandman'.	Byron, the Shelleys, and John Polidori holiday at the Villa Diodati; Charlotte Brontë born; Walter Scott, *Old Mortality*.
1817	Hoffmann, *Night Pieces*.	Death of Jane Austen; Scott, *Rob Roy*; Byron, *Manfred*; *Blackwood's Magazine* founded.
1818		Invention of the bicycle; Karl Marx born; Mary Shelley, *Frankenstein*; Austen, *Northanger Abbey* and *Persuasion*; Shelley, 'Ozymandias'.

Horror Writers	*Cultural and Historical Background*
1819	Herman Melville born in New York.	Peterloo Massacre; Queen Victoria, Prince Albert, Walt Whitman, and George Eliot born; Keats, *Odes*; Shelley, 'The Mask of Anarchy'; Scott, *Ivanhoe*; Polidori, *The Vampyre*.
1820		Regency ends with death of George III and coronation of George IV; Maturin, *Melmoth the Wanderer*; Shelley, *Prometheus Unbound*.
1821	Maginn, 'The Man in the Bell'.	Charles Baudelaire, Gustave Flaubert, and Fyodor Dostoevsky born; death of John Keats, Napoleon Bonaparte, and John Polidori; Thomas de Quincey, *Confessions of an English Opium Eater*.
1822	Death of E. T. A. Hoffmann.	Charles Babbage devises 'difference engine', the first computer; Matthew Arnold and Ulysses S. Grant born.
1824	Hogg, *Private Memoirs and Confessions of a Justified Sinner*.	Wilkie Collins born; death of Byron and Charles Maturin.
1826		Nicéphore Niépce takes first photograph; Mary Shelley, *The Last Man*.
1828	Fitz-James O'Brien born in Cork.	Kaspar Hauser, feral child, discovered in Nuremberg, Germany; Jules Verne, Henrik Ibsen, Dante Gabriel Rossetti, and Leo Tolstoy born.
1829	Hogg, *The Shepherd's Calendar*; Balzac, *Les Chouans*; Poe, *Al Araaf*.	Andrew Jackson becomes US president; Burke and Hare trial; Stephenson's *Rocket* built; first performance of Goethe's *Faust*.
1835	Death of James Hogg; Poe, 'Berenice—A Tale'.	Charles Darwin visits Galapagos Islands; Mark Twain born; Hans Christian Anderson, *Fairy Tales Told for Children*; Gogol, *Arabesques*; Tocqueville, *Democracy in America*.
1836	Dickens, *Sketches by Boz* and first serialization of *The Pickwick Papers*.	London and Greenwich Railway opens; Texas declares independence from US.
1838	Poe, *The Narrative of Arthur Gordon Pym of Nantucket*; Dickens, *Oliver Twist* and *Nicholas Nickleby*.	Brunel's SS *Great Western* makes transatlantic crossing; Henry Irving and Ferdinand von Zeppelin born.

	Horror Writers	Cultural and Historical Background
1839	Le Fanu, 'Schalken the Painter'; Poe, 'The Fall of the House of Usher' and 'William Wilson'.	Daguerreotype photography invented; Michael Faraday, 'Experimental Researches in Electricity'; Charles Darwin, *Voyage of the Beagle*; Stendhal, *The Charterhouse of Parma*.
1840	Émile Zola born in Paris; Poe, *Tales of the Grotesque and Arabesque*; Dickens, *The Old Curiosity Shop* and *Barnaby Rudge*.	Rowland Hill introduces penny post; Thomas Hardy, Auguste Rodin, and Claude Monet born; death of Caspar David Friedrich.
1842	Death of William Maginn; Ambrose Bierce born in Ohio; Poe, 'The Pit and the Pendulum'.	First Opium War ends with the Treaty of Nanking; death of Stendhal; Robert Browning, *Dramatic Lyrics*.
1843	Hawthorne, 'The Birth-Mark'; Dickens, 'A Christmas Carol' and *Martin Chuzzlewit*.	Battle of Hyderabad; Isambard Kingdom Brunel launches SS *Great Britain*; Henry James born; Søren Kierkegaard, *Fear and Trembling*; Tennyson, *Morte d'Arthur*.
1847	Bram Stoker born in Dublin; Melville, *Omoo*.	Chloroform first used as general anaesthetic; Thomas Edison and Alexander Graham Bell born; Charlotte Brontë, *Jane Eyre*; Emily Brontë, *Wuthering Heights*; Anne Brontë, *Agnes Grey*; William Makepeace Thackeray, *Vanity Fair*.
1849	Death of Edgar Allan Poe; Dickens, *David Copperfield*.	August Strindberg and Max Nordau born; death of Anne Brontë.
1850	Death of Honoré de Balzac; Robert Louis Stevenson born in Edinburgh; Hawthorne, *The Scarlet Letter*.	California becomes a US state; Samuel Pinkerton forms detective agency; death of William Wordsworth and Robert Peel; Wordsworth, *The Prelude*; Tennyson, *In Memoriam*.
1851	Melville, *Moby Dick*.	Henry Mayhew, *London Labour and the London Poor*.
1852	Mary E. Wilkins Freeman born in Massachusetts.	Harriet Beecher Stowe, *Uncle Tom's Cabin*.
1854	Francis Marion Crawford born in Italy; Dickens, *Hard Times*.	US Republican Party formed; Pope Pius IX declares doctrine of the Immaculate Conception; Oscar Wilde and Arthur Rimbaud born; Henry David Thoreau, *Walden*.

	Horror Writers	*Cultural and Historical Background*
1855	Melville, 'The Tartarus of Maids'; Dickens, *Little Dorrit*.	Lord Palmerston becomes British prime minister; death of Charlotte Brontë and Søren Kierkegaard; Henry Wadsworth Longfellow, *Song of Hiawatha*; Walt Whitman, *Leaves of Grass*; Elizabeth Gaskell, *North and South*.
1857	Ronald Ross born in India; Richard Marsh born in London.	Indian Mutiny; Elisha Otis installs first elevator, in New York City; Obscene Publications Act, UK; Edward Elgar and Joseph Conrad born; Flaubert, *Madame Bovary*; Thomas Hughes, *Tom Brown's Schooldays*; Anthony Trollope, *Barchester Towers*; Charles Baudelaire, *Les Fleurs du mal*.
1859	Arthur Conan Doyle born in Edinburgh; Fitz-James O'Brien, 'What Was It?'; Dickens, *A Tale of Two Cities*.	Work begins on Suez Canal; Henri Bergson, Knut Hamsen, and Alfred Dreyfus born; Charles Darwin, *On the Origin of Species*; George Eliot, *Adam Bede*; Edward Fitzgerald, *The Rubáiyát of Omar Khayyám*; John Stuart Mill, *On Liberty*; Samuel Smiles, *Self-Help*.
1860	Charlotte Perkins Gilman born in Connecticut; Dickens, *Great Expectations*.	Abraham Lincoln elected US president; death of Arthur Schopenhauer; Wilkie Collins, *The Woman in White*; George Eliot, *The Mill on the Floss*.
1862	Death of Fitz-James O'Brien; M. R. James born in Goodnestone, Kent.	Jefferson Davis inaugurated as president of Confederacy; US Civil War: Battles of Shiloh, Bull Run and Antietam; Otto von Bismarck becomes prime minister of Prussia; Victor Hugo, *Les Misérables*; Mary Elizabeth Braddon, *Lady Audley's Secret*.
1863	Arthur Machen born in Caerleon; W. W. Jacobs born in Wapping; Ambrose Bierce fights as Union officer at Battle of Chickamauga.	First US transcontinental railroad begins construction; Abraham Lincoln, Gettysburg Address; death of Thackeray; Charles Kingsley, *The Water-Babies*.
1864	Death of Nathaniel Hawthorne; Le Fanu, *Uncle Silas*; Dickens, *Our Mutual Friend*.	Dostoevsky, *Notes from Underground*; Verne, *Journey to the Centre of the Earth*.
1865	Rudyard Kipling born in India; Robert W. Chambers born in Brooklyn.	Assassination of Abraham Lincoln; surrender of Robert E. Lee ends American Civil War; Gregor Mendel formulates genetic theory; W. B. Yeats born; Lewis Carroll, *Alice's Adventures in Wonderland*.

	Horror Writers	Cultural and Historical Background
1867	E. F. Benson born in Wellington College, Berkshire.	Karl Marx, *Das Kapital*, vol. i; Arnold, 'Dover Beach'.
1868		Discovery of Cro-Magnon man; public hangings abolished in UK; Wilkie Collins, *The Moonstone*; Dostoevsky, *The Idiot*.
1869	Algernon Blackwood born in Shooter's Hill, Kent.	National Women's Suffrage Organization founded in New York; First Vatican Council opens; Leo Tolstoy, *War and Peace*; Matthew Arnold, *Culture and Anarchy*.
1870	Death of Charles Dickens.	Franco-Prussian War (1870–1); Verne, *Twenty-Thousand Leagues Under the Sea*; Sacher-Masoch, *Venus in Furs*.
1872	Le Fanu, *In a Glass Darkly*.	*Mary Celeste* mystery; Thomas Hardy, *Under the Greenwood Tree*.
1876		Alexander Graham Bell invents telephone; Cesare Lombroso, *The Criminal Man*.
1877	William Hope Hodgson born in Essex.	Queen Victoria proclaimed empress of India.
1879		Edison produces electric light bulb; Anglo-Zulu War; Twain, *Tom Sawyer*.
1881	Stevenson, 'The Body Snatcher' and *Treasure Island*; Ross, 'The Vivisector Vivisected' (1881–2).	Death of Dostoevsky and Benjamin Disraeli.
1885	W. F. Harvey born in York; Zola, *Germinal*.	Leopold II of Belgium establishes Congo Free State; Louis Pasteur produces rabies vaccine; General Charles Gordon killed in Khartoum; H. Rider Haggard, *King Solomon's Mines*; Mark Twain, *Huckleberry Finn*.
1886	Stevenson, *Strange Case of Dr Jekyll and Mr Hyde* and *Kidnapped*.	Hardy, *The Mayor of Casterbridge*.
1887	Doyle, *A Study in Scarlet* (first appearance of Sherlock Holmes).	Hermetic Order of the Golden Dawn founded; Rider Haggard, *She*; Boris Karloff born.
1889	Bierce, 'Chickamauga'; Stevenson, *The Master of Ballantrae*.	Eiffel Tower constructed; death of Wilkie Collins, Gerard Manley Hopkins, and Robert Browning.

	Horror Writers	Cultural and Historical Background
1890	Kipling, 'The Mark of the Beast'; Stevenson moves to Samoa.	H. P. Lovecraft born; William Morris, *News from Nowhere*; William James, *Principles of Psychology*.
1891	Death of Herman Melville; first Sherlock Holmes story published in the *Strand Magazine*.	Death of Madame Blavatsky; Wilde, *The Picture of Dorian Gray*; Huysmans, *Là-Bas*.
1892	Gilman, 'The Yellow Wall Paper'; Doyle, *The Adventures of Sherlock Holmes*; Kipling, *Barrack Room Ballads*.	Gladstone becomes prime minister for third time; Dimitri Ivanovski discovers the virus; Max Nordau, *Degeneration*.
1893	Doyle, 'The Adventure of the Final Problem' (death of Sherlock Holmes); M. R. James reads first ghost stories to Chitchat Society, Cambridge University.	Sigmund Freud and Josef Breuer, *Studies in Hysteria*.
1894	Death of Robert Louis Stevenson; Machen, *The Great God Pan*; Kipling, *Jungle Books*; Doyle, *The Memoirs of Sherlock Holmes*.	Alfred Dreyfus arrested and convicted of treason; Martial Bourdin attempts to blow up Greenwich Observatory.
1895	Machen, *The Three Impostors*; Chambers, *The King in Yellow*.	Oscar Wilde trial; discovery of the X-ray; Lumière brothers develop moving pictures; H. G. Wells, *The Time Machine*; Marie Corelli, *The Sorrows of Satan*.
1897	Stoker, *Dracula*; Marsh, *The Beetle*.	Wells, *The Invisible Man*.
1898	Marsh, 'The Adventure of Lady Wishaw's Hand'; Zola, 'J'accuse'.	Spanish–American War; Wells, *War of the Worlds*; Wilde, *The Ballad of Reading Gaol*; Henry James, *The Turn of the Screw*; Conrad's 'Heart of Darkness' in *Blackwood's Magazine*.
1899	Machen joins Order of the Golden Dawn.	Boer War; Boxer Rebellion; Sigmund Freud, *The Interpretation of Dreams*.
1902	Death of Émile Zola; Jacobs, 'The Monkey's Paw'; Freeman, 'Luella Miller'; Doyle, *The Hound of the Baskervilles*; Kipling, *Just So Stories*; Ronald Ross wins Nobel Prize for Medicine.	End of Boer War; coronation of Edward VII.

	Horror Writers	Cultural and Historical Background
1904	James, *Ghost Stories of an Antiquary*.	Theodore Roosevelt becomes US president; Conrad, *Nostromo*; J. M. Barrie, *Peter Pan*.
1905	Crawford, 'For the Blood is the Life'; Doyle, *The Return of Sherlock Holmes*; M. R. James becomes provost of King's College, Cambridge.	Trans-Siberian Railway opens; death of Jules Verne and Henry Irving; Albert Einstein, Theory of Special Relativity.
1907	Rudyard Kipling wins Nobel Prize for Literature; Machen, *The Hill of Dreams*.	W. H. Auden born; Conrad, *The Secret Agent*.
1908	Blackwood, *John Silence, Physician Extraordinary*; Hodgson, *The House on the Borderland*.	Ford Model T goes on sale; E. M. Forster, *A Room with a View*; Kenneth Grahame, *The Wind in the Willows*.
1909	Death of Francis Marion Crawford.	Louis Bleriot flies across English Channel; Wells, *Tono-Bungay*.
1910	Blackwood, 'The Wendigo'; Harvey, 'August Heat'.	Mexican Revolution; first horror film released, an adaptation of *Frankenstein*; death of Mark Twain and Leo Tolstoy; Gaston Leroux, *The Phantom of the Opera*; Forster, *Howards End*.
1911	Stoker, *The Lair of the White Worm*; James, *More Ghost Stories of an Antiquary*.	Conrad, *Under Western Eyes*.
1912	Death of Bram Stoker; Benson, 'The Room in the Tower'; Hodgson, 'The Derelict' and *The Night Land*; Doyle, *The Lost World*.	Republic of China formed; sinking of RMS *Titanic*; Woodrow Wilson elected US president; Scott expedition to South Pole ends in disaster; Carl Jung, *Psychology of the Unconscious*.
1913	Bierce travels to Mexico to cover revolution.	Freud, *Totem and Taboo*; D. H. Lawrence, *Sons and Lovers*; Marcel Proust, *Swann's Way*.
1914	Probable death of Ambrose Bierce.	Assassination of Archduke Franz Ferdinand of Austria; First World War begins; Irish Home Rule; James Joyce, *Dubliners*; Edgar Rice Burroughs, *Tarzan of the Apes*; Wyndham Lewis, *BLAST*, vol. i.

	Horror Writers	Cultural and Historical Background
1915	Death of Richard Marsh; Gilman, *Herland*.	First large-scale use of poison gas as a weapon; first Zeppelin raid on England; Albert Einstein, General Theory of Relativity; Joyce, *A Portrait of the Artist as a Young Man*; Lawrence, *The Rainbow*; T. S. Eliot, 'The Love Song of J. Alfred Prufrock'; Franz Kafka, *Metamorphosis*.
1918	Death of William Hope Hodgson; M. R. James becomes provost of Eton.	First World War ends; influenza pandemic kills *c*.100,000,000 worldwide; Lytton Strachey, *Eminent Victorians*.
1919	James, *A Thin Ghost and Others*.	Benito Mussolini founds Italian Fascist movement; Amritsar Massacre; Treaty of Versailles.
1925	James, *A Warning to the Curious*.	Mussolini becomes dictator of Italy; John Scopes tried and found guilty in Arkansas of teaching Darwinism; death of H. Rider Haggard; Hitler, *Mein Kampf*; F. Scott Fitzgerald, *The Great Gatsby*.
1928	Harvey, 'The Beast with Five Fingers'.	Frederick Griffith proves existence of DNA; John Logie Baird demonstrates colour television; Lawrence, *Lady Chatterley's Lover*.
1930	Death of Arthur Conan Doyle and Mary E. Wilkins Freeman.	Haile Selassie crowned emperor of Abyssinia; Mahatma Gandhi initiates Indian civil disobedience; death of D. H. Lawrence; William Faulkner, *As I Lay Dying*; Dashiell Hammett, *The Maltese Falcon*.
1933	Death of Robert W. Chambers.	Adolf Hitler becomes chancellor of Germany; Franklin Delano Roosevelt becomes US president; Leó Szilárd devises theory of nuclear chain reaction; Wells, *The Shape of Things to Come*; George Orwell, *Down and Out in Paris and London*; Cooper and Schoedsack, *King Kong*.
1935	Death of Charlotte Perkins Gilman.	Hitler announces German rearmament; Eliot, *Murder in the Cathedral*; James Whale, *The Bride of Frankenstein*.
1936	Death of Rudyard Kipling and M. R. James; Algernon Blackwood appears on *Picture Page*, first British TV programme.	Spanish Civil War begins; Berlin Olympics; abdication of Edward VIII; Daphne Du Maurier, *Jamaica Inn*; Dylan Thomas, *Twenty-five Poems*.

	Horror Writers	*Cultural and Historical Background*
1937	Death of W. F. Harvey.	Sino-Japanese War; death of H. P. Lovecraft; Agatha Christie, *Death on the Nile*; J. R. R. Tolkien, *The Hobbit*.
1940	Death of E. F. Benson.	Winston Churchill becomes British prime minister; Battle of Britain; Blitzkrieg bombing campaign begins; Leon Trotsky assassinated; Ernest Hemingway, *For Whom the Bell Tolls*; Alfred Hitchcock, *Rebecca*.
1943	Death of W. W. Jacobs.	Allied invasion of Italy; Warsaw Ghetto Uprising; first US bombing raids on Germany; Jean Paul Sartre, *Being and Nothingness*.
1947	Death of Arthur Machen.	Cold War begins; Partition of British Indian Empire into the independent states of India and Pakistan; Stephen King born; Albert Camus, *The Plague*; Ray Bradbury, *Dark Carnival*; Tennessee Williams, *A Streetcar Named Desire*; Powell and Pressburger, *Black Narcissus*.
1951	Death of Algernon Blackwood.	Korean War (1950–3); Festival of Britain; thermonuclear bomb developed; Ferranti Mark I becomes first commercially available computer; John Wyndham, *The Day of the Triffids*; J. D. Salinger, *The Catcher in the Rye*.

HORROR STORIES

E. T. A. HOFFMANN

The Sandman

❖

Nathanael to Lothar

YOU must all be very worried by my not having written for so long. Mother is probably angry, and Clara, I dare say, thinks that I am living in the lap of luxury and have completely forgotten the lovely, angelic image which is so deeply imprinted on my heart and mind. That is not so, however; I think of you all, daily and hourly, and in my sweet dreams the amiable figure of my lovely Clara passes, smiling at me with her bright eyes as charmingly as she used to whenever I called on you. Oh, how could I possibly have written to you in the tormented state of mind which has distracted all my thoughts until now! Something appalling has entered my life! Dark forebodings of a hideous, menacing fate are looming over me like the shadows of black clouds, impervious to any kindly ray of sunlight. It is time for me to tell you what has befallen me. I realize that I must, but at the very thought mad laughter bursts from within me. Oh, my dear Lothar, how am I ever to convey to you that what happened to me a few days ago has indeed managed to devastate my life so cruelly! If only you were here, you could see for yourself; but now you must undoubtedly consider me a crack-brained, superstitious fool. To cut a long story short, the appalling event that befell me, the fatal memory of which I am vainly struggling to escape, was simply this: a few days ago, at twelve noon on 30 October to be precise, a barometer-seller entered my room and offered me his wares. Instead of buying anything, I threatened to throw him downstairs, whereupon he departed of his own accord.

You will apprehend that this incident must gain its significance from associations peculiar to myself, reaching far back into my own life, and that it must have been the personality of this unfortunate tradesman that had such a repulsive effect on me. That is indeed the case. I am using all my strength to compose myself so that I may calmly and patiently tell you enough about my early youth for your lively imagination to visualize everything in distinct and luminous images. As I prepare to begin, I hear you laugh, while Clara says: 'What childish nonsense!' Laugh, I beg you, laugh and mock me as much as you please! But, God in heaven! the hair is rising on my scalp, and I feel as though I were begging you to mock me in mad despair, as Franz Moor begged Daniel.* Now, let me get on with the story!

During the day, except at lunch, my brothers and sisters and I saw little of our father. He was no doubt heavily occupied with his duties. After dinner, which was served at seven in accordance with the old custom, all of us, including our mother, would go into our father's study and sit at a round table. Our father would smoke tobacco and drink a big glass of beer with it. He would tell us many wondrous tales, and would become so excited over them that his pipe always went out; I would then have to light it again by holding out burning paper, which I greatly enjoyed. Often, however, he would give us picture-books and sit silent and motionless in his armchair, blowing such clouds of smoke that we all seemed to be swathed in mist. On such evenings our mother would be very melancholy, and hardly had the clock struck nine than she would say: 'Now, children, time for bed! The Sandman* is coming, I can tell.'

Whenever she said this, I would indeed hear something coming noisily upstairs with rather heavy, slow steps; it must be the Sandman. On one occasion I found this hollow trampling particularly alarming, and asked my mother as she was shepherding us away: 'Mother! who is the wicked Sandman who always chases us away from Papa? What does he look like?'

'There is no such person as the Sandman, dear child,' replied my mother; 'when I say the Sandman is coming, that just means that you are sleepy, and can't keep your eyes open, as though someone had thrown sand in them.'

My mother's answer did not satisfy me; indeed my childish mind formed the conviction that our mother was only denying the Sandman's existence so that we should not be afraid of him; after all, I could always hear him coming upstairs. Filled with curiosity about this Sandman and his relation to us children, I finally asked my youngest sister's old nurse what kind of man the Sandman was.

'Why, Natty,' replied the old woman, 'don't you know that yet?

He's a wicked man who comes to children when they don't want to go to bed and throws handfuls of sand into their eyes; that makes their eyes fill with blood and jump out of their heads, and he throws the eyes into his bag and takes them into the crescent moon to feed his own children, who are sitting in the nest there; the Sandman's children have crooked beaks, like owls, with which to peck the eyes of naughty human children.'

I now formed a hideous mental picture of the cruel Sandman, and as soon as the heavy steps came upstairs in the evening, I would tremble with fear and horror. My mother could extract nothing from me except the stammering, tearful cry: 'The Sandman! the Sandman!' I would then run to my bedroom and be tormented all night by the frightful apparition of the Sandman.

Soon I grew old enough to realize that the nurse's tale of the Sandman and his children's nest in the crescent moon could not be exactly true; yet the Sandman remained for me a fearsome spectre, and terror, indeed horror,* would seize upon me when I heard him not only coming upstairs but also pulling open the door of my father's room and entering. Sometimes he would stay away for a long period; then he would come several times in quick succession. This went on for years, during which I never became accustomed to these sinister happenings, and my image of the hideous Sandman lost nothing of its vividness. His dealings with my father began increasingly to occupy my imagination; I was prevented from asking my father about them by an unconquerable timidity, but the desire to investigate the mystery myself grew stronger as the years went by. The Sandman had aroused my interest in the marvellous and extraordinary, an interest that readily takes root in a child's mind. I liked nothing better than hearing or reading horrific stories about goblins, witches, dwarfs, and so forth; but pride of place always belonged to the Sandman, and I kept drawing him, in the strangest and most loathsome forms, with chalk or charcoal on tables, cupboards, and walls.

When I was ten, my mother made me move from my nursery to a little bedroom just along the corridor from my father's room. We were still obliged to go to bed whenever the clock struck nine and we heard the unknown being in the house. From my bedroom I could hear him entering my father's room, and soon afterwards a fine, strange-smelling vapour seemed to spread through the house. As my curiosity increased, so did my resolve to make the Sandman's acquaintance by some means or other. Often, when my mother had gone past, I would slip out of my bedroom into the corridor, but I never managed to discover anything; for the Sandman had always entered the room before I reached the spot at which he would have been visible. Finally, impelled by an irresistible urge, I decided to hide in my father's room and await the Sandman's arrival.

One evening I perceived from my father's silence and my mother's low spirits that the Sandman was coming; accordingly I pretended to be very tired, left the room before nine, and concealed myself in a recess just beside the door. The front door creaked and slow, heavy, rumbling steps approached the staircase. My mother hastened past me with my brothers and sisters. Gently, gently, I opened the door of my father's study. He was sitting, as usual, silent and motionless with his back to the door, and did not notice me; I slipped inside and hid behind the curtain which was drawn in front of an open wardrobe next to the door. The rumbling steps came closer and closer; strange sounds of coughing, scraping, and muttering could be heard. My heart was quaking with fear and anticipation. Right outside the door, a firm step, a violent tug at the latch, and the door sprang open with a clatter. Bracing myself with an effort, I peeped cautiously out. The Sandman was standing in the middle of the room, facing my father, with the lights shining brightly in his face. The Sandman, the frightful Sandman, was the old advocate Coppelius,* who sometimes had lunch with us!

But the most hideous of shapes could not have filled me with deeper horror than this same Coppelius. Imagine a big, broad-shouldered man with a massive, misshapen head, a pair of piercing, greenish, cat-like eyes sparkling from under bushy grey eyebrows, and a large beaky nose hanging over his upper lip. His crooked mouth was often distorted in a malicious smile, and then a couple of dark red spots appeared on his cheeks, and a strange hissing sound proceeded from between his clenched teeth. Coppelius was always seen wearing an ash-grey coat of old-fashioned cut, with waistcoat and breeches to match, but with black stockings and shoes with little jewelled buckles. His small wig scarcely covered more than the crown of his head, his greasy locks stood on end above his big red ears, and a large, tightly tied pigtail stuck out from the back of his neck, disclosing the silver buckle that fastened his crimped cravat. His entire appearance was repellent and disgusting; but we children had a particular aversion to his big, gnarled, hairy hands, and anything touched by them ceased at once to be appetizing. Once he noticed this, he took delight in finding some pretext for fingering a piece of cake or fruit that our kind mother had surreptitiously put on our plates, so that our loathing and disgust prevented us, with tears in our eyes, from enjoying the titbit that was supposed to give us pleasure. He behaved in just the same way on special days, when our father would pour out a small glass of sweet wine. Coppelius would then quickly pass his hand over it, or he would raise the glass to his blue lips and utter a fiendish laugh on seeing us unable to express our vexation other than by suppressed sobs. He used to refer to us only as 'the little beasts'; in his presence we were forbidden to utter a sound, and we cursed the ugly, unfriendly man, who was deliberately intent on spoiling our slightest pleasures. Our mother seemed to hate the odious Coppelius as much as we did; for as soon as he showed himself, her good spirits, her cheerful, relaxed manner, were transformed into sorrowful and gloomy gravity. Our father behaved towards him as though Coppelius were a higher being whose foibles must be endured and who had to be kept in a good mood at whatever cost. Coppelius had only to drop a hint, and his favourite dishes were cooked and rare wines opened.

On seeing Coppelius now, I realized with horror and alarm that he and none other must be the Sandman; but to me the Sandman was no longer the bogy man in the nursery story who brings children's eyes to feed his brood in their nest in the crescent moon. No! He was a hateful, spectral monster, bringing misery, hardship, and perdition, both temporal and eternal, wherever he went.

I was rooted to the spot. Despite the risk of being discovered and, as I was well aware, of being severely punished, I stayed there, listening, and poking my head between the curtains. My father welcomed Coppelius with much formality.

'Come on, let's get to work!' cried Coppelius in a hoarse, croaking voice, throwing off his coat.

My father, silent and frowning, took off his dressing-gown, and the two of them donned long black smocks. I did not notice where these came from. My father opened the folding doors of a cupboard; but I saw that what I had so long taken for a cupboard was instead a dark recess containing a small fireplace. Coppelius walked over to it, and a blue flame crackled up from the hearth. All manner of strange instruments were standing around. Merciful heavens! As my old father bent down to the fire, he looked quite different. A horrible, agonizing convulsion seemed to have contorted his gentle, honest face into the hideous, repulsive mask of a fiend. He looked like Coppelius. The latter, brandishing a pair of red-hot tongs, was lifting gleaming lumps from the thick smoke and then hammering at them industriously. It seemed to me that human faces were visible on all sides, but without eyes, and with ghastly, deep, black cavities instead.

'Bring the eyes! Bring the eyes!' cried Coppelius in a hollow rumbling voice.

Gripped by uncontrollable terror, I screamed out and dived from my hiding-place on to the floor. Coppelius seized me, gnashing his teeth and bleating, 'Little beast! Little beast!' He pulled me to my feet and hurled me on to the fireplace, where the flames began to singe my hair. 'Now we've got eyes—eyes—a fine pair of children's eyes', whispered Coppelius, thrusting his hands into the flames and pulling out fragments of red-hot coal which he was about to strew in my eyes. My father raised his hands imploringly and cried: 'Master! Master! Let my Nathanael keep his eyes! Let him keep them!'

With a piercing laugh, Coppelius cried: 'All right, the boy may keep his eyes and snivel his way through his lessons; but let's examine the mechanism of his hands and feet.' And with these words he seized me so hard that my joints made a cracking noise, dislocated my hands and feet, and put them back in various sockets. 'They don't fit properly! It was all right as it was! The Old Man knew what he was doing!' hissed and muttered Coppelius; but everything went black and dim before my eyes, a sudden convulsion shot through my nerves and my frame, and I felt nothing more. A warm, gentle breath passed over my face, and I awoke from a death-like sleep; my mother was bending over me.

'Is the Sandman still there?' I stammered.

'No, my dear child, he's been gone for a long, long time, he'll do you no harm!' said my mother, kissing and cuddling her darling boy who was thus restored to life.

Why should I weary you, my dear Lothar? Why should I dwell on minute details, when so much remains to be told? Suffice it to say that I was caught eavesdropping and was roughly treated by Coppelius. Fear and terror brought on a violent fever, with which I was laid low for several weeks. 'Is the Sandman still there?' These were my first coherent words and the sign that I was cured, that my life had been saved. Now I need only tell you about the most terrifying moment of my early life; you will then be convinced that it is not the weakness of my eyesight that makes everything appear colourless, but that a sombre destiny has indeed veiled my life in a murky cloud, which perhaps I shall not penetrate until I die.

Coppelius did not show his face again, and was said to have left the town.

A year, perhaps, had gone by, and we were sitting one evening round the table, according to the old, unaltered custom. My father was in excellent spirits and told many delightful stories about the journeys he had made in his youth. Then, as it struck nine, we suddenly heard the front door creaking on its hinges, and slow, leaden steps came rumbling through the hall and up the stairs.

'That's Coppelius,' said my mother, turning pale.

'Yes! It's Coppelius,' repeated my father, in a dull, spiritless voice.

Tears burst from my mother's eyes. 'But, father, father!' she cried, 'does this have to happen?'

'This is the last time he will visit me, I promise you!' replied my father. 'Go, take the children away! Go to bed! Good night!'

I felt as though I were being crushed under a heavy, cold stone; I could hardly breathe! As I stood motionless, my mother seized me by the arm: 'Come along, Nathanael!' I allowed her to lead me away, and went into my bedroom. 'Keep quiet, and go to bed! Go to sleep!' my mother called after me; but I was so tormented by indescribable inner terror and turmoil that I could not sleep a wink. Before me stood the hateful, loathsome Coppelius, his eyes sparkling, laughing at me maliciously, and I strove in vain to rid myself of his image. It must already have been midnight when a frightful crash was heard, as though a cannon had been fired. The whole house trembled, a rattling, rustling noise passed my door, and the front door was slammed with a clatter.

'That's Coppelius!' I cried in terror, leaping out of bed. Suddenly a piercing scream of lament was heard; I raced to my father's room; the door was open, a cloud of suffocating smoke billowed towards me, and the maidservant shrieked: 'Oh, the master! the master!' On the floor in front of the smoking fireplace my father was lying dead, his face burnt black and hideously contorted, while my sisters wailed and whimpered all round him and my mother lay in a dead faint.

'Coppelius, you abominable fiend, you've murdered my father!' I shouted; then I lost consciousness.

Two days later, when my father was laid in his coffin, his features were once again as mild and gentle as they had been during his life. I was comforted by the realization that his alliance with the devilish Coppelius could not have plunged him into eternal perdition.

The explosion had roused the neighbours; the incident got out and came to the attention of the authorities, who wanted to call Coppelius to account. He, however, had vanished from the town without leaving a trace.

If I now tell you, my cherished friend, that the barometer-seller who called on me was none other than the abominable Coppelius, you will not blame me for interpreting his malevolent appearance as a portent of dire misfortune. He was differently dressed, but Coppelius's figure and features are too deeply engraved on my mind for any mistake to be possible. Besides, Coppelius has not even changed his name. I am told that he claims to be a Piedmontese* mechanic called Giuseppe Coppola.*

I am determined to try conclusions with him and avenge my father's death, come what may.

Say nothing to my mother about the appearance of this hideous monster. Give my love to my dear Clara; I will write to her when my mind is calmer. Farewell!

Clara to Nathanael

IT is true that you haven't written to me for a long time, but I am still convinced that I am in your thoughts. For you must have been preoccupied with me when, intending to send off your last letter to my brother Lothar, you addressed it to me instead of to him. I opened the letter joyfully and realized your mistake only on reading the words: 'Oh, my dear Lothar!' I should of course have read no further, but given the letter to my brother. You have sometimes teasingly accused me of such womanly calm and deliberation that if the house were about to collapse I would pause before taking flight, like the woman in the story, to smooth out a fold in the curtains; however, I need hardly tell you that I was deeply shaken by the first few sentences of your letter. I could scarcely breathe, and my head was spinning. Oh, my precious Nathanael, what terrible thing could have entered your life! The idea of parting from you, never seeing you again, pierced my heart like a red-hot dagger. I read and read! Your description of the odious Coppelius is horrible. I did not know that your good old father had met such a terrible, violent death. When I gave Lothar back his rightful property, he tried to soothe me, but without success. The frightful barometer-seller Giuseppe Coppola followed me about wherever I went, and I'm almost ashamed to confess that he disturbed even my usually sound and healthy sleep with all manner of strange dreams. But soon, on the very next day, I regained my normal state of mind. Don't be cross, dearly beloved, if Lothar happens to tell you that, despite your strange notion that Coppelius will do you an injury, I am as cheerful and relaxed as ever.

I will confess frankly that in my opinion all the terrors and horrors you describe took place only inside your head, and had very little to do with the real world outside you. Old Coppelius may have been odious enough, but it was his hatred of children that bred such a loathing of him in you children.

It was quite natural that your childish mind should connect the terrible Sandman in the nursery tale with old Coppelius, and that even when you no longer believed in the Sandman, Coppelius should seem a sinister monster, particularly hostile to children. As for his uncanny nocturnal goings-on with your father, I expect the two of them were simply conducting secret alchemical experiments, which could hardly please your mother, since a lot of money must have been squandered and moreover, as is said always to happen to such inquirers, your father became obsessed with the delusive longing for higher wisdom and was estranged from his family. Your father must have brought about his death by his own carelessness, and Coppelius cannot be to blame. Would you believe that yesterday I asked our neighbour, an experienced chemist, whether it was possible for such an explosion which killed people on the spot to occur in chemical experiments? He said, 'Why, of course', and gave me a characteristically long-winded account of how this could happen, mentioning so many strange-sounding names that I couldn't remember any of them. Now I expect you'll be angry with your Clara. You'll say: 'Her cold temperament cannot accept the mystery that often enfolds man in invisible arms; she perceives only the varied surface of the world and takes pleasure in it as a childish infant does in a glittering fruit which has deadly poison concealed within it.'

Oh, my precious Nathanael! don't you think that even a cheerful, relaxed, carefree temperament may have premonitions of a dark power that tries malevolently to attack our inmost selves? But please forgive a simple girl like me for venturing to suggest what I think about such inner conflicts. I probably shan't be able to put it into words properly, and you'll laugh at me, not because what I'm trying to say is stupid, but because I'm so clumsy at saying it.

If there is a dark power which malevolently and treacherously places a thread within us, with which to hold us and draw us down a perilous and pernicious path that we would never otherwise have set foot on—if there is such a power, then it must take the same form as we do, it must become our very self; for only in this way can we believe in it and give it the scope it requires to accomplish its secret task. If our minds, strengthened by a cheerful life, are resolute enough to recognize alien and malevolent influences for what they are and to proceed tranquilly along the path to which our inclinations and our vocation have directed us, the uncanny power must surely perish in a vain struggle to assume the form which is our own reflection. Lothar also says there is no doubt that once we have surrendered ourselves to the dark psychic power, it draws alien figures, encountered by chance in the outside world, into our inner selves, so that we ourselves give life to the spirit which our strange delusion persuades us is speaking from such figures. It is the phantom of our own self which, thanks to its intimate relationship with us and its deep influence on our minds, casts us down to hell or transports us to heaven. You see, my darling Nathanael, that Lothar and I have talked at length about dark powers and forces, and now that I have, with some labour, written down the main points, it seems to me quite profound. I don't quite understand Lothar's last words, I only have a dim idea of what he means, and yet it all sounds very true. I beg you to forget all about the hateful advocate Coppelius and the barometer-man Giuseppe Coppola. Be assured that these alien figures have no power over you; only your belief in their malevolent power can make them truly malevolent to you. If every line of your letter did not reveal the deep perturbation of your spirits, if your state of mind did not cause me pain in my very soul, then, indeed, I could make jokes about the advocate Sandman and the barometer-seller Coppelius. Keep your spirits up! If the hateful Coppola should presume to annoy you in your dreams, I am determined to appear in your presence like your guardian angel and to drive him away with loud laughter. I am not the slightest bit afraid of him or his horrid hands; I wouldn't let him spoil my appetite as an advocate, nor hurt my eyes as a Sandman.

Eternally yours, my most dearly beloved Nathanael, etc.

Nathanael to Lothar

I AM very annoyed that Clara should have opened and read my recent letter to you, although admittedly the mistake was due to my own absent-mindedness. She has written me a most profound philosophical letter in which she demonstrates at great length that Coppelius and Coppola exist only in my mind and are phantoms emanating from myself which will crumble to dust the moment I acknowledge them as such. Really, who would have thought that the spirit which shines from such clear, gracious, smiling, child-like eyes, like a sweet and lovely dream, could draw such intellectual distinctions, worthy of a university graduate? She appeals to your opinion. You and she have talked about me. I suppose you have given her lectures on logic to teach her how to sift and search all problems with due subtlety. Well, stop it at once!

Anyway, it seems certain that the barometer-seller Giuseppe Coppola is not the same person as the old advocate Coppelius. I am attending the lectures given by the newly arrived professor of physics, who is called Spalanzani, like the famous naturalist,* and is likewise of Italian descent. He has known Coppola for many years, and besides, his accent makes it clear that he really is a Piedmontese. Coppelius was a German, though not an honest one, in my opinion. My mind is not completely at ease. You and Clara are welcome to think me a melancholy dreamer, but I cannot shake off the impression that Coppelius's accursed face made on me. I am glad he has left the town, as Spalanzani tells me.

This professor is an odd fish. A tubby little man with projecting cheek-bones, a delicate nose, thick lips, and small piercing eyes. But you will get a better idea of him than any description can convey if you take a look at Cagliostro* as he is depicted by Chodowiecki* in some Berlin magazine. That is what Spalanzani looks like.

Not long ago, as I was going up his stairs, I noticed that a narrow strip of the glass door was left unconcealed by the curtain which is normally drawn across it. I can't tell how it was that I peeped in

inquisitively. Inside the room a tall, very slim woman, beautifully proportioned and magnificently dressed, was sitting in front of a small
table on which she was leaning, with her hands folded. She was facing
the door, so that I had a full view of her angelic face. She seemed not
to notice me, and indeed there was something lifeless about her eyes,
as though they lacked the power of sight; she seemed to be asleep with
her eyes open. I had a rather uncanny feeling, and crept softly into
the lecture-hall next door. Afterwards I learnt that the figure I had
seen was Spalanzani's daughter Olimpia, whom, strangely and repre-
hensibly, he keeps locked up, so that nobody at all is allowed near her.
There must be something peculiar about her; perhaps she is feeble-
minded, for example. But why am I writing all this to you? I could
have told you all this better and more fully by word of mouth. For let
me tell you that in two weeks' time I shall be with you. I must see my
dear sweet angel, my Clara, again. Her presence will blow away the
mood of irritation which, I must confess, almost mastered me after
that damnably sensible letter. That's why I won't write to her today.

   Best wishes, etc.

No invention could be stranger or more extraordinary than the events
which befell my poor friend, the young student Nathanael, and which
I have undertaken to recount to you, dear reader. Have you, my kind
patron, ever had an experience that entirely absorbed your heart,
your mind, and your thoughts, banishing all other concerns? You
were seething and boiling inwardly; your fiery blood raced through
your veins and gave a richer colour to your cheeks. You had a strange,
fixed stare as though you were trying to make out forms, invisible to
any other eyes, in empty space, and your words faded into obscure
sighs. 'What's wrong, my dear fellow? Whatever's the matter, old
chap?' inquired your friends. And you, anxious to convey your inner
vision with all its glowing colours, its lights and shadows, laboured
in vain to find words with which to begin. But you felt as though you
must compress the entire wonderful, splendid, terrible, hilarious, and
hideous experience into your very first word, so that it should strike
your hearers like an electric shock; yet every word, all the resources of
language, seemed faded, frosty, and dead. You searched and searched,
and stammered and stuttered, and your friends' matter-of-fact questions were like gusts of icy air blowing on your inner glow and well-
nigh extinguishing it. But if, like a bold painter, you had first sketched

the outlines of your inner vision with a few careless strokes, you had little trouble in adding ever brighter colours until the swirling throng of multifarious figures seized hold of your friends' imagination, and they saw themselves, like you, in the midst of the picture that arose from your mind!

I must confess, kind reader, that nobody has actually asked me to tell the story of young Nathanael; you are aware, however, that I belong to the curious race of authors, who, if they are filled with such a vision as I have just described, feel as though everyone who approaches them, and all the world besides, were asking: 'Whatever's the matter? Tell me everything, my dear fellow!' Thus I felt powerfully impelled to tell you about Nathanael's calamitous life. Its strange and wondrous character absorbed my entire soul; but for that very reason, and because, dear reader, I have to put you in the right mood to endure an odd tale, which is no easy matter, I racked my brains to find a portentous, original, and arresting way of beginning Nathanael's story. 'Once upon a time . . .'—the best way to begin any story, but too down-to-earth! 'In the small provincial town of S. there lived . . .'—somewhat better: at least it provides some build-up to the climax. Or why not plunge *medias in res*:* ' "Go to the Devil!", cried the student Nathanael, wild-eyed with fury and terror, as the barometer-seller Giuseppe Coppola . . .'. I had in fact written this down, when I fancied there was something comical in the student Nathanael looking wild-eyed; this story, however, is no laughing matter. Unable to find words that seemed to reflect anything of the prismatic radiance of my inner vision, I decided not to begin at all. Be so good, dear reader, as to accept the three letters, kindly communicated to me by my friend Lothar, as the sketch for my portrayal; as I tell the story, I shall endeavour to add more and more colour to it. I may, like a good portraitist, succeed in depicting some figures so well that you find them good likenesses even without knowing the originals; indeed, you may feel as though you had often seen these persons with your very own eyes. Then, O my reader, you may come to believe that nothing can be stranger or weirder than real life, and that the poet can do no more than capture the strangeness of reality, like the dim reflection in a dull mirror.

In order to put you more fully in the picture, I must add that soon after the death of Nathanael's father, his mother had taken Clara and Lothar, the children of a distant relative who had likewise died and left them orphans, into the household. Clara and Nathanael became warmly attached to each other, and nobody could possibly have any objection to this; hence they were engaged by the time Nathanael left the town in order to continue his studies in G***. His last letter was written from G***, where he was attending lectures by the famous professor of physical sciences, Spalanzani.

I might now go on cheerfully with my story; but at this instant the image of Clara is so vividly present to me that I cannot look away, as always happened when she used to look at me with her lovely smile. Clara could by no means be called beautiful; that was the judgement of all professional authorities on beauty. Yet the architects praised her perfectly proportioned figure, while the painters raved about the chaste lines of her neck, her shoulders, and her breasts, fell in love with her wonderful hair, which reminded them of Battoni's Mary Magdalen,* and talked a lot of nonsense about Battoni's colouring techniques. One of them, however, a true fantasist, drew a very odd comparison between Clara's eyes and a lake by Ruysdael* which reflected the pure azure of the cloudless sky, the forests and flowery meadows, and the varied, happy life of the fertile landscape. Poets and musicians went further and said: 'Lake? Reflection? How can we look at the girl without perceiving wondrous, heavenly sounds and songs radiating from her gaze and penetrating and vivifying our very hearts? If we ourselves can't produce a decent song after that, we must be good for very little, and that indeed is the message of the sly smile that hovers around Clara's lips whenever we venture on some jingle that claims to be a song, though it consists only of a few incoherent notes.'

Such was the case. Clara had the vivid imagination of a cheerful, ingenuous, child-like child, a deep heart filled with womanly tenderness, and a very acute, discriminating mind. She was no friend to muddle-headed enthusiasts; for although she uttered few words, being taciturn by nature, her clear gaze and her sly, ironic smile said: 'Dear friends, how can you expect me to treat your shifting, shadowy images as real objects full of life and motion?' Many people accordingly criticized Clara for being cold, unresponsive, and prosaic; others, however, who saw life clearly and profoundly, were very fond of the warm-hearted, sensible, child-like girl, but none so much as Nathanael, who was energetic and cheerful in his approach to art and learning. Clara was intensely devoted to him, and their parting cast the first shadow on her life. With what rapture did she fly to his arms when he entered his mother's room, having returned home as he had promised in his last letter to Lothar. Nathanael's expectations were fulfilled; for on seeing Clara he thought neither about the advocate Coppelius nor about Clara's sensible letter, and all his irritation vanished.

Nathanael, however, was quite right when he told his friend Lothar that the figure of the repulsive barometer-seller Coppola had made a malevolent intrusion into his life. Even in the first few days of his visit, it was apparent to everyone that Nathanael's character had changed entirely. He fell into gloomy reveries and took to behaving in a strange and wholly unaccustomed way. To him, all life consisted of dreams and premonitions; he kept saying that each individual, fancying himself to be free, only served as a plaything for the cruelty of dark forces; that it was in vain to resist, and one must acquiesce humbly in the decrees of destiny. He went so far as to assert that artists and scholars were under a delusion when they believed that their creative endeavours were governed by the autonomy of their will: 'for', said he, 'the inspired state which is indispensable for creation does not arise from inside ourselves; it is due to the influence of a higher principle that lies outside us'.

The sensible Clara greatly disliked these mystical flights of fancy, but there seemed no point in trying to refute them. It was only when Nathanael maintained that Coppelius was the evil principle that had seized upon him when he was eavesdropping behind the curtain, and that this foul demon would wreak destruction upon their happy love, that Clara would become very serious and say: 'Yes, Nathanael, you're right! Coppelius is an evil, malevolent principle; he can do terrible harm, like the visible manifestation of a devilish power; but only if you fail to dismiss him from your mind. As long as you believe in him, he is real and active; his power consists only in your belief.'

Indignant that Clara conceded the existence of the demon only in his own mind, Nathanael would try to launch into the mystical doctrine of devils and evil forces, but Clara would irritably cut the conversation short by raising some trivial subject, to Nathanael's great annoyance. He concluded that such mysteries were inaccessible to cold and insensitive temperaments, without clearly realizing that he considered Clara's temperament to be such, and accordingly persevered in his attempts to initiate her into these mysteries. Early in the morning, when Clara was helping to make the breakfast, he would stand beside her, reading aloud from all manner of mystical books, until Clara asked: 'But, Nathanael dear, what if I were to scold *you* for being the evil principle exerting a malevolent influence on my coffee? For if I drop everything, as you demand, and gaze into your eyes while you read, the coffee will run over into the fire and none of you will get any breakfast!'

Nathanael would then clap the book shut and run angrily to his room.

In the past Nathanael had shown a special gift for composing charming and vivid stories which he would write down, and which Clara would listen to with heartfelt enjoyment. Now his compositions were gloomy, unintelligible, and formless, so that, even though Clara was too kind to say so, he was aware how little they appealed to her. Nothing had a more deadly effect on Clara than tedium; her unconquerable mental drowsiness would reveal itself in her expression and her speech. Nathanael's compositions were indeed very tedious. His annoyance with Clara's cold, prosaic temperament increased, while Clara could not overcome her irritation with Nathanael's dismal, obscure, tedious mysticism, and so, without noticing it, they became increasingly estranged from one another. Nathanael himself was obliged to confess that the figure of the hateful Coppelius had begun to fade from his imagination, and he often had difficulty in imparting lively colours to Coppelius in his compositions, where the latter appeared as a dreadful bogy man and emissary of fate. Finally he conceived the plan of writing a poem about his gloomy premonition that Coppelius would destroy his happy love. He portrayed himself and Clara as joined in true love, but every so often a black hand seemed to reach into their lives and tear out some newly discovered source of pleasure. Finally, when they are standing at the altar, the fearsome Coppelius appears and touches Clara's lovely eyes, which leap into Nathanael's breast, burning and singeing him; Coppelius seizes him and hurls him into a circle of flames which is rotating with the speed of a whirlwind, dragging him along in its fury. A tumult springs up, as when the savage hurricane lashes the ocean, whose foaming waves rear up like black giants with white heads, filled with the rage of combat. But through all the tumult he hears Clara's voice saying: 'Can't you see me? Coppelius deceived you; it wasn't my eyes that burned in your breast, but red-hot drops of your own heart's blood. I have my eyes, just look at me!' 'That is Clara', thinks Nathanael, 'and I am her own eternally.' At that moment his thought seems to reach down forcibly into the circle of flames, bringing it to a halt, and the tumult fades away in a black abyss. Nathanael gazes into Clara's eyes; but what looks at him from Clara's kindly eyes is death.

While composing this, Nathanael was calm and collected; he revised and polished every line, and, having submitted to the constraints of metre, he did not rest until the entire work was pure and melodious. Yet, when he had finished and read the poem aloud to himself, he was gripped by wild horror and terror, and shrieked: 'Whose hideous voice is this?' Before long, however, he again decided that it was a highly successful poem, which could not fail to animate Clara's cold temperament, though he had no clear idea what purpose this would serve or what might result from alarming her with hideous images prophesying the destruction of their love by a terrible fate.

They were sitting, Nathanael and Clara, in her mother's little garden. Clara was in good spirits, because during the past three days, while working on his poem, Nathanael had no longer tormented her with his dreams and premonitions. Besides, Nathanael talked in a lively, cheerful manner about pleasant matters, as in the past, so that Clara said: 'Now you're completely mine again. Do you see how we've driven that hateful Coppelius away?'

Only then did Nathanael remember that he had the poem in his pocket and had been meaning to read it aloud. He promptly drew it out and began reading, while Clara, resigned to the prospect of something tedious as usual, quietly began knitting. But as the cloud of gloom swelled up in ever-deepening blackness, she let her knitting fall from her hands and gazed fixedly at Nathanael. The latter was entirely carried away by his poem: his cheeks burned with the fire within him, tears gushed from his eyes. Finished at last, he gave a sigh of exhaustion. He seized Clara's hand and moaned miserably: 'Oh! Clara! Clara!'

Clara gave him a gentle hug and said in a low voice, but slowly and seriously: 'Nathanael, my darling Nathanael! Throw the crazy, senseless, insane story into the fire.'

Nathanael sprang up indignantly and exclaimed, thrusting Clara away: 'You accursed lifeless automaton!' He rushed away, while Clara, deeply hurt, shed bitter tears.

'Oh, he never loved me, because he doesn't understand me,' she wailed.

Lothar entered the bower, and Clara could not help telling him what had occurred. Since he loved his sister with all his heart, every accusing word she uttered threw sparks into his mind, so that the irritation he had long felt with the dreamy Nathanael was inflamed into furious anger. He ran to Nathanael and rebuked him harshly for his senseless behaviour towards Lothar's dearly loved sister. Nathanael flew into a passion and replied in kind. They called each other a mad, fantastical coxcomb and a wretched, vulgar philistine. A duel was inevitable. They decided to meet next morning behind the garden and fight with sharpened rapiers, as was customary among the local students. In the mean time, they crept about, silent and scowling. Clara overheard their violent quarrel and saw the fencing-master bringing the rapiers at daybreak. She guessed what was afoot. Lothar and Nathanael arrived at the scene of their duel in gloomy silence; they removed their coats and were about to assail each other, their eyes burning with the blood-thirsty fury of combat, when Clara rushed through the garden gate.

'You dreadful savages!' she cried amid her sobs, 'strike me down first before you attack each other; for how can I go on living if my lover has murdered my brother, or my brother has killed my lover!'

Lothar lowered his weapon and looked silently at the ground, but Nathanael, with a shock of heart-rending sorrow, recollected all the love he had felt for his adorable Clara in the most glorious days of his youth. The fatal implement fell from his hand and he threw himself at Clara's feet.

'Can you ever forgive me, my only, my beloved Clara! Can you forgive me, my beloved brother Lothar!'

Lothar was touched by his friend's agony; amid floods of tears, the three embraced in token of reconciliation and swore unfailing love and loyalty to one another.

Nathanael felt as though relieved of a heavy burden which had been crushing him, and as though, by resisting the dark forces which had ensnared him, he had saved his entire existence from the threat of annihilation. He spent three more blissful days among his dear ones, then returned to G***, where he intended to stay for another year before returning to his home town for good.

Everything relating to Coppelius was kept from his mother; for it was known that she could not think without horror of the man whom she, like Nathanael, held responsible for her husband's death.

On returning to his lodgings, Nathanael was astonished to discover that the whole house had been burnt to the ground. Nothing remained amid the ruins but the fire-walls separating it from the adjacent houses. Although the fire had broken out in the laboratory of the apothecary who lived on the ground floor, and the house had burnt from the bottom up, Nathanael's bold and energetic friends had managed to get into his upstairs room in time to save his books, manuscripts, and instruments. They had removed all these things, which were undamaged, to another house, and taken possession of a room there, which Nathanael immediately moved into. He paid no particular heed to the fact that he was now living opposite Professor Spalanzani; nor did he think it specially noteworthy that his window looked straight into the room where Olimpia often sat by herself, so that he could clearly make out her shape, although her features remained blurred and indistinct. He was eventually struck by the fact that Olimpia often spent hours sitting at a little table, just as he had previously glimpsed her through the glass door, without doing anything, but gazing rigidly across at him; he was also obliged to confess that he had never seen a more shapely woman, but, with Clara in his heart, he remained indifferent to the stiff and motionless Olimpia. Only occasionally did he glance up from his textbook at the beautiful statue: that was all.

Just as Nathanael was writing to Clara, there came a soft tap at the door. On his calling 'Come in!' it opened, and in peeped Coppola's repulsive face. Nathanael felt himself quaking inwardly; however, mindful of what Spalanzani had said about his fellow-countryman Coppola, and of his own sacred promise to Clara concerning the Sandman Coppelius, he felt ashamed of his childish superstition, pulled himself together with a great effort, and spoke as calmly and gently as he could: 'I don't wish to buy any barometers, my friend! Be off with you!'

Now, however, Coppola came right into the room; contorting his wide mouth into a hideous grin and giving a piercing look from under his long grey lashes, he said hoarsely: 'No barometer, no barometer! I 'ave beautiful eyes-a to sell you, beautiful eyes-a!'

'You madman,' cried Nathanael in horror, 'how can you have eyes to sell? Eyes?'

But Coppola had already put his barometers aside; he reached into the wide pockets of his coat and fetched out lorgnettes* and pairs of spectacles, which he placed on the table.

'Now, now, glass-a, glass-a to wear on your nose-a, dese are my eyes-a, beautiful eyes-a!' And with these words he pulled out more and more spectacles, so that the whole table began strangely gleaming and shining. Innumerable eyes flickered and winked and goggled at Nathanael; but he could not look away from the table, and Coppola put more and more spectacles on it, and their flaming eyes sprang to and fro ever more wildly, darting their blood-red rays into Nathanael's breast. Overcome by mad terror, he shrieked: 'Stop! stop, you frightful man!'—and seized Coppola by the arm as the latter was reaching into his pocket for yet more spectacles, even though the entire table was now covered with them. Coppola freed himself gently, uttering a horrible hoarse laugh, and with the words: 'No good for you—but here, beautiful glass-a!' he swept up all the spectacles, packed them away, and produced from the side-pocket of his coat a number of large and small spyglasses. As soon as the spectacles had been removed, Nathanael became perfectly calm; thinking of Clara, he realized that the hideous apparition could only have proceeded from within himself, and that Coppola must be a thoroughly honest mechanic and optician, who could not possibly be the accursed double or ghost of Coppelius. Besides, the spyglasses that Coppola had now placed on the table had nothing remarkable about them, let alone the sinister qualities of the spectacles, and, in order to make amends for his behaviour. Nathanael decided to buy something from Coppola after all. He picked up a small, beautifully made pocket spyglass and tested it by looking out of the window. Never before in his life had he come across a spyglass that brought objects before one's eyes with such clarity, sharpness, and distinctness. He involuntarily looked into Spalanzani's room; Olimpia was sitting as usual at the little table, with her arms on it and her hands folded.

Only now did Nathanael behold Olimpia's wondrously beautiful face. It was only her eyes that seemed to him strangely fixed and dead. As he peered ever more intently through the glass, however, he thought he saw moist moonbeams shining from Olimpia's eyes. It was as though her power of vision were only now being awakened; her eyes seemed to sparkle more and more vividly. Nathanael remained at the window, as though rooted to the spot by a spell, gazing uninterruptedly at Olimpia's heavenly beauty. He was aroused, like somebody lost in a dream, by the sound of foot-scraping and throat-clearing. Coppola was standing behind him.

'Tre zecchini—three ducat!'*

Nathanael, who had completely forgotten the optician, hastily paid the sum demanded.

'Beautiful glass-a, no? Beautiful glass-a?' asked Coppola in his repulsive hoarse voice, smiling maliciously.

'Yes, yes, yes!' replied Nathanael crossly. 'Good-bye, my friend!'

Coppola left the room, not without casting many strange side-glances at Nathanael, who heard him laughing loudly as he went downstairs.

'All right,' said Nathanael, 'he's laughing at me because I no doubt paid too high a price for the little spy-glass—too high a price!'

As he uttered these words in a low voice, a deep, deathly sigh seemed to send a grisly echo through the room. Nathanael caught his breath with fear. But no, it was he who had uttered the sigh, that was quite obvious.

'Clara', he said to himself, 'is probably right to think me tiresome and superstitious; but it's still a funny thing—oh, more than that, I suspect—that the silly idea that I paid too high a price for Coppola's spyglass makes me feel so oddly apprehensive; I can't think why this is.'

He then sat down in order to finish his letter to Clara, but one glance through the window convinced him that Olimpia was still sitting there, and at that instant, as though impelled by an irresistible force, he jumped up, seized Coppola's spyglass, and could not tear himself away from the alluring sight of Olimpia, until his friend and fellow-student Siegmund summoned him to Professor Spalanzani's lecture.

The curtain in front of the fateful room was drawn tight; Nathanael could neither glimpse Olimpia there nor, during the next two days, in her room, although he scarcely left his window and peered continually through Coppola's spyglass. On the third day the window was covered by drapery. In extreme despair, impelled by yearning and ardent desire, he ran out through the town gate. Olimpia's shape hovered in the air in front of him, stepped forth from the bushes, and looked at him with great radiant eyes from the clear water of the brook. The image of Clara had entirely departed from his mind; he thought only of Olimpia, and lamented out loud in a tearful voice: 'Oh, light of my life, you glorious, lofty star, did you rise upon me only to vanish again, leaving me in dark and hopeless night?'

Returning to his lodgings, he noticed a noisy upheaval going on in Spalanzani's house. The doors were open, all manner of utensils were being carried in, the first-floor windows had been taken off their hinges, busy maids were sweeping and dusting everywhere with large brooms, and inside joiners and decorators were tapping and hammering. Nathanael stood there in the street, beside himself with astonishment; Siegmund came up to him and said: 'Well, what do you think of our old Spalanzani?' Nathanael declared that he did not know what to think, since he knew nothing whatever about the Professor, but was extremely surprised to see such frantic activity going on in the quiet, gloomy house. Siegmund then informed him that Spalanzani was holding a ball and a concert the next day, and that half the university had been invited. It was rumoured abroad that Spalanzani would allow his daughter Olimpia, whom he had fearfully concealed from every human eye for so long, to make her first public appearance.

Nathanael obtained an invitation and went to the Professor's house at the appointed hour, his heart beating violently, as the carriages were rolling up and the lights were gleaming in the splendidly decorated rooms. A large and brilliant company was present. Olimpia made her appearance, sumptuously and tastefully dressed. Her beautifully moulded features and her shapely figure compelled general admiration. The slightly strange curve of her back and the wasp-like slenderness of her waist seemed to be the result of excessive tight-lacing. There was something stiff and measured about her gait and posture, which many people found displeasing; it was ascribed to the constraint imposed by such a large company.

The concert began. Olimpia played the piano with great skill and likewise performed a bravura aria in a clear, almost shrill voice, like a glass bell. Nathanael was enraptured; standing in the back row, he was unable to make out Olimpia's features clearly in the dazzling light of the candles. Without anybody noticing, he therefore took out Coppola's spyglass and looked through it at the fair Olimpia. Ah! then he perceived that she was gazing at him yearningly, and that every note she uttered found its full expression in the amorous look that pierced his heart and set it afire. The artificial roulades* seemed to Nathanael to be the heavenly jubilation of a heart transfigured by love, and when the cadenza* was at last followed by a long trill which rang and resounded through the room, he felt as though red-hot arms had suddenly seized him; unable to restrain himself, he shrieked out in agony and rapture: 'Olimpia!'

Everyone looked round at him, and many people laughed. The cathedral organist, however, scowled yet more darkly than before and said only: 'Now, now!'

The concert was over; the ball began. 'To dance with her, with *her*!'—that was now the goal of all Nathanael's wishes and desires; but how was he to find the courage to ask her, the queen of the ball, for a dance? And yet, he himself could not tell how it came about that when the dance had already begun he found himself standing close to Olimpia, who had not yet been asked for a dance, and, scarcely able to stammer out a few words, he seized her hand. Olimpia's hand was ice-cold: a shudder went through him like a hideous, deadly frost. He stared into Olimpia's eyes, which beamed at him full of love and yearning, and at that moment a pulse seemed to begin beating in her cold hand and her life's blood to flow in a glowing stream. Love and desire flared up in Nathanael's heart; he embraced the fair Olimpia and flew with her through the ranks of the dancers.

Nathanael considered himself a good dancer, but the peculiar rhythmic regularity with which Olimpia danced often disconcerted him and made him realize how badly he kept time. However, he was reluctant to dance with any other woman, and would gladly have murdered everyone who approached Olimpia to ask her to dance. Yet this only happened on two occasions; to his astonishment, Olimpia then remained without a partner, and he did not fail to draw her on to the dance-floor again and again. If Nathanael had been capable of seeing anything other than the fair Olimpia, all manner of quarrels and disputes would have been inevitable; for the young people in various corners of the room were having difficulty in suppressing their laughter, and their tittering was evidently directed at the fair Olimpia, whom they were looking at strangely for some unaccountable reason. Excited by the dance and by generous quantities of wine, Nathanael entirely cast off his usual bashfulness. He sat beside Olimpia, clasping her hand, and spoke of his love in fiery, enthusiastic words which neither he nor Olimpia understood. But perhaps *she* did; for she gazed fixedly into his eyes and sighed repeatedly: 'Oh! oh! oh!' whereupon Nathanael said: 'O you splendid, divine woman! You ray shining from the promised afterlife of love! You profound spirit, reflecting my whole existence!' and much more along the same lines; but Olimpia only sighed repeatedly: 'Oh! oh!'

Professor Spalanzani passed the happy couple once or twice and smiled upon them with an air of strange satisfaction. Although Nathanael was in the seventh heaven, he suddenly felt as though down on earth, in Professor Spalanzani's house, darkness were falling; he looked round and noticed, to his consternation, that the last two lights in the empty ballroom had burnt down to their sockets and were about to go out. The music and dancing had long since ceased. 'Parting! Parting!' he cried in frantic despair; he kissed Olimpia's hand, he bent down to her mouth, his burning lips met ice-cold ones! Just as he had done on touching Olimpia's cold hand, he felt himself gripped by inward horror, and the legend of the dead bride* suddenly flashed through his mind; but Olimpia was clasping him tightly, and his kiss seemed to bring warmth and life to her lips.

Professor Spalanzani walked slowly through the empty ballroom; his steps sounded hollow, and his figure, surrounded by flickering shadows, had an uncanny, ghostly appearance.

'Do you love me—do you love me, Olimpia? Just this word! Do you love me?' whispered Nathanael, but Olimpia, rising to her feet, only sighed: 'Oh! oh!'

'Yes, you lovely, magnificent light of my life,' said Nathanael, 'you will shine on me, transfiguring my heart for evermore!'

'Oh, oh!' responded Olimpia, moving away. Nathanael followed her. They stood before the Professor.

'You have had a remarkably animated conversation with my daughter,' said he with a smile. 'Well, my dear Nathanael, if you find pleasure in talking to the silly girl, I shall always welcome your visits.'

Nathanael was walking on air as he took his leave.

Spalanzani's ball was the main topic of conversation in the next few days. Although the Professor had endeavoured to display the utmost magnificence, the wags recounted all manner of oddities and improprieties, and criticism was levelled particularly at the rigid and silent Olimpia. Despite the beauty of her appearance, it was alleged that she was a complete imbecile, and that this was the reason why Spalanzani had kept her concealed for so long. Nathanael heard this with suppressed anger, but he held his peace; 'for', thought he, 'what would be the point of proving to these fellows that it is their own imbecility which prevents them from appreciating the wonderful depths of Olimpia's heart?'

'Do me a favour, old chap,' said Siegmund one day, 'and tell me how a sensible fellow like you could be besotted with that dummy, that wax doll?'

Nathanael was about to fly into a fury, but he controlled himself and replied: 'You tell me, Siegmund, how, with your sharp perceptions and your appreciation of beauty, you could fail to notice Olimpia's heavenly charms? But I thank the fates that, for that reason, I don't have you as a rival; otherwise one of us would have to perish.'

Observing his friend's state of mind, Siegmund backed down and remarked that in love there was no disputing about tastes. 'It's odd, though', he added, 'that many of us share the same opinion of Olimpia. We thought her—don't take this amiss, old chap!—strangely stiff and lacking in animation. Her figure is regular, certainly, and so is her face. She would be beautiful, but that her eyes seem to have no ray of life; they almost seem to lack the power of sight. Her gait is curiously measured, as though her every movement were produced by some mechanism like clockwork. She plays and sings with the disagreeably perfect, soulless timing of a machine, and she dances similarly. Olimpia gave us a very weird feeling; we wanted nothing to do with her; we felt that she was only pretending to be a living being, and that there was something very strange about her.'

Nathanael refrained from giving way to the bitterness that Siegmund's words aroused in him. He mastered his annoyance and only said, in grave tones: 'Olimpia may well inspire a weird feeling in cold, prosaic people like you. It is only to the poetic soul that a similarly organized soul reveals itself! I was the only one to arouse her loving gaze, which radiated through my heart and mind; only in Olimpia's love do I recognize myself. People like you may complain because she doesn't engage in trivial chit-chat, like other banal minds. She utters few words, certainly; but these few words are true hieroglyphs, disclosing an inner world filled with love and lofty awareness of the spiritual life led in contemplation of the everlasting Beyond. But you can't appreciate any of this, and I'm wasting my words.'

'God preserve you, my friend,' said Siegmund in very gentle, almost melancholy tones, 'but I feel you're in a bad way. Count on me if anything—no, I'd rather not say any more!' Nathanael suddenly felt that the cold, prosaic Siegmund was truly devoted to him, and when the latter extended his hand, Nathanael shook it very heartily.

Nathanael had entirely forgotten Clara's existence and his former love for her; his mother, Lothar, and everyone else had vanished from his memory; he lived only for Olimpia and spent several hours with her every day, holding forth about his love, the heartfelt rapport between them, and the elective affinities linking their souls, to all of which Olimpia listened with devout attention. From the darkest recesses of his desk Nathanael fetched everything he had ever written. Poems, fantasies, visions, novels, stories, were supplemented daily by all manner of incoherent sonnets, *ballades*, and *canzoni*,* which he read to Olimpia for hours on end without ever wearying. But then, he had never had such a perfect listener. She did not sew or knit, she never looked out of the window, she did not feed a cage-bird, she did not play with a lap-dog or a favourite cat, she did not fiddle with scraps of paper or anything else, she never needed to conceal her yawns by a slight artificial cough: in a word, she stared fixedly at her lover for hours on end, without moving a muscle, and her gaze grew ever more ardent and more animated. Only when Nathanael finally rose and kissed her hand, and also her lips, did she say: 'Oh! Oh!' and then: 'Good night, my dear friend!'

'Oh, you wonderful, profound soul,' cried Nathanael, back in his room, 'no one but you, you alone, understands me perfectly.'

He trembled with heartfelt rapture when he considered how the marvellous harmony between his soul and Olimpia's was becoming more manifest by the day; for he felt as though Olimpia had voiced his own thoughts about his works and about his poetic gift in general; indeed, her voice seemed to come from within himself. This must indeed have been the case, for the only words Olimpia ever spoke were those that have just been mentioned. Although Nathanael did have moments of lucidity and common sense, for example just after waking up in the morning, when he recalled how entirely passive and taciturn Olimpia was, he nevertheless said: 'Words? What are words! The look in her heavenly eyes says more than any terrestrial language. Can a child of heaven ever adjust itself to the narrow confines drawn by miserable earthly needs?'

Professor Spalanzani seemed highly delighted at his daughter's relationship with Nathanael; he gave the latter many unmistakable signs of his goodwill, and when Nathanael finally ventured to hint that he might ask for Olimpia's hand in marriage, the Professor smiled broadly and declared that his daughter should have a free choice. Encouraged by these words, his heart burning with desire, Nathanael resolved that on the very next day he would implore Olimpia to tell him in so many words what her lovely eyes had told him long since: that she was willing to be his for evermore. He looked for the ring which his mother had given him on his departure, so that he might present it to Olimpia as a symbol of his devotion and of the newly budding and blossoming life that he owed to her. As he searched, Clara's and Lothar's letters fell into his hands; he tossed them indifferently aside, found the ring, put it in his pocket, and dashed off to find Olimpia.

As soon as he climbed the stairs and approached the landing, he heard an extraordinary hubbub which seemed to be coming from Spalanzani's study. There were sounds of feet stamping, glass tinkling, and blows falling on the door, mingled with curses and imprecations.

'Let go! Let go! Scoundrel! Villain! You staked your whole life? Ha, ha, ha!—that wasn't part of our wager—I made the eyes, I did—I made the clockwork—stupid wretch, you and your clockwork—you confounded brute of a half-witted clock-maker—get out—Satan—stop—you tinker—you devilish creature—stop—get out—let go!'

The voices howling and raving in such confusion were those of Spalanzani and the horrible Coppelius. In rushed Nathanael, gripped by nameless fear. The Professor had seized a female figure by the shoulders, while the Italian Coppola was holding it by the feet, and both were tugging at it for dear life, while quarrelling violently over it. Nathanael started back, filled with deep horror, on recognizing the figure as Olimpia; wild fury flared up in him, and he tried to tear his beloved from the hands of the enraged combatants, but at that moment Coppola turned round with gigantic strength, wrested the figure from the Professor's hands, and struck him such a terrible blow with it that he staggered and fell backwards over the table covered with phials, retorts, bottles, and glass cylinders, all of which were broken to smithereens. Coppola then threw the figure over his shoulder and rushed downstairs with a frightful yell of laughter, so that the figure's feet, which were hanging down in an unsightly way, gave a wooden rattling and rumbling as they knocked against the steps.

Nathanael stood stock still. He had perceived only too clearly that Olimpia's deathly pale wax face had no eyes, just black caverns where eyes should be; she was a lifeless doll. Spalanzani was writhing on the floor; his head, chest, and arms had been cut by broken glass, and blood was gushing out as though from a fountain. But he summoned all his strength and cried:

'After him, after him! Why are you standing there? Coppelius—he's stolen my best automaton—twenty years' work—I staked my life on it—the clockwork—language—walk—all mine—the eyes—he stole your eyes. The cursed scoundrel, the damned villain—after him—fetch Olimpia—here are her eyes!'

Thereupon Nathanael noticed a pair of bloody eyes lying on the floor and staring at him. Spalanzani picked them up with his unscathed hand and threw them at Nathanael, so that they struck him on the chest. Madness seized him with its red-hot claws and entered his heart, tearing his mind to pieces. 'Hey, hey, hey! Fiery circle, fiery circle! Spin, spin, fiery circle! Come on! Spin, wooden dolly, hey, spin, pretty wooden dolly . . .' and with these words he flung himself on the Professor and clutched him by the throat. He would have throttled him, but the hubbub had attracted a large number of people who forced their way into the room and pulled the frenzied Nathanael to his feet, thus rescuing the Professor, whose wounds were promptly bandaged. Siegmund, despite his strength, was unable to restrain the lunatic, who kept bellowing in a frightful voice: 'Spin, wooden dolly', and brandishing his fists. At last the united efforts of several people managed to overcome Nathanael by throwing him to the ground and tying him up. His words were swallowed up in a horrible animal-like bellowing. Raving in a hideous frenzy, he was taken to the madhouse.

Before continuing, kind reader, with the story of the unfortunate Nathanael, let me assure you, just in case you should feel any sympathy for the skilful mechanic and automaton-maker Spalanzani, that he made a complete recovery from his wounds. He was, however, obliged to leave the University, since Nathanael's story had created a stir, and public opinion considered it monstrously deceitful to foist a wooden doll instead of a living person upon respectable tea-parties (Olimpia had attended some and made quite a hit). Legal scholars described it as a subtle fraud which deserved a condign punishment inasmuch as it had been practised upon the public, and so adroitly conducted that nobody (except for the sharpest students) had observed it, although everyone was now trying to display sagacity by referring to all kinds of suspicious-looking details. These details, however, threw virtually no light on the matter. For could anyone's suspicions have been aroused by the fact that, according to one elegant *habitué* of tea-parties, Olimpia had defied convention by sneezing more than she yawned? Her sneezing, explained this exquisite gentleman, was the sound of the concealed mechanism winding itself up, for there had been an audible creaking. The professor of poetry and eloquence took a pinch of snuff, snapped his box shut, cleared his throat, and said in solemn tones: 'My most esteemed ladies and gentlemen! Don't you see what lies behind all this? The entire matter is an allegory—an extended metaphor! You take my meaning! *Sapienti sat!*'* But many esteemed gentlemen were not so easily reassured: the story of the automaton had made a deep impression on their minds, and a detestable distrust of human figures became prevalent. In order to make quite sure that they were not in love with wooden dolls, several lovers demanded that their beloved should fail to keep time in singing and dancing, and that, when being read aloud to, she should sew, knit, or play with her pug-dog; above all, the beloved was required not merely to listen, but also, from time to time, to speak in a manner that revealed genuine thought and feeling. The bonds between some lovers thus became firmer and pleasanter; others quietly dissolved. 'One really can't take the risk', said some. At tea-parties there was an incredible amount of yawning, but no sneezing, in order to avert any suspicion.

As mentioned earlier, Spalanzani was obliged to disappear in order to evade a criminal prosecution for fraudulently introducing an automaton into human society. Coppola had likewise vanished.

Nathanael awoke, as though from a terrible nightmare; he opened his eyes and felt an indescribable sense of bliss permeating his being with mild, heavenly warmth. He was lying in bed in his room in his father's house. Clara was bending over him, and his mother and Lothar were standing nearby.

'At last, at last, oh my darling Nathanael, you've recovered from your dangerous illness, now you're mine again!' said Clara, from the depths of her heart, folding Nathanael in her arms. The latter was so overcome by rapture and sorrow that bright, hot tears gushed from his eyes, and he uttered a deep sigh: 'My own, my own Clara!'

Siegmund, who had faithfully stood by his friend in time of trouble, entered the room. Nathanael held out his hand to him: 'My loyal friend, you did not abandon me.'

All traces of madness had vanished. Nathanael soon regained his health and strength, tended as he was by his mother, his sweetheart, his friends. Good fortune, meanwhile, had entered their house; for a miserly old uncle, from whom nobody had expected anything, had died and left Nathanael's mother not only a substantial fortune but also a small estate in a pleasant spot not far from the town. They all planned to remove thither: Nathanael's mother, Nathanael himself, with his bride-to-be Clara, and Lothar. Nathanael was now more gentle and child-like than ever before, and appreciated the heavenly purity of Clara's glorious soul for the first time. Nobody reminded him of the past, even by the slightest allusion. Only when Siegmund was leaving him did Nathanael say: 'By God, my friend, I was in a bad way, but at the right moment an angel guided me on to the path of light! Ah, it was Clara!' Siegmund prevented him from saying any more, fearing that painful memories might return with excessive clarity.

The four happy people were about to move to the estate. It was midday, and they were walking through the streets of the town. They had done plenty of shopping, and the lofty tower of the town hall was casting its gigantic shadow over the market-place.

'Why!' said Clara, 'let's climb up there one last time, and gaze at the distant mountains!'

No sooner said than done! Nathanael and Clara began the ascent, their mother went home with the maidservant, and Lothar, reluctant to climb the many steps, decided to remain below. Soon afterwards the two lovers were standing arm in arm on the highest gallery of the tower, gazing into the dim forests beyond which the blue mountains rose like a giant city.

'Look at that funny little grey bush, which really seems to be walking towards us,' said Clara.

Nathanael reached mechanically into his side-pocket; he found Coppola's spyglass, he looked sideways—Clara was standing before the glass! A convulsion ran through his every vein, he stared at Clara in deathly pallor, but an instant later rivers of fire were glowing and sparkling in his rolling eyes, and he uttered a horrible bellow, like a tormented animal; then he sprang aloft and cried in a piercing voice, interspersed with hideous laughter: 'Spin, wooden dolly! Spin, wooden dolly'—and with superhuman strength he seized Clara and was about to dash her to the ground below, but Clara clung firmly to the parapet in the desperation born of terror. Lothar heard the madman raving, he heard Clara's shriek of fright, a horrible suspicion shot through his mind, he rushed up the stairs, the door leading to the second flight of stairs was locked. Clara's shrieks grew louder. Beside himself with fury and fear, he hurled himself against the door, which flew open. Clara's cries were growing fainter and fainter: 'Help! Save me! save me!' she moaned, her voice dying away. 'She's dead—the madman has murdered her,' shrieked Lothar. The door leading to the gallery was locked as well. Desperation endowed him with prodigious strength; he pushed the door off its hinges. God in heaven! Clara, in the grip of the frenzied Nathanael, was suspended in the air, over the edge of the gallery—only one hand still clung to its iron railings. With lightning speed Lothar seized his sister, pulled her to safety, and dashed his fist in the madman's face, forcing the latter to reel back and relinquish his intended victim.

Lothar rushed downstairs, his sister unconscious in his arms. She was saved.

Meanwhile Nathanael was raving in the gallery, leaping into the air and shrieking 'Fiery circle, spin! Fiery circle, spin!'

People gathered below, attracted by his wild yells; in their midst loomed the gigantic figure of the advocate Coppelius, who had just arrived in the town and made directly for the market-place. As people began to climb the stairs in order to seize the lunatic, Coppelius laughed and said: 'Ha, ha—just wait, he'll soon come down by himself', and looked up, like the others. Suddenly Nathanael paused and stood stock still; he bent down, perceived Coppelius, and, with a piercing shriek of 'Beautiful eyes-a! Beautiful eyes-a!' he jumped over the parapet.

By the time Nathanael was lying on the pavement, his head shattered. Coppelius had vanished into the throng.

It is reported that several years later, in a distant part of the country, Clara was seen sitting hand in hand with an affectionate husband outside the door of a handsome country dwelling, with two merry boys playing in front of her. This would seem to suggest that Clara succeeded in finding the quiet domestic happiness which suited her cheerful, sunny disposition, and which she could never have enjoyed with the tormented, self-divided Nathanael.

WILLIAM MAGINN

The Man in the Bell

❧

I N my younger days, bell-ringing was much more in fashion among
the young men of ——, than it is now. Nobody, I believe, practises
it there at present except the servants of the church, and the melody
has been much injured in consequence. Some fifty years ago, about
twenty of us who dwelt in the vicinity of the Cathedral, formed a club,
which used to ring every peal that was called for; and, from continual
practice and a rivalry which arose between us and a club attached to
another steeple, and which tended considerably to sharpen our zeal,
we became very Mozarts on our favourite instruments. But my bell-
ringing practice was shortened by a singular accident, which not only
stopt my performance, but made even the sound of a bell terrible to
my ears.

One Sunday, I went with another into the belfry to ring for noon
prayers, but the second stroke we had pulled shewed us that the clapper of the bell we were at was muffled. Some one had been buried
that morning, and it had been prepared, of course, to ring a mournful note. We did not know of this, but the remedy was easy. 'Jack,'
said my companion, 'step up to the loft, and cut off the hat;' for
the way we had of muffling was by tying a piece of an old hat, or of
cloth (the former was preferred) to one side of the clapper, which
deadened every second toll. I complied, and mounting into the belfry, crept as usual into the bell, where I began to cut away. The hat
had been tied on in some more complicated manner than usual, and
I was perhaps three or four minutes in getting it off; during which
time my companion below was hastily called away, by a message from
his sweetheart I believe, but that is not material to my story. The
person who called him was a brother of the club, who, knowing that
the time had come for ringing for service, and not thinking that any
one was above, began to pull. At this moment I was just getting out,
when I felt the bell moving; I guessed the reason at once—it was
a moment of terror; but by a hasty, and almost convulsive effort,

I succeeded in jumping down, and throwing myself on the flat of my back under the bell.

The room in which it was, was little more than sufficient to contain it, the bottom of the bell coming within a couple of feet of the floor of lath. At that time I certainly was not so bulky as I am now, but as I lay it was within an inch of my face. I had not laid myself down a second, when the ringing began.—It was a dreadful situation. Over me swung an immense mass of metal, one touch of which would have crushed me to pieces; the floor under me was principally composed of crazy laths, and if they gave way, I was precipitated to the distance of about fifty feet upon a loft, which would, in all probability, have sunk under the impulse of my fall, and sent me to be dashed to atoms upon the marble floor of the chancel,* an hundred feet below. I remembered—for fear is quick in recollection—how a common clock-wright, about a month before, had fallen, and bursting through the floors of the steeple, driven in the ceilings of the porch, and even broken into the marble tombstone of a bishop who slept beneath. This was my first terror, but the ringing had not continued a minute, before a more awful and immediate dread came on me. The deafening sound of the bell smote into my ears with a thunder which made me fear their drums would crack.—There was not a fibre of my body it did not thrill through: it entered my very soul; thought and reflection were almost utterly banished; I only retained the sensation of agonizing terror. Every moment I saw the bell sweep within an inch of my face; and my eyes—I could not close them, though to look at the object was bitter as death—followed it instinctively in its oscillating progress until it came back again. It was in vain I said to myself that it could come no nearer at any future swing than it did at first; every time it descended, I endeavoured to shrink into the very floor to avoid being buried under the down-sweeping mass; and then reflecting on the danger of pressing too weightily on my frail support, would cower up again as far as I dared.

At first my fears were mere matter of fact. I was afraid the pullies above would give way, and let the bell plunge on me. At another time, the possibility of the clapper being shot out in some sweep, and dashing through my body, as I had seen a ramrod glide through a door, flitted across my mind. The dread also, as I have already mentioned, of the crazy floor, tormented me, but these soon gave way to fears not more unfounded, but more visionary, and of course more tremendous. The roaring of the bell confused my intellect, and my fancy soon began to teem with all sort of strange and terrifying ideas. The bell pealing above, and opening its jaws with a hideous clamour, seemed to me at one time a ravening monster, raging to devour me; at another, a whirlpool ready to suck me into its bellowing abyss. As I gazed on it, it assumed all shapes; it was a flying eagle, or rather a roc of the Arabian story-tellers,* clapping its wings and screaming over me. As I looked upward into it, it would appear sometimes to lengthen into indefinite extent, or to be twisted at the end into the spiral folds of the tail of a flying-dragon. Nor was the flaming breath, or fiery glance of that fabled animal, wanting to complete the picture. My eyes inflamed, bloodshot, and glaring, invested the supposed monster with a full proportion of unholy light.

It would be endless were I to merely hint at all the fancies that possessed my mind. Every object that was hideous and roaring presented itself to my imagination. I often thought that I was in a hurricane at sea, and that the vessel in which I was embarked tossed under me with the most furious vehemence. The air, set in motion by the swinging of the bell, blew over me, nearly with the violence, and more than the thunder of a tempest; and the floor seemed to reel under me, as under a drunken man. But the most awful of all the ideas that seized on me were drawn from the supernatural. In the vast cavern of the bell hideous faces appeared, and glared down on me with terrifying frowns, or with grinning mockery, still more appalling. At last, the devil himself, accoutred, as in the common description of the evil spirit, with hoof, horn, and tail, and eyes of infernal lustre, made his appearance, and called on me to curse God and worship him, who was powerful to save me. This dread suggestion he uttered with the full-toned clangour of the bell. I had him within an inch of me, and I thought on the fate of the Santon Barsisa.* Strenuously and desperately I defied him, and bade him be gone. Reason, then, for a moment, resumed her sway, but it was only to fill me with fresh terror, just as the lightning dispels the gloom that surrounds the benighted mariner, but to shew him that his vessel is driving on a rock, where she must inevitably be dashed to pieces. I found I was becoming delirious, and trembled lest reason should utterly desert me. This is at all times an agonizing thought, but it smote me then with tenfold agony. I feared lest, when utterly deprived of my senses, I should rise, to do which I was every moment tempted by that strange feeling which calls on a man, whose head is dizzy from standing on the battlement of a lofty castle, to precipitate himself from it, and then death would be instant and tremendous. When I thought of this, I became desperate. I caught the floor with a grasp which drove the blood from my nails; and I yelled with the cry of despair. I called for help, I prayed, I shouted, but all the efforts of my voice were, of course, drowned in the bell. As it passed over my mouth, it occasionally echoed my cries, which mixed not with its own sound, but preserved their distinct character. Perhaps this was but fancy. To me, I know, they then sounded as if they were the shouting, howling, or laughing of the fiends with which my imagination had peopled the gloomy cave which swung over me.

You may accuse me of exaggerating my feelings; but I am not. Many a scene of dread have I since passed through, but they are nothing to the self-inflicted terrors of this half hour. The ancients have doomed one of the damned, in their Tartarus, to lie under a rock, which every moment seems to be descending to annihilate him,*—and an awful punishment it would be. But if to this you add a clamour as loud as if ten thousand furies were howling about you—a deafening uproar banishing reason, and driving you to madness, you must allow that the bitterness of the pang was rendered more terrible. There is no man, firm as his nerves may be, who could retain his courage in this situation.

In twenty minutes the ringing was done. Half of that time passed over me without power of computation,—the other half appeared an age. When it ceased, I became gradually more quiet, but a new fear retained me. I knew that five minutes would elapse without ringing, but, at the end of that short time, the bell would be rung a second time for five minutes more. I could not calculate time. A minute and an hour were of equal duration. I feared to rise, lest the five minutes should have elapsed, and the ringing be again commenced, in which case I should be crushed, before I could escape, against the walls or frame-work of the bell. I therefore still continued to lie down, cautiously shifting myself, however, with a careful gliding, so that my eye no longer looked into the hollow. This was of itself a considerable relief. The cessation of the noise had, in a great measure, the effect of stupifying me, for my attention, being no longer occupied by the chimeras* I had conjured up, began to flag. All that now distressed me was the constant expectation of the second ringing, for which, however, I settled myself with a kind of stupid resolution. I closed my eyes, and clenched my teeth as firmly as if they were screwed in a vice. At last the dreaded moment came, and the first swing of the bell extorted a groan from me, as they say the most resolute victim screams at the sight of the rack, to which he is for a second time destined. After this, however, I lay silent and lethargic, without a thought. Wrapt in the defensive armour of stupidity, I defied the bell and its intonations. When it ceased, I was roused a little by the hope of escape. I did not, however, decide on this step hastily, but, putting up my hand with the utmost caution, I touched the rim. Though the ringing had ceased, it still was tremulous from the sound, and shook under my hand, which instantly recoiled as from an electric jar.* A quarter of an hour probably elapsed before I again dared to make the experiment, and then I found it at rest. I determined to lose no time, fearing that I might have lain then already too long, and that the bell for evening service would catch me. This dread stimulated me, and I slipped out with the utmost rapidity, and arose. I stood, I suppose, for a minute, looking with silly wonder on the place of my imprisonment, penetrated with joy at escaping, but then rushed down the stony and irregular stair with the velocity of lightning, and arrived in the bell-ringer's room. This was the last act I had power to accomplish. I leant against the wall, motionless and deprived of thought, in which posture my companions found me, when, in the course of a couple of hours, they returned to their occupation.

They were shocked, as well they might, at the figure before them. The wind of the bell had excoriated my face, and my dim and stupified eyes were fixed with a lack-lustre gaze in my raw eye-lids. My hands were torn and bleeding; my hair dishevelled; and my clothes tattered. They spoke to me, but I gave no answer. They shook me, but I remained insensible. They then became alarmed, and hastened to remove me. He who had first gone up with me in the forenoon, met them as they carried me through the church-yard, and through him, who was shocked at having, in some measure, occasioned the accident, the cause of my misfortune was discovered. I was put to bed at home, and remained for three days delirious, but gradually recovered my senses. You may be sure the bell formed a prominent topic of my ravings, and if I heard a peal, they were instantly increased to the utmost violence. Even when the delirium abated, my sleep was continually disturbed by imagined ringings, and my dreams were haunted by the fancies which almost maddened me while in the steeple. My friends removed me to a house in the country, which was sufficiently distant from any place of worship, to save me from the apprehensions of hearing the church-going bell; for what Alexander Selkirk, in Cowper's poem,* complained of as a misfortune, was then to me as a blessing. Here I recovered; but, even long after recovery, if a gale wafted the notes of a peal towards me, I started with nervous apprehension. I felt a Mahometan hatred to all the bell tribe, and envied the subjects of the Commander of the Faithful the sonorous voice of their Muezzin.* Time cured this, as it does the most of our follies; but, even at the present day, if, by chance, my nerves be unstrung, some particular tones of the cathedral bell have power to surprise me into a momentary start.

JAMES HOGG

George Dobson's Expedition to Hell

❦❦

THERE is no phenomenon in nature less understood, and about which greater nonsense is written, than dreaming. It is a strange thing. For my part, I do not understand it, nor have I any desire to do so; and I firmly believe that no philosopher that ever wrote* knows a particle more about it than I do, however elaborate and subtle the theories he may advance concerning it. He knows not even what sleep is, nor can he define its nature, so as to enable any common mind to comprehend him; and how, then, can he define that ethereal part of it, wherein the soul holds intercourse with the external world?—how, in that state of abstraction, some ideas force themselves upon us, in spite of all our efforts to get rid of them; while others, which we have resolved to bear about with us by night as well as by day, refuse us their fellowship, even at periods when we most require their aid?

No, no; the philosopher knows nothing about either; and if he says he does, I entreat you not to believe him. He does not know what mind is;* even his own mind, to which one would think he has the most direct access: far less can he estimate the operations and powers of that of any other intelligent being. He does not even know, with all his subtlety, whether it be a power distinct from his body, or essentially the same, and only incidentally and temporarily endowed with different qualities. He sets himself to discover at what period of his existence the union was established. He is baffled; for Consciousness refuses the intelligence, declaring, that she cannot carry him far enough back to ascertain it. He tries to discover the precise moment when it is dissolved, but on this Consciousness is altogether silent; and all is darkness and mystery; for the origin, the manner of continuance, and the time and mode of breaking up of the union between soul and body, are in reality undiscoverable by our natural faculties— are not patent, beyond the possibility of mistake: but whosoever can read his Bible, and solve a dream,* can do either, without being subjected to any material error.

It is on this ground that I like to contemplate, not the theory of dreams, but the dreams themselves; because they prove to the unlettered man, in a very forcible manner, a distinct existence of the soul, and its lively and rapid intelligence with external nature, as well as with a world of spirits with which it has no acquaintance, when the body is lying dormant, and the same to the soul as if sleeping in death.

I account nothing of any dream that relates to the actions of the day; the person is not sound asleep who dreams about these things; there is no division between matter and mind, but they are mingled together in a sort of chaos—what a farmer would call compost—fermenting and disturbing one another. I find that in all dreams of that kind, men of every profession have dreams peculiar to their own occupations; and, in the country, at least, their import is generally understood. Every man's body is a barometer. A thing made up of the elements must be affected by their various changes and convulsions; and so the body assuredly is. When I was a shepherd,* and all the comforts of my life depended so much on good or bad weather, the first thing I did every morning was strictly to overhaul the dreams of the night; and I found that I could calculate better from them than from the appearance and changes of the sky. I know a keen sportsman, who pretends that his dreams never deceive him. If he dream of angling, or pursuing salmon in deep waters, he is sure of rain; but if fishing on dry ground, or in waters so low that the fish cannot get from him, it forebodes drought; hunting or shooting hares, is snow, and moorfowl, wind, &c. But the most extraordinary professional dream on record is, without all doubt, that well-known one of George Dobson, coach-driver in Edinburgh, which I shall here relate; for though it did not happen in the shepherd's cot, it has often been recited there.

George was part proprietor and driver of a hackney-coach in Edinburgh, when such vehicles were scarce; and one day a gentleman, whom he knew, came to him and said:—'George, you must drive me and my son here out to ——,' a certain place that he named, somewhere in the vicinity of Edinburgh.

'Sir,' said George, 'I never heard tell of such a place, and I cannot drive you to it unless you give me very particular directions.'

'It is false,' returned the gentleman; 'there is no man in Scotland who knows the road to that place better than you do. You have never driven on any other road all your life; and I insist on your taking us.'

'Very well, sir,' said George, 'I'll drive you to hell, if you have a mind; only you are to direct me on the road.'

'Mount and drive on, then,' said the other; 'and no fear of the road.'

George did so, and never in his life did he see his horses go at such a noble rate; they snorted, they pranced, and they flew on; and as the whole road appeared to lie down-hill, he deemed that he should soon come to his journey's end. Still he drove on at the same rate, far, far down-hill,—and so fine an open road he never travelled,—till by degrees it grew so dark that he could not see to drive any farther. He called to the gentleman, inquiring what he should do; who answered, that this was the place they were bound to, so he might draw up, dismiss them, and return. He did so, alighted from the dickie,* wondered at his foaming horses, and forthwith opened the coach-door, held the rim of his hat with the one hand, and with the other demanded his fare.

'You have driven us in fine style, George,' said the elder gentleman, 'and deserve to be remembered; but it is needless for us to settle just now, as you must meet us here again to-morrow precisely at twelve o'clock.'

'Very well, sir,' said George; 'there is likewise an old account, you know, and some toll-money;' which indeed there was.

'It shall be all settled to-morrow, George, and moreover, I fear there will be some toll-money to-day.'

'I perceived no tolls to-day, your honour,' said George.

'But I perceived one, and not very far back neither, which I suspect you will have difficulty in repassing without a regular ticket.* What a pity I have no change on me!'

'I never saw it otherwise with your honour,' said George, jocularly; 'what a pity it is you should always suffer yourself to run short of change!'

'I will give you that which is as good, George,' said the gentleman; and he gave him a ticket written with red ink, which the honest coachman could not read. He, however, put it into his sleeve, and inquired of his employer where that same toll was which he had not observed, and how it was that they did not ask toll from him as he came through? The gentleman replied, by informing George that there was no road out of that domain, and that whoever entered it must either remain in it, or return by the same path; so they never asked any toll till the person's return, when they were at times highly capricious; but that the ticket he had given him would answer his turn. And he then asked George if he did not perceive a gate, with a number of men in black standing about it.

'Oho! Is yon the spot?' says George; 'then, I assure your honour, yon is no toll-gate, but a private entrance into a great man's mansion; for do not I know two or three of the persons yonder to be gentlemen of the law, whom I have driven often and often? and as good fellows they are, too, as any I know—men who never let themselves run short of change! Good day—Twelve o'clock to-morrow?'

'Yes, twelve o'clock noon, precisely;' and with that, George's employer vanished in the gloom, and left him to wind his way out of that dreary labyrinth the best way he could. He found it no easy matter, for his lamps were not lighted, and he could not see an ell* before him—he could not even perceive his horses' ears; and what was worse, there was a rushing sound, like that of a town on fire, all around him, that stunned his senses, so that he could not tell whether his horses were moving or standing still. George was in the greatest distress imaginable, and was glad when he perceived the gate before him, with his two identical friends, men of the law, still standing. George drove boldly up, accosted them by their names, and asked what they were doing there; they made him no answer, but pointed to the gate and the keeper. George was terrified to look at this latter personage, who now came up and seized his horses by the reins, refusing to let him pass. In order to introduce himself, in some degree, to this austere toll-man, George asked him, in a jocular manner, how he came to employ his two eminent friends as assistant gate-keepers?

'Because they are among the last comers,' replied the ruffian, churlishly. 'You will be an assistant here, to-morrow.'

'The devil I will, sir?'

'Yes, the devil you will, sir.'

'I'll be d—d if I do then—that I will.'

'Yes, you'll be d—d if you do—that you will.'

'Let my horses go in the meantime, then, sir, that I may proceed on my journey.'

'Nay.'

'Nay?—Dare you say nay to me, sir? My name is George Dobson, of the Pleasance,* Edinburgh, coach-driver, and coach-proprietor too; and no man shall say *nay* to me, as long as I can pay my way.

I have his Majesty's license,* and I'll go and come as I choose—and that I will. Let go my horses there, and tell me what is your demand.'

'Well, then, I'll let your horses go,' said the keeper; 'but I'll keep yourself for a pledge.' And with that he let go the horses, and seized honest George by the throat, who struggled in vain to disengage himself, and swore, and threatened, according to his own confession, most bloodily. His horses flew off like the wind, so swift, that the coach seemed flying in the air, and scarcely bounding on the earth once in a quarter of a mile. George was in furious wrath, for he saw that his grand coach and harness would all be broken to pieces, and his gallant pair of horses maimed or destroyed; and how was his family's bread now to be won!—He struggled, threatened, and prayed in vain;—the intolerable toll-man was deaf to all remonstrances. He once more appealed to his two genteel acquaintances of the law, reminding them how he had of late driven them to Roslin* on a Sunday, along with two ladies, who, he supposed, were their sisters, from their familiarity, when not another coachman in town would engage with them. But the gentlemen, very ungenerously, only shook their heads, and pointed to the gate. George's circumstances now became desperate, and again he asked the hideous toll-man what right he had to detain him, and what were his charges.

'What right have I to detain you, sir, say you? Who are you that make such a demand here? Do you know where you are, sir?'

'No, faith, I do not,' returned George; 'I wish I did. But I *shall* know, and make you repent your insolence too. My name, I told you, is George Dobson, licensed coach-hirer in Pleasance, Edinburgh; and to get full redress of you for this unlawful interruption, I only desire to know where I am.'

'Then, sir, if it can give you so much satisfaction to know where you are,' said the keeper, with a malicious grin, 'you *shall* know, and you may take instruments by the hands of your two friends there, instituting a legal prosecution. Your redress, you may be assured, will be most ample, when I inform you that you are in HELL! and out at this gate you pass no more.'

This was rather a damper to George, and he began to perceive that nothing would be gained in such a place by the strong hand, so he addressed the inexorable toll-man, whom he now dreaded more than ever, in the following terms: 'But I must go home at all events, you know, sir, to unyoke my two horses, and put them up, and to inform Chirsty Halliday, my wife, of my engagement. And, bless me! I never recollected till this moment, that I am engaged to be back here to-morrow at twelve o'clock, and see, here is a free ticket for my passage this way.'

The keeper took the ticket with one hand, but still held George with the other. 'Oho! were you in with our honourable friend, Mr R—— of L——y?' said he. 'He has been on our books for a long while;—however, this will do, only you must put your name to it likewise; and the engagement is this—You, by this instrument, engage your soul, that you will return here by to-morrow at noon.'

'Catch me there, billy!' says George. 'I'll engage no such thing, depend on it;—that I will not.'

'Then remain where you are,' said the keeper, 'for there is no other alternative. We like best for people to come here in their own way,—in the way of their business;' and with that he flung George backward, heels-over-head down hill, and closed the gate.

George, finding all remonstrance vain, and being desirous once more to see the open day, and breathe the fresh air, and likewise to see Chirsty Halliday, his wife, and set his house and stable in some order, came up again, and in utter desperation, signed the bond, and was suffered to depart. He then bounded away on the track of his horses, with more than ordinary swiftness, in hopes to overtake them; and always now and then uttered a loud Wo! in hopes they might hear and obey, though he could not come in sight of them. But George's grief was but beginning; for at a well-known and dangerous spot, where there was a tan-yard on the one hand, and a quarry on the other, he came to his gallant steeds overturned, the coach smashed to pieces, Dawtie with two of her legs broken, and Duncan dead. This was more than the worthy coachman could bear, and many degrees worse than being in hell. There, his pride and manly spirit bore him up against the worst of treatment; but here, his heart entirely failed him, and he laid himself down, with his face on his two hands, and wept bitterly, bewailing, in the most deplorable terms, his two gallant horses, Dawtie and Duncan.

While lying in this inconsolable state, some one took hold of his shoulder, and shook it; and a well-known voice said to him, 'Geordie! what is the matter wi' ye, Geordie?' George was provoked beyond measure at the insolence of the question, for he knew the voice to be that of Chirsty Halliday, his wife. 'I think you needna ask that, seeing what you see,' said George. 'O, my poor Dawtie, where are a' your jinkings and prancings now, your moopings and your wincings? I'll ne'er be a proud man again—bereaved o' my bonny pair!'

'Get up, George; get up, and bestir yourself,' said Chirsty Halliday, his wife. 'You are wanted directly, to bring in the Lord President to the Parliament House.* It is a great storm, and he must be there by nine o'clock.—Get up—rouse yourself, and make ready—his servant is waiting for you.'

'Woman, you are demented!' cried George. 'How can I go and bring in the Lord President, when my coach is broken in pieces, my poor Dawtie lying with twa of her legs broken, and Duncan dead? And, moreover, I have a previous engagement, for I am obliged to be in hell before twelve o'clock.'

Chirsty Halliday now laughed outright, and continued long in a fit of laughter; but George never moved his head from the pillow, but lay and groaned,—for, in fact, he was all this while lying snug in his bed; while the tempest without was roaring with great violence, and which circumstance may perhaps account for the rushing and deafening sound which astounded him so much in hell. But so deeply was he impressed with the idea of the reality of his dream, that he would do nothing but lie and moan, persisting and believing in the truth of all he had seen. His wife now went and informed her neighbours of her husband's plight, and of his singular engagement with Mr R—— of L——y at twelve o'clock. She persuaded one friend to harness the horses, and go for the Lord President; but all the rest laughed immoderately at poor coachy's predicament. It was, however, no laughing to him; he never raised his head, and his wife becoming at last uneasy about the frenzied state of his mind, made him repeat every circumstance of his adventure to her, (for he would never believe or admit that it was a dream,) which he did in the terms above narrated; and she perceived, or dreaded, that he was becoming somewhat feverish. She went out, and told Dr Wood of her husband's malady, and of his solemn engagement to be in hell at twelve o'clock.

'He maunna* keep it, dearie. He maunna keep that engagement at no rate,' said Dr Wood. 'Set back the clock an hour or twa, to drive him past the time, and I'll ca' in the course of my rounds. Are ye sure he hasna been drinking hard?'—She assured him he had not.—'Weel, weel, ye maun tell him that he maunna keep that engagement at no rate. Set back the clock, and I'll come and see him. It is a frenzy that maunna be trifled with. Ye maunna laugh at it, dearie,—maunna laugh at it. Maybe a nervish fever, wha kens.'*

The Doctor and Chirsty left the house together, and as their road lay the same way for a space, she fell a-telling him of the two young lawyers whom George saw standing at the gate of hell, and whom the porter had described as two of the last comers. When the Doctor heard this, he stayed his hurried, stooping pace in one moment, turned full round on the woman, and fixing his eyes on her, that gleamed with a deep, unstable lustre, he said, 'What's that ye were saying, dearie? What's that ye were saying? Repeat it again to me, every word.' She did so. On which the Doctor held up his hands, as if palsied with astonishment, and uttered some fervent ejaculations. 'I'll go with you straight,' said he, 'before I visit another patient. This is wonderfu'! it is terrible! The young gentlemen are both at rest—both lying corpses at this time! Fine young men—I attended them both—died of the same exterminating disease—Oh, this is wonderful; this is wonderful!'

The Doctor kept Chirsty half running all the way down the High Street and St Mary's Wynd,* at such a pace did he walk, never lifting his eyes from the pavement, but always exclaiming now and then, 'It is wonderfu'! most wonderfu'!' At length, prompted by woman's natural curiosity, Chirsty inquired at the Doctor if he knew any thing of their friend Mr R—— of L——y. But he shook his head, and replied, 'Na, na, dearie,—ken naething about him. He and his son are baith in London,—ken naething about him; but the tither is awfu'—it is perfectly awfu'!'

When Dr Wood reached his patient, he found him very low, but only a little feverish; so he made all haste to wash his head with vinegar and cold water, and then he covered the crown with a treacle plaster, and made the same application to the soles of his feet, awaiting the issue. George revived a little, when the Doctor tried to cheer him up by joking him about his dream; but on mention of that he groaned, and shook his head. 'So you are convinced, dearie, that it is nae dream?' said the Doctor.

'Dear sir, how could it be a dream?' said the patient. 'I was there in person, with Mr R—— and his son; and see, here are the marks of the porter's fingers on my throat.'—Dr Wood looked, and distinctly saw two or three red spots on one side of his throat, which confounded him not a little.—'I assure you, sir,' continued George, 'it was no dream, which I know to my sad experience. I have lost my coach and horses,—and what more have I?—signed the bond with my own hand, and in person entered into the most solemn and terrible engagement.'

'But ye're no to keep it, I tell ye,' said Dr Wood; 'ye're no to keep it at no rate. It is a sin to enter into a compact wi' the deil, but it is a far greater ane to keep it. Sae let Mr R—— and his son bide where they are yonder, for ye sanna stir a foot to bring them out the day.'

'Oh, oh, Doctor!' groaned the poor fellow, 'this is not a thing to be made a jest o'! I feel that it is an engagement that I cannot break. Go I must, and that very shortly. Yes, yes, go I must, and go I will, although I should borrow David Barclay's pair.' With that he turned his face towards the wall, groaned deeply, and fell into a lethargy, while Dr Wood caused them to let him alone, thinking if he would sleep out the appointed time, which was at hand, he would be safe; but all the time he kept feeling his pulse, and by degrees showed symptoms of uneasiness. His wife ran for a clergyman of famed abilities, to pray and converse with her husband, in hopes by that means to bring him to his senses; but after his arrival, George never spoke more, save calling to his horses, as if encouraging them to run with great speed; and thus in imagination driving at full career to keep his appointment, he went off in a paroxysm, after a terrible struggle, precisely within a few minutes of twelve o'clock.

A circumstance not known at the time of George's death made this singular professional dream the more remarkable and unique in all its parts. It was a terrible storm on the night of the dream, as has been already mentioned, and during the time of the hurricane,

London smack went down off Wearmouth* about three in the morning. Among the sufferers were the Hon. Mr R—— of L——y, and his son! George could not know aught of this at break of day, for it was not known in Scotland till the day of his interment; and as little knew he of the deaths of the two young lawyers, who both died of the small-pox the evening before.

HONORÉ DE BALZAC

La Grande Bretêche

❧

'AH! madame,' replied the doctor, 'I have some appalling stories in
my collection. But each one has its proper hour in a conversation—you know the pretty jest recorded by Chamfort, and said to
the Duc de Fronsac:* "Between your sally and the present moment lie
ten bottles of champagne."'

'But it is two in the morning, and the story of Rosina has prepared
us,' said the mistress of the house.

'Tell us, Monsieur Bianchon!' was the cry on every side.

The obliging doctor bowed, and silence reigned.

'At about a hundred paces from Vendôme, on the banks of the
Loir,'* said he, 'stands an old brown house, crowned with very high
roofs, and so completely isolated that there is nothing near it, not even
a fetid tannery or a squalid tavern, such as are commonly seen outside small towns. In front of this house is a garden down to the river,
where the box shrubs, formerly clipped close to edge the walks, now
straggle at their own will. A few willows, rooted in the stream, have
grown up quickly like an enclosing fence, and half hide the house.
The wild plants we call weeds have clothed the bank with their beautiful luxuriance. The fruit-trees, neglected for these ten years past,
no longer bear a crop, and their suckers have formed a thicket. The
espaliers* are like a copse. The paths, once gravelled, are overgrown
with purslane;* but, to be accurate, there is no trace of a path.

'Looking down from the hilltop, to which cling the ruins of the
old castle of the Dukes of Vendôme, the only spot whence the eye
can see into this enclosure, we think that at a time, difficult now to
determine, this spot of earth must have been the joy of some country
gentleman devoted to roses and tulips, in a word, to horticulture, but
above all a lover of choice fruit. An arbor is visible, or rather the wreck
of an arbor, and under it a table still stands not entirely destroyed by
time. At the aspect of this garden that is no more, the negative joys
of the peaceful life of the provinces may be divined as we divine the

history of a worthy tradesman when we read the epitaph on his tomb. To complete the mournful and tender impressions which seize the soul, on one of the walls there is a sundial graced with this homely Christian motto, "*Ultimam cogita.*"*

'The roof of this house is dreadfully dilapidated; the outside shutters are always closed; the balconies are hung with swallows' nests; the doors are for ever shut. Straggling grasses have outlined the flagstones of the steps with green; the ironwork is rusty. Moon and sun, winter, summer, and snow have eaten into the wood, warped the boards, peeled off the paint. The dreary silence is broken only by birds and cats, polecats, rats, and mice, free to scamper round, and fight, and eat each other. An invisible hand has written over it all: "Mystery."

'If, prompted by curiosity, you go to look at this house from the street, you will see a large gate, with a round-arched top; the children have made many holes in it. I learned later that this door had been blocked for ten years. Through these irregular breaches you will see that the side towards the courtyard is in perfect harmony with the side towards the garden. The same ruin prevails. Tufts of weeds outline the paving-stones; the walls are scored by enormous cracks, and the blackened coping is laced with a thousand festoons of pellitory. The stone steps are disjointed; the bell-cord is rotten; the gutter-spouts broken. What fire from heaven can have fallen there? By what decree has salt been sown on this dwelling? Has God been mocked here? Or was France betrayed? These are the questions we ask ourselves. Reptiles crawl over it, but give no reply. This empty and deserted house is a vast enigma of which the answer is known to none.

'It was formerly a little domain, held in fief,* and is known as La Grande Bretêche. During my stay at Vendôme, where Despleins had left me in charge of a rich patient, the sight of this strange dwelling became one of my keenest pleasures. Was it not far better than a ruin? Certain memories of indisputable authenticity attach themselves to a ruin; but this house, still standing, though being slowly destroyed by an avenging hand, contained a secret, an unrevealed thought. At the very least, it testified to a caprice. More than once in the evening I boarded the hedge, run wild, which surrounded the enclosure. I braved scratches, I got into this ownerless garden, this plot which was no longer public or private; I lingered there for hours gazing at the disorder. I would not, as the price of the story to which this strange scene no doubt was due, have asked a single question of any gossiping native. On that spot I wove delightful romances, and abandoned myself to little debauches of melancholy which enchanted me. If I had known the reason—perhaps quite commonplace—of this neglect, I should have lost the unwritten poetry which intoxicated me. To me this refuge represented the most various phases of human life, shadowed by misfortune; sometimes the calm of a cloister without the monks; sometimes the peace of the graveyard without the dead, who speak in the language of epitaphs; one day I saw in it the home of lepers; another, the house of the Atridæ;* but, above all, I found there provincial life, with its contemplative ideas, its hour-glass existence. I often wept there, I never laughed.

'More than once I felt involuntary terrors as I heard overhead the dull hum of the wings of some hurrying woodpigeon. The earth is dank; you must be on the watch for lizards, vipers, and frogs, wandering about with the wild freedom of nature; above all, you must have no fear of cold, for in a few moments you feel an icy cloak settle on your shoulders, like the Commendatore's hand on Don Giovanni's neck.*

'One evening I felt a shudder; the wind had turned an old rusty weathercock, and the creaking sounded like a cry from the house, at the very moment when I was finishing a gloomy drama to account for this monumental embodiment of woe. I returned to my inn, lost in gloomy thoughts. When I had supped, the hostess came into my room with an air of mystery, and said, "Monsieur, here is Monsieur Regnault."

'"Who is Monsieur Regnault?"

'"What, sir, do you not know Monsieur Regnault?—Well, that's odd," said she, leaving the room.

'On a sudden I saw a man appear, tall, slim, dressed in black, hat in hand, who came in like a ram ready to butt his opponent, showing a receding forehead, a small pointed head, and a colourless face of the hue of a glass of dirty water. You would have taken him for an usher. The stranger wore an old coat, much worn at the seams; but he had a diamond in his shirt frill, and gold rings in his ears.

'"Monsieur," said I, "whom have I the honour of addressing?"— He took a chair, placed himself in front of my fire, put his hat on my table, and answered while he rubbed his hands: "Dear me, it is very cold.—Monsieur, I am Monsieur Regnault."

'I was encouraging myself by saying to myself, "*Il bondo cani!**
Seek!"

'"I am," he went on, "notary at Vendôme."

'"I am delighted to hear it, monsieur," I exclaimed. "But I am not
in a position to make a will for reasons best known to myself."

'"One moment!" said he, holding up his hand as though to gain
silence. "Allow me, monsieur, allow me! I am informed that you
sometimes go to walk in the garden of la Grande Bretêche."

'"Yes, monsieur."

'"One moment!" said he, repeating his gesture. "That constitutes
a misdemeanour. Monsieur, as executor under the will of the late
Comtesse de Merret, I come in her name to beg you to discontinue
the practice. One moment! I am not a Turk, and do not wish to make
a crime of it. And besides, you are free to be ignorant of the circumstances which compel me to leave the finest mansion in Vendôme to
fall into ruin. Nevertheless, monsieur, you must be a man of education, and you should know that the laws forbid, under heavy penalties, any trespass on enclosed property. A hedge is the same as a wall.
But, the state in which the place is left may be an excuse for your
curiosity. For my part, I should be quite content to make you free to
come and go in the house; but being bound to respect the will of the
testatrix,* I have the honour, monsieur, to beg that you will go into
the garden no more. I myself, monsieur, since the will was read, have
never set foot in the house, which, as I had the honour of informing
you, is part of the estate of the late Madame de Merret. We have done
nothing there but verify the number of doors and windows to assess
the taxes* I have to pay annually out of the funds left for that purpose
by the late Madame de Merret. Ah! my dear sir, her will made a great
commotion in the town."

'The good man paused to blow his nose. I respected his volubility, perfectly understanding that the administration of Madame de
Merret's estate had been the most important event of his life, his
reputation, his glory, his Restoration.* As I was forced to bid farewell
to my beautiful reveries and romances, I was to reject learning the
truth on official authority.

'"Monsieur," said I, "would it be indiscreet if I were to ask you the
reasons for such eccentricity?"

'At these words an expression, which revealed all the pleasure which
men feel who are accustomed to ride a hobby, overspread the lawyer's

countenance. He pulled up the collar of his shirt with an air, took out his snuffbox, opened it, and offered me a pinch; on my refusing, he took a large one. He was happy! A man who has no hobby does not know all the good to be got out of life. A hobby is the happy medium between a passion and a monomania. At this moment I understood the whole bearing of Sterne's charming passion, and had a perfect idea of the delight with which my uncle Toby, encouraged by Trim, bestrode his hobby-horse.*

' "Monsieur," said Monsieur Regnault, "I was head-clerk in Monsieur Roguin's office, in Paris. A first-rate house, which you may have heard mentioned? No! An unfortunate bankruptcy made it famous.——Not having money enough to purchase a practice in Paris at the price to which they were run up in 1816, I came here and bought my predecessor's business. I had relations in Vendôme; among others, a wealthy aunt, who allowed me to marry her daughter.——Monsieur," he went on after a little pause, "three months after being licensed by the Keeper of the Seals,* one evening, as I was going to bed—it was before my marriage—I was sent for by Madame la Comtesse de Merret, to her Château of Merret. Her maid, a good girl, who is now a servant in this inn, was waiting at my door with the Countess's own carriage. Ah! one moment! I ought to tell you that Monsieur le Comte de Merret had gone to Paris to die two months before I came here. He came to a miserable end, flinging himself into every kind of dissipation. You understand?

' "On the day when he left, Madame la Comtesse had quitted la Grande Bretêche, having dismantled it. Some people even say that she had burnt all the furniture, the hangings—in short, all the chattels and furniture whatever used in furnishing the premises now let by the said M.—— (Dear! what am I saying? I beg your pardon, I thought I was dictating a lease.)—In short, that she burnt everything in the meadow at Merret. Have you been to Merret, monsieur?—No," said he, answering himself. "Ah, it is a very fine place."

' "For about three months previously," he went on, with a jerk of his head, "the Count and Countess had lived in a very eccentric way; they admitted no visitors; Madame lived on the ground-floor, and Monsieur on the first floor. When the Countess was left alone, she was never seen excepting at church. Subsequently, at home, at the château, she refused to see the friends, whether gentlemen or ladies, who went to call on her. She was already very much altered when she left la Grande Bretêche to go to Merret. That dear lady—I say dear lady, for it was she who gave me this diamond, but indeed I saw her but once—that kind lady was very ill; she had, no doubt, given up all hope, for she died without choosing to send for a doctor; indeed, many of our ladies fancied she was not quite right in her head. Well, sir, my curiosity was strangely excited by hearing that Madame de Merret had need of my services. Nor was I the only person who took an interest in the affair. That very night, though it was already late, all the town knew that I was going to Merret.

' "The waiting-woman replied but vaguely to the questions I asked her on the way; nevertheless, she told me that her mistress had received the Sacrament* in the course of the day at the hands of the Curé of Merret, and seemed unlikely to live through the night. It was about eleven when I reached the château. I went up the great staircase. After crossing some large, lofty, dark rooms, diabolically cold and damp, I reached the state bedroom where the Countess lay. From the rumours that were current concerning this lady (monsieur, I should never end if I were to repeat all the tales that were told about her), I had imagined her a coquette. Imagine, then, that I had great difficulty in seeing her in the great bed where she was lying. To be sure, to light this enormous room, with old-fashioned heavy cornices, and so thick with dust that merely to see it was enough to make you sneeze, she had only an old Argand lamp.* Ah! but you have not been to Merret. Well, the bed is one of those old-world beds, with a high tester* hung with flowered chintz. A small table stood by the bed, on which I saw an 'Imitation of Christ,'* which, by the way, I bought for my wife, as well as the lamp. There were also a deep armchair for her confidential maid, and two small chairs. There was no fire. That was all the furniture, not enough to fill ten lines in an inventory.

' "My dear sir, if you had seen, as I then saw, that vast room, papered and hung with brown, you would have felt yourself transported into a scene of a romance. It was icy, nay more, funereal," and he lifted his hand with a theatrical gesture and paused.

' "By dint of seeking, as I approached the bed, at last I saw Madame de Merret, under the glimmer of the lamp, which fell on the pillows. Her face was as yellow as wax, and as narrow as two folded hands. The Countess had a lace cap showing abundant hair, but as white as linen thread. She was sitting up in bed, and seemed to keep upright with great difficulty. Her large black eyes, dimmed by fever, no doubt, and half-dead already, hardly moved under the bony arch of her eye-brows.—There," he added, pointing to his own brow. "Her forehead was clammy; her fleshless hands were like bones covered with soft skin; the veins and muscles were perfectly visible. She must have been very handsome; but at this moment I was startled into an indescrib-able emotion at the sight. Never, said those who wrapped her in her shroud, had any living creature been so emaciated and lived. In short, it was awful to behold! Sickness had so consumed that woman, that she was no more than a phantom. Her lips, which were pale violet, seemed to me not to move when she spoke to me.

' "Though my profession has familiarized me with such spectacles, by calling me not infrequently to the bedside of the dying to record their last wishes, I confess that families in tears and the agonies I have seen were as nothing in comparison with this lonely and silent woman in her vast château. I heard not the least sound, I did not perceive the movement which the sufferer's breathing ought to have given to the sheets that covered her, and I stood motionless, absorbed in looking at her in a sort of stupor. In fancy I am there still. At last her large eyes moved; she tried to raise her right hand, but it fell back on the bed, and she uttered these words, which came like a breath, for her voice was no longer a voice: 'I have waited for you with the greatest impatience.' A bright flush rose to her cheeks. It was a great effort to her to speak.

' " 'Madame,' I began. She signed to me to be silent. At that moment the old housekeeper rose and said in my ear, 'Do not speak; Madame la Comtesse is not in a state to bear the slightest noise, and what you would say might agitate her.'

' "I sat down. A few instants after, Madame de Merret collected all her remaining strength to move her right hand, and slipped it, not without infinite difficulty, under the bolster; she then paused a moment. With a last effort she withdrew her hand; and when she brought out a sealed paper, drops of perspiration rolled from her brow. 'I place my will in your hands—Oh! God! Oh!' and that was all. She clutched a crucifix that lay on the bed, lifted it hastily to her lips, and died.

' "The expression of her eyes still makes me shudder as I think of it. She must have suffered much! There was joy in her last glance, and it remained stamped on her dead eyes.

' "I brought away the will, and when it was opened I found that

Madame de Merret had appointed me her executor. She left the whole of her property to the hospital at Vendôme excepting a few legacies. But these were her instructions as relating to la Grande Bretèche: She ordered me to leave the place, for fifty years counting from the day of her death, in the state in which it might be at the time of her decease, forbidding any one, whoever he might be, to enter the apartments, prohibiting any repairs whatever, and even settling a salary to pay watchmen if it were needful to secure the absolute fulfilment of her intentions. At the expiration of that term, if the will of the testatrix has been duly carried out, the house is to become the property of my heirs, for, as you know, a notary cannot take a bequest. Otherwise la Grande Bretèche reverts to the heirs-at-law, but on condition of fulfilling certain conditions set forth in a codicil* to the will, which is not to be opened till the expiration of the said term of fifty years. The will has not been disputed, so——" And without finishing his sentence, the lanky notary looked at me with an air of triumph; I made him quite happy by offering him my congratulations.

'"Monsieur," I said in conclusion, "you have so vividly impressed me that I fancy I see the dying woman whiter than her sheets; her glittering eyes frighten me; I shall dream of her to-night.—But you must have formed some idea as to the instructions contained in that extraordinary will."

'"Monsieur," said he, with comical reticence, "I never allow myself to criticise the conduct of a person who honours me with the gift of a diamond."

'However, I soon loosened the tongue of the discreet notary of Vendôme, who communicated to me, not without long digressions, the opinions of the deep politicians of both sexes whose judgments are law in Vendôme. But these opinions were so contradictory, so diffuse, that I was near falling asleep in spite of the interest I felt in this authentic history. The notary's ponderous voice and monotonous accent, accustomed no doubt to listen to himself and to make himself listened to by his clients or fellow-townsmen, were too much for my curiosity. Happily, he soon went away.

'"Ah, ha, monsieur," said he on the stairs, "a good many persons would be glad to live five-and-forty years longer; but—one moment!" and he laid the first finger of his right hand to his nostril with a cunning look, as much as to say, "Mark my words!—To last as long as that—as long as that," said he, "you must not be past sixty now."

'I closed my door, having been roused from my apathy by this last speech, which the notary thought very funny; then I sat down in my armchair, with my feet on the fire-dogs. I had lost myself in a romance *à la* Radcliffe,* constructed on the juridical base given me by Monsieur Regnault, when the door, opened by a woman's cautious hand, turned on the hinges. I saw my landlady come in, a buxom, florid dame, always good-humoured, who had missed her calling in life. She was a Fleming,* who ought to have seen the light in a picture by Teniers.*

'"Well, monsieur," said she, "Monsieur Regnault has no doubt been giving you his history of la Grande Bretêche?"

'"Yes, Madame Lepas."

'"And what did he tell you?"

'I repeated in a few words the creepy and sinister story of Madame de Merret. At each sentence my hostess put her head forward, looking at me with an innkeeper's keen scrutiny, a happy compromise between the instinct of a police constable, the astuteness of a spy, and the cunning of a dealer.

'"My good Madame Lepas," said I as I ended, "you seem to know more about it. Heh? If not, why have you come up to me?"

'"On my word, as an honest woman——"

'"Do not swear; your eyes are big with a secret. You knew Monsieur de Merret; what sort of man was he?"

'"Monsieur de Merret—well, you see he was a man you never could see the top of, he was so tall! A very good gentleman, from Picardy,* and who had, as we say, his head close to his cap. He paid for everything down, so as never to have difficulties with any one. He was hot-tempered, you see! All our ladies liked him very much."

'"Because he was hot-tempered?" I asked her.

'"Well, may be," said she; "and you may suppose, sir, that a man had to have something to show for a figurehead before he could marry Madame de Merret, who, without any reflection on others, was the handsomest and richest heiress in our parts. She had about twenty thousand francs a year. All the town was at the wedding; the bride was pretty and sweet-looking, quite a gem of a woman. Oh, they were a handsome couple in their day!"

'"And were they happy together?"

'"Hm, hm! so-so—so far as can be guessed, for, as you may suppose, we of the common sort were not hail-fellow-well-met with them.—Madame de Merret was a kind woman and very pleasant, who had no doubt sometimes to put up with her husband's tantrums. But though he was rather haughty, we were fond of him. After all, it was his place to behave so. When a man is a born nobleman, you see——"

' "Still, there must have been some catastrophe for Monsieur and Madame de Merret to part so violently?"

' "I did not say there was any catastrophe, sir. I know nothing about it."

' "Indeed. Well, now, I am sure you know everything."

' "Well, sir, I will tell you the whole story.—When I saw Monsieur Regnault go up to see you, it struck me that he would speak to you about Madame de Merret as having to do with la Grande Bretêche. That put it into my head to ask your advice, sir, seeming to me that you are a man of good judgment and incapable of playing a poor woman like me false—for I never did any one a wrong, and yet I am tormented by my conscience. Up to now I have never dared to say a word to the people of these parts; they are all chatter-mags,* with tongues like knives. And never till now, sir, have I had any traveller here who stayed so long in the inn as you have, and to whom I could tell the history of the fifteen thousand francs——"

' "My dear Madame Lepas, if there is anything in your story of a nature to compromise me," I said, interrupting the flow of her words, "I would not hear it for all the world."

' "You need have no fears," said she; "you will see."

'Her eagerness made me suspect that I was not the only person to whom my worthy landlady had communicated the secret of which I was to be sole possessor, but I listened.

' "Monsieur," said she, "when the Emperor sent the Spaniards here, prisoners of war and others,* I was required to lodge at the charge of the Government a young Spaniard sent to Vendôme on parole. Notwithstanding his parole, he had to show himself every day to the sub-prefect. He was a Spanish grandee—neither more nor less. He had a name in *os* and *dia*, something like Bagos de Férédia. I wrote his name down in my books, and you may see it if you like. Ah! he was a handsome young fellow for a Spaniard, who are all ugly they say. He was not more than five feet two or three in height, but so well made; and he had little hands that he kept so beautifully! Ah! you should have seen them. He had as many brushes for his hands as a woman has for her toilet. He had thick, black hair, a flame in his eye, a somewhat coppery complexion, but which I admired all the same. He wore the finest linen I have ever seen, though I have had princesses to lodge here, and, among others, General Bertrand, the Duc and Duchesse d'Abrantés, Monsieur Descazes, and the King of Spain. He did not eat much, but he had such polite and amiable ways that it was impossible to owe him a grudge for that. Oh! I was very fond of him, though he did not say four words to me in a day, and it was impossible to have the least bit of talk with him; if he was spoken to, he did not answer; it is a way, a mania they all have, it would seem.

'"He read his breviary* like a priest, and went to mass and all the services quite regularly. And where did he post himself?—we found this out later.—Within two yards of Madame de Merret's chapel. As he took that place the very first time he entered the church, no one imagined that there was any purpose in it. Besides, he never raised his nose above his book, poor young man! And then, monsieur, of an evening he went for a walk on the hill among the ruins of the old castle. It was his only amusement, poor man; it reminded him of his native land. They say that Spain is all hills!

'"One evening, a few days after he was sent here, he was out very late. I was rather uneasy when he did not come in till just on the stroke of midnight; but we all got used to his whims; he took the key of the door, and we never sat up for him. He lived in a house belonging to us in the Rue des Casernes. Well, then, one of our stable-boys told us one evening that, going down to wash the horses in the river, he fancied he had seen the Spanish Grandee swimming some little way off, just like a fish. When he came in, I told him to be careful of the weeds, and he seemed put out at having been seen in the water.

'"At last, monsieur, one day, or rather one morning, we did not find him in his room; he had not come back. By hunting through his things, I found a written paper in the drawer of his table, with fifty pieces of Spanish gold of the kind they call doubloons,* worth about five thousand francs; and in a little sealed box ten thousand francs worth of diamonds. The paper said that in case he should not return, he left us this money and these diamonds in trust to found masses to thank God for his escape and for his salvation.

'"At that time I still had my husband, who ran off in search of him. And this is the queer part of the story: he brought back the Spaniard's clothes, which he had found under a big stone on a sort of break-water along the river bank, nearly opposite la Grande Bretêche. My husband went so early that no one saw him. After reading the letter, he burnt the clothes, and, in obedience to Count Férédia's wish, we announced that he had escaped.

'"The sub-prefect set all the constabulary at his heels; but, pshaw! he was never caught. Lepas believed that the Spaniard had drowned himself. I, sir, have never thought so; I believe, on the contrary, that he had something to do with the business about Madame de Merret, seeing that Rosalie told me that the crucifix her mistress was so fond of that she had it buried with her, was made of ebony and silver; now in the early days of his stay here, Monsieur Férédia had one of ebony and silver which I never saw later.—And now, monsieur, do not you say that I need have no remorse about the Spaniard's fifteen thousand francs? Are they not really and truly mine?"

'"Certainly.—But have you never tried to question Rosalie?" said I.

'"Oh, to be sure I have, sir. But what is to be done? That girl is like a wall. She knows something, but it is impossible to make her talk."

'After chatting with me for a few minutes, my hostess left me a prey to vague and sinister thoughts, to romantic curiosity, and a religious dread, not unlike the deep emotion which comes upon us when we go into a dark church at night and discern a feeble light glimmering under a lofty vault—a dim figure glides across—the sweep of a gown or of a priest's cassock is audible—and we shiver! La Grande Bretêche, with its rank grasses, its shuttered windows, its rusty iron-work, its locked doors, it deserted rooms, suddenly rose before me in fantastic vividness. I tried to get into the mysterious dwelling to search out the heart of this solemn story, this drama which had killed three persons.

'Rosalie became in my eyes the most interesting being in Vendôme. As I studied her, I detected signs of an inmost thought, in spite of the blooming health that glowed in her dimpled face. There was in her soul some element of truth or of hope; her manner suggested a secret, like the expression of devout souls who pray in excess, or of a girl who has killed her child and for ever hears its last cry. Nevertheless, she was simple and clumsy in her ways; her vacant smile had nothing criminal in it, and you would have pronounced her innocent only from seeing the large red and blue checked kerchief that covered her stalwart bust, tucked into the tight-laced square bodice of a lilac- and white-striped gown. "No," said I to myself, "I will not quit Vendôme without knowing the whole history of la Grande Bretêche. To achieve this end, I will make love to Rosalie if it proves necessary."

' "Rosalie!" said I one evening.

' "Your servant, sir?"

' "You are not married?" She started a little.

' "Oh! there is no lack of men if ever I take a fancy to be miserable!" she replied, laughing. She got over her agitation at once; for every woman, from the highest lady to the inn-servant inclusive, has a native presence of mind.

' "Yes; you are fresh and good-looking enough never to lack lovers! But tell me, Rosalie, why did you become an inn-servant on leaving Madame de Merret? Did she not leave you some little annuity?"

' "Oh yes, sir. But my place here is the best in all the town of Vendôme."

'This reply was such an one as judges and attorneys call evasive. Rosalie, as it seemed to me, held in this romantic affair the place of the middle square of the chess-board; she was at the very centre of the interest and of the truth; she appeared to me to be tied into the knot of it. It was not a case for ordinary love-making; this girl contained the last chapter of a romance, and from that moment all my attentions were devoted to Rosalie. By dint of studying the girl, I observed in her, as in every woman whom we make our ruling thought, a variety of good qualities; she was clean and neat; she was handsome, I need not say; she soon was possessed of every charm that desire can lend to a woman in whatever rank of life. A fortnight after the notary's visit, one evening, or rather one morning, in the small hours, I said to Rosalie:

' "Come, tell me all you know about Madame de Merret."

' "Oh!" she cried in terror, "do not ask me that, Monsieur Horace!"

'Her handsome features clouded over, her bright colouring grew pale, and her eyes lost their artless, liquid brightness.

' "Well," she said, "I will tell you; but keep the secret carefully."

' "All right, my child; I will keep all your secrets with a thief's honour, which is the most loyal known."

' "If it is all the same to you," said she, "I would rather it should be with your own."

'Thereupon she set her head-kerchief straight, and settled herself to tell the tale; for there is no doubt a particular attitude of confidence and security is necessary to the telling of a narrative. The best tales are told at a certain hour—just as we are all here at table. No one ever told a story well standing up, or fasting.

'If I were to reproduce exactly Rosalie's diffuse eloquence, a whole volume would scarcely contain it. Now, as the event of which she gave me a confused account stands exactly midway between the notary's gossip and that of Madame Lepas, as precisely as the middle term of a rule-of-three sum stands between the first and third, I have only to relate it in as few words as may be. I shall therefore be brief.

'The room at La Grande Bretêche in which Madame de Merret slept was on the ground floor; a little cupboard in the wall, about four feet deep, served her to hang her dresses in. Three months before the evening of which I have to relate the events, Madame de Merret had been seriously ailing, so much so that her husband had left her to herself, and had his own bedroom on the first floor. By one of those accidents which it is impossible to foresee, he came in that evening two hours later than usual from the club, where he went to read the papers and talk politics with the residents in the neighbourhood. His wife supposed him to have come in, to be in bed and asleep. But the invasion of France* had been the subject of a very animated discussion; the game of billiards had waxed vehement; he had lost forty francs, an enormous sum at Vendôme, where everybody is thrifty, and where social habits are restrained within the bounds of a simplicity worthy of all praise, and the foundation perhaps of a form of true happiness which no Parisian would care for.

'For some time past Monsieur de Merret had been satisfied to ask Rosalie whether his wife was in bed; on the girl's replying always in the affirmative, he at once went to his own room, with the good faith that comes of habit and confidence. But this evening, on coming in, he took it into his head to go to see Madame de Merret, to tell her of his ill-luck, and perhaps to find consolation. During dinner he had observed that his wife was very becomingly dressed; he reflected as he came home from the club that his wife was certainly much better, that convalescence had improved her beauty, discovering it, as husbands discover everything, a little too late. Instead of calling Rosalie, who was in the kitchen at the moment watching the cook and the coachman playing a puzzling hand at cards, Monsieur de Merret made his way to his wife's room by the light of his lantern, which he set down on the lowest step of the stairs. His step, easy to recognize, rang under the vaulted passage.

'At the instant when the gentleman turned the key to enter his wife's room, he fancied he heard the door shut of the closet of which I have spoken; but when he went in, Madame de Merret was alone, standing in front of the fireplace. The unsuspecting husband fancied that Rosalie was in the cupboard; nevertheless, a doubt, ringing in his ears like a peal of bells, put him on his guard; he looked at his wife, and read in her eyes an indescribably anxious and haunted expression.

'"You are very late," said she.—Her voice, usually so clear and sweet, struck him as being slightly husky.

'Monsieur de Merret made no reply, for at this moment Rosalie came in. This was like a thunder-clap. He walked up and down the room, going from one window to another at a regular pace, his arms folded.

'"Have you had bad news, or are you ill?" his wife asked him timidly, while Rosalie helped her to undress. He made no reply.

'"You can go, Rosalie," said Madame de Merret to her maid; "I can put in my curl-papers myself."—She scented disaster at the mere aspect of her husband's face, and wished to be alone with him. As soon as Rosalie was gone, or supposed to be gone, for she lingered a few minutes in the passage, Monsieur de Merret came and stood facing his wife, and said coldly, "Madame, there is some one in your cupboard!" She looked at her husband calmly, and replied quite simply, "No, monsieur."

'This "No" wrung Monsieur de Merret's heart; he did not believe it; and yet his wife had never appeared purer or more saintly than she seemed to be at this moment. He rose to go and open the closet door. Madame de Merret took his hand, stopped him, looked at him sadly, and said in a voice of strange emotion, "Remember, if you should find no one there, everything must be at an end between you and me."

'The extraordinary dignity of his wife's attitude filled him with deep esteem for her, and inspired him with one of those resolves which need only a grander stage to become immortal.

'"No, Josephine," he said, "I will not open it. In either event we should be parted for ever. Listen; I know all the purity of your soul, I know you lead a saintly life, and would not commit a deadly sin to save your life."—At these words Madame de Merret looked at her husband with a haggard stare.—"See, here is your crucifix," he went on. "Swear to me before God that there is no one in there; I will believe you—I will never open that door."

'Madame de Merret took up the crucifix and said, "I swear it."

'"Louder," said her husband; "and repeat: 'I swear before God that there is nobody in that closet.'" She repeated the words without flinching.

' "That will do," said Monsieur de Merret coldly. After a moment's silence: "You have there a fine piece of work which I never saw before," said he, examining the crucifix of ebony and silver, very artistically wrought.

' "I found it at Duvivier's; last year when that troop of Spanish prisoners came through Vendôme, he bought it of a Spanish monk."

' "Indeed," said Monsieur de Merret, hanging the crucifix on its nail; and he rang the bell.

'He had not to wait for Rosalie. Monsieur de Merret went forward quickly to meet her, led her into the bay of the window that looked on to the garden, and said to her in an undertone:

' "I know that Gorenflot wants to marry you, that poverty alone prevents your setting up house, and that you told him you would not be his wife till he found means to become a master mason.—Well, go and fetch him; tell him to come here with his trowel and tools. Contrive to wake no one in his house but himself. His reward will be beyond your wishes. Above all, go out without saying a word—or else!" and he frowned.

'Rosalie was going, and he called her back. "Here, take my latch-key," said he.

' "Jean!" Monsieur de Merret called in a voice of thunder down the passage. Jean, who was both coachman and confidential servant, left his cards and came.

' "Go to bed, all of you," said his master, beckoning him to come close; and the gentleman added in a whisper, "When they are all asleep—mind, *asleep*—you understand?—come down and tell me."

'Monsieur de Merret, who had never lost sight of his wife while giving his orders, quietly came back to her at the fireside, and began to tell her the details of the game of billiards and the discussion at the club. When Rosalie returned she found Monsieur and Madame de Merret conversing amiably.

'Not long before this Monsieur de Merret had had new ceilings made to all the reception-rooms on the ground floor. Plaster is very scarce at Vendôme; the price is enhanced by the cost of carriage; the gentleman had therefore had a considerable quantity delivered to him, knowing that he could always find purchasers for what might be left. It was this circumstance which suggested the plan he carried out.

' "Gorenflot is here, sir," said Rosalie in a whisper.

' "Tell him to come in," said her master aloud.

'Madame de Merret turned paler when she saw the mason.

'"Gorenflot," said her husband, "go and fetch some bricks from the coach-house; bring enough to wall up the door of this cupboard; you can use the plaster that is left for cement." Then, dragging Rosalie and the workman close to him—"Listen, Gorenflot," said he, in a low voice, "you are to sleep here to-night; but to-morrow morning you shall have a passport to take you abroad to a place I will tell you of. I will give you six thousand francs for your journey. You must live in that town for ten years; if you find you do not like it, you may settle in another, but it must be in the same country. Go through Paris and wait there till I join you. I will there give you an agreement for six thousand francs more, to be paid to you on your return, provided you have carried out the conditions of the bargain. For that price you are to keep perfect silence as to what you have to do this night. To you, Rosalie, I will secure ten thousand francs, which will not be paid to you till your wedding day, and on condition of your marrying Gorenflot; but, to get married, you must hold your tongue. If not, no wedding gift!"

'"Rosalie," said Madame de Merret, "come and brush my hair."

'Her husband quietly walked up and down the room, keeping an eye on the door, on the mason, and on his wife, but without any insulting display of suspicion. Gorenflot could not help making some noise. Madame de Merret seized a moment when he was unloading some bricks, and when her husband was at the other end of the room, to say to Rosalie: "My dear child, I will give you a thousand francs a year if only you will tell Gorenflot to leave a crack at the bottom." Then she added aloud quite coolly: "You had better help him."

'Monsieur and Madame de Merret were silent all the time while Gorenflot was walling up the door. This silence was intentional on the husband's part; he did not wish to give his wife the opportunity of saying anything with a double meaning. On Madame de Merret's side it was pride or prudence. When the wall was half built up the cunning mason took advantage of his master's back being turned to break one of the two panes in the top of the door with a blow of his pick. By this Madame de Merret understood that Rosalie had spoken to Gorenflot. They all three then saw the face of a dark, gloomy-looking man, with black hair and flaming eyes.

'Before her husband turned round again the poor woman had nodded to the stranger, to whom the signal was meant to convey, "Hope."

'At four o'clock, as day was dawning, for it was the month of September, the work was done. The mason was placed in charge of Jean, and Monsieur de Merret slept in his wife's room.

'Next morning when he got up he said with apparent carelessness, "Oh, by the way, I must go to the Mairie for the passport." He put on his hat, took two or three steps towards the door, paused, and took the crucifix. His wife was trembling with joy.

'"He will go to Duvivier's," thought she.

'As soon as he had left, Madame de Merret rang for Rosalie, and then in a terrible voice she cried: "The pick! Bring the pick! and set to work. I saw how Gorenflot did it yesterday; we shall have time to make a gap and build it up again."

'In an instant Rosalie had brought her mistress a sort of cleaver; she, with a vehemence of which no words can give an idea, set to work to demolish the wall. She had already got out a few bricks, when, turning to deal a stronger blow than before, she saw behind her Monsieur de Merret. She fainted away.

'"Lay madame on her bed," said he coldly.

'Foreseeing what would certainly happen in his absence, he had laid this trap for his wife; he had merely written to the Mairie and sent for Duvivier. The jeweller arrived just as the disorder in the room had been repaired.

'"Duvivier," asked Monsieur de Merret, "did not you buy some crucifixes of the Spaniards who passed through the town?"

'"No, monsieur."

'"Very good; thank you," said he, flashing a tiger's glare at his wife. "Jean," he added, turning to his confidential valet, "you can serve my meals here in Madame de Merret's room. She is ill, and I shall not leave her till she recovers."

'The cruel man remained in his wife's room for twenty days. During the earlier time, when there was some little noise in the closet, and Josephine wanted to intercede for the dying man, he said, without allowing her to utter a word, "You swore on the Cross that there was no one there."'

After this story all the ladies rose from table, and thus the spell under which Bianchon had held them was broken. But there were some among them who had almost shivered at the last words.

EDGAR ALLAN POE

Berenice—A Tale

❧❧

MISERY is manifold. The wretchedness of earth is multiform. Overreaching the wide horizon like the rainbow, its hues are as various as the hues of that arch, as distinct too, yet as intimately blended. Overreaching the wide horizon like the rainbow! How is it that from Beauty I have derived a type of unloveliness?—from the covenant of Peace a simile of sorrow? But thus is it. And as, in ethics, Evil is a consequence of Good, so, in fact, out of Joy is sorrow born. Either the memory of past bliss is the anguish of to-day, or the agonies which *are*, have their origin in the ecstasies which *might have been*. I have a tale to tell in its own essence rife with horror—I would suppress it were it not a record more of feelings than of facts.*

My baptismal name is Egæus*—that of my family I will not mention. Yet there are no towers in the land more time-honored than my gloomy, grey, hereditary halls. Our line has been called a race of visionaries: and in many striking particulars—in the character of the family mansion—in the frescos of the chief saloon—in the tapestries of the dormitories—in the chiseling of some buttresses in the armory—but more especially in the gallery of antique paintings—in the fashion of the library chamber—and, lastly, in the very peculiar nature of the library's contents, there is more than sufficient evidence to warrant the belief.

The recollections of my earliest years are connected with that chamber, and with its volumes—of which latter I will say no more. Here died my mother. Herein was I born. But it is mere idleness to say that I had not lived before—that the soul has no previous existence. You deny it. Let us not argue the matter. Convinced myself I seek not to convince. There is, however, a remembrance of ærial forms—of spiritual and meaning eyes—of sounds musical yet sad—a remembrance which will not be excluded: a memory like a shadow, vague, variable, indefinite, unsteady—and like a shadow too, in the impossibility of my getting rid of it, while the sunlight of my reason shall exist.

In that chamber was I born. Thus awaking, as it were, from the long night of what seemed, but was not, nonentity at once into the very regions of fairy land—into a palace of imagination—into the wild dominions of monastic thought and erudition—it is not singular that I gazed around me with a startled and ardent eye—that I loitered away my boyhood in books, and dissipated my youth in reverie—but it is singular that as years rolled away, and the noon of manhood found me still in the mansion of my fathers—it is wonderful what stagnation there fell upon the springs of my life—wonderful how total an inversion took place in the character of my common thoughts. The realities of the world affected me as visions, and as visions only, while the wild ideas of the land of dreams became, in turn,—not the material of my every-day existence—but in very deed that existence utterly and solely in itself.

* * * * *

Berenice* and I were cousins, and we grew up together in my paternal halls—Yet differently we grew. I ill of health and buried in gloom—she agile, graceful, and overflowing with energy. Hers the ramble on the hill side—mine the studies of the cloister. I living within my own heart, and addicted body and soul to the most intense and painful meditation—she roaming carelessly through life with no thought of the shadows in her path, or the silent flight of the raven-winged hours. Berenice!—I call upon her name—Berenice!—and from the grey ruins of memory a thousand tumultuous recollections are startled at the sound! Ah! vividly is her image before me now, as in the early days of her light-heartedness and joy! Oh! gorgeous yet fantastic beauty! Oh! Sylph amid the shrubberies of Arnheim!—Oh! Naiad* among her fountains!—and then—then all is mystery and terror, and a tale which should not be told. Disease—a fatal disease—fell like the Simoom* upon her frame, and, even while I gazed upon her, the spirit of change swept over her, pervading her mind, her habits, and her character, and, in a manner the most subtle and terrible, disturbing even the very identity of her person! Alas! the destroyer came and went, and the victim—where was she? I knew her not—or knew her no longer as Berenice.

Among the numerous train of maladies, superinduced by that fatal and primary one which effected a revolution of so horrible a kind in the moral and physical being of my cousin, may be mentioned as the most distressing and obstinate in its nature, a species of epilepsy not unfrequently terminating in *trance* itself—trance very nearly resembling positive dissolution, and from which her manner of recovery was, in most instances, startlingly abrupt. In the meantime my own disease—for I have been told that I should call it by no other appellation—my own disease, then, grew rapidly upon me, and, aggravated in its symptoms by the immoderate use of opium, assumed finally a monomaniac* character of a novel and extraordinary form—hourly and momentarily gaining vigor—and at length obtaining over me the most singular and incomprehensible ascendancy. This monomania—if I must so term it—consisted in a morbid irritability of the nerves immediately affecting those properties of the mind, in metaphysical science termed the *attentive*. It is more than probable that I am not understood—but I fear that it is indeed in no manner possible to convey to the mind of the merely general reader, an adequate idea of that nervous *intensity of interest* with which, in my case, the powers of meditation (not to speak technically) busied, and, as it were, buried themselves in the contemplation of even the most common objects of the universe.

To muse for long unwearied hours with my attention rivetted to some frivolous device upon the margin, or in the typography of a book—to become absorbed for the better part of a summer's day in a quaint shadow falling aslant upon the tapestry, or upon the floor—to lose myself for an entire night in watching the steady flame of a lamp, or the embers of a fire—to dream away whole days over the perfume of a flower—to repeat monotonously some common word, until the sound, by dint of frequent repetition, ceased to convey any idea whatever to the mind—to lose all sense of motion or physical existence in a state of absolute bodily quiescence long and obstinately persevered in—Such were a few of the most common and least pernicious vagaries induced by a condition of the mental faculties, not, indeed, altogether unparalleled, but certainly bidding defiance to any thing like analysis or explanation.

Yet let me not be misapprehended. The undue, intense, and morbid attention thus excited by objects in their own nature frivolous, must not be confounded in character with that ruminating propensity common to all mankind, and more especially indulged in by persons of ardent imagination. By no means. It was not even, as might be at first supposed, an extreme condition, or exaggeration of such propensity, but primarily and essentially distinct and different. In the one instance the dreamer, or enthusiast, being interested by an object usually *not* frivolous, imperceptibly loses sight of this object in a wilderness of deductions and suggestions issuing therefrom, until, at the conclusion of a day-dream *often replete with luxury*, he finds the *incitamentum** or first cause of his musings utterly vanished and forgotten. In my case the primary object was *invariably frivolous*, although assuming, through the medium of my distempered vision, a refracted and unreal importance. Few deductions—if any—were made; and those few pertinaciously returning in, so to speak, upon the original object as a centre. The meditations were *never* pleasurable; and, at the termination of the reverie, the first cause, so far from being out of sight, had attained that supernaturally exaggerated interest which was the prevailing feature of the disease. In a word, the powers of mind more particularly exercised were, with me, as I have said before, the *attentive*, and are, with the day-dreamer, the *speculative*.

My books, at this epoch, if they did not actually serve to irritate the disorder, partook, it will be perceived, largely, in their imaginative, and inconsequential nature, of the characteristic qualities of the disorder itself. I well remember, among others, the treatise of the noble Italian Cœlius Secundus Curio '*de amplitudine beati regni Dei*'*—St Austin's great work the 'City of God'*—and Tertullian '*de Carne Christi*,' in which the unintelligible sentence '*Mortuus est Dei filius; credibile est quia ineptum est: et sepultus resurrexit; certum est quia impossibile est*'* occupied my undivided time, for many weeks of laborious and fruitless investigation.

Thus it will appear that, shaken from its balance only by trivial things, my reason bore resemblance to that ocean-crag spoken of by Ptolemy Hephestion, which steadily resisting the attacks of human violence, and the fiercer fury of the waters and the winds, trembled only to the touch of the flower called Asphodel.* And although, to a careless thinker, it might appear a matter beyond doubt, that the fearful alteration produced by her unhappy malady, in the *moral* condition of Berenice, would afford me many objects for the exercise of that intense and morbid meditation whose nature I have been at some trouble in explaining, yet such was not by any means the case. In the lucid intervals of my infirmity, her calamity indeed gave me pain, and, taking deeply to heart that total wreck of her fair and gentle life, I did not fail to ponder frequently and bitterly upon the wonder-working means by which so strange a revolution had been so suddenly brought to pass. But these reflections partook not of the idiosyncrasy of my disease, and were such as would have occurred, under similar circumstances, to the ordinary mass of mankind. True to its own character, my disorder revelled in the less important but more startling changes wrought in the *physical* frame of Berenice, and in the singular and most appalling distortion of her personal identity.

During the brightest days of her unparalleled beauty, most surely I had never loved her. In the strange anomaly of my existence, feelings, with me, *had never been* of the heart, and my passions *always were* of the mind. Through the grey of the early morning—among the trellissed shadows of the forest at noon-day—and in the silence of my library at night, she had flitted by my eyes, and I had seen her—not as the living and breathing Berenice, but as the Berenice of a dream—not as a being of the earth—earthly—but as the abstraction of such a being—not as a thing to admire, but to analyze—not as an object of love, but as the theme of the most abstruse although desultory speculation. And *now*—now I shuddered in her presence, and grew pale at her approach; yet, bitterly lamenting her fallen and desolate condition, I knew that she had loved me long, and, in an evil moment, I spoke to her of marriage.

And at length the period of our nuptials was approaching, when, upon an afternoon in the winter of the year, one of those unseasonably warm, calm, and misty days which are the nurse of the beautiful Halcyon,[1]* I sat, and sat, as I thought alone, in the inner apartment of the library. But uplifting my eyes Berenice stood before me.

Was it my own excited imagination—or the misty influence of the atmosphere—or the uncertain twilight of the chamber—or the grey draperies which fell around her figure—that caused it to loom up in so unnatural a degree? I could not tell. Perhaps she had grown taller since her malady. She spoke, however, no word, and I—not for worlds could I have uttered a syllable. An icy chill ran through my frame; a sense of insufferable anxiety oppressed me; a consuming curiosity pervaded my soul; and, sinking back upon the chair, I remained for some time breathless, and motionless, and with my eyes rivetted upon her person. Alas! its emaciation was excessive, and not one vestige of the former being lurked in any single line of the contour. My burning glances at length fell upon her face.

[1] For as Jove, during the winter season, gives twice seven days of warmth, men have called this clement and temperate time the nurse of the beautiful Halcyon.—*Simonides.**

The forehead was high, and very pale, and singularly placid; and the once golden hair fell partially over it, and overshadowed the hollow temples with ringlets now black as the raven's ring, and jarring discordantly, in their fantastic character, with the reigning melancholy of the countenance. The eyes were lifeless, and lustreless, and I shrunk involuntarily from their glassy stare to the contemplation of the thin and shrunken lips. They parted: and, in a smile of peculiar meaning, the teeth of the changed Berenice disclosed themselves slowly to my view. Would to God that I had never beheld them, or that, having done so, I had died!

* * * * *

The shutting of a door disturbed me, and, looking up, I found my cousin had departed from the chamber. But from the disordered chamber of my brain, had not, alas! departed, and would not be driven away, the white and ghastly *spectrum** of the teeth. Not a speck upon their surface—not a shade on their enamel—not a line in their configuration—not an indenture in their edges—but what that brief period of her smile had sufficed to brand in upon my memory. I saw them now even more unequivocally than I beheld them *then*. The teeth!—the teeth!—they were here, and there, and every where, and visibly, and palpably before me, long, narrow, and excessively white, with the pale lips writhing about them, as in the very moment of their first terrible development. Then came the full fury of my *monomania*, and I struggled in vain against its strange and irresistible influence. In the multiplied objects of the external world I had no thoughts but for the teeth. All other matters and all different interests became absorbed in their single contemplation. They—they alone were present to the mental eye, and they, in their sole individuality, became the essence of my mental life. I held them in every light—I turned them in every attitude. I surveyed their characteristics—I dwelt upon their peculiarities—I pondered upon their conformation—I mused upon the alteration in their nature—and shuddered as I assigned to them in imagination a sensitive and sentient power, and even when unassisted by the lips, a capability of moral expression. Of Mad'selle Sallé* it has been said, '*que tous ses pas etoient des sentiments,*' and of Berenice I more seriously believed *que tous ses dents etoient des idées.**

And the evening closed in upon me thus—and then the darkness came, and tarried, and went—and the day again dawned—and the mists of a second night were now gathering around—and still I sat motionless in that solitary room, and still I sat buried in meditation, and still the *phantasma** of the teeth maintained its terrible ascendancy as, with the most vivid and hideous distinctness, it floated about amid the changing lights and shadows of the chamber. At length there broke forcibly in upon my dreams a wild cry as of horror and dismay; and thereunto, after a pause, succeeded the sound of troubled voices intermingled with many low meanings of sorrow, or of pain. I arose hurriedly from my seat, and, throwing open one of the doors of the library, there stood out in the antechamber a servant maiden, all in tears, and she told me that Berenice was—no more.* Seized with an epileptic fit she had fallen dead in the early morning, and now, at the closing in of the night, the grave was ready for its tenant, and all the preparations for the burial were completed.

With a heart full of grief, yet reluctantly, and oppressed with awe, I made my way to the bed-chamber of the departed. The room was large, and very dark, and at every step within its gloomy precincts I encountered the paraphernalia of the grave. The coffin, so a menial told me, lay surrounded by the curtains of yonder bed, and in that coffin, he whisperingly assured me, was all that remained of Berenice. Who was it asked me would I not look upon the corpse? I had seen the lips of no one move, yet the question had been demanded, and the echo of the syllables still lingered in the room. It was impossible to refuse; and with a sense of suffocation I dragged myself to the side of the bed. Gently I uplifted the sable draperies of the curtains.

As I let them fall they descended upon my shoulders, and shutting me thus out from the living, enclosed me in the strictest communion with the deceased.

The very atmosphere was redolent of death. The peculiar smell of the coffin sickened me; and I fancied a deleterious odor was already exhaling from the body. I would have given worlds to escape—to fly from the pernicious influence of mortality—to breathe once again the pure air of the eternal heavens. But I had no longer the power to move—my knees tottered beneath me—and I remained rooted to the spot, and gazing upon the frightful length of the rigid body as it lay outstretched in the dark coffin without a lid.

God of heaven!—is it possible? Is it my brain that reels—or was it indeed the finger of the enshrouded dead that stirred in the white cerement that bound it? Frozen with unutterable awe I slowly raised my eyes to the countenance of the corpse. There had been a band around the jaws, but, I know not how, it was broken asunder. The livid lips were wreathed into a species of smile, and, through the enveloping gloom, once again there glared upon me in too palpable reality, the while and glistening, and ghastly teeth of Berenice. I sprang convulsively from the bed, and, uttering no word, rushed forth a maniac from that apartment of triple horror, and mystery, and death.*

* * * * *

I found myself again sitting in the library, and again sitting there alone. It seemed that I had newly awakened from a confused and exciting dream. I knew that it was now midnight, and I was well aware that since the setting of the sun Berenice had been interred. But of that dreary period which had intervened I had no positive, at least no definite comprehension. Yet its memory was rife with horror—horror more horrible from being vague, and terror more terrible from ambiguity. It was a fearful page in the record of my existence, written all over with dim, and hideous, and unintelligible recollections. I strived to decypher them, but in vain—while ever and anon, like the spirit of a departed sound, the shrill and piercing shriek of a female voice seemed to be ringing in my ears. I had done a deed—what was it? And the echoes of the chamber answered me 'what was it?'

On the table beside me burned a lamp, and near it lay a little box of ebony. It was a box of no remarkable character, and I had seen it frequently before, it being the property of the family physician; but how came it *there* upon my table, and why did I shudder in regarding it? These were things in no manner to be accounted for, and my eyes at length dropped to the open pages of a book, and to a sentence underscored therein. The words were the singular, but simple words of the poet Ebn Zaiat.* '*Dicebant mihi sodales si sepulchrum amicœ visit arem curas meas aliquantulum fore levatas.*'[2] Why then, as I perused them, did the hairs of my head erect themselves on end, and the blood of my body congeal within my veins?

There came a light tap at the library door, and, pale as the tenant of a tomb, a menial entered upon tiptoe. His looks were wild with terror, and he spoke to me in a voice tremulous, husky, and very low. What said he?—some broken sentences I heard. He told of a wild

---

[2] My companions told me I might find some little alleviation of my misery, in visiting the grave of my beloved.

cry heard in the silence of the night—of the gathering together of the household—of a search in the direction of the sound—and then his tones grew thrillingly distinct as he whispered me of a violated grave—of a disfigured body discovered upon its margin—a body enshrouded, yet still breathing, still palpitating, still alive!*

He pointed to my garments—they were muddy and clotted with gore. I spoke not, and he took me gently by the hand—but it was indented with the impress of human nails. He directed my attention to some object against the wall—I looked at it for some minutes— it was a spade. With a shriek I bounded to the table, and grasped the ebony box that lay upon it. But I could not force it open, and in my tremor it slipped from out my hands, and fell heavily, and burst into pieces, and from it, with a rattling sound, there rolled out some instruments of dental surgery, intermingled with many white and glistening substances that were scattered to and fro about the floor.

SHERIDAN LE FANU

Strange Event in the Life of
Schalken the Painter

Being a Seventh Extract from the Legacy of the late
Francis Purcell, P.P. of Drumcoolagh*

❧❦

YOU will no doubt be surprised, my dear friend, at the subject
of the following narrative.* What had I to do with Schalken, or
Schalken with me? He had returned to his native land, and was
probably dead and buried, before I was born; I never visited Holland
nor spoke with a native of that country. So much I believe you already
know. I must, then, give you my authority, and state to you frankly the
ground upon which rests the credibility of the strange story which
I am about to lay before you.

I was acquainted, in my early days, with a Captain Vandael, whose
father had served King William in the Low Countries, and also in
my own unhappy land during the Irish campaigns.* I know not how
it happened that I liked this man's society, spite of his politics and
religion: but so it was; and it was by means of the free intercourse to
which our intimacy gave rise that I became possessed of the curious
tale which you are about to hear.

I had often been struck, while visiting Vandael, by a remarkable
picture, in which, though no *connoisseur* myself, I could not fail to
discern some very strong peculiarities, particularly in the distribution
of light and shade, as also a certain oddity in the design itself, which
interested my curiosity. It represented the interior of what might be
a chamber in some antique religious building—the foreground was
occupied by a female figure, arrayed in a species of white robe, part
of which is arranged so as to form a veil. The dress, however, is not
strictly that of any religious order. In its hand the figure bears a lamp,
by whose light alone the form and face are illuminated; the features are
marked by an arch smile, such as pretty women wear when engaged

in successfully practising some roguish trick; in the background, and, excepting where the dim red light of an expiring fire serves to define the form, totally in the shade, stands the figure of a man equipped in the old fashion, with doublet* and so forth, in an attitude of alarm, his hand being placed upon the hilt of his sword, which he appears to be in the act of drawing.

'There are some pictures,' said I to my friend, 'which impress one, I know not how, with a conviction that they represent not the mere ideal shapes and combinations which have floated through the imagination of the artist, but scenes, faces, and situations which have actually existed. When I look upon that picture, something assures me that I behold the representation of a reality.'

Vandael smiled, and, fixing his eyes upon the painting musingly, he said:

'Your fancy has not deceived you, my good friend, for that picture is the record, and I believe a faithful one, of a remarkable and mysterious occurrence. It was painted by Schalken, and contains, in the face of the female figure, which occupies the most prominent place in the design, an accurate portrait of Rose Velderkaust, the niece of Gerard Douw,* the first and, I believe, the only love of Godfrey Schalken. My father knew the painter well, and from Schalken himself he learned the story of the mysterious drama, one scene of which the picture has embodied. This painting, which is accounted a fine specimen of Schalken's style, was bequeathed to my father by the artist's will, and, as you have observed, is a very striking and interesting production.'

I had only to request Vandael to tell the story of the painting in order to be gratified; and thus it is that I am enabled to submit to you a faithful recital of what I heard myself, leaving you to reject or to allow the evidence upon which the truth of the tradition depends, with this one assurance, that Schalken was an honest, blunt Dutchman, and, I believe, wholly incapable of committing a flight of imagination; and further, that Vandael, from whom I heard the story, appeared firmly convinced of its truth.

There are few forms upon which the mantle of mystery and romance could seem to hang more ungracefully than upon that of the uncouth and clownish Schalken—the Dutch boor—the rude and dogged, but most cunning worker in oils, whose pieces delight the initiated of the present day almost as much as his manners disgusted the refined of his own; and yet this man, so rude, so dogged, so slovenly, I had almost said so savage, in mien* and manner, during his after successes, had been selected by the capricious goddess, in his early life, to figure as the hero of a romance by no means devoid of interest or of mystery.

Who can tell how meet he may have been in his young days to play the part of the lover or of the hero—who can say that in early life he had been the same harsh, unlicked, and rugged boor that, in his maturer age, he proved—or how far the neglected rudeness which afterwards marked his air, and garb, and manners, may not have been the growth of that reckless apathy not unfrequently produced by bitter misfortunes and disappointments in early life?

These questions can never now be answered.

We must content ourselves, then, with a plain statement of facts, or what have been received and transmitted as such, leaving matters of speculation to those who like them.

When Schalken studied under the immortal Gerard Douw, he was a young man; and in spite of the phlegmatic constitution and unexcitable manner which he shared, we believe, with his countrymen, he was not incapable of deep and vivid impressions, for it is an established fact that the young painter looked with considerable interest upon the beautiful niece of his wealthy master.

Rose Velderkaust was very young, having, at the period of which we speak, not yet attained her seventeenth year, and, if tradition speaks truth, possessed all the soft dimpling charms of the fair, light-haired Flemish maidens. Schalken had not studied long in the school of Gerard Douw, when he felt this interest deepening into something of a keener and intenser feeling than was quite consistent with the tranquillity of his honest Dutch heart; and at the same time he perceived, or thought he perceived, flattering symptoms of a reciprocity of liking, and this was quite sufficient to determine whatever indecision he might have heretofore experienced, and to lead him to devote exclusively to her every hope and feeling of his heart. In short, he was as much in love as a Dutchman could be. He was not long in making his passion known to the pretty maiden herself, and his declaration was followed by a corresponding confession upon her part.

Schalken, however, was a poor man, and he possessed no counterbalancing advantages of birth or position to induce the old man to consent to a union which must involve his niece and ward in the strugglings and difficulties of a young and nearly friendless artist. He was, therefore, to wait until time had furnished him with opportunity, and accident with success; and then, if his labours were found sufficiently lucrative, it was to be hoped that his proposals might at least be listened to by her jealous guardian. Months passed away, and, cheered by the smiles of the little Rose, Schalken's labours were redoubled, and with such effect and improvement as reasonably to promise the realisation of his hopes, and no contemptible eminence in his art, before many years should have elapsed.

The even course of this cheering prosperity was, however, destined to experience a sudden and formidable interruption, and that, too, in a manner so strange and mysterious as to baffle all investigation, and throw upon the events themselves a shadow of almost supernatural horror.

Schalken had one evening remained in the master's studio considerably longer than his more volatile companions, who had gladly availed themselves of the excuse which the dusk of evening afforded, to withdraw from their several tasks, in order to finish a day of labour in the jollity and conviviality of the tavern.

But Schalken worked for improvement, or rather for love. Besides, he was now engaged merely in sketching a design, an operation which, unlike that of colouring, might be continued as long as there was light sufficient to distinguish between canvas and charcoal. He had not then, nor, indeed, until long after, discovered the peculiar powers of his pencil, and he was engaged in composing a group of extremely roguish-looking and grotesque imps and demons, who were inflicting various ingenious torments upon a perspiring and pot-bellied St Anthony,* who reclined in the midst of them, apparently in the last stage of drunkenness.

The young artist, however, though incapable of executing, or even of appreciating, anything of true sublimity, had nevertheless discernment enough to prevent his being by any means satisfied with his work; and many were the patient erasures and corrections which the limbs and features of saint and devil underwent, yet all without producing in their new arrangement anything of improvement or increased effect.

The large, old-fashioned room was silent, and, with the exception of himself, quite deserted by its usual inmates. An hour had passed—nearly two—without any improved result. Daylight had already

declined, and twilight was fast giving way to the darkness of night.
The patience of the young man was exhausted, and he stood before
his unfinished production, absorbed in no very pleasing ruminations,
one hand buried in the folds of his long dark hair, and the other
holding the piece of charcoal which had so ill executed its office,
and which he now rubbed, without much regard to the sable streaks
which it produced, with irritable pressure upon his ample Flemish
inexpressibles.

'Pshaw!' said the young man aloud, 'would that picture, devils,
saint, and all, were where they should be—in hell!'

A short, sudden laugh, uttered startlingly close to his ear, instantly
responded to the ejaculation.

The artist turned sharply round, and now for the first time became
aware that his labours had been overlooked by a stranger.

Within about a yard and a half, and rather behind him, there stood
what was, or appeared to be, the figure of an elderly man: he wore
a short cloak, and broad-brimmed hat with a conical crown, and in
his hand, which was protected with a heavy, gauntlet-shaped glove, he
carried a long ebony walking-stick, surmounted with what appeared,
as it glittered dimly in the twilight, to be a massive head of gold, and
upon his breast, through the folds of the cloak, there shone what
appeared to be the links of a rich chain of the same metal.

The room was so obscure that nothing further of the appearance of
the figure could be ascertained, and the face was altogether overshadowed by the heavy flap of the beaver* which overhung it, so that not
a feature could be discerned. A quantity of dark hair escaped from
beneath this sombre hat, a circumstance which, connected with the
firm, upright carriage of the intruder, proved that his years could not
yet exceed threescore or thereabouts.

There was an air of gravity and importance about the garb of this
person, and something indescribably odd, I might say awful, in the
perfect, stone-like movelessness of the figure, that effectually checked
the testy comment which had at once risen to the lips of the irritated
artist. He therefore, as soon as he had sufficiently recovered the surprise, asked the stranger, civilly, to be seated, and desired to know if
he had any message to leave for his master.

'Tell Gerard Douw,' said the unknown, without altering his
attitude in the smallest degree, 'that Mynher* Vanderhausen, of
Rotterdam, desires to speak with him to-morrow evening at this

hour, and, if he please, in this room, upon matters of weight—that is all. Goodnight.'

The stranger, having finished this message, turned abruptly, and, with a quick but silent step, quitted the room, before Schalken had time to say a word in reply.

The young man felt a curiosity to see in what direction the burgher of Rotterdam would turn on quitting the studio, and for that purpose he went directly to the window which commanded the door.

A lobby of considerable extent intervened between the inner door of the painter's room and the street entrance, so that Schalken occupied the post of observation before the old man could possibly have reached the street.

He watched in vain, however. There was no other mode of exit.

Had the old man vanished, or was he lurking about the recesses of the lobby for some bad purpose? This last suggestion filled the mind of Schalken with a vague horror, which was so unaccountably intense as to make him alike afraid to remain in the room alone and reluctant to pass through the lobby.

However, with an effort which appeared very disproportioned to the occasion, he summoned resolution to leave the room, and, having double-locked the door and thrust the key in his pocket, without looking to the right or left, he traversed the passage which had so recently, perhaps still, contained the person of his mysterious visitant, scarcely venturing to breathe till he had arrived in the open street.

'Mynher Vanderhausen,' said Gerard Douw within himself, as the appointed hour approached, 'Mynher Vanderhausen of Rotterdam! I never heard of the man till yesterday. What can he want of me? A portrait, perhaps, to be painted; or a younger son or a poor relation to be apprenticed; or a collection to be valued; or—pshaw! there's no one in Rotterdam to leave me a legacy. Well, whatever the business may be, we shall soon know it all.'

It was now the close of day, and every easel, except that of Schalken, was deserted. Gerard Douw was pacing the apartment with the restless step of impatient expectation, every now and then humming a passage from a piece of music which he was himself composing; for, though no great proficient, he admired the art; sometimes pausing to glance over the work of one of his absent pupils, but more frequently placing himself at the window, from whence he might observe the passengers who threaded the obscure by-street in which his studio was placed.

'Said you not, Godfrey,' exclaimed Douw, after a long and fruitless gaze from his post of observation, and turning to Schalken—'said you not the hour of appointment was at about seven by the clock of the Stadhouse?'*

'It had just told seven when I first saw him, sir,' answered the student.

'The hour is close at hand, then,' said the master, consulting a horologe* as large and as round as a full-grown orange. 'Mynher Vanderhausen, from Rotterdam—is it not so?'

'Such was the name.'

'And an elderly man, richly clad?' continued Douw.

'As well as I might see,' replied his pupil; 'he could not be young, nor yet very old neither, and his dress was rich and grave, as might become a citizen of wealth and consideration.'

At this moment the sonorous boom of the Stadhouse clock told, stroke after stroke, the hour of seven; the eyes of both master and student were directed to the door; and it was not until the last peal of the old bell had ceased to vibrate, that Douw exclaimed:

'So, so; we shall have his worship presently—that is, if he means to keep his hour; if not, thou mayst wait for him, Godfrey, if you court the acquaintance of a capricious burgomaster.* As for me, I think our old Leyden* contains a sufficiency of such commodities, without an importation from Rotterdam.'

Schalken laughed, as in duty bound; and after a pause of some minutes, Douw suddenly exclaimed:

'What if it should all prove a jest, a piece of mummery got up by Vankarp, or some such worthy! I wish you had run all risks, and cudgelled the old burgomaster, stadholder,* or whatever else he may be, soundly. I would wager a dozen of Rhenish,* his worship would have pleaded old acquaintance before the third application.'

'Here he comes, sir,' said Schalken, in a low admonitory tone; and instantly, upon turning towards the door, Gerard Douw observed the same figure which had, on the day before, so unexpectedly greeted the vision of his pupil Schalken.

There was something in the air and mien of the figure which at once satisfied the painter that there was no *mummery* in the case, and that he really stood in the presence of a man of worship; and so, without hesitation, he doffed his cap, and courteously saluting the stranger, requested him to be seated.

The visitor waved his hand slightly, as if in acknowledgment of the courtesy, but remained standing.

'I have the honour to see Mynher Vanderhausen, of Rotterdam?' said Gerard Douw.

'The same,' was the laconic reply of his visitant.

'I understand your worship desires to speak with me,' continued Douw, 'and I am here by appointment to wait your commands.'

'Is that a man of trust?' said Vanderhausen, turning towards Schalken, who stood at a little distance behind his master.

'Certainly,' replied Gerard.

'Then let him take this box and get the nearest jeweller or gold-smith to value its contents, and let him return hither with a certificate of the valuation.'

At the same time he placed a small case, about nine inches square, in the hands of Gerard Douw, who was as much amazed at its weight as at the strange abruptness with which it was handed to him.

In accordance with the wishes of the stranger, he delivered it into the hands of Schalken, and repeating *his* directions, despatched him upon the mission.

Schalken disposed his precious charge securely beneath the folds of his cloak, and rapidly traversing two or three narrow streets, he stopped at a corner house, the lower part of which was then occupied by the shop of a Jewish goldsmith.

Schalken entered the shop, and calling the little Hebrew into the obscurity of its back recesses, he proceeded to lay before him Vanderhausen's packet.

On being examined by the light of a lamp, it appeared entirely cased with lead, the outer surface of which was much scraped and soiled, and nearly white with age. This was with difficulty partially removed, and disclosed beneath a box of some dark and singularly hard wood; this, too, was forced, and after the removal of two or three folds of linen, its contents proved to be a mass of golden ingots, close packed, and, as the Jew declared, of the most perfect quality.

Every ingot underwent the scrutiny of the little Jew, who seemed to feel an epicurean delight in touching and testing these morsels of the glorious metal; and each one of them was replaced in the box with the exclamation:

'*Mein Gott*, how very perfect! not one grain of alloy—beautiful, beautiful!'

The task was at length finished, and the Jew certified under his hand the value of the ingots submitted to his examination to amount to many thousand rix-dollars.*

With the desired document in his bosom, and the rich box of gold carefully pressed under his arm, and concealed by his cloak, he retraced his way, and entering the studio, found his master and the stranger in close conference.

Schalken had no sooner left the room, in order to execute the commission he had taken in charge, than Vanderhausen addressed Gerard Douw in the following terms:

'I may not tarry with you to-night more than a few minutes, and so I shall briefly tell you the matter upon which I come. You visited the town of Rotterdam some four months ago, and then I saw in the church of St Lawrence* your niece, Rose Velderkaust. I desire to marry her, and if I satisfy you as to the fact that I am very wealthy—more wealthy than any husband you could dream of for her—I expect that you will forward my views to the utmost of your authority. If you approve my proposal, you must close with it at once, for I cannot command time enough to wait for calculations and delays.'

Gerard Douw was, perhaps, as much astonished as anyone could be by the very unexpected nature of Mynher Vanderhausen's communication; but he did not give vent to any unseemly expression of surprise, for besides the motives supplied by prudence and politeness, the painter experienced a kind of chill and oppressive sensation, something like that which is supposed to affect a man who is placed unconsciously in immediate contact with something to which he has a natural antipathy—an undefined horror and dread while standing in the presence of the eccentric stranger, which made him very unwilling to say anything which might reasonably prove offensive.

'I have no doubt,' said Gerard, after two or three prefatory hems, 'that the connection which you propose would prove alike advantageous and honourable to my niece; but you must be aware that she has a will of her own, and may not acquiesce in what *we* may design for her advantage.'

'Do not seek to deceive me, Sir Painter,' said Vanderhausen; 'you are her guardian—she is your ward. She is mine if *you* like to make her so.'

The man of Rotterdam moved forward a little as he spoke, and Gerard Douw, he scarce knew why, inwardly prayed for the speedy return of Schalken.

'I desire,' said the mysterious gentleman, 'to place in your hands at once an evidence of my wealth, and a security for my liberal dealing with your niece. The lad will return in a minute or two with a sum in value five times the fortune which she has a right to expect from a husband. This shall lie in your hands, together with her dowry, and you may apply the united sum as suits her interest best; it shall be all exclusively hers while she lives. Is that liberal?'

Douw assented, and inwardly thought that fortune had been extraordinarily kind to his niece. The stranger, he thought, must be both wealthy and generous, and such an offer was not to be despised, though made by a humourist, and one of no very prepossessing presence.

Rose had no very high pretensions, for she was almost without dowry; indeed, altogether so, excepting so far as the deficiency had been supplied by the generosity of her uncle. Neither had she any right to raise any scruples against the match on the score of birth, for her own origin was by no means elevated; and as to other objections, Gerard resolved, and, indeed, by the usages of the time was warranted in resolving, not to listen to them for a moment.

'Sir,' said he, addressing the stranger, 'your offer is most liberal, and whatever hesitation I may feel in closing with it immediately, arises solely from my not having the honour of knowing anything of your family or station. Upon these points you can, of course, satisfy me without difficulty?'

'As to my respectability,' said the stranger, drily, 'you must take that for granted at present; pester me with no inquiries; you can discover nothing more about me than I choose to make known. You shall have sufficient security for my respectability—my word, if you are honourable: if you are sordid, my gold.'

'A testy old gentleman,' thought Douw; 'he must have his own way. But, all things considered, I am justified in giving my niece to him. Were she my own daughter, I would do the like by her. I will not pledge myself unnecessarily, however.'

'You will not pledge yourself unnecessarily,' said Vanderhausen, strangely uttering the very words which had just floated through the mind of his companion; 'but you will do so if it *is* necessary, I presume; and I will show you that I consider it indispensable. If the gold

I mean to leave in your hands satisfy you, and if you desire that my proposal shall not be at once withdrawn, you must, before I leave this room, write your name to this engagement.'

Having thus spoken, he placed a paper in the hands of Gerard, the contents of which expressed an engagement entered into by Gerard Douw, to give to Wilken Vanderhausen, of Rotterdam, in marriage, Rose Velderkaust, and so forth, within one week of the date hereof.

While the painter was employed in reading this covenant, Schalken, as we have stated, entered the studio, and having delivered the box and the valuation of the Jew into the hands of the stranger, he was about to retire, when Vanderhausen called to him to wait; and, presenting the case and the certificate to Gerard Douw, he waited in silence until he had satisfied himself by an inspection of both as to the value of the pledge left in his hands. At length he said:

'Are you content?'

The painter said he would fain have another day to consider.

'Not an hour,' said the suitor, coolly.

'Well, then,' said Douw, 'I am content; it is a bargain.'

'Then sign at once,' said Vanderhausen; 'I am weary.'

At the same time he produced a small case of writing materials, and Gerard signed the important document.

'Let this youth witness the covenant,' said the old man; and Godfrey Schalken unconsciously signed the instrument which bestowed upon another that hand which he had so long regarded as the object and reward of all his labours.

The compact being thus completed, the strange visitor folded up the paper, and stowed it safely in an inner pocket.

'I will visit you to-morrow night, at nine of the clock, at your house, Gerard Douw, and will see the subject of our contract. Farewell.' And so saying, Wilken Vanderhausen moved stiffly, but rapidly out of the room.

Schalken, eager to resolve his doubts, had placed himself by the window in order to watch the street entrance; but the experiment served only to support his suspicions, for the old man did not issue from the door. This was very strange, very odd, very fearful. He and his master returned together, and talked but little on the way, for each had his own subjects of reflection, of anxiety, and of hope.

Schalken, however, did not know the ruin which threatened his cherished schemes.

Gerard Douw knew nothing of the attachment which had sprung up between his pupil and his niece; and even if he had, it is doubtful whether he would have regarded its existence as any serious obstruction to the wishes of Mynher Vanderhausen.

Marriages were then and there matters of traffic and calculation; and it would have appeared as absurd in the eyes of the guardian to make a mutual attachment an essential element in a contract of marriage, as it would have been to draw up his bonds and receipts in the language of chivalrous romance.

The painter, however, did not communicate to his niece the important step which he had taken in her behalf, and his resolution arose not from any anticipation of opposition on her part, but solely from a ludicrous consciousness that if his ward were, as she very naturally might do, to ask him to describe the appearance of the bridegroom whom he destined for her, he would be forced to confess that he had not seen his face, and, if called upon, would find it impossible to identify him.

Upon the next day, Gerard Douw having dined, called his niece to him, and having scanned her person with an air of satisfaction, he took her hand, and looking upon her pretty, innocent face with a smile of kindness, he said:

'Rose, my girl, that face of yours will make your fortune.' Rose blushed and smiled. 'Such faces and such tempers seldom go together, and, when they do, the compound is a love-potion which few heads or hearts can resist. Trust me, thou wilt soon be a bride, girl. But this is trifling, and I am pressed for time, so make ready the large room by eight o'clock to-night, and give directions for supper at nine. I expect a friend to-night; and observe me, child, do thou trick thyself out handsomely. I would not have him think us poor or sluttish.'

With these words he left the chamber, and took his way to the room to which we have already had occasion to introduce our readers—that in which his pupils worked.

When the evening closed in, Gerard called Schalken, who was about to take his departure to his obscure and comfortless lodgings, and asked him to come home and sup with Rose and Vanderhausen.

The invitation was of course accepted, and Gerard Douw and his pupil soon found themselves in the handsome and somewhat antique-looking room which had been prepared for the reception of the stranger.

A cheerful wood-fire blazed in the capacious hearth; a little at one side an old-fashioned table, with richly-carved legs, was placed—destined, no doubt, to receive the supper, for which preparations were going forward; and ranged with exact regularity, stood the tall-backed chairs, whose ungracefulness was more than counterbalanced by their comfort.

The little party, consisting of Rose, her uncle, and the artist, awaited the arrival of the expected visitor with considerable impatience.

Nine o'clock at length came, and with it a summons at the street-door, which, being speedily answered, was followed by a slow and emphatic tread upon the staircase; the steps moved heavily across the lobby, the door of the room in which the party which we have described were assembled slowly opened, and there entered a figure which startled, almost appalled, the phlegmatic Dutchmen, and nearly made Rose scream with affright; it was the form, and arrayed in the garb, of Mynher Vanderhausen; the air, the gait, the height was the same, but the features had never been seen by any of the party before.

The stranger stopped at the door of the room, and displayed his form and face completely. He wore a dark-coloured cloth cloak, which was short and full, not falling quite to the knees; his legs were cased in dark purple silk stockings, and his shoes were adorned with roses of the same colour. The opening of the cloak in front showed the under-suit to consist of some very dark, perhaps sable material, and his hands were enclosed in a pair of heavy leather gloves which ran up considerably above the wrist, in the manner of a gauntlet. In one hand he carried his walking-stick and his hat, which he had removed, and the other hung heavily by his side. A quantity of grizzled hair descended in long tresses from his head, and its folds rested upon the plaits of a stiff ruff, which effectually concealed his neck.

So far all was well; but the face!—all the flesh of the face was coloured with the bluish leaden hue which is sometimes produced by the operation of metallic medicines administered in excessive quantities; the eyes were enormous, and the white appeared both above and below the iris, which gave to them an expression of insanity, which was heightened by their glassy fixedness; the nose was well enough, but the mouth was writhed considerably to one side, where it opened in order to give egress to two long, discoloured fangs, which projected from the upper jaw, far below the lower lip; the hue of the lips themselves bore the usual relation to that of the face, and was consequently nearly black. The character of the face was malignant, even satanic, to the last degree; and, indeed, such a combination of horror could hardly be accounted for, except by supposing the corpse of some atrocious malefactor, which had long hung blackening upon the gibbet, to have at length become the habitation of a demon—the frightful sport of Satanic possession.

It was remarkable that the worshipful stranger suffered as little as possible of his flesh to appear, and that during his visit he did not once remove his gloves.

Having stood for some moments at the door, Gerard Douw at length found breath and collectedness to bid him welcome, and, with a mute inclination of the head, the stranger stepped forward into the room.

There was something indescribably odd, even horrible, about all his motions, something undefinable, that was unnatural, unhuman— it was as if the limbs were guided and directed by a spirit unused to the management of bodily machinery.

The stranger said hardly anything during his visit, which did not exceed half an hour; and the host himself could scarcely muster courage enough to utter the few necessary salutations and cour- tesies: and, indeed, such was the nervous terror which the presence of Vanderhausen inspired, that very little would have made all his entertainers fly bellowing from the room.

They had not so far lost all self-possession, however, as to fail to observe two strange peculiarities of their visitor.

During his stay he did not once suffer his eyelids to close, nor even to move in the slightest degree; and further, there was a death-like stillness in his whole person, owing to the total absence of the heaving motion of the chest, caused by the process of respiration.

These two peculiarities, though when told they may appear trif- ling, produced a very striking and unpleasant effect when seen and observed. Vanderhausen at length relieved the painter of Leyden of his inauspicious presence; and with no small gratification the little party heard the street-door close after him.

'Dear uncle,' said Rose, 'what a frightful man! I would not see him again for the wealth of the States!'

'Tush, foolish girl!' said Douw, whose sensations were anything but comfortable. 'A man may be as ugly as the devil, and yet if his heart and actions are good, he is worth all the pretty-faced, perfumed puppies that walk the Mall. Rose, my girl, it is very true he has not thy pretty face, but I know him to be wealthy and liberal; and were he ten times more ugly——'

'Which is inconceivable,' observed Rose.

'These two virtues would be sufficient,' continued her uncle, 'to counterbalance all his deformity; and if not of power sufficient actually to alter the shape of the features, at least of efficacy enough to prevent one thinking them amiss.'

'Do you know, uncle,' said Rose, 'when I saw him standing at the door, I could not get it out of my head that I saw the old, painted, wooden figure that used to frighten me so much in the church of St Laurence of Rotterdam.'

Gerard laughed, though he could not help inwardly acknowledging the justness of the comparison. He was resolved, however, as far as he could, to check his niece's inclination to ridicule the ugliness of her intended bridegroom, although he was not a little pleased to observe that she appeared totally exempt from that mysterious dread of the stranger which, he could not disguise it from himself, considerably affected him, as also his pupil Godfrey Schalken.

Early on the next day there arrived, from various quarters of the town, rich presents of silks, velvets, jewellery, and so forth, for Rose; and also a packet directed to Gerard Douw, which, on being opened, was found to contain a contract of marriage, formally drawn up, between Wilken Vanderhausen of the Boom-quay,* in Rotterdam, and Rose Velderkaust of Leyden, niece to Gerard Douw, master in the art of painting, also of the same city; and containing engagements on the part of Vanderhausen to make settlements upon his bride, far more splendid than he had before led her guardian to believe likely, and which were to be secured to her use in the most unexceptionable manner possible—the money being placed in the hands of Gerard Douw himself.

I have no sentimental scenes to describe, no cruelty of guardians, or magnanimity of wards, or agonies of lovers. The record I have to make is one of sordidness, levity,* and interest. In less than a week after the first interview which we have just described, the contract of marriage was fulfilled, and Schalken saw the prize which he would have risked anything to secure, carried off triumphantly by his formidable rival.

For two or three days he absented himself from the school; he then returned and worked, if with less cheerfulness, with far more dogged resolution than before; the dream of love had given place to that of ambition.

Months passed away, and, contrary to his expectation, and, indeed, to the direct promise of the parties, Gerard Douw heard nothing of his niece, or her worshipful spouse. The interest of the money, which was to have been demanded in quarterly sums, lay unclaimed in his hands. He began to grow extremely uneasy.

Mynher Vanderhausen's direction in Rotterdam he was fully possessed of. After some irresolution he finally determined to journey thither—a trifling undertaking, and easily accomplished—and thus to satisfy himself of the safety and comfort of his ward, for whom he entertained an honest and strong affection.

His search was in vain, however. No one in Rotterdam had ever heard of Mynher Vanderhausen.

Gerard Douw left not a house in the Boom-quay untried; but all in vain. No one could give him any information whatever touching the object of his inquiry; and he was obliged to return to Leyden, nothing wiser than when he had left it.

On his arrival he hastened to the establishment from which Vanderhausen had hired the lumbering though, considering the times, most luxurious vehicle which the bridal party had employed to convey them to Rotterdam. From the driver of this machine he learned, that having proceeded by slow stages, they had late in the evening approached Rotterdam; but that before they entered the city, and while yet nearly a mile from it, a small party of men, soberly clad, and after the old fashion, with peaked beards and moustaches, standing in the centre of the road, obstructed the further progress of the carriage. The driver reined in his horses, much fearing, from the obscurity of the hour, and the loneliness of the road, that some mischief was intended.

His fears were, however, somewhat allayed by his observing that these strange men carried a large litter, of an antique shape, and which they immediately set down upon the pavement, whereupon the bridegroom, having opened the coach-door from within, descended, and having assisted his bride to do likewise, led her, weeping bitterly and wringing her hands, to the litter, which they both entered. It was then raised by the men who surrounded it, and speedily carried towards the city, and before it had proceeded many yards the darkness concealed it from the view of the Dutch charioteer.

In the inside of the vehicle he found a purse, whose contents more than thrice paid the hire of the carriage and man. He saw and could tell nothing more of Mynher Vanderhausen and his beautiful lady. This mystery was a source of deep anxiety and almost of grief to Gerard Douw.

There was evidently fraud in the dealing of Vanderhausen with him, though for what purpose committed he could not imagine. He greatly doubted how far it was possible for a man possessing in his countenance so strong an evidence of the presence of the most demoniac feelings, to be in reality anything but a villain; and every day that passed without his hearing from or of his niece, instead of inducing him to forget his fears, on the contrary tended more and more to exasperate them.

The loss of his niece's cheerful society tended also to depress his spirits; and in order to dispel this despondency, which often crept upon his mind after his daily employment was over, he was wont frequently to prevail upon Schalken to accompany him home, and by his presence to dispel, in some degree, the gloom of his otherwise solitary supper.

One evening, the painter and his pupil were sitting by the fire, having accomplished a comfortable supper, and had yielded to that silent pensiveness sometimes induced by the process of digestion, when their reflections were disturbed by a loud sound at the street-door, as if occasioned by some person rushing forcibly and repeatedly against it. A domestic had run without delay to ascertain the cause of the disturbance, and they heard him twice or thrice interrogate the applicant for admission, but without producing an answer or any cessation of the sounds.

They heard him then open the hall-door, and immediately there followed a light and rapid tread upon the staircase. Schalken laid his hand on his sword, and advanced towards the door. It opened before he reached it, and Rose rushed into the room. She looked wild and haggard, and pale with exhaustion and terror; but her dress surprised them as much even as her unexpected appearance. It consisted of a kind of white woollen wrapper, made close about the neck, and descending to the very ground. It was much deranged and travel-soiled. The poor creature had hardly entered the chamber when she fell senseless on the floor. With some difficulty they succeeded in reviving her, and on recovering her senses she instantly exclaimed, in a tone of eager, terrified impatience:

'Wine, wine, quickly, or I'm lost!'

Much alarmed at the strange agitation in which the call was made, they at once administered to her wishes, and she drank some wine with a haste and eagerness which surprised them. She had hardly swallowed it, when she exclaimed, with the same urgency:

'Food, food, at once, or I perish!'

A considerable fragment of a roast joint was upon the table, and Schalken immediately proceeded to cut some, but he was anticipated; for no sooner had she become aware of its presence than she darted at it with the rapacity of a vulture, and, seizing it in her hands she tore off the flesh with her teeth and swallowed it.

When the paroxysm of hunger had been a little appeased, she appeared suddenly to become aware how strange her conduct had been, or it may have been that other more agitating thoughts recurred to her mind, for she began to weep bitterly and to wring her hands.

'Oh! send for a minister of God,' said she; 'I am not safe till he comes; send for him speedily.'

Gerard Douw despatched a messenger instantly, and prevailed on his niece to allow him to surrender his bedchamber to her use; he also persuaded her to retire to it at once and to rest; her consent was extorted upon the condition that they would not leave her for a moment.

'Oh that the holy man were here!' she said; 'he can deliver me. The dead and the living can never be one—God has forbidden it.'

With these mysterious words she surrendered herself to their guidance, and they proceeded to the chamber which Gerard Douw had assigned to her use.

'Do not—do not leave me for a moment,' said she. 'I am lost for ever if you do.'

Gerard Douw's chamber was approached through a spacious apartment, which they were now about to enter. Gerard Douw and Schalken each carried a wax candle, so that a sufficient degree of light was cast upon all surrounding objects. They were now entering the large chamber, which, as I have said, communicated with Douw's apartment, when Rose suddenly stopped, and, in a whisper which seemed to thrill with horror, she said:

'O God! he is here—he is here! See, see—there he goes!'

She pointed towards the door of the inner room, and Schalken thought he saw a shadowy and ill-defined form gliding into that apartment. He drew his sword, and raising the candle so as to throw its light with increased distinctness upon the objects in the room, he entered the chamber into which the shadow had glided. No figure was there—nothing but the furniture which belonged to the room, and yet he could not be deceived as to the fact that something had moved before them into the chamber.

A sickening dread came upon him, and the cold perspiration broke out in heavy drops upon his forehead; nor was he more composed when he heard the increased urgency, the agony of entreaty, with which Rose implored them not to leave her for a moment.

'I saw him,' said she. 'He's here! I cannot be deceived—I know him. He's by me—he's with me—he's in the room. Then, for God's sake, as you would save, do not stir from beside me!'

They at length prevailed upon her to lie down upon the bed, where she continued to urge them to stay by her. She frequently uttered incoherent sentences, repeating again and again, 'The dead and the living cannot be one—God has forbidden it!' and then again, 'Rest to the wakeful—sleep to the sleep-walkers.'

These and such mysterious and broken sentences she continued to utter until the clergyman arrived.

Gerard Douw began to fear, naturally enough, that the poor girl, owing to terror or ill-treatment, had become deranged; and he half suspected, by the suddenness of her appearance, and the unseasonableness of the hour, and, above all, from the wildness and terror of her manner, that she had made her escape from some place of confinement for lunatics, and was in immediate fear of pursuit. He resolved to summon medical advice as soon as the mind of his niece had been in some measure set at rest by the offices of the clergyman whose attendance she had so earnestly desired; and until this object had been attained, he did not venture to put any questions to her, which might possibly, by reviving painful or horrible recollections, increase her agitation.

The clergyman soon arrived—a man of ascetic countenance and venerable age—one whom Gerard Douw respected much, forasmuch as he was a veteran polemic,* though one, perhaps, more dreaded as a combatant than beloved as a Christian—of pure morality, subtle

brain, and frozen heart. He entered the chamber which communicated with that in which Rose reclined, and immediately on his arrival
she requested him to pray for her, as for one who lay in the hands of
Satan, and who could hope for deliverance—only from heaven.

That our readers may distinctly understand all the circumstances
of the event which we are about imperfectly to describe, it is necessary to state the relative position of the parties who were engaged in
it. The old clergyman and Schalken were in the anteroom of which we
have already spoken; Rose lay in the inner chamber, the door of which
was open; and by the side of the bed, at her urgent desire, stood her
guardian; a candle burned in the bedchamber, and three were lighted
in the outer apartment.

The old man now cleared his voice, as if about to commence; but
before he had time to begin, a sudden gust of air blew out the candle
which served to illuminate the room in which the poor girl lay, and
she, with hurried alarm, exclaimed:

'Godfrey, bring in another candle; the darkness is unsafe.'

Gerard Douw, forgetting for the moment her repeated injunctions
in the immediate impulse, stepped from the bedchamber into the
other, in order to supply what she desired.

'O God! do not go, dear uncle!' shrieked the unhappy girl; and at
the same time she sprang from the bed and darted after him, in order,
by her grasp, to detain him.

But the warning came too late, for scarcely had he passed the
threshold, and hardly had his niece had time to utter the startling
exclamation, when the door which divided the two rooms closed violently after him, as if swung to by a strong blast of wind.

Schalken and he both rushed to the door, but their united and desperate efforts could not avail so much as to shake it.

Shriek after shriek burst from the inner chamber, with all the piercing loudness of despairing terror. Schalken and Douw applied every
energy and strained every nerve to force open the door; but all in vain.

There was no sound of struggling from within, but the screams
seemed to increase in loudness, and at the same time they heard the
bolts of the latticed window withdrawn, and the window itself grated
upon the sill as if thrown open.

One *last* shriek, so long and piercing and agonised as to be scarcely
human, swelled from the room, and suddenly there followed a death-
like silence.

A light step was heard crossing the floor, as if from the bed to the window; and almost at the same instant the door gave way, and, yielding to the pressure of the external applicants, they were nearly precipitated into the room. It was empty. The window was open, and Schalken sprang to a chair and gazed out upon the street and canal below. He saw no form, but he beheld, or thought he beheld, the waters of the broad canal beneath settling ring after ring in heavy circular ripples, as if a moment before disturbed by the immersion of some large and heavy mass.

No trace of Rose was ever after discovered, nor was anything certain respecting her mysterious wooer detected or even suspected; no clue whereby to trace the intricacies of the labyrinth and to arrive at a distinct conclusion was to be found. But an incident occurred, which, though it will not be received by our rational readers as at all approaching to evidence upon the matter, nevertheless produced a strong and a lasting impression upon the mind of Schalken.

Many years after the events which we have detailed, Schalken, then remotely situated, received an intimation of his father's death, and of his intended burial upon a fixed day in the church of Rotterdam. It was necessary that a very considerable journey should be performed by the funeral procession, which, as it will readily be believed, was not very numerously attended. Schalken with difficulty arrived in Rotterdam late in the day upon which the funeral was appointed to take place. The procession had not then arrived. Evening closed in, and still it did not appear.

Schalken strolled down to the church—he found it open—notice of the arrival of the funeral had been given, and the vault in which the body was to be laid had been opened. The official who corresponds to our sexton, on seeing a well-dressed gentleman, whose object was to attend the expected funeral, pacing the aisle of the church, hospitably invited him to share with him the comforts of a blazing wood fire, which, as was his custom in winter time upon such occasions, he had kindled on the hearth of a chamber which communicated, by a flight of steps, with the vault below.

In this chamber Schalken and his entertainer seated themselves, and the sexton, after some fruitless attempts to engage his guest in conversation, was obliged to apply himself to his tobacco-pipe and can to solace his solitude.

In spite of his grief and cares, the fatigues of a rapid journey of nearly forty hours gradually overcame the mind and body of Godfrey Schalken, and he sank into a deep sleep, from which he was awakened by some one shaking him gently by the shoulder. He first thought that the old sexton had called him, but *he* was no longer in the room.

He roused himself, and as soon as he could clearly see what was around him, he perceived a female form, clothed in a kind of light robe of muslin, part of which was so disposed as to act as a veil, and in her hand she carried a lamp. She was moving rather away from him, and towards the flight of steps which conducted towards the vaults.

Schalken felt a vague alarm at the sight of this figure, and at the same time an irresistible impulse to follow its guidance. He followed it towards the vaults, but when it reached the head of the stairs, he paused; the figure paused also, and, turning gently round, displayed, by the light of the lamp it carried, the face and features of his first love, Rose Velderkaust. There was nothing horrible, or even sad, in the countenance. On the contrary, it wore the same arch smile which used to enchant the artist long before in his happy days.

A feeling of awe and of interest, too intense to be resisted, prompted him to follow the spectre, if spectre it were. She descended the stairs—he followed; and, turning to the left, through a narrow passage, she led him, to his infinite surprise, into what appeared to be an old-fashioned Dutch apartment, such as the pictures of Gerard Douw have served to immortalise.

Abundance of costly antique furniture was disposed about the room, and in one corner stood a four-post bed, with heavy black-cloth curtains around it; the figure frequently turned towards him with the same arch smile; and when she came to the side of the bed, she drew the curtains, and by the light of the lamp which she held towards its contents, she disclosed to the horror-stricken painter, sitting bolt upright in the bed, the livid and demoniac form of Vanderhausen. Schalken had hardly seen him when he fell senseless upon the floor, where he lay until discovered, on the next morning, by persons employed in closing the passages into the vaults. He was lying in a cell of considerable size, which had not been disturbed for a long time, and he had fallen beside a large coffin which was supported upon small stone pillars, a security against the attacks of vermin.

To his dying day Schalken was satisfied of the reality of the vision which he had witnessed, and he has left behind him a curious evidence of the impression which it wrought upon his fancy, in a painting executed shortly after the event we have narrated, and which is valuable as exhibiting not only the peculiarities which have made Schalken's pictures sought after, but even more so as presenting a portrait, as close and faithful as one taken from memory can be, of his early love, Rose Velderkaust, whose mysterious fate must ever remain matter of speculation.

The picture represents a chamber of antique masonry, such as might be found in most old cathedrals, and is lighted faintly by a lamp carried in the hand of a female figure, such as we have above attempted to describe; and in the background, and to the left of him who examines the painting, there stands the form of a man apparently aroused from sleep, and by his attitude, his hand being laid upon his sword, exhibiting considerable alarm: this last figure is illuminated only by the expiring glare of a wood or charcoal fire.

The whole production exhibits a beautiful specimen of that artful and singular distribution of light and shade which has rendered the name of Schalken immortal among the artists of his country. This tale is traditionary, and the reader will easily perceive, by our studiously omitting to heighten many points of the narrative, when a little additional colouring might have added effect to the recital, that we have desired to lay before him, not a figment of the brain, but a curious tradition connected with, and belonging to, the biography of a famous artist.

NATHANIEL HAWTHORNE

The Birth-Mark

❧❧

I N the latter part of the last century there lived a man of science, an eminent proficient in every branch of natural philosophy, who not long before our story opens had made experience of a spiritual affinity more attractive than any chemical one. He had left his laboratory to the care of an assistant, cleared his fine countenance from the furnace smoke, washed the stain of acids from his fingers, and persuaded a beautiful woman to become his wife. In those days, when the comparatively recent discovery of electricity* and other kindred mysteries of Nature seemed to open paths into the region of miracle, it was not unusual for the love of science to rival the love of woman in its depth and absorbing energy. The higher intellect, the imagination, the spirit, and even the heart might all find their congenial aliment in pursuits which, as some of their ardent votaries believed, would ascend from one step of powerful intelligence to another, until the philosopher should lay his hand on the secret of creative force and perhaps make new worlds for himself. We know not whether Aylmer possessed this degree of faith in man's ultimate control over Nature. He had devoted himself, however, too unreservedly to scientific studies ever to be weaned from them by any second passion. His love for his young wife might prove the stronger of the two; but it could only be by intertwining itself with his love of science and uniting the strength of the latter to his own.

Such a union accordingly took place, and was attended with truly remarkable consequences and a deeply impressive moral. One day, very soon after their marriage, Aylmer sat gazing at his wife with a trouble in his countenance that grew stronger until he spoke.

'Georgiana,' said he, 'has it never occurred to you that the mark upon your cheek might be removed?'

'No, indeed,' said she, smiling; but, perceiving the seriousness of his manner, she blushed deeply. 'To tell you the truth, it has been so often called a charm that I was simple enough to imagine it might be so.'

'Ah, upon another face perhaps it might,' replied her husband; 'but never on yours. No, dearest Georgiana, you came so nearly perfect from the hand of Nature that this slightest possible defect, which we hesitate whether to term a defect or a beauty, shocks me, as being the visible mark of earthly imperfection.'

'Shocks you, my husband!' cried Georgiana, deeply hurt; at first reddening with momentary anger, but then bursting into tears. 'Then why did you take me from my mother's side? You cannot love what shocks you!'

To explain this conversation, it must be mentioned that in the centre of Georgiana's left cheek there was a singular mark, deeply interwoven, as it were, with the texture and substance of her face. In the usual state of her complexion—a healthy though delicate bloom—the mark wore a tint of deeper crimson, which imperfectly defined its shape amid the surrounding rosiness. When she blushed it gradually became more indistinct, and finally vanished amid the triumphant rush of blood that bathed the whole cheek with its brilliant glow. But if any shifting motion caused her to turn pale there was the mark again, a crimson stain upon the snow, in what Aylmer sometimes deemed an almost fearful distinctness. Its shape bore not a little similarity to the human hand, though of the smallest pygmy size. Georgiana's lovers were wont to say that some fairy at her birth hour had laid her tiny hand upon the infant's cheek, and left this impress there in token of the magic endowments that were to give her such sway over all hearts. Many a desperate swain would have risked life for the privilege of pressing his lips to the mysterious hand. It must not be concealed, however, that the impression wrought by this fairy sign manual varied exceedingly according to the difference of temperament in the beholders. Some fastidious persons—but they were exclusively of her own sex—affirmed that the bloody hand, as they chose to call it, quite destroyed the effect of Georgiana's beauty and rendered her countenance even hideous. But it would be as reasonable to say that one of those small blue stains which sometimes occur in the purest statuary marble would convert the Eve of Powers* to a monster. Masculine observers, if the birthmark did not heighten their admiration, contented themselves with wishing it away, that the world might possess one living specimen of ideal loveliness without the semblance of a flaw. After his marriage,—for he thought little or nothing of the matter before,—Aylmer discovered that this was the case with himself.

Had she been less beautiful,—if Envy's self could have found aught else to sneer at,—he might have felt his affection heightened by the prettiness of this mimic hand, now vaguely portrayed, now lost, now stealing forth again and glimmering to and fro with every pulse of emotion that throbbed within her heart; but, seeing her otherwise so perfect, he found this one defect grow more and more intolerable with every moment of their united lives. It was the fatal flaw of humanity which Nature, in one shape or another, stamps ineffaceably on all her productions, either to imply that they are temporary and finite, or that their perfection must be wrought by toil and pain. The crimson hand expressed the ineludible* gripe in which mortality clutches the highest and purest of earthly mould, degrading them into kindred with the lowest, and even with the very brutes, like whom their visible frames return to dust. In this manner, selecting it as the symbol of his wife's liability to sin, sorrow, decay, and death, Aylmer's sombre imagination was not long in rendering the birthmark a frightful object, causing him more trouble and horror than ever Georgiana's beauty, whether of soul or sense, had given him delight.

At all the seasons which should have been their happiest he invariably, and without intending it, nay, in spite of a purpose to the contrary, reverted to this one disastrous topic. Trifling as it at first appeared, it so connected itself with innumerable trains of thought and modes of feeling that it became the central point of all. With the morning twilight Aylmer opened his eyes upon his wife's face and recognized the symbol of imperfection; and when they sat together at the evening hearth his eyes wandered stealthily to her cheek, and beheld, flickering with the blaze of the wood fire, the spectral hand that wrote mortality where he would fain have worshipped. Georgiana soon learned to shudder at his gaze. It needed but a glance with the peculiar expression that his face often wore to change the roses of her cheek into a deathlike paleness, amid which the crimson hand was brought strongly out, like a bass relief* of ruby on the whitest marble.

Late one night, when the lights were growing dim so as hardly to betray the stain on the poor wife's cheek, she herself, for the first time, voluntarily took up the subject.

'Do you remember, my dear Aylmer,' said she, with a feeble attempt at a smile, 'have you any recollection, of a dream last night about this odious hand?'

'None! none whatever!' replied Aylmer, starting; but then he added, in a dry, cold tone, affected for the sake of concealing the real depth of his emotion, 'I might well dream of it; for, before I fell asleep, it had taken a pretty firm hold of my fancy.'

'And you did dream of it?' continued Georgiana, hastily; for she dreaded lest a gush of tears should interrupt what she had to say. 'A terrible dream! I wonder that you can forget it. Is it possible to forget this one expression?—"It is in her heart now; we must have it out!" Reflect, my husband; for by all means I would have you recall that dream.'

The mind is in a sad state when Sleep, the all-involving, cannot confine her spectres within the dim region of her sway, but suffers them to break forth, affrighting this actual life with secrets that perchance belong to a deeper one. Aylmer now remembered his dream. He had fancied himself with his servant Aminadab* attempting an operation for the removal of the birthmark; but the deeper went the knife, the deeper sank the hand, until at length its tiny grasp appeared to have caught hold of Georgiana's heart; whence, however, her husband was inexorably resolved to cut or wrench it away.

When the dream had shaped itself perfectly in his memory Aylmer sat in his wife's presence with a guilty feeling. Truth often finds its way to the mind close muffled in robes of sleep, and then speaks with uncompromising directness of matters in regard to which we practise an unconscious self-deception during our waking moments. Until now he had not been aware of the tyrannizing influence acquired by one idea over his mind, and of the lengths which he might find in his heart to go for the sake of giving himself peace.

'Aylmer,' resumed Georgiana, solemnly, 'I know not what may be the cost to both of us to rid me of this fatal birthmark. Perhaps its removal may cause cureless deformity; or it may be the stain goes as deep as life itself. Again: do we know that there is a possibility, on any terms, of unclasping the firm gripe of this little hand which was laid upon me before I came into the world?'

'Dearest Georgiana, I have spent much thought upon the subject,' hastily interrupted Aylmer. 'I am convinced of the perfect practicability of its removal.'

'If there be the remotest possibility of it,' continued Georgiana, 'let the attempt be made, at whatever risk. Danger is nothing to me; for life, while this hateful mark makes me the object of your horror and disgust,—life is a burden which I would fling down with joy. Either remove this dreadful hand, or take my wretched life! You have deep science. All the world bears witness of it. You have achieved great wonders. Cannot you remove this little, little mark, which I cover with the tips of two small fingers? Is this beyond your power, for the sake of your own peace, and to save your poor wife from madness?'

'Noblest, dearest, tenderest wife,' cried Aylmer, rapturously, 'doubt not my power. I have already given this matter the deepest thought—thought which might almost have enlightened me to create a being less perfect than yourself. Georgiana, you have led me deeper than ever into the heart of science. I feel myself fully competent to render this dear cheek as faultless as its fellow; and then, most beloved, what will be my triumph when I shall have corrected what Nature left imperfect in her fairest work! Even Pygmalion,* when his sculptured woman assumed life, felt not greater ecstasy than mine will be.'

'It is resolved, then,' said Georgiana, faintly smiling. 'And, Aylmer, spare me not, though you should find the birthmark take refuge in my heart at last.'

Her husband tenderly kissed her cheek—her right cheek—not that which bore the impress of the crimson hand.

The next day Aylmer apprised his wife of a plan that he had formed whereby he might have opportunity for the intense thought and constant watchfulness which the proposed operation would require; while Georgiana, likewise, would enjoy the perfect repose essential to its success. They were to seclude themselves in the extensive apartments occupied by Aylmer as a laboratory, and where, during his toilsome youth, he had made discoveries in the elemental powers of Nature that had roused the admiration of all the learned societies in Europe. Seated calmly in this laboratory, the pale philosopher had investigated the secrets of the highest cloud region and of the profoundest mines; he had satisfied himself of the causes that kindled and kept alive the fires of the volcano; and had explained the mystery of fountains, and how it is that they gush forth, some so bright and pure, and others with such rich medicinal virtues, from the dark bosom of the earth.* Here, too, at an earlier period, he had studied the wonders of the human frame, and attempted to fathom the very process by which Nature assimilates all her precious influences from earth and air, and from the spiritual world, to create and foster man, her masterpiece. The latter pursuit, however, Aylmer had long laid aside in unwilling recognition of the truth—against which all seekers sooner or later stumble—that our great creative Mother, while she amuses us with apparently working in the broadest sunshine, is yet severely careful to keep her own secrets, and, in spite of her pretended openness, shows us nothing but results. She permits us, indeed, to mar, but seldom to mend, and, like a jealous patentee, on no account to make. Now, however, Aylmer resumed these half-forgotten investigations; not, of course, with such hopes or wishes as first suggested them; but because they involved much physiological truth and lay in the path of his proposed scheme for the treatment of Georgiana.

As he led her over the threshold of the laboratory, Georgiana was cold and tremulous. Aylmer looked cheerfully into her face, with intent to reassure her, but was so startled with the intense glow of the birthmark upon the whiteness of her cheek that he could not restrain a strong convulsive shudder. His wife fainted.

'Aminadab! Aminadab!' shouted Aylmer, stamping violently on the floor.

Forthwith there issued from an inner apartment a man of low stature, but bulky frame, with shaggy hair hanging about his visage, which was grimed with the vapors of the furnace. This personage had been Aylmer's underworker during his whole scientific career, and was admirably fitted for that office by his great mechanical readiness, and the skill with which, while incapable of comprehending a single principle, he executed all the details of his master's experiments. With his vast strength, his shaggy hair, his smoky aspect, and the indescribable earthiness that incrusted him, he seemed to represent man's physical nature; while Aylmer's slender figure, and pale, intellectual face, were no less apt a type of the spiritual element.

'Throw open the door of the boudoir, Aminadab,' said Aylmer, 'and burn a pastil.'*

'Yes, master,' answered Aminadab, looking intently at the lifeless form of Georgiana; and then he muttered to himself, 'If she were my wife, I'd never part with that birthmark.'

When Georgiana recovered consciousness she found herself breathing an atmosphere of penetrating fragrance, the gentle potency of which had recalled her from her deathlike faintness. The scene around her looked like enchantment. Aylmer had converted those smoky, dingy, sombre rooms, where he had spent his brightest years in recondite pursuits, into a series of beautiful apartments not unfit to be the secluded abode of a lovely woman. The walls were hung with gorgeous curtains, which imparted the combination of grandeur and grace that no other species of adornment can achieve; and, as they fell from the ceiling to the floor, their rich and ponderous folds, concealing all angles and straight lines, appeared to shut in the scene from infinite space. For aught Georgiana knew, it might be a pavilion among the clouds. And Aylmer, excluding the sunshine, which would have interfered with his chemical processes, had supplied its place with perfumed lamps, emitting flames of various hue, but all uniting in a soft, impurpled radiance. He now knelt by his wife's side, watching her earnestly, but without alarm; for he was confident in his science, and felt that he could draw a magic circle* round her within which no evil might intrude.

'Where am I? Ah, I remember,' said Georgiana, faintly; and she placed her hand over her cheek to hide the terrible mark from her husband's eyes.

'Fear not, dearest!' exclaimed he. 'Do not shrink from me! Believe me, Georgiana, I even rejoice in this single imperfection, since it will be such a rapture to remove it.'

'O, spare me!' sadly replied his wife. 'Pray do not look at it again. I never can forget that convulsive shudder.'

In order to soothe Georgiana, and, as it were, to release her mind from the burden of actual things, Aylmer now put in practice some of the light and playful secrets which science had taught him among its profounder lore. Airy figures, absolutely bodiless ideas, and forms of unsubstantial beauty came and danced before her, imprinting their momentary footsteps on beams of light. Though she had some indistinct idea of the method of these optical phenomena, still the illusion was almost perfect enough to warrant the belief that her husband possessed sway over the spiritual world. Then again, when she felt a wish to look forth from her seclusion, immediately, as if her thoughts were answered, the procession of external existence flitted across a screen. The scenery and the figures of actual life were perfectly represented, but with that bewitching yet indescribable difference which always makes a picture, an image, or a shadow so much more attractive than the original. When wearied of this, Aylmer bade her cast her eyes upon a vessel containing a quantity of earth. She did so, with little interest at first; but was soon startled to perceive the germ of a plant shooting upward from the soil. Then came the slender stalk; the leaves gradually unfolded themselves; and amid them was a perfect and lovely flower.

'It is magical!' cried Georgiana. 'I dare not touch it.'

'Nay, pluck it,' answered Aylmer,—'pluck it, and inhale its brief perfume while you may. The flower will wither in a few moments and leave nothing save its brown seed vessels; but thence may be perpetuated a race as ephemeral as itself.'

But Georgiana had no sooner touched the flower than the whole plant suffered a blight, its leaves turning coal-black as if by the agency of fire.

'There was too powerful a stimulus,' said Aylmer, thoughtfully.

To make up for this abortive experiment, he proposed to take her portrait by a scientific process of his own invention. It was to be effected by rays of light striking upon a polished plate of metal.* Georgiana assented; but, on looking at the result, was affrighted to find the features of the portrait blurred and indefinable; while the minute figure of a hand appeared where the cheek should have been. Aylmer snatched the metallic plate and threw it into a jar of corrosive acid.

Soon, however, he forgot these mortifying failures. In the intervals of study and chemical experiment he came to her flushed and exhausted, but seemed invigorated by her presence, and spoke in glowing language of the resources of his art. He gave a history of the long dynasty of the alchemists, who spent so many ages in quest of the universal solvent by which the golden principle might be elicited from all things vile and base. Aylmer appeared to believe that, by the plainest scientific logic, it was altogether within the limits of possibility to discover this long-sought medium; 'but,' he added, 'a philosopher who should go deep enough to acquire the power would attain too lofty a wisdom to stoop to the exercise of it.' Not less singular were his opinions in regard to the elixir vitæ.* He more than intimated that it was at his option to concoct a liquid that should prolong life for years, perhaps interminably; but that it would produce a discord in Nature which all the world, and chiefly the quaffer of the immortal nostrum,* would find cause to curse.

'Aylmer, are you in earnest?' asked Georgiana, looking at him with amazement and fear. 'It is terrible to possess such power, or even to dream of possessing it.'

'O, do not tremble, my love,' said her husband. 'I would not wrong either you or myself by working such inharmonious effects upon our lives; but I would have you consider how trifling, in comparison, is the skill requisite to remove this little hand.'

At the mention of the birthmark, Georgiana, as usual, shrank as if a redhot iron had touched her cheek.

Again Aylmer applied himself to his labors. She could hear his voice in the distant furnace room giving directions to Aminadab, whose harsh, uncouth, misshapen tones were audible in response, more like the grunt or growl of a brute than human speech. After hours of absence, Aylmer reappeared and proposed that she should now examine his cabinet of chemical products and natural treasures of the earth. Among the former he showed her a small vial, in which, he remarked, was contained a gentle yet most powerful fragrance, capable of impregnating all the breezes that blow across a kingdom. They were of inestimable value, the contents of that little vial; and, as he said so, he threw some of the perfume into the air and filled the room with piercing and invigorating delight.

'And what is this?' asked Georgiana, pointing to a small crystal globe containing a gold-colored liquid. 'It is so beautiful to the eye that I could imagine it the elixir of life.'

'In one sense it is,' replied Aylmer; 'or rather, the elixir of immortality. It is the most precious poison that ever was concocted in this world. By its aid I could apportion the lifetime of any mortal at whom you might point your finger. The strength of the dose would determine whether he were to linger out years, or drop dead in the midst of a breath. No king on his guarded throne could keep his life if I, in my private station, should deem that the welfare of millions justified me in depriving him of it.'

'Why do you keep such a terrific drug?' inquired Georgiana in horror.

'Do not mistrust me, dearest,' said her husband, smiling; 'its virtuous potency is yet greater than its harmful one. But see! here is a powerful cosmetic. With a few drops of this in a vase of water, freckles may be washed away as easily as the hands are cleansed. A stronger infusion would take the blood out of the cheek, and leave the rosiest beauty a pale ghost.'

'Is it with this lotion that you intend to bathe my cheek?' asked Georgiana, anxiously.

'O, no,' hastily replied her husband; 'this is merely superficial. Your case demands a remedy that shall go deeper.'

In his interviews with Georgiana, Aylmer generally made minute inquiries as to her sensations and whether the confinement of the rooms and the temperature of the atmosphere agreed with her. These questions had such a particular drift that Georgiana began to conjecture that she was already subjected to certain physical influences, either breathed in with the fragrant air or taken with her food. She fancied likewise, but it might be altogether fancy, that there was a stirring up of her system—a strange, indefinite sensation creeping through her veins, and tingling, half painfully, half pleasurably, at her heart. Still, whenever she dared to look into the mirror, there she beheld herself pale as a white rose and with the crimson birthmark stamped upon her cheek. Not even Aylmer now hated it so much as she.

To dispel the tedium of the hours which her husband found it necessary to devote to the processes of combination and analysis, Georgiana turned over the volumes of his scientific library. In many dark old tomes she met with chapters full of romance and poetry. They were the works of the philosophers of the middle ages, such as Albertus Magnus, Cornelius Agrippa, Paracelsus, and the famous friar who created the prophetic Brazen Head.* All these antique naturalists stood in advance of their centuries, yet were imbued with some of their credulity, and therefore were believed, and perhaps imagined themselves to have acquired from the investigation of Nature a power above Nature, and from physics a sway over the spiritual world. Hardly less curious and imaginative were the early volumes of the Transactions of the Royal Society,* in which the members, knowing little of the limits of natural possibility, were continually recording wonders or proposing methods whereby wonders might be wrought.

But, to Georgiana, the most engrossing volume was a large folio from her husband's own hand, in which he had recorded every experiment of his scientific career, its original aim, the methods adopted for its development, and its final success or failure, with the circumstances to which either event was attributable. The book, in truth, was both the history and emblem of his ardent, ambitious, imaginative, yet practical and laborious life. He handled physical details as if there were nothing beyond them; yet spiritualized them all, and redeemed himself from materialism by his strong and eager aspiration towards the infinite. In his grasp the veriest clod of earth assumed a soul. Georgiana, as she read, reverenced Aylmer and loved him more profoundly than ever, but with a less entire dependence on his judgment than heretofore. Much as he had accomplished, she could not but observe that his most splendid successes were almost invariably failures, if compared with the ideal at which he aimed. His brightest diamonds were the merest pebbles, and felt to be so by himself, in comparison with the inestimable gems which lay hidden beyond his reach. The volume, rich with achievements that had won renown for its author, was yet as melancholy a record as ever mortal hand had penned. It was the sad confession and continual exemplification of the shortcomings of the composite man, the spirit burdened with clay and working in matter, and of the despair that assails the higher nature at finding itself so miserably thwarted by the earthly part. Perhaps every man of genius, in whatever sphere, might recognize the image of his own experience in Aylmer's journal.

So deeply did these reflections affect Georgiana that she laid her face upon the open volume and burst into tears. In this situation she was found by her husband.

'It is dangerous to read in a sorcerer's books,' said he with a smile, though his countenance was uneasy and displeased. 'Georgiana, there are pages in that volume which I can scarcely glance over and keep my senses. Take heed lest it prove as detrimental to you.'

'It has made me worship you more than ever,' said she.

'Ah, wait for this one success,' rejoined he, 'then worship me if you will. I shall deem myself hardly unworthy of it. But come, I have sought you for the luxury of your voice. Sing to me, dearest.'

So she poured out the liquid music of her voice to quench the thirst of his spirit. He then took his leave with a boyish exuberance of gayety, assuring her that her seclusion would endure but a little longer, and that the result was already certain. Scarcely had he departed when Georgiana felt irresistibly impelled to follow him. She had forgotten to inform Aylmer of a symptom which for two or three hours past had begun to excite her attention. It was a sensation in the fatal birthmark, not painful, but which induced a restlessness throughout her system. Hastening after her husband, she intruded for the first time into the laboratory.

The first thing that struck her eye was the furnace, that hot and feverish worker, with the intense glow of its fire, which by the quantities of soot clustered above it seemed to have been burning for ages. There was a distilling apparatus in full operation. Around the room were retorts, tubes, cylinders, crucibles, and other apparatus of chemical research. An electrical machine* stood ready for immediate use.

The atmosphere felt oppressively close, and was tainted with gaseous odors which had been tormented forth by the processes of science. The severe and homely simplicity of the apartment, with its naked walls and brick pavement, looked strange, accustomed as Georgiana had become to the fantastic elegance of her boudoir. But what chiefly, indeed almost solely, drew her attention, was the aspect of Aylmer himself.

He was pale as death, anxious and absorbed, and hung over the furnace as if it depended upon his utmost watchfulness whether the liquid which it was distilling should be the draught of immortal happiness or misery. How different from the sanguine and joyous mien that he had assumed for Georgiana's encouragement!

'Carefully now, Aminadab; carefully, thou human machine; carefully, thou man of clay,'* muttered Aylmer, more to himself than his assistant. 'Now, if there be a thought too much or too little, it is all over.'

'Ho! ho!' mumbled Aminadab. 'Look, master! look!'

Aylmer raised his eyes hastily, and at first reddened, then grew paler than ever, on beholding Georgiana. He rushed towards her and seized her arm with a grip that left the print of his fingers upon it.

'Why do you come hither? Have you no trust in your husband?' cried he, impetuously. 'Would you throw the blight of that fatal birthmark over my labors? It is not well done. Go, prying woman! go!'

'Nay, Aylmer,' said Georgiana with the firmness of which she possessed no stinted endowment, 'it is not you that have a right to complain. You mistrust your wife; you have concealed the anxiety with which you watch the development of this experiment. Think not so unworthily of me, my husband. Tell me all the risk we run, and fear not that I shall shrink; for my share in it is far less than your own.'

'No, no, Georgiana!' said Aylmer, impatiently; 'it must not be.'

'I submit,' replied she, calmly. 'And, Aylmer, I shall quaff whatever draught you bring me; but it will be on the same principle that would induce me to take a dose of poison if offered by your hand.'

'My noble wife,' said Aylmer, deeply moved, 'I knew not the height and depth of your nature until now. Nothing shall be concealed. Know, then, that this crimson hand, superficial as it seems, has clutched its grasp into your being with a strength of which I had no previous conception. I have already administered agents powerful enough to do aught except to change your entire physical system. Only one thing remains to be tried. If that fail us we are ruined.'

'Why did you hesitate to tell me this?' asked she.

'Because, Georgiana,' said Aylmer, in a low voice, 'there is danger.'

'Danger? There is but one danger—that this horrible stigma shall be left upon my cheek!' cried Georgiana. 'Remove it, remove it, whatever be the cost, or we shall both go mad!'

'Heaven knows your words are too true,' said Aylmer, sadly. 'And now, dearest, return to your boudoir. In a little while all will be tested.'

He conducted her back and took leave of her with a solemn tenderness which spoke far more than his words how much was now at stake. After his departure Georgiana became rapt in musings. She considered the character of Aylmer and did it completer justice than at any previous moment. Her heart exulted, while it trembled, at his honorable love—so pure and lofty that it would accept nothing less than perfection nor miserably make itself contented with an earthlier nature than he had dreamed of. She felt how much more precious was such a sentiment than that meaner kind which would have borne with the imperfection for her sake, and have been guilty of treason to holy love by degrading its perfect idea to the level of the actual; and with her whole spirit she prayed that, for a single moment, she might satisfy his highest and deepest conception. Longer than one moment she well knew it could not be; for his spirit was ever on the march, ever ascending, and each instant required something that was beyond the scope of the instant before.

The sound of her husband's footsteps aroused her. He bore a crystal goblet containing a liquor colorless as water, but bright enough to be the draught of immortality. Aylmer was pale; but it seemed rather the consequence of a highly-wrought state of mind and tension of spirit than of fear or doubt.

'The concoction of the draught has been perfect,' said he, in answer to Georgiana's look. 'Unless all my science have deceived me, it cannot fail.'

'Save on your account, my dearest Aylmer,' observed his wife, 'I might wish to put off this birthmark of mortality by relinquishing mortality itself in preference to any other mode. Life is but a sad possession to those who have attained precisely the degree of moral advancement at which I stand. Were I weaker and blinder, it might be happiness. Were I stronger, it might be endured hopefully. But, being what I find myself, methinks I am of all mortals the most fit to die.'

'You are fit for heaven without tasting death!' replied her husband.

'But why do we speak of dying? The draught cannot fail. Behold its effect upon this plant.'

On the window seat there stood a geranium* diseased with yellow blotches which had overspread all its leaves. Aylmer poured a small quantity of the liquid upon the soil in which it grew. In a little time, when the roots of the plant had taken up the moisture, the unsightly blotches began to be extinguished in a living verdure.

'There needed no proof,' said Georgiana, quietly. 'Give me the goblet. I joyfully stake all upon your word.'

'Drink, then, thou lofty creature!' exclaimed Aylmer, with fervid admiration. 'There is no taint of imperfection on thy spirit. Thy sensible frame, too, shall soon be all perfect.'

She quaffed the liquid and returned the goblet to his hand.

'It is grateful,' said she, with a placid smile. 'Methinks it is like water from a heavenly fountain; for it contains I know not what of unobtrusive fragrance and deliciousness. It allays a feverish thirst that had parched me for many days. Now, dearest, let me sleep. My earthly senses are closing over my spirit like the leaves around the heart of a rose at sunset.'

She spoke the last words with a gentle reluctance, as if it required almost more energy than she could command to pronounce the faint and lingering syllables. Scarcely had they loitered through her lips ere she was lost in slumber. Aylmer sat by her side, watching her aspect with the emotions proper to a man the whole value of whose existence was involved in the process now to be tested. Mingled with this mood, however, was the philosophic investigation characteristic of the man of science. Not the minutest symptom escaped him. A heightened flush of the cheek, a slight irregularity of breath, a quiver of the eyelid, a hardly perceptible tremor through the frame,—such were the details which, as the moments passed, he wrote down in his folio volume. Intense thought had set its stamp upon every previous page of that volume; but the thoughts of years were all concentrated upon the last.

While thus employed, he failed not to gaze often at the fatal hand, and not without a shudder. Yet once, by a strange and unaccountable impulse, he pressed it with his lips. His spirit recoiled, however, in the very act; and Georgiana, out of the midst of her deep sleep, moved uneasily and murmured as if in remonstrance. Again Aylmer resumed his watch. Nor was it without avail. The crimson hand, which at first had been strongly visible upon the marble paleness of Georgiana's cheek, now grew more faintly outlined. She remained not less pale than ever; but the birthmark, with every breath that came and went, lost somewhat of its former distinctness. Its presence had been awful; its departure was more awful still. Watch the stain of the rainbow fading out of the sky, and you will know how that mysterious symbol passed away.

'By Heaven! it is well nigh gone!' said Aylmer to himself, in almost irrepressible ecstasy. 'I can scarcely trace it now. Success! success! And now it is like the faintest rose color. The lightest flush of blood across her cheek would overcome it. But she is so pale!'

He drew aside the window curtain and suffered the light of natural day to fall into the room and rest upon her cheek. At the same time he heard a gross, hoarse chuckle, which he had long known as his servant Aminadab's expression of delight.

'Ah, clod! ah, earthly mass!' cried Aylmer, laughing in a sort of frenzy, 'you have served me well! Matter and spirit—earth and heaven—have both done their part in this! Laugh, thing of the senses! You have earned the right to laugh.'

These exclamations broke Georgiana's sleep. She slowly unclosed her eyes and gazed into the mirror which her husband had arranged for that purpose. A faint smile flitted over her lips when she recognized how barely perceptible was now that crimson hand which had once blazed forth with such disastrous brilliancy as to scare away all their happiness. But then her eyes sought Aylmer's face with a trouble and anxiety that he could by no means account for.

'My poor Aylmer!' murmured she.

'Poor? Nay, richest, happiest, most favored!' exclaimed he. 'My peerless bride, it is successful! You are perfect!'

'My poor Aylmer,' she repeated, with a more than human tenderness, 'you have aimed loftily; you have done nobly. Do not repent that, with so high and pure a feeling, you have rejected the best the earth could offer. Aylmer, dearest Aylmer, I am dying!'

Alas! it was too true! The fatal hand had grappled with the mystery of life, and was the bond by which an angelic spirit kept itself in union with a mortal frame. As the last crimson tint of the birthmark—that sole token of human imperfection—faded from her cheek, the parting breath of the now perfect woman passed into the atmosphere, and her soul, lingering a moment near her husband, took its heavenward flight. Then a hoarse, chuckling laugh was heard again! Thus ever does the gross fatality of earth exult in its invariable triumph over the immortal essence which, in this dim sphere of half development, demands the completeness of a higher state. Yet, had Aylmer reached a profounder wisdom, he need not thus have flung away the happiness which would have woven his mortal life of the selfsame texture with the celestial. The momentary circumstance was too strong for him; he failed to look beyond the shadowy scope of time, and, living once for all in eternity, to find the perfect future in the present.

HERMAN MELVILLE

The Tartarus of Maids

❊

I T lies not far from Woedolor Mountain* in New England. Turning
to the east, right out from among bright farms and sunny meadows,
nodding in early June with odorous grasses, you enter ascendingly
among bleak hills. These gradually close in upon a dusky pass, which,
from the violent Gulf Stream* of air unceasingly driving between its
cloven walls of haggard rock, as well as from the tradition of a crazy
spinster's hut having long ago stood somewhere hereabout, is called
the Mad Maid's Bellows'-pipe.

Winding along at the bottom of the gorge is a dangerously narrow
wheel-road, occupying the bed of a former torrent. Following this road
to its highest point, you stand as within a Dantean gateway. From the
steepness of the walls here, their strangely ebon hue, and the sudden
contraction of the gorge, this particular point is called the Black Notch.
The ravine now expandingly descends into a great, purple, hopper-
shaped* hollow, far sunk among many Plutonian,* shaggy-wooded
mountains. By the country people this hollow is called the Devil's
Dungeon. Sounds of torrents fall on all sides upon the ear. These rapid
waters unite at last in one turbid, brick-colored stream, boiling through
a flume among enormous boulders. They call this strange-colored
torrent Blood River. Gaining a dark precipice it wheels suddenly to
the west, and makes one maniac spring of sixty feet into the arms of
a stunted wood of gray-haired pines, between which it thence eddies
on its further way down to the invisible lowlands.

Conspicuously crowning a rocky bluff high to one side, at the cataract's verge, is the ruin of an old saw-mill, built in those primitive
times when vast pines and hemlocks superabounded throughout the
neighboring region. The black-mossed bulk of those immense, rough-
hewn, and spike-knotted logs, here and there tumbled all together, in
long abandonment and decay, or left in solitary, perilous projection
over the cataract's gloomy brink, impart to this rude wooden ruin
not only much of the aspect of one of rough-quarried stone, but also

a sort of feudal, Rhineland, and Thurmberg* look, derived from the pinnacled wildness of the neighborhood scenery.

Not far from the bottom of the Dungeon stands a large whitewashed building, relieved, like some great white sepulchre, against the sullen background of mountain-side firs, and other hardy evergreens, inaccessibly rising in grim terraces for some two thousand feet.

The building is a paper-mill.

Having embarked on a large scale in the seedsman's business (so extensively and broadcast, indeed, that at length my seeds were distributed through all the Eastern and Northern States, and even fell into the far soil of Missouri and the Carolinas), the demand for paper at my place became so great, that the expenditure soon amounted to a most important item in the general account. It need hardly be hinted how paper comes into use with seedsmen, as envelopes. These are mostly made of yellowish paper, folded square; and when filled, are all but flat, and being stamped, and superscribed with the nature of the seeds contained, assume not a little the appearance of business letters ready for the mail. Of these small envelopes I used an incredible quantity—several hundred of thousands in a year. For a time I had purchased my paper from the wholesale dealers in a neighboring town. For economy's sake, and partly for the adventure of the trip, I now resolved to cross the mountains, some sixty miles, and order my future paper at the Devil's Dungeon paper-mill.

The sleighing being uncommonly fine toward the end of January, and promising to hold so for no small period, in spite of the bitter cold I started one gray Friday noon in my pung,* well fitted with buffalo and wolf robes; and, spending one night on the road, next noon came in sight of Woedolor Mountain.

The far summit fairly smoked with frost; white vapors curled up from its white-wooded top, as from a chimney. The intense congelation made the whole country look like one petrification.* The steel shoes of my pung craunched and gritted over the vitreous, chippy snow, as if it had been broken glass. The forests here and there skirting the route, feeling the same all-stiffening influence, their inmost fibres penetrated with the cold, strangely groaned—not in the swaying branches merely, but likewise in the vertical trunk—as the fitful gusts remorseless swept through them. Brittle with excessive frost, many colossal tough-grained maples, snapped in twain like pipestems, cumbered the unfeeling earth.

Flaked all over with frozen sweat, white as a milky ram, his nostrils at each breath sending forth two horn-shaped shoots of heated respiration, Black, my good horse, but six years old, started at a sudden turn, where, right across the track—not ten minutes fallen—an old distorted hemlock lay, darkly undulatory as an anaconda.

Gaining the Bellows'-pipe, the violent blast, dead from behind, all but shoved my high-backed pung up-hill. The gust shrieked through the shivered pass, as if laden with lost spirits bound to the unhappy world. Ere gaining the summit, Black, my horse, as if exasperated by the cutting wind, slung out with his strong hind legs, tore the light pung straight up-hill, and sweeping grazingly through the narrow notch, sped downward madly past the ruined saw-mill. Into the Devil's Dungeon horse and cataract rushed together.

With might and main, quitting my seat and robes, and standing backward, with one foot braced against the dashboard, I rasped and churned the bit, and stopped him just in time to avoid collision, at a turn, with the bleak nozzle of a rock, couchant like a lion in the way—a road-side rock.

At first I could not discover the paper-mill.

The whole hollow gleamed with the white, except, here and there, where a pinnacle of granite showed one wind-swept angle bare. The mountains stood pinned in shrouds—a pass of Alpine corpses. Where stands the mill? Suddenly a whirling, humming sound broke upon my ear. I looked, and there, like an arrested avalanche, lay the large whitewashed factory. It was subordinately surrounded by a cluster of other and smaller buildings, some of which, from their cheap, blank air, great length, gregarious windows, and comfortless expression, no doubt were boarding-houses of the operatives. A snow-white hamlet amidst the snows. Various rude, irregular squares and courts resulted from the somewhat picturesque clusterings of these buildings, owing to the broken, rocky nature of the ground, which forbade all method in their relative arrangement. Several narrow lanes and alleys, too, partly blocked with snow fallen from the roof, cut up the hamlet in all directions.

When, turning from the traveled highway, jingling with bells of numerous farmers—who, availing themselves of the fine sleighing, were dragging their wood to market—and frequently diversified with swift cutters dashing from inn to inn of the scattered villages—when, I say, turning from that bustling main-road, I by degrees wound into the Mad Maid's Bellows'-pipe, and saw the grim Black Notch beyond, then something latent, as well as something obvious in the time and scene, strangely brought back to my mind my first sight of dark and grimy Temple Bar. And when Black, my horse, went darting through the Notch, perilously grazing its rocky wall, I remembered being in a runaway London omnibus, which in much the same sort of style, though by no means at an equal rate, dashed through the ancient arch of Wren.* Though the two objects did by no means correspond, yet this partial inadequacy but served to tinge the similitude not less with the vividness than the disorder of a dream. So that, when upon reining up at the protruding rock I at last caught sight of the quaint groupings of the factory-buildings, and with the traveled highway and the Notch behind, found myself all alone, silently and privily stealing through deep-cloven passages into this sequestered spot, and saw the long, high-gabled main factory edifice, with a rude tower—for hoisting heavy boxes—at one end, standing among its crowded outbuildings and boarding-houses, as the Temple Church* amidst the surrounding offices and dormitories, and when the marvelous retirement of this mysterious mountain nook fastened its whole spell upon me, then, what memory lacked, all tributary imagination furnished, and I said to myself, This is the very counterpart of the Paradise of Bachelors, but snowed upon, and frost-painted in a sepulchre.

Dismounting, and warily picking my way down the dangerous declivity—horse and man both sliding now and then upon the icy ledges—at length I drove, or the blast drove me, into the largest square, before one side of the main edifice. Piercingly and shrilly the shotted blast blew by the corner; and redly and demoniacally boiled Blood River at one side. A long woodpile, of many scores of cords, all glittering in mail of crusted ice, stood crosswise in the square. A row of horse-posts, their north sides plastered with adhesive snow, flanked the factory wall. The bleak frost packed and paved the square as with some ringing metal.

The inverted similitude recurred—'The sweet, tranquil Temple garden, with the Thames bordering its green beds,' strangely meditated I.

But where are the gay bachelors?

Then, as I and my horse stood shivering in the wind-spray, a girl ran from a neighboring dormitory door, and throwing her thin apron over her bare head, made for the opposite building.

'One moment, my girl; is there no shed hereabouts which I may drive into?'

Pausing, she turned upon me a face pale with work, and blue with cold; an eye supernatural with unrelated misery.

'Nay,' faltered I, 'I mistook you. Go on; I want nothing.'

Leading my horse close to the door from which she had come, I knocked. Another pale, blue girl appeared, shivering in the doorway as, to prevent the blast, she jealously held the door ajar.

'Nay, I mistake again. In God's name shut the door. But hold, is there no man about?'

That moment a dark-complexioned well-wrapped personage passed, making for the factory door, and spying him coming, the girl rapidly closed the other one.

'Is there no horse-shed here, Sir?'

'Yonder, the wood-shed,' he replied, and disappeared inside the factory.

With much ado I managed to wedge in horse and pung between scattered piles of wood all sawn and split. Then, blanketing my horse, and piling my buffalo on the blanket's top, and tucking in its edges well around the breast-band and breeching,* so that the wind might not strip him bare, I tied him fast, and ran lamely for the factory door, still with frost, and cumbered with my driver's dread-naught.*

Immediately I found myself standing in a spacious place, intolerably lighted by long rows of windows, focusing inward the snowy scene without.

At rows of blank-looking counters sat rows of blank-looking girls, white folders in their blank hands, all blankly folding blank paper.

In one corner stood some huge frame of ponderous iron, with a vertical thing like a piston periodically rising and falling upon a heavy wooden block. Before it—its tame minister—stood a tall girl, feeding the iron animal with half-quires of rose-hued note paper, which, at every downward dab of the piston-like machine, received in the corner the impress of a wreath of roses. I looked from the rosy paper to the pallid cheek, but said nothing.

Seated before a long apparatus, strung with long, slender strings like any harp, another girl was feeding it with foolscap sheets, which, so soon as they curiously traveled from her on the cords, were withdrawn at the opposite end of the machine by a second girl. They came to the first girl blank; they went to the second girl ruled.

I looked upon the first girl's brow, and saw it was young and fair; I looked upon the second girl's brow, and saw it was ruled and wrinkled. Then, as I still looked, the two—for some small variety to the monotony—changed places; and where had stood the young, fair brow, now stood the ruled and wrinkled one.

Perched high upon a narrow platform, and still higher upon a high stool crowning it, sat another figure serving some other iron animal; while below the platform sat her mate in some sort of reciprocal attendance.

Not a syllable was breathed. Nothing was heard but the low, steady overruling hum of the iron animals. The human voice was banished from the spot. Machinery—that vaunted slave of humanity—here stood menially served by human beings, who served mutely and cringingly as the slave serves the Sultan. The girls did not so much seem accessory wheels to the general machinery as mere cogs to the wheels.

All this scene around me was instantaneously taken in at one sweeping glance—even before I had proceeded to unwind the heavy fur tippet* from around my neck. But as soon as this fell from me the dark-complexioned man, standing close by, raised a sudden cry, and seizing my arm, dragged me out into the open air, and without pausing for a word instantly caught up some congealed snow and began rubbing both my cheeks.

'Two white spots like the whites of your eyes,' he said; 'man, your cheeks are frozen.'

'That may well be,' muttered I; ''tis some wonder the frost of the Devil's Dungeon strikes in no deeper. Rub away.'

Soon a horrible, tearing pain caught at my reviving cheeks. Two gaunt blood-hounds, one on either side, seemed mumbling them. I seemed Actæon.*

Presently, when all was over, I re-entered the factory, made known my business, concluded it satisfactorily, and then begged to be conducted throughout the place to view it.

'Cupid* is the boy for that,' said the dark-complexioned man. 'Cupid!' and by this odd fancy-name calling a dimpled, red-cheeked, spirited-looking, forward little fellow, who was rather impudently, I thought, gliding about among the passive-looking girls—like a gold fish through hueless waves—yet doing nothing in particular that I could see, the man bade him lead the stranger through the edifice.

'Come first and see the water-wheel,' said this lively lad, with the air of boyishly-brisk importance.

Quitting the folding-room, we crossed some damp, cold boards, and stood beneath a great wet shed, incessantly showered with foam, like the green barnacled bow of some East Indiaman* in a gale. Round and round here went the enormous revolutions of the dark colossal water-wheel, grim with its one immutable purpose.

'This sets our whole machinery a-going, Sir; in every part of all these buildings; where the girls work and all.'

I looked, and saw that the turbid waters of Blood River had not changed their hue by coming under the use of man.

'You make only blank paper; no printing of any sort, I suppose? All blank paper, don't you?'

'Certainly; what else should a paper-factory make?'

The lad here looked at me as if suspicious of my common-sense.

'Oh, to be sure!' said I, confused and stammering; 'it only struck me as so strange that red waters should turn out pale chee—paper, I mean.'*

He took me up a wet and rickety stair to a great light room, furnished with no visible thing but rude, manger-like receptacles running all round its sides; and up to these mangers, like so many mares haltered to the rack stood rows of girls. Before each was vertically thrust up a long, glittering scythe, immovably fixed at bottom to the manger-edge. The curve of the scythe, and its having no snath* to it, made it look exactly like a sword. To and fro, across the sharp edge, the girls forever dragged long strips of rags, washed white, picked from baskets at one side; thus ripping asunder every seam, and converting the tatters almost into lint. The air swam with the fine, poisonous particles, which from all sides darted, subtilely, as motes in sunbeams, into the lungs.

'This is the rag-room,' coughed the boy.

'You find it rather stifling here,' coughed I, in answer; 'but the girls don't cough.'

'Oh, they are used to it.'

'Where do you get such hosts of rags?' picking up a handful from a basket.

'Some from the country round about; some from far over sea— Leghorn* and London.'

''Tis not unlikely, then,' murmured I, 'that among these heaps of rags there may be some old shirts, gathered from the dormitories of the Paradise of Bachelors. But the buttons are all dropped off. Pray, my lad, do you ever find any bachelor's buttons hereabouts?'

'None grow in this part of the country. The Devil's Dungeon is no place for flowers.'

'Oh! you mean the *flowers* so called—the Bachelor's Buttons?'*

'And was not that what you asked about? Or did you mean the gold bosom-buttons of our boss, Old Bach, as our whispering girls all call him?'

'The man, then, I saw below is a bachelor, is he?'

'Oh, yes, he's a Bach.'

'The edges of those swords, they are turned outward from the girls, if I see right; but their rags and fingers fly so, I can not distinctly see.'

'Turned outward.'

Yes, murmured I to myself; I see it now; turned outward; and each erected sword is so borne, edge-outward, before each girl. If my reading fails me not, just so, of old, condemned state-prisoners went from the hall of judgment to their doom; an officer before, bearing a sword, its edge turned outward, in significance of their fatal sentence. So, through consumptive pallors of this blank, raggy life, go these white girls to death.

'Those scythes look very sharp,' again turning toward the boy.

'Yes; they have to keep them so. Look!'

That moment two of the girls, dropping their rags, plied each a whetstone up and down the sword-blade. My unaccustomed blood curdled at the sharp shriek of the tormented steel.

Their own executioners; themselves whetting the very swords that slay them; meditated I.

'What makes those girls so sheet-white, my lad?'

'Why'—with a roguish twinkle, pure ignorant drollery, not knowing heartlessness—'I suppose the handling of such white bits of sheets all the time makes them so sheety.'

'Let us leave the rag-room now, my lad.'

More tragical and more inscrutably mysterious than any mystic sight, human or machine, throughout the factory, was the strange innocence of cruel-heartedness in this usage-hardened boy.

'And now,' said he, cheerily, 'I suppose you want to see our great machine, which cost us twelve thousand dollars only last autumn. That's the machine that makes the paper, too. This way, Sir.'

Following him I crossed a large, bespattered place, with two great round vats in it, full of a white, wet, woolly-looking stuff, not unlike the albuminous part of an egg,* soft-boiled.

'There,' said Cupid, tapping the vats carelessly, 'these are the first beginning of the paper; this white pulp you see. Look how it swims bubbling round and round, moved by the paddle here. From hence it pours from both vats into the one common channel yonder; and so goes, mixed up and leisurely, to the great machine. And now for that.'

He led me into a room, stifling with a strange, blood-like, abdominal heat, as if here, true enough, were being finally developed the germinous* particles lately seen.

Before me, rolled out like some long Eastern manuscript, lay stretched one continuous length of iron framework—multitudinous and mystical, with all sorts of rollers, wheels, and cylinders, in slowly-measured and unceasing motion.

'Here first comes the pulp now,' said Cupid, pointing to the nighest end of the machine.

'See; first it pours out and spreads itself upon this wide, sloping board; and then—look—slides, thin and quivering, beneath the first roller there. Follow on now, and see it as it slides from under that to the next cylinder. There; see how it has become just a very little less pulpy now. One step more, and it grows still more to some slight consistence. Still another cylinder, and it is so knitted—though as yet mere dragon-fly wing—that it forms an air-bridge here, like a suspended cobweb, between two more separated rollers; and flowing over the last one, and under again, and doubling about there out of sight for a minute among all those mixed cylinders you indistinctly see, it reappears here, looking now at last a little less like pulp and more like paper, but still quite delicate and defective yet awhile. But—a little further onward, Sir, if you please—here now, at this further point, it puts on something of a real look, as if it might turn out to be something you might possibly handle in the end. But it's not yet done, Sir. Good way to travel yet, and plenty more of cylinders must roll it.'

'Bless my soul!' said I, amazed at the elongation, interminable convolutions, and deliberate slowness of the machine. 'It must take a long time for the pulp to pass from end to end, and come out paper.'

'Oh, not so long,' smiled the precocious lad, with a superior and patronizing air; 'only nine minutes. But look; you may try it for yourself. Have you a bit of paper? Ah! here's a bit on the floor. Now mark that with any word you please, and let me dab it on here, and we'll see how long before it comes out at the other end.'

'Well, let me see,' said I, taking out my pencil. 'Come, I'll mark it with your name.'

Bidding me take out my watch, Cupid adroitly dropped the inscribed slip on an exposed part of the incipient mass.

Instantly my eye marked the second-hand on my dial-plate.

Slowly I followed the slip, inch by inch: sometimes pausing for full half a minute as it disappeared beneath inscrutable groups of the lower cylinders, but only gradually to emerge again; and so, on, and on, and on—inch by inch; now in open sight, sliding along like a freckle on the quivering sheet; and then again wholly vanished; and so, on, and on, and on—inch by inch; all the time the main sheet growing more and more to final firmness—when, suddenly, I saw a sort of paper-fall, not wholly unlike a water-fall; a scissory sound smote my ear, as of some cord being snapped; and down dropped an unfolded sheet of perfect foolscap,* with my 'Cupid' half faded out of it, and still moist and warm.

My travels were at an end, for here was the end of the machine.

'Well, how long was it?' said Cupid.

'Nine minutes to a second,' replied I, watch in hand.

'I told you so.'

For a moment a curious emotion filled me, not wholly unlike that which one might experience at the fulfillment of some mysterious prophecy. But how absurd, thought I again; the thing is a mere machine, the essence of which is unvarying punctuality and precision.

Previously absorbed by the wheels and cylinders, my attention was now directed to a sad-looking woman standing by.

'That is rather an elderly person so silently tending the machine-end here. She would not seem wholly used to it either.'

'Oh,' knowingly whispered Cupid, through the din, 'she only came last week. She was a nurse formerly. But the business is poor in these parts, and she's left it. But look at the paper she is piling there.'

'Ay, foolscap,' handling the piles of moist, warm sheets, which continually were being delivered into the woman's waiting hands. 'Don't you turn out anything but foolscap at this machine?'

'Oh, sometimes, but not often, we turn out finer work—cream-laid and royal sheets, we call them. But foolscap being in chief demand we turn out foolscap most.'

It was very curious. Looking at that blank paper continually dropping, dropping, dropping, my mind ran on in wonderings of those strange uses to which those thousand sheets eventually would be put. All sorts of writings would be writ on those now vacant things— sermons, lawyers' briefs, physicians' prescriptions, love-letters, marriage certificates, bills of divorce, registers of births, death-warrants, and so on, without end. Then, recurring back to them as they here lay all blank, I could not but bethink me of that celebrated comparison of John Locke,* who, in demonstration of his theory that man had no innate ideas, compared the human mind at birth to a sheet of blank paper, something destined to be scribbled on, but what sort of characters no soul might tell.

Pacing slowly to and fro along the involved machine, still humming with its play, I was struck as well by the inevitability as the evolvement-power in all its motions.

'Does that thin cobweb there,' said I, pointing to the sheet in its more imperfect stage, 'does that never tear or break? It is marvelous fragile, and yet this machine it passes through is so mighty.'

'It never is known to tear a hair's point.'

'Does it never stop—get clogged?'

'No. It *must* go. The machinery makes it go just *so*; just that very way, and at that very pace you there plainly *see* it go. The pulp can't help going.'

Something of awe now stole over me, as I gazed upon this inflexible iron animal. Always, more or less, machinery of this ponderous, elaborate sort strikes, in some moods, strange dread into the human heart, as some living, panting Behemoth* might. But what made the thing I saw so specially terrible to me was the metallic necessity, the unbudging fatality which governed it. Though, here and there, I could not follow the thin, gauzy vail of pulp in the course of its more mysterious or entirely invisible advance, yet it was indubitable that, at those points where it eluded me, it still marched on in unvarying docility to the autocratic cunning of the machine. A fascination fastened on me. I stood spellbound and wandering in my soul. Before my eyes—there, passing in slow procession along the wheeling cylinders, I seemed to see, glued to the pallid incipience of the pulp, the yet more pallid faces of all the pallid girls I had eyed that heavy day. Slowly, mournfully, beseechingly, yet unresistingly, they gleamed along, their agony dimly outlined on the imperfect paper, like the print of the tormented face on the handkerchief of Saint Veronica.*

'Halloa! the heat of the room is too much for you,' cried Cupid, staring at me.

'No—I am rather chill, if anything.'

'Come out, Sir—out—out,' and, with the protecting air of a careful father, the precocious lad hurried me outside.

In a few moments, feeling revived a little, I went into the folding-room—the first room I had entered, and where the desk for transacting business stood, surrounded by the blank counters and blank girls engaged at them.

'Cupid here has led me a strange tour,' said I to the dark-complexioned man before mentioned, whom I had ere this discovered not only to be an old bachelor, but also the principal proprietor. 'Yours is a most wonderful factory. Your great machine is a miracle of inscrutable intricacy.'

'Yes, all our visitors think it so. But we don't have many. We are in a very out-of-the-way corner here. Few inhabitants, too. Most of our girls come from far-off villages.'

'The girls,' echoed I, glancing round at their silent forms. 'Why is it, Sir, that in most factories, female operatives, of whatever age, are indiscriminately called girls, never women?'

'Oh! as to that—why, I suppose, the fact of their being generally unmarried—that's the reason, I should think. But it never struck me before. For our factory here, we will not have married women; they are apt to be off-and-on too much. We want none but steady workers; twelve hours to the day, day after day, through the three hundred and sixty-five days, excepting Sundays, Thanksgiving, and Fast-days. That's our rule. And so, having no married women, what females we have are rightly enough called girls.'

'Then these are all maids,' said I, while some pained homage to their pale virginity made me involuntarily bow.

'All maids.'

Again the strange emotion filled me.

'Your cheeks look whitish yet, Sir,' said the man, gazing at me narrowly. 'You must be careful going home. Do they pain you at all now? It's a bad sign, if they do.'

'No doubt, Sir,' answered I, 'when once I have got out of the Devil's Dungeon I shall feel them mending.'

'Ah, yes; the winter air in valleys, or gorges, or any sunken place, is far colder and more bitter than elsewhere. You would hardly believe it now, but it is colder here than at the top of Woedolor Mountain.'

'I dare say it is, Sir. But time presses me; I must depart.'

With that, remuffling myself in dread-naught and tippet, thrusting my hands into my huge seal-skin mittens, I sallied out into the nipping air, and found poor Black, my horse, all cringing and doubled up with the cold.

Soon, wrapped in furs and meditations, I ascended from the Devil's Dungeon.

At the Black Notch I paused, and once more bethought me of Temple-Bar. Then, shooting through the pass, all alone with inscrutable nature, I exclaimed—Oh! Paradise of Bachelors! and oh! Tartarus of Maids!

FITZ-JAMES O'BRIEN

What Was It?

❧❧

I T is, I confess, with considerable diffidence that I approach the strange narrative which I am about to relate. The events which I purpose detailing are of so extraordinary a character that I am quite prepared to meet with an unusual amount of incredulity and scorn. I accept all such beforehand. I have, I trust, the literary courage to face unbelief. I have, after mature consideration, resolved to narrate, in as simple and straightforward a manner as I can compass, some facts that passed under my observation, in the month of July last, and which, in the annals of the mysteries of physical science, are wholly unparalleled.

I live at No. — Twenty-sixth Street, in New York.* The house is in some respects a curious one. It has enjoyed for the last two years the reputation of being haunted. It is a large and stately residence, surrounded by what was once a garden, but which is now only a green enclosure used for bleaching clothes. The dry basin of what has been a fountain, and a few fruit-trees ragged and unpruned, indicate that this spot in past days was a pleasant, shady retreat, filled with fruits and flowers and the sweet murmur of waters.

The house is very spacious. A hall of noble size leads to a large spiral staircase winding through its centre, while the various apartments are of imposing dimensions. It was built some fifteen or twenty years since by Mr A——, the well-known New York merchant, who five years ago threw the commercial world into convulsions by a stupendous bank fraud. Mr A——, as every one knows, escaped to Europe, and died not long after, of a broken heart. Almost immediately after the news of his decease reached this country and was verified, the report spread in Twenty-sixth Street that No. — was haunted. Legal measures had dispossessed the widow of its former owner, and it was inhabited merely by a care-taker and his wife, placed there by the house-agent into whose hands it had passed for purposes of renting or sale. These people declared that they were troubled with unnatural noises. Doors were opened without any visible agency. The remnants of furniture scattered through the various rooms were, during the night, piled one upon the other by unknown hands. Invisible feet passed up and down the stairs in broad daylight, accompanied by the rustle of unseen silk dresses, and the gliding of viewless hands along the massive balusters.* The care-taker and his wife declared they would live there no longer. The house-agent laughed, dismissed them, and put others in their place. The noises and supernatural manifestations continued. The neighborhood caught up the story, and the house remained untenanted for three years. Several persons negotiated for it; but, somehow, always before the bargain was closed they heard the unpleasant rumors and declined to treat any further.

It was in this state of things that my landlady, who at that time kept a boarding-house in Bleecker Street,* and who wished to move further up town, conceived the bold idea of renting No. — Twenty-sixth Street. Happening to have in her house rather a plucky and philosophical set of boarders, she laid her scheme before us, stating candidly everything she had heard respecting the ghostly qualities of the establishment to which she wished to remove us. With the exception of two timid persons,—a sea-captain and a returned Californian, who immediately gave notice that they would leave,—all of Mrs Moffat's guests declared that they would accompany her in her chivalric incursion into the abode of spirits.

Our removal was effected in the month of May, and we were charmed with our new residence. The portion of Twenty-sixth Street where our house is situated, between Seventh and Eighth Avenues, is one of the pleasantest localities in New York. The gardens back of the houses, running down nearly to the Hudson,* form, in the summer time, a perfect avenue of verdure. The air is pure and invigorating, sweeping, as it does, straight across the river from the Weehawken* heights, and even the ragged garden which surrounded the house, although displaying on washing days rather too much clothes-line, still gave us a piece of greensward to look at, and a cool retreat in the summer evenings, where we smoked our cigars in the dusk, and watched the fire-flies flashing their dark-lanterns in the long grass.

Of course we had no sooner established ourselves at No. — than we began to expect the ghosts. We absolutely awaited their advent with eagerness. Our dinner conversation was supernatural. One of the boarders, who had purchased Mrs Crowe's 'Night Side of Nature'* for his own private delectation, was regarded as a public enemy by the entire household for not having bought twenty copies. The man led a life of supreme wretchedness while he was reading this volume. A system of espionage was established, of which he was the victim. If he incautiously laid the book down for an instant and left the room, it was immediately seized and read aloud in secret places to a select few. I found myself a person of immense importance, it having leaked out that I was tolerably well versed in the history of supernaturalism, and had once written a story the foundation of which was a ghost.* If a table or a wainscot panel happened to warp when we were assembled in the large drawing-room, there was an instant silence, and every one was prepared for an immediate clanking of chains and a spectral form.

After a month of psychological excitement, it was with the utmost dissatisfaction that we were forced to acknowledge that nothing in the remotest degree approaching the supernatural had manifested itself. Once the black butler asseverated* that his candle had been blown out by some invisible agency while he was undressing himself for the night; but as I had more than once discovered this colored gentleman in a condition when one candle must have appeared to him like two, I thought it possible that, by going a step further in his potations,* he might have reversed this phenomenon, and seen no candle at all where he ought to have beheld one.

Things were in this state when an incident took place so awful and inexplicable in its character that my reason fairly reels at the bare memory of the occurrence. It was the tenth of July. After dinner was over I repaired, with my friend Dr Hammond, to the garden to smoke my evening pipe. Independent of certain mental sympathies which existed between the Doctor and myself, we were linked together by a vice. We both smoked opium. We knew each other's secret, and respected it. We enjoyed together that wonderful expansion of thought, that marvellous intensifying of the perceptive faculties, that boundless feeling of existence when we seem to have points of contact with the whole universe,—in short, that unimaginable spiritual bliss, which I would not surrender for a throne, and which I hope you, reader, will never—never taste.

Those hours of opium happiness which the Doctor and I spent together in secret were regulated with a scientific accuracy. We did not blindly smoke the drug of paradise,* and leave our dreams to chance.

While smoking, we carefully steered our conversation through the brightest and calmest channels of thought. We talked of the East, and endeavored to recall the magical panorama of its glowing scenery. We criticised the most sensuous poets,—those who painted life ruddy with health, brimming with passion, happy in the possession of youth and strength and beauty. If we talked of Shakespeare's 'Tempest,' we lingered over Ariel, and avoided Caliban.* Like the Guebers,* we turned our faces to the east, and saw only the sunny side of the world.

This skilful coloring of our train of thought produced in our subsequent visions a corresponding tone. The splendors of Arabian fairy-land dyed our dreams. We paced that narrow strip of grass with the tread and port of kings. The song of the *rana arborea*,* while he clung to the bark of the ragged plum-tree, sounded like the strains of divine musicians. Houses, walls, and streets melted like rain-clouds, and vistas of unimaginable glory stretched away before us. It was a rapturous companionship. We enjoyed the vast delight more perfectly because, even in our most ecstatic moments, we were conscious of each other's presence. Our pleasures, while individual, were still twin, vibrating and moving in musical accord.

On the evening in question, the tenth of July, the Doctor and myself drifted into an unusually metaphysical mood. We lit our large meerschaums,* filled with fine Turkish tobacco, in the core of which burned a little black nut of opium, that, like the nut in the fairy tale,* held within its narrow limits wonders beyond the reach of kings; we paced to and fro, conversing. A strange perversity dominated the currents of our thought. They would *not* flow through the sun-lit channels into which we strove to divert them. For some unaccountable reason, they constantly diverged into dark and lonesome beds, where a continual gloom brooded. It was in vain that, after our old fashion, we flung ourselves on the shores of the East, and talked of its gay bazaars, of the splendors of the time of Haroun,* of harems and golden palaces. Black afreets continually arose from the depths of our talk, and expanded, like the one the fisherman released from the copper vessel,* until they blotted everything bright from our vision. Insensibly, we yielded to the occult force that swayed us, and indulged in gloomy speculation. We had talked some time upon the proneness of the human mind to mysticism, and the almost universal love of the terrible, when Hammond suddenly said to me, 'What do you consider to be the greatest element of terror?'

The question puzzled me. That many things were terrible, I knew. Stumbling over a corpse in the dark; beholding, as I once did, a woman floating down a deep and rapid river, with wildly lifted arms, and awful, upturned face, uttering, as she drifted, shrieks that rent one's heart, while we, the spectators, stood frozen at a window which overhung the river at a height of sixty feet, unable to make the slightest effort to save her, but dumbly watching her last supreme agony and her disappearance. A shattered wreck, with no life visible, encountered floating listlessly on the ocean, is a terrible object, for it suggests a huge terror, the proportions of which are veiled. But it now struck me, for the first time, that there must be one great and ruling embodiment of fear,—a King of Terrors, to which all others must succumb. What might it be? To what train of circumstances would it owe its existence?

'I confess, Hammond,' I replied to my friend, 'I never considered the subject before. That there must be one Something more terrible than any other thing, I feel. I cannot attempt, however, even the most vague definition.'

'I am somewhat like you, Harry,' he answered. 'I feel my capacity to experience a terror greater than anything yet conceived by the human mind;—something combining in fearful and unnatural amalgamation hitherto supposed incompatible elements. The calling of the voices in Brockden Brown's novel of "Wieland" is awful; so is the picture of the Dweller of the Threshold, in Bulwer's "Zanoni";* but,' he added, shaking his head gloomily, 'there is something more horrible still than these.'

'Look here, Hammond,' I rejoined, 'let us drop this kind of talk, for heaven's sake! We shall suffer for it, depend on it.'

'I don't know what's the matter with me to-night,' he replied, 'but my brain is running upon all sorts of weird and awful thoughts. I feel as if I could write a story like Hoffman, to-night, if I were only master of a literary style.'

'Well, if we are going to be Hoffmanesque* in our talk, I'm off to bed. Opium and nightmares should never be brought together. How sultry it is! Good-night, Hammond.'

'Good-night, Harry. Pleasant dreams to you.'

'To you, gloomy wretch, afreets, ghouls, and enchanters.'

We parted, and each sought his respective chamber. I undressed quickly and got into bed, taking with me, according to my usual custom, a book, over which I generally read myself to sleep. I opened the volume as soon as I had laid my head upon the pillow, and instantly flung it to the other side of the room. It was Goudon's 'History of Monsters,'*—a curious French work, which I had lately imported from Paris, but which, in the state of mind I had then reached, was anything but an agreeable companion. I resolved to go to sleep at once; so, turning down my gas until nothing but a little blue point of light glimmered on the top of the tube, I composed myself to rest.

The room was in total darkness. The atom of gas that still remained alight did not illuminate a distance of three inches round the burner. I desperately drew my arm across my eyes, as if to shut out even the darkness, and tried to think of nothing. It was in vain. The confounded themes touched on by Hammond in the garden kept obtruding themselves on my brain. I battled against them. I erected ramparts of would-be blankness of intellect to keep them out. They still crowded upon me. While I was lying still as a corpse, hoping that by a perfect physical inaction I should hasten mental repose, an awful incident occurred. A Something dropped, as it seemed, from the ceiling, plumb upon my chest, and the next instant I felt two bony hands encircling my throat, endeavoring to choke me.

I am no coward, and am possessed of considerable physical strength. The suddenness of the attack, instead of stunning me, strung every nerve to its highest tension. My body acted from instinct, before my brain had time to realize the terrors of my position. In an instant I wound two muscular arms around the creature, and squeezed it, with all the strength of despair, against my chest. In a few seconds the bony hands that had fastened on my throat loosened their hold, and I was free to breathe once more. Then commenced a struggle of awful intensity. Immersed in the most profound darkness, totally ignorant of the nature of the Thing by which I was so suddenly attacked, finding my grasp slipping every moment, by reason, it seemed to me, of the entire nakedness of my assailant, bitten with sharp teeth in the shoulder, neck, and chest, having every moment to protect my throat against a pair of sinewy, agile hands, which my utmost efforts could not confine,—these were a combination of circumstances to combat which required all the strength, skill, and courage that I possessed.

At last, after a silent, deadly, exhausting struggle, I got my assailant under by a series of incredible efforts of strength. Once pinned, with my knee on what I made out to be its chest, I knew that I was victor. I rested for a moment to breathe. I heard the creature beneath me panting in the darkness, and felt the violent throbbing of a heart. It was apparently as exhausted as I was; that was one comfort. At this moment I remembered that I usually placed under my pillow, before going to bed, a large yellow silk pocket-handkerchief. I felt for it instantly; it was there. In a few seconds more I had, after a fashion, pinioned the creature's arms.

I now felt tolerably secure. There was nothing more to be done but to turn on the gas, and, having first seen what my midnight assailant was like, arouse the household. I will confess to being actuated by a certain pride in not giving the alarm before; I wished to make the capture alone and unaided.

Never losing my hold for an instant, I slipped from the bed to the floor, dragging my captive with me. I had but a few steps to make to reach the gas-burner; these I made with the greatest caution, holding the creature in a grip like a vice. At last I got within arm's-length of the tiny speck of blue light which told me where the gas-burner lay. Quick as lightning I released my grasp with one hand and let on the full flood of light. Then I turned to look at my captive.

I cannot even attempt to give any definition of my sensations the instant after I turned on the gas. I suppose I must have shrieked with terror, for in less than a minute afterward my room was crowded with the inmates of the house. I shudder now as I think of that awful moment. *I saw nothing!* Yes; I had one arm firmly clasped round a breathing, panting, corporeal shape, my other hand gripped with all its strength a throat as warm, and apparently fleshly, as my own; and yet, with this living substance in my grasp, with its body pressed against my own, and all in the bright glare of a large jet of gas, I absolutely beheld nothing! Not even an outline,—a vapor!

I do not, even at this hour, realize the situation in which I found myself. I cannot recall the astounding incident thoroughly. Imagination in vain tries to compass the awful paradox.

It breathed. I felt its warm breath upon my cheek. It struggled fiercely. It had hands. They clutched me. Its skin was smooth, like my own. There it lay, pressed close up against me, solid as stone,—and yet utterly invisible!

I wonder that I did not faint or go mad on the instant. Some wonderful instinct must have sustained me; for, absolutely, in place of loosening my hold on the terrible Enigma, I seemed to gain an additional strength in my moment of horror, and tightened my grasp with such wonderful force that I felt the creature shivering with agony.

Just then Hammond entered my room at the head of the household. As soon as he beheld my face—which, I suppose, must have been an awful sight to look at—he hastened forward, crying, 'Great heaven, Harry! what has happened?'

'Hammond! Hammond!' I cried, 'come here. O, this is awful! I have been attacked in bed by something or other, which I have hold of; but I can't see it,—I can't see it!'

Hammond, doubtless struck by the unfeigned horror expressed in my countenance, made one or two steps forward with an anxious yet puzzled expression. A very audible titter burst from the remainder of my visitors. This suppressed laughter made me furious. To laugh at a human being in my position! It was the worst species of cruelty. *Now*, I can understand why the appearance of a man struggling violently, as it would seem, with an airy nothing, and calling for assistance against a vision, should have appeared ludicrous. *Then*, so great was my rage against the mocking crowd that had I the power I would have stricken them dead where they stood.

'Hammond! Hammond!' I cried again, despairingly, 'for God's sake come to me. I can hold the—the thing but a short while longer. It is overpowering me. Help me! Help me!'

'Harry,' whispered Hammond, approaching me, 'you have been smoking too much opium.'

'I swear to you, Hammond, that this is no vision,' I answered, in the same low tone. 'Don't you see how it shakes my whole frame with its struggles? If you don't believe me, convince yourself. Feel it,—touch it.'

Hammond advanced and laid his hand in the spot I indicated. A wild cry of horror burst from him. He had felt it!

In a moment he had discovered somewhere in my room a long piece of cord, and was the next instant winding it and knotting it about the body of the unseen being that I clasped in my arms.

'Harry,' he said, in a hoarse, agitated voice, for, though he preserved his presence of mind, he was deeply moved, 'Harry, it's all safe now. You may let go, old fellow, if you're tired. The Thing can't move.'

I was utterly exhausted, and I gladly loosed my hold.

Hammond stood holding the ends of the cord that bound the Invisible, twisted round his hand, while before him, self-supporting as it were, he beheld a rope laced and interlaced, and stretching tightly around a vacant space. I never saw a man look so thoroughly stricken with awe. Nevertheless his face expressed all the courage and determination which I knew him to possess. His lips, although white, were set firmly, and one could perceive at a glance that, although stricken with fear, he was not daunted.

The confusion that ensued among the guests of the house who were witnesses of this extraordinary scene between Hammond and myself,—who beheld the pantomime of binding this struggling Something,—who beheld me almost sinking from physical exhaustion when my task of jailer was over,—the confusion and terror that took possession of the bystanders, when they saw all this, was beyond description. The weaker ones fled from the apartment. The few who remained clustered near the door and could not be induced to approach Hammond and his Charge. Still incredulity broke out through their terror. They had not the courage to satisfy themselves, and yet they doubted. It was in vain that I begged of some of the men to come near and convince themselves by touch of the existence in that room of a living being which was invisible. They were incredulous, but did not dare to undeceive themselves. How could a solid, living, breathing body be invisible, they asked. My reply was this. I gave a sign to Hammond, and both of us—conquering our fearful repugnance to touch the invisible creature—lifted it from the ground, manacled as it was, and took it to my bed. Its weight was about that of a boy of fourteen.

'Now, my friends,' I said, as Hammond and myself held the creature suspended over the bed, 'I can give you self-evident proof that here is a solid, ponderable body, which, nevertheless, you cannot see. Be good enough to watch the surface of the bed attentively.'

I was astonished at my own courage in treating this strange event so calmly; but I had recovered from my first terror, and felt a sort of scientific pride in the affair, which dominated every other feeling.

The eyes of the bystanders were immediately fixed on my bed. At a given signal Hammond and I let the creature fall. There was the dull sound of a heavy body alighting on a soft mass. The timbers of the bed creaked. A deep impression marked itself distinctly on the pillow, and on the bed itself. The crowd who witnessed this gave a low cry, and rushed from the room. Hammond and I were left alone with our Mystery.

We remained silent for some time, listening to the low, irregular breathing of the creature on the bed, and watching the rustle of the bed-clothes as it impotently struggled to free itself from confinement. Then Hammond spoke.

'Harry, this is awful.'

'Ay, awful.'

'But not unaccountable.'

'Not unaccountable! What do you mean? Such a thing has never occurred since the birth of the world. I know not what to think, Hammond. God grant that I am not mad, and that this is not an insane fantasy!'

'Let us reason a little, Harry. Here is a solid body which we touch, but which we cannot see. The fact is so unusual that it strikes us with terror. Is there no parallel, though, for such a phenomenon? Take a piece of pure glass. It is tangible and transparent. A certain chemical coarseness is all that prevents its being so entirely transparent as to be totally invisible. It is not *theoretically impossible*, mind you, to make a glass which shall not reflect a single ray of light,—a glass so pure and homogeneous in its atoms that the rays from the sun will pass through it as they do through the air, refracted but not reflected. We do not see the air, and yet we feel it.'

'That's all very well, Hammond, but these are inanimate substances. Glass does not breathe, air does not breathe. *This* thing has a heart that palpitates,—a will that moves it,—lungs that play, and inspire and respire.'

'You forget the phenomena of which we have so often heard of late,' answered the Doctor, gravely. 'At the meetings called "spirit circles,"* invisible hands have been thrust into the hands of those persons round the table,—warm, fleshly hands that seemed to pulsate with mortal life.'

'What? Do you think, then, that this thing is—'

'I don't know what it is,' was the solemn reply; 'but please the gods I will, with your assistance, thoroughly investigate it.'

We watched together, smoking many pipes, all night long, by the bedside of the unearthly being that tossed and panted until it was apparently wearied out. Then we learned by the low, regular breathing that it slept.

The next morning the house was all astir. The boarders congregated on the landing outside my room, and Hammond and myself were lions. We had to answer a thousand questions as to the state of our extraordinary prisoner, for as yet not one person in the house except ourselves could be induced to set foot in the apartment.

The creature was awake. This was evidenced by the convulsive manner in which the bed-clothes were moved in its efforts to escape. There was something truly terrible in beholding, as it were, those second-hand indications of the terrible writhings and agonized struggles for liberty which themselves were invisible.

Hammond and myself had racked our brains during the long night to discover some means by which we might realize the shape and general appearance of the Enigma. As well as we could make out by passing our hands over the creature's form, its outlines and lineaments were human. There was a mouth; a round, smooth head without hair; a nose, which, however, was little elevated above the cheeks; and its hands and feet felt like those of a boy. At first we thought of placing the being on a smooth surface and tracing its outline with chalk, as shoemakers trace the outline of the foot. This plan was given up as being of no value. Such an outline would give not the slightest idea of its conformation.

A happy thought struck me. We would take a cast of it in plaster of Paris. This would give us the solid figure, and satisfy all our wishes. But how to do it? The movements of the creature would disturb the setting of the plastic covering, and distort the mould. Another thought. Why not give it chloroform?* It had respiratory organs,—that was evident by its breathing. Once reduced to a state of insensibility, we could do with it what we would. Doctor X——— was sent for; and after the worthy physician had recovered from the first shock of amazement, he proceeded to administer the chloroform. In three minutes afterward we were enabled to remove the fetters from the creature's body, and a modeller was busily engaged in covering the invisible form with the moist clay. In five minutes more we had a mould, and before evening a rough fac-simile of the Mystery. It was shaped like a man,—distorted, uncouth, and horrible, but still a man. It was small, not over four feet and some inches in height, and its limbs revealed a muscular development that was unparalleled. Its face surpassed in hideousness anything I had ever seen. Gustave Doré, or Callot, or Tony Johannot, never conceived anything so horrible. There is a face in one of the latter's illustrations to *Un Voyage où il vous plaira*,* which somewhat approaches the countenance of this creature, but does not equal it. It was the physiognomy of what I should fancy a ghoul might be. It looked as if it was capable of feeding on human flesh.

Having satisfied our curiosity, and bound every one in the house to secrecy, it became a question what was to be done with our Enigma? It was impossible that we should keep such a horror in our house; it was equally impossible that such an awful being should be let loose upon the world. I confess that I would have gladly voted for the creature's destruction. But who would shoulder the responsibility? Who would undertake the execution of this horrible semblance of a human being? Day after day this question was deliberated gravely. The boarders all left the house. Mrs Moffat was in despair, and threatened Hammond and myself with all sorts of legal penalties if we did not remove the Horror. Our answer was, 'We will go if you like, but we decline taking this creature with us. Remove it yourself if you please. It appeared in your house. On you the responsibility rests.' To this there was, of course, no answer. Mrs Moffat could not obtain for love or money a person who would even approach the Mystery.

The most singular part of the affair was that we were entirely ignorant of what the creature habitually fed on. Everything in the way of nutriment that we could think of was placed before it, but was never touched. It was awful to stand by, day after day, and see the clothes toss, and hear the hard breathing, and know that it was starving.

Ten, twelve days, a fortnight passed, and it still lived. The pulsations of the heart, however, were daily growing fainter, and had now nearly ceased. It was evident that the creature was dying for want of sustenance. While this terrible life-struggle was going on, I felt miserable. I could not sleep. Horrible as the creature was, it was pitiful to think of the pangs it was suffering.

At last it died. Hammond and I found it cold and stiff one morning in the bed. The heart had ceased to beat, the lungs to inspire. We hastened to bury it in the garden. It was a strange funeral, the dropping of that viewless corpse into the damp hole. The cast of its form I gave to Doctor X——, who keeps it in his museum in Tenth Street.

As I am on the eve of a long journey from which I may not return, I have drawn up this narrative of an event the most singular that has ever come to my knowledge.

CHARLES DICKENS

No. 1 Branch Line: The Signal-Man

⊰⊱

'HALLOA! Below there!'
When he heard a voice thus calling to him, he was standing at the door of his box, with a flag in his hand, furled round its short pole. One would have thought, considering the nature of the ground, that he could not have doubted from what quarter the voice came; but, instead of looking up to where I stood on the top of the steep cutting nearly over his head, he turned himself about and looked down the Line. There was something remarkable in his manner of doing so, though I could not have said, for my life, what. But, I know it was remarkable enough to attract my notice, even though his figure was foreshortened and shadowed, down in the deep trench, and mine was high above him, so steeped in the glow of an angry sunset that I had shaded my eyes with my hand before I saw him at all.

'Halloa! Below!'

From looking down the Line, he turned himself about again, and, raising his eyes, saw my figure high above him.

'Is there any path by which I can come down and speak to you?'

He looked up at me without replying, and I looked down at him without pressing him too soon with a repetition of my idle question. Just then, there came a vague vibration in the earth and air, quickly changing into a violent pulsation, and an oncoming rush that caused me to start back, as though it had force to draw me down. When such vapour as rose to my height from this rapid train, had passed me and was skimming away over the landscape, I looked down again, and saw him re-furling the flag he had shown while the train went by.

I repeated my inquiry. After a pause, during which he seemed to regard me with fixed attention, he motioned with his rolled-up flag towards a point on my level, some two or three hundred yards distant. I called down to him, 'All right!' and made for that point. There, by dint of looking closely about me, I found a rough zig-zag descending path notched out: which I followed.

The cutting was extremely deep, and unusually precipitate. It was made through a clammy stone that became oozier and wetter as I went down. For these reasons, I found the way long enough to give me time to recal a singular air of reluctance or compulsion with which he had pointed out the path.

When I came down low enough upon the zigzag descent, to see him again, I saw that he was standing between the rails on the way by which the train had lately passed, in an attitude as if he were waiting for me to appear. He had his left hand at his chin, and that left elbow rested on his right hand crossed over his breast. His attitude was one of such expectation and watchfulness, that I stopped a moment, wondering at it.

I resumed my downward way, and, stepping out upon the level of the railroad and drawing nearer to him, saw that he was a dark sallow man, with a dark beard and rather heavy eyebrows. His post was in as solitary and dismal a place as ever I saw. On either side, a dripping-wet wall of jagged stone, excluding all view but a strip of sky; the perspective one way, only a crooked prolongation of this great dungeon; the shorter perspective in the other direction, terminating in a gloomy red light, and the gloomier entrance to a black tunnel, in whose massive architecture there was a barbarous, depressing, and forbidding air. So little sunlight ever found its way to this spot, that it had an earthy deadly smell; and so much cold wind rushed through it, that it struck chill to me, as if I had left the natural world.

Before he stirred, I was near enough to him to have touched him. Not even then removing his eyes from mine, he stepped back one step, and lifted his hand.

This was a lonesome post to occupy (I said), and it had riveted my attention when I looked down from up yonder. A visitor was a rarity, I should suppose; not an unwelcome rarity, I hoped? In me, he merely saw a man who had been shut up within narrow limits all his life, and who, being at last set free, had a newly awakened interest in these great works. To such purpose I spoke to him; but I am far from sure of the terms I used, for, besides that I am not happy in opening any conversation, there was something in the man that daunted me.

He directed a most curious look towards the red light near the tunnel's mouth, and looked all about it, as if something were missing from it, and then looked at me.

That light was part of his charge? Was it not?

He answered in a low voice: 'Don't you know it is?'

The monstrous thought came into my mind as I perused the fixed eyes and the saturnine face, that this was a spirit, not a man. I have speculated since, whether there may have been infection in his mind.

In my turn, I stepped back. But in making the action, I detected in his eyes some latent fear of me. This put the monstrous thought to flight.

'You look at me,' I said, forcing a smile, 'as if you had a dread of me.'

'I was doubtful,' he returned, 'whether I had seen you before.'

'Where?'

He pointed to the red light he had looked at.

'There?' I said.

Intently watchful of me, he replied (but without sound), Yes.

'My good fellow, what should I do there? However, be that as it may, I never was there, you may swear.'

'I think I may,' he rejoined. 'Yes. I am sure I may.'

His manner cleared, like my own. He replied to my remarks with readiness, and in well-chosen words. Had he much to do there? Yes; that was to say, he had enough responsibility to bear; but exactness and watchfulness were what was required of him, and of actual work—manual labour—he had next to none. To change that signal, to trim those lights, and to turn this iron handle now and then, was all he had to do under that head. Regarding those many long and lonely hours of which I seemed to make so much, he could only say that the routine of his life had shaped itself into that form, and he had grown used to it. He had taught himself a language down here—if only to know it by sight, and to have formed his own crude ideas of its pronunciation, could be called learning it. He had also worked at fractions and decimals, and tried a little algebra; but he was, and had been as a boy, a poor hand at figures. Was it necessary for him when on duty, always to remain in that channel of damp air, and could he never rise into the sunshine from between those high stone walls? Why, that depended upon times and circumstances. Under some conditions there would be less upon the Line than under others, and the same held good as to certain hours of the day and night. In bright weather, he did choose occasions for getting a little above these lower shadows; but, being at all times liable to be called by his electric bell, and at such times listening for it with redoubled anxiety, the relief was less than I would suppose.

He took me into his box, where there was a fire, a desk for an official book in which he had to make certain entries, a telegraphic instrument with its dial face and needles, and the little bell of which he had spoken. On my trusting that he would excuse the remark that he had been well educated, and (I hoped I might say without offence), perhaps educated above that station, he observed that instances of slight incongruity in such-wise would rarely be found wanting among large bodies of men; that he had heard it was so in workhouses, in the police force, even in that last desperate resource, the army; and that he knew it was so, more or less, in any great railway staff. He had been, when young (if I could believe it, sitting in that hut; he scarcely could), a student of natural philosophy, and had attended lectures; but he had run wild, misused his opportunities, gone down, and never risen again. He had no complaint to offer about that. He had made his bed, and he lay upon it. It was far too late to make another.

All that I have here condensed, he said in a quiet manner, with his grave dark regards divided between me and the fire. He threw in the word 'Sir,' from time to time, and especially when he referred to his youth: as though to request me to understand that he claimed to be nothing but what I found him. He was several times interrupted by the little bell, and had to read off messages, and send replies. Once, he had to stand without the door, and display a flag as a train passed, and make some verbal communication to the driver. In the discharge of his duties I observed him to be remarkably exact and vigilant, breaking off his discourse at a syllable, and remaining silent until what he had to do was done.

In a word, I should have set this man down as one of the safest of men to be employed in that capacity, but for the circumstance that while he was speaking to me he twice broke off with a fallen colour, turned his face towards the little bell when it did NOT ring, opened the door of the hut (which was kept shut to exclude the unhealthy damp), and looked out towards the red light near the mouth of the tunnel. On both of those occasions, he came back to the fire with the inexplicable air upon him which I had remarked, without being able to define, when we were so far asunder.

Said I when I rose to leave him: 'You almost make me think that I have met with a contented man.'

(I am afraid I must acknowledge that I said it to lead him on.)

'I believe I used to be so,' he rejoined, in the low voice in which he had first spoken; 'but I am troubled, sir, I am troubled.'

He would have recalled the words if he could. He had said them, however, and I took them up quickly.

'With what? What is your trouble?'

'It is very difficult to impart, sir. It is very, very, difficult to speak of. If ever you make me another visit, I will try to tell you.'

'But I expressly intend to make you another visit. Say, when shall it be?'

'I go off early in the morning, and I shall be on again at ten to-morrow night, sir.'

'I will come at eleven.'

He thanked me, and went out at the door with me. 'I'll show my white light, sir,' he said, in his peculiar low voice, 'till you have found the way up. When you have found it, don't call out! And when you are at the top, don't call out!'

His manner seemed to make the place strike colder to me, but I said no more than 'Very well.'

'And when you come down to-morrow night, don't call out! Let me ask you a parting question. What made you cry "Halloa! Below there!" to-night?'

'Heaven knows,' said I. 'I cried something to that effect——'

'Not to that effect, sir. Those were the very words. I know them well.'

'Admit those were the very words. I said them, no doubt, because I saw you below.'

'For no other reason?'

'What other reason could I possibly have!'

'You had no feeling that they were conveyed to you in any super-natural way?'

'No.'

He wished me good night, and held up his light. I walked by the side of the down Line of rails (with a very disagreeable sensation of a train coming behind me), until I found the path. It was easier to mount than to descend, and I got back to my inn without any adventure.

Punctual to my appointment, I placed my foot on the first notch of the zig-zag next night, as the distant clocks were striking eleven. He was waiting for me at the bottom, with his white light on. 'I have not called out,' I said, when we came close together; 'may I speak now?'

'By all means, sir.' 'Good night then, and here's my hand.' 'Good night, sir, and here's mine.' With that, we walked side by side to his box, entered it, closed the door, and sat down by the fire.

'I have made up my mind, sir,' he began, bending forward as soon as we were seated, and speaking in a tone but a little above a whisper, 'that you shall not have to ask me twice what troubles me. I took you for some one else yesterday evening. That troubles me.'

'That mistake?'

'No. That someone else.'

'Who is it?'

'I don't know.'

'Like me?'

'I don't know. I never saw the face. The left arm is across the face, and the right arm is waved. Violently waved. This way.'

I followed his action with my eyes, and it was the action of an arm gesticulating with the utmost passion and vehemence: 'For God's sake clear the way!'

'One moonlight night,' said the man, 'I was sitting here, when I heard a voice cry "Halloa! Below there!" I started up, looked from that door, and saw this Some one else standing by the red light near the tunnel, waving as I just now showed you. The voice seemed hoarse with shouting, and it cried, "Look out! Look out!" And then again "Halloa! Below there! Look out!" I caught up my lamp, turned it on red, and ran towards the figure, calling, "What's wrong? What has happened? Where?" It stood just outside the blackness of the tunnel. I advanced so close upon it that I wondered at its keeping the sleeve across its eyes. I ran right up at it, and had my hand stretched out to pull the sleeve away, when it was gone.'

'Into the tunnel,' said I.

'No. I ran on into the tunnel, five hundred yards. I stopped and held my lamp above my head, and saw the figures of the measured distance, and saw the wet stains stealing down the walls and trickling through the arch. I ran out again, faster than I had run in (for I had a mortal abhorrence of the place upon me), and I looked all round the red light with my own red light, and I went up the iron ladder to the gallery atop of it, and I came down again, and ran back here. I telegraphed both ways: "An alarm has been given. Is anything wrong?" The answer came back, both ways: "All well."'

Resisting the slow touch of a frozen finger tracing out my spine,

I showed him how that this figure must be a deception of his sense of sight, and how that figures, originating in disease of the delicate nerves that minister to the functions of the eye, were known to have often troubled patients, some of whom had become conscious of the nature of their affliction, and had even proved it by experiments upon themselves. 'As to an imaginary cry,' said I, 'do but listen for a moment to the wind in this unnatural valley while we speak so low, and to the wild harp it makes of the telegraph wires!'

That was all very well, he returned, after we had sat listening for a while, and he ought to know something of the wind and the wires, he who so often passed long winter nights there, alone and watching. But he would beg to remark that he had not finished.

I asked his pardon, and he slowly added these words, touching my arm:

'Within six hours after the Appearance, the memorable accident on this Line happened, and within ten hours the dead and wounded were brought along through the tunnel over the spot where the figure had stood.'

A disagreeable shudder crept over me, but I did my best against it. It was not to be denied, I rejoined, that this was a remarkable coincidence, calculated deeply to impress his mind. But, it was unquestionable that remarkable coincidences did continually occur, and they must be taken into account in dealing with such a subject. Though to be sure I must admit, I added (for I thought I saw that he was going to bring the objection to bear upon me), men of common sense did not allow much for coincidences in making the ordinary calculations of life.

He again begged to remark that he had not finished.

I again begged his pardon for being betrayed into interruptions.

'This,' he said, again laying his hand upon my arm, and glancing over his shoulder with hollow eyes, 'was just a year ago. Six or seven months passed, and I had recovered from the surprise and shock, when one morning, as the day was breaking, I, standing at that door, looked towards the red light, and saw the spectre again.' He stopped, with a fixed look at me.

'Did it cry out?'

'No. It was silent.'

'Did it wave its arm?'

'No. It leaned against the shaft of the light, with both hands before the face. Like this.'

Once more, I followed his action with my eyes. It was an action of mourning. I have seen such an attitude in stone figures on tombs.

'Did you go up to it?'

'I came in and sat down, partly to collect my thoughts, partly because it had turned me faint. When I went to the door again, daylight was above me, and the ghost was gone.'

'But nothing followed? Nothing came of this?'

He touched me on the arm with his forefinger twice or thrice, giving a ghastly nod each time:

'That very day, as a train came out of the tunnel, I noticed, at a carriage window on my side, what looked like a confusion of hands and heads, and something waved. I saw it, just in time to signal the driver, Stop! He shut off, and put his brake on, but the train drifted past here a hundred and fifty yards or more. I ran after it, and, as I went along, heard terrible screams and cries. A beautiful young lady had died instantaneously in one of the compartments, and was brought in here, and laid down on this floor between us.'

Involuntarily, I pushed my chair back, as I looked from the boards at which he pointed, to himself.

'True, sir. True. Precisely as it happened, so I tell it you.'

I could think of nothing to say, to any purpose, and my mouth was very dry. The wind and the wires took up the story with a long lamenting wail.

He resumed. 'Now, sir, mark this, and judge how my mind is troubled. The spectre came back, a week ago. Ever since, it has been there, now and again, by fits and starts.'

'At the light?'

'At the Danger-light.'

'What does it seem to do?'

He repeated, if possible with increased passion and vehemence, that former gesticulation of 'For God's sake clear the way!'

Then, he went on. 'I have no peace or rest for it. It calls to me, for many minutes together, in an agonised manner, 'Below there! Look out! Look out!' It stands waving to me. It rings my little bell——'

I caught at that. 'Did it ring your bell yesterday evening when I was here, and you went to the door?'

'Twice.'

'Why, see,' said I, 'how your imagination misleads you. My eyes were on the bell, and my ears were open to the bell, and if I am a living man, it did NOT ring at those times. No, nor at any other time, except when it was rung in the natural course of physical things by the station communicating with you.'

He shook his head. 'I have never made a mistake as to that, yet, sir. I have never confused the spectre's ring with the man's. The ghost's ring is a strange vibration in the bell that it derives from nothing else, and I have not asserted that the bell stirs to the eye. I don't wonder that you failed to hear it. But I heard it.'

'And did the spectre seem to be there, when you looked out?'

'It WAS there.'

'Both times?'

He repeated firmly: 'Both times.'

'Will you come to the door with me, and look for it now?'

He bit his under-lip as though he were somewhat unwilling, but arose. I opened the door, and stood on the step, while he stood in the doorway. There, was the Danger-light. There, was the dismal mouth of the tunnel. There, were the high wet stone walls of the cutting. There, were the stars above them.

'Do you see it?' I asked him, taking particular note of his face. His eyes were prominent and strained; but not very much more so, perhaps, than my own had been when I had directed them earnestly towards the same spot.

'No,' he answered. 'It is not there.'

'Agreed,' said I.

We went in again, shut the door, and resumed our seats. I was thinking how best to improve this advantage, if it might be called one, when he took up the conversation in such a matter of course way, so assuming that there could be no serious question of fact between us, that I felt myself placed in the weakest of positions.

'By this time you will fully understand, sir,' he said, 'that what troubles me so dreadfully, is the question, What does the spectre mean?'

I was not sure, I told him, that I did fully understand.

'What is its warning against?' he said, ruminating, with his eyes on the fire, and only by times turning them on me. 'What is the danger? Where is the danger? There is danger overhanging, somewhere on the Line. Some dreadful calamity will happen. It is not to be doubted this third time, after what has gone before. But surely this is a cruel haunting of *me*. What can I do!'

He pulled out his handkerchief, and wiped the drops from his heated forehead.

'If I telegraph Danger, on either side of me, or on both, I can give no reason for it,' he went on, wiping the palms of his hands. 'I should get into trouble, and do no good. They would think I was mad. This is the way it would work:—Message: "Danger! Take care!" Answer: "What Danger? Where?" Message: "Don't know. But for God's sake take care!" They would displace me. What else could they do?'

His pain of mind was most pitiable to see. It was the mental torture of a conscientious man, oppressed beyond endurance by an unintelligible responsibility involving life.

'When it first stood under the Danger-light,' he went on, putting his dark hair back from his head, and drawing his hands outward across and across his temples in an extremity of feverish distress, 'why not tell me where that accident was to happen—if it must happen? Why not tell me how it could be averted—if it could have been averted? When on its second coming it hid its face, why not tell me instead: "She is going to die. Let them keep her at home"? If it came, on those two occasions, only to show me that its warnings were true, and so to prepare me for the third, why not warn me plainly now? And I, Lord help me! A mere poor signalman on this solitary station! Why not go to somebody with credit to be believed, and power to act!'

When I saw him in this state, I saw that for the poor man's sake, as well as for the public safety, what I had to do for the time was, to compose his mind. Therefore, setting aside all question of reality or unreality between us, I represented to him that whoever thoroughly discharged his duty, must do well, and that at least it was his comfort that he understood his duty, though he did not understand these confounding Appearances. In this effort I succeeded far better than in the attempt to reason him out of his conviction. He became calm; the occupations incidental to his post as the night advanced, began to make larger demands on his attention; and I left him at two in the morning. I had offered to stay through the night, but he would not hear of it.

That I more than once looked back at the red light as I ascended the pathway, that I did not like the red light, and that I should have slept but poorly if my bed had been under it, I see no reason to conceal. Nor, did I like the two sequences of the accident and the dead girl. I see no reason to conceal that, either.

But, what ran most in my thoughts was the consideration how ought I to act, having become the recipient of this disclosure? I had proved the man to be intelligent, vigilant, painstaking, and exact; but how long might he remain so, in his state of mind? Though in a subordinate position, still he held a most important trust, and would I (for instance) like to stake my own life on the chances of his continuing to execute it with precision?

Unable to overcome a feeling that there would be something treacherous in my communicating what he had told me, to his superiors in the Company, without first being plain with himself and proposing a middle course to him, I ultimately resolved to offer to accompany him (otherwise keeping his secret for the present) to the wisest medical practitioner we could hear of in those parts, and to take his opinion. A change in his time of duty would come round next night, he had apprised me, and he would be off an hour or two after sunrise, and on again soon after sunset. I had appointed to return accordingly.

Next evening was a lovely evening, and I walked out early to enjoy it. The sun was not yet quite down when I traversed the field-path near the top of the deep cutting. I would extend my walk for an hour, I said to myself, half an hour on and half an hour back, and it would then be time to go to my signalman's box.

Before pursuing my stroll, I stepped to the brink, and mechanically looked down, from the point from which I had first seen him. I cannot describe the thrill that seized upon me, when, close at the mouth of the tunnel, I saw the appearance of a man, with his left sleeve across his eyes, passionately waving his right arm.

The nameless horror that oppressed me, passed in a moment, for in a moment I saw that this appearance of a man was a man indeed, and that there was a little group of other men standing at a short distance, to whom he seemed to be rehearsing the gesture he made. The Danger-light was not yet lighted. Against its shaft, a little low hut, entirely new to me, had been made of some wooden supports and tarpaulin. It looked no bigger than a bed.

With an irresistible sense that something was wrong—with a flashing self-reproachful fear that fatal mischief had come of my leaving the man there, and causing no one to be sent to overlook or correct what he did—I descended the notched path with all the speed I could make.

'What is the matter?' I asked the men.

'Signalman killed this morning, sir.'

'Not the man belonging to that box?'

'Yes, sir.'

'Not the man I know?'

'You will recognise him, sir, if you knew him,' said the man who spoke for the others, solemnly uncovering his own head and raising an end of the tarpaulin, 'for his face is quite composed.'

'O! how did this happen, how did this happen?' I asked, turning from one to another as the hut closed in again.

'He was cut down by an engine, sir. No man in England knew his work better. But somehow he was not clear of the outer rail. It was just at broad day. He had struck the light, and had the lamp in his hand. As the engine came out of the tunnel, his back was towards her, and she cut him down. That man drove her, and was showing how it happened. Show the gentleman, Tom.'

The man, who wore a rough dark dress, stepped back to his former place at the mouth of the tunnel:

'Coming round the curve in the tunnel, sir,' he said, 'I saw him at the end, like as if I saw him down a perspective-glass.* There was no time to check speed, and I knew him to be very careful. As he didn't seem to take heed of the whistle, I shut it off when we were running down upon him, and called to him as loud as I could call.'

'What did you say?'

'I said, Below there! Look out! Look out! For God's sake clear the way!'

I started.

'Ah! it was a dreadful time, sir. I never left off calling to him. I put this arm before my eyes, not to see, and I waved this arm to the last; but it was no use.'

Without prolonging the narrative to dwell on any one of its curious circumstances more than on any other, I may, in closing it, point out the coincidence that the warning of the Engine-Driver included, not only the words which the unfortunate Signalman had repeated to me as haunting him, but also the words which I myself—not he—had attached, and that only in my own mind, to the gesticulation he had imitated.

ÉMILE ZOLA

The Death of Olivier Bécaille

❧

I

IT was a Saturday morning, at six o'clock, that I died. I had been
ill for three days. My poor wife had just been rummaging through
a trunk, looking for some clean linen, and when she turned, she
saw me lying there stiff, eyes staring, not breathing; she rushed over
to me, thinking that I must have fainted; she touched my hands,
bent down to look at my face. Terror-stricken, she burst into tears,
repeating in broken tones: 'Dear God, he's dead, Olivier's dead.'

I could hear everything, although the sounds were muffled, as if
they were coming from a long way off . . . With my left eye I could
just distinguish a dull glimmer of light, a white haze into which all
the objects in the room merged; my right eye was totally paralysed.
My entire body had been affected by the fit; it was as though a thun-
derbolt had struck me down. My will-power had died, and there was
not a nerve in my body which would respond. The only thing that
remained in this state of non-being, above my lifeless limbs, was my
ability to think, somewhat dull and sluggish, but still intact.

Poor Marguerite was on her knees at my bedside, weeping and
wailing, 'He's dead, oh God, he's dead.'

Was this, then, death? this strange state of torpor, the flesh suddenly condemned to immobility, while the mind remained as active as
ever? Or was it that my soul was still lingering in my body, and about
to fly off? I had been a prey to nervous attacks since childhood. Twice
when I was still very young, I had nearly died of an acute fever. So
people had become used to my being sickly; it had indeed been I who
had told Marguerite not to fetch a doctor on the day we arrived in
Paris, when I had had to take to my bed in the boarding house in the
rue Dauphine.* What I needed was a little rest, I was just worn out
after the journey. In fact, though, I was extremely worried. We had
left our country home very suddenly; we were poor and had scarcely

enough to cope before we'd receive the first month's pay for the clerical job I had taken on. And on top of all those worries, now this attack looked as though it was going to carry me off!

Was it really death? I had thought it would be darker, that the silence would be heavier. I had been scared of death since I was a child. Because I was weakly, people were always pitying me, and I was permanently afraid that I did not have long to live, that they'd have to bury me at an early age. The idea of the earth terrified me, and although it obsessed my waking and my sleeping hours, I had never been able to accept it. As I grew older I never outgrew the obsession. From time to time, after long days spent thinking of nothing else, I could almost believe that I had finally conquered my fear. After all, each one of us died; everything came to an end; there was an end to everything; we all had to die sooner or later; there was nothing more appropriate, nothing better. I would even manage to laugh at it; I could look death in the face. But then an icy shudder would run down my spine and my terror would return in full, just as though some giant hand had picked me up and swung me over a bottomless black hole. It was always the thought of the earth that came back to me and prevented me thinking straight. How many times, at night, have I woken up with a start, not knowing what ghostly breath had brushed over me as I slept, and clasped my hands in despair, jabbering that we all have to die. Fear tightened my chest; the inevitability of death was even more inhuman in this half-sleeping state. It was hard, after that, to go back to sleep; sleep itself scared me, because it was so akin to death. Supposing I were to sleep for ever! Supposing I were to close my eyes never to open them again!

I do not know if other people experience this anguish. It had certainly made my life a lonely one. Death has come between me and everything I have ever loved. I can recall now the happiest moments of my life with Marguerite. During the first few months of our marriage, when she lay sleeping alongside me at night; and as I thought of her, while dreaming of the future, inevitably the idea of being separated from her would spoil my joy and ruin all my dreams. We would have to leave each other maybe the following day, maybe in just an hour's time. An unbearable hopelessness would overcome me; I'd wonder what was the point of ever being happy together, since it was bound to end in so tragic a separation. My imagination would indulge itself in the morbid. Who would be the first to go, she or I?

At both possibilities, my eyes would fill with tears of self-pity, as the scene of our broken lives would unfold before me. At each one of the best moments of my life, I have had similar attacks of melancholy, which no one has ever been able to understand. Whenever I had a piece of good luck, people would be surprised at how gloomily I would react. It was because I would suddenly be struck, in the middle of my joy, with the thought of being no longer. The awful words 'What's the point?' would ring out in my ears like the voice of doom. The worst thing about such suffering is that it has to be endured like a secret vice. You can't tell anyone else about it. Frequently husband and wife must lie side by side in a darkened room, feeling the same fear, yet neither of them speaking about it, because one cannot talk about death any more readily than one can use obscene words. We are so afraid of it that we dare not name it; we hide it, just as we hide our sexual organs.

Such were the thoughts that went through my mind, as Marguerite continued her sobbing beside me. It hurt me not to be able to soothe her and tell her that I was not in pain. If death were merely this numbing of the body, I had been quite mistaken to dread it so. There was a feeling of personal well-being, a total calm in which I could cast my worries aside. My memory, in particular, seemed to have become extraordinarily acute. The whole of my past life rushed past me like a show in which I was no longer an actor. The feeling was a bizarre one, and somewhat amusing; it was as though some distant speaker was telling me the story of my own life.

The memory of the countryside near Guérande, on the Piriac road,* kept coming back to me. The road bends, and a pine wood sprawls over the rocky slopes. When I was seven, I used to go there with my father to a tumbledown old house where we would partake of pancakes with Marguerite's family. They were having a hard time trying to make a living out of the nearby salt works. Then I recalled the school in Nantes* where I grew up in the restriction of the old walls, constantly longing for the open spaces of Guérande with its endless salt marshes just below the town, and the vast expanses of the sea and sky. At that point, darkness descended on my life—my father died, and I got a clerical job in the local hospital; I began a wretched life in which the only bright spot was the Sunday visits I would make to the old house on the Piriac road. Things were going from bad to worse there, as the salt marshes were not producing much and the whole area was increasingly poverty-stricken. Marguerite was still just a child. She liked me because I used to give her wheelbarrow rides. Later, when I asked her to marry me, I realized from the movement of repulsion she made that she found me unprepossessing. Her parents gave her to me immediately; they were better off without her. She was a dutiful daughter, and didn't complain. As she got used to the idea of becoming my wife, she did not seem too upset. On our wedding day at Guérande, I remember how it poured with rain and how, when we got home, she had to stay in her petticoats because her dress had been soaked.

That, then, was my youth. We went on living there for a while, till one day, when I got home from work, I came across my wife in floods of tears. She was apparently unhappy, wanted to move somewhere else. After six months, I had managed to scrimp and save some money by doing extra work, and an old family friend found me a job; I was able to take my little love off to Paris to stop her shedding any more tears. In the train, she laughed. The third-class benches were hard and I sat her on my lap so that she could sleep more comfortably.

That is the past. And now I have just died, on this narrow bed in the boarding house, and my wife is kneeling there, bemoaning her fate. The white blur I could see with my left eye was growing hazier but I could still remember the room clearly. The chest of drawers to the left; to the right the fireplace, with, in the centre, the clock which no longer told the right time because its pendulum was broken; it stood at six minutes past ten. The window looked out over the dark street. The whole of Paris seemed to pass by and with so much clatter that I could hear the window-panes creaking.

We did not know a soul in Paris. As we had left earlier than intended, I was not expected in the office till the following Monday. Ever since I had taken to my bed I had had the strange feeling of being imprisoned in this room where our journey had led us, still bemused by our fifteen hours in the train, and bewildered by the bustle of the streets of Paris. My wife had looked after me in her usual gentle, smiling way, but I sensed how perturbed she must be. From time to time, she would go over to the window, look out at the street, and come back pale and upset by the sheer size of Paris, which she did not know at all and which constantly made so terrifying a noise. What could she do, if I didn't wake up? What would become of her in this huge city, alone, without help, not knowing anyone or anything?

Marguerite had now taken one of my hands in hers, as it lay there lifeless on the edge of the bed. She kissed it over and over again, imploring me thus: 'Oh, say something . . . Dear God, he's dead . . .'

Death, then, couldn't be nothingness, since I could still hear and think. But not being had terrified me since I was a child. I couldn't conceive of myself disappearing; the total suppression of all that I was, for ever, for all eternity, without my life ever being able to begin again. I sometimes used to tremble if I came across a date in some newspaper of a future century; I would no longer be alive at that time, and the idea of a year in a future that I would not know and when I would no longer be filled me with anguish. Was not I the world, and wouldn't everything end when I left it?

I had always hoped to dream of life in death. But this probably wasn't death, after all. I would doubtless wake up in an hour or two. Yes, that was it; I would soon be able to bend over Marguerite and take her into my arms, and dry her tears. What bliss to be together again! and how we would love each other more deeply than ever! I would take two more days off, then I'd go to work. A new life would begin for us, happier, more open. Though I wasn't in a hurry for it yet. In a while; for the time being I was too tired. Marguerite was wrong to despair, and I didn't have the energy to turn my head and give her a smile. In a minute, when she again lamented 'He's dead', I would kiss her and murmur in her ear, so as not to frighten her too much, 'It's all right, my love. I was just asleep. See! I'm alive and I love you.'

II

BECAUSE of all Marguerite's wailing, the door suddenly opened and someone's voice said: 'What's the matter? Has he had another attack?'

I recognized the voice. It was an old lady, Mme Gabin, who had a room on the same landing as us. As soon as we had arrived, she had been very kind to us, and sorry for our plight. She had told us her story immediately. Some wretch of a landlord had sold her furniture the previous winter, since which she had been living in the boarding house with her daughter Adèle who was ten. They both cut out lampshades and scraped together about forty sous.*

'Dear God, it's all over, then?' she asked in a whisper.

I realized that she was coming over to me. She looked at me, touched me, then said, in a hushed tone, 'You poor little thing.'

At the end of her tether now, Marguerite burst into tears like a child. Mme Gabin picked her up and made her sit down in the rickety armchair next to the fireplace; she did her best to comfort her.

'Well, if you go on like that you'll do yourself an injury. You don't have to kill yourself just because your husband has died. Of course, I felt just like you do when I lost Gabin; three days, I was, without being able to swallow a morsel of food. But it didn't get me anywhere; quite the opposite, it just made matters worse . . . Come along, now, for goodness' sake. Be a good girl.'

Gradually, Marguerite calmed down. She was exhausted, and from time to time another burst of sobbing would rack her. Meanwhile the old woman took control of the whole room with stern determination.

'Don't you bother about anything,' she said. 'Dédé has gone off with some lampshades and anyway neighbours ought to help each other. Now then, your trunks aren't all unpacked, are they? but there should be some linen in the cupboard, shouldn't there?'

I heard her opening the cupboard. She must have got out a towel, and came over and laid it out on the table. She then struck a match, which made me think she must be lighting one of the candles on the fireplace. I was able to follow every one of the movements she made in the room, every one of her actions.

'Poor man,' she muttered. 'It's a good job I heard you, my dear.'

Suddenly, the white light that I had been able to see with my left eye disappeared. Mme Gabin had closed my eyes, although I had not felt the touch of her finger on my lids. When I realized what had happened, a chill ran down my spine.

The door opened again. Dédé, the ten-year-old daughter, came in, saying, in her high-pitched voice: 'Mummy, mummy, ah, I knew you must be here! Here's the money, three francs forty. I've brought back twenty dozen lampshades.'

'Sh! be quiet, will you,' her mother tried to stop her.

When her daughter still went on, she pointed to the bed. Dédé stopped and I could feel how worried she was, as she moved backwards towards the door.

'Is the gentleman asleep?' she whispered.

'Yes, so just you go off and play,' answered Mme Gabin.

The child, however, did not go off. She must have been watching me wide-eyed, scared and only half understanding what was happening. Suddenly, she was panic-stricken and ran off, knocking a chair on her way.

The silence was total. Marguerite, huddled in a chair, was no longer crying. Mme Gabin was walking to and fro about the room. She started muttering through her teeth again. 'Children always know everything nowadays. Just look at her. God knows, I bring her up as best I can. When she goes out on an errand for me, or if I send her off to bring some work back, I count the minutes so that I can be sure she's not up to anything bad. It doesn't make any difference, she always knows everything. She saw it then, she realized in a second what was the matter. Yet she's only ever seen one dead person; that was her Uncle François, and she was only four when that happened. Children aren't children any longer, are they?'

She broke off and went on immediately on a different tack. 'Now then, my dear, you'll have to start thinking about all the formalities, registering the death, and then the funeral. You really aren't in any fit state to bother about all that. And I don't want to leave you by yourself. I'll just go and see if M. Simoneau is in, if you don't mind.'

Marguerite did not reply. I watched all this as though I was many miles away. Sometimes I felt as though I was flying, like a will-o'-the-wisp, through the room while some foreign body was lying on the bed. I should, however, have preferred Marguerite to refuse the offer of M. Simoneau's services. I had had three or four glimpses of him during my illness. He had one of the neighbouring rooms and seemed kind enough. Mme Gabin had told us that he was just passing through Paris, sorting out the financial affairs of his father, who lived in the country and had recently died. He was a tall, good-looking, well-built fellow. I loathed him, perhaps because of his rude health. He had been in the evening before, and it had hurt to see him so close to Marguerite. She was so pretty and so fair next to him!

He looked at her so closely and she had smiled up at him, telling him how kind it was of him to come and see how I was!

'Here is M. Simoneau,' said Mme Gabin, as she came back in.

He pushed the door open carefully and, as soon as she saw him, Marguerite burst into tears. Seeing this friend, the only person she knew, brought back her grief. He did not attempt to comfort her.

I could not see him, but, in the shadows engulfing me, I could recall his face and imagine it clearly, upset and concerned to find my wife suffering. She must have looked so beautiful, with her fair hair loose, her pale face and her tiny little hands feverish.

'I'll do anything I can,' Simoneau murmured, 'anything. Just let me take charge.'

She could only reply in broken sentences. As the young man withdrew, Mme Gabin accompanied him, and I could hear them mentioning money as they passed by me. It was always so expensive and she didn't think the poor little thing could have a penny to her name; they'd have to ask her. Simoneau told the old woman to be quiet. He didn't want Marguerite to be upset; he would go himself to the town hall and sort out the funeral arrangements.

When the silence began again, I wondered whether the nightmare was going to last long. I was alive, since I was aware of the least significant external fact. And I was beginning to understand more exactly what my state was. It was doubtless one of these cases of catalepsy* of which I had heard. Even when I was a child I had been subject to fits which could last several hours. It was presumably something of a similar nature which was holding me thus, stiff as a corpse, and which was misleading everyone around me. But surely my heart would start beating again, and my blood would pump through my veins; I would awaken and be able to comfort Marguerite. By such arguments I managed to encourage myself to keep calm.

Hours passed. Mme Gabin had brought her food in. Marguerite refused to eat anything. The afternoon went by. Through the window, which had been left open, the noises rose from the rue Dauphine. The faint sound of the copper candlestick chinking against the marble table indicated that the candle had been changed. Finally Simoneau came back.

'Well?' the old lady inquired softly.

'Everything is organized,' he replied. 'The funeral will start tomorrow at eleven o'clock. Don't worry yourself about anything, and don't start talking about it in front of this poor lady.'

Mme Gabin replied nevertheless. 'The death doctor hasn't come yet.'

Simoneau went and sat down beside Marguerite, comforted her, then fell quiet. The procession was to start the next day at eleven; the news resounded in my head like a death knell. What with that and the death doctor, as Mme Gabin called him, not coming! He would be sure to see immediately that I was simply in a deep sleep. He would do everything that was necessary; he would know how to rouse me. I awaited him in an agony of worry.

Meanwhile, the day went on. Mme Gabin had brought up her lampshades, so as not to waste any time. She had even got Dédé to come up, once she had asked Marguerite's permission, because, she said, she didn't like leaving a child alone for too long at a time.

'Come along, come in,' she said to the girl, 'and don't be silly. Don't look away like that or you'll be having me to deal with.'

She would not let her look at me; she felt it would not be fitting. Dédé obviously took a peep from time to time, because I could hear her mother slapping her arm. She would then say, angrily, 'Work, or you'll have to go out. And then the gentlemen will come and pester you tonight.'

Mother and daughter were settled at our table. The sound of their scissors slitting the material of the lampshades came to me clearly; it was delicate work and the cutting had to be done very carefully; they couldn't rush it. I began counting them one by one, my despair increasing.

In the room the only sound was that of the scissors. Marguerite, overcome with exhaustion, must have gone to sleep. Twice, Simoneau got up. The awful suspicion that he was taking advantage of her being asleep to brush her hair with his lips tormented me. I did not know the man, yet I felt that he was in love with her. The sound of Dédé's laughter annoyed me.

'What are you laughing for, silly?' asked her mother. 'Come along, tell me, why are you laughing?'

The child blurted out that she hadn't been laughing, she'd just been coughing. I imagined that what she had seen was Simoneau leaning over Marguerite, and that she'd found it funny.

The light was lit. Someone knocked.

'Ah, the doctor at last,' said the old lady.

It was, indeed, the doctor. He did not bother to apologize for arriving so late. He had doubtless had many steps to climb during his day's work. The light was very dim, and he asked: 'The body is here?'

'Yes, sir,' Simoneau replied.

Marguerite had stood up, shivering. Mme Gabin had made Dédé go out to the landing because children should not be present at such a scene. She made my wife go over to the window, so as to spare her the sight.

The doctor came over towards me quickly. I knew he was tired, in a hurry, anxious to be off. Did he touch me? Did he place his hand on my heart? I could not tell. But he did seem to have bent over me in a somewhat negligent manner.

'Would you like me to hold the lamp closer for you?' asked Simoneau.

'No, it's not worth it,' the doctor replied calmly.

What! Not worth it? This man had my life in his hands and didn't think it worth while taking a careful look at me. But I wasn't dead! I would have given anything to shout out that I wasn't dead.

'When did he die?' he asked.

'At six this morning,' replied Simoneau.

A surge of revolt rose through me, from within the dreadful rigidity that bound me. Oh! The terror of not being able to utter a word, or move a muscle.

The doctor added, 'The weather is very heavy. There's nothing so tiring as these early spring days.'

He moved away. It was my life that was moving away. Shouts, tears, insults rose in me, tore at my stricken throat—from which not even the slightest breath came. The wretch! The habit of his profession had turned him into a machine and he could turn up at someone's deathbed with the mere thought of a formality to go through. He knew nothing, the idiot. All his learning was a lie—he couldn't even tell the difference between life and death. And he was going away, going away.

'Good night, doctor,' Simoneau said.

There was a silence. The doctor was probably taking his leave of Marguerite, who had moved from the window which Mme Gabin was now closing. He then went from the room and I could hear him going down the stairs.

So it was all over. I was a condemned man. My last hope had disappeared along with the doctor. If I didn't come to before tomorrow at eleven I would be buried alive. The idea was so terrifying that I lost all consciousness of what was going on around me. It was like fainting within death. The last noise I heard was that of Mme Gabin's and Dédé's scissors. The funeral wake began. No one spoke. Marguerite had refused to go to bed in the next room; she remained there, half lying in the chair, with her lovely pale face, her eyes closed and her lashes still wet with tears; meanwhile, seated in front of her, silent in the darkness, Simoneau watched.

III

I CANNOT find words to describe my anguish of the following morning. It has remained with me like some nightmarish dream; my feelings were so bizarre, so confused that it would be almost impossible for me to recount them accurately. What made my agony so dreadful was that I was constantly hoping to awake. As the time of the funeral procession drew nearer, my terror increased.

It was only towards dawn that I became aware of people and things around me again. The creaking of the bolt awoke me. Mme Gabin had opened the window. It was about seven o'clock, for I could hear the shopkeepers in the street below, the high voice of the girl selling chickweed and the deeper one of the carrot seller. The noise of Paris waking up soothed me for a moment or two; it seemed impossible that I could be buried underground while all this life was going on around me. Something I recalled made me even calmer. I remembered having seen a case similar to mine when I worked at the hospital in Guérande. A man had slept for a full twenty-eight hours and his sleep had been so deep that the doctors had been unable to come to any decision; suddenly the man had sat up on his backside and been able to leave his bed immediately. I had now been asleep for twenty-five hours; if I were to awake before ten, there would still be time.

I attempted to work out who was in the room and what they were all doing. Little Dédé was doubtless playing, because the door was open and a child's voice could be heard. Simoneau was probably no longer about, at least, no sound I could hear indicated that he was there. Mme Gabin's clogs clattered across the tiled floor. At last someone spoke.

'My dear,' the old lady said, 'you are wrong not to have some while it's still hot, it will do you good.'

She was talking to Marguerite and the drip, drip from the filter, on the mantelpiece, told me she was making coffee.

'I needed that, I can tell you,' she went on. 'I can't take these long nights at my age. It's worse at night-time, too, when there's a death in the house. Just have a drop of this coffee, there's a good girl.'

She made Marguerite have a cup.

'There, it's nice and hot, you can feel the good it's doing you. You'll need all your strength today. Now, if you were really good, you'd go and wait in my room.'

'No,' replied Marguerite, firmly. 'I want to stay here.'

Her voice, which I hadn't heard since the evening before, touched me to the quick. It had changed, it was grief-stricken. Ah, my love; I could feel her close to me, my final comfort. I knew her eyes were constantly fixed on me and that she was weeping her heart out.

The minutes, meanwhile, were ticking by. There was a noise at the door which I did not at first recognize. It sounded like a piece of furniture being banged against the walls of the narrow staircase. Then I understood. I heard Marguerite's sobbings. It was the coffin.

'You're too early,' said Mme Gabin crossly. 'Put it down by the bed.'

What time could it be? Nine, perhaps. And the coffin was already here. I could see it through the shadows, bright and shiny, the wood still rough from the saw. Dear God, was everything going to end now? Was I really going to be carried off in this box that I could feel at my feet?

I did however have one great pleasure left. Marguerite, despite her exhaustion, was determined to lay out my body. It was she, aided by the old woman, who dressed me, with the gentleness of a sister and wife. I could feel that I was in her arms again as she put on each of my clothes. She stopped, overcome with emotion; she hugged me to her, bathed me in her tears. I longed to return her embrace, to tell her I was alive; but I was powerless, I had to lie there, an inert mass.

'Don't do that. It's useless,' chided Mme Gabin.

Marguerite replied, her voice choked with tears, 'Let me be. I want him to have the best things we had.'

I realized that she was dressing me up as I had been for our wedding day. I still had the clothes which I intended to use in Paris only on high days and holidays. She fell back in the chair, exhausted by her efforts.

Suddenly I heard Simoneau's voice. He must have just come in.

'They are downstairs,' he said.

'Just as well, not too soon,' said Mme Gabin, lowering her voice as he had. 'Tell them to come up, we must get this over with.'

'I am worried about how much it will upset this poor lady.'

The old lady thought for a minute. She then went on, 'Listen,

M. Simoneau, you make her go into my room. I don't want her to stay here. It's a kindness we'll be doing her. While you do that, we'll get everything sewn up here as quick as a flash.'

The words were like a knife in my heart. Worse still, as I listened to the struggle that then ensued, Simoneau went over to Marguerite imploring her not to stay in the room.

'For pity's sake,' he said. 'Come along with me, spare yourself any unnecessary suffering.'

'No, no,' said my wife. 'I am staying here, I want to stay till the last possible moment. Just imagine, he is all I have in the world. When he is no longer here, I shall be quite alone.'

Mme Gabin, just by the bed, whispered in the young man's ear: 'Go off, take her by the arm, carry her if needs be.'

Would Simoneau take Marguerite in his arms and carry her off? I heard her sudden cry. Filled with fury I wanted to leap to my feet. There wasn't an ounce of strength left in my body. I had to stay there, stiff, not able even to lift an eyelid to see what was happening there, in front of me. The struggle went on. My wife was clutching the furniture, saying again and again, 'Please don't. Leave me, leave me.'

He must now have taken her in his strong arms, and her only cries were the whimpers of a child. He carried her away, the sobs became fainter and I imagined the two of them, he so strong and tall, bearing her off, her arms round his neck; she in tears, shattered, letting herself go, ready to follow him anywhere he wished.

'Goodness, that took some doing,' murmured Mme Gabin. 'Well, now they are out of the way, I can get things done.'

I was consumed with jealousy and could only see his act as a despicable intrusion. I hadn't been able to see Marguerite since the previous evening but at least I could hear her. Now even that was over: she had been taken from me; a man had captured her, even before I was under the ground. And he was with her, just on the other side of the wall; he alone could comfort her, even kiss her . . .

The door had opened again, heavy steps moved round the room.

'Hurry up now, get a move on,' urged Mme Gabin. 'Before the poor lady comes back.'

She was speaking to strangers who replied only in grunts.

'After all, I'm not one of the family. I'm only a neighbour. I haven't got anything to gain from all this. It's out of the kindness of my heart I'm doing it. And it's not much fun I can tell you. Yes, I spent the whole night here. And it wasn't very warm at four in the morning. But then I've always been a bit soft-hearted. I'm too kind for my own good.'

At that point, the coffin was pulled into the centre of the room and I understood. I was condemned; I wasn't going to wake up. My thoughts became muddled; everything turned into a fuzzy darkness; I felt so tired that it was almost a comfort no longer to hope for anything.

'They were generous with the wood,' croaked one of the undertakers. 'The box is too long.'

'Well, he'll be travelling in comfort,' said another, cheerfully.

I didn't weigh too much, which they were pleased about because there were three flights of stairs to go down. When they took me by the elbows and feet, Mme Gabin suddenly started shouting, 'You wretched child! Has to put her nose round every corner, doesn't she? I'll teach you to peep and pry, just you wait.'

Dédé had pushed the door half open and poked her tousled head through. She wanted to see the gentleman put in the box. A couple of slaps rang out, followed by the sound of tears. When her mother returned, she started chatting to the men about her daughter as they arranged me in the coffin.

'Ten years old, she is. A good girl, but too nosy by half. I don't often smack her, but she must learn to do what she's told.'

'Oh,' replied one of the men, 'little girls are all the same. As soon as someone dies, they're there nosing around.'

I was now lying down comfortably and it was almost as though I was still in my bed, apart from my left arm hurting a bit where it was squashed against the wood. Just as they had said, I fitted quite easily because I wasn't too big.

'Wait a minute,' said Mme Gabin. 'I promised his wife I'd put a cushion under his head.'

The men were in a hurry, however, and stuffed the pillow in, without thought for me. One was looking for the hammer, swearing away; they had left it downstairs and had to go and get it. The lid was put in place and I felt a shudder throughout my body as two blows of the hammer nailed it down. It had happened, I had lived. The nails went in, one after the other, and the hammer banged away rhythmically. It was like packers nailing up a box of dried fruits, with thoughtless efficiency . . . From then on, the noises from above were muffled and indistinct, echoing in a curious way as if the pine coffin had become a sound box. The last words to reach me in the room in rue Dauphine were those of Mme Gabin: 'Go down carefully, mind the banister on the second floor. It's giving way.'

I was being carried; it felt like drifting over a stormy sea . . .

From that time on, my memories are shrouded in a mist. I can, though, remember that the sole thought which occupied my mind— a senseless, automatic one—was to work out the route we were taking to the cemetery. I didn't know a single road in Paris and was totally ignorant of where the main cemeteries were, though I had heard their names often enough, but none of this prevented me from concentrat- ing all my mental efforts on working out whether we were turning right or left. The hearse bumped me around over the cobbled streets. All around me, the noise of traffic and passing feet made a sort of rumbling noise which echoed in the coffin. At first I was able to follow the way we took quite clearly. Then we stopped and I was lifted out; I thought we must be at the church. When the hearse set off again, I lost consciousness of where we were. Bells ringing meant we had passed a church; a softer more continuous sound made me think we were going along a wide avenue. I was a condemned man being taken to his execution, my senses dulled, awaiting the final blow which was slow in coming . . .

We stopped and I was taken out of the hearse. It was all over. All sound ceased, I knew I was in some deserted place, beneath the trees, the open sky above my head. Obviously there were several people fol- lowing the hearse, people from the boarding house, Simoneau and others, because I could hear their muffled voices. There was a psalm, and the priest muttered away in Latin. They stood around for sev- eral seconds. Suddenly I was aware that I was being lowered; ropes were rubbing against the sides of the coffin, scraping like the bow of a cracked 'cello. It was the end. A dreadful noise like the rumbling of a cannon burst over my head to the left; another one came from around my feet; a third, even worse, over my belly; I thought the cof- fin had split in two. I fainted.

IV

I DON'T know how long I remained like this. An eternity and a second are the same in nothingness. I was no longer. Gradually, confusedly, the awareness of life came back to me. I was still asleep, but I had begun to dream. A nightmare started to emerge in the dark, blocking the horizon of my thoughts. The dream I had was a strange fantasy, one that had often tormented me before when, eyes open, with my tendency to conjure up the most dreadful pictures, I used to indulge in the morbid pleasure of inventing disasters.

I thus started dreaming that my wife was expecting me somewhere—in Guérande, I think—and that I had taken the train to go and meet her. As the train was going through a tunnel, suddenly a dreadful noise thundered out. Two falls of earth had occurred. Our train hadn't been touched by a single stone and the coaches were still intact; but at each end of the tunnel, behind us and in front, the roof had caved in and we were in the middle of a mountain, walled in by blocks of rock. A long and terrible wait then began. There was no hope of help; it would have taken a month to unblock the tunnel and would have required extremely powerful machines and great care. We were prisoners in a cave with no way out. Our death was only a matter of hours.

I had often, as I said, imagined this scene. I used to concoct different variations on the theme. I'd create men, women and children as actors in the drama, more than a hundred people, a great crowd, and they would provide me with all sorts of different episodes. There were a few provisions in the train, but they soon ran out and, although they didn't actually end up eating each other, they had the most vicious arguments about who would have the last crumb of bread. Should it be an old man, pushed aside, already half dead, or a mother who fought like a dragon to keep a few morsels for her child? In my compartment, a young newly wed couple suffered in agony in each other's arms, no hope left, till they died. The track was empty and people got out, prowled along the length of the train, like wild animals on the run, desperate for food. The different classes mixed together, a wealthy man, possibly some high-up civil servant, would weep on the shoulders of a labourer, calling him brother. The lights had gone out very shortly after the disaster, and the engine fires had died. As people passed from one coach to the next, they had to feel their way along, so as not to bump into anything; they knew when they got to the engine because of the ice-cold connecting rod, the huge, sleeping flanks; all that energy gone to waste, still and motionless under the ground, as though buried alive with its passengers all dying off one by one.

I revelled in dreaming up the most lurid of details. Screams rending the dark. All of a sudden, someone you had not realized was there
and whom you could not see fell against you. This time, however,
what was worst was the cold and the lack of air. I had never in my
life felt so cold; a blanket of ice was covering me, heavy dankness
wrapping my head. I couldn't breathe properly and it seemed as if the
stone ceiling was falling on my chest, the whole mountain weighing
me down and crushing me. Suddenly, a shout of joy rang out. For
some time we had been imagining that we could hear a distant sound,
comforting ourselves that someone was working close by to us. Help
did not, however, arrive. One of us had found a shaft within the tunnel and we all ran there to see it—at the top flickered a blue light,
scarcely bigger than a piece of sealing wax. What joy it gave us. It was
the sky; we reached out to breathe it in; we could make out little black
dots moving, probably workmen setting up a winch to try to get us
out. A frantic cry went up—'We're safe, we're safe.' We all cried, our
arms stretching out towards the tiny blue spot.

The loudness of this shout woke me up. Where could I be? Still in
the tunnel, maybe. I was lying flat out and could feel on either side
something hard imprisoning me. I tried to get up but bumped my
head. Was the rock all around me? The blue spot had disappeared,
and the sky was no more. I was being smothered, my teeth chattering
with cold, shaking in all my limbs.

Suddenly it all came back to me. My hair stood on end and I felt
the whole of the terror shudder through me from top to toe, icy. Had
I finally come out of the fit which had imprisoned me for so many
long hours in a corpse-like trance? Yes, I could move, I could run my
hands along the edges of the coffin. One last test remained—I opened
my mouth and started talking, calling on Marguerite, instinctively.
But I had in fact shouted aloud, and my voice, within the pine box,
took on so terrifying a tone that I frightened myself. Dear God, so it
was true! I could talk, I could shout out loud that I was alive, but my
voice would not be heard; I was shut in, crushed under the earth.

I made a superhuman effort to calm down and think. Was there
no way of escaping? My dream came back; I did not yet have the
all-too-solid coffin; I started mixing the fantasy of the shaft of air and
the spot of sunlight with the reality of the hole in which I was suffocating. My eyes wide open, I watched the shadows. Perhaps I would
see some hole, a crack of light, a glimpse of day! But only sparks of

flame passed through the night—red lights blazing and dying away. Nothing—a black void—impenetrable. Finally, I recovered my sanity and pushed aside the nightmare; I needed to be completely clear-headed if I wanted to escape.

At first, the greatest danger seemed to be that of suffocating to death. I had probably been able to last so long without air because of the fit which had meant that all my functions had slowed down. Now that my heart had begun beating again, however, and that my lungs were gulping in air, I would die of asphyxia if I didn't get out soon. I was also acutely aware of how cold I was and was afraid lest numbness proved fatal, as happens when someone slips in the snow, never to rise again.

Although I kept telling myself to keep calm, at the same time waves of fear kept rising in me. So I summoned all my strength, attempting to recall what I knew of burial procedures. I was probably in a private five-year plot.* This deprived me of one hope; I had noticed years ago at Nantes that in the public graves, because of the constant coming and going, the feet of the most recently buried biers often could be seen. If that had been my case, I could simply have broken a plank or two and got out; whereas if I were in a properly filled hole, there would be a complete layer of earth over me, which would probably prove an insurmountable obstacle. Hadn't I heard someone saying that in Paris people were buried under six feet of earth? How would I ever be able to get through? Even were I able to pierce through the lid of my coffin, the earth would filter through, seep through like sand, filling my eyes and mouth. And there would be death, another dreadful death, drowning in mud.

Nevertheless, I felt around me carefully. The coffin was wide and I could move my arms quite freely. I couldn't feel any crack in the lid. To my right and left, the planks were roughly planed, but they were strong and tough. I bent my arm inwards over my chest and felt towards my head. There I found a knot of wood in the end plank which gave a little if I pushed; I worked away carefully and pressed out the knot; on the other side I could feel the earth, rich, damp clay. It didn't help me at all. I even regretted having pushed out the knot, as though the earth was going to start coming through the hole. I then tried something else—tapping at the edges of the coffin to find out whether there was by any remote chance a gap somewhere. It sounded exactly the same all over. When I tried tapping with my toes, it did seem, though, that the sound at the end was different. Though it could just have been the sound effects in the box.

I then started pushing gently with clenched fists, arms braced. The wood did not give. I next used my knees, arching my back. Not the slightest crack. I finally put all my strength into such a push that all the bones in my body seemed to screech with pain. It was then that I went mad.

Till that moment, I had not succumbed to panic, nor to the force of anger which coursed through my veins like drink. I was particularly careful to restrain my shouts; I realized that were I to shout I would be lost. But suddenly, now, I started screaming my head off. It was stronger than I; the cries came from my throat, using all the breath in my body. I yelled for help in a voice which I did not recognize, becoming more and more panic-stricken with each shout, screaming that I did not want to die. I scratched at the wood with my nails, twisted and turned like some wild animal in a cage. I do not know how long this went on, but I can still remember the hard feel of the unbending wood as I struggled, still hear the storm of shouts and tears which filled my four walls. A final flash of reason told me to restrain myself, but I could not.

I was overcome with tiredness. I awaited death in a painful half-consciousness. The coffin was made of stone; I should never be able to open it; convinced of my impending doom, I lay there motionless, incapable of making the slightest movement. I had now begun suffering the pangs of hunger in addition to those of cold and being suffocated. I weakened fast. The agony soon became intolerable. I tried to finger out bits of earth through the knot of wood I had loosened and eat them; this only increased my torment. I bit my arms, but not till they bled, and sucked my skin, longing to plunge my teeth into it.

How I longed to die, now. I had feared not being all my life, now I wanted it, I called for it—nothing could be black enough for me. How childish I had been to fear this dreamless sleep, this eternity of silence and shadows. Death was good only if it stopped being in one fell swoop, for ever. Oh to sleep like the stones, to disappear into the clay, to be no longer!

Meanwhile my hands went on mechanically feeling the wood. Suddenly I pinched my left thumb, and the pain shook me from my numbness. What could it be? I felt again, found a nail which the undertakers had not knocked in straight and which was loose in the wood of the coffin. It was very long and sharp. The head was fast in the lid but I could move it. From that moment onward, I had but one idea in my head: to get hold of this nail. I moved my right hand over my stomach and began shaking it. It was incredibly hard to loosen it. I often had to change hands, and my left hand, which I couldn't position very well, got tired very quickly. As I worked away, a plan started forming in my head. The nail was my salvation. I needed it. But would I be in time? I was famished and I had to stop when I became so dizzy that my hands wouldn't obey me and my mind was wandering. I had sucked the drops of blood from my thumb. I then bit my arm and drank my blood. Encouraged by my pain and warmed by this bitter taste of tepid wine in my mouth, I went back to tackle the nail with both hands and finally managed to get it out.

From then on, I believed I would be successful. My plan was quite simple. I dug the tip of the nail into the lid, and ran it down in a long straight line so as to make a crack. My hands were getting stiff but I went on stubbornly. When I reckoned I had made a deep enough hole in the wood, I turned over on to my stomach then, raising myself on my knees and my elbows, I pushed my back against the lid. It split but still did not come open. The hole was not deep enough. I had to turn over on to my back once more and start all over again, which sapped my strength. A final effort and the lid cracked from one end to the other.

I had not yet escaped but hope filled my heart. I stopped pushing, didn't move for fear of disturbing the earth and having it cave in on me. I wanted to be able to use the lid as a shield while I made a shaft in the clay. Unfortunately, this turned out to be hard work; the clods of earth got in the way of the planks of wood and I couldn't manipulate them easily; I would never get to ground level; the earth was already falling in and pressing against my spine and almost burying my face. Fear overcame me again when suddenly, as I stretched out to find some support, I thought I felt the plank holding the coffin at the feet give way. I kicked with all my might, hoping there might be some kind of hole being dug.

My feet kicked into nothingness. My idea had been right. A new grave was being dug and there was only a thin layer of earth to kick away before I was able to wriggle over into it. Great God! I was saved!

I lay there for a second, my eyes raised, at the bottom of the hole. It was dark. Stars were twinkling in the velvet blue of the sky above. An occasional breeze wafted the warmth of spring over me, and the scent of the trees. Dear God, I had escaped, I was breathing. I was warm, I could cry and offer my thanks, hands raised to infinity. How good it was to be alive!

V

THE first idea I had was to go to see the cemetery-keeper and ask him to take me home. But some vague presentiment held me back. I would frighten everyone. Why hurry, since I was in control of everything? I felt my body; all that was wrong with me was the bite on my left arm; even the slight temperature I had pleased me, gave me an unexpected strength. I should certainly be able to walk unaided.

So I took my time. All kinds of vague thoughts crossed my mind. I had felt the gravediggers' tools next to me and wanted to make good the damage I had done, and fill up the hole again so that no one would know anything about my rising from the dead. At that particular time I had no precise idea in my head as to what I was going to do; I simply thought that it was not a good idea to advertise the incident too widely, feeling somewhat ashamed to be alive when everyone believed me to be dead. After half an hour's work I had completely covered any trace of what had happened. And I jumped out of the ditch.

What a lovely evening it was! The cemetery was in total silence. The black trees cast motionless shadows among the white tombs. As I attempted to get my bearings, I noticed that one half of the sky seemed to be ablaze with light. Paris was over there. I walked towards it along a path, through the shadows of the branches. After only fifty paces I had to stop for breath. I sat down on a gravestone. I looked down at myself and realized that I was fully dressed, only lacking a hat. How grateful I was for the pious care with which Marguerite had dressed me! The sudden thought of Marguerite made me get to my feet again. I wanted to see her.

At the end of the lane, there was a wall in the way. I climbed up on to a gravestone, hung on to the coping on the other side and let myself drop. The jolt was hard. I then walked for a few minutes down a deserted road which encircled the cemetery. I had no idea where I was but I kept telling myself obsessively that I would soon be back in Paris and be able to find the rue Dauphine. People passed but I did not question them; I was too suspicious and refused to trust anyone. I now know that I was already racked with fever and my mind was wandering. As I turned into a wider road, I lost consciousness and fell heavily to the pavement.

The next three weeks of my life are a blank; I remained unconscious. When I finally came to I found myself in some unknown room. A man was there, looking after me. He told me how he had picked me up one morning on the Boulevard Montparnasse* and taken me to his home. He was a doctor but no longer practising. When I thanked him, he answered shortly that he had found my case interesting and wanted the chance of studying it further. For the early days of my convalescence, he refused to allow me to ask him any questions. Later on, he asked me none. I had to stay in bed for another week and continued to feel very weak, not wishing to try to remember anything, because the effort hurt too much. I felt timid and diffident. I'd see when I was able to get about. I might have mentioned a name during my fever but the doctor never once alluded to anything I might have said. He was discreet in his kindness.

Meanwhile, summer had come. One June day I finally obtained permission to take a short walk. It was a lovely morning, with one of those bright suns which liven up the old streets of Paris. I walked slowly, asking people at each crossroads the whereabouts of the rue Dauphine. I reached it, but scarcely recognized the old boarding house where we had been. A childish fear held me back. If I were to show myself without warning to Marguerite the shock could well kill her. It might be preferable to tell our old neighbour, Mme Gabin, first. But I didn't like the idea of someone coming between us. I couldn't make up my mind. Deep down, I felt a great emptiness, as though I had made the sacrifice long ago.

The house shone yellow in the sun. I knew which one it was because of a somewhat seedy restaurant on the ground floor from which they sent us up food. I looked up at the third-floor window on the left. It was wide open. Suddenly a young woman, hair tousled and with her camisole awry, came and leant at the window. Behind her came a young man, he bent over and kissed her neck. It was not Marguerite. I felt no surprise. It seemed to me as if I had dreamt it all, this and other things I was to learn.

I stayed there for a while, in the street, unable to make up my mind whether or not to go up and talk to the young couple who were still there, laughing in the sun. Then I decided to go into the restaurant below. I could not be recognized; my beard had grown during my illness and my face had got much thinner. As I sat down, I saw Mme Gabin bringing across a cup to buy herself a drop of coffee; she stood at the counter and began gossiping with the women behind the counter. I listened hard.

'So,' asked the woman, 'has that poor little thing on the third floor come to a decision yet?'

'What do you expect?' replied Mme Gabin. 'It was best for her. M. Simoneau has been so kind to her. He's finished his business here, something to do with coming into a fortune and he was proposing to take her away with him to live with his aunt who needs "someone she can trust".'

The lady at the counter laughed. I had buried my face in a paper, pale-faced, and my hands were trembling.

'It will probably end up with them getting married,' Mme Gabin continued. 'But I can honestly say to you that things have been all clean and above board. She was very upset about her husband and that young man has behaved like a perfect gentleman. Anyway, they went off yesterday. As soon as she's come out of mourning, they'll be able to do as they please.'

At that point, the door of the restaurant opened wide and Dédé came in.

'Mum, aren't you coming up? I've been waiting for you. Hurry up.'

'I'll come in a minute. You get on my nerves,' said her mother.

The child stayed there, listening to the two women with that look she had of a precocious child who had to grow up on the streets of Paris.

'Gracious me!' said Mme Gabin. 'After all, the late husband wasn't a patch on M. Simoneau. I didn't take to him at all, such a runt of a man! Always moaning! And not a penny to his name. No, having a husband like that is no fun for a woman with red blood in her veins. But M. Simoneau, now, he's a wealthy man and as strong as a horse.'

'I saw him one day,' interjected Dédé, 'when he was washing. He's got such hairy arms!'

'Will you leave us alone,' shouted the old woman, pushing her daughter out. 'You always have to poke your nose into business that doesn't concern you.'

Then she went on: 'The first one did her a good turn, dying when he did.'

When I was back out in the street, I walked slowly, my legs almost giving way beneath me. Yet I wasn't suffering too much. I even managed a smile when I saw my shadow in the sun. Yes, I wasn't much of a figure of a man; it had been an odd idea to marry Marguerite. I thought of all her problems in Guérande, how upset she'd got, how miserable and tiring her life was. She had been good to me. But I had never been a lover to her; it was more of a brother whom she had mourned. Why upset her life again? A dead man can't be jealous. I looked up and saw the Jardins du Luxembourg* in front of me; I went in and sat there in the sun, dreaming peacefully. The thought of Marguerite filled me with tenderness. I envisaged her in the country, a lady in a small town, happy, loved, cosseted; getting more and more beautiful, bearing three sons and two daughters. Yes, it had been nice of me to die and I wasn't prepared to be fool enough to rise from the dead.

I have travelled a lot since that time, lived here, there and everywhere. I am a normal man, working and eating like everyone else. Death no longer frightens me; but it doesn't seem to want me any more, whereas I have no reason to go on living; I am afraid that it may pass me by ...

RONALD ROSS

The Vivisector Vivisected

⊰⊱

I N the year 1860, I, having completed my medical studies in London, and being a man of some small independence, determined upon visiting the various universities and scientific societies of the world. I travelled through Germany, France, Spain, Italy, Russia, Persia, Turkey, India and China. Having seen much physic poured down many throats, and having listened to the opposing views of five thousand professors, I became in the end assured that for most diseases the best medicine is water, taken internally.* I was also convinced of the necessity for a better knowledge of Physiology; for unless we know the working of a watch or machine, how can we hope to mend it? Truly hot oil poured in *may* do good; but it can also possibly clog the wheels. Hygiene is the better part of medicine; physiology, the best part of both: for without it we put on spectacles in the dark. Those great mysteries of Life and Death, birth, maintenance, action and thought were to me Mexicos, their solution El Dorados.* Accordingly I set foot in America, the land of experiment, with enthusiasm. I passed eastward, calling on persons long known to me through their works; but I was not satisfied.

At the large city of Snogginsville* I met the well-known Dr Silcutt, famous for his excellent work on the encephalon* of politicians. He was as ardent a physiologist as myself; and was at the time much excited by his recent excellent discovery that gold produces effects different from those of copper when approached to the different nerves of those engaged in public services. Titillation of the palm with the former metal produces contraction of the flexors, with the latter, contraction of the extensors.* He was personally tall, sombre, and not of a humorous disposition. He lived in his private chambers at the Infirmary where I stayed with him so long that we became friends. With him there resided an old gentleman, suffering from dementia, whom at first I took to be his father.

The day before the one on which I intended leaving Snogginsville, Silcutt exhibited to me his private museum of medical curiosities.

I remember that when we entered the room, he, being interested in argument, left the door ajar. Passing from specimen to specimen we at last arrived before a most curious contrivance. Roughly described, one would have considered it a double kind of pump with four tubes (two tubes from each pump) leading to a central mechanism. Each pump was a heavy square mass meant to be placed on the ground, with a piston action; the piston being so disposed as to require pushing down and pulling up without a lever. Silcutt seemed inclined to pass it, but I inquired its use; no sooner, however, were the words out of my mouth, than I heard a kind of scream behind me, muffled in laughter. The above-mentioned old gentleman was standing looking at the construction which had interested me. A quick frown passed over Silcutt's face, and he clutched the other by the arm. The old man lifted his right foot and placed it on a low bench close by. His face became tumid with blood until his white hair, eye-brows and scanty whiskers started out, as it were, in contrast. The veins of his neck swelled, and perspiration broke out on his forehead. His teeth were clenched and his eyes bloodshot; and though all this transformation occurred in a few seconds, yet he had every appearance of a man who had undergone severe bodily exercise. He stooped down as if to lift a heavy weight with both hands, and began to pull up and push down with his arms, as if, as I thought, he was working one of the pumps described above. He laughed and screamed alternately; until, after a few seconds more, a foam gathered on his lips, he shrieked, and fell down in an epileptic seizure.

Silcutt said, 'He is not my father. He is accustomed to these fits. He has been located with me for twenty years. To-night, I will give you a manuscript, fully describing this occurrence and that machine; upon the condition that you do not divulge its contents until the death of both of us.'

Upon retiring to rest, I found on my bedroom table a manuscript signed 'William Silcutt, U.Sc. Phil.'* Opening it, I read:—

'I attended Snogginsville Infirmary as a medical student from 1838 to 1840. Patrick Maculligan, a man of about forty years of age, was resident medical officer. He was at the time deeply engaged in experimental research on both physiology and therapeutics; and needing an assistant, he fixed on me. I was intensely fond of both these subjects; and we were often engaged together in the laboratory for the whole

day. The Infirmary is situated on a hill, and is a long building, tur-
reted at either end. At the time I speak of only one half of the structure was occupied by patients. At the top of the turret belonging to
the empty wing, our laboratory was situated. Here we worked, ate,
and often slept without seeing anyone but ourselves for twenty-four
hours at a stretch. The laboratory consisted of five rooms; an animal's
room for keeping live-stock; a chemical room; a miscroscopical room;
a workshop for making implements; and the operation room. This
last chamber was the top central one of the turret and had a window
facing westward. It was painted black so as not to show the blood that
was often spurted upon its walls. In a corner were a basin and ewer.*
Tables with various knives, tweezers, forceps, saws, etc., stood round.
At a yard from one wall there was the usual stove with a pipe leading
through the roof. In the middle stood the operating-table, which we
called the altar of science. It was a complicated contrivance, padded
and covered with leather, with a waterproof over all. It could be so
drawn out, or pushed in, as to afford room for holding either a donkey
or a guinea-pig at will. Numbers of fastening straps were attached.
The door and window were padded to prevent the egress of any sound
which might disturb the patients below.

'Maculligan was an Irish immigrant.* He was of middle stature,
pale of complexion, with light sandy hair. He was very grave and had
large white front teeth. His hands were long and hairy; and owing to
his studies, he was slightly bowed and weakly. A long scar cut from
his left eye to the mouth, and the deformity made him the more shy.
He was a Protestant, and when not engaged in vivisection, it was his
great delight to read over a book of hymns, which he often hummed
to himself. He told me that he was the son of an Irish physician and
had left home owing to family quarrels, when a lad of seventeen.

'We had often discussed the awful problem of death. Could it
be prevented? May not science hope to find its antidote? He said:
"Seeing that most tissues are repairable, like bone, re-formable, or
like skin to be mended by another structure, I believe that death does
not originate in these parts which may be called rather the appur-
tenances of life than life itself. The older the man, the less able is
he to obtain healing of wounds. Why? Because the healing power
is older and less vigorous. What is the healing power? Where is it?
Either in the nervous system or in the blood, I should say. A man
dies, not because his muscles and organs decay; but because either

the mechanism of his brain, cord, or ganglia is so attrite,* and worn out, or his blood is so changed by continual use, as to be of no further service to the body. We cannot give an animal a new brain; but we can provide him with fresh blood. Let us try then whether the blood be not the seat of life. The plan we will adopt is this: I have constructed an artificial heart which may be filled with the fresh blood of an animal recently killed. Now we must obtain a corpse which has died of loss of blood alone: we must quickly after death cut down to his heart, and apply the apparatus to his blood-vessels, pour in a fresh circulation. By this means," he ended, rubbing his hands, "I hope to bring the dead to life." '

To understand the rest of Dr Silcutt's narrative, the reader should know the course of the circulation. This is very simple. The heart is divided into two partitions, a right and a left one. The blood enters the right partition, whence it is squirted into the lungs; from the lungs it returns to the left partition, whence it is squirted all over the body; and from the body it finally returns back to the right partition, and so on *ad infinitum*. The apparatus now shown to Silcutt, described without the use of anatomical words, was an artificial heart, only the two partitions were quite separate, and to be worked by different pressure. The chest was opened and into the large blood-vessels, which convey the blood to and from the heart, long india-rubber tubes were inserted: so that the blood from the body was carried to the right artificial heart or pump, and thence squirted back to the lungs; from the lungs it passed to the left artificial heart or pump, and thence to the body, and so on. These artificial hearts were mere ordinary double-action pumps, with valves, which sucked in the fluid from one direction and expelled it in another; but having to be completely air-tight they were heavily constructed and the pistons were worked only with considerable difficulty. Each pump was placed in a hot-water bath to maintain the blood at the temperature of 100°;* and one was to be put on either side of the dead body. To resume the manuscript:—

'It was some time before a fit subject was brought into the hospital. What was required was a person who had simply bled to death without much serious injury except the wound of the blood-vessels. A donkey was kept in readiness to supply the required fluid. We often practised the insertion of the india-rubber tubes into the blood-vessel on dead patients; and had become so skilful as to be able to finish the operation in five minutes.

'At last, on the morning of 5th October 1840, a patient was brought into the Infirmary with a cut wound on the head from which he had bled profusely. He had been cut with a knife in a street row. He was a tall, vigorous man, with an immense amount of red hair and beard and with a vicious leering kind of expression. When I saw him he was fast sinking; for the evident drunken habits of the patient did not predispose him to recovery. I only saw him and attended him (except the nurses); and had him removed to a private ward when he died at 2 p.m. Having previously acquainted Maculligan of the case, I waited below while that gentleman was preparing the apparatus. I sent the nurses out of the ward after the patient's death. I wrapt him in a blanket and drawing his hands over my shoulders carried him out. A violent storm, which had just broken, gave me greater security. I locked the door of the private ward and struggled as I best could with my burden up the narrow stairs of the turret. When I arrived in the laboratory, the apparatus was ready, and the pumps were stand-ing in their baths of hot-water (which was procured from the stove boiler). The donkey had been killed, and his fresh blood was in the cavities of our machine.

'Maculligan was flushed with excitement: "Now," he exclaimed, "we shall get at least some knowledge; either a useful negative result, or a world-reforming fact."

'I placed the body on the bed: on his left side was the pump which I was to work and which sent the blood all over his body; on his right side Maculligan supplied his lungs. In a minute I had fastened the limbs, and made bare the chest of the man. Maculligan seized the knife, and at one swoop cut down to the heart. I held apart the sev-eral parts. Almost immediately it seemed he had inserted the tubes into the arteries and veins, and a few seconds sufficed to sew up the chest again, joining the cartilages as well as the skin, and covering all the incision with a quickly congealing gum to exclude the air, and permit breathing. The whole was done by ten minutes after death. The corpse was pale, slightly cold, the eyelids half-open, and the eyes turned upwards beneath them. Blankets were thrown upon it to retain the heat. The storm outside had increased in fury; the rain drenched the window-panes, and the violence of the wind was such that the whole tower seemed to rock. Most unearthly noises, too, were caused by it; and the darkness was so great that we could barely see to do our experiment. I could observe Maculligan trembling with excitement. I myself, though generally stolid, was much moved.

'"Are you ready," said he, taking hold of his pump and speaking hoarsely. "Then away," and down went the pistons simultaneously.

'We told twelve strokes—no blood had oozed from the cut in the chest—all was satisfactory. Another twelve—a slight flushing the cheeks. Maculligan stopped, and we both took off our coats, the wind howling with tenfold fury. We resumed—suddenly the eyes closed. We went on for fully quarter of an hour.

'"He is breathing," cried my companion.

'Most certainly there was some slight action of the diaphragm. Maculligan suddenly motioned me to stop, and going up to the patient listened to hear the breathing. While he looked into the man's face the eyes suddenly opened, following my friend, who sprang back to his pump, trembling violently. We went on silently; the man, all the while, watching Maculligan whose hair seemed stiff, and whose face was so changed that I should hardly have known him. I myself was so astounded that I could not conceive the occurrence as real. We had never expected that there would be any recovery beyond a comatose condition.

'Suddenly the man, who appeared as if recovering from chloroform, said aloud, "Lave it, will you."

'"Lave what?" asked Maculligan, hoarsely.

'"Lave pulling that out of the ground, for sure it goes bang through the wurrld, and is clamped on the other side. It's o' no use."

'"Bedad," he continued, "but ye're the rummiest egg-flip iver I came across."

'"Egg-flip! Eh, boy?" cried Maculligan, laughing excitedly; "You're another."

'"What!" said the man, smiling with one side of his mouth, "you air a wag, you air—a kind o' wag as tells loodicrus tales to tay-totallers at taymatins, you air."

'"No, I ain't now," exclaimed my friend, lifting his chin, and winking in an excited, ready-boy kind of manner.

'"Wal, friend," continued the patient, "kep your 'air on, an' nobody 'ud tell you warn't a Quaker. But you're too quaky for your occupation—I tak it you're a water-works man, with that 'ere pump, eh? friend." He then spat into the air.

' "What makes you think that, boy," answered my companion, putting his tongue in his cheek, and pumping vigorously.

' "Wal," returned the other, laughing roughly, "I guessed you war by your complexion. I say," he continued, winking, "you don't often git your pipes bunged in these parts by vivisections does yer—no vivisected babbies, now—eh?"

' "Not I, lad, not I," laughed Maculligan boisterously.

' "That's odd now! och! man, sure, an wasn't I a vivisector in ould Ireland, an a phesycian."

' "I hope you got many of 'em," laughed the other.

' "Many o' wot?"

' "Fees—you said you were a feesycian."

' "Wal," laughed the man, winking, "just you write that 'ere goak in yer diary and have a dinner on the annivassery of it, ivery year. Yes, sir, I was a physician, and, sure, an eminent one and got me thousand a year, and lived in Merion Square,* bedad. But I went in for physiology—I went in for physiology, and so got ruined. I say! won't the devil give me hot for my vivisecting—for the cutting—eh? For the fastening up—eh? 'You should have taken the trouble to give chloroform,' he'll say. But I don't care a doight for the devil—eh?—till I am dead—eh? snifflewink?"

' "But what if you are," cried Maculligan, loudly. "Eh, boy, what if you are?"

' "Hey? Wal, stranger, I guess you air goin' it with that 'ere pump. I say," he called out suddenly, "stop it, will you! Every push sends a throb in me chist, you skippin' spalpeen."

'The patient seemed to become alarmed. He had kept his eyes fixed on my associate; he now turned them upon me, and I saw that he recognized me.

'He began to pull at his wrists and ankles, when Maculligan, not knowing what he was saying, kept on repeating, "But, what if you *are* dead?"

'All this while we were both pumping without intermission.

' "Aha!" hissed the man, his face wearing a horrible expression, "what is this? What is this? I am dead! Begorra, I died just now— I died of a cut on the head, and drank a bottle o' whiskey upon it to die drunk! Oh, Lord! I see it—ochone! I am in hell, and I am drunk still!" He wrenched again at his wrists, screaming.

' "So you are, Pat," cried my friend. "So you are."

'"Ah! Lord! What 'ull they say if I come up to court drunk! Maybe I have been in court already, but was so inebriate I did not know it, and have got dammed out o' hand, with never a bit of a voice in the matter."

'"So you have, Pat, so you have. You were dead drunk in the dock, you were."

'"Ah! krimy," groaned the man, his eye wandering down to the instrument stuck in his chest, the stitches in his skin and the tubes leading to the pumps. "Och! St Pathrick, I see it! And my punishment is, to be done to as I have been done by. And you are a couple of devils, and I a vivisection; and I shall be vivisected for iver and iver, wurrld without end—Oh! Lord—damn—damn—damn——"

'Here Maculligan inadvertently missed a stroke which caused the patient to gasp violently.

'"Now, don't do it again, honey," he continued. "I'll swear no more, purty deevil that ye are, I did not mane to chaffer ye just now—but ye're the wittiest devil, truly speaking, that I iver saw on earth, or in h—— or anywhere. You'll not be studyin' much on me now, will yer, dear?"

'"We shall not do more than tie up your bile duct and establish a fistula* in your side to-day, friend," said Maculligan, winking at me.

'"And will you do that? Oh! crikey?"

'"To-morrow we are going to lay out a piece of your mesentery* under the microscope to see the blood circulate."

'"Oh, sammy! And what 'ull yer do the day arter?"

'"See how much of your brains we can slice off without stopping your thinking."

'"Why, yer don't imagine I think with the pit of my stomach, do yer? One blessing yer'll have to lave it soon, for there 'ull never be a pickin' place left on me carcase."

'"Not a bit of it, my dear sir," roared Maculligan, who seemed mad from excitement. "You heal up in one place as soon as we go on to another."

'"Well, that knocks all hope out of me. But what are ye doin' now?"

'"Injecting you with donkey's blood to see if you will bray."

'"I'll not do that, anyway, but I tell you what, I feel uncommon sharp and witty like. I 'ud advise you to try a little of the same mixture. Yer not agoin' to have any alcoholic experiments on me, friend, air ye?"

' "No—why?"

' "Wal, yer might find out how much whuskey it 'ull take to make me drunk, anyhow, honey. O Lord!" he ejaculated, looking round, "how well I know them scalpels, directors, retractors, bone-forceps, aneurism needles* and the like, and I have often done all the experiments you have mentioned."

'At times the man dropped the coarser Irish brogue, and at other times used a Californian slang.

' "You see," he continued, "I was a man of some eminence in the medical profession."

' "And how did you lose that eminence?"

' "One day I was up to the ears in thought about me theory of diabetes, when a poodle happening to bark about me heels, instead of kicking it away, sure enough I put it in me pocket, thoughtlessly."

' "Well?"

' "Well, that poodle belonged to the vice-queen, or the vice-royess,* who offered a hundred pound for it. Now a rapscallion saw me pockit the poodle, tould a policeman, who followed me as I went home one day, entered me house, got up to the laboratory and found the identical poodle with a pay in its fourth ventricle, and a pin in its curvickle ganglion.* They had me up for dog-stealing, jist as I had complated me work on the subject in hand, and instid of putting me in the Royal Society,* put me in a common prison. When I got out I took to drinking and went to America and the dogs; and I've got there now, begorra!—Yer will not give me chloroform, thin, honey; or a gin-cocktail now? Be Jesus, how the devils are howlin' round about!"

'During this extraordinary conversation the wind had risen still more, and the turret was plainly felt to rock to and fro. The evening, too, began to hasten in, aided by the black, scurrying rack that obscured the sky. We had been toiling for more than an hour, having to keep time like rowers. My arms were getting tired, and I was profusely perspiring. Maculligan was shouting and laughing like a maniac or drunkard, his face bloated with exertion and his long light hair hanging over his eyes. Suddenly I cast my eyes on the thermometer in the bath which maintained the heat of the blood at the necessary 100°. It stood at 97.4°. The fire in the stove was getting low.

'I said: "The fire is getting low; it must be replenished."

' "You pile it up then," said Maculligan; "we must both leave off together."

'At a signal from him we both ceased pumping and I, who was nearest, rushed to the stove, knocked the lid off and poured in, in my haste, the whole scuttle full of coals. When I returned the patient had fainted: we immediately resumed.

'I said: "He was nearly out then, Maculligan."

' "Wot's that?" muttered the patient, coming round. "Tarnation take you deevils, how did you gumption that my name was Maculligan?"

' "Is that so?" inquired Maculligan.

' "Is that so! I guess it is—Josephus Maculligan av Maculligan Castle, County Lietrim,* son av old Maculligan av the same, and be dammed to yer!"

'No sooner were these words uttered than my companion uttered the most horrible yell I ever heard.

' "You are my brother," he shrieked; "Ha! ha! look at this!" showing the long scar on his face. The patient's jaw dropped, and he violently struggled; but when my friend relaxed the speed of pumping he fell back, and began to groan.

' "Oh! oh! Is it me brother they have put to plague me, me twin brother, who I knocked about and gashed down the cheek because he was after bein' five munutes older than myself and had got all the proparty? Ye are not dead, Pathrick dear? Ye are no ghost, avic? Ye will not tormint me though your father and me druv you to Ameriky?"

' "No, no," shouted Maculligan. "I am alive! You are alive! We are all alive! I am surgeon of the Snogginsville Infirmary. I have made an invention for reviving the dead by means of injecting hot, fresh blood into his veins. I required a case for experiment, which had merely bled to death. You were the first that presented. If we leave off pumping for five minutes, or the stove goes out, letting the hot-water cool, the blood will clot in the machine and you will die immediately."

'I cannot describe the face of Josephus Maculligan during this recital. He burst forth into oaths, upbraiding his brother for attempting such an experiment, and shrieking for help. But the wind out-shrieked him. He prayed and cried alternately. My arms were getting intensely tired, and my back was aching, owing to the necessary stoop of the body. Suddenly the setting sun, which was almost touching the horizon, gleamed out from the clouds, and poured a red glow on Patrick Maculligan's face. I shall never forget its expression: he seemed to have become more like an ape than a man. His face was turbid and red; his mouth drawn back at the corners, showing all his teeth and the very gums. His tongue hung out, the large veins of the throat and forehead stood prominent, the long scar on the cheek glistened white, and seemed to have contracted in length, drawing up the upper lip, and showing the canine tooth of that side. His necktie and collar had burst open, and he panted quickly like a dog; while his eyes, round and lidless, glared on his brother, not with anger or fear, but without any expression at all. The one beam of blood-red light, streaming in from the window seemed to rest upon him on purpose, and, as it were, moved and twined amongst his hair. He alone was visible: all the rest of the room was dark; for the ray, after touching him passed into the workshop beyond. I could see that his hands which were working the pump were swollen and veined.

'He said: "You have wronged me. We are twin-brothers, and I being the weaker should have been protected by you, rather than bullied. We both loved Lucy Hagan; but she preferred me. One day I said: 'I have brains; I don't want the property; I will ask Lucy to marry me, and we will go to Amerika!' I went to ask her passing through a wood. You were there felling trees. You threw the hatchet at me, saying: 'I'll knock the Polly Beloy dear out of you!' The steel cut my cheek. A week afterwards I presented myself to Lucy. She said she would think about it, and in the evening sent me a refusal written in French and a hymn-book with her favourite hymns marked. She informed me that she was going to marry you. I called upon her to thank her for the hymn-book, and murdered her on the spot. I then proceeded to America when I heard that my father was found dead in bed. I said: 'My brother Joseph has murdered him.' Both of us being murderers, it was natural enough that we should go a step further and become vivisectors, and this is our punishment."

' "Wal," returned the other, spitting into the ray of light, "I guess I'd rayther be you than me in this here investigation of nature. You are payin' interest and principal together of that 'ere loan across the cheek I gave yer. If yer cannot kep up that elber-jiggerin work much longer, I will be much obleeged if you will ax someone to come up and relieve yer, and bring up a drop or two o' somethin' cooling, cas I am feeling tarnation warrum."

' "If either of us stop for two minutes you are dead, clear; and there are no more donkeys in the establishment," answered Patrick. "It won't do for only one to pump, because that will burst up your vessels. And it won't do to call, because no one will hear. It would take at least four minutes to get to the occupied wing of the building and back and by that time clots would be sure to form, any one of which getting in your brain would kill you slick."

'"Wal," asked Josephus, "and cud not both of you go and divide the distance atween yer? I am getting as hot as a tay-pot."

'Looking at the thermometer in the waterbath of my pump, I observed it stood at 102°. The fire in the stove, drawn by the violent wind, was beginning to roar through the heap of coals.

'"Turn on the cold water," said Patrick.

'It came from the tap with a gush, then stopped—*the water-pipe had been broken by the storm.* The thermometer was rising—if it passed 120° the blood would be heated to the same temperature, and would certainly become coagulated, or would coagulate the nervous matter of the patient. We left off, and I rushed to the stove—*the poker and shovel had both been sent to be mended.* The patient was gasping.

'"If you stop me circulation again, yer spalpeens, I'll skin yer," he said.

'We resumed. The light had left Patrick's face, but the stove glowed out in the darkness, and we heard the roaring of the flames. Patrick was staggering like a drunkard, and breathing stertorously.* His tongue was hanging further out; the corners of his mouth were drawn more and more backwards; and at every stroke he pulled, his ears twitched. In my hands there was no feeling left, for as said before, the pumps were very stiff. I pushed and pulled mechanically; there was a dead pain at my heart; I could think of nothing, my eyes were glazed; all I saw was the thermometer slowly rising. Josephus was struggling and howling.

'"Arrah, now," he cried, "ye're running fire into me. Lave it will yer. I guess I'll get up and pummel yer both."

'We stopped for a second, when he yelled out, "Go on yer hell-sparks, or I'll report yer behaviour to the deevil. O Lord," he groaned, "here's faver and no ague."

'The thermometer had reached 106°.

'"Wal," continued Josephus, "this 'ull put me in the very best trainin' for hell cud be imagined. I shall ask for a place as head stoker after this, for I shan't flinch at no fire agin."

'Patrick tried to speak but could not. The flames in the stove shot up through the coaling-hole at top. The thermometer stood at 108°, a temperature seldom reached by the most violent fevers.

' "Josephus said, 'I poisoned me father with opium and drove me brother to murder his sweetheart, but they ought to let me into heaven arter this, for it's punishment enough sure. It's plaguey hard on a poor boy to make him die twice—to make him pay over agin for his ticket to tarnation. Ah! lads kep it up, lads. Though ye're a runnin' the red-hot blood o' ten thousand jackasses biled in the boilers av the cintre of the wurrld into me Ah-orta, kep it up! Though ye are a sweatin' away yerselves, till there is nothin' left av yer but yer skilitons, and a little ile in yer boots, yet kep it up, lads, kep it up! Brayvo, brayvo! oh! but the warrmth—the warrmth! I'll tak me whusky cold, I thank you. Ice! Thanks, I wull jist tak a limp o' the same."

'He then ceased talking and struggled violently. The last he said was, "Good-bye, Pathrick; I'll vivisect yer, t' other side o' Jourdan!"

'The thermometer had reached 116.5°. The howling of the wind was awful. Patrick was rolling from side to side. The perspiration ran down over my eyes. I could not feel my arms below the shoulders. Patrick suddenly drew in his breath sharply, gave a yell, threw up his arms and fell on his face. Josephus by a last effort wrenched his arms loose, sat up, clutched at his throat and fell back. At the same moment the storm blew in the window with a crash. In came the tempest and rain, a spiral of flame shot up from the stove, and I was hurled to the ground.

'It was morning when I woke. The stove was out and Patrick sleeping soundly. I could not stand, nor move the arms below the elbows. As best I could I crawled downstairs for assistance.

'Josephus Maculligan was stone dead, and was soon buried. Patrick lives, but he is demented and suffers from attacks of epilepsy. I am myself quite well.

'(Signed) WILLIAM SILCUTT.'

Such was the remarkable manuscript I read, and I may well be believed when I state that so great was the horror of vivisection which I derived from the perusal of this account of the impaling and exhaustion to death of living beings, that I took to collecting butterflies in the summer, and hunting in the winter, neglecting the medical profession altogether. After the death of Silcutt and Maculligan, I related the story to the President of the Club for the Total Abolition of Vivisection.* He asked me down to the country branch of that club, where I was to read the manuscript.

After our interesting pigeon battue,* where more than two hundred birds were killed, we dined. I then read the work; which filled the members with such horror that they passed forty-five resolutions upon the spot, and finished the day with an oyster and white-bait supper. I am sure that the reader who believes this atrocious and fearful tale cannot become anything but a *Total Anti-vivisectionist.*

ROBERT LOUIS STEVENSON

The Body-Snatcher

-᯽-

EVERY night in the year, four of us sat in the small parlour of the George at Debenham*—the undertaker, and the landlord, and Fettes,* and myself. Sometimes there would be more; but blow high, blow low, come rain or snow or frost, we four would be each planted in his own particular arm-chair. Fettes was an old drunken Scotchman, a man of education obviously, and a man of some property, since he lived in idleness. He had come to Debenham years ago, while still young, and by a mere continuance of living had grown to be an adopted townsman. His blue camlet* cloak was a local antiquity, like the church-spire. His place in the parlour at the George, his absence from church, his old, crapulous,* disreputable vices, were all things of course in Debenham. He had some vague Radical opinions and some fleeting infidelities, which he would now and again set forth and emphasise with tottering slaps upon the table. He drank rum—five glasses regularly every evening; and for the greater portion of his nightly visit to the George sat, with his glass in his right hand, in a state of melancholy alcoholic saturation. We called him the Doctor, for he was supposed to have some special knowledge of medicine, and had been known, upon a pinch, to set a fracture or reduce a dislocation; but beyond these slight particulars, we had no knowledge of his character and antecedents.

One dark winter night—it had struck nine some time before the landlord joined us—there was a sick man in the George, a great neighbouring proprietor suddenly struck down with apoplexy on his way to Parliament; and the great man's still greater London doctor had been telegraphed to his bedside. It was the first time that such a thing had happened in Debenham, for the railway was but newly open, and we were all proportionately moved by the occurrence.

'He's come,' said the landlord, after he had filled and lighted his pipe.

'He?' said I. 'Who?—not the doctor?'

'Himself,' replied our host.

'What is his name?'

'Dr Macfarlane,' said the landlord.

Fettes was far through his third tumbler, stupidly fuddled, now nodding over, now staring mazily around him; but at the last word he seemed to awaken, and repeated the name 'Macfarlane' twice, quietly enough the first time, but with sudden emotion at the second.

'Yes,' said the landlord, 'that's his name, Doctor Wolfe Macfarlane.'

Fettes became instantly sober; his eyes awoke, his voice became clear, loud, and steady, his language forcible and earnest. We were all startled by the transformation, as if a man had risen from the dead.

'I beg your pardon,' he said. 'I am afraid I have not been paying much attention to your talk. Who is this Wolfe Macfarlane?' And then, when he had heard the landlord out, 'It cannot be, it cannot be,' he added; 'and yet I would like well to see him face to face.'

'Do you know him, Doctor?' asked the undertaker, with a gasp.

'God forbid!' was the reply. 'And yet the name is a strange one; it were too much to fancy two. Tell me, landlord, is he old?'

'Well,' said the host, 'he's not a young man, to be sure, and his hair is white; but he looks younger than you.'

'He is older, though; years older. But,' with a slap upon the table, 'it's the rum you see in my face—rum and sin. This man, perhaps, may have an easy conscience and a good digestion. Conscience! Hear me speak. You would think I was some good, old, decent Christian, would you not? But no, not I; I never canted. Voltaire* might have canted if he'd stood in my shoes; but the brains'—with a rattling fillip on his bald head—'the brains were clear and active, and I saw and made no deductions.'

'If you know this doctor,' I ventured to remark, after a somewhat awful pause, 'I should gather that you do not share the landlord's good opinion.'

Fettes paid no regard to me.

'Yes,' he said, with sudden decision, 'I must see him face to face.'

There was another pause, and then a door was closed rather sharply on the first floor, and a step was heard upon the stair.

'That's the doctor,' cried the landlord. 'Look sharp, and you can catch him.'

It was but two steps from the small parlour to the door of the old George Inn; the wide oak staircase landed almost in the street; there was room for a Turkey rug and nothing more between the threshold and the last round of the descent; but this little space was every evening brilliantly lit up, not only by the light upon the stair and the great signal-lamp below the sign, but by the warm radiance of the barroom window. The George thus brightly advertised itself to passers-by in the cold street. Fettes walked steadily to the spot, and we, who were hanging behind, beheld the two men meet, as one of them had phrased it, face to face. Dr Macfarlane was alert and vigorous. His white hair set off his pale and placid, although energetic, countenance. He was richly dressed in the finest of broadcloth* and the whitest of linen, with a great gold watch-chain, and studs and spectacles of the same precious material. He wore a broad-folded tie, white and speckled with lilac, and he carried on his arm a comfortable driving-coat of fur. There was no doubt but he became his years, breathing, as he did, of wealth and consideration; and it was a surprising contrast to see our parlour sot—bald, dirty, pimpled, and robed in his old camlet cloak—confront him at the bottom of the stairs.

'Macfarlane!' he said somewhat loudly, more like a herald than a friend.

The great doctor pulled up short on the fourth step, as though the familiarity of the address surprised and somewhat shocked his dignity.

'Toddy Macfarlane!' repeated Fettes.

The London man almost staggered. He stared for the swiftest of seconds at the man before him, glanced behind him with a sort of scare, and then in a startled whisper, 'Fettes!' he said, 'you!'

'Ay,' said the other, 'me! Did you think I was dead too? We are not so easy shut of our acquaintance.'

'Hush, hush!' exclaimed the doctor. 'Hush, hush! this meeting is so unexpected—I can see you are unmanned. I hardly knew you, I confess, at first; but I am overjoyed—overjoyed to have this opportunity. For the present it must be how-d'ye-do and good-by in one, for my fly is waiting, and I must not fail the train; but you shall—let me see—yes—you shall give me your address, and you can count on early news of me. We must do something for you, Fettes. I fear you are out at elbows; but we must see to that for auld lang syne,* as once we sang at suppers.'

'Money!' cried Fettes; 'money from you! The money that I had from you is lying where I cast it in the rain.'

Dr Macfarlane had talked himself into some measure of superiority and confidence, but the uncommon energy of this refusal cast him back into his first confusion.

A horrible, ugly look came and went across his almost venerable countenance. 'My dear fellow,' he said, 'be it as you please; my last thought is to offend you. I would intrude on none. I will leave you my address however——'

'I do not wish it—I do not wish to know the roof that shelters you,' interrupted the other. 'I heard your name; I feared it might be you; I wished to know if, after all, there were a God; I know now that there is none. Begone!'

He still stood in the middle of the rug, between the stair and doorway; and the great London physician, in order to escape, would be forced to step to one side. It was plain that he hesitated before the thought of this humiliation. White as he was, there was a dangerous glitter in his spectacles; but while he still paused uncertain, he became aware that the driver of his fly was peering in from the street at this unusual scene, and caught a glimpse at the same time of our little body from the parlour, huddled by the corner of the bar. The presence of so many witnesses decided him at once to flee. He crouched together, brushing on the wainscot, and made a dart like a serpent, striking for the door. But his tribulation was not yet entirely at an end, for even as he was passing Fettes clutched him by the arm and these words came in a whisper, and yet painfully distinct, 'Have you seen it again?'

The great rich London doctor cried out aloud with a sharp, throttling cry; he dashed his questioner across the open space, and, with his hands over his head, fled out of the door like a detected thief. Before it had occurred to one of us to make a movement the fly was already rattling toward the station. The scene was over like a dream, but the dream had left proofs and traces of its passage. Next day the servant found the fine gold spectacles broken on the threshold, and that very night we were all standing breathless by the barroom window, and Fettes at our side, sober, pale and resolute in look.

'God protect us, Mr Fettes!' said the landlord, coming first into possession of his customary senses. 'What in the universe is all this? These are strange things you have been saying.'

Fettes turned toward us; he looked us each in succession in the face. 'See if you can hold your tongues,' said he. 'That man Macfarlane is not safe to cross; those that have done so already have repented it too late.'

And then, without so much as finishing his third glass, far less waiting for the other two, he bade us good-by and went forth, under the lamp of the hotel, into the black night.

We three turned to our places in the parlour, with the big red fire and four clear candles; and as we recapitulated what had passed the first chill of our surprise soon changed into a glow of curiosity. We sat late; it was the latest session I have known in the old George. Each man, before we parted, had his theory that he was bound to prove; and none of us had any nearer business in this world than to track out the past of our condemned companion, and surprise the secret that he shared with the great London doctor. It is no great boast, but I believe I was a better hand at worming out a story than either of my fellows at the George; and perhaps there is now no other man alive who could narrate to you the following foul and unnatural events.

In his young days Fettes studied medicine in the schools of Edinburgh. He had talent of a kind, the talent that picks up swiftly what it hears and readily retails it for its own. He worked little at home; but he was civil, attentive, and intelligent in the presence of his masters. They soon picked him out as a lad who listened closely and remembered well; nay, strange as it seemed to me when I first heard it, he was in those days well favoured, and pleased by his exterior. There was, at that period, a certain extramural teacher of anatomy, whom I shall here designate by the letter K.* His name was subsequently too well known. The man who bore it skulked through the streets of Edinburgh in disguise, while the mob that applauded at the execution of Burke* called loudly for the blood of his employer. But Mr K—— was then at the top of his vogue; he enjoyed a popularity due partly to his own talent and address, partly to the incapacity of his rival, the university professor. The students, at least, swore by his name, and Fettes believed himself, and was believed by others, to have laid the foundations of success when he had acquired the favour of this meteorically famous man. Mr K—— was a *bon vivant** as well as an accomplished teacher; he liked a sly allusion no less than a careful preparation. In both capacities Fettes enjoyed and deserved his notice, and by the second year of his attendance he held the half-regular position of second demonstrator or sub-assistant in his class.

In this capacity, the charge of the theatre and lecture-room devolved in particular upon his shoulders. He had to answer for the cleanliness of the premises and the conduct of the other students, and it was a part of his duty to supply, receive, and divide the various subjects. It was with a view to this last—at that time very delicate—affair that he was lodged by Mr K—— in the same wynd,* and at last in the same building, with the dissecting-room. Here, after a night of turbulent pleasures, his hand still tottering, his sight still misty and confused, he would be called out of bed in the black hours before the winter dawn by the unclean and desperate interlopers who supplied the table. He would open the door to these men, since infamous throughout the land. He would help them with their tragic burden, pay them their sordid price, and remain alone, when they were gone, with the unfriendly relics of humanity. From such a scene he would return to snatch another hour or two of slumber, to repair the abuses of the night, and refresh himself for the labours of the day.

Few lads could have been more insensible to the impressions of a life thus passed among the ensigns of mortality. His mind was closed against all general considerations. He was incapable of interest in the fate and fortunes of another, the slave of his own desires and low ambitions. Cold, light, and selfish in the last resort, he had that modicum of prudence, miscalled morality, which keeps a man from inconvenient drunkenness or punishable theft. He coveted, besides, a measure of consideration from his masters and his fellow-pupils, and he had no desire to fail conspicuously in the external parts of life. Thus he made it his pleasure to gain some distinction in his studies, and day after day rendered unimpeachable eye-service to his employer, Mr K——. For his day of work he indemnified himself by nights of roaring, blackguardly enjoyment; and when that balance had been struck, the organ that he called his conscience declared itself content.

The supply of subjects was a continual trouble to him as well as to his master. In that large and busy class, the raw material of the anatomists kept perpetually running out; and the business thus rendered necessary was not only unpleasant in itself, but threatened dangerous consequences to all who were concerned. It was the policy of Mr K—— to ask no questions in his dealings with the trade. 'They bring the body, and we pay the price,' he used to say, dwelling on the alliteration—'*quid pro quo*.'* And again, and somewhat profanely,

'Ask no questions,' he would tell his assistants, 'for conscience sake.' There was no understanding that the subjects were provided by the crime of murder. Had that idea been broached to him in words, he would have recoiled in horror; but the lightness of his speech upon so grave a matter was, in itself, an offence against good manners, and a temptation to the men with whom he dealt. Fettes, for instance, had often remarked to himself upon the singular freshness of the bodies. He had been struck again and again by the hang-dog, abominable looks of the ruffians who came to him before the dawn; and putting things together clearly in his private thoughts, he perhaps attributed a meaning too immoral and too categorical to the unguarded counsels of his master. He understood his duty, in short, to have three branches: to take what was brought, to pay the price, and to avert the eye from any evidence of crime.

One November morning this policy of silence was put sharply to the test. He had been awake all night with a racking toothache—pacing his room like a caged beast or throwing himself in fury on his bed—and had fallen at last into that profound, uneasy slumber that so often follows on a night of pain, when he was awakened by the third or fourth angry repetition of the concerted signal. There was a thin, bright moonshine; it was bitter cold, windy, and frosty; the town had not yet awakened, but an indefinable stir already preluded the noise and business of the day. The ghouls had come later than usual, and they seemed more than usually eager to be gone. Fettes, sick with sleep, lighted them upstairs. He heard their grumbling Irish voices through a dream; and as they stripped the sack from their sad merchandise he leaned dozing, with his shoulder propped against the wall; he had to shake himself to find the men their money. As he did so his eyes lighted on the dead face. He started; he took two steps nearer, with the candle raised.

'God Almighty!' he cried. 'That is Jane Galbraith!'

The men answered nothing, but they shuffled nearer the door.

'I know her, I tell you,' he continued. 'She was alive and hearty yesterday. It's impossible she can be dead; it's impossible you should have got this body fairly.'

'Sure, sir, you're mistaken entirely,' said one of the men.

But the other looked Fettes darkly in the eyes, and demanded the money on the spot.

It was impossible to misconceive the threat or to exaggerate the danger. The lad's heart failed him. He stammered some excuses, counted out the sum, and saw his hateful visitors depart. No sooner were they gone than he hastened to confirm his doubts. By a dozen unquestionable marks he identified the girl he had jested with the day before. He saw, with horror, marks upon her body that might well betoken violence. A panic seized him, and he took refuge in his room. There he reflected at length over the discovery that he had made; considered soberly the bearing of Mr K——'s instructions and the danger to himself of interference in so serious a business, and at last, in sore perplexity, determined to wait for the advice of his immediate superior, the class assistant.

This was a young doctor, Wolfe Macfarlane, a high favourite among all the reckless students, clever, dissipated, and unscrupulous to the last degree. He had travelled and studied abroad. His manners were agreeable and a little forward. He was an authority on the stage, skilful on the ice or the links with skate or golf-club; he dressed with nice audacity, and, to put the finishing touch upon his glory, he kept a gig and a strong trotting-horse. With Fettes he was on terms of intimacy; indeed, their relative positions called for some community of life; and when subjects were scarce the pair would drive far into the country in Macfarlane's gig, visit and desecrate some lonely graveyard, and return before dawn with their booty to the door of the dissecting-room.

On that particular morning Macfarlane arrived somewhat earlier than his wont. Fettes heard him, and met him on the stairs, told him his story, and showed him the cause of his alarm. Macfarlane examined the marks on her body.

'Yes,' he said with a nod, 'it looks fishy.'

'Well, what should I do?' asked Fettes.

'Do?' repeated the other. 'Do you want to do anything? Least said soonest mended, I should say.'

'Some one else might recognise her,' objected Fettes. 'She was as well known as the Castle Rock.'*

'We'll hope not,' said Macfarlane, 'and if anybody does—well, you didn't, don't you see, and there's an end. The fact is, this has been going on too long. Stir up the mud, and you'll get K—— into the most unholy trouble; you'll be in a shocking box yourself. So will I, if you come to that. I should like to know how any one of us would look, or what the devil we should have to say for ourselves in any Christian witness-box. For me, you know there's one thing certain—that, practically speaking, all our subjects have been murdered.'

'Macfarlane!' cried Fettes.

'Come now!' sneered the other. 'As if you hadn't suspected it yourself!'

'Suspecting is one thing——'

'And proof another. Yes, I know; and I'm as sorry as you are this should have come here,' tapping the body with his cane. 'The next best thing for me is not to recognise it; and,' he added coolly, 'I don't. You may, if you please. I don't dictate, but I think a man of the world would do as I do; and I may add, I fancy that is what K—— would look for at our hands. The question is, Why did he choose us two for his assistants? And I answer, because he didn't want old wives.'

This was the tone of all others to affect the mind of a lad like Fettes. He agreed to imitate Macfarlane. The body of the unfortunate girl was duly dissected, and no one remarked or appeared to recognize her.

One afternoon, when his day's work was over, Fettes dropped into a popular tavern and found Macfarlane sitting with a stranger. This was a small man, very pale and dark, with coal-black eyes. The cut of his features gave a promise of intellect and refinement which was but feebly realised in his manners, for he proved, upon a nearer acquaintance, coarse, vulgar, and stupid. He exercised, however, a very remarkable control over Macfarlane; issued orders like the Great Bashaw;* became inflamed at the least discussion or delay, and commented rudely on the servility with which he was obeyed. This most offensive person took a fancy to Fettes on the spot, plied him with drinks, and honoured him with unusual confidences on his past career. If a tenth part of what he confessed were true, he was a very loathsome rogue; and the lad's vanity was tickled by the attention of so experienced a man.

'I'm a pretty bad fellow myself,' the stranger remarked, 'but Macfarlane is the boy—Toddy Macfarlane, I call him. Toddy, order your friend another glass.' Or it might be, 'Toddy, you jump up and shut the door.' 'Toddy hates me,' he said again. 'Oh, yes, Toddy, you do!'

'Don't you call me that confounded name,' growled Macfarlane.

'Hear him! Did you ever see the lads play knife? He would like to do that all over my body,' remarked the stranger.

'We medicals have a better way than that,' said Fettes. 'When we dislike a dead friend of ours, we dissect him.'

Macfarlane looked up sharply, as though this jest was scarcely to his mind.

The afternoon passed. Gray, for that was the stranger's name, invited Fettes to join them at dinner, ordered a feast so sumptuous that the tavern was thrown in commotion, and when all was done commanded Macfarlane to settle the bill. It was late before they separated; the man Gray was incapably drunk. Macfarlane, sobered by his fury, chewed the cud of the money he had been forced to squander and the slights he had been obliged to swallow. Fettes, with various liquors singing in his head, returned home with devious footsteps and a mind entirely in abeyance. Next day Macfarlane was absent from the class, and Fettes smiled to himself as he imagined him still squiring the intolerable Gray from tavern to tavern. As soon as the hour of liberty had struck he posted from place to place in quest of his last night's companions. He could find them, however, nowhere; so returned early to his rooms, went early to bed, and slept the sleep of the just.

At four in the morning he was awakened by the well-known signal. Descending to the door, he was filled with astonishment to find Macfarlane with his gig, and in the gig one of those long and ghastly packages with which he was so well acquainted.

'What?' he cried. 'Have you been out alone? How did you manage?'

But Macfarlane silenced him roughly, bidding him turn to business. When they had got the body upstairs and laid it on the table, Macfarlane made at first as if he were going away. Then he paused and seemed to hesitate; and then, 'You had better look at the face,' said he, in tones of some constraint. 'You had better,' he repeated, as Fettes only stared at him in wonder.

'But where, and how, and when did you come by it?' cried the other.

'Look at the face,' was the only answer.

Fettes was staggered; strange doubts assailed him. He looked from the young doctor to the body, and then back again. At last, with a start, he did as he was bidden. He had almost expected the sight that met his eyes, and yet the shock was cruel. To see, fixed in the rigidity of death and naked on that coarse layer of sackcloth, the man whom he had left well clad and full of meat and sin upon the threshold of a tavern, awoke, even in the thoughtless Fettes, some of the terrors of the conscience. It was a *cras tibi** which re-echoed in his soul, that two whom he had known should have come to lie upon these icy tables. Yet these were only secondary thoughts. His first concern regarded Wolfe. Unprepared for a challenge so momentous, he knew not how to look his comrade in the face. He durst not meet his eye, and he had neither words nor voice at his command.

It was Macfarlane himself who made the first advance. He came up quietly behind and laid his hand gently but firmly on the other's shoulder.

'Richardson,' said he, 'may have the head.'

Now Richardson was a student who had long been anxious for that portion of the human subject to dissect. There was no answer, and the murderer resumed: 'Talking of business, you must pay me; your accounts, you see, must tally.'

Fettes found a voice, the ghost of his own: 'Pay you!' he cried. 'Pay you for that?'

'Why, yes, of course you must. By all means and on every possible account, you must,' returned the other. 'I dare not give it for nothing, you dare not take it for nothing; it would compromise us both. This is another case like Jane Galbraith's. The more things are wrong the more we must act as if all were right. Where does old K—— keep his money?'

'There,' answered Fettes hoarsely, pointing to a cupboard in the corner.

'Give me the key, then,' said the other, calmly, holding out his hand.

There was an instant's hesitation, and the die was cast. Macfarlane could not suppress a nervous twitch, the infinitesimal mark of an immense relief, as he felt the key between his fingers. He opened the cupboard, brought out pen and ink and a paper-book that stood in one compartment, and separated from the funds in a drawer a sum suitable to the occasion.

'Now, look here,' he said, 'there is the payment made—first proof of your good faith: first step to your security. You have now to clinch it by a second. Enter the payment in your book, and then you for your part may defy the devil.'

The next few seconds were for Fettes an agony of thought; but in balancing his terrors it was the most immediate that triumphed. Any future difficulty seemed almost welcome if he could avoid a present quarrel with Macfarlane. He set down the candle which he had been carrying all this time, and with a steady hand entered the date, the nature, and the amount of the transaction.

'And now,' said Macfarlane, 'it's only fair that you should pocket the lucre. I've had my share already. By the bye, when a man of the world falls into a bit of luck, has a few shillings extra in his pocket— I'm ashamed to speak of it, but there's a rule of conduct in the case. No treating, no purchase of expensive class-books, no squaring of old debts; borrow, don't lend.'

'Macfarlane,' began Fettes, still somewhat hoarsely, 'I have put my neck in a halter to oblige you.'

'To oblige me?' cried Wolfe. 'Oh, come! You did, as near as I can see the matter, what you downright had to do in self-defence. Suppose I got into trouble, where would you be? This second little matter flows clearly from the first. Mr Gray is the continuation of Miss Galbraith. You can't begin and then stop. If you begin, you must keep on beginning; that's the truth. No rest for the wicked.'

A horrible sense of blackness and the treachery of fate seized hold upon the soul of the unhappy student.

'My God!' he cried, 'but what have I done? and when did I begin? To be made a class assistant—in the name of reason, where's the harm in that? Service wanted the position; Service might have got it. Would *he* have been where I am now?'

'My dear fellow,' said Macfarlane, 'what a boy you are! What harm *has* come to you? What harm *can* come to you if you hold your tongue? Why, man, do you know what this life is? There are two squads of us—the lions, and the lambs. If you're a lamb, you'll come to lie upon these tables like Gray or Jane Galbraith; if you're a lion, you'll live and drive a horse like me, like K——, like all the world with any wit or courage. You're staggered at the first. But look at K——! My dear fellow, you're clever, you have pluck. I like you, and K—— likes you. You were born to lead the hunt; and I tell you, on my honour and my experience of life, three days from now you'll laugh at all these scarecrows like a high-school boy at a farce.'

And with that Macfarlane took his departure and drove off up the wynd in his gig to get under cover before daylight. Fettes was thus left alone with his regrets. He saw the miserable peril in which he stood involved. He saw, with inexpressible dismay, that there was no limit to his weakness, and that, from concession to concession, he had

fallen from the arbiter of Macfarlane's destiny to his paid and helpless accomplice. He would have given the world to have been a little
braver at the time, but it did not occur to him that he might still be
brave. The secret of Jane Galbraith and the cursed entry in the day-
book closed his mouth.

Hours passed; the class began to arrive; the members of the
unhappy Gray were dealt out to one and to another, and received
without remark. Richardson was made happy with the head; and
before the hour of freedom rang Fettes trembled with exultation to
perceive how far they had already gone toward safety.

For two days he continued to watch, with increasing joy, the dreadful process of disguise.

On the third day Macfarlane made his appearance. He had been
ill, he said; but he made up for lost time by the energy with which he
directed the students. To Richardson in particular he extended the
most valuable assistance and advice, and that student, encouraged by
the praise of the demonstrator, burned high with ambitious hopes,
and saw the medal already in his grasp.

Before the week was out Macfarlane's prophecy had been fulfilled.
Fettes had outlived his terrors and had forgotten his baseness. He
began to plume himself upon his courage, and had so arranged the
story in his mind that he could look back on these events with an
unhealthy pride. Of his accomplice he saw but little. They met, of
course, in the business of the class; they received their orders together
from Mr K——. At times they had a word or two in private, and
Macfarlane was from first to last particularly kind and jovial. But it
was plain that he avoided any reference to their common secret; and
even when Fettes whispered to him that he had cast in his lot with the
lions and forsworn the lambs, he only signed to him smilingly to hold
his peace.

At length an occasion arose which threw the pair once more into
a closer union. Mr K—— was again short of subjects; pupils were
eager, and it was a part of this teacher's pretensions to be always well
supplied. At the same time there came the news of a burial in the
rustic graveyard of Glencorse.* Time has little changed the place
in question. It stood then, as now, upon a cross road,* out of call
of human habitations, and buried fathoms deep in the foliage of six
cedar trees. The cries of the sheep upon the neighbouring hills, the
streamlets upon either hand, one loudly singing among pebbles, the

other dripping furtively from pond to pond, the stir of the wind in mountainous old flowering chestnuts, and once in seven days the voice of the bell and the old tunes of the precentor,* were the only sounds that disturbed the silence around the rural church. The Resurrection Man*—to use a byname of the period—was not to be deterred by any of the sanctities of customary piety. It was part of his trade to despise and desecrate the scrolls and trumpets of old tombs, the paths worn by the feet of worshippers and mourners, and the offerings and the inscriptions of bereaved affection. To rustic neighbourhoods, where love is more than commonly tenacious, and where some bonds of blood or fellowship unite the entire society of a parish, the body-snatcher, far from being repelled by natural respect, was attracted by the ease and safety of the task. To bodies that had been laid in earth, in joyful expectation of a far different awakening, there came that hasty, lamp-lit, terror-haunted resurrection of the spade and mattock.* The coffin was forced, the cerements torn, and the melancholy relics, clad in sackcloth, after being rattled for hours on moonless byways, were at length exposed to uttermost indignities before a class of gaping boys.

Somewhat as two vultures may swoop upon a dying lamb, Fettes and Macfarlane were to be let loose upon a grave in that green and quiet resting-place. The wife of a farmer, a woman who had lived for sixty years, and been known for nothing but good butter and a godly conversation, was to be rooted from her grave at midnight and carried, dead and naked to that far-away city that she had always honoured with her Sunday's best; the place beside her family was to be empty till the crack of doom; her innocent and almost venerable members to be exposed to that last curiosity of the anatomist.

Late one afternoon the pair set forth, well wrapped in cloaks and furnished with a formidable bottle. It rained without remission— a cold, dense, lashing rain. Now and again there blew a puff of wind, but these sheets of falling water kept it down. Bottle and all, it was a sad and silent drive as far as Penicuik,* where they were to spend the evening. They stopped once, to hide their implements in a thick bush not far from the churchyard, and once again at the Fisher's Tryst, to have a toast before the kitchen fire and vary their nips of whisky with a glass of ale. When they reached their journey's end the gig was housed, the horse was fed and comforted, and the two young doctors in a private room sat down to the best dinner and the best wine the house afforded. The lights, the fire, the beating rain upon the window, the cold, incongruous work that lay before them, added zest to their enjoyment of the meal. With every glass their cordiality increased. Soon Macfarlane handed a little pile of gold to his companion.

'A compliment,' he said. 'Between friends these little d——d accommodations ought to fly like pipe-lights.'

Fettes pocketed the money, and applauded the sentiment to the echo. 'You are a philosopher,' he cried. 'I was an ass till I knew you. You and K—— between you, by the Lord Harry! but you'll make a man of me.'

'Of course, we shall,' applauded Macfarlane. 'A man? I tell you, it required a man to back me up the other morning. There are some big, brawling, forty-year-old cowards who would have turned sick at the look of the d——d thing; but not you—you kept your head. I watched you.'

'Well, and why not?' Fettes thus vaunted himself. 'It was no affair of mine. There was nothing to gain on the one side but disturbance, and on the other I could count on your gratitude, don't you see?' And he slapped his pocket till the gold pieces rang.

Macfarlane somehow felt a certain touch of alarm at these unpleasant words. He may have regretted that he had taught his young companion so successfully, but he had no time to interfere, for the other noisily continued in this boastful strain:

'The great thing is not to be afraid. Now, between you and me, I don't want to hang—that's practical; but for all cant, Macfarlane, I was born with a contempt. Hell, God, Devil, right, wrong, sin, crime, and all the old gallery of curiosities—they may frighten boys, but men of the world, like you and me, despise them. Here's to the memory of Gray!'

It was by this time growing somewhat late. The gig, according to order, was brought round to the door with both lamps brightly shining, and the young men had to pay their bill and take the road. They announced that they were bound for Peebles,* and drove in that direction till they were clear of the last houses of the town; then, extinguishing the lamps, returned upon their course, and followed a by-road toward Glencorse. There was no sound but that of their own passage, and the incessant, strident pouring of the rain. It was pitch dark; here and there a white gate or a white stone in the wall guided them for a short space across the night; but for the most part it was at a foot pace, and almost groping, that they picked their way through that resonant blackness to their solemn and isolated destination. In the sunken woods that traverse the neighbourhood of the burying-ground the last glimmer failed them, and it became necessary to kindle a match and reillumine one of the lanterns of the gig. Thus, under the dripping trees, and environed by huge and moving shadows, they reached the scene of their unhallowed labours.

They were both experienced in such affairs, and powerful with the spade; and they had scarce been twenty minutes at their task before they were rewarded by a dull rattle on the coffin lid. At the same moment Macfarlane, having hurt his hand upon a stone, flung it carelessly above his head. The grave, in which they now stood almost to the shoulders, was close to the edge of the plateau of the graveyard; and the gig lamp had been propped, the better to illuminate their labours, against a tree, and on the immediate verge of the steep bank descending to the stream. Chance had taken a sure aim with the stone. Then came a clang of broken glass; night fell upon them; sounds alternately dull and ringing announced the bounding of the lantern down the bank, and its occasional collision with the trees. A stone or two, which it had dislodged in its descent, rattled behind it into the profundities of the glen; and then silence, like night, resumed its sway; and they might bend their hearing to its utmost pitch, but naught was to be heard except the rain, now marching to the wind, now steadily falling over miles of open country.

They were so nearly at an end of their abhorred task that they judged it wisest to complete it in the dark. The coffin was exhumed and broken open; the body inserted in the dripping sack and carried between them to the gig; one mounted to keep it in its place, and the other, taking the horse by the mouth, groped along by wall and bush until they reached the wider road by the Fisher's Tryst. Here was a faint, diffused radiancy, which they hailed like daylight; by that they pushed the horse to a good pace and began to rattle along merrily in the direction of the town.

They had both been wetted to the skin during their operations, and now, as the gig jumped among the deep ruts, the thing that stood propped between them fell now upon one and now upon the other. At every repetition of the horrid contact each instinctively repelled it with the greater haste; and the process, natural although it was, began to tell upon the nerves of the companions. Macfarlane made some ill-favoured jest about the farmer's wife, but it came hollowly from his lips, and was allowed to drop in silence. Still their unnatural burden bumped from side to side; and now the head would be laid, as if in confidence, upon their shoulders, and now the drenching sackcloth would flap icily about their faces. A creeping chill began to possess the soul of Fettes. He peered at the bundle, and it seemed somehow larger than at first. All over the countryside, and from every degree of distance, the farm dogs accompanied their passage with tragic ululations;* and it grew and grew upon his mind that some unnatural miracle had been accomplished, that some nameless change had befallen the dead body, and that it was in fear of their unholy burden that the dogs were howling.

'For God's sake,' said he, making a great effort to arrive at speech, 'for God's sake, let's have a light!'

Seemingly Macfarlane was affected in the same direction; for, though he made no reply, he stopped the horse, passed the reins to his companion, got down, and proceeded to kindle the remaining lamp. They had by that time got no farther than the cross-road down to Auchenclinny.* The rain still poured as though the deluge were returning, and it was no easy matter to make a light in such a world of wet and darkness. When at last the flickering blue flame had been transferred to the wick and began to expand and clarify, and shed a wide circle of misty brightness round the gig, it became possible for the two young men to see each other and the thing they had along with them. The rain had moulded the rough sacking to the outlines of the body underneath; the head was distinct from the trunk, the shoulders plainly modelled; something at once spectral and human riveted their eyes upon the ghastly comrade of their drive.

For some time Macfarlane stood motionless, holding up the lamp. A nameless dread was swathed, like a wet sheet, about the body, and tightened the white skin upon the face of Fettes; a fear that was meaningless, a horror of what could not be, kept mounting to his brain. Another beat of the watch, and he had spoken. But his comrade forestalled him.

'That is not a woman,' said Macfarlane in a hushed voice.

'It was a woman when we put her in,' whispered Fettes.

'Hold that lamp,' said the other. 'I must see her face.'

And as Fettes took the lamp his companion untied the fastenings of the sack and drew down the cover from the head. The light fell very clear upon the dark, well-moulded features and smooth-shaven cheeks of a too familiar countenance, often beheld in dreams of both of these young men. A wild yell rang up into the night; each leaped from his own side into the roadway; the lamp fell, broke, and was extinguished; and the horse, terrified by this unusual commotion, bounded and went off toward Edinburgh at a gallop, bearing along with it, sole occupant of the gig, the body of the dead and long-dissected Gray.

RUDYARD KIPLING

The Mark of the Beast

❧❧

> Your Gods and my Gods—do you or I know which are the stronger?
>
> *Native Proverb*

E AST of Suez,* some hold, the direct control of Providence ceases;
Man being there handed over to the power of the Gods and Devils
of Asia, and the Church of England Providence only exercising
an occasional and modified supervision in the case of Englishmen.

This theory accounts for some of the more unnecessary horrors of
life in India: it may be stretched to explain my story.

My friend Strickland of the Police, who knows as much of natives
of India as is good for any man, can bear witness to the facts of the
case. Dumoise, our doctor, also saw what Strickland and I saw. The
inference which he drew from the evidence was entirely incorrect.
He is dead now; he died in a rather curious manner, which has been
elsewhere described.*

When Fleete came to India he owned a little money and some land
in the Himalayas, near a place called Dharmsala.* Both properties
had been left him by an uncle, and he came out to finance them.
He was a big, heavy, genial, and inoffensive man. His knowledge of
natives was, of course, limited, and he complained of the difficulties
of the language.

He rode in from his place in the hills to spend New Year in the
station, and he stayed with Strickland. On New Year's Eve there
was a big dinner at the club, and the night was excusably wet.
When men foregather from the uttermost ends of the Empire, they
have a right to be riotous. The Frontier had sent down a contin-
gent o' Catch'em-Alive-O's* who had not seen twenty white faces
for a year, and were used to ride fifteen miles to dinner at the next
Fort at the risk of a Khyberee* bullet where their drinks should lie.
They profited by their new security, for they tried to play pool with
a curled-up hedgehog found in the garden, and one of them carried

the marker round the room in his teeth. Half a dozen planters had come in from the south and were talking 'horse'* to the Biggest Liar in Asia, who was trying to cap all their stories at once. Everybody was there, and there was a general closing up of ranks and taking stock of our losses in dead or disabled that had fallen during the past year. It was a very wet night, and I remember that we sang 'Auld Lang Syne'* with our feet in the Polo Championship Cup, and our heads among the stars, and swore that we were all dear friends. Then some of us went away and annexed Burma,* and some tried to open up the Soudan and were opened up by Fuzzies in that cruel scrub outside Suakim,* and some found stars and medals, and some were married, which was bad, and some did other things which were worse, and the others of us stayed in our chains and strove to make money on insufficient experiences.

Fleete began the night with sherry and bitters, drank champagne steadily up to dessert, then raw, rasping Capri with all the strength of whisky, took Benedictine* with his coffee, four or five whiskies and sodas to improve his pool strokes, beer and bones at half-past two, winding up with old brandy. Consequently, when he came out, at half-past three in the morning, into fourteen degrees of frost, he was very angry with his horse for coughing, and tried to leapfrog into the saddle. The horse broke away and went to his stables; so Strickland and I formed a Guard of Dishonour to take Fleete home.

Our road lay through the bazaar, close to a little temple of Hanuman,* the Monkey-god, who is a leading divinity worthy of respect. All gods have good points, just as have all priests. Personally, I attach much importance to Hanuman, and am kind to his people— the great gray apes of the hills. One never knows when one may want a friend.

There was a light in the temple, and as we passed, we could hear voices of men chanting hymns. In a native temple, the priests rise at all hours of the night to do honour to their god. Before we could stop him, Fleete dashed up the steps, patted two priests on the back, and was gravely grinding the ashes of his cigar-butt in to the forehead of the red, stone image of Hanuman. Strickland tried to drag him out, but he sat down and said solemnly:

'Shee that? 'Mark of the B—beasht! *I* made it. Ishn't it fine?'

In half a minute the temple was alive and noisy, and Strickland, who knew what came of polluting gods, said that things might occur.

He, by virtue of his official position, long residence in the country, and weakness for going among the natives, was known to the priests and he felt unhappy. Fleete sat on the ground and refused to move. He said that 'good old Hanuman' made a very soft pillow.

Then, without any warning, a Silver Man came out of a recess behind the image of the god. He was perfectly naked in that bitter, bitter cold, and his body shone like frosted silver, for he was what the Bible calls 'a leper as white as snow.'* Also he had no face, because he was a leper of some years' standing, and his disease was heavy upon him. We two stooped to haul Fleete up, and the temple was filling and filling with folk who seemed to spring from the earth, when the Silver Man ran in under our arms, making a noise exactly like the mewing of an otter, caught Fleete round the body and dropped his head on Fleete's breast before we could wrench him away. Then he retired to a corner and sat mewing while the crowd blocked all the doors.

The priests were very angry until the Silver Man touched Fleete. That nuzzling seemed to sober them.

At the end of a few minutes' silence one of the priests came to Strickland and said, in perfect English, 'Take your friend away. He has done with Hanuman but Hanuman has not done with him.' The crowd gave room and we carried Fleete into the road.

Strickland was very angry. He said that we might all three have been knifed, and that Fleete should thank his stars that he had escaped without injury.

Fleete thanked no one. He said that he wanted to go to bed. He was gorgeously drunk.

We moved on, Strickland silent and wrathful, until Fleete was taken with violent shivering fits and sweating. He said that the smells of the bazaar were overpowering, and he wondered why slaughter-houses were permitted so near English residences. 'Can't you smell the blood?' said Fleete.

We put him to bed at last, just as the dawn was breaking, and Strickland invited me to have another whisky and soda. While we were drinking he talked of the trouble in the temple, and admitted that it baffled him completely. Strickland hates being mystified by natives, because his business in life is to overmatch them with their own weapons. He has not yet succeeded in doing this, but in fifteen or twenty years he will have made some small progress.

'They should have mauled us,' he said, 'instead of mewing at us. I wonder what they meant. I don't like it one little bit.'

I said that the Managing Committee of the temple would in all probability bring a criminal action against us for insulting their religion. There was a section of the Indian Penal Code* which exactly met Fleete's offence. Strickland said he only hoped and prayed that they would do this. Before I left I looked into Fleete's room, and saw him lying on his right side, scratching his left breast. Then I went to bed cold, depressed, and unhappy, at seven o'clock in the morning.

At one o'clock I rode over to Strickland's house to inquire after Fleete's head. I imagined that it would be a sore one. Fleete was breakfasting and seemed unwell. His temper was gone, for he was abusing the cook for not supplying him with an underdone chop. A man who can eat raw meat after a wet night is a curiosity. I told Fleete this and he laughed.

'You breed queer mosquitoes in these parts,' he said. 'I've been bitten to pieces, but only in one place.'

'Let's have a look at the bite,' said Strickland. 'It may have gone down since this morning.'

While the chops were being cooked, Fleete opened his shirt and showed us, just over his left breast, a mark, the perfect double of the black rosettes—the five or six irregular blotches arranged in a circle—on a leopard's hide. Strickland looked and said, 'It was only pink this morning. It's grown black now.'

Fleete ran to a glass.

'By Jove!' he said, 'this is nasty. What is it?'

We could not answer. Here the chops came in, all red and juicy, and Fleete bolted three in a most offensive manner. He ate on his right grinders only, and threw his head over his right shoulder as he snapped the meat. When he had finished, it struck him that he had been behaving strangely, for he said apologetically, 'I don't think I ever felt so hungry in my life. I've bolted like an ostrich.'

After breakfast Strickland said to me, 'Don't go. Stay here, and stay for the night.'

Seeing that my house was not three miles from Strickland's, this request was absurd. But Strickland insisted, and was going to say something when Fleete interrupted by declaring in a shamefaced way that he felt hungry again. Strickland sent a man to my house to fetch over my bedding and a horse, and we three went down to Strickland's stables to pass the hours until it was time to go out for a ride. The man who has a weakness for horses never wearies of inspecting them; and when two men are killing time in this way they gather knowledge and lies the one from the other.

There were five horses in the stables, and I shall never forget the scene as we tried to look them over. They seemed to have gone mad. They reared and screamed and nearly tore up their pickets; they sweated and shivered and lathered and were distraught with fear. Strickland's horses used to know him as well as his dogs; which made the matter more curious. We left the stable for fear of the brutes throwing themselves in their panic. Then Strickland turned back and called me. The horses were still frightened, but they let us 'gentle' and make much of them, and put their heads in our bosoms.

'They aren't afraid of *us*,' said Strickland. 'D' you know, I'd give three months' pay if *Outrage* here could talk.'

But *Outrage* was dumb, and could only cuddle up to his master and blow out his nostrils, as is the custom of horses when they wish to explain things but can't. Fleete came up when we were in the stalls, and as soon as the horses saw him, their fright broke out afresh. It was all that we could do to escape from the place unkicked. Strickland said, 'They don't seem to love you, Fleete.'

'Nonsense,' said Fleete; 'my mare will follow me like a dog.' He went to her; she was in a loose-box; but as he slipped the bars she plunged, knocked him down, and broke away into the garden. I laughed, but Strickland was not amused. He took his moustache in both fists and pulled at it till it nearly came out. Fleete, instead of going off to chase his property, yawned, saying that he felt sleepy. He went to the house to lie down, which was a foolish way of spending New Year's Day.

Strickland sat with me in the stables and asked if I had noticed anything peculiar in Fleete's manner. I said that he ate his food like a beast; but that this might have been the result of living alone in the hills out of the reach of society as refined and elevating as ours for instance. Strickland was not amused. I do not think that he listened to me, for his next sentence referred to the mark on Fleete's breast, and I said that it might have been caused by blister-flies,* or that it was possibly a birth-mark newly born and now visible for the first time. We both agreed that it was unpleasant to look at, and Strickland found occasion to say that I was a fool.

'I can't tell you what I think now,' said he, 'because you would call me a madman; but you must stay with me for the next few days, if you can. I want you to watch Fleete, but don't tell me what you think till I have made up my mind.'

'But I am dining out to-night,' I said.

'So am I,' said Strickland, 'and so is Fleete. At least if he doesn't change his mind.'

We walked about the garden smoking, but saying nothing—because we were friends, and talking spoils good tobacco—till our pipes were out. Then we went to wake up Fleete. He was wide awake and fidgeting about his room.

'I say, I want some more chops,' he said. 'Can I get them?'

We laughed and said, 'Go and change. The ponies will be round in a minute.'

'All right,' said Fleete. 'I'll go when I get the chops—underdone ones, mind.'

He seemed to be quite in earnest. It was four o'clock, and we had had breakfast at one; still, for a long time, he demanded those underdone chops. Then he changed into riding clothes and went out into the verandah. His pony—the mare had not been caught—would not let him come near. All three horses were unmanageable—mad with fear—and finally Fleete said that he would stay at home and get something to eat. Strickland and I rode out wondering. As we passed the temple of Hanuman, the Silver Man came out and mewed at us.

'He is not one of the regular priests of the temple,' said Strickland. 'I think I should peculiarly like to lay my hands on him.'

There was no spring in our gallop on the racecourse that evening. The horses were stale, and moved as though they had been ridden out.

'The fright after breakfast has been too much for them,' said Strickland.

That was the only remark he made through the remainder of the ride. Once or twice I think he swore to himself; but that did not count.

We came back in the dark at seven o'clock, and saw that there were no lights in the bungalow. 'Careless ruffians my servants are!' said Strickland.

My horse reared at something on the carriage drive, and Fleete stood up under its nose.

'What are you doing, grovelling about the garden?' said Strickland.

But both horses bolted and nearly threw us. We dismounted by the stables and returned to Fleete, who was on his hands and knees under the orange-bushes.

'What the devil's wrong with you?' said Strickland.

'Nothing, nothing in the world,' said Fleete, speaking very quickly and thickly. 'I've been gardening—botanising you know. The smell of the earth is delightful. I think I'm going for a walk—a long walk—all night.'

Then I saw that there was something excessively out of order somewhere, and I said to Strickland, 'I am not dining out.'

'Bless you!' said Strickland. 'Here, Fleete, get up. You'll catch fever there. Come in to dinner and let's have the lamps lit. We'll all dine at home.'

Fleete stood up unwillingly, and said, 'No lamps—no lamps. It's much nicer here. Let's dine outside and have some more chops—lots of 'em and underdone—bloody ones with gristle.'

Now a December evening* in Northern India is bitterly cold, and Fleete's suggestion was that of a maniac.

'Come in,' said Strickland sternly. 'Come in at once.'

Fleete came, and when the lamps were brought, we saw that he was literally plastered with dirt from head to foot. He must have been rolling in the garden. He shrank from the light and went to his room. His eyes were horrible to look at. There was a green light behind them, not in them, if you understand, and the man's lower lip hung down.

Strickland said, 'There is going to be trouble—big trouble—tonight. Don't you change your riding-things.'

We waited and waited for Fleete's reappearance, and ordered dinner in the meantime. We could hear him moving about his own room, but there was no light there. Presently from the room came the long-drawn howl of a wolf.

People write and talk lightly of blood running cold and hair standing up and things of that kind. Both sensations are too horrible to be trifled with. My heart stopped as though a knife had been driven through it, and Strickland turned as white as the tablecloth.

The howl was repeated, and was answered by another howl far across the fields.

That set the gilded roof on the horror. Strickland dashed into Fleete's room. I followed, and we saw Fleete getting out of the window.

He made beast-noises in the back of his throat. He could not answer us when we shouted at him. He spat.

I don't quite remember what followed, but I think that Strickland must have stunned him with the long boot-jack* or else I should never have been able to sit on his chest. Fleete could not speak, he could only snarl, and his snarls were those of a wolf, not of a man. The human spirit must have been giving way all day and have died out with the twilight. We were dealing with a beast that had once been Fleete.

The affair was beyond any human and rational experience. I tried to say 'Hydrophobia,'* but the word wouldn't come, because I knew that I was lying.

We bound this beast with leather thongs of the punkah-rope,* and tied its thumbs and big toes together, and gagged it with a shoe-horn, which makes a very efficient gag if you know how to arrange it. Then we carried it into the dining-room, and sent a man to Dumoise, the doctor, telling him to come over at once. After we had despatched the messenger and were drawing breath, Strickland said, 'It's no good. This isn't any doctor's work.' I, also, knew that he spoke the truth.

The beast's head was free, and it threw it about from side to side. Any one entering the room would have believed that we were curing a wolf's pelt.* That was the most loathsome accessory of all.

Strickland sat with his chin in the heel of his fist, watching the beast as it wriggled on the ground, but saying nothing. The shirt had been torn open in the scuffle and showed the black rosette mark on the left breast. It stood out like a blister.

In the silence of the watching we heard something without mewing like a she-otter. We both rose to our feet, and, I answer for myself, not Strickland, felt sick—actually and physically sick. We told each other, as did the men in *Pinafore*, that it was the cat.*

Dumoise arrived, and I never saw a little man so unprofessionally shocked. He said that it was a heartrending case of hydrophobia, and that nothing could be done. At least any palliative measures would only prolong the agony. The beast was foaming at the mouth. Fleete, as we told Dumoise, had been bitten by dogs once or twice. Any man who keeps half a dozen terriers must expect a nip now and again. Dumoise could offer no help. He could only certify that Fleete was dying of hydrophobia. The beast was then howling, for it had managed to spit out the shoe-horn. Dumoise said that he would be ready to certify to the cause of death, and that the end was certain. He was a good little man, and he offered to remain with us; but Strickland refused the kindness. He did not wish to poison Dumoise's New Year. He would only ask him not to give the real cause of Fleete's death to the public.

So Dumoise left, deeply agitated; and as soon as the noise of the cart-wheels had died away, Strickland told me, in a whisper, his suspicions. They were so wildly improbable that he dared not say them out aloud; and I, who entertained all Strickland's beliefs, was so ashamed of owning to them that I pretended to disbelieve.

'Even if the Silver Man had bewitched Fleete for polluting the image of Hanuman, the punishment could not have fallen so quickly.'

As I was whispering this the cry outside the house rose again, and the beast fell into a fresh paroxysm of struggling till we were afraid that the thongs that held it would give way.

'Watch!' said Strickland. 'If this happens six times I shall take the law into my own hands. I order you to help me.'

He went into his room and came out in a few minutes with the barrels of an old shot-gun, a piece of fishing-line, some thick cord, and his heavy wooden bedstead. I reported that the convulsions had followed the cry by two seconds in each case, and the beast seemed perceptibly weaker.

Strickland muttered, 'But he can't take away the life! He can't take away the life!'

I said, though I knew that I was arguing against myself, 'It may be a cat. It must be a cat. If the Silver Man is responsible, why does he dare to come here?'

Strickland arranged the wood on the hearth, put the gun-barrels into the glow of the fire, spread the twine on the table and broke a walking stick in two. There was one yard of fishing line, gut, lapped with wire, such as is used for *mahseer*-fishing,* and he tied the two ends together in a loop.

Then he said, 'How can we catch him? He must be taken alive and unhurt.'

I said that we must trust in Providence, and go out softly with polo-sticks into the shrubbery at the front of the house. The man or animal that made the cry was evidently moving round the house as regularly as a night-watchman. We could wait in the bushes till he came by and knock him over.

Strickland accepted this suggestion, and we slipped out from a bath-room window into the front verandah and then across the carriage drive into the bushes.

In the moonlight we could see the leper coming round the corner of the house. He was perfectly naked, and from time to time he mewed and stopped to dance with his shadow. It was an unattractive sight, and thinking of poor Fleete, brought to such degradation by so foul a creature, I put away all my doubts and resolved to help Strickland from the heated gun-barrels to the loop of twine—from the loins to the head and back again—with all tortures that might be needful.

The leper halted in the front porch for a moment and we jumped out on him with the sticks. He was wonderfully strong, and we were afraid that he might escape or be fatally injured before we caught him. We had an idea that lepers were frail creatures, but this proved to be incorrect. Strickland knocked his legs from under him and I put my foot on his neck. He mewed hideously, and even through my riding-boots I could feel that his flesh was not the flesh of a clean man.

He struck at us with his hand and feet-stumps. We looped the lash of a dog-whip round him, under the armpits, and dragged him backwards into the hall and so into the dining-room where the beast lay. There we tied him with trunk-straps. He made no attempt to escape, but mewed.

When we confronted him with the beast the scene was beyond description. The beast doubled backwards into a bow as though he had been poisoned with strychnine,* and moaned in the most pitiable fashion. Several other things happened also, but they cannot be put down here.

'I think I was right,' said Strickland. 'Now we will ask him to cure this case.'

But the leper only mewed. Strickland wrapped a towel round his hand and took the gun-barrels out of the fire. I put the half of the broken walking stick through the loop of fishing-line and buckled the leper comfortably to Strickland's bedstead I understood then how men and women and little children can endure to see a witch burnt alive; for the beast was moaning on the floor, and though the Silver Man had no face, you could see horrible feelings passing through the slab that took its place, exactly as waves of heat play across red-hot iron—gun-barrels for instance.

Strickland shaded his eyes with his hands for a moment and we got to work. This part is not to be printed.

* * *

The dawn was beginning to break when the leper spoke. His mewings had not been satisfactory up to that point. The beast had fainted from exhaustion and the house was very still. We unstrapped the leper and told him to take away the evil spirit. He crawled to the beast and laid his hand upon the left breast. That was all. Then he fell face down and whined, drawing in his breath as he did so.

We watched the face of the beast, and saw the soul of Fleete coming back into the eyes. Then a sweat broke out on the forehead and the eyes—they were human eyes—closed. We waited for an hour but Fleete still slept. We carried him to his room and bade the leper go, giving him the bedstead, and the sheet on the bedstead to cover his nakedness, the gloves and the towels with which we had touched him, and the whip that had been hooked round his body. He put the sheet about him and went out into the early morning without speaking or mewing.

Strickland wiped his face and sat down. A night-gong, far away in the city, made seven o'clock.

'Exactly four-and-twenty hours!' said Strickland. 'And I've done enough to ensure my dismissal from the service, besides permanent quarters in a lunatic asylum. Do you believe that we are awake?'

The red-hot gun-barrel had fallen on the floor and was singeing the carpet. The smell was entirely real.

That morning at eleven we two together went to wake up Fleete. We looked and saw that the black leopard-rosette on his chest had disappeared. He was very drowsy and tired, but as soon as he saw us, he said, 'Oh! Confound you fellows. Happy New Year to you. Never mix your liquors. I'm nearly dead.'

'Thanks for your kindness, but you're over time,' said Strickland. 'To-day is the morning of the second. You've slept the clock round with a vengeance.'

The door opened, and little Dumoise put his head in. He had come on foot, and fancied that we were laying out Fleete.

'I've brought a nurse,' said Dumoise. 'I suppose that she can come in for . . . what is necessary.'

'By all means,' said Fleete cheerily, sitting up in bed. 'Bring on your nurses.'

Dumoise was dumb. Strickland led him out and explained that there must have been a mistake in the diagnosis. Dumoise remained dumb and left the house hastily. He considered that his professional reputation had been injured, and was inclined to make a personal matter of the recovery. Strickland went out too. When he came back, he said that he had been to call on the Temple of Hanuman to offer redress for the pollution of the god, and had been solemnly assured that no white man had ever touched the idol and that he was an incarnation of all the virtues labouring under a delusion. 'What do you think?' said Strickland.

I said, 'There are more things . . .'*

But Strickland hates that quotation. He says that I have worn it threadbare.

One other curious thing happened which frightened me as much as anything in all the night's work. When Fleete was dressed he came into the dining-room and sniffed. He had a quaint trick of moving his nose when he sniffed. 'Horrid doggy smell, here,' said he. 'You should really keep those terriers of yours in better order. Try sulphur, Strick.'

But Strickland did not answer. He caught hold of the back of a chair, and, without warning, went into an amazing fit of hysterics. It is terrible to see a strong man overtaken with hysteria. Then it struck me that we had fought for Fleete's soul with the Silver Man in that room, and had disgraced ourselves as Englishmen for ever, and I laughed and gasped and gurgled just as shamefully as Strickland, while Fleete thought that we had both gone mad. We never told him what we had done.

Some years later, when Strickland had married and was a church-going member of society for his wife's sake, we reviewed the incident dispassionately, and Strickland suggested that I should put it before the public.

I cannot myself see that this step is likely to clear up the mystery; because, in the first place, no one will believe a rather unpleasant story, and, in the second, it is well known to every right-minded man that the gods of the heathen are stone and brass, and any attempt to deal with them otherwise is justly condemned.

AMBROSE BIERCE

Chickamauga

⁂

ONE sunny autumn afternoon a child strayed away from its rude home in a small field and entered a forest unobserved. It was happy in a new sense of freedom from control—happy in the opportunity of exploration and adventure; for this child's spirit, in bodies of its ancestors, had for many thousands of years been trained to memorable feats of discovery and conquest—victories in battles whose critical moments were centuries, whose victors' camps were cities of hewn stone. From the cradle of its race it had conquered its way through two continents, and, passing a great sea, had penetrated a third, there to be born to war and dominance as a heritage.

The child was a boy, aged about six years, the son of a poor planter. In his younger manhood the father had been a soldier, had fought against naked savages, and followed the flag of his country into the capital of a civilized race to the far South.* In the peaceful life of a planter the warrior-fire survived; once kindled it is never extinguished. The man loved military books and pictures, and the boy had understood enough to make himself a wooden sword, though even the eye of his father would hardly have known it for what it was. This weapon he now bore bravely, as became the son of an heroic race, and, pausing now and again in the sunny spaces of the forest, assumed, with some exaggeration, the postures of aggression and defense that he had been taught by the engraver's art. Made reckless by the ease with which he overcame invisible foes attempting to stay his advance, he committed the common enough military error of pushing the pursuit to a dangerous extreme, until he found himself upon the margin of a wide but shallow brook, whose rapid waters barred his direct advance against the flying foe who had crossed with illogical ease. But the intrepid victor was not to be baffled; the spirit of the race which had passed the great sea burned unconquerable in that small breast and would not be denied. Finding a place where some bowlders in the bed of the stream lay but a step or a leap apart, he made his way across and fell again upon the rear guard of his imaginary foe, putting all to the sword.

Now that the battle had been won, prudence required that he withdraw to his base of operations. Alas! like many a mightier conquerer, and like one, the mightiest, he could not

> curb the lust for war,
> Nor learn that tempted Fate will leave the loftiest star.*

Advancing from the bank of the creek, he suddenly found himself confronted with a new and more formidable enemy; in the path that he was following, bolt upright, with ears erect and paws suspended before it, sat a rabbit. With a startled cry the child turned and fled, he knew not in what direction, calling with inarticulate cries for his mother, weeping, stumbling, his tender skin cruelly torn by brambles, his little heart beating hard with terror—breathless, blind with tears—lost in the forest! Then, for more than an hour, he wandered with erring feet through the tangled undergrowth, till at last, overcome with fatigue, he lay down in a narrow space between two rocks, within a few yards of the stream, and, still grasping his toy sword, no longer a weapon but a companion, sobbed himself to sleep. The wood birds sang merrily above his head; the squirrels, whisking their bravery of tail, ran barking from tree to tree, unconscious of the pity of it, and somewhere far away was a strange, muffled thunder, as if the partridges were drumming in celebration of nature's victory over the son of her immemorial enslavers. And back at the little plantation, where white men and black were hastily searching the fields and hedgerows in alarm, a mother's heart was breaking for her missing child.

Hours passed, and then the little sleeper rose to his feet. The chill of the evening was in his limbs, the fear of the gloom in his heart. But he had rested, and he no longer wept. With some blind instinct which impelled to action, he struggled through the undergrowth about him and came to a more open ground—on his right the brook, to the left a gentle acclivity* studded with infrequent trees; over all the gathering gloom of twilight. A thin, ghostly mist rose along the water. It frightened and repelled him; instead of recrossing, in the direction whence he had come, he turned his back upon it and went forward toward the dark inclosing wood. Suddenly he saw before him a strange moving object which he took to be some large animal—a dog, a pig—he could not name it; perhaps it was a bear. He had seen pictures of bears, but knew of nothing to their discredit, and had vaguely wished to meet one. But something in form or movement of this object—something in the awkwardness of its approach—told him that it was not a bear, and curiosity was stayed by fear. He stood still, and as it came slowly on, gained courage every moment, for he saw that at least it had not the long, menacing ears of the rabbit. Possibly his impression-able mind was half conscious of something familiar in its shambling, awkward gait. Before it had approached near enough to resolve his doubts, he saw that it was followed by another and another. To right and to left were many more; the whole open space about him was alive with them—all moving forward toward the brook.

They were men. They crept upon their hands and knees. They used their hands only, dragging their legs. They used their knees only, their arms hanging useless at their sides. They strove to rise to their feet, but fell prone in the attempt. They did nothing naturally, and nothing alike, save only to advance foot by foot in the same direc-tion. Singly, in pairs, and in little groups, they came on through the gloom, some halting now and again while others crept slowly past them, then resuming their movement. They came by dozens and by hundreds; as far on either hand as one could see in the deepening gloom they extended, and the black wood behind them appeared to be inexhaustible. The very ground seemed in motion toward the creek. Occasionally one who had paused did not again go on, but lay motionless. He was dead. Some, pausing, made strange gestures with their hands, erected their arms and lowered them again, clasped their heads; spread their palms upward, as men are sometimes seen to do in public prayer.

Not all of this did the child note; it is what would have been noted by an older observer; he saw little but that these were men, yet crept like babes. Being men, they were not terrible, though some of them were unfamiliarly clad. He moved among them freely, going from one to another and peering into their faces with childish curiosity. All their faces were singularly white and many were streaked and gouted with red. Something in this—something too, perhaps, in their grotesque attitudes and movements—reminded him of the painted clown whom he had seen last summer in the circus, and he laughed as he watched them. But on and ever on they crept, these maimed and bleeding men, as heedless as he of the dramatic contrast between his laughter and their own ghastly gravity. To him it was a merry spectacle. He had seen his father's negroes creep upon their hands and knees for his amusement—had ridden them so, 'making believe' they were his horses. He now approached one of these crawling figures from behind and with an agile movement mounted it astride. The man sank upon his breast, recovered, flung the small boy fiercely to the ground as an unbroken colt might have done, then turned upon him a face that lacked a lower jaw—from the upper teeth to the throat was a great red gap fringed with hanging shreds of flesh and splinters of bone. The unnatural prominence of nose, the absence of chin, the fierce eyes, gave this man the appearance of a great bird of prey crimsoned in throat and breast by the blood of its quarry. The man rose to his knees, the child to his feet. The man shook his fist at the child; the child, terrified at last, ran to a tree near by, got upon the farther side of it, and took a more serious view of the situation. And so the uncanny multitude dragged itself slowly and painfully along in hideous pantomime—moved forward down the slope like a swarm of great black beetles, with never a sound of going—in silence profound, absolute.

Instead of darkening, the haunted landscape began to brighten. Through the belt of trees beyond the brook shone a strange red light, the trunks and branches of the trees making a black lacework against it. It struck the creeping figures and gave them monstrous shadows, which caricatured their movements on the lit grass. It fell upon their faces, touching their whiteness with a ruddy tinge, accentuating the stains with which so many of them were freaked and maculated.* It sparkled on buttons and bits of metal in their clothing. Instinctively the child turned toward the growing splendor and moved down the slope with his horrible companions; in a few moments had passed the foremost of the throng—not much of a feat, considering his advantages. He placed himself in the lead, his wooden sword still in hand, and solemnly directed the march, conforming his pace to theirs and occasionally turning as if to see that his forces did not straggle. Surely such a leader never before had such a following.

Scattered about upon the ground now slowly narrowing by the encroachment of this awful march to water, were certain articles to which, in the leader's mind, were coupled no significant associations; an occasional blanket, tightly rolled lengthwise, doubled and the ends bound together with a string; a heavy knapsack here, and there a broken musket—such things, in short, as are found in the rear of retreating troops, the 'spoor'* of men flying from their hunters. Everywhere near the creek, which here had a margin of lowland, the earth was trodden into mud by the feet of men and horses. An observer of better experience in the use of his eyes would have noticed that these footprints pointed in both directions; the ground had been twice passed over—in advance and in retreat. A few hours before, these desperate, stricken men, with their more fortunate and now distant comrades, had penetrated the forest in thousands. Their successive battalions, breaking into swarms and reforming in lines, had passed the child on every side—had almost trodden on him as he slept. The rustle and murmur of their march had not awakened him. Almost within a stone's throw of where he lay they had fought a battle; but all unheard by him were the roar of the musketry, the shock of the cannon, 'the thunder of the captains and the shouting.'* He had slept through it all, grasping his little wooden sword with perhaps a tighter clutch in unconscious sympathy with his martial environment, but as heedless of the grandeur of the struggle as the dead who died to make the glory.

The fire beyond the belt of woods on the farther side of the creek, reflected to earth from the canopy of its own smoke, was now suffusing the whole landscape. It transformed the sinuous line of mist to the vapor of gold. The water gleamed with dashes of red, and red, too, were many of the stones protruding above the surface. But that was blood; the less desperately wounded had stained them in crossing. On them, too, the child now crossed with eager steps; he was going to the fire. As he stood upon the farther bank, he turned about to look at the companions of his march. The advance was arriving at the creek. The stronger had already drawn themselves to the brink and plunged their faces in the flood. Three or four who lay without motion appeared to have no heads. At this the child's eyes expanded with wonder; even his hospitable understanding could not accept a phenomenon implying such vitality as that. After slaking their thirst these men had not the strength to back away from the water, nor to keep their heads above it. They were drowned. In rear of these the open spaces of the forest showed the leader as many formless figures of his grim command as at first; but not nearly so many were in motion. He waved his cap for their encouragement and smilingly pointed with his weapon in the direction of the guiding light—a pillar of fire to this strange exodus.*

Confident of the fidelity of his forces, he now entered the belt of woods, passed through it easily in the red illumination, climbed a fence, ran across a field, turning now and again to coquette with his responsive shadow, and so approached the blazing ruin of a dwelling. Desolation everywhere. In all the wide glare not a living thing was visible. He cared nothing for that; the spectacle pleased, and he danced with glee in imitation of the wavering flames. He ran about collecting fuel, but every object that he found was too heavy for him to cast in from the distance to which the heat limited his approach. In despair he flung in his sword—a surrender to the superior forces of nature. His military career was at an end.

Shifting his position, his eyes fell upon some outbuildings which had an oddly familiar appearance, as if he had dreamed of them. He stood considering them with wonder, when suddenly the entire plantation, with its inclosing forest, seemed to turn as if upon a pivot. His little world swung half around; the points of the compass were reversed. He recognized the blazing building as his own home!

For a moment he stood stupefied by the power of the revelation, then ran with stumbling feet, making a half circuit of the ruin. There, conspicuous in the light of the conflagration, lay the dead body of a woman—the white face turned upward, the hands thrown out and clutched full of grass, the clothing deranged, the long dark hair in tangles and full of clotted blood. The greater part of the forehead was torn away, and from the jagged hole the brain protruded, over-flowing the temple, a frothy mass of gray, crowned with clusters of crimson bubbles—the work of a shell!

The child moved his little hands, making wild, uncertain gestures. He uttered a series of inarticulate and indescribable cries—something between the chattering of an ape and the gobbling of a turkey—a startling, soulless, unholy sound, the language of a devil. The child was a deaf mute.

Then he stood motionless, with quivering lips, looking down upon the wreck.

CHARLOTTE PERKINS GILMAN

The Yellow Wall Paper

❧❧

I
T is very seldom that mere ordinary people like John and myself secure ancestral halls for the summer.

A colonial mansion, a hereditary estate, I would say a haunted house, and reach the height of romantic felicity,—but that would be asking too much of fate!

Still I will proudly declare that there is something queer about it.

Else, why should it be let so cheaply? And why have stood so long untenanted?

John laughs at me, of course, but one expects that in marriage.

John is practical in the extreme. He has no patience with faith, an intense horror of superstition, and he scoffs openly at any talk of things not to be felt and seen and put down in figures.

John is a physician, and *perhaps*—(I would not say it to a living soul, of course, but this is dead paper and a great relief to my mind)—*perhaps* that is one reason I do not get well faster.

You see, he does not believe I am sick!

And what can one do?

If a physician of high standing, and one's own husband, assures friends and relatives that there is really nothing the matter with one but temporary nervous depression,—a slight hysterical tendency,*— what is one to do?

My brother is also a physician, and also of high standing, and he says the same thing.

So I take phosphates or phosphites,*—whichever it is,—and tonics, and journeys, and air, and exercise, and am absolutely forbidden to 'work' until I am well again.

Personally I disagree with their ideas.

Personally I believe that congenial work, with excitement and change, would do me good.

But what is one to do?

I did write for a while in spite of them; but it *does* exhaust me a good deal—having to be so sly about it, or else meet with heavy opposition.

I sometimes fancy that in my condition if I had less opposition and more society and stimulus—but John says the very worst thing I can do is to think about my condition, and I confess it always makes me feel bad.

So I will let it alone and talk about the house.

The most beautiful place! It is quite alone, standing well back from the road, quite three miles from the village. It makes me think of English places that you read about, for there are hedges and walls and gates that lock, and lots of separate little houses for the gardeners and people.

There is a *delicious* garden! I never saw such a garden—large and shady, full of box-bordered paths, and lined with long grape-covered arbors with seats under them.

There were greenhouses, too, but they are all broken now.

There was some legal trouble, I believe, something about the heirs and co-heirs; anyhow, the place has been empty for years.

That spoils my ghostliness, I am afraid; but I don't care—there is something strange about the house—I can feel it.

I even said so to John one moonlight evening, but he said what I felt was a *draught*, and shut the window.

I get unreasonably angry with John sometimes. I'm sure I never used to be so sensitive. I think it is due to this nervous condition.

But John says if I feel so I shall neglect proper self-control; so I take pains to control myself,—before him, at least,—and that makes me very tired.

I don't like our room a bit. I wanted one downstairs that opened on the piazza and had roses all over the window, and such pretty, old-fashioned chintz hangings! but John would not hear of it.

He said there was only one window and not room for two beds, and no near room for him if he took another.

He is very careful and loving, and hardly lets me stir without special direction.

I have a schedule prescription for each hour in the day; he takes all care from me, and so I feel basely ungrateful not to value it more.

He said we came here solely on my account, that I was to have perfect rest and all the air I could get. 'Your exercise depends on your strength, my dear,' said he, 'and your food somewhat on your appetite; but air you can absorb all the time.' So we took the nursery, at the top of the house.

It is a big, airy room, the whole floor nearly, with windows that look all ways, and air and sunshine galore. It was nursery first and then playground and gymnasium, I should judge; for the windows are barred for little children, and there are rings and things in the walls.

The paint and paper look as if a boys' school had used it. It is stripped off—the paper—in great patches all around the head of my bed, about as far as I can reach, and in a great place on the other side of the room low down. I never saw a worse paper in my life.

One of those sprawling flamboyant patterns committing every artistic sin.

It is dull enough to confuse the eye in following, pronounced enough to constantly irritate, and provoke study, and when you follow the lame, uncertain curves for a little distance they suddenly commit suicide—plunge off at outrageous angles, destroy themselves in unheard-of contradictions.

The color is repellant, almost revolting; a smouldering, unclean yellow, strangely faded by the slow-turning sunlight.

It is a dull yet lurid orange in some places, a sickly sulphur tint in others.

No wonder the children hated it! I should hate it myself if I had to live in this room long.

There comes John, and I must put this away,—he hates to have me write a word.

We have been here two weeks, and I haven't felt like writing before, since that first day.

I am sitting by the window now, up in this atrocious nursery, and there is nothing to hinder my writing as much as I please, save lack of strength.

John is away all day, and even some nights when his cases are serious.

I am glad my case is not serious!

But these nervous troubles are dreadfully depressing.

John does not know how much I really suffer. He knows there is no *reason* to suffer, and that satisfies him.

Of course it is only nervousness. It does weigh on me so not to do my duty in any way!

I meant to be such a help to John, such a real rest and comfort, and here I am a comparative burden already!

Nobody would believe what an effort it is to do what little I am able—to dress and entertain, and order things.

It is fortunate Mary is so good with the baby. Such a dear baby!

And yet I *cannot* be with him, it makes me so nervous.

I suppose John never was nervous in his life. He laughs at me so about this wall paper!

At first he meant to repaper the room, but afterwards he said that I was letting it get the better of me, and that nothing was worse for a nervous patient than to give way to such fancies.

He said that after the wall paper was changed it would be the heavy bedstead, and then the barred windows, and then that gate at the head of the stairs, and so on.

'You know the place is doing you good,' he said, 'and really, dear, I don't care to renovate the house just for a three months' rental.'

'Then do let us go downstairs,' I said, 'there are such pretty rooms there.'

Then he took me in his arms and called me a blessed little goose, and said he would go down cellar if I wished, and have it whitewashed into the bargain.

But he is right enough about the beds and windows and things.

It is as airy and comfortable a room as any one need wish, and, of course, I would not be so silly as to make him uncomfortable just for a whim.

I'm really getting quite fond of the big room, all but that horrid paper.

Out of one window I can see the garden, those mysterious deep-shaded arbors, the riotous old-fashioned flowers, and bushes and gnarly trees.

Out of another I get a lovely view of the bay and a little private wharf belonging to the estate. There is a beautiful shaded lane that runs down there from the house. I always fancy I see people walking in these numerous paths and arbors, but John has cautioned me not to give way to fancy in the least. He says that with my imaginative power and habit of story-making a nervous weakness like mine is sure to lead to all manner of excited fancies, and that I ought to use my will and good sense to check the tendency. So I try.

I think sometimes that if I were only well enough to write a little it would relieve the press of ideas and rest me.

But I find I get pretty tired when I try.

It is so discouraging not to have any advice and companionship about my work. When I get really well John says we will ask Cousin Henry and Julia down for a long visit; but he says he would as soon put fire-works in my pillow-case as to let me have those stimulating people about now.

I wish I could get well faster.

But I must not think about that. This paper looks to me as if it *knew* what a vicious influence it had!

There is a recurrent spot where the pattern lolls like a broken neck and two bulbous eyes stare at you upside-down.

I got positively angry with the impertinence of it and the everlastingness. Up and down and sideways they crawl, and those absurd, unblinking eyes are everywhere. There is one place where two breadths didn't match, and the eyes go all up and down the line, one a little higher than the other.

I never saw so much expression in an inanimate thing before, and we all know how much expression they have! I used to lie awake as a child and get more entertainment and terror out of blank walls and plain furniture than most children could find in a toystore.

I remember what a kindly wink the knobs of our big old bureau used to have, and there was one chair that always seemed like a strong friend.

I used to feel that if any of the other things looked too fierce I could always hop into that chair and be safe.

The furniture in this room is no worse than inharmonious, however, for we had to bring it all from downstairs. I suppose when this was used as a playroom they had to take the nursery things out, and no wonder! I never saw such ravages as the children have made here.

The wall paper, as I said before, is torn off in spots, and it sticketh closer than a brother*—they must have had perseverance as well as hatred.

Then the floor is scratched and gouged and splintered, the plaster itself is dug out here and there, and this great heavy bed, which is all we found in the room, looks as if it had been through the wars.

But I don't mind it a bit—only the paper.

There comes John's sister. Such a dear girl as she is, and so careful of me! I must not let her find me writing.

She is a perfect, an enthusiastic housekeeper, and hopes for no better profession. I verily believe she thinks it is the writing which made me sick!

But I can write when she is out, and see her a long way off from these windows.

There is one that commands the road, a lovely, shaded, winding road, and one that just looks off over the country. A lovely country, too, full of great elms and velvet meadows.

This wall paper has a kind of sub-pattern in a different shade, a particularly irritating one, for you can only see it in certain lights, and not clearly then.

But in the places where it isn't faded, and where the sun is just so, I can see a strange, provoking, formless sort of figure, that seems to sulk about behind that silly and conspicuous front design.

There's sister on the stairs!

Well, the Fourth of July is over! The people are all gone and I am tired out. John thought it might do me good to see a little company, so we just had mother and Nellie and the children down for a week.

Of course I didn't do a thing. Jennie sees to everything now.

But it tired me all the same.

John says if I don't pick up faster he shall send me to Weir Mitchell* in the fall.

But I don't want to go there at all. I had a friend who was in his hands once, and she says he is just like John and my brother, only more so!

Besides, it is such an undertaking to go so far.

I don't feel as if it was worth while to turn my hand over for anything, and I'm getting dreadfully fretful and querulous.

I cry at nothing, and cry most of the time.

Of course I don't when John is here, or anybody else, but when I am alone.

And I am alone a good deal just now. John is kept in town very often by serious cases, and Jennie is good and lets me alone when I want her to.

So I walk a little in the garden or down that lovely lane, sit on the porch under the roses, and lie down up here a good deal.

I'm getting really fond of the room in spite of the wall paper. Perhaps *because* of the wall paper.

It dwells in my mind so!

I lie here on this great immovable bed—it is nailed down, I believe—and follow that pattern about by the hour. It is as good as gymnastics, I assure you. I start, we'll say, at the bottom, down in the corner over there where it has not been touched, and I determine for the thousandth time that I *will* follow that pointless pattern to some sort of a conclusion.

I know a little of the principles of design,* and I know this thing was not arranged on any laws of radiation, or alternation, or repetition, or symmetry, or anything else that I ever heard of.

It is repeated, of course, by the breadths, but not otherwise.

Looked at in one way, each breadth stands alone, the bloated curves and flourishes—a kind of 'debased Romanesque' with *delirium tremens**—go waddling up and down in isolated columns of fatuity.

But, on the other hand, they connect diagonally, and the sprawling outlines run off in great slanting waves of optic horror, like a lot of wallowing seaweeds in full chase.

The whole thing goes horizontally, too, at least it seems so, and I exhaust myself in trying to distinguish the order of its going in that direction.

They have used a horizontal breadth for a frieze,* and that adds wonderfully to the confusion.

There is one end of the room where it is almost intact, and there, when the cross-lights fade and the low sun shines directly upon it, I can almost fancy radiation, after all,—the interminable grotesques seem to form around a common centre and rush off in headlong plunges of equal distraction.

It makes me tired to follow it. I will take a nap, I guess.

I don't know why I should write this.

I don't want to.

I don't feel able.

And I know John would think it absurd. But I *must* say what I feel and think in some way—it is such a relief!

But the effort is getting to be greater than the relief.

Half the time now I am awfully lazy, and lie down ever so much.

John says I mustn't lose my strength, and has me take cod-liver oil and lots of tonics and things, to say nothing of ale and wine and rare meat.*

Dear John! He loves me very dearly, and hates to have me sick. I tried to have a real earnest reasonable talk with him the other day, and tell him how I wished he would let me go and make a visit to Cousin Henry and Julia.

But he said I wasn't able to go, nor able to stand it after I got there; and I did not make out a very good case for myself, for I was crying before I had finished.

It is getting to be a great effort for me to think straight. Just this nervous weakness, I suppose.

And dear John gathered me up in his arms, and just carried me upstairs and laid me on the bed, and sat by me and read to me till he tired my head.

He said I was his darling and his comfort and all he had, and that I must take care of myself for his sake, and keep well.

He says no one but myself can help me out of it, that I must use my will and self-control and not let my silly fancies run away with me.

There's one comfort, the baby is well and happy, and does not have to occupy this nursery with the horrid wall paper.

If we had not used it that blessed child would have! What a fortunate escape! Why, I wouldn't have a child of mine, an impressionable little thing, live in such a room for worlds.

I never thought of it before, but it is lucky that John kept me here, after all. I can stand it so much easier than a baby, you see.

Of course I never mention it to them any more,—I am too wise,—but I keep watch of it all the same.

There are things in that paper that nobody knows but me, or ever will.

Behind that outside pattern the dim shapes get clearer every day.

It is always the same shape, only very numerous.

And it is like a woman stooping down and creeping about behind that pattern. I don't like it a bit. I wonder—I begin to think—I wish John would take me away from here!

It is so hard to talk with John about my case, because he is so wise, and because he loves me so.

But I tried it last night.

It was moonlight. The moon shines in all around, just as the sun does.

I hate to see it sometimes, it creeps so slowly, and always comes in by one window or another.

John was asleep and I hated to waken him, so I kept still and watched the moonlight on that undulating wall paper till I felt creepy.

The faint figure behind seemed to shake the pattern, just as if she wanted to get out.

I got up softly and went to feel and see if the paper *did* move, and when I came back John was awake.

'What is it, little girl?' he said. 'Don't go walking about like that— you'll get cold.'

I thought it was a good time to talk, so I told him that I really was not gaining here, and that I wished he would take me away.

'Why, darling!' said he, 'our lease will be up in three weeks, and I can't see how to leave before.

'The repairs are not done at home, and I cannot possibly leave town just now. Of course if you were in any danger I could and would, but you really are better, dear, whether you can see it or not. I am a doctor, dear, and I know. You are gaining flesh and color, your appetite is better. I feel really much easier about you.'

'I don't weigh a bit more,' said I, 'nor as much; and my appetite may be better in the evening, when you are here, but it is worse in the morning, when you are away.'

'Bless her little heart!' said he with a big hug; 'she shall be as sick as she pleases. But now let's improve the shining hours by going to sleep, and talk about it in the morning.'

'And you won't go away?' I asked gloomily.

'Why, how can I, dear? It is only three weeks more and then we will take a nice little trip of a few days while Jennie is getting the house ready. Really, dear, you are better!'

'Better in body, perhaps'—I began, and stopped short, for he sat up straight and looked at me with such a stern, reproachful look that I could not say another word.

'My darling,' said he, 'I beg of you, for my sake and for our child's sake, as well as for your own, that you will never for one instant let that idea enter your mind! There is nothing so dangerous, so fascinating, to a temperament like yours. It is a false and foolish fancy. Can you not trust me as a physician when I tell you so?'

So of course I said no more on that score, and we went to sleep before long. He thought I was asleep first, but I wasn't,—I lay there for hours trying to decide whether that front pattern and the back pattern really did move together or separately.

On a pattern like this, by daylight, there is a lack of sequence, a defiance of law, that is a constant irritant to a normal mind.

The color is hideous enough, and unreliable enough, and infuriating enough, but the pattern is torturing.

You think you have mastered it, but just as you get well under way in following, it turns a back somersault, and there you are. It slaps you in the face, knocks you down, and tramples upon you. It is like a bad dream.

The outside pattern is a florid arabesque,* reminding one of a fungus. If you can imagine a toadstool in joints, an interminable string of toadstools, budding and sprouting in endless convolutions,—why, that is something like it.

That is, sometimes!

There is one marked peculiarity about this paper, a thing nobody seems to notice but myself, and that is that it changes as the light changes.

When the sun shoots in through the east window—I always watch for that first long, straight ray—it changes so quickly that I never can quite believe it.

That is why I watch it always.

By moonlight—the moon shines in all night when there is a moon—I wouldn't know it was the same paper.

At night in any kind of light, in twilight, candlelight, lamplight, and worst of all by moonlight, it becomes bars! The outside pattern, I mean, and the woman behind it is as plain as can be.

I didn't realize for a long time what the thing was that showed behind,—that dim sub-pattern,—but now I am quite sure it is a woman.

By daylight she is subdued, quiet. I fancy it is the pattern that keeps her so still. It is so puzzling. It keeps me quiet by the hour.

I lie down ever so much now. John says it is good for me, and to sleep all I can.

Indeed, he started the habit by making me lie down for an hour after each meal.

It is a very bad habit, I am convinced, for, you see, I don't sleep.

And that cultivates deceit, for I don't tell them I'm awake,—oh, no! The fact is, I am getting a little afraid of John.

He seems very queer sometimes, and even Jennie has an inexplicable look.

It strikes me occasionally, just as a scientific hypothesis, that perhaps it is the paper!

I have watched John when he did not know I was looking, and come into the room suddenly on the most innocent excuses, and I've caught him several times *looking at the paper!* And Jennie too. I caught Jennie with her hand on it once.

She didn't know I was in the room, and when I asked her in a quiet, a very quiet voice, with the most restrained manner possible, what she was doing with the paper she turned around as if she had been caught stealing, and looked quite angry—asked me why I should frighten her so!

Then she said that the paper stained everything it touched, that she had found yellow smooches* on all my clothes and John's, and she wished we would be more careful!

Did not that sound innocent? But I know she was studying that pattern, and I am determined that nobody shall find it out but myself!

Life is very much more exciting now than it used to be. You see I have something more to expect, to look forward to, to watch. I really do eat better, and am more quiet than I was.

John is so pleased to see me improve! He laughed a little the other day, and said I seemed to be flourishing in spite of my wall paper.

I turned it off with a laugh. I had no intention of telling him it was *because* of the wall paper—he would make fun of me. He might even want to take me away.

I don't want to leave now until I have found it out. There is a week more, and I think that will be enough.

I'm feeling ever so much better! I don't sleep much at night, for it is so interesting to watch developments; but I sleep a good deal in the daytime.

In the daytime it is tiresome and perplexing.

There are always new shoots on the fungus, and new shades of yellow all over it. I cannot keep count of them, though I have tried conscientiously.

It is the strangest yellow, that wall paper! It makes me think of all the yellow things I ever saw—not beautiful ones like buttercups, but old foul, bad yellow things.

But there is something else about that paper—the smell! I noticed it the moment we came into the room, but with so much air and sun it was not bad. Now we have had a week of fog and rain, and whether the windows are open or not the smell is here.

It creeps all over the house.

I find it hovering in the dining-room, skulking in the parlor, hiding in the hall, lying in wait for me on the stairs.

It gets into my hair.

Even when I go to ride, if I turn my head suddenly and surprise it—there is that smell!

Such a peculiar odor, too! I have spent hours in trying to analyze it, to find what it smelled like.

It is not bad—at first, and very gentle, but quite the subtlest, most enduring odor I ever met.

In this damp weather it is awful. I wake up in the night and find it hanging over me.

It used to disturb me at first. I thought seriously of burning the house—to reach the smell.

But now I am used to it. The only thing I can think of that it is like is the *color* of the paper—a yellow smell!

There is a very funny mark on this wall, low down, near the mop-board. A streak that runs around the room. It goes behind every piece of furniture, except the bed, a long, straight, even *smooch*, as if it had been rubbed over and over.

I wonder how it was done and who did it, and what they did it for. Round and round and round—round and round and round—it makes me dizzy!

I really have discovered something at last.

Through watching so much at night, when it changes so, I have finally found out.

The front pattern *does* move—and no wonder! The woman behind shakes it!

Sometimes I think there are a great many women behind, and sometimes only one, and she crawls around fast, and her crawling shakes it all over.

Then in the very bright spots she keeps still, and in the very shady spots she just takes hold of the bars and shakes them hard.

And she is all the time trying to climb through. But nobody could climb through that pattern—it strangles so; I think that is why it has so many heads.*

They get through, and then the pattern strangles them off and turns them upside-down, and makes their eyes white!

If those heads were covered or taken off it would not be half so bad.

I think that woman gets out in the daytime!

And I'll tell you why—privately—I've seen her!

I can see her out of every one of my windows!

It is the same woman, I know, for she is always creeping, and most women do not creep by daylight.

I see her in that long shaded lane, creeping up and down. I see her in those dark grape arbors, creeping all around the garden.

I see her on that long road under the trees, creeping along, and when a carriage comes she hides under the blackberry vines.

I don't blame her a bit. It must be very humiliating to be caught creeping by daylight!

I always lock the door when I creep by daylight. I can't do it at night, for I know John would suspect something at once.

And John is so queer, now, that I don't want to irritate him. I wish he would take another room! Besides, I don't want anybody to get that woman out at night but myself.

I often wonder if I could see her out of all the windows at once.

But, turn as fast as I can, I can only see out of one at one time.

And though I always see her she *may* be able to creep faster than I can turn!

I have watched her sometimes away off in the open country, creeping as fast as a cloud shadow in a high wind.

If only that top pattern could be gotten off from the under one! I mean to try it, little by little.

I have found out another funny thing, but I shan't tell it this time! It does not do to trust people too much.

There are only two more days to get this paper off, and I believe John is beginning to notice. I don't like the look in his eyes.

And I heard him ask Jennie a lot of professional questions about me. She had a very good report to give.

She said I slept a good deal in the daytime.

John knows I don't sleep very well at night, for all I'm so quiet!

He asked me all sorts of questions, too, and pretended to be very loving and kind.

As if I couldn't see through him!

Still, I don't wonder he acts so, sleeping under this paper for three months.

It only interest me, but I feel sure John and Jennie are secretly affected by it.

Hurrah! This is the last day, but it is enough. John is to stay in town over night, and won't be out until this evening.

Jennie wanted to sleep with me—the sly thing! but I told her I should undoubtedly rest better for a night all alone.

That was clever, for really I wasn't alone a bit! As soon as it was moonlight, and that poor thing began to crawl and shake the pattern, I got up and ran to help her.

I pulled and she shook, I shook and she pulled, and before morning we had peeled off yards of that paper.

A strip about as high as my head and half around the room.

And then when the sun came and that awful pattern began to laugh at me I declared I would finish it today!

We go away to-morrow, and they are moving all my furniture down again to leave things as they were before.

Jennie looked at the wall in amazement, but I told her merrily that I did it out of pure spite at the vicious thing.

She laughed and said she wouldn't mind doing it herself, but I must not get tired.

How she betrayed herself that time!

But I am here, and no person touches this paper but me—not *alive!*

She tried to get me out of the room—it was too patent! But I said it was so quiet and empty and clean now that I believed I would lie down again and sleep all I could; and not to wake me even for dinner—I would call when I woke.

So now she is gone, and the servants are gone, and the things are gone, and there is nothing left but that great bedstead nailed down, with the canvas mattress we found on it.

We shall sleep downstairs to-night, and take the boat home to-morrow.

I quite enjoy the room, now it is bare again.

How those children did tear about here!

This bedstead is fairly gnawed!

But I must get to work.

I have locked the door and thrown the key down into the front path.

I don't want to go out, and I don't want to have anybody come in, till John comes.

I want to astonish him.

I've got a rope up here that even Jennie did not find. If that woman does get out, and tries to get away, I can tie her!

But I forgot I could not reach far without anything to stand on!

This bed will *not* move!

I tried to lift and push it until I was lame, and then I got so angry I bit off a little piece at one corner—but it hurt my teeth.

Then I peeled off all the paper I could reach standing on the floor. It sticks horribly and the pattern just enjoys it! All those strangled heads and bulbous eyes and waddling fungus growths just shriek with derision!

I am getting angry enough to do something desperate. To jump out of the window would be admirable exercise, but the bars are too strong even to try.

Besides, I wouldn't do it. Of course not. I know well enough that a step like that is improper and might be misconstrued.

I don't like to *look* out of the windows even—there are so many of those creeping women, and they creep so fast.

I wonder if they all come out of that wall paper, as I did?

But I am securely fastened now by my well-hidden rope—you don't get *me* out in the road there!

I suppose I shall have to get back behind the pattern when it comes night, and that is hard!

It is so pleasant to be out in this great room and creep around as I please!

I don't want to go outside. I won't, even if Jennie asks me to.

For outside you have to creep on the ground, and everything is green instead of yellow.

But here I can creep smoothly on the floor, and my shoulder just fits in that long smooch around the wall, so I cannot lose my way.

Why, there's John at the door!

It is no use, young man, you can't open it!

How he does call and pound!

Now he's crying for an axe.

It would be a shame to break down that beautiful door!

'John, dear!' said I in the gentlest voice, 'the key is down by the front steps, under a plantain leaf!'

That silenced him for a few moments.

Then he said—very quietly indeed, 'Open the door, my darling!'

'I can't,' said I. 'The key is down by the front door, under a plantain leaf!'

And then I said it again, several times, very gently and slowly, and said it so often that he had to go and see, and he got it, of course, and came in. He stopped short by the door.

'What is the matter?' he cried. 'For God's sake, what are you doing?'

I kept on creeping just the same, but I looked at him over my shoulder.

'I've got out at last,' said I, 'in spite of you and Jane! And I've pulled off most of the paper, so you can't put me back!'

Now why should that man have fainted? But he did, and right across my path by the wall, so that I had to creep over him every time!

ARTHUR CONAN DOYLE

The Case of Lady Sannox

꧂

THE relations between Douglas Stone and the notorious Lady Sannox were very well known both among the fashionable circles of which she was a brilliant member, and the scientific bodies which numbered him among their most illustrious *confrères*.* There was naturally, therefore, a very widespread interest when it was announced one morning that the lady had absolutely and for ever taken the veil, and that the world would see her no more. When, at the very tail of this rumour, there came the assurance that the celebrated operating surgeon, the man of steel nerves, had been found in the morning by his valet, seated on one side of his bed, smiling pleasantly upon the universe, with both legs jammed into one side of his breeches and his great brain about as valuable as a cap full of porridge, the matter was strong enough to give quite a little thrill of interest to folk who had never hoped that their jaded nerves were capable of such a sensation.

Douglas Stone in his prime was one of the most remarkable men in England. Indeed, he could hardly be said to have ever reached his prime, for he was but nine-and-thirty at the time of this little incident. Those who knew him best were aware that famous as he was as a surgeon, he might have succeeded with even greater rapidity in any of a dozen lines of life. He could have cut his way to fame as a soldier, struggled to it as an explorer, bullied for it in the courts, or built it out of stone and iron as an engineer. He was born to be great, for he could plan what another man dare not do, and he could do what another man dare not plan. In surgery none could follow him. His nerve, his judgment, his intuition, were things apart. Again and again his knife cut away death, but grazed the very springs of life in doing it, until his assistants were as white as the patient. His energy, his audacity, his full-blooded self-confidence—does not the memory of them still linger to the south of Marylebone Road and the north of Oxford Street?*

His vices were as magnificent as his virtues, and infinitely more picturesque. Large as was his income, and it was the third largest of all professional men in London, it was far beneath the luxury of his living. Deep in his complex nature lay a rich vein of sensualism, at the sport of which he placed all the prizes of his life. The eye, the ear, the touch, the palate, all were his masters. The bouquet of old vintages, the scent of rare exotics, the curves and tints of the daintiest potteries of Europe, it was to these that the quick-running stream of gold was transformed. And then there came his sudden mad passion for Lady Sannox, when a single interview with two challenging glances and a whispered word set him ablaze. She was the loveliest woman in London, and the only one to him. He was one of the handsomest men in London, but not the only one to her. She had a liking for new experiences, and was gracious to most men who wooed her. It may have been cause or it may have been effect that Lord Sannox looked fifty, though he was but six-and-thirty.

He was a quiet, silent, neutral-tinted man this lord, with thin lips and heavy eyelids, much given to gardening, and full of home-like habits. He had at one time been fond of acting, had even rented a theatre in London, and on its boards had first seen Miss Marion Dawson, to whom he had offered his hand, his title, and the third of a county. Since his marriage this early hobby had become distasteful to him. Even in private theatricals it was no longer possible to persuade him to exercise the talent which he had often shown that he possessed. He was happier with a spud* and a watering can among his orchids and chrysanthemums.

It was quite an interesting problem whether he was absolutely devoid of sense, or miserably wanting in spirit. Did he know his lady's ways and condone them, or was he a mere blind, doting fool? It was a point to be discussed over the teacups in snug little drawing-rooms, or with the aid of a cigar in the bow windows of clubs. Bitter and plain were the comments among men upon his conduct. There was but one who had a good word to say for him, and he was the most silent member in the smoking-room. He had seen him break in a horse at the University, and it seemed to have left an impression upon his mind.

But when Douglas Stone became the favourite all doubts as to Lord Sannox's knowledge or ignorance were set for ever at rest. There was no subterfuge about Stone. In his high-handed, impetuous fashion, he set all caution and discretion at defiance. The scandal became notorious. A learned body intimated that his name had been struck from the list of its vice-presidents. Two friends implored him to consider his professional credit. He cursed them all three, and spent forty guineas on a bangle to take with him to the lady. He was at her house every evening, and she drove in his carriage in the afternoons. There was not an attempt on either side to conceal their relations; but there came at last a little incident to interrupt them.

It was a dismal winter's night, very cold and gusty, with the wind whooping in the chimneys and blustering against the window-panes. A thin spatter of rain tinkled on the glass with each fresh sough of the gale, drowning for the instant the dull gurgle and drip from the eaves. Douglas Stone had finished his dinner, and sat by his fire in the study, a glass of rich port upon the malachite* table at his elbow. As he raised it to his lips, he held it up against the lamplight, and watched with the eye of a connoisseur the tiny scales of beeswing* which floated in its rich ruby depths. The fire, as it spurted up, threw fitful lights upon his bold, clear-cut face, with its widely-opened grey eyes, its thick and yet firm lips, and the deep, square jaw, which had something Roman in its strength and its animalism. He smiled from time to time as he nestled back in his luxurious chair. Indeed, he had a right to feel well pleased, for, against the advice of six colleagues, he had performed an operation that day of which only two cases were on record, and the result had been brilliant beyond all expectation. No other man in London would have had the daring to plan, or the skill to execute, such a heroic measure.

But he had promised Lady Sannox to see her that evening and it was already half-past eight. His hand was outstretched to the bell to order the carriage when he heard the dull thud of the knocker. An instant later there was the shuffling of feet in the hall, and the sharp closing of a door.

'A patient to see you, sir, in the consulting room,' said the butler.

'About himself?'

'No, sir; I think he wants you to go out.'

'It is too late,' cried Douglas Stone peevishly. 'I won't go.'

'This is his card, sir.'

The butler presented it upon the gold salver which had been given to his master by the wife of a Prime Minister.

'"Hamil Ali, Smyrna."* Hum! The fellow is a Turk, I suppose.'

'Yes, sir. He seems as if he came from abroad, sir. And he's in a terrible way.'

'Tut, tut! I have an engagement. I must go somewhere else. But I'll see him. Show him in here, Pim.'

A few moments later the butler swung open the door and ushered in a small and decrepid man, who walked with a bent back and with the forward push of the face and blink of the eyes which goes with extreme short sight. His face was swarthy, and his hair and beard of the deepest black. In one hand he held a turban of white muslin striped with red, in the other a small chamois leather bag.

'Good evening,' said Douglas Stone, when the butler had closed the door. 'You speak English, I presume?'

'Yes, sir. I am from Asia Minor,* but I speak English when I speak slow.'

'You wanted me to go out, I understand?'

'Yes, sir. I wanted very much that you should see my wife.'

'I could come in the morning, but I have an engagement which prevents me from seeing your wife to-night.'

The Turk's answer was a singular one. He pulled the string which closed the mouth of the chamois leather bag, and poured a flood of gold on to the table.

'There are one hundred pounds there,' said he, 'and I promise you that it will not take you an hour. I have a cab ready at the door.'

Douglas Stone glanced at his watch. An hour would not make it too late to visit Lady Sannox. He had been there later. And the fee was an extraordinarily high one. He had been pressed by his creditors lately, and he could not afford to let such a chance pass. He would go.

'What is the case?' he asked,

'Oh, it is so sad a one! So sad a one! You have not, perhaps, heard of the daggers of the Almohades?'*

'Never.'

'Ah, they are Eastern daggers of a great age and of a singular shape, with the hilt like what you call a stirrup. I am a curiosity dealer, you understand, and that is why I have come to England from Smyrna, but next week I go back once more. Many things I brought with me, and I have a few things left, but among them, to my sorrow, is one of these daggers.'

'You will remember that I have an appointment, sir,' said the surgeon, with some irritation; 'pray confine yourself to the necessary details.'

'You will see that it is necessary. To-day my wife fell down in a faint in the room in which I keep my wares, and she cut her lower lip upon this cursed dagger of Almohades.'

'I see,' said Douglas Stone, rising. 'And you wish me to dress the wound?'

'No, no, it is worse than that.'

'What then?'

'These daggers are poisoned.'

'Poisoned!'

'Yes, and there is no man, East or West, who can tell now what is the poison or what the cure. But all that is known I know, for my father was in this trade before me, and we have had much to do with these poisoned weapons.'

'What are the symptoms?'

'Deep sleep, and death in thirty hours.'

'And you say there is no cure. Why then should you pay me this considerable fee?'

'No drug can cure, but the knife may.'

'And how?'

'The poison is slow of absorption. It remains for hours in the wound.'

'Washing, then, might cleanse it?'

'No more than in a snake bite. It is too subtle and too deadly.'

'Excision of the wound, then?'

'That is it. If it be on the finger, take the finger off. So said my father always. But think of where this wound is, and that it is my wife. It is dreadful!'

But familiarity with such grim matters may take the finer edge from a man's sympathy. To Douglas Stone this was already an interesting case, and he brushed aside as irrelevant the feeble objections of the husband.

'It appears to be that or nothing,' said he brusquely. 'It is better to lose a lip than a life.'

'Ah, yes, I know that you are right. Well, well, it is kismet,* and it must be faced. I have the cab, and you will come with me and do this thing.'

Douglas Stone took his case of bistouries* from a drawer, and placed it with a roll of bandage and a compress of lint in his pocket. He must waste no more time if he were to see Lady Sannox.

'I am ready,' said he, pulling on his overcoat. 'Will you take a glass of wine before you go out into this cold air?'

His visitor shrank away, with a protesting hand upraised.

'You forget that I am a Mussulman,* and a true follower of the Prophet,' said he. 'But tell me what is the bottle of green glass which you have placed in your pocket?'

'It is chloroform.'*

'Ah, that also is forbidden to us. It is a spirit, and we make no use of such things.'

'What! You would allow your wife to go through an operation without an anæsthetic?'

'Ah! she will feel nothing, poor soul. The deep sleep has already come on, which is the first working of the poison. And then I have given her of our Smyrna opium. Come, sir, for already an hour has passed.'

As they stepped out into the darkness, a sheet of rain was driven in upon their faces, and the hall lamp, which dangled from the arm of a marble Caryatid,* went out with a fluff. Pim, the butler, pushed the heavy door to, straining hard with his shoulder against the wind, while the two men groped their way towards the yellow glare which showed where the cab was waiting. An instant later they were rattling upon their journey.

'Is it far?' asked Douglas Stone.

'Oh, no. We have a very little quiet place off the Euston Road.'*

The surgeon pressed the spring of his repeater* and listened to the little tings which told him the hour. It was a quarter past nine. He calculated the distances, and the short time which it would take him to perform so trivial an operation. He ought to reach Lady Sannox by ten o'clock. Through the fogged windows he saw the blurred gas lamps dancing past, with occasionally the broader glare of a shop front. The rain was pelting and rattling upon the leathern top of the carriage, and the wheels swashed as they rolled through puddle and mud. Opposite to him the white headgear of his companion gleamed faintly through the obscurity. The surgeon felt in his pockets and arranged his needles, his ligatures and his safety-pins, that no time might be wasted when they arrived. He chafed with impatience and drummed his foot upon the floor.

But the cab slowed down at last and pulled up. In an instant Douglas Stone was out, and the Smyrna merchant's toe was at his very heel.

'You can wait,' said he to the driver.

It was a mean-looking house in a narrow and sordid street. The surgeon, who knew his London well, cast a swift glance into the shadows, but there was nothing distinctive,—no shop, no movement, nothing but a double line of dull, flat-faced houses, a double stretch of wet flagstones which gleamed in the lamplight, and a double rush of water in the gutters which swirled and gurgled towards the sewer gratings. The door which faced them was blotched and discoloured, and a faint light in the fan pane above it served to show the dust and the grime which covered it. Above, in one of the bedroom windows, there was a dull yellow glimmer. The merchant knocked loudly, and, as he turned his dark face towards the light, Douglas Stone could see that it was contracted with anxiety. A bolt was drawn, and an elderly woman with a taper stood in the doorway, shielding the thin flame with her gnarled hand.

'Is all well?' gasped the merchant.

'She is as you left her, sir.'

'She has not spoken?'

'No, she is in a deep sleep.'

The merchant closed the door, and Douglas Stone walked down the narrow passage, glancing about him in some surprise as he did so. There was no oilcloth, no mat, no hat-rack. Deep grey dust and heavy festoons of cobwebs met his eyes everywhere. Following the old woman up the winding stair, his firm footfall echoed harshly through the silent house. There was no carpet.

The bedroom was on the second landing. Douglas Stone followed the old nurse into it, with the merchant at his heels. Here, at least, there was furniture and to spare. The floor was littered and the corners piled with Turkish cabinets, inlaid tables, coats of chain mail, strange pipes, and grotesque weapons. A single small lamp stood upon a bracket on the wall. Douglas Stone took it down, and picking his way among the lumber, walked over to a couch in the corner, on which lay a woman dressed in the Turkish fashion, with yashmak and veil. The lower part of the face was exposed, and the surgeon saw a jagged cut which zigzagged along the border of the under lip.

'You will forgive the yashmak,' said the Turk. 'You know our views about woman in the East.'

But the surgeon was not thinking about the yashmak. This was no longer a woman to him. It was a case. He stooped and examined the wound carefully.

'There are no signs of irritation,' said he. 'We might delay the operation until local symptoms develop.'

The husband wrung his hands in incontrollable agitation.

'Oh! sir, sir,' he cried. 'Do not trifle. You do not know. It is deadly. I know, and I give you my assurance that an operation is absolutely necessary. Only the knife can save her.'

'And yet I am inclined to wait,' said Douglas Stone.

'That is enough,' the Turk cried, angrily. 'Every minute is of importance, and I cannot stand here and see my wife allowed to sink. It only remains for me to give you my thanks for having come, and to call in some other surgeon before it is too late.'

Douglas Stone hesitated. To refund that hundred pounds was no pleasant matter. But of course if he left the case he must return the money. And if the Turk were right and the woman died, his position before a coroner might be an embarrassing one.

'You have had personal experience of this poison?' he asked.

'I have.'

'And you assure me that an operation is needful.'

'I swear it by all that I hold sacred.'

'The disfigurement will be frightful.'

'I can understand that the mouth will not be a pretty one to kiss.'

Douglas Stone turned fiercely upon the man. The speech was a brutal one. But the Turk has his own fashion of talk and of thought, and there was no time for wrangling. Douglas Stone drew a bistoury from his case, opened it and felt the keen straight edge with his fore-finger. Then he held the lamp closer to the bed. Two dark eyes were gazing up at him through the slit in the yashmak. They were all iris, and the pupil was hardly to be seen.

'You have given her a very heavy dose of opium.'

'Yes, she has had a good dose.'

He glanced again at the dark eyes which looked straight at his own. They were dull and lustreless, but, even as he gazed, a little shifting sparkle came into them, and the lips quivered.

'She is not absolutely unconscious,' said he.

'Would it not be well to use the knife while it will be painless?'

The same thought had crossed the surgeon's mind. He grasped the wounded lip with his forceps, and with two swift cuts he took out a broad V-shaped piece. The woman sprang up on the couch with a dreadful gurgling scream. Her covering was torn from her face. It was a face that he knew. In spite of that protruding upper lip and that slobber of blood, it was a face that he knew. She kept on putting her hand up to the gap and screaming. Douglas Stone sat down at the foot of the couch with his knife and his forceps. The room was whirling round, and he had felt something go like a ripping seam behind his ear. A bystander would have said that his face was the more ghastly of the two. As in a dream, or as if he had been looking at something at the play, he was conscious that the Turk's hair and beard lay upon the table, and that Lord Sannox was leaning against the wall with his hand to his side, laughing silently. The screams had died away now, and the dreadful head had dropped back again upon the pillow, but Douglas Stone still sat motionless, and Lord Sannox still chuckled quietly to himself.

'It was really very necessary for Marion, this operation,' said he, 'not physically, but morally, you know, morally.'

Douglas Stone stooped forwards and began to play with the fringe of the coverlet. His knife tinkled down upon the ground, but he still held the forceps and something more.

'I had long intended to make a little example,' said Lord Sannox, suavely. 'Your note of Wednesday miscarried, and I have it here in my pocket-book. I took some pains in carrying out my idea. The wound, by the way, was from nothing more dangerous than my signet ring.'

He glanced keenly at his silent companion, and cocked the small revolver which he held in his coat pocket. But Douglas Stone was still picking at the coverlet.

'You see you have kept your appointment after all,' said Lord Sannox.

And at that Douglas Stone began to laugh. He laughed long and loudly. But Lord Sannox did not laugh now. Something like fear sharpened and hardened his features. He walked from the room, and he walked on tiptoe. The old woman was waiting outside.

'Attend to your mistress when she awakes,' said Lord Sannox.

Then he went down to the street. The cab was at the door, and the driver raised his hand to his hat.

'John,' said Lord Sannox, 'you will take the doctor home first. He will want leading downstairs, I think. Tell his butler that he has been taken ill at a case.'

'Very good, sir.'

'Then you can take Lady Sannox home.'

'And how about yourself, sir?'

'Oh, my address for the next few months will be Hotel di Roma, Venice.* Just see that the letters are sent on. And tell Stevens to exhibit all the purple chrysanthemums next Monday, and to wire me the result.'

BRAM STOKER

The Squaw

❧❧

NURNBERG* at the time was not so much exploited as it has been since then. Irving had not been playing *Faust*,* and the very name of the old town was hardly known to the great bulk of the travelling public. My wife and I being in the second week of our honeymoon, naturally wanted someone else to join our party, so that when the cheery stranger, Elias P. Hutcheson, hailing from Isthmian City, Bleeding Gulch, Maple Tree County, Neb.,* turned up at the station at Frankfort,* and casually remarked that he was going on to see the most all-fired old Methusaleh of a town in Yurrup,* and that he guessed that so much travelling alone was enough to send an intelligent, active citizen into the melancholy ward of a daft house, we took the pretty broad hint and suggested that we should join forces. We found, on comparing notes afterwards, that we had each intended to speak with some diffidence or hesitation so as not to appear too eager, such not being a good compliment to the success of our married life; but the effect was entirely marred by our both beginning to speak at the same instant—stopping simultaneously and then going on together again. Anyhow, no matter how, it was done; and Elias P. Hutcheson became one of our party. Straightway Amelia and I found the pleasant benefit; instead of quarrelling, as we had been doing, we found that the restraining influence of a third party was such that we now took every opportunity of spooning in odd corners. Amelia declares that ever since she has, as the result of that experience, advised all her friends to take a friend on the honeymoon. Well, we 'did' Nurnberg together, and much enjoyed the racy remarks of our Transatlantic friend, who, from his quaint speech and his wonderful stock of adventures, might have stepped out of a novel. We kept for the last object of interest in the city to be visited the Burg,* and on the day appointed for the visit strolled round the outer wall of the city by the eastern side.

The Burg is seated on a rock dominating the town, and an immensely deep fosse guards it on the northern side. Nurnberg has been happy in that it was never sacked; had it been it would certainly not be so spick and span perfect as it is at present. The ditch has not been used for centuries, and now its base is spread with tea-gardens and orchards, of which some of the trees are of quite respectable growth. As we wandered round the wall, dawdling in the hot July sunshine, we often paused to admire the views spread before us, and in especial the great plain covered with towns and villages and bounded with a blue line of hills, like a landscape of Claude Lorraine.* From this we always turned with new delight to the city itself, with its myriad of quaint old gables and acre-wide red roofs dotted with dormer windows, tier upon tier. A little to our right rose the towers of the Burg, and nearer still, standing grim, the Torture Tower, which was, and is, perhaps, the most interesting place in the city. For centuries the tradition of the Iron Virgin* of Nurnberg has been handed down as an instance of the horrors of cruelty of which man is capable; we had long looked forward to seeing it; and here at last was its home.

In one of our pauses we leaned over the wall of the moat and looked down. The garden seemed quite fifty or sixty feet below us, and the sun pouring into it with an intense, moveless heat like that of an oven. Beyond rose the grey, grim wall seemingly of endless height, and losing itself right and left in the angles of bastion and counterscarp.* Trees and bushes crowned the wall, and above again towered the lofty houses on whose massive beauty Time has only set the hand of approval. The sun was hot and we were lazy; time was our own, and we lingered, leaning on the wall. Just below us was a pretty sight— a great black cat lying stretched in the sun, whilst round her gambolled prettily a tiny black kitten. The mother would wave her tail for the kitten to play with, or would raise her feet and push away the little one as an encouragement to further play. They were just at the foot of the wall, and Elias P. Hutcheson, in order to help the play, stooped and took from the walk a moderate sized pebble.

'See!' he said, 'I will drop it near the kitten, and they will both wonder where it came from.'

'Oh, be careful,' said my wife; 'you might hit the dear little thing!'

'Not me, ma'am,' said Elias P. 'Why, I'm as tender as a Maine cherry-tree.* Lor, bless ye, I wouldn't hurt the poor pooty* little critter more'n I'd scalp a baby. An' you may bet your variegated socks on that! See, I'll drop it fur away on the outside so's not to go near her!' Thus saying, he leaned over and held his arm out at full length and dropped the stone. It may be that there is some attractive force which draws lesser matters to greater; or more probably that the wall was not plumb but sloped to its base—we not noticing the inclination from above; but the stone fell with a sickening thud that came up to us through the hot air, right on the kitten's head, and shattered out its little brains then and there. The black cat cast a swift upward glance, and we saw her eyes like green fire fixed an instant on Elias P. Hutcheson; and then her attention was given to the kitten, which lay still with just a quiver of her tiny limbs, whilst a thin red stream trickled from a gaping wound. With a muffled cry, such as a human being might give, she bent over the kitten, licking its wound and moaning. Suddenly she seemed to realise that it was dead, and again threw her eyes up at us. I shall never forget the sight, for she looked the perfect incarnation of hate. Her green eyes blazed with lurid fire, and the white, sharp teeth seemed to almost shine through the blood which dabbled her mouth and whiskers. She gnashed her teeth, and her claws stood out stark and at full length on every paw. Then she made a wild rush up the wall as if to reach us, but when the momentum ended fell back, and further added to her horrible appearance for she fell on the kitten, and rose with her black fur smeared with its brains and blood. Amelia turned quite faint, and I had to lift her back from the wall. There was a seat close by in shade of a spreading plane-tree, and here I placed her whilst she composed herself. Then I went back to Hutcheson, who stood without moving, looking down on the angry cat below.

As I joined him, he said:

'Wall, I guess that air the savagest beast I ever see—'cept once when an Apache squaw had an edge on a half-breed what they nicknamed "Splinters" 'cos of the way he fixed up her papoose* which he stole on a raid just to show that he appreciated the way they had given his mother the fire torture. She got that kinder look so set on her face that it jest seemed to grow there. She followed Splinters more'n three year till at last the braves got him and handed him over to her. They did say that no man, white or Injun, had ever been so long a-dying under the tortures of the Apaches. The only time I ever see her smile was when I wiped her out. I kem on the camp just in time to see Splinters pass in his checks, and he wasn't sorry to go either. He was a hard citizen, and though I never could shake with him after that papoose business—for it was bitter bad, and he should have been a white man, for he looked like one—I see he had got paid out in full. Durn me, but I took a piece of his hide from one of his skinnin' posts an' had it made into a pocket-book. It's here now!' and he slapped the breast pocket of his coat.

Whilst he was speaking the cat was continuing her frantic efforts to get up the wall. She would take a run back and then charge up, sometimes reaching an incredible height. She did not seem to mind the heavy fall which she got each time but started with renewed vigour; and at every tumble her appearance became more horrible. Hutcheson was a kind-hearted man—my wife and I had both noticed little acts of kindness to animals as well as to persons—and he seemed concerned at the state of fury to which the cat had wrought herself.

'Wall, now!' he said, 'I du declare that that poor critter seems quite desperate. There! there! poor thing, it was all an accident—though that won't bring back your little one to you. Say! I wouldn't have had such a thing happen for a thousand! Just shows what a clumsy fool of a man can do when he tries to play! Seems I'm too darned slipper-handed* to even play with a cat. Say Colonel!' it was a pleasant way he had to bestow titles freely—'I hope your wife don't hold no grudge against me on account of this unpleasantness? Why, I wouldn't have had it occur on no account.'

He came over to Amelia and apologised profusely, and she with her usual kindness of heart hastened to assure him that she quite understood that it was an accident. Then we all went again to the wall and looked over.

The cat missing Hutcheson's face had drawn back across the moat, and was sitting on her haunches as though ready to spring. Indeed, the very instant she saw him she did spring, and with a blind unreasoning fury, which would have been grotesque, only that it was so frightfully real. She did not try to run up the wall, but simply launched herself at him as though hate and fury could lend her wings to pass straight through the great distance between them. Amelia, womanlike, got quite concerned, and said to Elias P. in a warning voice:

'Oh! you must be very careful. That animal would try to kill you if she were here; her eyes look like positive murder.'

He laughed out jovially. 'Excuse me, ma'am,' he said, 'but I can't help laughin'. Fancy a man that has fought grizzlies an' Injuns bein' careful of bein' murdered by a cat!'

When the cat heard him laugh, her whole demeanour seemed to

change. She no longer tried to jump or run up the wall, but went quietly over, and sitting again beside the dead kitten began to lick and fondle it as though it were alive.

'See!' said I, 'the effect of a really strong man. Even that animal in the midst of her fury recognises the voice of a master, and bows to him!'

'Like a squaw!' was the only comment of Elias P. Hutcheson, as we moved on our way round the city fosse. Every now and then we looked over the wall and each time saw the cat following us. At first she had kept going back to the dead kitten, and then as the distance grew greater took it in her mouth and so followed. After a while, however, she abandoned this, for we saw her following all alone; she had evidently hidden the body somewhere. Amelia's alarm grew at the cat's persistence, and more than once she repeated her warning; but the American always laughed with amusement, till finally, seeing that she was beginning to be worried, he said:

'I say, ma'am, you needn't be skeered over that cat. I go heeled,* I du!' Here he slapped his pistol pocket at the back of his lumbar region. 'Why sooner'n have you worried, I'll shoot the critter, right here, an' risk the police interferin' with a citizen of the United States for carryin' arms contrairy to reg'lations!' As he spoke he looked over the wall, but the cat, on seeing him, retreated, with a growl, into a bed of tall flowers, and was hidden. He went on: 'Blest if that ar critter ain't got more sense of what's good for her than most Christians. I guess we've seen the last of her! You bet, she'll go back now to that busted kitten and have a private funeral of it, all to herself!'

Amelia did not like to say more, lest he might, in mistaken kindness to her, fulfil his threat of shooting the cat: and so we went on and crossed the little wooden bridge leading to the gateway whence ran the steep paved roadway between the Burg and the pentagonal Torture Tower. As we crossed the bridge we saw the cat again down below us. When she saw us her fury seemed to return, and she made frantic efforts to get up the steep wall. Hutcheson laughed as he looked down at her, and said:

'Good-bye, old girl. Sorry I in-jured your feelin's, but you'll get over it in time! So long!' And then we passed through the long, dim archway and came to the gate of the Burg.

When we came out again after our survey of this most beautiful old place which not even the well-intentioned efforts of the Gothic restorers of forty years ago* have been able to spoil—though their restoration was then glaring white—we seemed to have quite forgotten the unpleasant episode of the morning. The old lime tree with its great trunk gnarled with the passing of nearly nine centuries, the deep well cut through the heart of the rock by those captives of old, and the lovely view from the city wall whence we heard, spread over almost a full quarter of an hour, the multitudinous chimes of the city, had all helped to wipe out from our minds the incident of the slain kitten.

We were the only visitors who had entered the Torture Tower that morning—so at least said the old custodian—and as we had the place all to ourselves were able to make a minute and more satisfactory survey than would have otherwise been possible. The custodian, looking to us as the sole source of his gains for the day, was willing to meet our wishes in any way. The Torture Tower is truly a grim place, even now when many thousands of visitors have sent a stream of life, and the joy that follows life, into the place; but at the time I mention it wore its grimmest and most gruesome aspect. The dust of ages seemed to have settled on it, and the darkness and the horror of its memories seem to have become sentient in a way that would have satisfied the Pantheistic souls of Philo or Spinoza.* The lower chamber where we entered was seemingly, in its normal state, filled with incarnate darkness; even the hot sunlight streaming in through the door seemed to be lost in the vast thickness of the walls, and only showed the masonry rough as when the builder's scaffolding had come down, but coated with dust and marked here and there with patches of dark stain which, if walls could speak, could have given their own dread memories of fear and pain. We were glad to pass up the dusty wooden staircase, the custodian leaving the outer door open to light us somewhat on our way; for to our eyes the one long-wick'd, evil-smelling candle stuck in a sconce on the wall gave an inadequate light. When we came up through the open trap in the corner of the chamber overhead, Amelia held on to me so tightly that I could actually feel her heart beat. I must say for my own part that I was not surprised at her fear, for this room was even more gruesome than that below. Here there was certainly more light, but only just sufficient to realise the horrible surroundings of the place. The builders of the tower had evidently intended that only they who should gain the top should have any of the joys of light and prospect.

There, as we had noticed from below, were ranges of windows, albeit of mediæval smallness, but elsewhere in the tower were only a very few narrow slits such as were habitual in places of mediæval defence. A few of these only lit the chamber, and these so high up in the wall that from no part could the sky be seen through the thickness of the walls. In racks, and leaning in disorder against the walls, were a number of headsmen's swords,* great double-handed weapons with broad blade and keen edge. Hard by were several blocks whereon the necks of the victims had lain, with here and there deep notches where the steel had bitten through the guard of flesh and shored into the wood. Round the chamber, placed in all sorts of irregular ways, were many implements of torture which made one's heart ache to see—chairs full of spikes which gave instant and excruciating pain; chairs and couches with dull knobs whose torture was seemingly less, but which, though slower, were equally efficacious; racks, belts, boots, gloves, collars, all made for compressing at will; steel baskets in which the head could be slowly crushed into a pulp if necessary; watchmen's hooks with long handle and knife that cut at resistance—this a specialty of the old Nurnberg police system; and many, many other devices for man's injury to man. Amelia grew quite pale with the horror of the things, but fortunately did not faint, for being a little overcome she sat down on a torture chair, but jumped up again with a shriek, all tendency to faint gone. We both pretended that it was the injury done to her dress by the dust of the chair, and the rusty spikes which had upset her, and Mr Hutcheson acquiesced in accepting the explanation with a kind-hearted laugh.

But the central object in the whole of this chamber of horrors was the engine known as the Iron Virgin, which stood near the centre of the room. It was a rudely-shaped figure of a woman, something of the bell order, or, to make a closer comparison, of the figure of Mrs Noah in the children's Ark, but without that slimness of waist and perfect *rondeur** of hip which marks the æsthetic type of the Noah family. One would hardly have recognised it as intended for a human figure at all had not the founder shaped on the forehead a rude semblance of a woman's face. This machine was coated with rust without, and covered with dust; a rope was fastened to a ring in the front of the figure, about where the waist should have been, and was drawn through a pulley, fastened on the wooden pillar which sustained the flooring above. The custodian pulling this rope showed that a section of the front was hinged like a door at one side; we then saw that the engine was of considerable thickness, leaving just room enough inside for a man to be placed. The door was of equal thickness and of great weight, for it took the custodian all his strength, aided though he was by the contrivance of the pulley, to open it. This weight was partly due to the fact that the door was of manifest purpose hung so as to throw its weight downwards, so that it might shut of its own accord when the strain was released. The inside was honeycombed with rust—nay more, the rust alone that comes through time would hardly have eaten so deep into the iron walls; the rust of the cruel stains was deep indeed! It was only, however, when we came to look at the inside of the door that the diabolical intention was manifest to the full. Here were several long spikes, square and massive, broad at the base and sharp at the points, placed in such a position that when the door should close the upper ones would pierce the eyes of the victim, and the lower ones his heart and vitals. The sight was too much for poor Amelia, and this time she fainted dead off, and I had to carry her down the stairs, and place her on a bench outside till she recovered. That she felt it to the quick was afterwards shown by the fact that my eldest son bears to this day a rude* birthmark on his breast, which has, by family consent, been accepted as representing the Nurnberg Virgin.

When we got back to the chamber we found Hutcheson still opposite the Iron Virgin; he had been evidently philosophising, and now gave us the benefit of his thought in the shape of a sort of exordium.*

'Wall, I guess I've been learnin' somethin' here while madam has been gettin' over her faint. 'Pears to me that we're a long way behind the times on our side of the big drink. We uster think out on the plains that the Injun could give us points in tryin' to make a man oncomfortable; but I guess your old mediæval law-and-order party could raise him every time. Splinters was pretty good in his bluff on the squaw, but this here young miss held a straight flush all high on him. The points of them spikes air sharp enough still, though even the edges air eaten out by what uster be on them. It'd be a good thing for our Indian section to get some specimens of this here play-toy to send round to the Reservations jest to knock the stuffin' out of the bucks, and the squaws too, by showing them as how old civilisation lays over them at their best. Guess but I'll get in that box a minute jest to see how it feels!'

'Oh no! no!' said Amelia. 'It is too terrible!'

'Guess, ma'am, nothin's too terrible to the explorin' mind. I've been in some queer places in my time. Spent a night inside a dead horse while a prairie fire swept over me in Montana Territory—an' another time slept inside a dead buffler* when the Comanches was on the war path an' I didn't keer to leave my kyard on them. I've been two days in a caved-in tunnel in the Billy Broncho gold mine in New Mexico, an' was one of the four shut up for three parts of a day in the caisson what slid over on her side when we was settin' the foundations of the Buffalo Bridge.* I've not funked an odd experience yet, an' I don't propose to begin now!'

We saw that he was set on the experiment, so I said: 'Well, hurry up, old man, and get through it quick?'

'All right, General,' said he, 'but I calculate we ain't quite ready yet. The gentlemen, my predecessors, what stood in that thar canister, didn't volunteer for the office—not much! And I guess there was some ornamental tyin' up before the big stroke was made. I want to go into this thing fair and square, so I must get fixed up proper first. I dare say this old galoot can rise some string and tie me up accordin' to sample?'

This was said interrogatively to the old custodian, but the latter, who understood the drift of his speech, though perhaps not appreciating to the full the niceties of dialect and imagery, shook his head. His protest was, however, only formal and made to be overcome. The American thrust a gold piece into his hand, saying, 'Take it, pard! it's your pot; and don't be skeer'd. This ain't no necktie party that you're asked to assist in!' He produced some thin frayed rope and proceeded to bind our companion with sufficient strictness for the purpose. When the upper part of his body was bound, Hutcheson said:

'Hold on a moment, Judge. Guess I'm too heavy for you to tote into the canister. You jest let me walk in, and then you can wash up regardin' my legs!'

Whilst speaking he had backed himself into the opening which was just enough to hold him. It was a close fit and no mistake. Amelia looked on with fear in her eyes, but she evidently did not like to say anything. Then the custodian completed his task by tying the American's feet together so that he was now absolutely helpless and fixed in his voluntary prison. He seemed to really enjoy it, and the incipient smile which was habitual to his face blossomed into actuality as he said:

'Guess this here Eve was made out of the rib of a dwarf!* There ain't much room for a full-grown citizen of the United States to hustle. We uster make our coffins more roomier in Idaho territory. Now, Judge, you jest begin to let this door down, slow, on to me. I want to feel the same pleasure as the other jays had when those spikes began to move toward their eyes!'

'Oh no! no! no!' broke in Amelia hysterically. 'It is too terrible! I can't bear to see it!—I can't! I can't!'

But the American was obdurate. 'Say, Colonel,' said he, 'Why not take Madame for a little promenade? I wouldn't hurt her feelin's for the world; but now that I am here, havin' kem eight thousand miles, wouldn't it be too hard to give up the very experience I've been pinin' an' pantin' fur? A man can't get to feel like canned goods every time! Me and the Judge here'll fix up this thing in no time, an' then you'll come back, an' we'll all laugh together!'

Once more the resolution that is born of curiosity triumphed, and Amelia stayed holding tight to my arm and shivering whilst the custodian began to slacken slowly inch by inch the rope that held back the iron door. Hutcheson's face was positively radiant as his eyes followed the first movement of the spikes.

'Wall!' he said, 'I guess I've not had enjoyment like this since I left Noo York. Bar a scrap with a French sailor at Wapping*—an' that warn't much of a picnic neither—I've not had a show fur real pleasure in this dod-rotted* Continent, where there ain't no b'ars nor no Injuns, an' wheer nary man goes heeled. Slow there, Judge! Don't you rush this business! I want a show for my money this game—I du!'

The custodian must have had in him some of the blood of his predecessors in that ghastly tower, for he worked the engine with a deliberate and excruciating slowness which after five minutes, in which the outer edge of the door had not moved half as many inches, began to overcome Amelia. I saw her lips whiten, and felt her hold upon my arm relax. I looked around an instant for a place whereon to lay her, and when I looked at her again found that her eye had become fixed on the side of the Virgin. Following its direction I saw the black cat crouching out of sight. Her green eyes shone like danger lamps in the gloom of the place, and their colour was heightened by the blood which still smeared her coat and reddened her mouth. I cried out:

'The cat! look out for the cat!' for even then she sprang out before the engine. At this moment she looked like a triumphant demon. Her eyes blazed with ferocity, her hair bristled out till she seemed twice her normal size, and her tail lashed about as does a tiger's when the quarry is before it. Elias P. Hutcheson when he saw her was amused, and his eyes positively sparkled with fun as he said:

'Darned if the squaw hain't got on all her war paint! Jest give her a shove off if she comes any of her tricks on me, for I'm so fixed ever-lastingly by the boss, that durn my skin if I can keep my eyes from her if she wants them! Easy there, Judge! don't you slack that ar rope or I'm euchered!'*

At this moment Amelia completed her faint, and I had to clutch hold of her round the waist or she would have fallen to the floor. Whilst attending to her I saw the black cat crouching for a spring, and jumped up to turn the creature out.

But at that instant, with a sort of hellish scream, she hurled her-self, not as we expected at Hutcheson, but straight at the face of the custodian. Her claws seemed to be tearing wildly as one sees in the Chinese drawings of the dragon rampant, and as I looked I saw one of them light on the poor man's eye, and actually tear through it and down his cheek, leaving a wide band of red where the blood seemed to spurt from every vein.

With a yell of sheer terror which came quicker than even his sense of pain, the man leaped back, dropping as he did so the rope which held back the iron door. I jumped for it, but was too late, for the cord ran like lightning through the pulley-block, and the heavy mass fell forward from its own weight.

As the door closed I caught a glimpse of our poor companion's face. He seemed frozen with terror. His eyes stared with a horrible anguish as if dazed, and no sound came from his lips.

And then the spikes did their work. Happily the end was quick, for when I wrenched open the door they had pierced so deep that they had locked in the bones of the skull through which they had crushed, and actually tore him—it—out of his iron prison till, bound as he was, he fell at full length with a sickly thud upon the floor, the face turning upward as he fell.

I rushed to my wife, lifted her up and carried her out, for I feared for her very reason if she should wake from her faint to such a scene. I laid her on the bench outside and ran back. Leaning against the wooden column was the custodian moaning in pain whilst he held his reddening handkerchief to his eyes. And sitting on the head of the poor American was the cat, purring loudly as she licked the blood which trickled through the gashed socket of his eyes.

I think no one will call me cruel because I seized one of the old executioner's swords and shore her in two as she sat.

ROBERT W. CHAMBERS

The Repairer of Reputations

❦

'Along the shore the cloud waves break,
The twin suns sink behind the lake,
The shadows lengthen
                    In Carcosa.*

Strange is the night where black stars rise,
And strange moons circle through the skies,
But stranger still is
                    Lost Carcosa.

Songs that the Hyades* shall sing,
Where flap the tatters of the King,
Must die unheard in
                    Dim Carcosa.

Song of my soul, my voice is dead,
Die thou, unsung, as tears unshed
Shall dry and die in
                    Lost Carcosa.'

Cassilda's Song in 'The King in Yellow.'
Act 1. Scene 2.

I

'Ne raillons pas les fous; leur folie dure plus longtemps que la
nôtre . . . Voilà toute la différence.'*

TOWARD the end of the year 1920 the Government of the United
States had practically completed the programme, adopted during
the last months of President Winthrop's administration. The
country was apparently tranquil. Everybody knows how the Tariff
and Labor questions were settled. The war with Germany,* incident
on that country's seizure of the Samoan Islands,* had left no visible
scars upon the republic, and the temporary occupation of Norfolk*
by the invading army had been forgotten in the joy over repeated
naval victories and the subsequent ridiculous plight of General

Von Gartenlaube's forces in the State of New Jersey. The Cuban
and Hawaiian investments had paid one hundred per cent, and the
territory of Samoa was well worth its cost as a coaling station.* The
country was in a superb state of defence. Every coast city had been
well supplied with land fortifications; the army under the parental
eye of the General Staff, organized according to the Prussian
system,* had been increased to 300,000 men with a territorial reserve
of a million; and six magnificent squadrons of cruisers and battle-
ships patrolled the six stations of the navigable seas, leaving a steam
reserve amply fitted to control home waters. The gentlemen from the
West had at last been constrained to acknowledge that a college for
the training of diplomats was as necessary as law schools are for the
training of barristers; consequently we were no longer represented
abroad by incompetent patriots. The nation was prosperous. Chicago,
for a moment paralyzed after a second great fire,* had risen from
its ruins, white and imperial, and more beautiful than the white city
which had been built for its plaything in 1893. Everywhere good
architecture was replacing bad, and even in New York, a sudden
craving for decency had swept away a great portion of the existing
horrors. Streets had been widened, properly paved and lighted, trees
had been planted, squares laid out, elevated structures demolished
and underground roads built to replace them. The new government
buildings and barracks were fine bits of architecture, and the long
system of stone quays which completely surrounded the island had
been turned into parks which proved a godsend to the population.
The subsidizing of the state theatre and state opera brought its own
reward. The United States National Academy of Design was much like
European institutions of the same kind. Nobody envied the Secretary
of Fine Arts, either his cabinet position or his portfolio. The Secretary
of Forrestry and Game Preservation had a much easier time thanks to
the new system of National Mounted Police. We had profited well by
the latest treaties with France and England; the exclusion of foreign-
born Jews* as a measure of national self-preservation, the settlement
of the new independent negro state of Suanee,* the checking of
immigration, the new laws concerning naturalization, and the
gradual centralization of power in the executive all contributed to
national calm and prosperity. When the Government solved the
Indian problem and squadrons of Indian cavalry scouts in native
costume were substituted for the pitiable organizations tacked on to

the tail of skeletonized regiments by a former Secretary of War, the nation drew a long sigh of relief. When, after the colossal Congress of Religions, bigotry and intolerance were laid in their graves and kindness and charity began to draw warring sects together, many thought the millennium had arrived, at least in the new world, which after all is a world by itself.

But self-preservation is the first law, and the United States had to look on in helpless sorrow as Germany, Italy, Spain and Belgium writhed in the throes of Anarchy, while Russia, watching from the Caucasus, stooped and bound them one by one.

In the city of New York the summer of 1899 was signalized by the dismantling of the Elevated Railroads.* The summer of 1900 will live in the memories of New York people for many a cycle; the Dodge Statue* was removed in that year. In the following winter began that agitation for the repeal of the laws prohibiting suicide which bore its final fruit in the month of April, 1920, when the first Government Lethal Chamber was opened on Washington Square.*

I had walked down that day from Dr Archer's house on Madison Avenue, where I had been as a mere formality. Ever since that fall from my horse, four years before, I had been troubled at times with pains in the back of my head and neck, but now for months they had been absent, and the doctor sent me away that day saying there was nothing more to be cured in me. It was hardly worth his fee to be told that; I knew it myself. Still I did not grudge him the money. What I minded was the mistake which he made at first. When they picked me up from the pavement where I lay unconscious, and somebody had mercifully sent a bullet through my horse's head, I was carried to Doctor Archer, and he, pronouncing my brain affected, placed me in his private asylum where I was obliged to endure treatment for insanity. At last he decided that I was well, and I, knowing that my mind had always been as sound as his, if not sounder, 'paid my tuition' as he jokingly called it, and left. I told him, smiling, that I would get even with him for his mistake, and he laughed heartily, and asked me to call once in a while. I did so, hoping for a chance to even up accounts, but he gave me none, and I told him I would wait.

The fall from my horse had fortunately left no evil results; on the contrary it had changed my whole character for the better. From a lazy young man about town, I had become active, energetic, temperate, and above all—oh, above all else—ambitious. There was only one thing which troubled me, I laughed at my own uneasiness, and yet it troubled me.

During my convalescence I had bought and read for the first time, 'The King in Yellow.' I remember after finishing the first act that it occurred to me that I had better stop. I started up and flung the book into the fireplace; the volume struck the barred grate and fell open on the hearth in the fire-light. If I had not caught a glimpse of the opening words in the second act I should never have finished it, but as I stooped to pick it up, my eyes became riveted to the open page, and with a cry of terror, or perhaps it was of joy so poignant that I suffered in every nerve, I snatched the thing out of the coals and crept shaking to my bedroom, where I read it and reread it, and wept and laughed and trembled with a horror which at times assails me yet. This is the thing that troubles me, for I cannot forget Carcosa where black stars hang in the heavens; where the shadows of men's thoughts lengthen in the afternoon, when the twin suns sink into the Lake of Hali; and my mind will bear forever the memory of the Pallid Mask. I pray God will curse the writer, as the writer has cursed the world with this beautiful, stupendous creation, terrible in its simplicity, irresistible in its truth—a world which now trembles before the King in Yellow. When the French Government seized the translated copies which had just arrived in Paris, London, of course, became eager to read it. It is well known how the book spread like an infectious disease, from city to city, from continent to continent, barred out here, confiscated there, denounced by press and pulpit, censured even by the most advanced of literary anarchists. No definite principles had been violated in those wicked pages, no doctrine promulgated, no convictions outraged. It could not be judged by any known standard, yet, although it was acknowledged that the supreme note of art had been struck in 'The King in Yellow,' all felt that human nature could not bear the strain, nor thrive on words in which the essence of purest poison lurked. The very banality and innocence of the first act only allowed the blow to fall afterward with more awful effect.

It was, I remember, the 13th day of April, 1920, that the first Government Lethal Chamber was established on the south side of Washington Square, between Wooster Street* and South Fifth Avenue. The block which had formerly consisted of a lot of shabby old buildings, used as cafés and restaurants for foreigners, had been acquired by the Government in the winter of 1898. The French and

Italian cafés and restaurants were torn down; the whole block was enclosed by a gilded iron railing, and converted into a lovely garden with lawns, flowers and fountains. In the centre of the garden stood a small, white building, severely classical in architecture, and surrounded by thickets of flowers. Six Ionic columns* supported the roof, and the single door was of bronze. A splendid marble group of 'The Fates' stood before the door, the work of a young American sculptor, Boris Yvain,* who had died in Paris when only twenty-three years old.

The inauguration ceremonies were in progress as I crossed University Place and entered the square. I threaded my way through the silent throng of spectators, but was stopped at Fourth Street by a cordon of police. A regiment of United States lancers were drawn up in a hollow square around the Lethal Chamber. On a raised tribune facing Washington Park stood the Governor of New York, and behind him were grouped the Mayor of New York and Brooklyn, the Inspector-General of Police, the Commandant of the state troops, Colonel Livingston, military aid to the President of the United States, General Blount, commanding at Governor's Island, Major-General Hamilton, commanding the garrison of New York and Brooklyn, Admiral Buffby of the fleet in the North River, Surgeon General Lanceford, the staff of the National Free Hospital, Senators Wyse and Franklin of New York, and the Commissioner of Public Works. The tribune was surrounded by a squadron of hussars of the National Guard.

The Governor was finishing his reply to the short speech of the Surgeon-General. I heard him say: 'The laws prohibiting suicide and providing punishment for any attempt at self-destruction have been repealed. The Government has seen fit to acknowledge the right of man to end an existence which may have become intolerable to him, through physical suffering or mental despair. It is believed that the community will be benefited by the removal of such people from their midst. Since the passage of this law, the number of suicides in the United States has not increased. Now that the Government has determined to establish a Lethal Chamber in every city, town and village in the country, it remains to be seen whether or not that class of human creatures from whose desponding ranks new victims of self-destruction fall daily will accept the relief thus provided.' He paused, and turned to the white Lethal Chamber. The silence in the street was absolute. 'There a painless death awaits him who can no longer bear the sorrows of this life. If death is welcome let him seek it there.' Then quickly turning to the military aid of the President's household, he said, 'I declare the Lethal Chamber open,' and again facing the vast crowd he cried in a clear voice: 'Citizens of New York and of the United States of America, through me the Government declares the Lethal Chamber to be open.'

The solemn hush was broken by a sharp cry of command, the squadron of hussars filed after the Governor's carriage, the lancers wheeled and formed along Fifth Avenue to wait for the commandant of the garrison, and the mounted police followed them. I left the crowd to gape and stare at the white marble Death Chamber, and, crossing South Fifth Avenue, walked along the western side of that thoroughfare to Bleecker Street.* Then I turned to the right and stopped before a dingy shop which bore the sign,

HAWBERK, ARMORER.

I glanced in at the doorway and saw Hawberk* busy in his little shop at the end of the hall. He looked up, and catching sight of me cried in his deep, hearty voice, 'Come in, Mr Castaigne!' Constance, his daughter, rose to meet me as I crossed the threshold, and held out her pretty hand, but I saw the blush of disappointment on her cheeks, and knew that it was another Castaigne she had expected, my Cousin Louis. I smiled at her confusion and complimented her on the banner which she was embroidering from a colored plate. Old Hawberk sat riveting the worn greaves* of some ancient suit of armor, and the ting! ting! ting! of his little hammer sounded pleasantly in the quaint shop. Presently he dropped his hammer, and fussed about for a moment with a tiny wrench. The soft clash of the mail sent a thrill of pleasure through me. I loved to hear the music of steel brushing against steel, the mellow shock of the mallet on thigh pieces, and the jingle of chain armor. That was the only reason I went to see Hawberk. He had never interested me personally, nor did Constance, except for the fact of her being in love with Louis. This did occupy my attention, and some-times even kept me awake at night. But I knew in my heart that all would come right, and that I should arrange their future as I expected to arrange that of my kind doctor, John Archer. However, I should never have troubled myself about visiting them just then, had it not been, as I say, that the music of the tinkling hammer had for me this strong fascination. I would sit for hours, listening and listening, and when a stray sunbeam struck the inlaid steel, the sensation it gave me was almost too keen to endure. My eyes would become fixed, dilating with a pleasure that stretched every nerve almost to breaking, until some movement of the old armorer cut off the ray of sunlight, then, still thrilling secretly, I leaned back and listened again to the sound of the polishing rag, swish! swish! rubbing rust from the rivets.

Constance worked with the embroidery over her knees, now and then pausing to examine more closely the pattern in the colored plate from the Metropolitan Museum.*

'Who is this for?' I asked.

Hawberk explained, that in addition to the treasures of armor in the Metropolitan Museum of which he had been appointed armorer, he also had charge of several collections belonging to rich amateurs. This was the missing greave of a famous suit which a client of his had traced to a little shop in Paris on the Quai d'Orsay.* He, Hawberk, had negotiated for and secured the greave, and now the suit was complete. He laid down his hammer and read me the history of the suit, traced since 1450 from owner to owner until it was acquired by Thomas Stainbridge. When his superb collection was sold, this client of Hawberk's bought the suit, and since then the search for the missing greave had been pushed until it was, almost by accident, located in Paris.

'Did you continue the search so persistently without any certainty of the greave being still in existence?' I demanded.

'Of course,' he replied coolly.

Then for the first time I took a personal interest in Hawberk.

'It was worth something to you,' I ventured.

'No,' he replied, laughing, 'my pleasure in finding it was my reward.'

'Have you no ambition to be rich?' I asked smiling.

'My one ambition is to be the best armorer in the world,' he answered gravely.

Constance asked me if I had seen the ceremonies at the Lethal Chamber. She herself had noticed cavalry passing up Broadway that morning, and had wished to see the inauguration, but her father wanted the banner finished, and she had stayed at his request.

'Did you see your cousin, Mr Castaigne, there?' she asked, with the slighest tremor of her soft eyelashes.

'No,' I replied carelessly. 'Louis' regiment is manœuvreing out in Westchester County.'* I rose and picked up my hat and cane.

'Are you going upstairs to see the lunatic again?' laughed old Hawberk. If Hawberk knew how I loathe that word 'lunatic,' he would never use it in my presence. It rouses certain feelings within me which I do not care to explain. However, I answered him quietly: 'I think I shall drop in and see Mr Wilde* for a moment or two.'

'Poor fellow,' said Constance, with a shake of her head, 'it must be hard to live alone year after year, poor, crippled and almost demented. It is very good of you, Mr Castaigne, to visit him as often as you do.'

'I think he is vicious,' observed Hawberk, beginning again with his hammer. I listened to the golden tinkle on the greave plates; when he had finished I replied:

'No, he is not vicious, nor is he in the least demented. His mind is a wonder chamber, from which he can extract treasures that you and I would give years of our lives to acquire.'

Hawberk laughed.

I continued a little impatiently: 'He knows history as no one else could know it. Nothing, however trivial, escapes his search, and his memory is so absolute, so precise in details, that were it known in New York that such a man existed, the people could not honor him enough.'

'Nonsense,' muttered Hawberk, searching on the floor for a fallen rivet.

'Is it nonsense,' I asked, managing to suppress what I felt, 'is it nonsense when he says that the tassets and cuissards* of the enamelled suit of armor commonly known as the "Prince's Emblazoned" can be found among a mass of rusty theatrical properties, broken stoves and ragpicker's refuse in a garret in Pell Street?'*

Hawberk's hammer fell to the ground, but he picked it up and asked, with a great deal of calm, how I knew that the tassets and left cuissard were missing from the 'Prince's Emblazoned.'

'I did not know until Mr Wilde mentioned it to me the other day. He said they were in the garret of 998 Pell Street.'

'Nonsense,' he cried, but I noticed his hand trembling under his leathern apron.

'Is this nonsense too?' I asked pleasantly. 'Is it nonsense when Mr Wilde continually speaks of you as the Marquis of Avonshire and of Miss Constance——'

I did not finish, for Constance had started to her feet with terror written on every feature. Hawberk looked at me and slowly smoothed his leathern apron. 'That is impossible,' he observed, 'Mr Wilde may know a great many things——'

'About armor, for instance, and the "Prince's Emblazoned,"' I interposed, smiling.

'Yes,' he continued, slowly, 'about armor also—may be—but he is wrong in regard to the Marquis of Avonshire, who, as you know, killed his wife's traducer years ago, and went to Australia where he did not long survive his wife.'

'Mr Wilde is wrong,' murmured Constance. Her lips were blanched but her voice was sweet and calm.

'Let us agree, if you please, that in this one circumstance Mr Wilde is wrong,' I said.

II

I CLIMBED the three dilapidated flights of stairs, which I had so often climbed before, and knocked at a small door at the end of the corridor. Mr Wilde opened the door and I walked in.

When he had double-locked the door and pushed a heavy chest against it, he came and sat down beside me, peering up into my face with his little light-colored eyes. Half a dozen new scratches covered his nose and cheeks, and the silver wires which supported his artificial ears had become displaced. I thought I had never seen him so hideously fascinating. He had no ears. The artificial ones, which now stood out at an angle from the fine wire, were his one weakness. They were made of wax and painted a shell pink, but the rest of his face was yellow. He might better have revelled in the luxury of some artificial fingers for his left hand, which was absolutely fingerless, but it seemed to cause him no inconvenience, and he was satisfied with his wax ears. He was very small, scarcely higher than a child of ten, but his arms were magnificently developed, and his thighs as thick as any athlete's. Still, the most remarkable thing about Mr Wilde was that a man of his marvellous intelligence and knowledge should have such a head. It was flat and pointed, like the heads of many of those unfortunates whom people imprison in asylums for the weak-minded. Many called him insane but I knew him to be as sane as I was.

I do not deny that he was eccentric; the mania he had for keeping that cat and teasing her until she flew at his face like a demon, was certainly eccentric. I never could understand why he kept the creature, nor what pleasure he found in shutting himself up in his room with the surly, vicious beast. I remember once, glancing up from the manuscript I was studying by the light of some tallow dips, and seeing Mr Wilde squatting motionless on his high chair, his eyes fairly blazing with excitement, while the cat, which had risen from her place before the stove, came creeping across the floor right at him. Before I could move she flattened her belly to the ground, crouched, trembled, and sprang into his face. Howling and foaming they rolled over and over on the floor, scratching and clawing, until the cat screamed and fled under the cabinet, and Mr Wilde turned over on his back, his limbs contracting and curling up like the legs of a dying spider. He *was* eccentric.

Mr Wilde had climbed into his high chair, and, after studying my face, picked up a dog's-eared ledger and opened it.

'Henry B. Matthews,' he read, 'book-keeper with Whysot Whysot and Company, dealers in church ornaments. Called April 3d. Reputation damaged on the race-track. Known as a welcher.* Reputation to be repaired by August 1st. Retainer Five Dollars.' He turned the page and ran his fingerless knuckles down the closely-written columns.

'P. Greene Dusenberry, Minister of the Gospel, Fairbeach, New Jersey. Reputation damaged in the Bowery.* To be repaired as soon as possible. Retainer $100.'

He coughed and added, 'Called, April 6th.'

'Then you are not in need of money, Mr Wilde,' I inquired.

'Listen,' he coughed again.

'Mrs C. Hamilton Chester, of Chester Park, New York City, Called April 7th. Reputation damaged at Dieppe,* France. To be repaired by October 1st. Retainer $500.

'Note.—C. Hamilton Chester, Captain U. S. S. "Avalanche" ordered home from South Sea Squadron October 1st.'

'Well,' I said, 'the profession of a Repairer of Reputations is lucrative.'

His colorless eyes sought mine. 'I only wanted to demonstrate that I was correct. You said it was impossible to succeed as a Repairer of Reputations; that even if I did succeed in certain cases it would cost me more than I would gain by it. To-day I have five hundred men in my employ, who are poorly paid, but who pursue the work with an enthusiasm which possibly may be born of fear. These men enter every shade and grade of society; some even are pillars of the most exclusive social temples; others are the prop and pride of the financial world; still others, hold undisputed sway among the 'Fancy and the Talent.'* I choose them at my leisure from those who reply to my advertisements. It is easy enough, they are all cowards. I could treble the number in twenty days if I wished. So you see, those who have in their keeping the reputations of their fellow-citizens, I have in my pay.'

'They may turn on you,' I suggested.

He rubbed his thumb over his cropped ears, and adjusted the wax substitutes. 'I think not,' he murmured thoughtfully, 'I seldom have to apply the whip, and then only once. Besides they like their wages.'

'How do you apply the whip?' I demanded.

His face for a moment was awful to look upon. His eyes dwindled to a pair of green sparks.

'I invite them to come and have a little chat with me,' he said in a soft voice.

A knock at the door interrupted him, and his face resumed its amiable expression.

'Who is it?' he inquired.

'Mr Steylette,' was the answer.

'Come to-morrow,' replied Mr Wilde.

'Impossible,' began the other, but was silenced by a sort of bark from Mr Wilde.

'Come to-morrow,' he repeated.

We heard somebody move away from the door and turn the corner by the stairway.

'Who is that?' I asked.

'Arnold Steylette, Owner and Editor in Chief of the great New York daily.'

He drummed on the ledger with his fingerless hand adding: 'I pay him very badly, but he thinks it a good bargain.'

'Arnold Steylette!' I repeated amazed.

'Yes,' said Mr Wilde with a self-satisfied cough.

The cat, which had entered the room as he spoke, hesitated, looked up at him and snarled. He climbed down from the chair and squatting on the floor, took the creature into his arms and caressed her. The cat ceased snarling and presently began a loud purring which seemed to increase in timbre as he stroked her.

'Where are the notes?' I asked. He pointed to the table, and for the hundredth time I picked up the bundle of manuscript entitled

'THE IMPERIAL DYNASTY OF AMERICA.'

One by one I studied the well-worn pages, worn only by my own handling, and although I knew all by heart, from the beginning, 'When from Carcosa, the Hyades, Hastur,* and Aldebaran,' to 'Castaigne, Louis de Calvados, born December 19th, 1877,' I read it with an eager rapt attention, pausing to repeat parts of it aloud, and dwelling especially on 'Hildred de Calvados, only son of Hildred Castaigne and Edythe Landes Castaigne, first in succession,' etc., etc.

When I finished, Mr Wilde nodded and coughed.

'Speaking of your legitimate ambition,' he said, 'how do Constance and Louis get along?'

'She loves him,' I replied simply.

The cat on his knee suddenly turned and struck at his eyes, and he flung her off and climbed on to the chair opposite me.

'And Doctor Archer! But that's a matter you can settle any time you wish,' he added.

'Yes,' I replied, 'Doctor Archer can wait, but it is time I saw my cousin Louis.'

'It is time,' he repeated. Then he took another ledger from the table and ran over the leaves rapidly.

'We are now in communication with ten thousand men,' he muttered. 'We can count on one hundred thousand within the first twenty-eight hours, and in forty-eight hours the state will rise *en masse*. The country follows the state, and the portion that will not, I mean California and the Northwest, might better never have been inhabited. I shall not send them the Yellow Sign.'

The blood rushed to my head, but I only answered, 'A new broom sweeps clean.'

'The ambition of Cæsar and of Napoleon pales before that which could not rest until it had seized the minds of men and controlled even their unborn thoughts,' said Mr Wilde.

'You are speaking of the King in Yellow,' I groaned with a shudder.

'He is a king whom Emperors have served.'

'I am content to serve him,' I replied.

Mr Wilde sat rubbing his ears with his crippled hand. 'Perhaps Constance does not love him,' he suggested.

I started to reply, but a sudden burst of military music from the street below drowned my voice. The twentieth dragoon regiment, formerly in garrison at Mount St Vincent,* was returning from the manœuvres in Westchester County, to its new barracks on East Washington Square. It was my cousin's regiment. They were a fine lot of fellows, in their pale-blue, tight-fitting jackets, jaunty busbys and white riding breeches with the double yellow stripe, into which their limbs seemed molded. Every other squadron was armed with lances, from the metal points of which fluttered yellow and white pennons. The band passed, playing the regimental march, then came the colonel and staff, the horses crowding and trampling, while their heads bobbed in unison, and the pennons fluttered from their lance points. The troopers, who rode with the beautiful English seat,* looked brown as berries from their bloodless campaign among the farms of Westchester, and the music of their sabres against the stirrups, and the jingle of spurs and carbines was delightful to me. I saw Louis riding with his squadron. He was as handsome an officer as I have ever seen. Mr Wilde, who had mounted a chair by the window, saw him too, but said nothing. Louis turned and looked straight at Hawberk's shop as he passed, and I could see the flush on his brown cheeks. I think Constance must have been at the window. When the last troopers had clattered by, and the last pennons vanished into South 5th Avenue, Mr Wilde clambered out of his chair and dragged the chest away from the door.

'Yes,' he said, 'it is time that you saw your cousin Louis.'

He unlocked the door and I picked up my hat and stick and stepped into the corridor. The stairs were dark. Groping about, I set my foot on something soft, which snarled and spit, and I aimed a murderous blow at the cat, but my cane shivered to splinters against the balustrade, and the beast scurried back into Mr Wilde's room.

Passing Hawberk's door again I saw him still at work on the armor, but I did not stop, and stepping out into Bleecker Street, I followed it to Wooster, skirted the grounds of the Lethal Chamber, and crossing Washington Park went straight to my rooms in the Benedick. Here I lunched comfortably, read the *Herald* and the *Meteor*,* and finally went to the steel safe in my bedroom and set the time combination. The three and three-quarter minutes which it is necessary to wait, while the time lock is opening, are to me golden moments. From the instant I set the combination to the moment when I grasp the knobs and swing back the solid steel doors, I live in an ecstasy of expectation. Those moments must be like moments passed in Paradise. I know what I am to find at the end of the time limit. I know what the massive safe holds secure for me, for me alone, and the exquisite pleasure of waiting is hardly enhanced when the safe opens and I lift, from its velvet crown, a diadem of purest gold, blazing with diamonds. I do this every day, and yet the joy of waiting and at last touching again the diadem, only seems to increase as the days pass. It is a diadem fit for a King among kings, an Emperor among emperors. The King in Yellow might scorn it, but it shall be worn by his royal servant.

I held it in my arms until the alarm on the safe rang harshly, and then tenderly, proudly, I replaced it and shut the steel doors. I walked slowly back into my study, which faces Washington Square, and leaned on the window-sill. The afternoon sun poured into my windows, and a gentle breeze stirred the branches of the elms and maples in the park, now covered with buds and tender foliage. A flock of pigeons circled about the tower of the Memorial Church; sometimes alighting on the purple tiled roof, sometimes wheeling downward to the lotos fountain in front of the marble arch.* The gardeners were busy with the flower beds around the fountain, and the freshly-turned earth smelled sweet and spicy. A lawn mower, drawn by a fat white horse, clinked across the green sward, and watering carts poured showers of spray over the asphalt drives. Around the statue of Peter Stuyvesant,* which in 1897 had replaced the monstrosity supposed to represent Garibaldi,* children played in the spring sunshine, and nurse girls wheeled elaborate baby-carriages with a reckless disregard for the pasty-faced occupants, which could probably be explained by the presence of half a dozen trim dragoon troopers languidly lolling on the benches. Through the trees, the Washington Memorial Arch glistened like silver in the sunshine, and beyond, on the eastern extremity of the square the gray stone barracks of the dragoons, and the white granite artillery stables were alive with color and motion.

I looked at the Lethal Chamber on the corner of the square opposite. A few curious people still lingered about the gilded iron railing, but inside the grounds the paths were deserted. I watched the fountains ripple and sparkle; the sparrows had already found this new bathing nook, and the basins were crowded with the dusty-feathered little things. Two or three white peacocks picked their way across the lawns, and a drab-colored pigeon sat so motionless on the arm of one of the Fates, that it seemed to be a part of the sculptured stone.

As I was turning carelessly away, a slight commotion in the group of curious loiterers around the gates attracted my attention. A young man had entered, and was advancing with nervous strides along the gravel path which leads to the bronze doors of the Lethal Chamber. He paused a moment before the Fates, and as he raised his head to those three mysterious faces, the pigeon rose from its sculptured perch, circled about for a moment and wheeled to the east. The young man pressed his hands to his face, and then with an undefinable gesture sprang up the marble steps, the bronze doors closed behind him, and half an hour later the loiterers slouched away, and the frightened pigeon returned to its perch in the arms of Fate.

I put on my hat and went out into the park for a little walk before dinner. As I crossed the central driveway a group of officers passed, and one of them called out, 'Hello, Hildred,' and came back to shake hands with me. It was my Cousin Louis, who stood smiling and tapping his spurred heels with his riding-whip.

'Just back from Westchester,' he said; 'been doing the bucolic; milk and curds, you know, dairy-maids in sunbonnets, who say "haeow" and "I don't think" when you tell them they are pretty. I'm nearly dead for a square meal at Delmonico's.* What's the news?'

'There is none,' I replied pleasantly. 'I saw your regiment coming in this morning.'

'Did you? I didn't see you. Where were you?'

'In Mr Wilde's window.'

'Oh, hell!' he began impatiently, 'that man is stark mad! I don't understand why you——'

He saw how annoyed I felt by this outburst, and begged my pardon.

'Really, old chap,' he said, 'I don't mean to run down a man you like, but for the life of me I can't see what the deuce you find in common with Mr Wilde. He's not well-bred, to put it generously; he's hideously deformed; his head is the head of a criminally insane person. You know yourself he's been in an asylum——'

'So have I,' I interrupted calmly.

Louis looked startled and confused for a moment, but recovered and slapped me heartily on the shoulder.

'You were completely cured,' he began, but I stopped him again.

'I suppose you mean that I was simply acknowledged never to have been insane.'

'Of course that—that's what I meant,' he laughed.

I disliked his laugh because I knew it was forced, but I nodded gaily and asked him where he was going. Louis looked after his brother officers who had now almost reached Broadway.

'We had intended to sample a Brunswick cocktail,* but to tell you the truth I was anxious for an excuse to go and see Hawberk instead. Come along, I'll make you my excuse.'

We found old Hawberk, neatly attired in a fresh spring suit, standing at the door of his shop and sniffing the air.

'I had just decided to take Constance for a little stroll before dinner,' he replied to the impetuous volley of questions from Louis. 'We thought of walking on the park terrace along the North River.'*

At that moment Constance appeared and grew pale and rosy by turns as Louis bent over her small gloved fingers. I tried to excuse myself, alleging an engagement up-town, but Louis and Constance would not listen, and I saw I was expected to remain and engage old Hawberk's attention. After all it would be just as well if I kept my eye on Louis, I thought, and when they hailed a Spring Street* horsecar, I got in after them and took my seat beside the armorer.

The beautiful line of parks and granite terraces overlooking the wharves along the North River, which were built in 1910 and finished in the autumn of 1917, had become one of the most popular promenades in the metropolis. They extended from the battery to 190th Street,* overlooking the noble river and affording a fine view of the Jersey shore and the Highlands opposite. Cafés and restaurants were scattered here and there among the trees, and twice a week military bands from the garrison played in the kiosks on the parapets.

We sat down in the sunshine on the bench at the foot of the equestrian statue of General Sheridan.* Constance tipped her sunshade to shield her eyes, and she and Louis began a murmuring conversation which was impossible to catch. Old Hawberk, leaning on his ivory-headed cane, lighted an excellent cigar, the mate to which I politely refused, and smiled at vacancy. The sun hung low above the Staten Island* woods, and the bay was dyed with golden hues reflected from the sun-warmed sails of the shipping in the harbor.

Brigs, schooners, yachts, clumsy ferry-boats, their decks swarming with people, railroad transports carrying lines of brown, blue and

white freight cars, stately sound steamers, *de-classé* tramp steamers,*
coasters, dredgers, scows, and everywhere pervading the entire bay
impudent little tugs puffing and whistling officiously;—these were the
crafts which churned the sunlit waters as far as the eye could reach. In
calm contrast to the hurry of sailing vessel and steamer a silent fleet
of white warships lay motionless in midstream.

Constance's merry laugh aroused me from my reverie.

'What *are* you staring at?' she inquired.

'Nothing—the fleet,' I smiled.

Then Louis told us what the vessels were, pointing out each by its
relative position to the old Red Fort on Governor's Island.*

'That little cigar-shaped thing is a torpedo boat,' he explained;
'there are four more lying close together. They are the "Tarpon," the
"Falcon," the "Sea Fox" and the "Octopus." The gun-boats just above
are the "Princeton," the "Champlain," the "Still Water" and the
"Erie." Next to them lie the cruisers "Farragut" and "Los Angeles,"
and above them the battle-ships "California" and "Dakota," and the
"Washington" which is the flag-ship. Those two squatty-looking
chunks of metal which are anchored there off Castle William are the
double-turreted monitors "Terrible" and "Magnificent"; behind
them lies the ram, "Osceola." ' *

Constance looked at him with deep approval in her beautiful eyes.
'What loads of things you know for a soldier,' she said, and we all
joined in the laugh which followed.

Presently Louis rose with a nod to us and offered his arm to
Constance, and they strolled away along the river wall. Hawberk
watched them for a moment and then turned to me.

'Mr Wilde was right,' he said. 'I have found the missing tassets and
left cuissard of the 'Prince's Emblazoned,' in a vile old junk garret in
Pell Street.'

'998?' I inquired, with a smile.

'Yes.'

'Mr Wilde is a very intelligent man,' I observed.

'I want to give him the credit of this most important discovery,'
continued Hawberk. 'And I intend it shall be known that he is entitled
to the fame of it.'

'He won't thank you for that,' I answered sharply; 'please say nothing about it.'

'Do you know what it is worth?' said Hawberk.

'No, fifty dollars, perhaps.'

'It is valued at five hundred, but the owner of the "Prince's Emblazoned" will give two thousand dollars to the person who completes his suit; that reward also belongs to Mr Wilde.'

'He doesn't want it! He refuses it!' I answered angrily. 'What do you know about Mr Wilde? He doesn't need the money. He is rich—or will be—richer than any living man except myself. What will we care for money then—what will we care, he and I, when—when——'

'When what?' demanded Hawberk, astonished.

'You will see,' I replied, on my guard again.

He looked at me narrowly, much as Doctor Archer used to, and I knew he thought I was mentally unsound. Perhaps it was fortunate for him that he did not use the word lunatic just then.

'No,' I replied to his unspoken thought, 'I am not mentally weak; my mind is as healthy as Mr Wilde's. I do not care to explain just yet what I have on hand, but it is an investment which will pay more than mere gold, silver and precious stones. It will secure the happiness and prosperity of a continent—yes, a hemisphere!'

'Oh,' said Hawberk.

'And eventually,' I continued more quietly, 'it will secure the happiness of the whole world.'

'And incidentally your own happiness and prosperity as well as Mr Wilde's?'

'Exactly,' I smiled. But I could have throttled him for taking that tone.

He looked at me in silence for a while and then said very gently, 'Why don't you give up your books and studies, Mr Castaigne, and take a tramp among the mountains somewhere or other? You used to be fond of fishing. Take a cast or two at the trout in the Rangelys.'*

'I don't care for fishing any more,' I answered, without a shade of annoyance in my voice.

'You used to be fond of everything,' he continued; 'athletics, yachting, shooting, riding——'

'I have never cared to ride since my fall,' I said quietly.

'Ah, yes, your fall,' he repeated, looking away from me.

I thought this nonsense had gone far enough, so I turned the conversation back to Mr Wilde; but he was scanning my face again in a manner highly offensive to me.

'Mr Wilde,' he repeated, 'do you know what he did this afternoon?

He came down stairs and nailed a sign over the hall door next to mine; it read:

MR WILDE,

REPAIRER OF REPUTATIONS.

3d Bell.

Do you know what a Repairer of Reputations can be?'

'I do,' I replied, suppressing the rage within.

'Oh,' he said again.

Louis and Constance came strolling by and stopped to ask if we would join them. Hawberk looked at his watch. At the same moment a puff of smoke shot from the casemates of Castle William,* and the boom of the sunset gun rolled across the water and was re-echoed from the Highlands opposite. The flag came running down from the flag-pole, the bugles sounded on the white decks of the warships, and the first electric light sparkled out from the Jersey shore.

As I turned into the city with Hawberk I heard Constance murmur something to Louis which I did not understand; but Louis whispered 'My darling,' in reply; and again, walking ahead with Hawberk through the square I heard a murmur of 'sweetheart,' and 'my own Constance,' and I knew the time had nearly arrived when I should speak of important matters with my Cousin Louis.

III

ONE morning early in May I stood before the steel safe in my bedroom, trying on the golden jewelled crown. The diamonds flashed fire as I turned to the mirror, and the heavy beaten gold burned like a halo about my head. I remembered Camilla's agonized scream and the awful words echoing through the dim streets of Carcosa. They were the last lines in the first act, and I dared not think of what followed—dared not, even in the spring sunshine, there in my own room, surrounded with familiar objects, reassured by the bustle from the street and the voices of the servants in the hallway outside. For those poisoned words had dropped slowly into my heart, as death-sweat drops upon a bed-sheet and is absorbed. Trembling, I put the diadem from my head and wiped my forehead, but I thought of Hastur and of my own rightful ambition, and I remembered

Mr Wilde as I had last left him, his face all torn and bloody from the claws of that devil's creature, and what he said—ah, what he said! The alarm bell in the safe began to whirr harshly, and I knew my time was up; but I would not heed it, and replacing the flashing circlet upon my head I turned defiantly to the mirror. I stood for a long time absorbed in the changing expression of my own eyes. The mirror reflected a face which was like my own, but whiter, and so thin that I hardly recognized it. And all the time I kept repeating between my clenched teeth, 'The day has come! the day has come!' while the alarm in the safe whirred and clamored, and the diamonds sparkled and flamed above my brow. I heard a door open but did not heed it. It was only when I saw two faces in the mirror;—it was only when another face rose over my shoulder, and two other eyes met mine. I wheeled like a flash and seized a long knife from my dressing-table, and my cousin sprang back very pale, crying: 'Hildred! for God's sake!' then as my hand fell, he said: 'It is I, Louis, don't you know me?' I stood silent. I could not have spoken for my life. He walked up to me and took the knife from my hand.

'What is all this?' he inquired, in a gentle voice. 'Are you ill?'

'No,' I replied. But I doubt if he heard me.

'Come, come, old fellow,' he cried, 'take off that brass crown and toddle into the study. Are you going to a masquerade? What's all this theatrical tinsel anyway?'

I was glad he thought the crown was made of brass and paste, yet I didn't like him any the better for thinking so. I let him take it from my hand, knowing it was best to humor him. He tossed the splendid diadem in the air, and catching it, turned to me smiling.

'It's dear at fifty cents,' he said. 'What's it for?'

I did not answer, but took the circlet from his hands, and placing it in the safe shut the massive steel door. The alarm ceased its infernal din at once. He watched me curiously, but did not seem to notice the sudden ceasing of the alarm. He did, however, speak of the safe as a biscuit box. Fearing lest he might examine the combination I led the way into my study. Louis threw himself on the sofa and flicked at flies with his eternal riding-whip. He wore his fatigue uniform with the braided jacket and jaunty cap, and I noticed that his riding-boots were all splashed with red mud.

'Where have you been,' I inquired.

'Jumping mud creeks in Jersey,' he said, 'I haven't had time to change yet; I was rather in a hurry to see you. Haven't you got a glass of something? I'm dead tired; been in the saddle twenty-four hours.'

I gave him some brandy from my medicinal store, which he drank with a grimace.

'Damned bad stuff,' he observed. 'I'll give you an address where they sell brandy that is brandy.'

'It's good enough for my needs,' I said indifferently. 'I use it to rub my chest with.' He stared and flicked at another fly.

'See here, old fellow,' he began, 'I've got something to suggest to you. It's four years now that you've shut yourself up here like an owl, never going anywhere, never taking any healthy exercise, never doing a damn thing but poring over those books up there on the mantelpiece.'

He glanced along the row of shelves. 'Napoleon, Napoleon, Napoleon!' he read. For heaven sake, have you nothing but Napoleons there?'

'I wish they were bound in gold,' I said. 'But wait, yes, there is another book, "The King in Yellow."' I looked him steadily in the eye.

'Have you never read it?' I asked.

'I? No, thank God! I don't want to be driven crazy.'

I saw he regretted his speech as soon as he had uttered it. There is only one word which I loathe more than I do lunatic and that word is crazy. But I controlled myself and asked him why he thought 'The King in Yellow' dangerous.

'Oh, I don't know,' he said, hastily. 'I only remember the excitement it created and the denunciations from pulpit and press. I believe the author shot himself after bringing forth this monstrosity, didn't he?'

'I understand he is still alive,' I answered.

'That's probably true,' he muttered; 'bullets couldn't kill a fiend like that.'

'It is a book of great truths,' I said.

'Yes,' he replied, 'of "truths" which send men frantic and blast their lives. I don't care if the thing is, as they say, the very supreme essence of art. It's a crime to have written it, and I for one shall never open its pages.'

'Is that what you have come to tell me?' I asked.

'No,' he said, 'I came to tell you that I am going to be married.'

I believe for a moment my heart ceased to beat, but I kept my eyes on his face.

'Yes,' he continued, smiling happily, 'married to the sweetest girl on earth.'

'Constance Hawberk,' I said mechanically.

'How did you know?' he cried, astonished. 'I didn't know it myself until that evening last April, when we strolled down to the embankment before dinner.'

'When is it to be?' I asked.

'It was to have been next September, but an hour ago a despatch came ordering our regiment to the Presidio,* San Francisco. We leave at noon to-morrow. To-morrow,' he repeated. 'Just think, Hildred, to-morrow I shall be the happiest fellow that ever drew breath in this jolly world, for Constance will go with me.'

I offered him my hand in congratulation, and he seized and shook it like the good-natured fool he was—or pretended to be.

'I am going to get my squadron as a wedding present,' he rattled on. 'Captain and Mrs Louis Castaigne, eh, Hildred?'

Then he told me where it was to be and who were to be there, and made me promise to come and be best man. I set my teeth and listened to his boyish chatter without showing what I felt, but—

I was getting to the limit of my endurance, and when he jumped up, and, switching his spurs till they jingled, said he must go, I did not detain him.

'There's one thing I want to ask of you,' I said quietly.

'Out with it, it's promised,' he laughed.

'I want you to meet me for a quarter of an hour's talk to-night.'

'Of course, if you wish,' he said, somewhat puzzled. 'Where?'

'Anywhere, in the park there.'

'What time, Hildred?'

'Midnight.'

'What in the name of ——' he began, but checked himself and laughingly assented. I watched him go down the stairs and hurry away, his sabre banging at every stride. He turned into Bleecker Street, and I knew he was going to see Constance. I gave him ten minutes to disappear and then followed in his footsteps, taking with me the jewelled crown and the silken robe embroidered with the Yellow Sign. When I turned into Bleecker Street, and entered the doorway which bore the sign,

Mr Wilde,
Repairer of Reputations.
3d Bell.

I saw old Hawberk moving about in his shop, and imagined I heard Constance's voice in the parlor; but I avoided them both and hurried up the trembling stairways to Mr Wilde's apartment. I knocked, and entered without ceremony. Mr Wilde lay groaning on the floor, his face covered with blood, his clothes torn to shreds. Drops of blood were scattered about over the carpet, which had also been ripped and frayed in the evidently recent struggle.

'It's that cursed cat,' he said, ceasing his groans, and turning his colorless eyes to me; 'she attacked me while I was asleep. I believe she will kill me yet.'

This was too much, so I went into the kitchen and seizing a hatchet from the pantry, started to find the infernal beast and settle her then and there. My search was fruitless, and after a while I gave it up and came back to find Mr Wilde squatting on his high chair by the table. He had washed his face and changed his clothes. The great furrows which the cat's claws had ploughed up in his face he had filled with collodion,* and a rag hid the wound in his throat. I told him I should kill the cat when I came across her, but he only shook his head and turned to the open ledger before him. He read name after name of the people who had come to him in regard to their reputation, and the sums he had amassed were startling.

'I put on the screws now and then.' he explained.

'One day or other some of these people will assassinate you,' I insisted.

'Do you think so?' he said, rubbing his mutilated ears.

It was useless to argue with him, so I took down the manuscript entitled Imperial Dynasty of America, for the last time I should ever take it down in Mr Wilde's study. I read it through, thrilling and trembling with pleasure. When I had finished Mr Wilde took the manuscript and, turning to the dark passage which leads from his study to his bedchamber, called out in a loud voice, 'Vance.' Then for the first time, I noticed a man crouching there in the shadow. How I had overlooked him during my search for the cat, I cannot imagine.

'Vance, come in,' cried Mr Wilde.

The figure rose and crept toward us, and I shall never forget the face that he raised to mine, as the light from the window illuminated it.

'Vance, this is Mr Castaigne,' said Mr Wilde. Before he had finished speaking, the man threw himself on the ground before the table, crying and gasping, 'Oh, God! Oh, my God! Help me. Forgive me—Oh, Mr Castaigne, keep that man away. You cannot, you cannot mean it! You are different—save me! I am broken down—I was in a madhouse and now—when all was coming right—when I had forgotten the King—the King in Yellow and—but I shall go mad again—I shall go mad——'

His voice died into a choking rattle, for Mr Wilde had leapt on him and his right hand encircled the man's throat. When Vance fell in a heap on the floor, Mr Wilde clambered nimbly into his chair again, and rubbing his mangled ears with the stump of his hand, turned to me and asked me for the ledger. I reached it down from the shelf and he opened it. After a moment's searching among the beautifully written pages, he coughed complacently, and pointed to the name Vance.

'Vance,' he read aloud, 'Osgood Oswald Vance.' At the sound of his name, the man on the floor raised his head and turned a convulsed face to Mr Wilde. His eyes were injected with blood, his lips tumefied. 'Called April 28th,' continued Mr Wilde. 'Occupation, cashier in the Seaforth National Bank; has served a term of forgery at Sing Sing,* from whence he was transferred to the Asylum for the Criminal Insane. Pardoned by the Governor of New York, and discharged from the Asylum, January 19, 1918. Reputation damaged at Sheepshead Bay.* Rumors that he lives beyond his income. Reputation to be repaired at once. Retainer $1,500.

'Note.—Has embezzled sums amounting to $30,000 since March 20th, 1919, excellent family, and secured present position through uncle's influence. Father, President of Seaforth Bank.'

I looked at the man on the floor.

'Get up, Vance,' said Mr Wilde in a gentle voice. Vance rose as if hypnotized. 'He will do as we suggest now,' observed Mr Wilde, and opening the manuscript, he read the entire history of the Imperial Dynasty of America. Then in a kind and soothing murmur he ran over the important points with Vance, who stood like one stunned. His eyes were so blank and vacant that I imagined he had become half-witted, and remarked it to Mr Wilde who replied that it was of no consequence anyway. Very patiently we pointed out to Vance what his share in the affair would be, and he seemed to understand after a while. Mr Wilde explained the manuscript, using several volumes on Heraldry, to substantiate the result of his researches. He mentioned the establishment of the Dynasty in Carcosa, the lakes which connected Hastur, Aldebaran and the mystery of the Hyades. He spoke of Cassilda and Camilla, and sounded the cloudy depths of Demhe, and the Lake of Hali. 'The scolloped tatters of the King in Yellow must hide Yhtill forever,' he muttered, but I do not believe Vance heard him. Then by degrees he led Vance along the ramifications of the Imperial family, to Uoht and Thale, from Naotalba and Phantom of Truth, to Aldones, and then tossing aside his manuscript and notes, he began the wonderful story of the Last King. Fascinated and thrilled I watched him. He threw up his head, his long arms were stretched out in a magnificent gesture of pride and power, and his eyes blazed deep in their sockets like two emeralds. Vance listened stupefied. As for me, when at last Mr Wilde had finished, and pointing to me, cried, 'The cousin of the King!' my head swam with excitement.

Controlling myself with a superhuman effort, I explained to Vance why I alone was worthy of the crown and why my cousin must be exiled or die. I made him understand that my cousin must never marry, even after renouncing all his claims, and how that least of all he should marry the daughter of the Marquis of Avonshire and bring England into the question. I showed him a list of thousands of names which Mr Wilde had drawn up; every man whose name was there had received the Yellow Sign which no living human being dared disregard. The city, the state, the whole land, were ready to rise and tremble before the Pallid Mask.

The time had come, the people should know the son of Hastur, and the whole world bow to the Black Stars which hang in the sky over Carcosa.

Vance leaned on the table, his head buried in his hands. Mr Wilde drew a rough sketch on the margin of yesterday's *Herald* with a bit of lead pencil. It was a plan of Hawberk's rooms. Then he wrote out the order and affixed the seal, and shaking like a palsied man I signed my first writ of execution with my name Hildred-Rex.

Mr Wilde clambered to the floor and unlocking the cabinet, took a long square box from the first shelf. This he brought to the table and opened. A new knife lay in the tissue paper inside and I picked it up and handed it to Vance, along with the order and the plan of

Hawberk's apartment. Then Mr Wilde told Vance he could go; and he went, shambling like an outcast of the slums.

I sat for a while watching the daylight fade behind the square tower of the Judson Memorial Church, and finally, gathering up the manuscript and notes, took my hat and started for the door.

Mr Wilde watched me in silence. When I had stepped into the hall I looked back. Mr Wilde's small eyes were still fixed on me. Behind him, the shadows gathered in the fading light. Then I closed the door behind me and went out into the darkening streets.

I had eaten nothing since breakfast, but I was not hungry. A wretched half-starved creature, who stood looking across the street at the Lethal Chamber, noticed me and came up to tell me a tale of misery. I gave him money, I don't know why, and he went away without thanking me. An hour later another outcast approached and whined his story. I had a blank bit of paper in my pocket, on which was traced the Yellow Sign and I handed it to him. He looked at it stupidly for a moment, and then with an uncertain glance at me, folded it with what seemed to me exaggerated care and placed it in his bosom.

The electric lights were sparkling among the trees, and the new moon shone in the sky above the Lethal Chamber. It was tiresome waiting in the square; I wandered from the Marble Arch to the artillery stables, and back again to the lotos fountain. The flowers and grass exhaled a fragrance which troubled me. The jet of the fountain played in the moonlight, and the musical splash of falling drops reminded me of the tinkle of chained mail in Hawberk's shop. But it was not so fascinating, and the dull sparkle of the moonlight on the water brought no such sensations of exquisite pleasure, as when the sunshine played over the polished steel of a corselet on Hawberk's knee. I watched the bats darting and turning above the water plants in the fountain basin, but their rapid, jerky flight set my nerves on edge, and I went away again to walk aimlessly to and fro among the trees.

The artillery stables were dark, but in the cavalry barracks the officer's windows were brilliantly lighted, and the sallyport* was constantly filled with troopers in fatigue, carrying straw and harness and baskets filled with tin dishes.

Twice the mounted sentry at the gates was changed, while I wandered up and down the asphalt walk. I looked at my watch. It was nearly time. The lights in the barracks went out one by one, the barred gate was closed, and every minute or two an officer passed in through the side wicket, leaving a rattle of accoutrements and a jingle of spurs on the night air. The square had become very silent. The last homeless loiterer had been driven away by the gray-coated park policeman, the car tracks along Wooster Street were deserted, and the only sound which broke the stillness was the stamping of the sentry's horse and the ring of his sabre against the saddle pommel. In the barracks, the officer's quarters were still lighted, and military servants passed and repassed before the bay windows. Twelve o'clock sounded from the new spire of St Francis Xavier,* and at the last stroke of the sad-toned bell a figure passed through the wicket beside the portcullis, returned the salute of the sentry, and crossing the street entered the square and advanced toward the Benedick apartment house.

'Louis,' I called.

The man pivoted on his spurred heels and came straight toward me.

'Is that you, Hildred?'

'Yes, you are on time.'

I took his offered hand, and we strolled toward the Lethal Chamber.

He rattled on about his wedding and the graces of Constance, and their future prospects, calling my attention to his captain's shoulder-straps, and the triple gold arabesque on his sleeve and fatigue cap. I believe I listened as much to the music of his spurs and sabre as I did to his boyish babble, and at last we stood under the elms on the Fourth Street corner of the square opposite the Lethal Chamber. Then he laughed and asked me what I wanted with him. I motioned him to a seat on a bench under the electric light, and sat down beside him. He looked at me curiously, with that same searching glance which I hate and fear so in doctors. I felt the insult of his look, but he did not know it, and I carefully concealed my feelings.

'Well, old chap,' he enquired, 'what can I do for you?'

I drew from my pocket the manuscript and notes of the Imperial Dynasty of America, and looking him in the eye said:

'I will tell you. On your word as a soldier, promise me to read this manuscript from beginning to end, without asking me a question. Promise me to read these notes in the same way, and promise me to listen to what I have to tell later.'

'I promise, if you wish it,' he said pleasantly, 'Give me the paper, Hildred.'

He began to read, raising his eyebrows with a puzzled whimsical air, which made me tremble with suppressed anger. As he advanced, his eyebrows contracted, and his lips seemed to form the word, 'rubbish.' Then he looked slightly bored, but apparently for my sake read, with an attempt at interest, which presently ceased to be an effort. He started when in the closely-written pages he came to his own name, and when he came to mine he lowered the paper, and looked sharply at me for a moment. But he kept his word, and resumed his reading, and I let the half-formed question die on his lips unanswered. When he came to the end and read the signature of Mr Wilde, he folded the paper carefully and returned it to me. I handed him the notes, and he settled back, pushing his fatigue cap up to his forehead, with a boyish gesture, which I remembered so well in school. I watched his face as he read, and when he finished I took the notes with the manuscript, and placed them in my pocket. Then I unfolded a scroll marked with the Yellow Sign. He saw the sign, but he did not seem to recognize it, and I called his attention to it somewhat sharply.

'Well,' he said, 'I see it. What is it?'

'It is the Yellow Sign,' I said, angrily.

'Oh, that's it, is it?' said Louis, in that flattering voice, which Doctor Archer used to employ with me, and would probably have employed again, had I not settled his affair for him.

I kept my rage down and answered as steadily as possible, 'Listen, you have engaged your word?'

'I am listening, old chap,' he replied soothingly.

I began to speak very calmly.

'Dr Archer, having by some means become possessed of the secret of the Imperial Succession, attempted to deprive me of my right, alleging that because of a fall from my horse four years ago, I had become mentally deficient. He presumed to place me under restraint in his own house in hopes of either driving me insane or poisoning me. I have not forgotten it. I visited him last night and the interview was final.'

Louis turned quite pale, but did not move. I resumed triumphantly, 'There are yet three people to be interviewed in the interests of Mr Wilde and myself. They are my cousin Louis, Mr Hawberk, and his daughter Constance.'

Louis sprang to his feet and I arose also, and flung the paper marked with the Yellow Sign to the ground.

'Oh, I don't need that to tell you what I have to say,' I cried with a laugh of triumph. 'You must renounce the crown to me, do you hear, to *me*.'

Louis looked at me with a startled air, but recovering himself said kindly, 'Of course I renounce the—what is it I must renounce?'

'The crown,' I said angrily.

'Of course,' he answered, 'I renounce it. Come, old chap, I'll walk back to your rooms with you.'

'Don't try any of your doctor's tricks on me,' I cried, trembling with fury. 'Don't act as if you think I am insane.'

'What nonsense,' he replied. 'Come, it's getting late, Hildred.'

'No,' I shouted, 'you must listen. You cannot marry, I forbid it. Do you hear? I forbid it. You shall renounce the crown, and in reward I grant you exile, but if you refuse you shall die.'

He tried to calm me but I was roused at last, and drawing my long knife barred his way.

Then I told him how they would find Dr Archer in the cellar with his throat open, and I laughed in his face when I thought of Vance and his knife, and the order signed by me.

'Ah, you are the King,' I cried, 'but I shall be King. Who are you to keep me from Empire over all the habitable earth! I was born the cousin of a king, but I shall be King!'

Louis stood white and rigid before me. Suddenly a man came running up Fourth Street, entered the gate of the Lethal Temple, traversed the path to the bronze doors at full speed, and plunged into the death chamber with the cry of one demented, and I laughed until I wept tears, for I had recognized Vance, and knew that Hawberk and his daughter were no longer in my way.

'Go,' I cried to Louis, 'you have ceased to be a menace. You will never marry Constance now, and if you marry any one else in your exile, I will visit you as I did my doctor last night. Mr Wilde takes charge of you to-morrow.' Then I turned and darted into South Fifth Avenue, and with a cry of terror Louis dropped his belt and sabre and followed me like the wind. I heard him close behind me at the corner of Bleecker Street, and I dashed into the doorway under Hawberk's sign. He cried, 'Halt, or I fire!' but when he saw that I flew up the stairs leaving Hawberk's shop below, he left me, and I heard him hammering and shouting at their door as though it were possible to arouse the dead.

Mr Wilde's door was open, and I entered crying, 'It is done, it is done! Let the nations rise and look upon their King!' but I could not find Mr Wilde, so I went to the cabinet and took the splendid diadem from its case. Then I drew on the white silk robe, embroidered with the yellow sign, and placed the crown upon my head. At last I was King, King by my right in Hastur, King because I knew the mystery of the Hyades, and my mind had sounded the depths of the Lake of Hali. I was King! The first gray pencillings of dawn would raise a tempest which would shake two hemispheres. Then as I stood, my every nerve pitched to the highest tension, faint with the joy and splendor of my thought, without, in the dark passage, a man groaned.

I seized the tallow dip and sprang to the door. The cat passed me like a demon, and the tallow dip went out, but my long knife flew swifter than she, and I heard her screech, and I knew that my knife had found her. For a moment I listened to her tumbling and thumping about in the darkness, and then when her frenzy ceased, I lighted a lamp and raised it over my head. Mr Wilde lay on the floor with his throat torn open. At first I thought he was dead, but as I looked, a green sparkle came into his sunken eyes, his mutilated hand trembled, and then a spasm stretched his mouth from ear to ear. For a moment my terror and despair gave place to hope, but as I bent over him his eyeballs rolled clean around in his head, and he died. Then while I stood, transfixed with rage and despair, seeing my crown, my empire, every hope and every ambition, my very life, lying prostrate there with the dead master, *they* came, seized me from behind, and bound me until my veins stood out like cords, and my voice failed with the paroxysms of my frenzied screams. But I still raged, bleeding and infuriated among them, and more than one policeman felt my sharp teeth. Then when I could no longer move they came nearer; I saw old Hawberk, and behind him my cousin Louis' ghastly face, and farther away, in the corner, a woman, Constance, weeping softly.

'Ah! I see it now!' I shrieked. 'You have seized the throne and the empire. Woe! woe to you who are crowned with the crown of the King in Yellow!'

[EDITOR'S NOTE.—Mr Castaigne died yesterday in the Asylum for Criminal Insane.]

ARTHUR MACHEN

Novel of the White Powder

❧❧

MY name is Leicester;* my father, Major-General Wyn Leicester, a distinguished officer of artillery, succumbed five years ago to a complicated liver complaint acquired in the deadly climate of India. A year later my only brother, Francis, came home after an exceptionally brilliant career at the University, and settled down with the resolution of a hermit to master what has been well called the great legend of the law. He was a man who seemed to live in utter indifference to everything that is called pleasure; and though he was handsomer than most men, and could talk as merrily and wittily, as if he were a mere vagabond, he avoided society, and shut himself up in a large room at the top of the house to make himself a lawyer. Ten hours a day of hard reading was at first his allotted portion; from the first light in the east to the late afternoon he remained shut up with his books, taking a hasty half-hour's lunch with me as if he grudged the wasting of the moments, and going out for a short walk when it began to grow dusk. I thought that such relentless application must be injurious, and tried to cajole him from the crabbed textbooks, but his ardour seemed to grow rather than diminish, and his daily tale of hours increased. I spoke to him seriously, suggesting some occasional relaxation, if it were but an idle afternoon with a harmless novel; but he laughed, and said that he read about feudal tenures* when he felt in need of amusement, and scoffed at the notion of theatres, or a month's fresh air. I confessed that he looked well, and seemed not to suffer from his labours, but I knew that such unnatural toil would take revenge at last, and I was not mistaken. A look of anxiety began to lurk about his eyes, and he seemed languid, and at last he avowed that he was no longer in perfect health; he was troubled, he said, with a sensation of dizziness, and awoke now and then of nights from fearful dreams, terrified and cold with icy sweats. 'I am taking care of myself,' he said, 'so you must not trouble; I passed the whole of yesterday afternoon in idleness, leaning back in that comfortable chair you gave me, and scribbling nonsense on a sheet of paper. No, no; I will not overdo my work; I shall be well enough in a week or two, depend upon it.'

Yet in spite of his assurances I could see that he grew no better, but rather worse; he would enter the drawing-room with a face all miserably wrinkled and despondent, and endeavour to look gaily when my eyes fell on him, and I thought such symptoms of evil omen, and was frightened sometimes at the nervous irritation of his movements, and at glances which I could not decipher. Much against his will, I prevailed on him to have medical advice, and with an ill grace he called in our old doctor.

Dr Haberden cheered me after examination of his patient.

'There is nothing really much amiss,' he said to me. 'No doubt he reads too hard, and eats hastily, and then goes back again to his books in too great a hurry, and the natural consequence is some digestive trouble and a little mischief in the nervous system. But I think— I do indeed, Miss Leicester—that we shall be able to set this all right. I have written him a prescription which ought to do great things. So you have no cause for anxiety.'

My brother insisted on having the prescription made up by a chemist in the neighbourhood; it was an odd, old-fashioned shop, devoid of the studied coquetry and calculated glitter that make so gay a show on the counters and shelves of the modern apothecary; but Francis liked the old chemist, and believed in the scrupulous purity of his drugs. The medicine was sent in due course, and I saw that my brother took it regularly after lunch and dinner. It was an innocent-looking white powder, of which a little was dissolved in a glass of cold water; I stirred it in, and it seemed to disappear, leaving the water clear and colourless. At first Francis seemed to benefit greatly; the weariness vanished from his face, and he became more cheerful than he had ever been since the time when he left school; he talked gaily of reforming himself, and avowed to me that he had wasted his time.

'I have given too many hours to law,' he said, laughing; 'I think you have saved me in the nick of time. Come, I shall be Lord Chancellor* yet, but I must not forget life. You and I will have a holiday together before long; we will go to Paris and enjoy ourselves, and keep away from the Bibliothèque Nationale.'*

I confessed myself delighted with the prospect.

'When shall we go?' I said. 'I can start the day after to-morrow if you like.'

'Ah! that is perhaps a little too soon; after all, I do not know London yet, and I suppose a man ought to give the pleasures of his own country the first choice. But we will go off together in a week or two, so try and furbish up your French. I only know law French myself, and I am afraid that wouldn't do.'

We were just finishing dinner, and he quaffed off his medicine with a parade of carousal as if it had been wine from some choicest bin.

'Has it any particular taste?' I said.

'No; I should not know I was not drinking water,' and he got up from his chair and began to pace up and down the room as if he were undecided as to what he should do next.

'Shall we have coffee in the drawing-room?' I said; 'or would you like to smoke?'

'No, I think I will take a turn; it seems a pleasant evening. Look at the afterglow; why, it is as if a great city were burning in flames, and down there between the dark houses it is raining blood fast, fast. Yes, I will go out; I may be in soon, but I shall take my key; so good-night, dear, if I don't see you again.'

The door slammed behind him, and I saw him walk lightly down the street, swinging his malacca cane,* and I felt grateful to Dr Haberden for such an improvement.

I believe my brother came home very late that night, but he was in a merry mood the next morning.

'I walked on without thinking where I was going,' he said, 'enjoying the freshness of the air, and livened by the crowds as I reached more frequented quarters. And then I met an old college friend, Orford, in the press of the pavement, and then—well, we enjoyed ourselves. I have felt what it is to be young and a man; I find I have blood in my veins, as other men have. I made an appointment with Orford for to-night; there will be a little party of us at the restaurant. Yes; I shall enjoy myself for a week or two, and hear the chimes at midnight, and then we will go for our little trip together.'

Such was the transmutation of my brother's character that in a few days he became a lover of pleasure, a careless and merry idler of western pavements, a hunter out of snug restaurants, and a fine critic of fantastic dancing; he grew fat before my eyes, and said no more of Paris, for he had clearly found his paradise in London. I rejoiced, and yet wondered a little; for there was, I thought, something in his gaiety that indefinitely displeased me, though I could not have defined my feeling. But by degrees there came a change; he returned still in the cold hours of the morning, but I heard no more about his pleasures, and one morning as we sat at breakfast together I looked suddenly into his eyes and saw a stranger before me.

'O Francis!' I cried. 'O Francis, Francis, what have you done?' and rending sobs cut the words short. I went weeping out of the room; for though I knew nothing, yet I knew all, and by some odd play of thought I remembered the evening when he first went abroad to prove his manhood, and the picture of the sunset sky glowed before me; the clouds like a city in burning flames, and the rain of blood. Yet I did battle with such thoughts, resolving that perhaps, after all, no great harm had been done, and in the evening at dinner I resolved to press him to fix a day for our holiday in Paris. We had talked easily enough, and my brother had just taken his medicine, which he had continued all the while. I was about to begin my topic, when the words forming in my mind vanished, and I wondered for a second what icy and intolerable weight oppressed my heart and suffocated me as with the unutterable horror of the coffin-lid nailed down on the living.

We had dined without candles; the room had slowly grown from twilight to gloom, and the walls and corners were indistinct in the shadow. But from where I sat I looked out into the street; and as I thought of what I would say to Francis, the sky began to flush and shine, as it had done on a well-remembered evening, and in the gap between two dark masses that were houses an awful pageantry of flame appeared—lurid whorls of writhed cloud, and utter depths burning, grey masses like the fume blown from a smoking city, and an evil glory blazing far above shot with tongues of more ardent fire, and below as if there were a deep pool of blood. I looked down to where my brother sat facing me, and the words were shaped on my lips, when I saw his hand resting on the table. Between the thumb and forefinger of the closed hand there was a mark, a small patch about the size of a sixpence, and somewhat of the colour of a bad bruise. Yet, by some sense I cannot define, I knew that what I saw was no bruise at all; oh, if human flesh could burn with flame, and if flame could be black as pitch, such was that before me. Without thought or fashioning of words grey horror shaped within me at the sight, and in an inner cell it was known to be a brand. For a moment the stained sky became dark as midnight, and when the light returned to me I was alone in the silent room, and soon after I heard my brother go out.

Late as it was, I put on my bonnet and went to Dr Haberden, and in his great consulting room, ill lighted by a candle which the doctor brought in with him, with stammering lips, and a voice that would break in spite of my resolve, I told him all, from the day on which my brother began to take the medicine down to the dreadful thing I had seen scarcely half an hour before.

When I had done, the doctor looked at me for a minute with an expression of great pity on his face.

'My dear Miss Leicester,' he said, 'you have evidently been anxious about your brother; you have been worrying over him, I am sure. Come, now, is it not so?'

'I have certainly been anxious,' I said. 'For the last week or two I have not felt at ease.'

'Quite so; you know, of course, what a queer thing the brain is?'

'I understand what you mean; but I was not deceived. I saw what I have told you with my own eyes.'

'Yes, yes, of course. But your eyes had been staring at that very curious sunset we had to-night. That is the only explanation. You will see it in the proper light to-morrow, I am sure. But, remember, I am always ready to give any help that is in my power; do not scruple to come to me, or to send for me if you are in any distress.'

I went away but little comforted, all confusion and terror and sorrow, not knowing where to turn. When my brother and I met the next day, I looked quickly at him, and noticed, with a sickening at heart, that the right hand, the hand on which I had clearly seen the patch as of a black fire, was wrapped up with a handkerchief.

'What is the matter with your hand, Francis?' I said in a steady voice.

'Nothing of consequence. I cut a finger last night, and it bled rather awkwardly. So I did it up roughly to the best of my ability.'

'I will do it neatly for you, if you like.'

'No, thank you, dear; this will answer very well. Suppose we have breakfast; I am quite hungry.'

We sat down, and I watched him. He scarcely ate or drank at all, but tossed his meat to the dog when he thought my eyes were turned away; there was a look in his eyes that I had never yet seen, and the thought flashed across my mind that it was a look that was scarcely human. I was firmly convinced that awful and incredible as was the thing I had seen the night before, yet it was no illusion, no glamour* of bewildered sense, and in the course of the morning I went again to the doctor's house.

He shook his head with an air puzzled and incredulous, and seemed to reflect for a few minutes.

'And you say he still keeps up the medicine? But why? As I understand, all the symptoms he complained of have disappeared long ago; why should he go on taking the stuff when he is quite well. And, by the bye, where did he get it made up? At Sayce's? I never send any one there; the old man is getting careless. Suppose you come with me to the chemist's; I should like to have some talk with him.'

We walked together to the shop; old Sayce knew Dr Haberden, and was quite ready to give any information.

'You have been sending that in to Mr Leicester for some weeks I think on my prescription,' said the doctor, giving the old man a pencilled scrap of paper.

The chemist put on his great spectacles with trembling uncertainty, and held up the paper with a shaking hand.

'Oh, yes,' he said, 'I have very little of it left; it is rather an uncommon drug, and I have had it in stock some time. I must get in some more, if Mr Leicester goes on with it.'

'Kindly let me have a look at the stuff,' said Haberden, and the chemist gave him a glass bottle. He took out the stopper and smelt the contents, and looked strangely at the old man.

'Where did you get this?' he said, 'and what is it? For one thing, Mr Sayce, it is not what I prescribed. Yes, yes, I see the label is right enough, but I tell you this is not the drug.'

'I have had it a long time,' said the old man in feeble terror; 'I got it from Burbage's in the usual way. It is not prescribed often, and I have had it on the shelf for some years. You see there is very little left.'

'You had better give it to me,' said Haberden. 'I am afraid something wrong has happened.'

We went out of the shop in silence, the doctor carrying the bottle neatly wrapped in paper under his arm.

'Dr Haberden,' I said when we had walked a little way—'Dr Haberden.'

'Yes,' he said, looking at me gloomily enough.

'I should like you to tell me what my brother has been taking twice a day for the last month or so.'

'Frankly, Miss Leicester, I don't know. We will speak of this when we get to my house.'

We walked on quickly without another word till we reached Dr Haberden's. He asked me to sit down, and began pacing up and down the room, his face clouded over, as I could see, with no common fears.

'Well,' he said at length, 'this is all very strange; it is only natural that you should feel alarmed, and I must confess that my mind is far from easy. We will put aside, if you please, what you told me last night and this morning, but the fact remains that for the last few weeks Mr Leicester has been impregnating his system with a drug which is completely unknown to me. I tell you, it is not what I ordered; and what that stuff in the bottle really is remains to be seen.'

He undid the wrapper, and cautiously tilted a few grains of the white powder on to a piece of paper, and peered curiously at it.

'Yes,' he said, 'it is like the sulphate of quinine,* as you say; it is flaky. But smell it.'

He held the bottle to me, and I bent over it. It was a strange, sickly smell, vaporous and overpowering, like some strong anæsthetic.

'I shall have it analysed,' said Haberden; 'I have a friend who has devoted his whole life to chemistry as a science. Then we shall have something to go upon. No, no; say no more about that other matter; I cannot listen to that; and take my advice and think no more about it yourself.'

That evening my brother did not go out as usual after dinner.

'I have had my fling,' he said with a queer laugh, 'and I must go back to my old ways. A little law will be quite a relaxation after so sharp a dose of pleasure,' and he grinned to himself, and soon after went up to his room. His hand was still all bandaged.

Dr Haberden called a few days later.

'I have no special news to give you,' he said. 'Chambers is out of town, so I know no more about that stuff than you do. But I should like to see Mr Leicester if he is in.'

'He is in his room,' I said; 'I will tell him you are here.'

'No, no, I will go up to him; we will have a little quiet talk together. I dare say that we have made a good deal of fuss about very little; for, after all, whatever the white powder may be, it seems to have done him good.'

The doctor went upstairs, and standing in the hall I heard his knock, and the opening and shutting of the door; and then I waited in the silent house for an hour, and the stillness grew more and more intense as the hands of the clock crept round. Then there sounded from above the noise of a door shut sharply, and the doctor was coming down the stairs. His footsteps crossed the hall, and there was a pause at the door; I drew a long, sick breath with difficulty, and saw my face white in a little mirror, and he came in and stood at the door. There was an unutterable horror shining in his eyes; he steadied himself by holding the back of a chair with one hand, his lower lip trembled like a horse's, and he gulped and stammered unintelligible sounds before he spoke.

'I have seen that man,' he began in a dry whisper. 'I have been sitting in his presence for the last hour. My God! And I am alive and in my senses! I, who have dealt with death all my life, and have dabbled with the melting ruins of the earthly tabernacle.* But not this, oh! not this,' and he covered his face with his hands as if to shut out the sight of something before him.

'Do not send for me again, Miss Leicester,' he said with more composure. 'I can do nothing in this house. Good-bye.'

As I watched him totter down the steps, and along the pavement towards his house, it seemed to me that he had aged by ten years since the morning.

My brother remained in his room. He called out to me in a voice I hardly recognised that he was very busy, and would like his meals brought to his door and left there, and I gave the order to the servants. From that day it seemed as if the arbitrary conception we call time had been annihilated for me; I lived in an ever-present sense of horror, going through the routine of the house mechanically, and only speaking a few necessary words to the servants. Now and then I went out and paced the streets for an hour or two and came home again; but whether I were without or within, my spirit delayed before the closed door of the upper room, and, shuddering, waited for it to open. I have said that I scarcely reckoned time; but I suppose it must have been a fortnight after Dr Haberden's visit that I came home from my stroll a little refreshed and lightened. The air was sweet and pleasant, and the hazy form of green leaves, floating cloudlike in the square, and the smell of blossoms, had charmed my senses, and I felt happier and walked more briskly. As I delayed a moment at the verge of the pavement, waiting for a van to pass by before crossing over to the house, I happened to look up at the windows, and instantly there was the rush and swirl of deep cold waters in my ears, my heart leapt up, and fell down, down as into a deep hollow, and I was amazed with a dread and terror without form or shape. I stretched out a hand blindly through folds of thick darkness, from the black and shadowy valley, and held myself from falling, while the stones beneath my feet rocked and swayed and tilted, and the sense of solid things seemed to sink away from under me. I had glanced up at the window of my brother's study, and at that moment the blind was drawn aside, and something that had life stared out into the world. Nay, I cannot say I saw a face or any human likeness; a living thing, two eyes of burning flame glared at me, and they were in the midst of something as form-less as my fear, the symbol and presence of all evil and all hideous cor-ruption. I stood shuddering and quaking as with the grip of ague, sick with unspeakable agonies of fear and loathing, and for five minutes I could not summon force or motion to my limbs. When I was within the door, I ran up the stairs to my brother's room, and knocked.

'Francis, Francis,' I cried, 'for Heaven's sake, answer me. What is the horrible thing in your room? Cast it out, Francis; cast it from you.'

I heard a noise as of feet shuffling slowly and awkwardly, and a choking, gurgling sound, as if some one was struggling to find utterance, and then the noise of a voice, broken and stifled, and words that I could scarcely understand.

'There is nothing here,' the voice said. 'Pray do not disturb me. I am not very well to-day.'

I turned away, horrified, and yet helpless. I could do nothing, and I wondered why Francis had lied to me, for I had seen the appearance beyond the glass too plainly to be deceived, though it was but the sight of a moment. And I sat still, conscious that there had been something else, something I had seen in the first flash of terror, before those burning eyes had looked at me. Suddenly I remembered; as I lifted my face the blind was being drawn back, and I had had an instant's glance of the thing that was moving it, and in my recollection I knew that a hideous image was engraved for ever on my brain. It was not a hand; there were no fingers that held the blind, but a black stump pushed it aside, the mouldering outline and the clumsy movement as of a beast's paw had glowed into my senses before the darkling waves of terror had overwhelmed me as I went down quick into the pit. My mind was aghast at the thought of this, and of the awful presence that dwelt with my brother in his room; I went to his door and cried to him again, but no answer came. That night one of the servants came up to me and told me in a whisper that for three days food had been regularly placed at the door and left untouched; the maid had knocked, but had received no answer; she had heard the noise of shuffling feet that I had noticed. Day after day went by, and still my brother's meals were brought to his door and left untouched; and though I knocked and called again and again, I could get no answer. The servants began to talk to me; it appeared they were as alarmed as I; the cook said that when my brother first shut himself up in his room she used to hear him come out at night and go about the house; and once, she said, the hall door had opened and closed again, but for several nights she had heard no sound. The climax came at last; it was in the dusk of the evening, and I was sitting in the darkening dreary room when a terrible shriek jarred and rang harshly out of the silence, and I heard a frightened scurry of feet dashing down the stairs. I waited, and the servant-maid staggered into the room and faced me, white and trembling.

'Oh, Miss Helen!' she whispered; 'oh! for the Lord's sake, Miss Helen, what has happened? Look at my hand, miss; look at that hand!'

I drew her to the window, and saw there was a black wet stain upon her hand.

'I do not understand you,' I said. 'Will you explain to me?'

'I was doing your room just now,' she began. 'I was turning down the bed-clothes, and all of a sudden there was something fell upon my hand, wet, and I looked up, and the ceiling was black and dripping on me.'

I looked hard at her and bit my lip.

'Come with me,' I said. 'Bring your candle with you.'

The room I slept in was beneath my brother's, and as I went in I felt I was trembling. I looked up at the ceiling, and saw a patch, all black and wet, and a dew of black drops upon it, and a pool of horrible liquor soaking into the white bed-clothes.

I ran upstairs, and knocked loudly.

'Oh, Francis, Francis, my dear brother,' I cried, 'what has happened to you?'

And I listened. There was a sound of choking, and a noise like water bubbling and regurgitating, but nothing else, and I called louder, but no answer came.

In spite of what Dr Haberden had said, I went to him; with tears streaming down my cheeks I told him of all that had happened, and he listened to me with a face set hard and grim.

'For your father's sake,' he said at last, 'I will go with you, though I can do nothing.'

We went out together; the streets were dark and silent, and heavy with heat and a drought of many weeks. I saw the doctor's face white under the gas-lamps, and when we reached the house his hand was shaking.

We did not hesitate, but went upstairs directly. I held the lamp, and he called out in a loud, determined voice—

'Mr Leicester, do you hear me? I insist on seeing you. Answer me at once.'

There was no answer, but we both heard that choking noise I have mentioned.

'Mr Leicester, I am waiting for you. Open the door this instant, or I shall break it down.' And he called a third time in a voice that rang and echoed from the walls—

'Mr Leicester! For the last time I order you to open the door.'

'Ah!' he said, after a pause of heavy silence, 'we are wasting time here. Will you be so kind as to get me a poker, or something of the kind.'

I ran into a little room at the back where odd articles were kept, and found a heavy adze*-like tool that I thought might serve the doctor's purpose.

'Very good,' he said, 'that will do, I dare say. I give you notice, Mr Leicester,' he cried loudly at the keyhole, 'that I am now about to break into your room.'

Then I heard the wrench of the adze, and the woodwork split and cracked under it; with a loud crash the door suddenly burst open, and for a moment we started back aghast at a fearful screaming cry, no human voice, but as the roar of a monster, that burst forth inarticulate and struck at us out of the darkness.

'Hold the lamp,' said the doctor, and we went in and glanced quickly round the room.

'There it is,' said Dr Haberden, drawing a quick breath; 'look, in that corner.'

I looked, and a pang of horror seized my heart as with a white-hot iron. There upon the floor was a dark and putrid mass, seething with corruption and hideous rottenness, neither liquid nor solid, but melting and changing before our eyes, and bubbling with unctuous oily bubbles like boiling pitch. And out of the midst of it shone two burning points like eyes, and I saw a writhing and stirring as of limbs, and something moved and lifted up that might have been an arm. The doctor took a step forward, raised the iron bar and struck at the burning points; he drove in the weapon, and struck again and again in a fury of loathing. At last the thing was quiet.

* * *

A week or two later, when I had to some extent recovered from the terrible shock, Dr Haberden came to see me.

'I have sold my practice,' he began, 'and tomorrow I am sailing on a long voyage. I do not know whether I shall ever return to England; in all probability I shall buy a little land in California, and settle there for the remainder of my life. I have brought you this packet, which you may open and read when you feel able to do so. It contains the report of Dr Chambers on what I submitted to him. Good-bye, Miss Leicester, good-bye.'

When he was gone I opened the envelope; I could not wait, and proceeded to read the papers within. Here is the manuscript, and if you will allow me, I will read you the astounding story it contains.

'My dear Haberden,' the letter began, 'I have delayed inexcusably in answering your questions as to the white substance you sent me. To tell you the truth, I have hesitated for some time as to what course I should adopt, for there is a bigotry and an orthodox standard in physical science as in theology, and I knew that if I told you the truth I should offend rooted prejudices which I once held dear myself. However, I have determined to be plain with you, and first I must enter into a short personal explanation.

'You have known me, Haberden, for many years as a scientific man; you and I have often talked of our profession together, and discussed the hopeless gulf that opens before the feet of those who think to attain to truth by any means whatsoever except the beaten way of experiment and observation in the sphere of material things. I remember the scorn with which you have spoken to me of men of science who have dabbled a little in the unseen, and have timidly hinted that perhaps the senses are not, after all, the eternal, impenetrable bounds of all knowledge, the everlasting walls beyond which no human being has ever passed. We have laughed together heartily, and I think justly, at the "occult" follies of the day, disguised under various names—the mesmerisms, spiritualisms, materialisations, theosophies,* all the rabble rant of imposture, with their machinery of poor tricks and feeble conjuring, the true back-parlour magic of shabby London streets. Yet, in spite of what I have said, I must confess to you that I am no materialist, taking the word of course in its usual signification. It is now many years since I have convinced myself, convinced myself—a sceptic remember—that the old iron-bound theory is utterly and entirely false. Perhaps this confession will not wound you so sharply as it would have done twenty years ago; for I think you cannot have failed to notice that for some time hypotheses have been advanced by men of pure science which are nothing less than transcendental,* and I suspect that most modern chemists and biologists of repute would not hesitate to subscribe the *dictum* of the old Schoolman, *Omnia exeunt in mysterium,** which means, I take it, that every branch of human knowledge, if traced up to its source and final principles, vanishes into mystery. I need not trouble you now with a detailed account of the painful steps which led me to my conclusions; a few simple experiments suggested a doubt as to my then standpoint, and a train of thought that rose from circumstances comparatively trifling brought me far; my old conception of the universe has been swept away, and I stand in a world that seems as strange and awful to me as the endless waves of the ocean seen for the first time, shining, from a peak in Darien.* Now I know that the walls of sense that seemed so impenetrable, that seemed to loom up above the heavens and to be founded below the depths, and to shut us in for evermore, are no such everlasting impassable barriers, as we fancied, but thinnest and most airy veils that melt away before the seeker, and dissolve as the early mist of the morning about the brooks. I know that you never adopted the extreme materialistic position; you did not go about trying to prove a universal negative, for your logical sense withheld you from that crowning absurdity; but I am sure that you will find all that I am saying strange and repellent to your habits of thought. Yet, Haberden, what I tell you is the truth, nay, to adopt our common language, the

sole and scientific truth, verified by experience; and the universe is
verily more splendid and more awful than we used to dream. The
whole universe, my friend, is a tremendous sacrament; a mystic,
ineffable force and energy, veiled by an outward form of matter; and
man, and the sun and the other stars, and the flower of the grass,
and the crystal in the test-tube, are each and every one as spiritual,
as material, and subject to an inner working.

'You will perhaps wonder, Haberden, whence all this tends; but
I think a little thought will make it clear. You will understand that
from such a standpoint the whole view of things is changed, and what
we thought incredible and absurd may be possible enough. In short,
we must look at legend and belief with other eyes, and be prepared to
accept tales that had become mere fables. Indeed, this is no such great
demand. After all, modern science will concede as much, in a hypo-
critical manner; you must not, it is true, believe in witchcraft, but you
may credit hypnotism; ghosts are out of date, but there is a good deal
to be said for the theory of telepathy.* Give a superstition a Greek
name, and believe in it, should almost be a proverb.

'So much for my personal explanation. You sent me, Haberden,
a phial, stoppered and sealed, containing a small quantity of a flaky
white powder, obtained from a chemist who has been dispensing it
to one of your patients. I am not surprised to hear that this powder
refused to yield any results to your analysis. It is a substance which
was known to a few many hundred years ago, but which I never
expected to have submitted to me from the shop of a modern apothecary. There seems no reason to doubt the truth of the man's tale; he
no doubt got, as he says, the rather uncommon salt you prescribed
from the wholesale chemist's; and it has probably remained on his
shelf for twenty years, or perhaps longer. Here what we call chance
and coincidence begin to work; during all these years the salt in the
bottle was exposed to certain recurring variations of temperature,
variations probably ranging from 40° to 80°. And, as it happens, such
changes, recurring year after year at irregular intervals, and with
varying degrees of intensity and duration, have constituted a process, and a process so complicated and so delicate, that I question
whether modern scientific apparatus directed with the utmost precision could produce the same result. The white powder you sent me
is something very different from the drug you prescribed; it is the
powder from which the wine of the Sabbath, the *Vinum Sabbati*,*

was prepared. No doubt you have read of the Witches' Sabbath, and have laughed at the tales which terrified our ancestors; the black cats, and the broomsticks, and dooms pronounced against some old woman's cow. Since I have known the truth I have often reflected that it is on the whole a happy thing that such burlesque as this is believed, for it serves to conceal much that it is better should not be known generally. However, if you care to read the appendix to Payne Knight's monograph,* you will find that the true Sabbath was something very different, though the writer has very nicely refrained from printing all he knew. The secrets of the true Sabbath were the secrets of remote times surviving into the Middle Ages, secrets of an evil science which existed long before Aryan* man entered Europe. Men and women, seduced from their homes on specious pretences, were met by beings well qualified to assume, as they did assume, the part of devils, and taken by their guides to some desolate and lonely place, known to the initiate by long tradition, and unknown to all else. Perhaps it was a cave in some bare and wind-swept hill, perhaps some inmost recess of a great forest, and there the Sabbath was held. There, in the blackest hour of night, the *Vinum Sabbati* was prepared, and this evil graal* was poured forth and offered to the neophytes, and they partook of an infernal sacrament; *sumentes calicem principis inferorum,** as an old author well expresses it. And suddenly, each one that had drunk found himself attended by a companion, a shape of glamour and unearthly allurement, beckoning him apart, to share in joys more exquisite, more piercing than the thrill of any dream, to the consummation of the marriage of the Sabbath. It is hard to write of such things as these, and chiefly because that shape that allured with loveliness was no hallucination, but, awful as it is to express, the man himself. By the power of that Sabbath wine, a few grains of white powder thrown into a glass of water, the house of life was riven asunder and the human trinity dissolved, and the worm which never dies, that which lies sleeping within us all, was made tangible and an external thing, and clothed with a garment of flesh. And then, in the hour of midnight, the primal fall was repeated and re-presented, and the awful thing veiled in the mythos of the Tree in the Garden was done anew. Such was the *nuptiæ Sabbati.**

'I prefer to say no more; you, Haberden, know as well as I do that the most trivial laws of life are not to be broken with impunity; and for so terrible an act as this, in which the very inmost place of the temple was broken open and defiled, a terrible vengeance followed. What began with corruption ended also with corruption.'

Underneath is the following in Dr Haberden's writing:—

'The whole of the above is unfortunately strictly and entirely true. Your brother confessed all to me on that morning when I saw him in his room. My attention was first attracted to the bandaged hand, and I forced him to show it me. What I saw made me, a medical man of many years standing, grow sick with loathing, and the story I was forced to listen to was infinitely more frightful than I could have believed possible. It has tempted me to doubt the Eternal Goodness which can permit nature to offer such hideous possibilities; and if you had not with your own eyes seen the end, I should have said to you—disbelieve it all. I have not, I think, many more weeks to live, but you are young, and may forget all this.

'JOSEPH HABERDEN, M.D.'

In the course of two or three months I heard that Dr Haberden had died at sea shortly after the ship left England.

RICHARD MARSH

The Adventure of Lady Wishaw's Hand

(Mr Pugh tells the story)

❧❧❧

CHAPTER I

THE LEGACY

IT was a woman's hand. In life, in its proper place at the end of a woman's arm, I could easily believe that it had been beautiful. But as it lay before me on the table, amidst the heap of papers in which it had been wrapped, I am bound to say that it was not its beauty that struck me first of all. One peculiar feature about it was its extraordinary state of preservation. Some embalming process must have been employed with which I was wholly unacquainted. It looked as if it were alive. Not only so!—when, after some not inconsiderable amount of hesitation, I ventured to pick it up, it felt warm to the touch. Almost unwittingly, I pressed it—as I might have pressed a friendly hand in greeting. It seemed to return my pressure. Of course, it was all imagination. But it was imagination of rather a ghastly kind. So vivid was the delusion, that I let it fall back on the table with a start that was sufficiently real.

The hand had been severed, with what had evidently been some sharp instrument, just above the wrist. A joint or some fraction of the bone—I am no anatomist—had apparently been withdrawn, so that the skin overlapped at the end. A white skin it was. I never saw a whiter. Yet it was not a bloodless white. Indeed, it was not difficult to believe that the warm blood was circulating underneath. It was a little hand. It struck me as being exquisitely shaped. A dainty hand. The fingers were long and slender, and tapered to a point. The finger-nails were perfect. They were pink, as are the finger-nails of some young girls. It was those almond-shaped, pink, well-kept finger-nails, which, as much as anything else, gave to the hand such a curious semblance of life. The fingers and thumb were close together, so that, as it lay palm downwards the thumb was in the air, and only the finger-tips pressing against the table, the whole hand formed a sort of arch. It was a right hand. On the fore-finger was a ring. So quaint a ring that, in itself, it was a curio. It was of plain gold, clumsily fashioned, and at the back it had been beaten out by some unskilled craftsman into what had probably been intended to represent a heart-shaped shield. On it were some roughly graven words, which, at any rate without a microscope, I was unable to decipher. I attributed the ring at a rough and ready estimate to perhaps the latter portion of the fourteenth century. It seemed odd to see that ill-shaped and ancient gewgaw* on the pretty finger of that dainty little hand.

It was an extraordinary legacy, even for a collector to receive. It appeared that it was a legacy—this woman's hand. From a man, too, who had been but a shadowy acquaintance. It had reached me by a singularly matter-of-fact route—the parcels post. I wondered if the post office officials would have said anything if they had known what it was that they were carrying. With it had come a letter, in which David Wishaw informed me that his brother, Colin, was dead, of which fact I had known nothing, and cared, if possible, still less; and that it had been one of Colin's very last requests that the hand which, according to David, had been known in the family as 'Lady Wishaw's hand,' should be sent me as a legacy. Very kind of Colin, and also of David, on my honour! David went on to say that Colin had been aware that I was a great collector of curiosities, and he had felt very strongly that 'Lady Wishaw's hand' was a curiosity that I should value. Had he indeed! Kinder still, and kinder! The hand, said David, had been an heirloom in the family. Then what on earth did the man mean by passing his family heirlooms on to me, an almost utter stranger? It had been in the family, in uninterrupted sequence, since 1382. When I read that, I wondered whether the man took me for an idiot. The hand—that hand which was lying before me on the table—had been in his family, or anybody's family, since 1382! I doubted very much if it had not been upon a living woman's arm, certainly, within the last six months.

What was I to do with such a legacy? I might be a collector of curiosities, a virtuoso, or a bric-à-brac hunter, which you please. But I was not a curator of an anatomical museum. The curiosities which I collected did not include detached portions of the human frame. The Messrs Colin and David Wishaw seemed both of them to have laboured under the same misapprehension. I knew a man who collected the ropes with which criminals had been hung. He was a virtuoso of a kind which I was not. Mr Colin Wishaw should have bequeathed and Mr David Wishaw should have despatched—by means of parcels post—this curiosity to him.

The ring on the finger did seem more in my way. Getting a magnifying glass, I endeavoured to make out the legend which was on the shield. The ring was old—there could be no doubt about that. It might date from 1382. The legend, in the first place, had been ill done, and in course of time it had become so worn that even with the aid of a good glass, it was difficult to decipher.

' "I take myne owne," that's what it is,' I finally decided. 'It's either "seke" or "take". I fancy it's "take"—"I take myne owne". I wonder if that is the motto of the Wishaws? I have a good mind to write to Mr David Wishaw, and to send him back the hand, and to tell him that, with his permission, as a mark of my appreciation of his brother's thought for me, I'll keep the ring. I might add that, in my judgment, it would be as well if the hand were decently interred. Let's see if I can take the ring off the lady's finger, so that I can have a look at it at closer quarters.'

With this idea and with the intention of putting the idea into execution, I once more picked up the hand—though I own I touched it with reluctance. Holding it with my left hand, grasping the ring with the fingers of my right, I prepared to work it loose. Instantly the hand shut up! It was clenched into a fist! I do not think I ever was so startled in my life. The action was so natural, so lifelike, that, though I was in my own drawing-room, and it was broad day, and there was no one present but the hand and myself, it seemed almost as if my heart had leapt into my mouth. It was no optical delusion—the open hand had become a tightened fist. No doubt, it was owing to some muscular contraction—but it was muscular contraction of a sort I did not like. So startled was I that for some moments I could do nothing else but stare. When I could I dropped the hand as if it had been a red-hot coal. I sprang to my feet.

'I'll send it back to Mr David Wishaw, directly after lunch, ring and all!'

I was momentarily expecting lunch to be announced. It would not do to leave the hand lying on the table open. So I hurriedly caught up the papers in which it had come, and, wrapping them about it anyhow, I put it in a cabinet which stood upon a small side table.

CHAPTER II

THE LEGEND

As I was finishing lunch, there came a knock at the hall door. Nalder went to see who it was. Nalder is a most excellent servant; one whom scarcely anything would induce to forget his place. Therefore, I was the more surprised, when, after a few minutes' absence, he reappeared with an expression of countenance which suggested both bewilderment and pain. He was rubbing his thigh, too, in a manner which, considering that he was standing in the presence of his master, was highly unbecoming.

'What's the matter, Nalder?'

'Well, sir, it's Mr Brasher, sir.'

'Mr Brasher? What do you mean? What's the matter with Mr Brasher?'

'Well, sir—nothing's the matter with Mr Brasher, that I am aware of but—a most extraordinary thing has happened. At least, I beg your pardon, sir, it seems to me a most extraordinary thing. When I showed Mr Brasher up into the drawing-room, I noticed that the ormolu-cabinet which stands on the Chippendale* tripod table was open.' This was the cabinet in which I placed Mr Colin Wishaw's legacy. I must unintentionally have omitted to close it when I left the room. 'I went to shut it, and directly I had done so, just as I was turning round, some one or something caught me in the fleshy part of the leg, and gave me such a nip, that, I do believe, there's a piece nipped out.'

'Some one or something? What do you mean by some one or something?'

'I don't know, sir, I really don't. There was no one or nothing, near me, that I could see, and that's why I say it's a most extraordinary thing. But I never did feel anything so painful—never.'

I left Nalder still rubbing his thigh in a manner which his previous conduct had certainly given me no reason to expect from him. When I went upstairs I found Martin Brasher standing in the centre of the room with a look on his face which might have been twin brother to the look I had seen on Nalder's.

'Pugh,' was his salutation to me as I went in, 'what on earth have you got in this room of yours?'

'I have a good many things in this room of mine, as, if you had eyes, you would be able to see. What is the matter with you?'

'Upon my word, I hardly know what is the matter with me. Do you know, I was just sitting on that armchair, waiting for you, when something—it felt like somebody's finger-nails—scratched my cheek from top to bottom. Isn't there a scratch to be seen?'

There was, unmistakably. On his left cheek there was what was, obviously, the mark of a recent scratch.

'You've been in dreamland, Brasher, and scratched yourself in your dream.'

'Nothing of the kind. I tell you what, Pugh, it's uncommonly queer! But never mind about that now; I have come to tell you that I've got a case at last.'

'A case of what?'

'A case for the society*—a genuine ghost. Have you ever heard of a man named Wishaw?' I had very much indeed, and very recently. But he didn't give me a chance. He was so very full of his subject, that he went dashing on, without noticing that he had not afforded me an opportunity to answer.

'They're a Scotch family, the Wishaws—one of those Scotch families which antedate the deluge. They have had some peculiar characters among them in their time, more peculiar than pleasant—as some of these Scotch families have had a way of having. One of the most peculiar was a woman, who lived somewhere about the close of the fourteenth century—a propitious period, especially in Scotland, for peculiar characters. She is known among them to this day, as "Lady Wishaw". You know how they have that sort of thing in stories. She was the most beautiful woman that ever was—that's of course. She was, also, the wickedest woman that ever was—that's equally of course. She does appear to have done something to deserve a niche, as the latter, in the temple of fame. She was a thief. Such a thief that she became notorious as a thief, even in that age and land of thieves. She stole from foes and friends alike. At last, in the house of a friend, she was caught redhanded, in some more astounding theft than usual. We should have called her a kleptomaniac, I suspect, in these latter days. The term was not invented then, nor the thing. To her host she appeared to have been guilty of an act of hideous treachery. Taking upon himself, as was not uncommon in those sweet and simple days, the offices of judge, jury and executioner, there and then he hacked off her hand at the wrist. The first intimation which the Wishaws received of the latest *petit faux pas** in which the lady had indulged came to them in rather grisly fashion. The lady's guilty, but, I understand, lovely member was sent to them by the host and by a special messenger. The lady herself they never saw again—at least in life. She felt, when she had lost her hand, that she had lost all that there was worth living for. She destroyed herself within the hour. Thus, as you perceive, there was ample ground why a pleasant little feud should exist, henceforth, between the whilom friends, the Wishaws and the Macfies—the host's name was, it seems, Macfie.

'The story goes that the dismembered lady managed to convey some sort of spiritual intimation to her relatives, to the effect that they were never to cease from killing while a Macfie still remained to cumber the ground.* Thenceforward, the first end and aim of the Wishaws was to kill the Macfies. And in order that they might not forget their high calling, a special injunction was laid on them that they were to keep the hacked-off hand ever with them as a sort of heirloom, and as a perpetual reminder, until the last of the Macfies was slain. Not only so. They were given clearly to understand, that should a Wishaw arise who, before the Macfies were wholly exterminated, proved unworthy, and ceased from killing, the dead hand would turn against the living man, and would measure out to him that measure which he should have measured out to the Macfies.'

'This is a queer story.' I felt that it was. 'But the queerest part is still to come. I am informed, on creditable authority, that the hand was never embalmed. That nothing has been done to preserve it, of any sort or kind. That it has continued, uninterruptedly, in the possession of the Wishaws. And that, after the passage of the centuries, it still looks as fresh and as lifelike as if its original owner still had it, in the proper place, at the end of her arm.'

As to the truth of this portion of his story, touching the appearance of life which the hand possessed, I could have gone to the cabinet, taken out its contents, and given him the proof on the spot; and I may add, that I should have done it, had it not been that a contraction of the muscles of my throat seemed to keep me a fixture in my chair.

'Pugh, I mean to see that hand.' He should have seen it, then and there, had not the sensation of which I had suddenly become conscious almost amounted to strangulation. 'It strikes me that there's a clear case for the Psychical Research Society at last. I have chanced, almost by accident, upon some extraordinary stories of Lady Wishaw's hand. It seems that the Wishaws did keep on killing the Macfies. But they were a prolific breed. As soon as a sire was struck down a son sprang up. There came a time when murder, even in Scotland, was not looked upon with such lenient eyes. Still the Wishaws pursued the even tenor of their way. More than one of them has brought himself within the clutches, and has suffered the last penalties of the law. Finally, even the Wishaws succumbed to the influence of the new spirit of the newer age. They declined to keep on murdering. In fact, they ceased to murder. When they ceased, the hand—the dead hand—Lady Wishaw's hand, began. Pugh, I have reason to believe that, literally, for generations, the head of the family, for the time being, has been found strangled in his bed.'

Brasher paused. He stood in front of me with a dramatic gesture. With an effort I found myself able to speak.

'Where did you get that piece of information from, may I inquire?'

'Never mind where I got it from, it is so. You may take it from me that the thing was kept hushed up. It was given out that they died from a spasmodic affection of the heart. Nothing of the kind. There never was a Wishaw with a weak heart yet. At last, only two of them were left, Colin Wishaw, the head of the house, and David, his younger brother. Colin was something like a madman.' From the little I had seen of him he had struck me as being about as mad as a man could be, without being pronounced, legally and medically, insane. 'He swore a great oath that he would rid himself and the family of Lady Wishaw's hand.'

'If what you have told me is correct, Brasher, I fail to see any signs of madness in his doing that.'

'The extraordinary part of the thing was the way in which he set himself to carry out his oath. He put the hand in a coffin and buried it, coffin and all. Lady Wishaw's hand returned to him from the grave.'

'Oh, Brasher, come!'

'So I am told. He took it with him across the Atlantic. In mid-ocean he dropped it into the sea. When he reached his hotel in New York he found it at his bedside in the morning. He cast it into a smelter's furnace. It was waiting for him when he got home. I am credibly assured that he cooked it and ate it, only to find it on his pillow when he went to bed.'

'Brasher, your story begins to remind me of a poem which I read in my childhood days, which, if I remember rightly, was called, and appropriately, called, "A Horrible Tale".'*

'Wait a bit. About a fortnight ago Colin Wishaw was found dead in his bed. There was no mistake about it this time—he had been strangled. It was impossible to hush it up. An inquest was held. The verdict was, that he had been strangled by some person or persons unknown.'

If that were so, what on earth did David Wishaw mean by saying that, almost with his last breath, Colin had bequeathed, what appeared to be, *par excellence*, the heirloom of the Wishaws, as a legacy to me. Mr David Wishaw was a nice man, upon my word!

'The present possessor of Lady Wishaw's hand,' continued Brasher, 'is David Wishaw, the last living representative of the Wishaw strain.' Was he? He would very soon be the possessor, though he was not then. 'I am going to call on Mr David Wishaw. I shall request him to allow me to examine the hand. I intend to make inquiries as to the truth of its extraordinary history. As I have told you, I have reason to believe that its truth will be made quite plain. Should that be so, I shall present the case for the immediate consideration of the Psychical Research Society. I think you will agree with me that a more remarkable case will hardly come its way.'

I quite agreed that, if—that little if—he could find evidence to prove it, it would be a remarkable case. And I was more than once on the point of informing him that, if he really desired to look at, and to examine Lady Wishaw's hand he need go no further than where he stood. But each time, as the words had already almost escaped my lips, I again became conscious of what I can only describe as that curious and distinctly involuntary suppression of the larynx.

CHAPTER III

THE HORROR

WHEN Martin Brasher went, he left, so to speak, his story behind. I heartily wished he had not. His story might sound incredible. It

might even sound absurd. But there are men, sane men, who are
entirely of opinion that it is quite within the bounds of reason to
suppose that there may be what the world commonly calls spiritual
manifestations—dealings between the seen and the unseen. Of such
men, I avowedly, am one. And the idea that there had come to me,
from such a deathbed as Colin Wishaw's appeared to have been, a gift
which was, in itself, a ghastly gift, and with which was associated such
a history—the mere idea to me was full of horror.

Besides, what had prevented me from speaking? What was it that
had caused that sensation of pressure about the region of my throat,
and so stayed me from telling Brasher that the thing for which he was
about to seek, all the time, was at his side, within reach of his arm?
What had pinched Nalder? It was a ridiculous inquiry, perhaps—but
what had? What had scratched Brasher's face? What had caused the
open hand to shut up into a clenched fist, before my very eyes? Was
it because the hand, though dead, was living, and was still attached to
a living form, though unseen?

Men are made in different fashions. Some men would have found
in my situation nothing but pleasurable excitement. For my part
I sat in my chair and sweated. I was unwilling to be left alone in
my own drawing-room, even though it was broad day. Nothing but
shame prevented me from summoning Nalder to come and keep me
company.

On one point I was resolved, that Lady Wishaw's hand would not
remain in my possession. For two hours I endeavoured to summon up
sufficient resolution to enable me to rise from my chair, and to go to
the cabinet, and to take out the hand, and to pack it up, and to return
it whence it came. As I look back upon those two hours, I am half
inclined to wonder how it was that, as they have it in the nightmare
stories, during their passage my hair did not turn grey. All the while
I had the consciousness that something was in the room with me.
Something seemed to keep stroking the back of my hand, something
with the delicate touch of a dainty woman. I knew that the starch was
coming out of my linen. I felt that my collar was becoming as limp
as a rag. At last, with what, positively, amounted to a frenzied effort,
I sprang from my seat, rushed to the cabinet, opened it, and reached
out for the hand, and found that it was—not there.

There could be no question as to whether its apparent disappearance was not one of the effects of being endowed with too vivid an

imagination. In the papers in which I had hastily wrapped Lady Wishaw's hand, before going down to lunch, there was nothing at all.

'Nalder! Nalder!'

I scarcely think that I expected him to hear me call. I am under the impression that I hardly spoke above a whisper. I began to stagger toward the door, intending to go out on to the landing and call him loudly. As I turned, something was placed against my mouth. Something which felt like the slender fingers of a woman's hand. And my lips were sealed!

CHAPTER IV

WHAT HAPPENED AT THE CLUB

I DINED at the club. I am unable to say how I reached it. I know that I did reach it. For me, at least, that is sufficient. I had a little table at the third window from the door. Perkins was my waiter. Perkins is not only an excellent waiter; he is, what is almost of as much importance, an excellent man. I am persuaded that Perkins and I have many things in common. He knows exactly what I like and how I like it. When he tells me what to eat, I eat it, without so much as a hint of an amendment. Never yet have I found that the house of my confidence has been builded on the sand.

I remember that, on that particular night, I had one of the finest woodcocks I ever tasted. Plain roast. I am almost inclined to believe that Perkins must have raised that bird himself, have shot it himself, have hung it himself, and have cooked it himself, he had its history so completely at his finger-ends. Brasher's story, and my two hours' agony, had almost faded from my mind. I do not say that the woodcock was wholly responsible, but it had certainly borne its part. I was just going to drink my second glass of champagne—I don't care what anybody says, everybody has his own taste, and with woodcock I like champagne. I daresay, in another half minute, I should have thanked God that I was alive. The glass was still on its way to my lips when, without any sort of a warning, in an instant, there returned to me that hideous consciousness which had been with me in the afternoon, that something was in the room. I do not mean the waiters, or the diners, and that sort of thing. I wish I did. I mean something intangible, unseen.

I put down my untasted glass. A cold shiver went over me. Then I began to perspire. My feeling was one of the acutest misery. My first impulse, in spite of the woodcock, was to wish that I was dead. In that brilliantly-lighted room, with all the people about me, I was afraid. Perkins was at my side. He had his back to me, for some cause or other, at the moment. All at once he faced round to me, with quite a little twirl. To be frank it was not the kind of movement which was becoming to Perkins. One of his great charms is that he never evinces what I consider indecorous signs of haste. Of an actual twirl, as if he had been a sort of human teetotum,* I do not think that he had ever been guilty before.

'I beg your pardon, sir?'

I have no doubt that I looked at him with what were a lack-lustre pair of eyes. I believe that I murmured 'Eh?'

'Did you touch me, sir?'

'Touch you? What do you mean?'

'I really must ask you to excuse me, sir,'—Perkins is an educated man—'but I certainly was under the impression, sir, that you pulled my coat-tails.'

I pulled his coat-tails! A waiter's! I had, after all, over-estimated Perkins' intellectual powers, if he could suppose that I could be capable of such an action as that. But I said nothing. I rose from the table there and then, and went away. I daresay that Perkins imagined I was bitterly offended. I should certainly have been justified in being so. Or, perhaps, he imagined that I had suddenly gone mad. I left my second glass of champagne untasted. I did not wait for the sweets—Perkins has an exquisite taste in sweets. His sweets never give me indigestion. I said nothing about his wife. (I always inquire after Perkins' wife—who I understand is paralysed, and as good as dead—when he has seen that I have had a creditable dinner.) I went into the smoking-room. I do not know why. I was in no mood to smoke. I take it that I went there simply because, with that intangible unseen something keeping me company, I could not go home.

Several men were in the smoking-room. Tolerably comfortable they seemed, as for a second, I stood at the door and looked round. I envied them. Their contentment with the position in life in which they found themselves placed was so transparently greater than mine. My moving to a seat seemed to create a slight sensation. Each man, as I passed him, gave a perceptible start. Again, I don't know why, I had scarcely seated myself before I became aware that something curious was going on. I seemed to have brought with me an element of discord into the room. Those who had seemed so wholly at their ease, as I viewed them from the door, seemed, all at once, to have been attacked by a fit of the fidgets. A most pronounced fit of the fidgets, too. The attack seemed to be passing from one smoker to the other, right round the room. Under cover of an evening paper I pretended to notice nothing. But I did. Man after man sprang up in his seat and looked about him with an air of startled surprise. Pranklyn was sitting in front of me. 'Plain' Pranklyn, as they call him, to distinguish him from the other Pranklyn—'Picture' Pranklyn—who has a chamber of horrors which he calls his picture gallery. Plain Pranklyn is in his seventies, and would turn the scale, I daresay, at eighteen stone. So when I say that suddenly he sprang up from his seat, as if he had been an india-rubber ball, I am aware that the language which I use is strong.

'Good God!' he exclaimed.

Everybody looked at him. All the room was in a stir.

'What is up, Pranklyn?' asked Sir Gerald Carr.

'Who was that caught hold of my hand?'

'Caught hold of your hand? What do you mean?'

'Hanged if I know what I do mean.' Pranklyn looked to me as if he were on the verge of an apoplectic fit. 'I know that some one caught hold of my hand and twisted it right round.'

A man whom I don't know spoke next:—

'That's odd. A moment before some one, or something, did exactly the same thing to me.'

'Be George!' cried old Jack Brett. 'But there's the devil in the room. I'll swear that some one nearly pulled me hand clean off me wrist.'

'And mine!' 'And mine!'

Nearly every person present claimed to have undergone a similar experience. There were a score of men turning the smoking-room into a Bedlam. I don't know what the committee would have said. I, for my part, sat as if I were glued to my chair. For, directly Pranklyn sprang from his seat, I felt a hand steal into mine, and fingers and a thumb clasp it about.

'Holloa,' said Carr, 'what's gone wrong with you? You don't look well.'

I rose from my seat with a palsied start. As I did so, the hand let go.

'I'm not feeling well. I—I think that I'll go home.' I went home, there and then. As I moved across the room, every man jack of them followed me with his eyes. I don't know if they thought that I had bewitched them, or played some hanky-panky trick. They looked as if they did.

As I went along the passage, and down the steps, into the street, I felt some one twitching at my coat sleeve. I hailed a cab. I bade the cabman drive me home. All the time, as he drove me through the streets, I felt as if there were some one seated beside me in the cab. Some one who continually twitched me by the arm. I doubt if there was ever a sane creature in such a state of mind as I then was. Nalder let me in. He started when he saw my face.

'I hope, sir, you are not ill?'

'To tell the truth, Nalder, I'm not feeling quite the thing. I think I'll have some brandy in my bedroom and go to bed.'

I had the strongest reluctance to go, unaccompanied, up my own staircase. I hung about in the hall until Nalder appeared with some brandy on a tray. Together we went up, he in front and I behind. I don't know what he thought of me. He is too well-trained a servant to betray his feelings in his face. At the same time, he is possessed of too much discernment to have failed to see that my indisposition was of a peculiar kind. Especially when, under one pretext and another, I kept him in my bedroom until I was actually between the sheets in bed.

'Shall I leave the light burning, sir?'

It is a peculiarity of mine that I never can sleep where there is a light in the room. On that occasion my choice seemed to lie between the devil and the deep sea. The idea of being left in the dark filled me with a paralysis of horror. On the other hand, what might I not be destined to witness, if the room was light. I chose, mechanically, what I could only hope would turn out to be the less evil of the two.

'Leave it burning. If I find that it keeps me from sleeping, I will get out of bed and put it out.'

I did not get out of bed to put it out. Queerly enough, scarcely had Nalder turned his back, than I fell asleep. I must have done, because I remember nothing after he left the room. Nothing, that is, until I awoke. I was not troubled with a dream. I must have slept the quiet dreamless sleep of tired childhood.

CHAPTER V

THE COMING OF THE GIFT

WHAT woke me I do not know, even to this hour. I know that I did wake, to find myself in a cold sweat of agony. Quivering under the overwhelming burden of some unknown horror. For some moments I was only conscious that the room was still lighted. At first, I seemed to have to gasp for breath. But, by degrees, the curtain of unconsciousness was partly lifted, and I became aware that something was with me in the room. What it was, I cannot say. It was something which touched me on the brow. With a light touch, such as we might use to waken a sleeper out of sleep. Only that touch was like the touch of death. I believe that it was the touch of death. Light though it was, under it I could not move. While it remained, I doubt if I breathed. I lay, as I have said, in a cold sweat of agony. When the touch was removed, I closed my eyes. I was afraid of what it was I might see. For what was a period of a few moments I suppose, nothing happened; though I never for an instant lost consciousness of the presence which was with me in the room. As I lay with my eyes fast closed, in agony, something—something tangible—fell on my cheek from above. It had something of the effect of an electric shock. With what I apprehend was an involuntary tension of the muscles of my body, I leaped out of bed on to the floor. I believe that, as I stood on the floor, I cried. Then I stretched out my arms on either side of me, as a blind man might do. Then, and only then, I opened my eyes and looked and saw. Leaning over the bed, I saw that on the pillow on which my head had just been lying was a ring.

I never had a moment's doubt as to the ring's identity. Having seen it once, it was one which I never could forget. It was the ring which had been on the forefinger of the hand which, according to David Wishaw, his brother Colin had bequeathed me as a legacy. The ring which the dead hand had seemed to resent my attempting to remove from its place by clenching itself into a fist. Was it possible that it was offered me as a present after all? Then, by whom? As the scriptural writers have it, my heart melted within me* as I realised that it was an offering from the presence which was with me in the room.

I shrunk away. I extended my arms as if to prevent the ring from coming to close quarters. As I did so I saw a hand advancing across the pillows from the opposite side of the bed. It was the hand which, having once been seen under such circumstances as I had seen it, was no more to be mistaken than the ring. It was, indeed, the hand to which it belonged. The hand of which Brasher had told such a horrible tale. The hand which according to him had urged to murder through the centuries, and then, when its urging had failed, had murdered on its own account.

I saw the hand coming slowly across the bed. It at no time touched the pillow, but, without any visible support, was in the air at a distance above the pillow, of, perhaps, a couple of inches. I saw the dainty fingers close upon the ring. When I saw that, with a spasmodic effort I turned my face away. My glance fell upon the clock which was on the mantelshelf. I noticed, with a singular degree of vividness that, according to that clock, the time was five and twenty minutes to four.

A touch came on my arm. I started round. In front of me was the hand. It was palm uppermost. On the open palm was the ring. It was being held out for me to take. But I would have none of it—although the chance of becoming the possessor of so genuine and unique a curio was hardly likely ever to come again in my way. I slunk back. The hand followed me. It moved quicker than I did. It caught me by the hand. It pressed the ring against my palm. But still I would have none of it. I made no attempt to close my hand so as to retain the ring within my grasp.

Suddenly the something which guided and ruled the hand—never, as I have said, for a moment did I lack consciousness of the something which was there—suddenly this something seemed to become annoyed. My persistent, automatic refusal of the proffered ring seemed, in some fantastic way, to give annoyance. All at once, the hand was withdrawn. It was clenched. It was held before me in the air. I saw the ring between the little dainty fingers. Then, with an extraordinary degree of violence, it was thrown against my face.

CHAPTER VI
THE PASSING OF DAVID WISHAW

'WHY are you lying there upon the floor?'

It was Brasher's voice. I found, as he said, that I was lying in my night-shirt on the floor. I sat up. I saw that the light still burned.

'Has it gone?'

'Has what gone? What has happened to your face?'

I put my hand up to my face. When I removed it, it was dabbled with blood. It all came back to me—the extreme violence of the movement with which the hand had hurled the ring at me through the air.

'The ring!' was all I said.

'The ring? What ring?' I rose to my feet. I dimly perceived that, for some cause, Brasher was almost as much disturbed as I myself.

We looked each other in the face. 'Pugh!' He caught me by the arm. His hand was shaking. 'Where is Lady Wishaw's hand?'

I looked around the room. 'Is it still here?'

'Here? Where? For God's sake don't speak like that. Your voice is as hoarse as a crow's.'

I felt him shiver.

'Why did you not tell me, yesterday, that you were the present fortunate possessor of Lady Wishaw's hand?'

I said nothing. He went on. Owing to his haste, or to some other cause, he seemed to pronounce his words as if he were temporarily afflicted with an impediment in his speech.

'It's been at its devil's tricks again. I've come straight from Wishaw's. David's dead.'

'Dead! David Wishaw! Brasher!'

'Don't look at me like that. You look at me as if you were looking at a ghost.' Taking out his handkerchief, he wiped his brow. 'Yes, David Wishaw's dead. He was the last of the breed. With him all of them have gone. It seems that this morning at a quarter after three——'

'When?'

'This morning, at a quarter after three, his servants heard him screaming in his room. When they went to his aid, they could not get to him, because the door was locked. They heard him fighting and yelling within. They called to him but could get no answer. All was still when the shrieking ceased. They found the door open. They found him dead. He had been strangled. He was a strong man. He must have fought furiously for his life, because they found him lying in a hideous heap on his bed.'

'Brasher, Lady Wishaw's hand was with me here at five and twenty minutes to four.'

'Pugh.' His jaw dropped down.

'Yes, Brasher, it was here, with me.'

'Are you sure that you are not mistaken?'

'And because I would not have the ring, which it endeavoured to force on my acceptance, it flung it in my face with such violence that it cut my face right open, as you see. I wonder if that ring is anywhere upon the floor.'

No. We searched everywhere. But it was nowhere to be found. After all, the hand had vanished with that ancient gewgaw of a ring. Acting up to the legend which seemed to me to have been inscribed upon it Lady Wishaw's hand had taken its own.

W. W. JACOBS

The Monkey's Paw

I

WITHOUT, the night was cold and wet, but in the small parlour of Laburnam Villa* the blinds were drawn and the fire burned brightly. Father and son were at chess, the former, who possessed ideas about the game involving radical changes, putting his king into such sharp and unnecessary perils that it even provoked comment from the white-haired old lady knitting placidly by the fire.

'Hark at the wind,' said Mr White, who, having seen a fatal mistake after it was too late, was amiably desirous of preventing his son from seeing it.

'I'm listening,' said the latter, grimly surveying the board as he stretched out his hand. 'Check.'

'I should hardly think that he'd come tonight,' said his father, with his hand poised over the board.

'Mate,' replied the son.

'That's the worst of living so far out,' bawled Mr White, with sudden and unlooked-for violence; 'of all the beastly, slushy, out-of-the-way places to live in, this is the worst. Pathway's a bog, and the road's a torrent. I don't know what people are thinking about. I suppose because only two houses in the road are let, they think it doesn't matter.'

'Never mind, dear,' said his wife, soothingly; 'perhaps you'll win the next one.'

Mr White looked up sharply, just in time to intercept a knowing glance between mother and son. The words died away on his lips, and he hid a guilty grin in his thin grey beard.

'There he is,' said Herbert White,* as the gate banged to loudly and heavy footsteps came toward the door.

The old man rose with hospitable haste, and opening the door, was heard condoling with the new arrival. The new arrival also condoled with himself, so that Mrs White said, 'Tut, tut!' and coughed gently as her husband entered the room, followed by a tall, burly man, beady of eye and rubicund* of visage.

'Sergeant-Major Morris,' he said, introducing him.

The sergeant-major shook hands, and taking the proffered seat by the fire, watched contentedly while his host got out whiskey and tumblers and stood a small copper kettle on the fire.

At the third glass his eyes got brighter, and he began to talk, the little family circle regarding with eager interest this visitor from distant parts, as he squared his broad shoulders in the chair and spoke of wild scenes and doughty deeds; of wars and plagues and strange peoples.

'Twenty-one years of it,' said Mr White, nodding at his wife and son. 'When he went away he was a slip of a youth in the warehouse. Now look at him.'

'He don't look to have taken much harm,' said Mrs White, politely.

'I'd like to go to India myself,' said the old man, 'just to look round a bit, you know.'

'Better where you are,' said the sergeant-major, shaking his head. He put down the empty glass, and sighing softly, shook it again.

'I should like to see those old temples and fakirs* and jugglers,' said the old man. 'What was that you started telling me the other day about a monkey's paw or something, Morris?'

'Nothing,' said the soldier, hastily. 'Leastways nothing worth hearing.'

'Monkey's paw?' said Mrs White, curiously.

'Well, it's just a bit of what you might call magic, perhaps,' said the sergeant-major, off-handedly.

His three listeners leaned forward eagerly. The visitor absent-mindedly put his empty glass to his lips and then set it down again. His host filled it for him.

'To look at,' said the sergeant-major, fumbling in his pocket, 'it's just an ordinary little paw, dried to a mummy.'

He took something out of his pocket and proffered it. Mrs White drew back with a grimace, but her son, taking it, examined it curiously.

'And what is there special about it?' inquired Mr White as he took it from his son, and having examined it, placed it upon the table.

'It had a spell put on it by an old fakir,' said the sergeant-major, 'a very holy man. He wanted to show that fate ruled people's lives, and that those who interfered with it did so to their sorrow. He put a spell on it so that three separate men could each have three wishes from it.'

His manner was so impressive that his hearers were conscious that their light laughter jarred somewhat.

'Well, why don't you have three, sir?' said Herbert White, cleverly.

The soldier regarded him in the way that middle age is wont to regard presumptuous youth. 'I have,' he said, quietly, and his blotchy face whitened.

'And did you really have the three wishes granted?' asked Mrs White.

'I did,' said the sergeant-major, and his glass tapped against his strong teeth.

'And has anybody else wished?' persisted the old lady.

'The first man had his three wishes. Yes,' was the reply; 'I don't know what the first two were, but the third was for death. That's how I got the paw.'

His tones were so grave that a hush fell upon the group.

'If you've had your three wishes, it's no good to you now, then, Morris,' said the old man at last. 'What do you keep it for?'

The soldier shook his head. 'Fancy, I suppose,' he said, slowly. 'I did have some idea of selling it, but I don't think I will. It has caused enough mischief already. Besides, people won't buy. They think it's a fairy tale; some of them, and those who do think anything of it want to try it first and pay me afterward.'

'If you could have another three wishes,' said the old man, eyeing him keenly, 'would you have them?'

'I don't know,' said the other. 'I don't know.'

He took the paw, and dangling it between his forefinger and thumb, suddenly threw it upon the fire. White, with a slight cry, stooped down and snatched it off.

'Better let it burn,' said the soldier, solemnly.

'If you don't want it, Morris,' said the other, 'give it to me.'

'I won't,' said his friend, doggedly. 'I threw it on the fire. If you keep it, don't blame me for what happens. Pitch it on the fire again like a sensible man.'

The other shook his head and examined his new possession closely. 'How do you do it?' he inquired.

'Hold it up in your right hand and wish aloud,' said the sergeant-major, 'but I warn you of the consequences.'

'Sounds like the *Arabian Nights*,'* said Mrs White, as she rose and began to set the supper. 'Don't you think you might wish for four pairs of hands for me?'

Her husband drew the talisman from pocket, and then all three burst into laughter as the sergeant-major, with a look of alarm on his face, caught him by the arm.

'If you must wish,' he said, gruffly, 'wish for something sensible.'

Mr White dropped it back in his pocket, and placing chairs, motioned his friend to the table. In the business of supper the talisman was partly forgotten, and afterward the three sat listening in an enthralled fashion to a second instalment of the soldier's adventures in India.

'If the tale about the monkey's paw is not more truthful than those he has been telling us,' said Herbert, as the door closed behind their guest, just in time for him to catch the last train, 'we sha'nt make much out of it.'

'Did you give him anything for it, father?' inquired Mrs White, regarding her husband closely.

'A trifle,' said he, colouring slightly. 'He didn't want it, but I made him take it. And he pressed me again to throw it away.'

'Likely,' said Herbert, with pretended horror. 'Why, we're going to be rich, and famous and happy. Wish to be an emperor, father, to begin with; then you can't be henpecked.'

He darted round the table, pursued by the maligned Mrs White armed with an antimacassar.

Mr White took the paw from his pocket and eyed it dubiously. 'I don't know what to wish for, and that's a fact,' he said, slowly. 'It seems to me I've got all I want.'

'If you only cleared the house, you'd be quite happy, wouldn't you?' said Herbert, with his hand on his shoulder. 'Well, wish for two hundred pounds, then; that'll just do it.'

His father, smiling shamefacedly at his own credulity, held up the talisman, as his son, with a solemn face, somewhat marred by a wink at his mother, sat down at the piano and struck a few impressive chords.

'I wish for two hundred pounds,' said the old man distinctly.

A fine crash from the piano greeted the words, interrupted by a shuddering cry from the old man. His wife and son ran toward him.

'It moved,' he cried, with a glance of disgust at the object as it lay on the floor. 'As I wished, it twisted in my hand like a snake.'

'Well, I don't see the money,' said his son as he picked it up and placed it on the table, 'and I bet I never shall.'

'It must have been your fancy, father,' said his wife, regarding him anxiously.

He shook his head. 'Never mind, though; there's no harm done, but it gave me a shock all the same.'

They sat down by the fire again while the two men finished their pipes. Outside, the wind was higher than ever, and the old man started nervously at the sound of a door banging upstairs. A silence unusual and depressing settled upon all three, which lasted until the old couple rose to retire for the night.

'I expect you'll find the cash tied up in a big bag in the middle of your bed,' said Herbert, as he bade them good-night, 'and something horrible squatting up on top of the wardrobe watching you as you pocket your ill-gotten gains.'

He sat alone in the darkness, gazing at the dying fire, and seeing faces in it. The last face was so horrible and so simian that he gazed at it in amazement. It got so vivid that, with a little uneasy laugh, he felt on the table for a glass containing a little water to throw over it. His hand grasped the monkey's paw, and with a little shiver he wiped his hand on his coat and went up to bed.

II

In the brightness of the wintry sun next morning as it streamed over the breakfast table he laughed at his fears. There was an air of prosaic wholesomeness about the room which it had lacked on the previous night, and the dirty, shrivelled little paw was pitched on the sideboard with a carelessness which betokened no great belief in its virtues.

'I suppose all old soldiers are the same,' said Mrs White. 'The idea of our listening to such nonsense! How could wishes be granted in these days? And if they could, how could two hundred pounds hurt you, father?'

'Might drop on his head from the sky,' said the frivolous Herbert.

'Morris said the things happened so naturally,' said his father, 'that you might if you so wished attribute it to coincidence.'

'Well, don't break into the money before I come back,' said Herbert as he rose from the table. 'I'm afraid it'll turn you into a mean, avaricious man, and we shall have to disown you.'

His mother laughed, and following him to the door, watched him down the road; and returning to the breakfast table, was very happy at the expense of her husband's credulity. All of which did not prevent her from scurrying to the door at the postman's knock, nor prevent her from referring somewhat shortly to retired sergeant-majors of bibulous habits when she found that the post brought a tailor's bill.

'Herbert will have some more of his funny remarks, I expect, when he comes home,' she said, as they sat at dinner.

'I dare say,' said Mr White, pouring himself out some beer; 'but for all that, the thing moved in my hand; that I'll swear to.'

'You thought it did,' said the old lady soothingly.

'I say it did,' replied the other. 'There was no thought about it; I had just—What's the matter?'

His wife made no reply. She was watching the mysterious movements of a man outside, who, peering in an undecided fashion at the house, appeared to be trying to make up his mind to enter. In mental connection with the two hundred pounds, she noticed that the stranger was well dressed, and wore a silk hat of glossy newness. Three times he paused at the gate, and then walked on again. The fourth time he stood with his hand upon it, and then with sudden resolution flung it open and walked up the path. Mrs White at the same moment placed her hands behind her, and hurriedly unfastening the strings of her apron, put that useful article of apparel beneath the cushion of her chair.

She brought the stranger, who seemed ill at ease, into the room. He gazed at her furtively, and listened in a preoccupied fashion as the old lady apologized for the appearance of the room, and her husband's coat, a garment which he usually reserved for the garden. She then waited as patiently as her sex would permit, for him to broach his business, but he was at first strangely silent.

'I—was asked to call,' he said at last, and stooped and picked a piece of cotton from his trousers. 'I come from "Maw and Meggins."'*

The old lady started. 'Is anything the matter?' she asked, breathlessly. 'Has anything happened to Herbert? What is it? What is it?'

Her husband interposed. 'There, there, mother,' he said, hastily.

'Sit down, and don't jump to conclusions. You've not brought bad news, I'm sure, sir;' and he eyed the other wistfully.

'I'm sorry——' began the visitor.

'Is he hurt?' demanded the mother, wildly.

The visitor bowed in assent. 'Badly hurt,' he said, quietly, 'but he is not in any pain.'

'Oh, thank God!' said the old woman, clasping her hands. 'Thank God for that! Thank——'

She broke off suddenly as the sinister meaning of the assurance dawned upon her and she saw the awful confirmation of her fears in the other's perverted face. She caught her breath, and turning to her slower-witted husband, laid her trembling old hand upon his. There was a long silence.

'He was caught in the machinery,' said the visitor at length in a low voice.

'Caught in the machinery,' repeated Mr White, in a dazed fashion, 'yes.'

He sat staring blankly out at the window, and taking his wife's hand between his own, pressed it as he had been wont to do in their old courting-days nearly forty years before.

'He was the only one left to us,' he said, turning gently to the visitor. 'It is hard.'

The other coughed, and rising, walked slowly to the window. 'The firm wished me to convey their sincere sympathy with you in your great loss,' he said, without looking round. 'I beg that you will understand I am only their servant and merely obeying orders.'

There was no reply; the old woman's face was white, her eyes staring, and her breath inaudible: on the husband's face was a look such as his friend the sergeant might have carried into his first action.

'I was to say that Maw and Meggins disclaim all responsibility,' continued the other. 'They admit no liability at all, but in consideration of your son's services, they wish to present you with a certain sum as compensation.'

Mr White dropped his wife's hand, and rising to his feet, gazed with a look of horror at his visitor. His dry lips shaped the words, 'How much?'

'Two hundred pounds,' was the answer.

Unconscious of his wife's shriek, the old man smiled faintly, put out his hands like a sightless man, and dropped, a senseless heap, to the floor.

III

IN the huge new cemetery, some two miles distant, the old people buried their dead, and came back to a house steeped in shadow and silence. It was all over so quickly that at first they could hardly realize it, and remained in a state of expectation as though of something else to happen—something else which was to lighten this load, too heavy for old hearts to bear.

But the days passed, and expectation gave place to resignation—the hopeless resignation of the old, sometimes miscalled, apathy. Sometimes they hardly exchanged a word, for now they had nothing to talk about, and their days were long to weariness.

It was about a week after that the old man, waking suddenly in the night, stretched out his hand and found himself alone. The room was in darkness, and the sound of subdued weeping came from the window. He raised himself in bed and listened.

'Come back,' he said, tenderly. 'You will be cold.'

'It is colder for my son,' said the old woman, and wept afresh.

The sound of her sobs died away on his ears. The bed was warm, and his eyes heavy with sleep. He dozed fitfully, and then slept until a sudden wild cry from his wife awoke him with a start.

'*The paw!*' she cried wildly. 'The monkey's paw!'

He started up in alarm. 'Where? Where is it? What's the matter?'

She came stumbling across the room toward him. 'I want it,' she said, quietly. 'You've not destroyed it?'

'It's in the parlour, on the bracket,' he replied, marvelling. 'Why?'

She cried and laughed together, and bending over, kissed his cheek.

'I only just thought of it,' she said, hysterically. 'Why didn't I think of it before? Why didn't *you* think of it?'

'Think of what?' he questioned.

'The other two wishes,' she replied, rapidly. 'We've only had one.'

'Was not that enough?' he demanded, fiercely.

'No,' she cried, triumphantly; 'we'll have one more. Go down and get it quickly, and wish our boy alive again.'

The man sat up in bed and flung the bed-clothes from his quaking limbs. 'Good God, you are mad!' he cried, aghast.

'Get it,' she panted; 'get it quickly, and wish—— Oh, my boy, my boy!'

Her husband struck a match and lit the candle. 'Get back to bed,' he said, unsteadily. 'You don't know what you are saying.'

'We had the first wish granted,' said the old woman, feverishly; 'why not the second?'

'A coincidence,' stammered the old man.

'Go and get it and wish,' cried his wife, quivering with excitement.

The old man turned and regarded her, and his voice shook. 'He has been dead ten days, and besides he—I would not tell you else, but—I could only recognize him by his clothing. If he was too terrible for you to see then, how now?'

'Bring him back,' cried the old woman, and dragged him toward the door. 'Do you think I fear the child I have nursed?'

He went down in the darkness, and felt his way to the parlour, and then to the mantelpiece. The talisman was in its place, and a horrible fear that the unspoken wish might bring his mutilated son before him ere he could escape from the room seized upon him, and he caught his breath as he found that he had lost the direction of the door. His brow cold with sweat, he felt his way round the table, and groped along the wall until he found himself in the small passage with the unwholesome thing in his hand.

Even his wife's face seemed changed as he entered the room. It was white and expectant, and to his fears seemed to have an unnatural look upon it. He was afraid of her.

'*Wish!*' she cried, in a strong voice.

'It is foolish and wicked,' he faltered.

'*Wish!*' repeated his wife.

He raised his hand. 'I wish my son alive again.'

The talisman fell to the floor, and he regarded it fearfully. Then he sank trembling into a chair as the old woman, with burning eyes, walked to the window and raised the blind.

He sat until he was chilled with the cold, glancing occasionally at the figure of the old woman peering through the window. The candle-end, which had burned below the rim of the china candle-stick, was throwing pulsating shadows on the ceiling and walls, until, with a flicker larger than the rest, it expired. The old man, with an unspeakable sense of relief at the failure of the talisman, crept back to his bed, and a minute or two afterward the old woman came silently and apathetically beside him.

Neither spoke, but lay silently listening to the ticking of the clock. A stair creaked, and a squeaky mouse scurried noisily through the wall. The darkness was oppressive, and after lying for some time screwing up his courage, he took the box of matches, and striking one, went downstairs for a candle.

At the foot of the stairs the match went out, and he paused to strike another; and at the same moment a knock, so quiet and stealthy as to be scarcely audible, sounded on the front door.

The matches fell from his hand and spilled in the passage. He stood motionless, his breath suspended until the knock was repeated. Then he turned and fled swiftly back to his room, and closed the door behind him. A third knock sounded through the house.

'What's that?' cried the old woman, starting up.

'A rat,' said the old man in shaking tones—'a rat. It passed me on the stairs.'

His wife sat up in bed listening. A loud knock resounded through the house.

'It's Herbert!' she screamed. 'It's Herbert!'

She ran to the door, but her husband was before her, and catching her by the arm, held her tightly.

'What are you going to do?' he whispered hoarsely.

'It's my boy; it's Herbert!' she cried, struggling mechanically. 'I forgot it was two miles away. What are you holding me for? Let go. I must open the door.'

'For God's sake don't let it in,' cried the old man, trembling.

'You're afraid of your own son,' she cried, struggling. 'Let me go. I'm coming, Herbert; I'm coming.'

There was another knock, and another. The old woman with a sudden wrench broke free and ran from the room. Her husband followed to the landing, and called after her appealingly as she hurried downstairs. He heard the chain rattle back and the bottom bolt drawn slowly and stiffly from the socket. Then the old woman's voice, strained and panting.

'The bolt,' she cried, loudly. 'Come down. I can't reach it.'

But her husband was on his hands and knees groping wildly on the floor in search of the paw. If he could only find it before the thing outside got in. A perfect fusillade* of knocks reverberated through the house, and he heard the scraping of a chair as his wife put it down in the passage against the door. He heard the creaking of the bolt as it came slowly back, and at the same moment he found the monkey's paw, and frantically breathed his third and last wish.

The knocking ceased suddenly, although the echoes of it were still in the house. He heard the chair drawn back, and the door opened. A cold wind rushed up the staircase, and a long loud wail of disappointment and misery from his wife gave him courage to run down to her side, and then to the gate beyond. The street lamp flickering opposite shone on a quiet and deserted road.

MARY E. WILKINS FREEMAN

Luella Miller

❧❧

CLOSE to the village street stood the one-story house in which
Luella Miller, who had an evil name in the village, had dwelt. She
had been dead for years, yet there were those in the village who,
in spite of the clearer light which comes on a vantage-point from
a long-past danger, half believed in the tale which they had heard
from their childhood. In their hearts, although they scarcely would
have owned it, was a survival of the wild horror and frenzied fear of
their ancestors who had dwelt in the same age with Luella Miller.
Young people even would stare with a shudder at the old house as
they passed, and children never played around it as was their wont
around an untenanted building. Not a window in the old Miller house
was broken: the panes reflected the morning sunlight in patches of
emerald and blue, and the latch of the sagging front door was never
lifted, although no bolt secured it. Since Luella Miller had been
carried out of it, the house had had no tenant except one friendless
old soul who had no choice between that and the far-off shelter of the
open sky. This old woman, who had survived her kindred and friends,
lived in the house one week, then one morning no smoke came out of
the chimney, and a body of neighbours, a score strong, entered and
found her dead in her bed. There were dark whispers as to the cause
of her death, and there were those who testified to an expression of
fear so exalted that it showed forth the state of the departing soul
upon the dead face. The old woman had been hale and hearty when
she entered the house, and in seven days she was dead; it seemed that
she had fallen a victim to some uncanny power. The minister talked
in the pulpit with covert severity against the sin of superstition; still
the belief prevailed. Not a soul in the village but would have chosen
the almshouse rather than that dwelling. No vagrant, if he heard the
tale, would seek shelter beneath that old roof, unhallowed by nearly
half a century of superstitious fear.

There was only one person in the village who had actually known

Luella Miller. That person was a woman well over eighty, but a marvel of vitality and unextinct youth. Straight as an arrow, with the spring of one recently let loose from the bow of life, she moved about the streets, and she always went to church, rain or shine. She had never married, and had lived alone for years in a house across the road from Luella Miller's.

This woman had none of the garrulousness of age, but never in all her life had she ever held her tongue for any will save her own, and she never spared the truth when she essayed to present it. She it was who bore testimony to the life, evil, though possibly wittingly or designedly so, of Luella Miller, and to her personal appearance. When this old woman spoke—and she had the gift of description, although her thoughts were clothed in the rude vernacular of her native village—one could seem to see Luella Miller as she had really looked. According to this woman, Lydia Anderson by name, Luella Miller had been a beauty of a type rather unusual in New England. She had been a slight, pliant sort of creature, as ready with a strong yielding to fate and as unbreakable as a willow. She had glimmering lengths of straight, fair hair, which she wore softly looped round a long, lovely face. She had blue eyes full of soft pleading, little slender, clinging hands, and a wonderful grace of motion and attitude.

'Luella Miller used to sit in a way nobody else could if they sat up and studied a week of Sundays,' said Lydia Anderson, 'and it was a sight to see her walk. If one of them willows over there on the edge of the brook could start up and get its roots free of the ground, and move off, it would go just the way Luella Miller used to. She had a green shot silk she used to wear, too, and a hat with green ribbon streamers, and a lace veil blowing across her face and out sideways, and a green ribbon flyin' from her waist. That was what she came out bride in when she married Erastus Miller. Her name before she was married was Hill. There was always a sight of "l's" in her name, married or single. Erastus Miller was good lookin', too, better lookin' than Luella. Sometimes I used to think that Luella wa'n't so handsome after all. Erastus just about worshiped her. I used to know him pretty well. He lived next door to me, and we went to school together. Folks used to say he was waitin' on me, but he wa'n't. I never thought he was except once or twice when he said things that some girls might have suspected meant somethin'. That was before Luella came here to teach the district school. It was funny how she came to get it, for folks said she hadn't any education, and that one of the big girls, Lottie Henderson, used to do all the teachin' for her, while she sat back and did embroidery work on a cambric pocket-handkerchief. Lottie Henderson was a real smart girl, a splendid scholar, and she just set her eyes by Luella, as all the girls did. Lottie would have made a real smart woman, but she died when Luella had been here about a year—just faded away and died: nobody knew what aided her. She dragged herself to that schoolhouse and helped Luella teach till the very last minute. The committee all knew how Luella didn't do much of the work herself, but they winked at it. It wa'n't long after Lottie died that Erastus married her. I always thought he hurried it up because she wa'n't fit to teach. One of the big boys used to help her after Lottie died, but he hadn't much government, and the school didn't do very well, and Luella might have had to give it up, for the committee couldn't have shut their eyes to things much longer. The boy that helped her was a real honest, innocent sort of fellow, and he was a good scholar, too. Folks said he overstudied, and that was the reason he was took crazy the year after Luella married, but I don't know. And I don't know what made Erastus Miller go into consumption of the blood the year after he was married: consumption wa'n't in his family. He just grew weaker and weaker, and went almost bent double when he tried to wait on Luella, and he spoke feeble, like an old man. He worked terrible hard till the last trying to save up a little to leave Luella. I've seen him out in the worst storms on a wood-sled—he used to cut and sell wood—and he was hunched up on top lookin' more dead than alive. Once I couldn't stand it: I went over and helped him pitch some wood on the cart—I was always strong in my arms. I wouldn't stop for all he told me to, and I guess he was glad enough for the help. That was only a week before he died. He fell on the kitchen floor while he was gettin' breakfast. He always got the breakfast and let Luella lay abed. He did all the sweepin' and the washin' and the ironin' and most of the cookin'. He couldn't bear to have Luella lift her finger, and she let him do for her. She lived like a queen for all the work she did. She didn't even do her sewin'. She said it made her shoulder ache to sew, and poor Erastus's sister Lily used to do all her sewin'. She wa'n't able to, either; she was never strong in her back, but she did it beautifully. She had to, to suit Luella, she was so dreadful particular. I never saw anythin' like the fagottin' and hemstitchin' that Lily Miller did for Luella. She made all Luella's weddin' outfit, and that green silk dress, after Maria Babbit cut it. Maria she cut it for nothin', and she did a lot more cuttin' and fittin' for nothin' for Luella, too. Lily Miller went to live with Luella after Erastus died. She gave up her home, though she was real attached to it and wa'n't a mite afraid to stay alone. She rented it and she went to live with Luella right away after the funeral.'

Then this old woman, Lydia Anderson, who remembered Luella Miller, would go on to relate the story of Lily Miller. It seemed that on the removal of Lily Miller to the house of her dead brother, to live with his widow, the village people first began to talk. This Lily Miller had been hardly past her first youth, and a most robust and blooming woman, rosy-cheeked, with curls of strong, black hair overshadowing round, candid temples and bright dark eyes. It was not six months after she had taken up her residence with her sister-in-law that her rosy colour faded and her pretty curves became wan hollows. White shadows began to show in the black rings of her hair, and the light died out of her eyes, her features sharpened, and there were pathetic lines at her mouth, which yet wore always an expression of utter sweetness and even happiness. She was devoted to her sister; there was no doubt that she loved her with her whole heart, and was perfectly content in her service. It was her sole anxiety lest she should die and leave her alone.

'The way Lily Miller used to talk about Luella was enough to make you mad and enough to make you cry,' said Lydia Anderson. 'I've been in there sometimes toward the last when she was too feeble to cook and carried her some blanc-mange or custard—somethin' I thought she might relish, and she'd thank me, and when I asked her how she was, say she felt better than she did yesterday, and asked me if I didn't think she looked better, dreadful pitiful, and say poor Luella had an awful time takin' care of her and doin' the work—she wa'n't strong enough to do anythin'—when all the time Luella wa'n't liftin' her finger and poor Lily didn't get any care except what the neighbours gave her, and Luella eat up everythin' that was carried in for Lily. I had it real straight that she did. Luella used to just sit and cry and do nothin'. She did act real fond of Lily, and she pined away considerable, too. There was those that thought she'd go into a decline herself. But after Lily died, her Aunt Abby Mixter came, and then Luella picked up and grew as fat and rosy as ever. But poor Aunt Abby begun to droop just the way Lily had, and I guess somebody wrote to her married daughter, Mrs Sam

Abbot, who lived in Barre, for she wrote her mother that she must leave right away and come and make her a visit, but Aunt Abby wouldn't go. I can see her now. She was a real good-lookin' woman, tall and large, with a big, square face and a high forehead that looked of itself kind of benevolent and good. She just tended out on Luella as if she had been a baby, and when her married daughter sent for her she wouldn't stir one inch. She'd always thought a lot of her daughter, too, but she said Luella needed her and her married daughter didn't. Her daughter kept writin' and writin', but it didn't do any good. Finally she came, and when she saw how bad her mother looked, she broke down and cried and all but went on her knees to have her come away. She spoke her mind out to Luella, too. She told her that she'd killed her husband and everybody that had anythin' to do with her, and she'd thank her to leave her mother alone. Luella went into hysterics, and Aunt Abby was so frightened that she called me after her daughter went. Mrs Sam Abbot she went away fairly cryin' out loud in the buggy, the neighbours heard her, and well she might, for she never saw her mother again alive. I went in that night when Aunt Abby called for me, standin' in the door with her little green-checked shawl over her head. I can see her now. "Do come over here, Miss Anderson," she sung out, kind of gasping for breath. I didn't stop for anythin'. I put over as fast as I could, and when I got there, there was Luella laughin' and cryin' all together, and Aunt Abby trying to hush her, and all the time she herself was white as a sheet and shakin' so she could hardly stand. "For the land sakes, Mrs Mixter," says I, "you look worse than she does. You ain't fit to be up out of your bed."

' "Oh, there ain't anythin' the matter with me," says she. Then she went on talkin' to Luella. "There, there, don't, don't, poor little lamb," says she. "Aunt Abby is here She ain't goin' away and leave you. Don't, poor little lamb."

' "Do leave her with me, Mrs Mixter, and you get back to bed," says I, for Aunt Abby had been layin' down considerable lately, though somehow she contrived to do the work.

' "I'm well enough," says she. "Don't you think she had better have the doctor, Miss Anderson?"

' "The doctor," says I, "I think *you* had better have the doctor. I think you need him much worse than some folks I could mention." And I looked right straight at Luella Miller laughin' and cryin' and goin' on as if she was the centre of all creation. All the time she was actin' so—seemed as if she was too sick to sense anythin'—she was keepin' a sharp lookout as to how we took it out of the corner of one eye. I see her. You could never cheat me about Luella Miller. Finally I got real mad and I run home and I got a bottle of valerian I had, and I poured some boilin' hot water on a handful of catnip,* and I mixed up that catnip tea with most half a wineglass of valerian, and I went with it over to Luella's. I marched right up to Luella, a-holdin' out of that cup, all smokin'. "Now," says I, "Luella Miller, *you swaller this!*"

'"What is—what is it, oh, what is it?" she sort of screeches out. Then she goes off a-laughin' enough to kill.

'"Poor lamb, poor little lamb," says Aunt Abby, standin' over her, all kind of tottery, and tryin' to bathe her head with camphor.

'"*You swaller this right down,*" says I. And I didn't waste any ceremony. I just took hold of Luella Miller's chin and I tipped her head back, and I caught her mouth open with laughin', and I clapped that cup to her lips, and I fairly hollered at her: "Swaller, swaller, swaller!" and she gulped it right down. She had to, and I guess it did her good. Anyhow, she stopped cryin' and laughin' and let me put her to bed, and she went to sleep like a baby inside of half an hour. That was more than poor Aunt Abby did. She lay awake all that night and I stayed with her, though she tried not to have me; said she wa'n't sick enough for watchers. But I stayed, and I made some good cornmeal gruel and I fed her a teaspoon every little while all night long. It seemed to me as if she was jest dyin' from bein' all wore out. In the mornin' as soon as it was light I run over to the Bisbees and sent Johnny Bisbee for the doctor. I told him to tell the doctor to hurry, and he come pretty quick. Poor Aunt Abby didn't seem to know much of anythin' when he got there. You couldn't hardly tell she breathed, she was so used up. When the doctor had gone, Luella came into the room lookin' like a baby in her ruffled nightgown. I can see her now. Her eyes were as blue and her face all pink and white like a blossom, and she looked at Aunt Abby in the bed sort of innocent and surprised. "Why," says she, "Aunt Abby ain't got up yet?"

'"No, she ain't," says I, pretty short.

'"I thought I didn't smell the coffee," says Luella.

'"Coffee," says I. "I guess if you have coffee this mornin' you'll make it yourself."

'"I never made the coffee in all my life," says she, dreadful astonished. "Erastus always made the coffee as long as he lived, and then

Lily she made it, and then Aunt Abby made it. I don't believe I *can* make the coffee, Miss Anderson."

' "You can make it or go without, jest as you please," says I.

' "Ain't Aunt Abby goin' to get up?" says she.

' "I guess she won't get up," says I, "sick as she is." I was gettin' madder and madder. There was somethin' about that little pink-and-white thing standin' there and talkin' about coffee, when she had killed so many better folks than she was, and had jest killed another, that made me feel 'most as if I wished somebody would up and kill her before she had a chance to do any more harm.

' "Is Aunt Abby sick?" says Luella, as if she was sort of aggrieved and injured.

' "Yes," says I, "she's sick, and she's goin' to die, and then you'll be left alone, and you'll have to do for yourself and wait on yourself, or do without things." I don't know but I was sort of hard, but it was the truth, and if I was any harder than Luella Miller had been I'll give up. I ain't never been sorry that I said it. Well, Luella, she up and had hysterics again at that, and I jest let her have 'em. All I did was to bundle her into the room on the other side of the entry where Aunt Abby couldn't hear her, if she wa'n't past it—I don't know but she was—and set her down hard in a chair and told her not to come back into the other room, and she minded. She had her hysterics in there till she got tired. When she found out that nobody was comin' to coddle her and do for her she stopped. At least I suppose she did. I had all I could do with poor Aunt Abby tryin' to keep the breath of life in her. The doctor had told me that she was dreadful low, and give me some very strong medicine to give to her in drops real often, and told me real particular about the nourishment. Well, I did as he told me real faithful till she wa'n't able to swaller any longer. Then I had her daughter sent for. I had begun to realize that she wouldn't last any time at all. I hadn't realized it before, though I spoke to Luella the way I did. The doctor he came, and Mrs Sam Abbot, but when she got there it was too late; her mother was dead. Aunt Abby's daughter just give one look at her mother layin' there, then she turned sort of sharp and sudden and looked at me.

' "Where is she?" says she, and I knew she meant Luella.

' "She's out in the kitchen," says I. "She's too nervous to see folks die. She's afraid it will make her sick."

'The Doctor he speaks up then. He was a young man. Old Doctor

Park had died the year before, and this was a young fellow just out of college. "Mrs Miller is not strong," says he, kind of severe, "and she is quite right in not agitating herself."

' "You are another, young man; she's got her pretty claw on you," thinks I, but I didn't say anythin' to him. I just said over to Mrs Sam Abbot that Luella was in the kitchen, and Mrs Sam Abbot she went out there, and I went, too, and I never heard anythin' like the way she talked to Luella Miller. I felt pretty hard to Luella myself, but this was more than I ever would have dared to say. Luella she was too scared to go into hysterics. She jest flopped. She seemed to jest shrink away to nothin' in that kitchen chair, with Mrs Sam Abbot standin' over her and talkin' and tellin' her the truth. I guess the truth was most too much for her and no mistake, because Luella presently actually did faint away, and there wa'n't any sham about it, the way I always suspected there was about them hysterics. She fainted dead away and we had to lay her flat on the floor, and the Doctor he came runnin' out and he said somethin' about a weak heart dreadful fierce to Mrs Sam Abbot, but she wa'n't a mite scared. She faced him jest as white as even Luella was layin' there lookin' like death and the Doctor feelin' of her pulse.

' "Weak heart," says she, "weak heart; weak fiddlesticks! There ain't nothin' weak about that woman. She's got strength enough to hang onto other folks till she kills 'em. Weak? It was my poor mother that was weak: this woman killed her as sure as if she had taken a knife to her."

'But the Doctor he didn't pay much attention. He was bendin' over Luella layin' there with her yellow hair all streamin' and her pretty pink-and-white face all pale, and her blue eyes like stars gone out, and he was holdin' onto her hand and smoothin' her forehead, and tellin' me to get the brandy in Aunt Abby's room, and I was sure as I wanted to be that Luella had got somebody else to hang onto, now Aunt Abby was gone, and I thought of poor Erastus Miller, and I sort of pitied the poor young Doctor, led away by a pretty face, and I made up my mind I'd see what I could do.

'I waited till Aunt Abby had been dead and buried about a month, and the Doctor was goin' to see Luella steady and folks were beginnin' to talk; then one evenin', when I knew the Doctor had been called out of town and wouldn't be round, I went over to Luella's. I found her all dressed up in a blue muslin with white polka dots on it, and her hair curled jest as pretty, and there wa'n't a young girl in the place could compare with her. There was somethin' about Luella Miller seemed to draw the heart right out of you, but she didn't draw it out of *me*. She was settin' rocking in the chair by her sittin'-room window, and Maria Brown had gone home. Maria Brown had been in to help her, or rather to do the work, for Luella wa'n't helped when she didn't do anythin'. Maria Brown was real capable and she didn't have any ties; she wa'n't married, and lived alone, so she'd offered. I couldn't see why she should do the work any more than Luella; she wa'n't any too strong; but she seemed to think she could and Luella seemed to think so, too, so she went over and did all the work—washed, and ironed, and baked, while Luella sat and rocked. Maria didn't live long afterward. She began to fade away just the same fashion the others had. Well, she was warned, but she acted real mad when folks said anythin': said Luella was a poor, abused woman, too delicate to help herself, and they'd ought to be ashamed, and if she died helpin' them that couldn't help themselves she would—and she did.

' "I s'pose Maria has gone home," says I to Luella, when I had gone in and sat down opposite her.

' "Yes, Maria went half an hour ago, after she had got supper and washed the dishes," says Luella, in her pretty way.

' "I suppose she has got a lot of work to do in her own house to-night," says I, kind of bitter, but that was all thrown away on Luella Miller. It seemed to her right that other folks that wa'n't any better able than she was herself should wait on her, and she couldn't get it through her head that anybody should think it *wa'n't* right.

' "Yes," says Luella, real sweet and pretty, "yes, she said she had to do her washin' to-night. She has let it go for a fortnight along of comin' over here."

' "Why don't she stay home and do her washin' instead of comin' over here and doin' *your* work, when you are just as well able, and enough sight more so, than she is to do it?" says I.

'Then Luella she looked at me like a baby who has a rattle shook at it. She sort of laughed as innocent as you please. "Oh, I can't do the work myself, Miss Anderson," says she. "I never did. Maria *has* to do it."

'Then I spoke out: "Has to do it!" says I. "Has to do it!" She don't have to do it, either. Maria Brown has her own home and enough to live on. She ain't beholden to you to come over here and slave for you and kill herself."

'Luella she jest set and stared at me for all the world like a doll-baby that was so abused that it was comin' to life.

'"Yes," says I, "she's killin' herself. She's goin' to die just the way Erastus did, and Lily, and your Aunt Abby. You're killin' her jest as you did them. I don't know what there is about you, but you seem to bring a curse," says I. "You kill everybody that is fool enough to care anythin' about you and do for you."

'She stared at me and she was pretty pale.

'"And Maria ain't the only one you're goin' to kill," says I. "You're goin' to kill Doctor Malcom before you're done with him."

'Then a red colour came flamin' all over her face. "I ain't goin' to kill him, either," says she, and she begun to cry.

'"Yes, you *be!*" says I. Then I spoke as I had never spoke before. You see, I felt it on account of Erastus. I told her that she hadn't any business to think of another man after she'd been married to one that had died for her: that she was a dreadful woman; and she was, that's true enough, but sometimes I have wondered lately if she knew it—if she wa'n't like a baby with scissors in its hand cuttin' everybody without knowin' what it was doin'.

'Luella she kept gettin' paler and paler, and she never took her eyes off my face. There was somethin' awful about the way she looked at me and never spoke one word. After awhile I quit talkin' and I went home. I watched that night, but her lamp went out before nine o'clock, and when Doctor Malcom came drivin' past and sort of slowed up he see there wa'n't any light and he drove along. I saw her sort of shy out of meetin' the next Sunday, too, so he shouldn't go home with her, and I begun to think mebbe she did have some conscience after all. It was only a week after that that Maria Brown died—sort of sudden at the last, though everybody had seen it was comin'. Well, then there was a good deal of feelin' and pretty dark whispers. Folks said the days of witchcraft* had come again, and they were pretty shy of Luella. She acted sort of offish to the Doctor and he didn't go there, and there wa'n't anybody to do anythin' for her. I don't know how she *did* get along. I wouldn't go in there and offer to help her—not because I was afraid of dyin' like the rest, but I thought she was just as well able to do her own work as I was to do it for her, and I thought it was about time that she did it and stopped killin' other folks. But it wa'n't very long before folks began to say that Luella herself was goin' into a decline jest the way her husband, and Lily, and Aunt Abby and the others had, and I saw myself that she looked pretty bad. I used to see her goin' past from the store with a bundle as if she could hardly crawl, but I remembered how Erastus used to wait and 'tend when he couldn't hardly put one foot before the other, and I didn't go out to help her.

'But at last one afternoon I saw the Doctor come drivin' up like mad with his medicine chest, and Mrs Babbit came in after supper and said that Luella was real sick.

'"I'd offer to go in and nurse her," says she, "but I've got my children to consider, and mebbe it ain't true what they say, but it's queer how many folks that have done for her have died."

'I didn't say anythin', but I considered how she had been Erastus's wife and how he had set his eyes by her, and I made up my mind to go in the next mornin', unless she was better, and see what I could do; but the next mornin' I see her at the window, and pretty soon she came steppin' out as spry as you please, and a little while afterward Mrs Babbit came in and told me that the Doctor had got a girl from out of town, a Sarah Jones, to come there, and she said she was pretty sure that the Doctor was goin' to marry Luella.

'I saw him kiss her in the door that night myself, and I knew it was true. The woman came that afternoon, and the way she flew around was a caution. I don't believe Luella had swept since Maria died. She swept and dusted, and washed and ironed; wet clothes and dusters and carpets were flyin' over there all day, and every time Luella set her foot out when the Doctor wa'n't there there was that Sarah Jones helpin' of her up and down the steps, as if she hadn't learned to walk.

'Well, everybody knew that Luella and the Doctor were goin' to be married, but it wa'n't long before they began to talk about his lookin' so poorly, jest as they had about the others; and they talked about Sarah Jones, too.

'Well, the Doctor did die, and he wanted to be married first, so as to leave what little he had to Luella, but he died before the minister could get there, and Sarah Jones died a week afterward.

'Well, that wound up everything for Luella Miller. Not another soul in the whole town would lift a finger for her. There got to be a sort of panic. Then she began to droop in good earnest. She used to have to go to the store herself, for Mrs Babbit was afraid to let Tommy go for her, and I've seen her goin' past and stoppin' every two or three steps to rest. Well, I stood it as long as I could, but one day I see her comin' with her arms full and stoppin' to lean against the Babbit fence, and I run out and took her bundles and carried them to her house. Then I went home and never spoke one word to her though she called after me dreadful kind of pitiful. Well, that night I was taken sick with a chill, and I was sick as I wanted to be for two weeks. Mrs Babbit had seen me run out to help Luella and she came in and told me I was goin' to die on account of it. I didn't know whether I was or not, but I considered I had done right by Erastus's wife.

'That last two weeks Luella she had a dreadful hard time, I guess. She was pretty sick, and as near as I could make out nobody dared go near her. I don't know as she was really needin' anythin' very much, for there was enough to eat in her house and it was warm weather, and she made out to cook a little flour gruel every day, I know, but I guess she had a hard time, she that had been so petted and done for all her life.

'When I got so I could go out, I went over there one morning. Mrs Babbit had just come in to say she hadn't seen any smoke and she didn't know but it was somebody's duty to go in, but she couldn't help thinkin' of her children, and I got right up, though I hadn't been out of the house for two weeks, and I went in there, and Luella she was layin' on the bed, and she was dyin'.

'She lasted all that day and into the night. But I sat there after the new doctor had gone away. Nobody else dared to go there. It was about midnight that I left her for a minute to run home and get some medicine I had been takin', for I begun to feel rather bad.

'It was a full moon that night, and just as I started out of my door to cross the street back to Luella's, I stopped short, for I saw something.'

Lydia Anderson at this juncture always said with a certain defiance that she did not expect to be believed, and then proceeded in a hushed voice:

'I saw what I saw, and I know I saw it, and I will swear on my death bed that I saw it. I saw Luella Miller and Erastus Miller, and Lily, and Aunt Abby, and Maria, and the Doctor, and Sarah, all goin' out of her door, and all but Luella shone white in the moonlight, and they were all helpin' her along till she seemed to fairly fly in the midst of them. Then it all disappeared. I stood a minute with my heart poundin', then I went over there. I thought of goin' for Mrs Babbit, but I thought she'd be afraid. So I went alone, though I knew what had happened. Luella was layin' real peaceful, dead on her bed.'

This was the story that the old woman, Lydia Anderson, told, but the sequel was told by the people who survived her, and this is the tale which has become folklore in the village.

Lydia Anderson died when she was eighty-seven. She had continued wonderfully hale and hearty for one of her years until about two weeks before her death.

One bright moonlight evening she was sitting beside a window in her parlour when she made a sudden exclamation, and was out of the house and across the street before the neighbour who was taking care of her could stop her. She followed as fast as possible and found Lydia Anderson stretched on the ground before the door of Luella Miller's deserted house, and she was quite dead.

The next night there was a red gleam of fire athwart the moonlight and the old house of Luella Miller was burned to the ground. Nothing is now left of it except a few old cellar stones and a lilac bush, and in summer a helpless trail of morning glories among the weeds, which might be considered emblematic of Luella herself.

M. R. JAMES

Count Magnus

❧❧

B Y what means the papers out of which I have made a connected
story came into my hands is the last point which the reader will
learn from these pages. But it is necessary to prefix to my extracts
from them a statement of the form in which I possess them.

They consist, then, partly of a series of collections for a book of
travels, such a volume as was a common product of the forties and fif-
ties. Horace Marryat's *Journal of a Residence in Jutland and the Danish
Isles** is a fair specimen of the class to which I allude. These books
usually treated of some unfamiliar district on the Continent. They
were illustrated with woodcuts or steel plates. They gave details of
hotel accommodation, and of means of communication, such as we
now expect to find in any well-regulated guide-book, and they dealt
largely in reported conversations with intelligent foreigners, racy
innkeepers and garrulous peasants. In a word, they were chatty.

Begun with the idea of furnishing material for such a book, my
papers as they progressed assumed the character of a record of one
single personal experience, and this record was continued up to the
very eve, almost, of its termination.

The writer was a Mr Wraxall. For my knowledge of him I have to
depend entirely on the evidence his writings afford, and from these
I deduce that he was a man past middle age, possessed of some private means, and very much alone in the world. He had, it seems, no
settled abode in England, but was a denizen of hotels and boarding-
houses. It is probable that he entertained the idea of settling down
at some future time which never came; and I think it also likely that
the Pantechnicon fire* in the early seventies must have destroyed
a great deal that would have thrown light on his antecedents, for he
refers once or twice to property of his that was warehoused at that
establishment.

It is further apparent that Mr Wraxall had published a book, and
that it treated of a holiday he had once taken in Brittany. More than

this I cannot say about his work, because a diligent search in biblio-graphical works has convinced me that it must have appeared either anonymously or under a pseudonym.

As to his character, it is not difficult to form some superficial opin-ion. He must have been an intelligent and cultivated man. It seems that he was near being a Fellow of his college at Oxford—Brasenose,* as I judge from the Calendar. His besetting fault was pretty clearly that of over-inquisitiveness, possibly a good fault in a traveller, cer-tainly a fault for which this traveller paid dearly enough in the end.

On what proved to be his last expedition, he was plotting another book. Scandinavia, a region not widely known to Englishmen forty years ago, had struck him as an interesting field. He must have lighted on some old books of Swedish history or memoirs, and the idea had struck him that there was room for a book descriptive of travel in Sweden, interspersed with episodes from the history of some of the great Swedish families. He procured letters of introduction, there-fore, to some persons of quality in Sweden, and set out thither in the early summer of 1863.

Of his travels in the North there is no need to speak, nor of his residence of some weeks in Stockholm. I need only mention that some *savant* resident there put him on the track of an important col-lection of family papers belonging to the proprietors of an ancient manor-house in Vestergothland,* and obtained for him permission to examine them.

The manor-house, or *herrgård*, in question is to be called Råbäck* (pronounced something like Roebeck), though that is not its name. It is one of the best buildings of its kind in all the country, and the picture of it in Dahlenberg's *Suecia antiqua et moderna*,* engraved in 1694, shows it very much as the tourist may see it to-day. It was built soon after 1600, and is, roughly speaking, very much like an English house of that period in respect of material—red-brick with stone facings—and style. The man who built it was a scion of the great house of De la Gardie,* and his descendants possess it still. De la Gardie is the name by which I will designate them when mention of them becomes necessary.

They received Mr Wraxall with great kindness and courtesy, and pressed him to stay in the house as long as his researches lasted. But, preferring to be independent, and mistrusting his powers of convers-ing in Swedish, he settled himself at the village inn, which turned out quite sufficiently comfortable, at any rate during the summer months. This arrangement would entail a short walk daily to and from the manor-house of something under a mile. The house itself stood in a park, and was protected—we should say grown up—with large old timber. Near it you found the walled garden, and then entered a close wood fringing one of the small lakes with which the whole country is pitted. Then came the wall of the demesne, and you climbed a steep knoll—a knob of rock lightly covered with soil—and on the top of this stood the church, fenced in with tall dark trees. It was a curious building to English eyes. The nave and aisles were low, and filled with pews and galleries. In the western gallery stood the handsome old organ, gaily painted, and with silver pipes. The ceiling was flat, and had been adorned by a seventeenth-century artist with a strange and hideous 'Last Judgment,' full of lurid flames, falling cities, burning ships, crying souls, and brown and smiling demons. Handsome brass coronæ hung from the roof; the pulpit was like a doll's-house, covered with little painted wooden cherubs and saints; a stand with three hour-glasses was hinged to the preacher's desk. Such sights as these may be seen in many a church in Sweden now, but what distinguished this one was an addition to the original building. At the eastern end of the north aisle the builder of the manor-house had erected a mausoleum* for himself and his family. It was a largish eight-sided building, lighted by a series of oval windows, and it had a domed roof, topped by a kind of pumpkin-shaped object rising into a spire, a form in which Swedish architects greatly delighted. The roof was of copper externally, and was painted black, while the walls, in common with those of the church, were staringly white. To this mausoleum there was no access from the church. It had a portal and steps of its own on the northern side.

Past the churchyard the path to the village goes, and not more than three or four minutes bring you to the inn door.

On the first day of his stay at Råbäck Mr Wraxall found the church door open, and made those notes of the interior which I have epitomized. Into the mausoleum, however, he could not make his way. He could by looking through the keyhole just descry that there were fine marble effigies and sarcophagi of copper, and a wealth of armorial ornament, which made him very anxious to spend some time in investigation.

The papers he had come to examine at the manor-house proved to be of just the kind he wanted for his book. There were family correspondence, journals, and account-books of the earliest owners of the estate, very carefully kept and clearly written, full of amusing and picturesque detail. The first De la Gardie appeared in them as a strong and capable man. Shortly after the building of the mansion there had been a period of distress in the district, and the peasants had risen and attacked several châteaux and done some damage. The owner of Råbäck took a leading part in suppressing the trouble, and there was reference to executions of ringleaders and severe punishments inflicted with no sparing hand.

The portrait of this Magnus de la Gardie was one of the best in the house, and Mr Wraxall studied it with no little interest after his day's work. He gives no detailed description of it, but I gather that the face impressed him rather by its power than by its beauty or goodness; in fact, he writes that Count Magnus was an almost phenomenally ugly man.

On this day Mr Wraxall took his supper with the family, and walked back in the late but still bright evening.

'I must remember,' he writes, 'to ask the sexton if he can let me into the mausoleum at the church. He evidently has access to it himself, for I saw him to-night standing on the steps, and, as I thought, locking or unlocking the door.'

I find that early on the following day Mr Wraxall had some conversation with his landlord. His setting it down at such length as he does surprised me at first; but I soon realized that the papers I was reading were, at least in their beginning, the materials for the book he was meditating, and that it was to have been one of those quasi-journalistic productions which admit of the introduction of an admixture of conversational matter.

His object, he says, was to find out whether any traditions of Count Magnus de la Gardie lingered on in the scenes of that gentleman's activity, and whether the popular estimate of him were favourable or not. He found that the Count was decidedly not a favourite. If his tenants came late to their work on the days which they owed to him as Lord of the Manor, they were set on the wooden horse, or flogged and branded in the manor-house yard. One or two cases there were of men who had occupied lands which encroached on the lord's domain, and whose houses had been mysteriously burnt on a winter's night, with the whole family inside. But what seemed to dwell on the innkeeper's mind most—for he returned to the subject more than once—was that the Count had been on the Black Pilgrimage,* and had brought something or someone back with him.

You will naturally inquire, as Mr Wraxall did, what the Black Pilgrimage may have been. But your curiosity on the point must remain unsatisfied for the time being, just as his did. The landlord was evidently unwilling to give a full answer, or indeed any answer, on the point, and, being called out for a moment, trotted off with obvious alacrity, only putting his head in at the door a few minutes afterwards to say that he was called away to Skara,* and should not be back till evening.

So Mr Wraxall had to go unsatisfied to his day's work at the manor-house. The papers on which he was just then engaged soon put his thoughts into another channel, for he had to occupy himself with glancing over the correspondence between Sophia Albertina in Stockholm and her married cousin Ulrica Leonora at Råbäck in the years 1705–1710. The letters were of exceptional interest from the light they threw upon the culture of that period in Sweden, as anyone can testify who has read the full edition of them in the publications of the Swedish Historical Manuscripts Commission.

In the afternoon he had done with these, and after returning the boxes in which they were kept to their places on the shelf, he proceeded, very naturally, to take down some of the volumes nearest to them, in order to determine which of them had best be his principal subject of investigation next day. The shelf he had hit upon was occupied mostly by a collection of account-books in the writing of the first Count Magnus. But one among them was not an account-book, but a book of alchemical and other tracts in another sixteenth-century hand. Not being very familiar with alchemical literature, Mr Wraxall spends much space which he might have spared in setting out the names and beginnings of the various treatises: The book of the Phœnix, book of the Thirty Words, book of the Toad, book of Miriam, Turba philosophorum, and so forth;* and then he announces with a good deal of circumstance his delight at finding, on a leaf originally left blank near the middle of the book, some writing of Count Magnus himself headed 'Liber nigræ peregrinationis.'* It is true that only a few lines were written, but there was quite enough to show that the landlord had that morning been referring to a belief at least as old as the time of Count Magnus, and probably shared by him. This is the English of what was written:

'If any man desires to obtain a long life, if he would obtain a faithful messenger and see the blood of his enemies, it is necessary that he should first go into the city of Chorazin,* and there salute the prince. . . .' Here there was an erasure of one word, not very thoroughly done, so that Mr Wraxall felt pretty sure that he was right in reading it as *aëris* ('of the air'*). But there was no more of the text copied, only a line in Latin: 'Quære reliqua hujus materiei inter secretiora' (See the rest of this matter among the more private things).

It could not be denied that this threw a rather lurid light upon the tastes and beliefs of the Count; but to Mr Wraxall, separated from him by nearly three centuries, the thought that he might have added to his general forcefulness alchemy, and to alchemy something like magic, only made him a more picturesque figure; and when, after a rather prolonged contemplation of his picture in the hall, Mr Wraxall set out on his homeward way, his mind was full of the thought of Count Magnus. He had no eyes for his surroundings, no perception of the evening scents of the woods or the evening light on the lake; and when all of a sudden he pulled up short, he was astonished to find himself already at the gate of the churchyard, and within a few minutes of his dinner. His eyes fell on the mausoleum.

'Ah,' he said, 'Count Magnus, there you are. I should dearly like to see you.'

'Like many solitary men,' he writes, 'I have a habit of talking to myself aloud; and, unlike some of the Greek and Latin particles, I do not expect an answer. Certainly, and perhaps fortunately in this case, there was neither voice nor any that regarded: only the woman who, I suppose, was cleaning up the church, dropped some metallic object on the floor, whose clang startled me. Count Magnus, I think, sleeps sound enough.'

That same evening the landlord of the inn, who had heard Mr Wraxall say that he wished to see the clerk or deacon (as he would be called in Sweden) of the parish, introduced him to that official in the inn parlour. A visit to the De la Gardie tomb-house was soon arranged for the next day, and a little general conversation ensued.

Mr Wraxall, remembering that one function of Scandinavian deacons is to teach candidates for Confirmation, thought he would refresh his own memory on a Biblical point.

'Can you tell me,' he said, 'anything about Chorazin?'

The deacon seemed startled, but readily reminded him how that village had once been denounced.

'To be sure,' said Mr Wraxall; 'it is, I suppose, quite a ruin now?'

'So I expect,' replied the deacon. 'I have heard some of our old priests say that Antichrist is to be born there; and there are tales——'

'Ah! what tales are those?' Mr Wraxall put in.

'Tales, I was going to say, which I have forgotten,' said the deacon; and soon after that he said good night.

The landlord was now alone, and at Mr Wraxall's mercy; and that inquirer was not inclined to spare him.

'Herr Nielsen,' he said, 'I have found out something about the Black Pilgrimage. You may as well tell me what you know. What did the Count bring back with him?'

Swedes are habitually slow, perhaps, in answering, or perhaps the landlord was an exception. I am not sure; but Mr Wraxall notes that the landlord spent at least one minute in looking at him before he said anything at all. Then he came close up to his guest, and with a good deal of effort he spoke:

'Mr Wraxall, I can tell you this one little tale, and no more—not any more. You must not ask anything when I have done. In my grand-father's time—that is, ninety-two years ago—there were two men who said: "The Count is dead; we do not care for him. We will go to-night and have a free hunt in his wood"—the long wood on the hill that you have seen behind Råbäck. Well, those that heard them say this, they said: "No, do not go; we are sure you will meet with persons walking who should not be walking. They should be resting, not walking." These men laughed. There were no forest-men to keep the wood, because no one wished to hunt there. The family were not here at the house. These men could do what they wished.

'Very well, they go to the wood that night. My grandfather was sitting here in this room. It was the summer, and a light night. With the window open, he could see out to the wood, and hear.

'So he sat there, and two or three men with him, and they listened. At first they hear nothing at all; then they hear someone—you know how far away it is—they hear someone scream, just as if the most inside part of his soul was twisted out of him. All of them in the room caught hold of each other, and they sat so for three-quarters of an hour. Then they hear someone else, only about three hundred ells off. They hear him laugh out loud: it was not one of those two men that laughed, and, indeed, they have all of them said that it was not any man at all. After that they hear a great door shut.

'Then, when it was just light with the sun, they all went to the priest. They said to him:

' "Father, put on your gown and your ruff, and come to bury these men, Anders Bjornsen and Hans Thorbjorn."

'You understand that they were sure these men were dead. So they went to the wood—my grandfather never forgot this. He said they were all like so many dead men themselves. The priest, too, he was in a white fear. He said when they came to him:

' "I heard one cry in the night, and I heard one laugh afterwards. If I cannot forget that, I shall not be able to sleep again."

'So they went to the wood, and they found these men on the edge of the wood. Hans Thorbjorn was standing with his back against a tree, and all the time he was pushing with his hands—pushing something away from him which was not there. So he was not dead. And they led him away, and took him to the house at Nykjoping, and he died before the winter; but he went on pushing with his hands. Also Anders Bjornsen was there; but he was dead. And I tell you this about Anders Bjornsen, that he was once a beautiful man, but now his face was not there, because the flesh of it was sucked away off the bones. You understand that? My grandfather did not forget that. And they laid him on the bier which they brought, and they put a cloth over his head, and the priest walked before; and they began to sing the psalm for the dead as well as they could. So, as they were singing the end of the first verse, one fell down, who was carrying the head of the bier, and the others looked back, and they saw that the cloth had fallen off, and the eyes of Anders Bjornsen were looking up, because there was nothing to close over them. And this they could not bear. Therefore the priest laid the cloth upon him, and sent for a spade, and they buried him in that place.'

The next day Mr Wraxall records that the deacon called for him soon after his breakfast, and took him to the church and mausoleum. He noticed that the key of the latter was hung on a nail just by the pulpit, and it occurred to him that, as the church door seemed to be left unlocked as a rule, it would not be difficult for him to pay a second and more private visit to the monuments if there proved to be more of interest among them than could be digested at first. The building, when he entered it, he found not unimposing. The monuments, mostly large erections of the seventeenth and eighteenth centuries, were dignified if luxuriant, and the epitaphs and heraldry were copious. The central space of the domed room was occupied by three copper sarcophagi, covered with finely-engraved ornament. Two of them had, as is commonly the case in Denmark and Sweden, a large metal crucifix on the lid. The third, that of Count Magnus, as it appeared, had, instead of that, a full-length effigy engraved upon it, and round the edge were several bands of similar ornament representing various scenes. One was a battle, with cannon belching out smoke, and walled towns, and troops of pikemen. Another showed an execution. In a third, among trees, was a man running at full speed, with flying hair and outstretched hands. After him followed a strange form; it would be hard to say whether the artist had intended it for a man, and was unable to give the requisite similitude, or whether it was intentionally made as monstrous as it looked. In view of the skill with which the rest of the drawing was done, Mr Wraxall felt inclined to adopt the latter idea. The figure was unduly short, and was for the most part muffled in a hooded garment which swept the ground. The only part of the form which projected from that shelter was not shaped like any hand or arm. Mr Wraxall compares it to the tentacle of a devil-fish,* and continues: 'On seeing this, I said to myself, "This, then, which is evidently an allegorical representation of some kind—a fiend pursuing a hunted soul—may be the origin of the story of Count Magnus and his mysterious companion. Let us see how the huntsman is pictured: doubtless it will be a demon blowing his horn." ' But, as it turned out, there was no such sensational figure, only the semblance of a cloaked man on a hillock, who stood leaning on a stick, and watching the hunt with an interest which the engraver had tried to express in his attitude.

Mr Wraxall noted the finely-worked and massive steel padlocks— three in number—which secured the sarcophagus. One of them, he saw, was detached, and lay on the pavement. And then, unwilling to delay the deacon longer or to waste his own working-time, he made his way onward to the manor-house.

'It is curious,' he notes, 'how on retracing a familiar path one's thoughts engross one to the absolute exclusion of surrounding objects. To-night, for the second time, I had entirely failed to notice where I was going (I had planned a private visit to the tomb-house to copy the epitaphs), when I suddenly, as it were, awoke to consciousness, and found myself (as before) turning in at the churchyard gate, and, I believe, singing or chanting some such words as, "Are you awake, Count Magnus? Are you asleep, Count Magnus?" and then something more which I have failed to recollect. It seemed to me that I must have been behaving in this nonsensical way for some time.'

He found the key of the mausoleum where he had expected to find it, and copied the greater part of what he wanted; in fact, he stayed until the light began to fail him.

'I must have been wrong,' he writes, 'in saying that one of the padlocks of my Count's sarcophagus was unfastened; I see to-night that two are loose. I picked both up, and laid them carefully on the window-ledge, after trying unsuccessfully to close them. The remaining one is still firm, and, though I take it to be a spring lock, I cannot guess how it is opened. Had I succeeded in undoing it, I am almost afraid I should have taken the liberty of opening the sarcophagus. It is strange, the interest I feel in the personality of this, I fear, somewhat ferocious and grim old noble.'

The day following was, as it turned out, the last of Mr Wraxall's stay at Råbäck. He received letters connected with certain investments which made it desirable that he should return to England; his work among the papers was practically done, and travelling was slow. He decided, therefore, to make his farewells, put some finishing touches to his notes, and be off.

These finishing touches and farewells, as it turned out, took more time than he had expected. The hospitable family insisted on his staying to dine with them—they dined at three—and it was verging on half-past six before he was outside the iron gates of Råbäck. He dwelt on every step of his walk by the lake, determined to saturate himself, now that he trod it for the last time, in the sentiment of the place and hour. And when he reached the summit of the churchyard knoll, he lingered for many minutes, gazing at the limitless prospect of woods near and distant, all dark beneath a sky of liquid green. When at last he turned to go, the thought struck him that surely he must bid farewell to Count Magnus as well as the rest of the De la Gardies. The church was but twenty yards away, and he knew where the key of the mausoleum hung. It was not long before he was standing over the great copper coffin, and, as usual, talking to himself aloud. 'You may have been a bit of a rascal in your time, Magnus,' he was saying, 'but for all that I should like to see you or, rather——'

'Just at that instant,' he says, 'I felt a blow on my foot. Hastily enough I drew it back, and something fell on the pavement with a clash. It was the third, the last of the three padlocks which had fastened the sarcophagus. I stooped to pick it up, and—Heaven is my witness that I am writing only the bare truth—before I had raised myself there was a sound of metal hinges creaking, and I distinctly saw the lid shifting upwards. I may have behaved like a coward, but I could not for my life stay for one moment. I was outside that dreadful building in less time than I can write—almost as quickly as I could have said—the words; and what frightens me yet more, I could not turn the key in the lock. As I sit here in my room noting these facts, I ask myself (it was not twenty minutes ago) whether that noise of creaking metal continued, and I cannot tell whether it did or not. I only know that there was something more than I have written that alarmed me, but whether it was sound or sight I am not able to remember. What is this that I have done?'

Poor Mr Wraxall! He set out on his journey to England on the next day, as he had planned, and he reached England in safety; and yet, as I gather from his changed hand and inconsequent jottings, a broken man. One of several small notebooks that have come to me with his papers gives, not a key to, but a kind of inkling of, his experiences. Much of his journey was made by canal-boat, and I find not less than six painful attempts to enumerate and describe his fellow-passengers. The entries are of this kind:

'24. Pastor of village in Skåne. Usual black coat and soft black hat.
'25. Commercial traveller from Stockholm going to Trollhättan.* Black cloak, brown hat.
'26. Man in long black cloak, broad-leafed hat, very old-fashioned.'

This entry is lined out, and a note added: 'Perhaps identical with No. 13. Have not yet seen his face.' On referring to No. 13, I find that he is a Roman priest in a cassock.

The net result of the reckoning is always the same. Twenty-eight people appear in the enumeration, one being always a man in a long black cloak and broad hat, and the other a 'short figure in dark cloak and hood.' On the other hand, it is always noted that only twenty-six passengers appear at meals, and that the man in the cloak is perhaps absent, and the short figure is certainly absent.

*

On reaching England, it appears that Mr Wraxall landed at Harwich,* and that he resolved at once to put himself out of the reach of some person or persons whom he never specifies, but whom he had evidently come to regard as his pursuers. Accordingly he took a vehicle—it was a closed fly—not trusting the railway, and drove across country to the village of Belchamp St Paul.* It was about nine o'clock on a moon-light August night when he neared the place. He was sitting forward, and looking out of the window at the fields and thickets—there was little else to be seen—racing past him. Suddenly he came to a cross-road. At the corner two figures were standing motionless; both were in dark cloaks; the taller one wore a hat, the shorter a hood. He had no time to see their faces, nor did they make any motion that he could discern. Yet the horse shied violently and broke into a gallop, and Mr Wraxall sank back into his seat in something like desperation. He had seen them before.

Arrived at Belchamp St Paul, he was fortunate enough to find a decent furnished lodging, and for the next twenty-four hours he lived, comparatively speaking, in peace. His last notes were written on this day. They are too disjointed and ejaculatory to be given here in full, but the substance of them is clear enough. He is expecting a visit from his pursuers—how or when he knows not—and his constant cry is 'What has he done?' and 'Is there no hope?' Doctors, he knows, would call him mad, policemen would laugh at him. The parson is away. What can he do but lock his door and cry to God?

People still remembered last year at Belchamp St Paul how a strange gentleman came one evening in August years back; and how the next morning but one he was found dead, and there was an inquest; and the jury that viewed the body fainted, seven of 'em did, and none of 'em wouldn't speak to what they see, and the verdict was visitation of God; and how the people as kep' the 'ouse moved out that same week, and went away from that part. But they do not, I think, know that any glimmer of light has ever been thrown, or could be thrown, on the mystery. It so happened that last year the little house came into my hands as part of a legacy. It had stood empty since 1863, and there seemed no prospect of letting it; so I had it pulled down, and the papers of which I have given you an abstract were found in a forgot-ten cupboard under the window in the best bedroom.

FRANCIS MARION CRAWFORD

For the Blood is the Life

❧❧❧

W E had dined at sunset on the broad roof of the old tower, because it was cooler there during the great heat of summer. Besides, the little kitchen was built at one corner of the great square platform, which made it more convenient than if the dishes had to be carried down the steep stone steps, broken in places and everywhere worn with age. The tower was one of those built all down the west coast of Calabria by the Emperor Charles V early in the sixteenth century, to keep off the Barbary pirates, when the unbelievers were allied with Francis I* against the Emperor and the Church. They have gone to ruin, a few still stand intact, and mine is one of the largest. How it came into my possession ten years ago, and why I spend a part of each year in it, are matters which do not concern this tale. The tower stands in one of the loneliest spots in Southern Italy, at the extremity of a curving rocky promontory, which forms a small but safe natural harbour at the southern extremity of the Gulf of Policastro, and just north of Cape Scalea,* the birthplace of Judas Iscariot, according to the old local legend. The tower stands alone on this hooked spur of the rock, and there is not a house to be seen within three miles of it. When I go there I take a couple of sailors, one of whom is a fair cook, and when I am away it is in charge of a gnome-like little being who was once a miner and who attached himself to me long ago.

My friend, who sometimes visits me in my summer solitude, is an artist by profession, a Scandinavian by birth, and a cosmopolitan by force of circumstances. We had dined at sunset; the sunset glow had reddened and faded again, and the evening purple steeped the vast chain of the mountains that embrace the deep gulf to eastward and rear themselves higher and higher toward the south. It was hot, and we sat at the landward corner of the platform, waiting for the night breeze to come down from the lower hills. The colour sank out of the air, there was a little interval of deep-grey twilight, and a lamp sent a yellow streak from the open door of the kitchen, where the men were getting their supper.

Then the moon rose suddenly above the crest of the promontory, flooding the platform and lighting up every little spur of rock and knoll of grass below us, down to the edge of the motionless water. My friend lighted his pipe and sat looking at a spot on the hillside. I knew that he was looking at it, and for a long time past I had wondered whether he would ever see anything there that would fix his attention. I knew that spot well. It was clear that he was interested at last, though it was a long time before he spoke. Like most painters, he trusts to his own eyesight, as a lion trusts his strength and a stag his speed, and he is always disturbed when he cannot reconcile what he sees with what he believes that he ought to see.

'It's strange,' he said. 'Do you see that little mound just on this side of the boulder?'

'Yes,' I said, and I guessed what was coming.

'It looks like a grave,' observed Holger.

'Very true. It does look like a grave.'

'Yes,' continued my friend, his eyes still fixed on the spot. 'But the strange thing is that I see the body lying on the top of it. Of course,' continued Holger, turning his head on one side as artists do, 'it must be an effect of light. In the first place, it is not a grave at all. Secondly, if it were, the body would be inside and not outside. Therefore, it's an effect of the moonlight. Don't you see it?'

'Perfectly; I always see it on moonlight nights.'

'It doesn't seem to interest you much,' said Holger.

'On the contrary, it does interest me, though I am used to it. You're not so far wrong, either. The mound is really a grave.'

'Nonsense!' cried Holger, incredulously. 'I suppose you'll tell me what I see lying on it is really a corpse!'

'No,' I answered, 'it's not. I know, because I have taken the trouble to go down and see.'

'Then what is it?' asked Holger.

'It's nothing.'

'You mean that it's an effect of light, I suppose?'

'Perhaps it is. But the inexplicable part of the matter is that it makes no difference whether the moon is rising or setting, or waxing or waning. If there's any moonlight at all, from east or west or overhead, so long as it shines on the grave you can see the outline of the body on top.'

Holger stirred up his pipe with the point of his knife, and then used his finger for a stopper. When the tobacco burned well he rose from his chair.

'If you don't mind,' he said, 'I'll go down and take a look at it.'

He left me, crossed the roof, and disappeared down the dark steps. I did not move, but sat looking down until he came out of the tower below. I heard him humming an old Danish song as he crossed the open space in the bright moonlight, going straight to the mysterious mound. When he was ten paces from it, Holger stopped short, made two steps forward, and then three or four backward, and then stopped again. I know what that meant. He had reached the spot where the Thing ceased to be visible—where, as he would have said, the effect of light changed.

Then he went on till he reached the mound and stood upon it. I could see the Thing still, but it was no longer lying down; it was on its knees now, winding its white arms round Holger's body and look-ing up into his face. A cool breeze stirred my hair at that moment, as the night wind began to come down from the hills, but it felt like a breath from another world.

The Thing seemed to be trying to climb to its feet, helping itself up by Holger's body while he stood upright, quite unconscious of it and apparently looking toward the tower, which is very picturesque when the moonlight falls upon it on that side.

'Come along!' I shouted. 'Don't stay there all night!'

It seemed to me that he moved reluctantly as he stepped from the mound, or else with difficulty. That was it. The Thing's arms were still round his waist, but its feet could not leave the grave. As he came slowly forward it was drawn and lengthened like a wreath of mist, thin and white, till I saw distinctly that Holger shook himself, as a man does who feels a chill. At the same instant a little wail of pain came to me on the breeze—it might have been the cry of the small owl that lives among the rocks—and the misty presence floated swiftly back from Holger's advancing figure and lay once more at its length upon the mound.

Again I felt the cool breeze in my hair, and this time an icy thrill of dread ran down my spine. I remembered very well that I had once gone down there alone in the moonlight; that presently, being near, I had seen nothing; that, like Holger, I had gone and had stood upon the mound; and I remembered how, when I came back, sure that there was nothing there, I had felt the sudden conviction that there was something after all if I would only look behind me. I remembered the strong temptation to look back, a temptation I had resisted as unworthy of a man of sense, until, to get rid of it, I had shaken myself just as Holger did.

And now I knew that those white, misty arms had been round me too; I knew it in a flash, and I shuddered as I remembered that I had heard the night owl then too. But it had not been the night owl. It was the cry of the Thing.

I refilled my pipe and poured out a cup of strong southern wine; in less than a minute Holger was seated beside me again.

'Of course there's nothing there,' he said, 'but it's creepy, all the same. Do you know, when I was coming back I was so sure that there was something behind me that I wanted to turn round and look? It was an effort not to.'

He laughed a little, knocked the ashes out of his pipe, and poured himself out some wine. For a while neither of us spoke, and the moon rose higher, and we both looked at the Thing that lay on the mound.

'You might make a story about that,' said Holger after a long time.

'There is one,' I answered. 'If you're not sleepy, I'll tell it to you.'

'Go ahead,' said Holger, who likes stories.

* * *

Old Alario was dying up there in the village behind the hill. You remember him, I have no doubt. They say that he made his money by selling sham jewellery in South America, and escaped with his gains when he was found out. Like all those fellows, if they bring anything back with them, he at once set to work to enlarge his house, and as there are no masons here, he sent all the way to Paola* for two workmen. They were a rough-looking pair of scoundrels—a Neapolitan who had lost one eye and a Sicilian with an old scar half an inch deep across his left cheek. I often saw them, for on Sundays they used to come down here and fish off the rocks. When Alario caught the fever that killed him the masons were still at work. As he had agreed that part of their pay should be their board and lodging, he made them sleep in the house. His wife was dead, and he had an only son called Angelo, who was a much better sort than himself. Angelo was to marry the daughter of the richest man in the village, and, strange to say, though the marriage was arranged by their parents, the young people were said to be in love with each other.

For that matter, the whole village was in love with Angelo, and among the rest a wild, good-looking creature called Cristina, who was more like a gipsy than any girl I ever saw about here. She had very red lips and very black eyes, she was built like a greyhound, and had the tongue of the devil. But Angelo did not care a straw for her. He was rather a simple-minded fellow, quite different from his old scoundrel of a father, and under what I should call normal circumstances I really believe that he would never have looked at any girl except the nice plump little creature, with a fat dowry, whom his father meant him to marry. But things turned up which were neither normal nor natural.

On the other hand, a very handsome young shepherd from the hills above Maratea* was in love with Cristina, who seems to have been quite indifferent to him. Cristina had no regular means of subsistence, but she was a good girl and willing to do any work or go on errands to any distance for the sake of a loaf of bread or a mess of beans, and permission to sleep under cover. She was especially glad when she could get something to do about the house of Angelo's father. There is no doctor in the village, and when the neighbours saw that old Alario was dying they sent Cristina to Scalea to fetch one. That was late in the afternoon, and if they had waited so long, it was because the dying miser refused to allow any such extravagance while he was able to speak. But while Cristina was gone matters grew rapidly worse, the priest was brought to the bedside, and when he had done what he could he gave it as his opinion to the bystanders that the old man was dead, and left the house.

You know these people. They have a physical horror of death. Until the priest spoke, the room had been full of people. The words were hardly out of his mouth before it was empty. It was night now. They hurried down the dark steps and out into the street.

Angelo, as I have said, was away, Cristina had not come back—the simple woman-servant who had nursed the sick man fled with the rest, and the body was left alone in the flickering light of the earthen oil lamp.

Five minutes later two men looked in cautiously and crept forward toward the bed. They were the one-eyed Neapolitan mason and his Sicilian companion. They knew what they wanted. In a moment they had dragged from under the bed a small but heavy iron-bound box, and long before any one thought of coming back to the dead man they had left the house and the village under cover of the darkness. It was easy enough, for Alario's house is the last toward the gorge which leads down here, and the thieves merely went out by the back door, got over the stone wall, and had nothing to risk after that except the possibility of meeting some belated countryman, which was very small indeed, since few of the people use that path. They had a mattock and shovel, and they made their way here without accident.

I am telling you this story as it must have happened, for, of course, there were no witnesses to this part of it. The men brought the box down by the gorge, intending to bury it until they should be able to come back and take it away in a boat. They must have been clever enough to guess that some of the money would be in paper notes, for they would otherwise have buried it on the beach in the wet sand, where it would have been much safer. But the paper would have rotted if they had been obliged to leave it there long, so they dug their hole down there, close to that boulder. Yes, just where the mound is now.

Cristina did not find the doctor in Scalea, for he had been sent for from a place up the valley, halfway to San Domenico.* If she had found him, he would have come on his mule by the upper road, which is smoother but much longer. But Cristina took the short cut by the rocks, which passes about fifty feet above the mound, and goes round that corner. The men were digging when she passed, and she heard them at work. It would not have been like her to go by without finding out what the noise was, for she was never afraid of anything in her life, and besides, the fishermen sometimes come ashore here at night to get a stone for an anchor or to gather sticks to make a little fire. The night was dark, and Cristina probably came close to the two men before she could see what they were doing. She knew them, of course, and they knew her, and understood instantly that they were in her power. There was only one thing to be done for their safety, and they did it. They knocked her on the head, they dug the hole deep, and they buried her quickly with the iron-bound chest. They must have understood that their only chance of escaping suspicion lay in getting back to the village before their absence was noticed, for they returned immediately, and were found half an hour later gossiping quietly with the man who was making Alario's coffin. He was a crony of theirs, and had been working at the repairs in the old man's house. So far as I have been able to make out, the only persons who were supposed to know where Alario kept his treasure were Angelo and the one woman-servant I have mentioned. Angelo was away; it was the woman who discovered the theft.

It is easy enough to understand why no one else knew where the money was. The old man kept his door locked and the key in his pocket when he was out, and did not let the woman enter to clean the place unless he was there himself. The whole village knew that he had money somewhere, however, and the masons had probably discovered the whereabouts of the chest by climbing in at the window in his absence. If the old man had not been delirious until he lost consciousness, he would have been in frightful agony of mind for his riches. The faithful woman-servant forgot their existence only for a few moments when she fled with the rest, overcome by the horror of death. Twenty minutes had not passed before she returned with the two hideous old hags who are always called in to prepare the dead for burial. Even then she had not at first the courage to go near the bed with them, but she made a pretence of dropping something, went down on her knees as if to find it, and looked under the bedstead. The walls of the room were newly whitewashed down to the floor, and she saw at a glance that the chest was gone. It had been there in the afternoon, it had therefore been stolen in the short interval since she had left the room.

There are no carabineers* stationed in the village; there is not so much as a municipal watchman, for there is no municipality. There never was such a place, I believe. Scalea is supposed to look after it in some mysterious way, and it takes a couple of hours to get anybody from there. As the old woman had lived in the village all her life, it did not even occur to her to apply to any civil authority for help. She simply set up a howl and ran through the village in the dark, screaming out that her dead master's house had been robbed. Many of the people looked out, but at first no one seemed inclined to help her. Most of them, judging her by themselves, whispered to each other that she had probably stolen the money herself. The first man to move was the father of the girl whom Angelo was to marry; having collected his household, all of whom felt a personal interest in the wealth which was to have come into the family, he declared it to be his opinion that the chest had been stolen by the two journeyman masons who lodged in the house. He headed a search for them, which naturally began in Alario's house and ended in the carpenter's workshop, where the thieves were found discussing a measure of wine with the carpenter over the half-finished coffin, by the light of one earthen lamp filled with oil and tallow. The search party at once accused the delinquents of the crime, and threatened to lock them up in the cellar till the carabineers could be fetched from Scalea. The two men looked at each other for one moment, and then without the slightest hesitation they put out the single light, seized the unfinished coffin between them, and using it as a sort of battering ram, dashed upon their assailants in the dark. In a few moments they were beyond pursuit.

That is the end of the first part of the story. The treasure had disappeared, and as no trace of it could be found the people naturally supposed that the thieves had succeeded in carrying it off. The old man was buried, and when Angelo came back at last he had to borrow money to pay for the miserable funeral, and had some difficulty in doing so. He hardly needed to be told that in losing his inheritance he had lost his bride. In this part of the world marriages are made on strictly business principles, and if the promised cash is not forthcoming on the appointed day the bride or the bridegroom whose parents have failed to produce it may as well take themselves off, for there will be no wedding. Poor Angelo knew that well enough. His father had been possessed of hardly any land, and now that the hard cash which he had brought from South America was gone, there was nothing left but debts for the building materials that were to have been used for enlarging and improving the old house. Angelo was beggared, and the nice plump little creature who was to have been his turned up her nose at him in the most approved fashion. As for Cristina, it was several days before she was missed, for no one remembered that she had been sent to Scalea for the doctor, who had never come. She often disappeared in the same way for days together, when she could find a little work here and there at the distant farms among the hills. But when she did not come back at all, people began to wonder, and at last made up their minds that she had connived with the masons and had escaped with them.

* * *

I paused and emptied my glass.

'That sort of thing could not happen anywhere else,' observed Holger, filling his everlasting pipe again. 'It is wonderful what a natural charm there is about murder and sudden death in a romantic country like this.

*Deeds that would be simply brutal and disgusting anywhere else become
dramatic and mysterious because this is Italy and we are living in a genuine tower of Charles V. built against genuine Barbary pirates.'*

'There's something in that,' I admitted. Holger is the most romantic
man in the world inside of himself, but he always thinks it necessary to
explain why he feels anything.

'I suppose they found the poor girl's body with the box,' he said presently.

'As it seems to interest you,' I answered, 'I'll tell you the rest of the
story.'

*The moon had risen high by this time; the outline of the Thing on the
mound was clearer to our eyes than before.*

* * *

The village very soon settled down to its small, dull life. No one
missed old Alario, who had been away so much on his voyages to
South America that he had never been a familiar figure in his native
place. Angelo lived in the half-finished house, and because he had no
money to pay the old woman-servant she would not stay with him, but
once in a long time she would come and wash a shirt for him for old
acquaintance' sake. Besides the house, he had inherited a small patch
of ground at some distance from the village; he tried to cultivate it,
but he had no heart in the work, for he knew he could never pay the
taxes on it and on the house, which would certainly be confiscated
by the Government, or seized for the debt of the building material,
which the man who had supplied it refused to take back.

Angelo was very unhappy. So long as his father had been alive and
rich, every girl in the village had been in love with him; but that was
all changed now. It had been pleasant to be admired and courted, and
invited to drink wine by fathers who had girls to marry. It was hard
to be stared at coldly, and sometimes laughed at because he had been
robbed of his inheritance. He cooked his miserable meals for himself,
and from being sad became melancholy and morose.

At twilight, when the day's work was done, instead of hanging
about in the open space before the church with young fellows of his
own age, he took to wandering in lonely places on the outskirts of
the village till it was quite dark. Then he slunk home and went to
bed to save the expense of a light. But in those lonely twilight hours
he began to have strange waking dreams. He was not always alone,
for often when he sat on the stump of a tree, where the narrow path

turns down the gorge, he was sure that a woman came up noiselessly over the rough stones, as if her feet were bare; and she stood under a clump of chestnut trees only half a dozen yards down the path, and beckoned to him without speaking. Though she was in the shadow he knew that her lips were red, and that when they parted a little and smiled at him she showed two small sharp teeth. He knew this at first rather than saw it, and he knew that it was Cristina, and that she was dead. Yet he was not afraid; he only wondered whether it was a dream, for he thought that if he had been awake he should have been frightened.

Besides, the dead woman had red lips, and that could only happen in a dream. Whenever he went near the gorge after sunset she was already there waiting for him, or else she very soon appeared, and he began to be sure that she came a little nearer to him every day. At first he had only been sure of her blood-red mouth, but now each feature grew distinct, and the pale face looked at him with deep and hungry eyes.

It was the eyes that grew dim. Little by little he came to know that some day the dream would not end when he turned away to go home, but would lead him down the gorge out of which the vision rose. She was nearer now when she beckoned to him. Her cheeks were not livid like those of the dead, but pale with starvation, with the furious and unappeased physical hunger of her eyes that devoured him. They feasted on his soul and cast a spell over him, and at last they were close to his own and held him. He could not tell whether her breath was as hot as fire or as cold as ice; he could not tell whether her red lips burned his or froze them, or whether her five fingers on his wrists seared scorching scars or bit his flesh like frost; he could not tell whether he was awake or asleep, whether she was alive or dead, but he knew that she loved him, she alone of all creatures, earthly or unearthly, and her spell had power over him.

When the moon rose high that night the shadow of that Thing was not alone down there upon the mound.

Angelo awoke in the cool dawn, drenched with dew and chilled through flesh, and blood, and bone. He opened his eyes to the faint grey light, and saw the stars still shining overhead. He was very weak, and his heart was beating so slowly that he was almost like a man fainting. Slowly he turned his head on the mound, as on a pillow, but the other face was not there. Fear seized him suddenly, a fear unspeakable and unknown; he sprang to his feet and fled up the gorge, and he never looked behind him until he reached the door of the house on the outskirts of the village. Drearily he went to his work that day, and wearily the hours dragged themselves after the sun, till at last he touched the sea and sank, and the great sharp hills above Maratea turned purple against the dove-coloured eastern sky.

Angelo shouldered his heavy hoe and left the field. He felt less tired now than in the morning when he had begun to work, but he promised himself that he would go home without lingering by the gorge, and eat the best supper he could get himself, and sleep all night in his bed like a Christian man. Not again would he be tempted down the narrow way by a shadow with red lips and icy breath; not again would he dream that dream of terror and delight. He was near the village now; it was half an hour since the sun had set, and the cracked church bell sent little discordant echoes across the rocks and ravines to tell all good people that the day was done. Angelo stood still a moment where the path forked, where it led toward the village on the left, and down to the gorge on the right, where a clump of chestnut trees overhung the narrow way. He stood still a minute, lifting his battered hat from his head and gazing at the fast-fading sea westward, and his lips moved as he silently repeated the familiar evening prayer. His lips moved, but the words that followed them in his brain lost their meaning and turned into others, and ended in a name that he spoke aloud—Cristina! With the name, the tension of his will relaxed suddenly, reality went out and the dream took him again, and bore him on swiftly and surely like a man walking in his sleep, down, down, by the steep path in the gathering darkness. And as she glided beside him, Cristina whispered strange, sweet things in his ear, which somehow, if he had been awake, he knew that he could not quite have understood; but now they were the most wonderful words he had ever heard in his life. And she kissed him also, but not upon his mouth. He felt her sharp kisses upon his white throat, and he knew that her lips were red. So the wild dream sped on through twilight and darkness and moonrise, and all the glory of the summer's night. But in the chilly dawn he lay as one half dead upon the mound down there, recalling and not recalling, drained of his blood, yet strangely longing to give those red lips more. Then came the fear, the awful nameless panic, the mortal horror that guards the confines of the world we see not, neither know of as we know of other things, but which we feel when its icy chill freezes our bones and stirs our hair with the touch of a ghostly hand. Once more Angelo sprang from the mound and fled up the gorge in the breaking day, but his step was less sure this time, and he panted for breath as he ran; and when he came to the bright spring of water that rises halfway up the hillside, he dropped upon his knees and hands and plunged his whole face in and drank as he had never drunk before—for it was the thirst of the wounded man who has lain bleeding all night long upon the battle-field.

She had him fast now, and he could not escape her, but would come to her every evening at dusk until she had drained him of his last drop of blood. It was in vain that when the day was done he tried to take another turning and to go home by a path that did not lead near the gorge. It was in vain that he made promises to himself each morning at dawn when he climbed the lonely way up from the shore to the village. It was all in vain, for when the sun sank burning into the sea, and the coolness of the evening stole out as from a hiding-place to delight the weary world, his feet turned toward the old way, and she was waiting for him in the shadow under the chestnut trees; and then all happened as before, and she fell to kissing his white throat even as she flitted lightly down the way, winding one arm about him. And as his blood failed, she grew more hungry and more thirsty every day, and every day when he awoke in the early dawn it was harder to rouse himself to the effort of climbing the steep path to the village; and when he went to his work his feet dragged painfully, and there was hardly strength in his arms to wield the heavy hoe. He scarcely spoke to any one now, but the people said he was 'consuming himself' for love of the girl he was to have married when he lost his inheritance; and they laughed heartily at the thought, for this is not a very romantic country. At this time, Antonio, the man who stays here to look after the tower, returned from a visit to his people, who live near Salerno.* He had been away all the time since before Alario's death and knew nothing of what had happened. He has told me that he came back late in the afternoon and shut himself up in the tower to eat and sleep, for he was very tired. It was past midnight when he awoke, and when he looked out the waning moon was rising over the shoulder of the hill. He looked out toward the mound, and he saw something, and he did not sleep again that night. When he went out again in the morning it was broad daylight, and there was nothing to be seen on the mound but loose stones and driven sand. Yet he did not go very near it; he went straight up the path to the village and directly to the house of the old priest.

'I have seen an evil thing this night,' he said; 'I have seen how the dead drink the blood of the living. And the blood is the life.'

'Tell me what you have seen,' said the priest in reply.

Antonio told him everything he had seen.

'You must bring your book and your holy water to-night,' he added. 'I will be here before sunset to go down with you, and if it pleases your reverence to sup with me while we wait, I will make ready.'

'I will come,' the priest answered, 'for I have read in old books of these strange beings which are neither quick nor dead,* and which lie ever fresh in their graves, stealing out in the dusk to taste life and blood.'

Antonio cannot read, but he was glad to see that the priest understood the business; for, of course, the books must have instructed him as to the best means of quieting the half-living Thing for ever.

So Antonio went away to his work, which consists largely in sitting on the shady side of the tower, when he is not perched upon a rock with a fishing-line catching nothing. But on that day he went twice to look at the mound in the bright sunlight, and he searched round and round it for some hole through which the being might get in and out; but he found none. When the sun began to sink and the air was cooler in the shadows, he went up to fetch the old priest, carrying a little wicker basket with him; and in this they placed a bottle of holy water, and the basin, and sprinkler, and the stole* which the priest would need; and they came down and waited in the door of the tower till it should be dark. But while the light still lingered very grey and faint, they saw something moving, just there, two figures, a man's that walked, and a woman's that flitted beside him, and while her head lay on his shoulder she kissed his throat. The priest has told me that, too, and that his teeth chattered and he grasped Antonio's arm. The vision passed and disappeared into the shadow. Then Antonio got the leathern flask of strong liquor, which he kept for great occasions, and poured such a draught as made the old man feel almost young again; and he got the lantern, and his pick and shovel, and gave the priest his stole to put on and the holy water to carry, and they went out together toward the spot where the work was to be done. Antonio says that in spite of the rum his own knees shook together, and the priest stumbled over his Latin. For when they were yet a few yards from the mound the flickering light of the lantern fell upon Angelo's white face, unconscious as if in sleep, and on his upturned throat, over which a very thin red line of blood trickled down into his collar; and the flickering light of the lantern played upon another face that looked up from the feast—upon two deep, dead eyes that saw in spite of death—upon parted lips redder than life itself—upon two gleaming teeth on which glistened a rosy drop. Then the priest, good old man, shut his eyes tight and showered holy water before him, and his cracked voice rose almost to a scream; and then Antonio, who is no coward after all, raised his pick in one hand and the lantern in the other, as he sprang forward, not knowing what the end should be; and then he swears that he heard a woman's cry, and the Thing was gone, and Angelo lay alone on the mound unconscious, with the red line on his throat and the beads of deathly sweat on his cold forehead. They lifted him, half-dead as he was, and laid him on the ground close by; then Antonio went to work, and the priest helped him, though he was old and could not do much; and they dug deep, and at last Antonio, standing in the grave, stooped down with his lantern to see what he might see.

His hair used to be dark brown, with grizzled streaks about the temples; in less than a month from that day he was as grey as a badger. He was a miner when he was young, and most of these fellows have seen ugly sights now and then, when accidents have happened, but he had never seen what he saw that night—that Thing which is neither alive nor dead, that Thing that will abide neither above ground nor in the grave. Antonio had brought something with him which the priest had not noticed. He had made it that afternoon—a sharp stake shaped from a piece of tough old driftwood. He had it with him now, and he had his heavy pick, and he had taken the lantern down into the grave. I don't think any power on earth could make him speak of what happened then, and the old priest was too frightened to look in. He says he heard Antonio breathing like a wild beast, and moving as if he were fighting with something almost as strong as himself; and he heard an evil sound also, with blows, as of something violently driven through flesh and bone; and then the most awful sound of all—a woman's shriek, the unearthly scream of a woman neither dead nor alive, but buried deep for many days. And he, the poor old priest, could only rock himself as he knelt there in the sand, crying aloud his prayers and exorcisms to drown these dreadful sounds. Then suddenly a small iron-bound chest was thrown up and rolled over against the old man's knee, and in a moment more Antonio was beside him, his face as white as tallow* in the flickering light of the lantern, shovelling the sand and pebbles into the grave with furious haste, and looking over the edge till the pit was half full; and the priest said that there was much fresh blood on Antonio's hands and on his clothes.

I had come to the end of my story. Holger finished his wine and leaned back in his chair.

'So Angelo got his own again,' he said. 'Did he marry the prim and plump young person to whom he had been betrothed?'

'No; he had been badly frightened. He went to South America, and has not been heard of since.'

'And that poor thing's body is there still, I suppose,' said Holger. 'Is it quite dead yet, I wonder?'

I wonder, too. But whether it be dead or alive, I should hardly care to see it, even in broad daylight. Antonio is as grey as a badger, and he has never been quite the same man since that night.

ALGERNON BLACKWOOD

The Wendigo

❦

I

A CONSIDERABLE number of hunting parties were out that year without finding so much as a fresh trail; for the moose were uncommonly shy, and the various Nimrods* returned to the bosoms of their respective families with the best excuses the facts or their imaginations could suggest. Dr Cathcart, among others, came back without a trophy; but he brought instead the memory of an experience which he declares was worth all the bull-moose that had ever been shot. But then Cathcart, of Aberdeen, was interested in other things besides moose—amongst them the vagaries of the human mind. This particular story, however, found no mention in his book on *Collective Hallucination* for the simple reason (so he confided once to a fellow colleague) that he himself played too intimate a part in it to form a competent judgment of the affair as a whole. . . .

Besides himself and his guide, Hank Davis, there was young Simpson, his nephew, a divinity student destined for the 'Wee Kirk'* (then on his first visit to Canadian backwoods), and the latter's guide, Défago. Joseph Défago was a French 'Canuck,'* who had strayed from his native Province of Quebec years before, and had got caught in Rat Portage when the Canadian Pacific Railway* was a-building; a man who, in addition to his unparalleled knowledge of woodcraft and bush-lore, could also sing the old *voyageur* songs and tell a capital hunting yarn into the bargain. He was deeply susceptible, moreover, to that singular spell which the wilderness lays upon certain lonely natures, and he loved the wild solitudes with a kind of romantic passion that amounted almost to an obsession. The life of the backwoods fascinated him—whence, doubtless, his surpassing efficiency in dealing with their mysteries.

On this particular expedition he was Hank's choice. Hank knew him and swore by him. He also swore at him, 'jest as a pal might,' and since he had a vocabulary of picturesque, if utterly meaningless, oaths, the conversation between the two stalwart and hardy woodsmen was often of a rather lively description. This river of expletives, however, Hank agreed to dam a little out of respect for his old 'hunting boss,' Dr Cathcart, whom of course he addressed after the fashion of the country as 'Doc'; and also because he understood that young Simpson was already a 'bit of a parson.' He had, however, one objection to Défago, and one only—which was, that the French Canadian sometimes exhibited what Hank described as 'the output of a cursed and dismal mind,' meaning apparently that he sometimes was true to type, Latin type, and suffered fits of a kind of silent moroseness when nothing could induce him to utter speech. Défago, that is to say, was imaginative and melancholy. And, as a rule, it was too long a spell of 'civilization' that induced the attacks, for a few days of the wilderness invariably cured them.

This, then, was the party of four that found themselves in camp the last week in October of that 'shy moose year' 'way up in the wilderness north of Rat Portage—a forsaken and desolate country. There was also Punk, an Indian, who had accompanied Dr Cathcart and Hank on their hunting trips in previous years, and who acted as cook. His duty was merely to stay in camp, catch fish, and prepare venison steaks and coffee at a few minutes' notice. He dressed in the worn-out clothes bequeathed to him by former patrons, and, except for his coarse black hair and dark skin, he looked in these city garments no more like a real redskin than a stage negro looks like a real African. For all that, however, Punk had in him still the instincts of his dying race; his taciturn silence and his endurance survived; also his superstition.

The party round the blazing fire that night were despondent, for a week had passed without a single sign of recent moose discovering itself. Défago had sung his song and plunged into a story, but Hank, in bad humour, reminded him so often that 'he kep' mussing-up the fac's so, that it was 'most all nothin' but a petred-out lie,' that the Frenchman had finally subsided into a sulky silence which nothing seemed likely to break. Dr Cathcart and his nephew were fairly done after an exhausting day. Punk was washing up the dishes, grunting to himself under the lean-to of branches, where he later also slept. No one troubled to stir the slowly dying fire. Overhead the stars were brilliant in a sky quite wintry, and there was so little wind that ice was already forming stealthily along the shores of the still lake behind them. The silence of the vast listening forest stole forward and enveloped them.

Hank broke in suddenly with his nasal voice.

'I'm in favour of breaking new ground to-morrow, Doc,' he observed with energy, looking across at his employer. 'We don't stand a dead Dago's chance about here.'

'Agreed,' said Cathcart, always a man of few words. 'Think the idea's good.'

'Sure pop, it's good,' Hank resumed with confidence. 'S'pose, now, you and I strike west, up Garden Lake* way for a change! None of us ain't touched that quiet bit o' land yet——'

'I'm with you.'

'And you, Défago, take Mr Simpson along in the small canoe, skip across the lake, portage over into Fifty Island Water,* and take a good squint down that thar southern shore. The moose 'yarded' there like hell last year, and for all we know they may be doin' it agin this year jest to spite us.'

Défago, keeping his eyes on the fire, said nothing by way of reply. He was still offended, possibly, about his interrupted story.

'No one's been up that way this year, an' I'll lay my bottom dollar on *that!*' Hank added with emphasis, as though he had a reason for knowing. He looked over at his partner sharply. 'Better take the little silk tent and stay away a couple o' nights,' he concluded, as though the matter were definitely settled. For Hank was recognized as general organizer of the hunt, and in charge of the party.

It was obvious to any one that Défago did not jump at the plan, but his silence seemed to convey something more than ordinary disapproval, and across his sensitive dark face there passed a curious expression like a flash of firelight—not so quickly, however, that the three men had not time to catch it. 'He funked for some reason, *I* thought,' Simpson said afterwards in the tent he shared with his uncle. Dr Cathcart made no immediate reply, although the look had interested him enough at the time for him to make a mental note of it. The expression had caused him a passing uneasiness he could not quite account for at the moment.

But Hank, of course, had been the first to notice it, and the odd thing was that instead of becoming explosive or angry over the other's reluctance, he at once began to humour him a bit.

'But there ain't no *speshul* reason why no one's been up there this year,' he said, with a perceptible hush in his tone; 'not the reason *you* mean, anyway! Las' year it was the fires that kep' folks out, and this year I guess—I guess it jest happened so, that's all!' His manner was clearly meant to be encouraging.

Joseph Défago raised his eyes a moment, then dropped them again. A breath of wind stole out of the forest and stirred the embers into a passing blaze. Dr Cathcart again noticed the expression in the guide's face, and again he did not like it. But this time the nature of the look betrayed itself. In those eyes, for an instant, he caught the gleam of a man scared in his very soul. It disquieted him more than he cared to admit.

'Bad Indians up that way?' he asked, with a laugh to ease matters a little, while Simpson, too sleepy to notice this subtle by-play, moved off to bed with a prodigious yawn; 'or—or anything wrong with the country?' he added, when his nephew was out of hearing.

Hank met his eye with something less than his usual frankness.

'He's jest skeered,' he replied good-humouredly, 'skeered stiff about some ole feery tale! That's all, ain't it, ole pard?' And he gave Défago a friendly kick on the moccasined foot that lay nearest the fire.

Défago looked up quickly, as from an interrupted reverie, a reverie, however, that had not prevented his seeing all that went on about him.

'Skeered—*nuthin'!*' he answered, with a flush of defiance. 'There's nuthin' in the Bush that can skeer Joseph Défago, and don't you forget it!' And the natural energy with which he spoke made it impossible to know whether he told the whole truth or only a part of it.

Hank turned towards the doctor. He was just going to add something when he stopped abruptly and looked round. A sound close behind them in the darkness made all three start. It was old Punk, who had moved up from his lean-to while they talked and now stood there just beyond the circle of fire-light—listening.

''Nother time, Doc!' Hank whispered, with a wink, 'when the gallery ain't stepped down into the stalls!' And, springing to his feet, he slapped the Indian on the back and cried noisily, 'Come up t' the fire an' warm yer dirty red skin a bit.' He dragged him towards the blaze and threw more wood on. 'That was a mighty good feed you give us an hour or two back,' he continued heartily, as though to set the man's thoughts on another scent, 'and it ain't Christian to let you stand out there freezin' yer ole soul to hell while we're gettin' all good an' toasted!' Punk moved in and warmed his feet, smiling darkly at the other's volubility which he only half understood, but saying nothing. And presently Dr Cathcart, seeing that further conversation was impossible, followed his nephew's example and moved off to the tent, leaving the three men smoking over the now blazing fire.

It is not easy to undress in a small tent without waking one's companion, and Cathcart, hardened and warm-blooded as he was in spite of his fifty odd years, did what Hank would have described as 'considerable of his twilight' in the open. He noticed, during the process, that Punk had meanwhile gone back to his lean-to, and that Hank and Défago were at it hammer and tongs, or, rather, hammer and anvil, the little French Canadian being the anvil. It was all very like the conventional stage picture of Western melodrama: the fire lighting up their faces with patches of alternate red and black; Défago, in slouch hat and moccasins in the part of the 'bad-lands'' villain; Hank, open-faced and hatless, with that reckless fling of his shoulders, the honest and deceived hero; and old Punk, eavesdropping in the background, supplying the atmosphere of mystery. The doctor smiled as he noticed the details; but at the same time something deep within him—he hardly knew what—shrank a little, as though an almost imperceptible breath of warning had touched the surface of his soul and was gone again before he could seize it. Probably it was traceable to that 'scared expression' he had seen in the eyes of Défago; 'probably'—for this hint of fugitive emotion otherwise escaped his usually so keen analysis. Défago, he was vaguely aware, might cause trouble somehow. . . . He was not as steady a guide as Hank, for instance. . . . Further than that he could not get . . .

He watched the men a moment longer before diving into the stuffy tent where Simpson already slept soundly. Hank, he saw, was swearing like a mad African in a New York nigger saloon; but it was the swearing of 'affection.' The ridiculous oaths flew freely now that the cause of their obstruction was asleep. Presently he put his arm almost tenderly upon his comrade's shoulder, and they moved off together into the shadows where their tent stood faintly glimmering. Punk, too, a moment later followed their example and disappeared between his odorous blankets in the opposite direction.

Dr Cathcart then likewise turned in, weariness and sleep still fighting in his mind with an obscure curiosity to know what it was had scared Défago about the country up Fifty Island Water way,—wondering, too, why Punk's presence had prevented the completion of what Hank had to say. Then sleep overtook him. He would know to-morrow. Hank would tell him the story while they trudged after the elusive moose.

Deep silence fell about the little camp, planted there so audaciously in the jaws of the wilderness. The lake gleamed like a sheet of black glass beneath the stars. The cold air pricked. In the draughts of night that poured their silent tide from the depths of the forest, with messages from distant ridges and from lakes just beginning to freeze, there lay already the faint, bleak odours of coming winter. White men, with their dull scent, might never have divined them; the fragrance of the wood-fire would have concealed from them these almost electrical hints of moss and bark and hardening swamp a hundred miles away. Even Hank and Défago, subtly in league with the soul of the woods as they were, would probably have spread their delicate nostrils in vain . . .

But an hour later, when all slept like the dead, old Punk crept from his blankets and went down to the shore of the lake like a shadow—silently, as only Indian blood can move. He raised his head and looked about him. The thick darkness rendered sight of small avail, but, like the animals, he possessed other senses that darkness could not mute. He listened—then sniffed the air. Motionless as a hemlock-stem he stood there. After five minutes again he lifted his head and sniffed, and yet once again. A tingling of the wonderful nerves that betrayed itself by no outer sign, ran through him as he tasted the keen air. Then, merging his figure into the surrounding blackness in a way that only wild men and animals understand, he turned, still moving like a shadow, and went stealthily back to his lean-to and his bed.

And soon after he slept, the change of wind he had divined stirred gently the reflection of the stars within the lake. Rising among the far ridges of the country beyond Fifty Island Water, it came from the direction in which he had stared, and it passed over the sleeping camp with a faint and sighing murmur through the tops of the big trees that was almost too delicate to be audible. With it, down the desert paths of night, though too faint, too high even for the Indian's hair-like nerves, there passed a curious, thin odour, strangely disquieting, an odour of something that seemed unfamiliar—utterly unknown.

The French Canadian and the man of Indian blood each stirred uneasily in his sleep just about this time, though neither of them woke. Then the ghost of that unforgettably strange odour passed away and was lost among the leagues of tenantless forest beyond.

II

IN the morning the camp was astir before the sun. There had been a light fall of snow during the night and the air was sharp. Punk had done his duty betimes, for the odours of coffee and fried bacon reached every tent. All were in good spirits.

'Wind's shifted!' cried Hank vigorously, watching Simpson and his guide already loading the small canoe. 'It's across the lake—dead right for you fellers. And the snow'll make bully trails! If there's any moose mussing around up thar, they'll not get so much as a tail-end scent of you with the wind as it is. Good luck, Monsieur Défago!' he added, facetiously giving the name its French pronunciation for once, '*bonne chance!*'

Défago returned the good wishes, apparently in the best of spirits, the silent mood gone. Before eight o'clock old Punk had the camp to himself, Cathcart and Hank were far along the trail that led westwards, while the canoe that carried Défago and Simpson, with silk tent and grub for two days, was already a dark speck bobbing on the bosom of the lake, going due east.

The wintry sharpness of the air was tempered now by a sun that topped the wooded ridges and blazed with a luxurious warmth upon the world of lake and forest below; loons flew skimming through the sparkling spray that the wind lifted; divers shook their dripping heads to the sun and popped smartly out of sight again; and as far as eye could reach rose the leagues of endless, crowding Bush, desolate in its lonely sweep and grandeur, untrodden by foot of man, and stretching its mighty and unbroken carpet right up to the frozen shores of Hudson Bay.

Simpson, who saw it all for the first time as he paddled hard in the bows of the dancing canoe, was enchanted by its austere beauty. His heart drank in the sense of freedom and great spaces just as his lungs drank in the cool and perfumed wind. Behind him in the stern seat, singing fragments of his native chanties, Défago steered the craft of birchbark like a thing of life, answering cheerfully all his companion's questions. Both were gay and light-hearted. On such occasions men lose the superficial, worldly distinctions; they become human beings working together for a common end. Simpson, the employer, and Défago the employed, among these primitive forces, were simply—two men, the 'guider' and the 'guided.' Superior knowledge, of course, assumed control, and the younger man fell without a second thought into the quasi-subordinate position. He never dreamed of objecting when Défago dropped the 'Mr,' and addressed him as 'Say, Simpson,' or 'Simpson, boss,' which was invariably the case before they reached the farther shore after a stiff paddle of twelve miles against a head wind. He only laughed, and liked it; then ceased to notice it at all.

For this 'divinity student' was a young man of parts and character, though as yet, of course, untravelled; and on this trip—the first time he had seen any country but his own and little Switzerland—the huge scale of things somewhat bewildered him. It was one thing, he realized, to hear about primeval forests, but quite another to see them. While to dwell in them and seek acquaintance with their wild life was, again, an initiation that no intelligent man could undergo without a certain shifting of personal values hitherto held for permanent and sacred.

Simpson knew the first faint indication of this emotion when he held the new .303 rifle* in his hands and looked along its pair of faultless, gleaming barrels. The three days' journey to their headquarters, by lake and portage, had carried the process a stage farther. And now that he was about to plunge beyond even the fringe of wilderness where they were camped into the virgin heart of uninhabited regions as vast as Europe itself, the true nature of the situation stole upon him with an effect of delight and awe that his imagination was fully capable of appreciating. It was himself and Défago against a multitude—at least, against a Titan!

The bleak splendours of these remote and lonely forests rather overwhelmed him with the sense of his own littleness. That stern quality of the tangled backwoods which can only be described as merciless and terrible, rose out of these far blue woods swimming upon the horizon, and revealed itself. He understood the silent warning. He realized his own utter helplessness. Only Défago, as a symbol of a distant civilization where man was master, stood between him and a pitiless death by exhaustion and starvation.

It was thrilling to him, therefore, to watch Défago turn over the canoe upon the shore, pack the paddles carefully underneath, and then proceed to 'blaze'* the spruce stems for some distance on either side of an almost invisible trail, with the careless remark thrown in, 'Say, Simpson, if anything happens to me, you'll find the canoe all correc' by these marks;—then strike doo west into the sun to hit the home camp agin, see?'

It was the most natural thing in the world to say, and he said it without any noticeable inflexion of the voice, only it happened to express the youth's emotions at the moment with an utterance that was symbolic of the situation and of his own helplessness as a factor in it. He was alone with Défago in a primitive world: that was all. The canoe, another symbol of man's ascendancy, was now to be left behind. Those small yellow patches, made on the trees by the axe, were the only indications of its hiding-place.

Meanwhile, shouldering the packs between them, each man carrying his own rifle, they followed the slender trail over rocks and fallen trunks and across half-frozen swamps; skirting numerous lakes that fairly gemmed the forest, their borders fringed with mist; and towards five o'clock found themselves suddenly on the edge of the woods, looking out across a large sheet of water in front of them, dotted with pine-clad islands of all describable shapes and sizes.

'Fifty Island Water,' announced Défago wearily, 'and the sun jest goin' to dip his bald old head into it!' he added, with unconscious poetry; and immediately they set about pitching camp for the night.

In a very few minutes, under those skilful hands that never made a movement too much or a movement too little, the silk tent stood taut and cosy, the beds of balsam* boughs ready laid, and a brisk cooking-fire burned with the minimum of smoke. While the young Scotchman cleaned the fish they had caught trolling behind the canoe, Défago 'guessed' he would 'jest as soon' take a turn through the Bush for indications of moose. '*May* come across a trunk where they bin and rubbed horns,' he said, as he moved off, 'or feedin' on the last of the maple leaves,'—and he was gone.

His small figure melted away like a shadow in the dusk, while Simpson noted with a kind of admiration how easily the forest absorbed him into herself. A few steps, it seemed, and he was no longer visible.

Yet there was little underbrush hereabouts; the trees stood somewhat apart, well spaced; and in the clearings grew silver-birch and maple, spear-like and slender, against the immense stems of spruce and hemlock. But for occasional prostrate monsters, and the boulders of grey rock that thrust uncouth shoulders here and there out of the ground, it might well have been a bit of park in the Old Country.

Almost, one might have seen in it the hand of man. A little to the right, however, began the great burnt section, miles in extent, proclaiming its real character—*brulé*,* as it is called, where the fires of the previous year had raged for weeks, and the blackened stumps now rose gaunt and ugly, bereft of branches, like gigantic match-heads stuck into the ground, savage and desolate beyond words. The perfume of charcoal and rain-soaked ashes still hung faintly about it.

The dusk rapidly deepened; the glades grew dark; the crackling of the fire and the wash of little waves along the rocky lake shore were the only sounds audible. The wind had dropped with the sun, and in all that vast world of branches nothing stirred. Any moment, it seemed, the woodland gods, who are to be worshipped in silence and loneliness, might sketch their mighty and terrific outlines among the trees. In front, through doorways pillared by huge straight stems, lay the stretch of Fifty Island Water, a crescent-shaped lake some fifteen miles from tip to tip, and perhaps five miles across where they were camped. A sky of rose and saffron, more clear than any atmosphere Simpson had ever known, still dropped its pale streaming fires across the waves, where the islands—a hundred, surely, rather than fifty—floated like the fairy barques of some enchanted fleet. Fringed with pines, whose crests fingered most delicately the sky, they almost seemed to move upwards as the light faded—about to weigh anchor and navigate the pathways of the heavens instead of the currents of their native and desolate lake.

And strips of coloured cloud, like flaunting pennons, signalled their departure to the stars. . . .

The beauty of the scene was strangely uplifting. Simpson smoked the fish and burnt his fingers into the bargain in his efforts to enjoy it and at the same time tend the frying-pan and the fire. Yet, ever at the back of his thoughts, lay that other aspect of the wilderness: the indifference to human life, the merciless spirit of desolation which took no note of man. The sense of his utter loneliness, now that even Défago had gone, came close as he looked about him and listened for the sound of his companion's returning footsteps.

There was pleasure in the sensation, yet with it a perfectly comprehensible alarm. And instinctively the thought stirred in him: 'What should I—*could* I, do—if anything happened and he did not come back——?'

They enjoyed their well-earned supper, eating untold quantities of

fish, and drinking unmilked tea strong enough to kill men who had
not covered thirty miles of hard 'going,' eating little on the way. And
when it was over, they smoked and told stories round the blazing fire,
laughing, stretching weary limbs, and discussing plans for the mor-
row. Défago was in excellent spirits, though disappointed at having
no signs of moose to report. But it was dark and he had not gone far.
The *brulé*, too, was bad. His clothes and hands were smeared with
charcoal. Simpson, watching him, realized with renewed vividness
their position—alone together in the wilderness.

'Défago,' he said presently, 'these woods, you know, are a bit too
big to feel quite at home in—to feel comfortable in, I mean! . . . Eh?'
He merely gave expression to the mood of the moment; he was hardly
prepared for the earnestness, the solemnity even, with which the
guide took him up.

'You've hit it right, Simpson, boss,' he replied, fixing his searching
brown eyes on his face, 'and that's the truth, sure. There's no end to
'em—no end at all.' Then he added in a lowered tone as if to himself,
'There's lots found out *that*, and gone plumb to pieces!'

But the man's gravity of manner was not quite to the other's liking;
it was a little too suggestive for this scenery and setting; he was sorry
he had broached the subject. He remembered suddenly how his uncle
had told him that men were sometimes stricken with a strange fever of
the wilderness, when the seduction of the uninhabited wastes caught
them so fiercely that they went forth, half fascinated, half deluded, to
their death. And he had a shrewd idea that his companion held something in sympathy with that queer type. He led the conversation on to
other topics, on to Hank and the doctor, for instance, and the natural
rivalry as to who should get the first sight of moose.

'If they went doo west,' observed Défago carelessly, 'there's sixty
miles between us now—with ole Punk at halfway house eatin' himself full to bustin' with fish and corfee.' They laughed together over
the picture. But the casual mention of those sixty miles again made
Simpson realize the prodigious scale of this land where they hunted;
sixty miles was a mere step; two hundred little more than a step.
Stories of lost hunters rose persistently before his memory. The passion and mystery of homeless and wandering men, seduced by the
beauty of great forests, swept his soul in a way too vivid to be quite
pleasant. He wondered vaguely whether it was the mood of his companion that invited the unwelcome suggestion with such persistence.

'Sing us a song, Défago, if you're not too tired,' he asked; 'one of those old *voyageur* songs you sang the other night.' He handed his tobacco pouch to the guide and then filled his own pipe, while the Canadian, nothing loth, sent his light voice across the lake in one of those plaintive, almost melancholy chanties with which lumbermen and trappers lessen the burden of their labour. There was an appealing and romantic flavour about it, something that recalled the atmosphere of the old pioneer days when Indians and wilderness were leagued together, battles frequent, and the Old Country farther off than it is to-day. The sound travelled pleasantly over the water, but the forest at their backs seemed to swallow it down with a single gulp that permitted neither echo nor resonance.

It was in the middle of the third verse that Simpson noticed something unusual—something that brought his thoughts back with a rush from far-away scenes. A curious change had come into the man's voice. Even before he knew what it was, uneasiness caught him, and looking up quickly, he saw that Défago, though still singing, was peering about him into the Bush, as though he heard or saw something. His voice grew fainter—dropped to a hush—then ceased altogether. The same instant, with a movement amazingly alert, he started to his feet and stood upright—*sniffing the air*. Like a dog scenting game, he drew the air into his nostrils in short, sharp breaths, turning quickly as he did so in all directions, and finally 'pointing' down the lake shore, eastwards. It was a performance unpleasantly suggestive and at the same time singularly dramatic. Simpson's heart fluttered disagreeably as he watched it.

'Lord, man! How you made me jump!' he exclaimed, on his feet beside him the same instant, and peering over his shoulder into the sea of darkness. 'What's up? Are you frightened——?'

Even before the question was out of his mouth he knew it was foolish, for any man with a pair of eyes in his head could see that the Canadian had turned white down to his very gills. Not even sunburn and the glare of the fire could hide that.

The student felt himself trembling a little, weakish in the knees. 'What's up?' he repeated quickly. 'D'you smell moose? Or anything queer, anything—wrong?' He lowered his voice instinctively.

The forest pressed round them with its encircling wall; the nearer tree-stems gleamed like bronze in the firelight; beyond that— blackness, and, so far as he could tell, a silence of death. Just behind them a passing puff of wind lifted a single leaf, looked at it, then laid it softly down again without disturbing the rest of the covey.* It seemed as if a million invisible causes had combined just to produce that single visible effect. *Other* life pulsed about them—and was gone.

Défago turned abruptly; the livid hue of his face had turned to a dirty grey.

'I never said I heered—or smelt—nuthin',' he said slowly and emphatically, in an oddly altered voice that conveyed somehow a touch of defiance. 'I was only—takin' a look round—so to speak. It's always a mistake to be too previous with yer questions.' Then he added suddenly with obvious effort, in his more natural voice, 'Have you got the matches, Boss Simpson?' and proceeded to light the pipe he had half filled just before he began to sing.

Without speaking another word they sat down again by the fire, Défago changing his side so that he could face the direction the wind came from. For even a tenderfoot* could tell that. Défago changed his position in order to hear and smell—all there was to be heard and smelt. And, since he now faced the lake with his back to the trees it was evidently nothing in the forest that had sent so strange and sudden a warning to his marvellously trained nerves.

'Guess now I don't feel like singing any,' he explained presently of his own accord. 'That song kinder brings back memories that's troublesome to me; I never oughter've begun it. It sets me on t' imagining things, see?'

Clearly the man was still fighting with some profoundly moving emotion. He wished to excuse himself in the eyes of the other. But the explanation, in that it was only a part of the truth, was a lie, and he knew perfectly well that Simpson was not deceived by it. For nothing could explain away the livid terror that had dropped over his face while he stood there sniffing the air. And nothing—no amount of blazing fire, or chatting on ordinary subjects—could make that camp exactly as it had been before. The shadow of an unknown horror, naked if unguessed, that had flashed for an instant in the face and gestures of the guide, had also communicated itself, vaguely and therefore more potently, to his companion. The guide's visible efforts to dissemble the truth only made things worse. Moreover, to add to the younger man's uneasiness, was the difficulty, nay, the impossibility he felt of asking questions, and also his complete ignorance as to the cause. . . . Indians, wild animals, forest fires—all these, he knew, were wholly out of the question. His imagination searched vigorously, but in vain. . . .

Yet, somehow or other, after another long spell of smoking, talking and roasting themselves before the great fire, the shadow that had so suddenly invaded their peaceful camp began to lift. Perhaps Défago's efforts, or the return of his quiet and normal attitude accomplished this; perhaps Simpson himself had exaggerated the affair out of all proportion to the truth; or possibly the vigorous air of the wilderness brought its own powers of healing. Whatever the cause, the feeling of immediate horror seemed to have passed away as mysteriously as it had come, for nothing occurred to feed it. Simpson began to feel that he had permitted himself the unreasoning terror of a child. He put it down partly to a certain subconscious excitement that this wild and immense scenery generated in his blood, partly to the spell of solitude, and partly to over fatigue. That pallor in the guide's face was, of course, uncommonly hard to explain, yet it *might* have been due in some way to an effect of firelight, or his own imagination. . . . He gave it the benefit of the doubt; he was Scotch.

When a somewhat unordinary emotion has disappeared, the mind always finds a dozen ways of explaining away its causes. . . . Simpson lit a last pipe and tried to laugh to himself. On getting home to Scotland it would make quite a good story. He did not realize that this laughter was a sign that terror still lurked in the recesses of his soul—that, in fact, it was merely one of the conventional signs by which a man, seriously alarmed, tries to persuade himself that he is *not* so.

Défago, however, heard that low laughter and looked up with surprise on his face. The two men stood, side by side, kicking the embers about before going to bed. It was ten o'clock—a late hour for hunters to be still awake.

'What's ticklin' yer?' he asked in his ordinary tone, yet gravely.

'I—I was thinking of our little toy woods at home, just at that moment,' stammered Simpson, coming back to what really dominated his mind, and startled by the question, 'and comparing them to—to all this,' and he swept his arm round to indicate the Bush.

A pause followed in which neither of them said anything.

'All the same I wouldn't laugh about it, if I was you,' Défago added, looking over Simpson's shoulder into the shadows. 'There's places in there nobody won't never see into—nobody knows what lives in there either.'

'Too big—too far off?' The suggestion in the guide's manner was immense and horrible.

Défago nodded. The expression on his face was dark. He, too, felt uneasy. The younger man understood that in a *hinterland* of this size there might well be depths of wood that would never in the life of the world be known or trodden. The thought was not exactly the sort he welcomed. In a loud voice, cheerfully, he suggested that it was time for bed. But the guide lingered, tinkering with the fire, arranging the stones needlessly, doing a dozen things that did not really need doing. Evidently there was something he wanted to say, yet found it difficult to 'get at.'

'Say, you, Boss Simpson,' he began suddenly, as the last shower of sparks went up into the air, 'you don't—smell nothing, do you— nothing pertickler, I mean?' The commonplace question, Simpson realized, veiled a dreadfully serious thought in his mind. A shiver ran down his back.

'Nothing but this burning wood,' he replied firmly, kicking again at the embers. The sound of his own foot made him start.

'And all the evenin' you ain't smelt—nothing?' persisted the guide, peering at him through the gloom; 'nothing extrordiny, and different to anything else you ever smelt before?'

'No, no, man; nothing at all!' he replied aggressively, half angrily.

Défago's face cleared. 'That's good!' he exclaimed, with evident relief. 'That's good to hear.'

'Have *you*?' asked Simpson sharply, and the same instant regretted the question.

The Canadian came closer in the darkness. He shook his head. 'I guess not,' he said, though without overwhelming conviction. 'It must 've been jest that song of mine that did it. It's the song they sing in lumber-camps and god-forsaken places like that, when they're skeered the Wendigo's somewheres around, doin' a bit of swift travellin'——'

'And what's the Wendigo, pray?' Simpson asked quickly, irritated because again he could not prevent that sudden shiver of the nerves. He knew that he was close upon the man's terror and the cause of it. Yet a rushing passionate curiosity overcame his better judgment, *and* his fear.

Défago turned swiftly and looked at him as though he were suddenly about to shriek. His eyes shone, his mouth was wide open. Yet all he said, or whispered rather, for his voice sank very low, was—

'It's nuthin'—nuthin' but what those lousy fellers believe when they've bin hittin' the bottle too long—a sort of great animal that lives up yonder,' he jerked his head northwards, 'quick as lightning in its tracks, an' bigger'n anything else in the Bush, an' ain't supposed to be very good to look at—*that's all!*'

'A backwoods' superstition——' began Simpson, moving hastily towards the tent in order to shake off the hand of the guide that clutched his arm. 'Come, come, hurry up for God's sake, and get the lantern going! It's time we were in bed and asleep if we're to be up with the sun to-morrow. . . .'

The guide was close on his heels. 'I'm coming,' he answered out of the darkness, 'I'm coming.' And after a slight delay he appeared with the lantern and hung it from a nail in the front pole of the tent. The shadows of a hundred trees shifted their places quickly as he did so, and when he stumbled over the rope, diving swiftly inside, the whole tent trembled as though a gust of wind struck it.

The two men lay down, without undressing, upon their beds of soft balsam boughs, cunningly arranged. Inside, all was warm and cosy, but outside the world of crowding trees pressed close about them, marshalling their million shadows, and smothering the little tent that stood there like a wee white shell facing the ocean of tremendous forest.

Between the two lonely figures within, however, there pressed another shadow that was *not* a shadow from the night. It was the Shadow cast by the strange Fear, never wholly exorcised, that had leaped suddenly upon Défago in the middle of his singing. And Simpson, as he lay there, watching the darkness through the open flap of the tent, ready to plunge into the fragrant abyss of sleep, knew first that unique and profound stillness of a primeval forest when no wind stirs . . . and when the night has weight and substance that enters into the soul to bind a veil about it. . . . Then sleep took him. . . .

III

THUS it seemed to him, at least. Yet it was true that the lap of the water, just beyond the tent door, still beat time with his lessening pulses when he realized that he was lying with his eyes open and that another sound had recently introduced itself with cunning softness between the splash and murmur of the little waves.

And, long before he understood what this sound was, it had stirred in him the centres of pity and alarm. He listened intently, though at first in vain, for the running blood beat all its drums too noisily in his ears. Did it come, he wondered, from the lake, or from the woods? . . .

Then, suddenly, with a rush and a flutter of the heart, he knew that it was close beside him in the tent; and, when he turned over for a better hearing, it focussed itself unmistakably not two feet away. It was a sound of weeping: Défago upon his bed of branches was sobbing in the darkness as though his heart would break, the blankets evidently stuffed against his mouth to stifle it.

And his first feeling, before he could think or reflect, was the rush of a poignant and searching tenderness. This intimate, human sound, heard amid the desolation about them, woke pity. It was so incongruous, so pitifully incongruous—and so vain! Tears—in this vast and cruel wilderness: of what avail? He thought of a little child crying in mid-Atlantic. . . . Then, of course, with fuller realization, and the memory of what had gone before, came the descent of the terror upon him, and his blood ran cold.

'Défago,' he whispered quickly, 'what's the matter?' He tried to make his voice very gentle. 'Are you in pain—unhappy——?' There was no reply, but the sounds ceased abruptly. He stretched his hand out and touched him. The body did not stir.

'Are you awake?' for it occurred to him that the man was crying in his sleep. 'Are you cold?' He noticed that his feet, which were uncovered, projected beyond the mouth of the tent. He spread an extra fold of his own blankets over them. The guide had slipped down in his bed, and the branches seemed to have been dragged with him. He was afraid to pull the body back again, for fear of waking him.

One or two tentative questions he ventured softly, but though he waited for several minutes there came no reply, nor any sign of movement. Presently he heard his regular and quiet breathing, and putting his hand again gently on the breast, felt the steady rise and fall beneath.

'Let me know if anything's wrong,' he whispered, 'or if I can do anything. Wake me at once if you feel—queer.'

He hardly knew quite what to say. He lay down again, thinking and wondering what it all meant. Défago, of course, had been crying in his sleep. Some dream or other had afflicted him. Yet never in his life would he forget that pitiful sound of sobbing, and the feeling that the whole awful wilderness of woods listened. . . .

His own mind busied itself for a long time with the recent events, of which *this* took its mysterious place as one, and though his reason successfully argued away all unwelcome suggestions, a sensation of uneasiness remained, resisting ejection, very deep-seated—peculiar beyond ordinary.

IV

BUT sleep, in the long run, proves greater than all emotions. His thoughts soon wandered again; he lay there, warm as a toast, exceedingly weary; the night soothed and comforted, blunting the edges of memory and alarm. Half-an-hour later he was oblivious of everything in the outer world about him.

Yet sleep, in this case, was his great enemy, concealing all approaches, smothering the warning of his nerves.

As, sometimes, in a nightmare events crowd upon each others' heels with a conviction of dreadfullest reality, yet some inconsistent detail accuses the whole display of incompleteness and disguise, so the events that now followed, though they actually happened, persuaded the mind somehow that the detail which could explain them had been overlooked in the confusion, and that therefore they were but partly true, the rest delusion. At the back of the sleeper's mind something remains awake, ready to let slip the judgment, 'All this is not *quite* real; when you wake up you'll understand.'

And thus, in a way, it was with Simpson. The events, not wholly inexplicable or incredible in themselves, yet remain for the man who saw and heard them a sequence of separate acts of cold horror, because the little piece that might have made the puzzle clear lay concealed or overlooked.

So far as he can recall, it was a violent movement, running downwards through the tent towards the door, that first woke him and made him aware that his companion was sitting bolt upright beside him—quivering. Hours must have passed, for it was the pale gleam of the dawn that revealed his outline against the canvas. This time the man was not crying; he was quaking like a leaf; the trembling he felt plainly through the blankets down the entire length of his own body. Défago had huddled down against him for protection, shrinking away from something that apparently concealed itself near the door-flaps of the little tent.

Simpson thereupon called out in a loud voice some question or other—in the first bewilderment of waking he does not remember exactly what—and the man made no reply. The atmosphere and feeling of true nightmare lay horribly about him, making movement and speech both difficult. At first, indeed, he was not sure where he was—whether in one of the earlier camps, or at home in his bed at Aberdeen. The sense of confusion was very troubling.

And next—almost simultaneous with his waking, it seemed—the profound stillness of the dawn outside was shattered by a most uncommon sound. It came without warning, or audible approach; and it was unspeakably dreadful. It was a voice, Simpson declares, possibly a human voice; hoarse yet plaintive—a soft, roaring voice close outside the tent, overhead rather than upon the ground, of immense volume, while in some strange way most penetratingly and seductively sweet. It rang out, too, in three separate and distinct notes, or cries, that bore in some odd fashion a resemblance, far-fetched yet recognizable, to the name of the guide: '*Dé—fa—go!*'

The student admits he is unable to describe it quite intelligently, for it was unlike any sound he had ever heard in his life, and combined a blending of such contrary qualities. 'A sort of windy, crying voice,' he calls it, 'as of something lonely and untamed, wild and of abominable power. . . .'

And, even before it ceased, dropping back into the great gulfs of silence, the guide beside him had sprung to his feet with an answering though unintelligible cry. He blundered against the tent-pole with violence, shaking the whole structure, spreading his arms out frantically for more room, and kicking his legs impetuously free of the clinging blankets. For a second, perhaps two, he stood upright by the door, his outline dark against the pallor of the dawn; then, with a furious, rushing speed, before his companion could move a hand to stop him, he shot with a plunge through the flaps of canvas—and was gone. And as he went—so astonishingly fast that the voice could actually be heard dying in the distance—he called aloud in tones of anguished terror that at the same time held something strangely like the frenzied exultation of delight—

'Oh! oh! My feet of fire! My burning feet of fire! Oh! oh! This height and fiery speed!'

And then the distance quickly buried it, and the deep silence of very early morning descended upon the forest as before.

It had all come about with such rapidity that, but for the evidence of the empty bed beside him, Simpson could almost have believed it to have been the memory of a nightmare carried over from sleep. He still felt the warm pressure of that vanished body against his side; there lay the twisted blankets in a heap; the very tent yet trembled with the vehemence of the impetuous departure. The strange words rang in his ears, as though he still heard them in the distance—wild language of a suddenly stricken mind. Moreover, it was not only the senses of sight and hearing that reported uncommon things to his brain, for even while the man cried and ran, he had become aware that a strange perfume, faint yet pungent, pervaded the interior of the tent. And it was at this point, it seems, brought to himself by the consciousness that his nostrils were taking this distressing odour down into his throat, that he found his courage, sprang quickly to his feet—and went out.

The grey light of dawn that dropped, cold and glimmering, between the trees revealed the scene tolerably well. There stood the tent behind him, soaked with dew; the dark ashes of the fire, still warm; the lake, white beneath a coating of mist, the islands rising darkly out of it like objects packed in wool; and patches of snow beyond among the clearer spaces of the Bush—everything cold, still, waiting for the sun. But nowhere a sign of the vanished guide—still, doubtless, flying at frantic speed through the frozen woods. There was not even the sound of disappearing footsteps, nor the echoes of the dying voice. He had gone—utterly.

There was nothing; nothing but the sense of his recent presence, so strongly left behind about the camp; *and*—this penetrating, all-pervading odour.

And even this was now rapidly disappearing in its turn. In spite of his exceeding mental perturbation, Simpson struggled hard to detect its nature, and define it, but the ascertaining of an elusive scent, not recognized subconsciously and at once, is a very subtle operation of the mind. And he failed. It was gone before he could properly seize or name it. Approximate description, even, seems to have been difficult, for it was unlike any smell he knew. Acrid rather, not unlike the odour of a lion, he thinks, yet softer and not wholly unpleasing, with something almost sweet in it that reminded him of the scent of decaying garden leaves, earth, and the myriad, nameless perfumes that make up the odour of a big forest. Yet the 'odour of lions' is the phrase with which he usually sums it all up.

Then—it was wholly gone, and he found himself standing by the ashes of the fire in a state of amazement and stupid terror that left him the helpless prey of anything that chose to happen. Had a muskrat poked its pointed muzzle over a rock, or a squirrel scuttled in that instant down the bark of a tree, he would most likely have collapsed without more ado and fainted. For he felt about the whole affair the touch somewhere of a great Outer Horror. . . . and his scattered powers had not as yet had time to collect themselves into a definite attitude of fighting self-control.

Nothing did happen, however. A great kiss of wind ran softly through the awakening forest, and a few maple leaves here and there rustled tremblingly to earth. The sky seemed to grow suddenly much lighter. Simpson felt the cool air upon his cheek and uncovered head; realized that he was shivering with the cold; and, making a great effort, realized next that he was alone in the Bush—*and* that he was called upon to take immediate steps to find and succour his vanished companion.

Make an effort, accordingly, he did, though an ill-calculated and futile one. With that wilderness of trees about him, the sheet of water cutting him off behind, and the horror of that wild cry in his blood, he did what any other inexperienced man would have done in similar bewilderment: he ran about, without any sense of direction, like a frantic child, and called loudly without ceasing the name of the guide—

'Défago! Défago! Défago!' he yelled, and the trees gave him back the name as often as he shouted, only a little softened—'Défago! Défago! Défago!'

He followed the trail that lay for a short distance across the patches of snow, and then lost it again where the trees grew too thickly for snow to lie. He shouted till he was hoarse, and till the sound of his own voice in all that unanswering and listening world began to frighten him. His confusion increased in direct ratio to the violence of his efforts. His distress became formidably acute, till at length his exertions defeated their own object, and from sheer exhaustion he headed back to the camp again. It remains a wonder that he ever found his way. It was with great difficulty, and only after numberless false clues, that he at last saw the white tent between the trees, and so reached safety.

Exhaustion then applied its own remedy, and he grew calmer. He made the fire and breakfasted. Hot coffee and bacon put a little sense and judgment into him again, and he realized that he had been behaving like a boy. He now made another, and more successful attempt to face the situation collectedly, and, a nature naturally plucky coming to his assistance, he decided that he must first make as thorough a search as possible, failing success in which, he must find his way to the home camp as best he could and bring help.

And this was what he did. Taking food, matches and rifle with him, and a small axe to blaze the trees against his return journey, he set forth. It was eight o'clock when he started, the sun shining over the tops of the trees in a sky without clouds. Pinned to a stake by the fire he left a note in case Défago returned while he was away.

This time, according to a careful plan, he took a new direction, intending to make a wide sweep that must sooner or later cut into indications of the guide's trail; and, before he had gone a quarter of a mile he came across the tracks of a large animal in the snow, and beside it the light and smaller tracks of what were beyond question human feet—the feet of Défago. The relief he at once experienced was natural, though brief; for at first sight he saw in these tracks a simple explanation of the whole matter: these big marks had surely been left by a bull moose that, wind against it, had blundered upon the camp, and uttered its singular cry of warning and alarm the moment its mistake was apparent. Défago, in whom the hunting instinct was developed to the point of uncanny perfection, had scented the brute coming down the wind hours before. His excitement and disappearance were due, of course, to—to his——

Then the impossible explanation at which he grasped faded, as common sense showed him mercilessly that none of this was true. No guide, much less a guide like Défago, could have acted in so irrational a way, going off even without his rifle. . . . ! The whole affair demanded a far more complicated elucidation, when he remembered the details of it all—the cry of terror, the amazing language, the grey face of horror when his nostrils first caught the new odour; that muffled sobbing in the darkness, and—for this, too, now came back to him dimly—the man's original aversion for this particular bit of country. . . .

Besides, now that he examined them closer, these were not the tracks of a moose at all! Hank had explained to him the outline of a bull's hoofs, of a cow's or calf's, too, for that matter; he had drawn them clearly on a strip of birch bark. And these were wholly different. They were big, round, ample, and with no pointed outline as of sharp hoofs. He wondered for a moment whether bear-tracks were like that. There was no other animal he could think of, for caribou did not come so far south at this season, and, even if they did, would leave hoof-marks.

They were ominous signs—these mysterious writings left in the snow by the unknown creature that had lured a human being away from safety—and when he coupled them in his imagination with that haunting sound that broke the stillness of the dawn, a momentary dizziness shook his mind, distressing him again beyond belief. He felt the *threatening* aspect of it all. And, stooping down to examine the marks more closely, he caught a faint whiff of that sweet yet pungent odour that made him instantly straighten up again, fighting a sensation almost of nausea.

Then his memory played him another evil trick. He suddenly recalled those uncovered feet projecting beyond the edge of the tent, and the body's appearance of having been dragged towards the opening; the man's shrinking from something by the door when he woke later. The details now beat against his trembling mind with concerted attack. They seemed to gather in those deep spaces of the silent forest about him, where the host of trees stood waiting, listening, watching to see what he would do. The woods were closing round him.

With the persistence of true pluck, however, Simpson went forward, following the tracks as best he could, smothering these ugly emotions that sought to weaken his will. He blazed innumerable trees as he went, ever fearful of being unable to find the way back, and calling aloud at intervals of a few seconds the name of the guide. The dull tapping of the axe upon the massive trunks, and the unnatural accents of his own voice became at length sounds that he even dreaded to make, dreaded to hear. For they drew attention without ceasing to his presence and exact whereabouts, and if it were really the case that something was hunting himself down in the same way that he was hunting down another——

With a strong effort, he crushed the thought out the instant it rose. It was the beginning, he realized, of a bewilderment utterly diabolical in kind that would speedily destroy him.

*

Although the snow was not continuous, lying merely in shallow flurries over the more open spaces, he found no difficulty in following the tracks for the first few miles. They went straight as a ruled line wherever the trees permitted. The stride soon began to increase in length, till it finally assumed proportions that seemed absolutely impossible for any ordinary animal to have made. Like huge flying leaps they became. One of these he measured, and though he knew that 'stretch' of eighteen feet must be somehow wrong, he was at a complete loss to understand why he found no signs on the snow between the extreme points. But what perplexed him even more, making him feel his vision had gone utterly awry, was that Défago's stride increased in the same manner, and finally covered the same incredible distances. It looked as if the great beast had lifted him with it and carried him across these astonishing intervals. Simpson, who was much longer in the limb, found that he could not compass even half the stretch by taking a running jump.

And the sight of these huge tracks, running side by side, silent evidence of a dreadful journey in which terror or madness had urged to impossible results, was profoundly moving. It shocked him in the secret depths of his soul. It was the most horrible thing his eyes had ever looked upon. He began to follow them mechanically, absent-mindedly almost, ever peering over his shoulder to see if he, too, were being followed by something with a gigantic tread. . . . And soon it came about that he no longer quite realized what it was they signified—these impressions left upon the snow by something nameless and untamed, always accompanied by the footmarks of the little French Canadian, his guide, his comrade, the man who had shared his tent a few hours before, chatting, laughing, even singing by his side. . . .

V

FOR a man of his years and inexperience, only a canny Scot, perhaps, grounded in common sense and established in logic, could have preserved even that measure of balance that this youth somehow or other did manage to preserve through the whole adventure. Otherwise, two things he presently noticed, while forging pluckily ahead, must have sent him headlong back to the comparative safety of his tent, instead of only making his hands close more tightly upon the rifle-stock, while his heart, trained for the Wee Kirk, sent a wordless prayer winging its way to heaven. Both tracks, he saw, had undergone a change, and this change, so far as it concerned the footsteps of the man, was in some undecipherable manner—appalling.

It was in the bigger tracks he first noticed this, and for a long time he could not quite believe his eyes. Was it the blown leaves that produced odd effects of light and shade, or that the dry snow, drifting like finely-ground rice about the edges, cast shadows and high lights? Or was it actually the fact that the great marks had become faintly coloured? For round about the deep, plunging holes of the animal there now appeared a mysterious, reddish tinge that was more like an effect of light than of anything that dyed the substance of the snow itself. Every mark had it, and had it increasingly—this indistinct fiery tinge that painted a new touch of ghastliness into the picture.

But when, wholly unable to explain or credit it, he turned his attention to the other tracks to discover if they, too, bore similar witness, he noticed that these had meanwhile undergone a change that was infinitely worse, and charged with far more horrible suggestion. For, in the last hundred yards or so, he saw that they had grown gradually into the semblance of the parent tread. Imperceptibly the change had come about, yet unmistakably. It was hard to see where the change first began. The result, however, was beyond question. Smaller, neater, more cleanly modelled, they formed now an exact and careful duplicate of the larger tracks beside them. The feet that produced them had, therefore, also changed. And something in his mind reared up with loathing and with terror as he saw it.

Simpson, for the first time, hesitated; then, ashamed of his alarm and indecision, took a few hurried steps ahead; the next instant stopped dead in his tracks. Immediately in front of him all signs of the trail ceased; both tracks came to an abrupt end. On all sides, for a hundred yards and more, he searched in vain for the least indication of their continuance. There was—nothing.

The trees were very thick just there, big trees all of them, spruce, cedar, hemlock; there was no underbrush. He stood, looking about him, all distraught; bereft of any power of judgment. Then he set to work to search again, and again, and yet again, but always with the same result: *nothing*. The feet that printed the surface of the snow thus far had now, apparently, left the ground!

And it was in that moment of distress and confusion that the whip of terror laid its most nicely calculated lash about his heart. It dropped with deadly effect upon the sorest spot of all, completely unnerving him. He had been secretly dreading all the time that it would come—and come it did.

Far overhead, muted by great height and distance, strangely thinned and wailing, he heard the crying voice of Défago, the guide.

The sound dropped upon him out of that still, wintry sky with an effect of dismay and terror unsurpassed. The rifle fell to his feet. He stood motionless an instant, listening as it were with his whole body, then staggered back against the nearest tree for support, disorganized hopelessly in mind and spirit. To him, in that moment, it seemed the most shattering and dislocating experience he had ever known, so that his heart emptied itself of all feeling whatsoever as by a sudden draught.

'Oh! oh! This fiery height! Oh, my feet of fire! My burning feet of fire. . . . !' ran in far, beseeching accents of indescribable appeal this voice of anguish down the sky. Once it called—then silence through all the listening wilderness of trees.

And Simpson, scarcely knowing what he did, presently found himself running wildly to and fro, searching, calling, tripping over roots and boulders, and flinging himself in a frenzy of undirected pursuit after the Caller. Behind the screen of memory and emotion with which experience veils events, he plunged, distracted and half-deranged, picking up false lights like a ship at sea, terror in his eyes and heart and soul. For the Panic of the Wilderness had called to him in that far voice—the Power of untamed Distance—the Enticement of the Desolation that destroys. He knew in that moment all the pains of some one hopelessly and irretrievably lost, suffering the lust and travail of a soul in the final Loneliness. A vision of Défago, eternally hunted, driven and pursued across the skiey vastness of those ancient forests, fled like a flame across the dark ruin of his thoughts. . . .

It seemed ages before he could find anything in the chaos of his disorganized sensations to which he could anchor himself steady for a moment, and think. . . .

The cry was not repeated; his own hoarse calling brought no response; the inscrutable forces of the Wild had summoned their victim beyond recall—and held him fast.

Yet he searched and called, it seems, for hours afterwards, for it was late in the afternoon when at length he decided to abandon a useless pursuit and return to his camp on the shores of Fifty Island Water. Even then he went with reluctance, that crying voice still echoing in his ears. With difficulty he found his rifle and the homeward trail. The concentration necessary to follow the badly blazed trees, and a biting hunger that gnawed, helped to keep his mind steady. Otherwise, he admits, the temporary aberration he had suffered might have been prolonged to the point of positive disaster. Gradually the ballast shifted back again, and he regained something that approached his normal equilibrium.

But for all that the journey through the gathering dusk was miserably haunted. He heard innumerable following footsteps; voices that laughed and whispered; and saw figures crouching behind trees and boulders, making signs to one another for a concerted attack the moment he had passed. The creeping murmur of the wind made him start and listen. He went stealthily, trying to hide where possible, and making as little sound as he could. The shadows of the woods, hitherto protective or covering merely, had now become menacing, challenging; and the pageantry in his frightened mind masked a host of possibilities that were all the more ominous for being obscure. The presentiment of a nameless doom lurked ill-concealed behind every detail of what had happened.

It was really admirable how he emerged victor in the end; men of riper powers and experience might have come through the ordeal with less success. He had himself tolerably well in hand, all things considered, and his plan of action proves it. Sleep being absolutely out of the question, and travelling an unknown trail in the darkness equally impracticable, he sat up the whole of that night, rifle in hand, before a fire he never for a single moment allowed to die down. The severity of the haunted vigil marked his soul for life; but it was successfully accomplished; and with the very first signs of dawn he set forth upon the long return journey to the home-camp to get help. As before, he left a written note to explain his absence, and to indicate where he had left a plentiful *cache* of food and matches—though he had no expectation that any human hands would find them!

How Simpson found his way alone by lake and forest might well make a story in itself, for to hear him tell it is to *know* the passionate loneliness of soul that a man can feel when the Wilderness holds him in the hollow of its illimitable hand—and laughs. It is also to admire his indomitable pluck.

He claims no skill, declaring that he followed the almost invisible trail mechanically, and without thinking. And this, doubtless, is the truth. He relied upon the guiding of the unconscious mind, which is instinct. Perhaps, too, some sense of orientation, known to animals and primitive men, may have helped as well, for through all that tangled region he succeeded in reaching the exact spot where Défago had hidden the canoe nearly three days before with the remark, 'Strike doo west across the lake into the sun to find the camp.'

There was not much sun left to guide him, but he used his compass to the best of his ability, embarking in the frail craft for the last twelve miles of his journey with a sensation of immense relief that the forest was at last behind him. And, fortunately, the water was calm; he took his line across the centre of the lake instead of coasting round the shores for another twenty miles. Fortunately, too, the other hunters were back. The light of their fires furnished a steering-point without which he might have searched all night long for the actual position of the camp.

It was close upon midnight all the same when his canoe grated on the sandy cove, and Hank, Punk and his uncle, disturbed in their sleep by his cries, ran quickly down and helped a very exhausted and broken specimen of Scotch humanity over the rocks towards a dying fire.

VI

THE sudden entrance of his prosaic uncle into this world of wizardry and horror that had haunted him without interruption now for two days and two nights, had the immediate effect of giving to the affair an entirely new aspect. The sound of that crisp 'Hulloa, my boy! And what's up *now?*' and the grasp of that dry and vigorous hand introduced another standard of judgment. A revulsion of feeling washed through him. He realized that he had let himself 'go' rather badly. He even felt vaguely ashamed of himself. The native hard-headedness of his race reclaimed him.

And this doubtless explains why he found it so hard to tell that group round the fire—everything. He told enough, however, for the immediate decision to be arrived at that a relief party must start at the earliest possible moment, and that Simpson, in order to guide it capably, must first have food and, above all, sleep. Dr Cathcart observing the lad's condition more shrewdly than his patient knew, gave him a very slight injection of morphine. For six hours he slept like the dead.

From the description carefully written out afterwards by this student of divinity, it appears that the account he gave to the astonished group omitted sundry vital and important details. He declares that, with his uncle's wholesome, matter-of-fact countenance staring him in the face, he simply had not the courage to mention them. Thus, all the search-party gathered, it would seem, was that Défago had suffered in the night an acute and inexplicable attack of mania, had imagined himself 'called' by some one or something, and had plunged into the bush after it without food or rifle, where he must die a horrible and lingering death by cold and starvation unless he could be found and rescued in time. 'In time,' moreover, meant 'at once.'

In the course of the following day, however—they were off by seven, leaving Punk in charge with instructions to have food and fire always ready—Simpson found it possible to tell his uncle a good deal more of the story's true inwardness, without divining that it was drawn out of him as a matter of fact by a very subtle form of cross-examination. By the time they reached the beginning of the trail, where the canoe was laid up against the return journey, he had mentioned how Défago spoke vaguely of 'something he called a "Wendigo"'; how he cried in his sleep; how he imagined an unusual scent about the camp; and had betrayed other symptoms of mental excitement. He also admitted the bewildering effect of 'that extraordinary odour' upon himself, 'pungent and acrid like the odour of lions.' And by the time they were within an easy hour of Fifty Island Water he had let slip the further fact—a foolish avowal of his own hysterical condition, as he felt afterwards—that he had heard the vanished guide call 'for help.' He omitted the singular phrases used, for he simply could not bring himself to repeat the preposterous language. Also, while describing how the man's footsteps in the snow had gradually assumed an exact miniature likeness of the animal's plunging tracks, he left out the fact that they measured a *wholly* incredible distance. It seemed a question, nicely balanced between individual pride and honesty, what he should reveal and what suppress. He mentioned the fiery tinge in the snow, for instance, yet shrank from telling that body and bed had been partly dragged out of the tent. . . .

With the net result that Dr Cathcart, adroit psychologist that he fancied himself to be, had assured him clearly enough exactly where his mind, influenced by loneliness, bewilderment and terror, had yielded to the strain and invited delusion. While praising his conduct, he managed at the same time to point out where, when, and how his mind had gone astray. He made his nephew think himself finer than he was by judicious praise, yet more foolish than he was by minimizing the value of his evidence. Like many another materialist, that is, he lied cleverly on the basis of insufficient knowledge, *because* the knowledge supplied seemed to his own particular intelligence inadmissible.

'The spell of these terrible solitudes,' he said, 'cannot leave any mind untouched, any mind, that is, possessed of the higher imaginative qualities. It has worked upon yours exactly as it worked upon my own when I was your age. The animal that haunted your little camp was undoubtedly a moose, for the 'belling' of a moose may have, sometimes, a very peculiar quality of sound. The coloured appearance of the big tracks was obviously a defect of vision in your own eyes produced by excitement. The size and stretch of the tracks we shall prove when we come to them. But the hallucination of an audible voice, of course, is one of the commonest forms of delusion due to mental excitement—an excitement, my dear boy, perfectly excusable, and, let me add, wonderfully controlled by you under the circumstances. For the rest, I am bound to say, you have acted with a splendid courage, for the terror of feeling oneself lost in this wilderness is nothing short of awful, and, had I been in your place, I don't for a moment believe I could have behaved with one quarter of your wisdom and decision. The only thing I find it uncommonly difficult to explain is—that—damned odour.'

'It made me feel sick, I assure you,' declared his nephew, 'positively dizzy!' His uncle's attitude of calm omniscience, merely because he knew more psychological formulæ, made him slightly defiant. It was so easy to be wise in the explanation of an experience one has not personally witnessed. 'A kind of desolate and terrible odour is the only way I can describe it,' he concluded, glancing at the features of the quiet, unemotional man beside him.

'I can only marvel,' was the reply, 'that under the circumstances it did not seem to you even worse.' The dry words, Simpson knew, hovered between the truth, and his uncle's interpretation of 'the truth.'

And so at last they came to the little camp and found the tent still standing, the remains of the fire, and the piece of paper pinned to a stake beside it—untouched. The *cache*, poorly contrived by inexperienced hands, however, had been discovered and opened—by musk rats, mink and squirrel. The matches lay scattered about the opening, but the food had been taken to the last crumb.

'Well, fellers, he ain't here,' exclaimed Hank loudly after his fashion, 'and that's as sartain as the coal supply down below! But whar he's got to by this time is 'bout as onsartain as the trade in crowns in t'other place.' The presence of a divinity student was no barrier to his language at such a time, though for the reader's sake it may be severely edited. 'I propose,' he added, 'that we start out at once an' hunt for'm like hell!'

The gloom of Défago's probable fate oppressed the whole party with a sense of dreadful gravity the moment they saw the familiar signs of recent occupancy. Especially the tent, with the bed of balsam branches still smoothed and flattened by the pressure of his body, seemed to bring his presence near to them. Simpson, feeling vaguely as if his word were somehow at stake, went about explaining particulars in a hushed tone. He was much calmer now, though overwearied with the strain of his many journeys. His uncle's method of explaining—'explaining away,' rather—the details still fresh in his haunted memory helped, too, to put ice upon his emotions.

'And that's the direction he ran off in,' he said to his two companions, pointing in the direction where the guide had vanished that morning in the grey dawn. 'Straight down there he ran like a deer, in between the birch and the hemlock. . . .'

Hank and Dr Cathcart exchanged glances.

'And it was about two miles down there, in a straight line,' continued the other, speaking with something of the former terror in his voice, 'that I followed his trail to the place where—it stopped—dead!'

'And where you heered him callin' an' caught the stench, an' all the rest of the wicked entertainment,' cried Hank, with a volubility that betrayed his keen distress.

'And where your excitement overcame you to the point of producing illusions,' added Dr Cathcart under his breath, yet not so low that his nephew did not hear it.

It was early in the afternoon, for they had travelled quickly, and there were still a good two hours of daylight left. Dr Cathcart and Hank lost no time in beginning the search, but Simpson was too exhausted to accompany them. They would follow the blazed marks on the trees, and where possible, his footsteps. Meanwhile the best thing he could do was to keep a good fire going, and rest.

But after something like three hours' search, the darkness already down, the two men returned to camp with nothing to report. Fresh snow had covered all signs, and though they had followed the blazed trees to the spot where Simpson had turned back, they had not discovered the smallest indications of a human being—or, for that matter, of an animal. There were no fresh tracks of any kind; the snow lay undisturbed.

It was difficult to know what was best to do, though in reality there was nothing more they *could* do. They might stay and search for weeks without much chance of success. The fresh snow destroyed their only hope, and they gathered round the fire for supper, a gloomy and despondent party. The facts, indeed, were sad enough, for Défago had a wife at Rat Portage, and his earnings were the family's sole means of support.

Now that the whole truth in all its ugliness was out, it seemed useless to deal in further disguise or pretence. They talked openly of the facts and probabilities. It was not the first time, even in the experience of Dr Cathcart, that a man had yielded to the singular seduction of the Solitudes and gone out of his mind; Défago, moreover, was predisposed to something of the sort, for he already had the touch of melancholia in his blood, and his fibre was weakened by bouts of drinking that often lasted for weeks at a time. Something on this trip—one might never know precisely what—had sufficed to push him over the line, that was all. And he had gone, gone off into the great wilderness of trees and lakes to die by starvation and exhaustion. The chances against his finding camp again were overwhelming; the delirium that was upon him would also doubtless have increased, and it was quite likely he might do violence to himself and so hasten his cruel fate. Even while they talked, indeed, the end had probably come. On the suggestion of Hank, his old pal, however, they proposed to wait a little longer and devote the whole of the following day, from dawn to darkness, to the most systematic search they could devise. They would divide the territory between them. They discussed their plan in great detail. All that men could do they would do.

And, meanwhile, they talked about the particular form in which the singular Panic of the Wilderness had made its attack upon the mind of the unfortunate guide. Hank, though familiar with the legend in its general outline, obviously did not welcome the turn the conversation had taken. He contributed little, though that little was illuminating. For he admitted that a story ran over all this section of country to the effect that several Indians had 'seen the Wendigo' along the shores of Fifty Island Water in the 'fall' of last year, and that this was the true reason of Défago's disinclination to hunt there. Hank doubtless felt that he had in a sense helped his old pal to death by over-persuading him. 'When an Indian goes crazy,' he explained, talking to himself more than to the others, it seemed, 'it's always put that he's "seen the Wendigo."' An' pore old Défaygo was superstitious down to his very heels . . . !'

And then Simpson, feeling the atmosphere more sympathetic, told over again the full story of his astonishing tale; he left out no details this time; he mentioned his own sensations and gripping fears. He only omitted the strange language used.

'But Défago surely had already told you all these details of the Wendigo legend, my dear fellow,' insisted the doctor. 'I mean, he had talked about it, and thus put into your mind the ideas which your own excitement afterwards developed?'

Whereupon Simpson again repeated the facts. Défago, he declared, had barely mentioned the beast. He, Simpson, knew nothing of the story, and, so far as he remembered, had never even read about it. Even the word was unfamiliar.

Of course he was telling the truth, and Dr Cathcart was reluctantly compelled to admit the singular character of the whole affair. He did not do this in words so much as in manner, however. He kept his back against a good, stout tree; he poked the fire into a blaze the moment it showed signs of dying down; he was quicker than any of them to notice the least sound in the night about them—a fish jumping in the lake, a twig snapping in the bush, the dropping of occasional fragments of frozen snow from the branches overhead where the heat loosened them. His voice, too, changed a little in quality, becoming a shade less confident, lower also in tone. Fear, to put it plainly, hovered close about that little camp, and though all three would have been glad to speak of other matters, the only thing they seemed able to discuss was this—the source of their fear. They tried other subjects in vain; there was nothing to say about them. Hank was the most honest of the group; he said next to nothing. He never once, however, turned his back to the darkness. His face was always to the forest, and when wood was needed he didn't go farther than was necessary to get it.

VII

A WALL of silence wrapped them in, for the snow, though not thick, was sufficient to deaden any noise, and the frost held things pretty tight besides. No sound but their voices and the soft roar of the flames made itself heard. Only, from time to time, something soft as the flutter of a pine-moth's wings went past them through the air. No one seemed anxious to go to bed. The hours slipped towards midnight.

'The legend is picturesque enough,' observed the doctor after one of the longer pauses, speaking to break it rather than because he had anything to say, 'for the Wendigo is simply the Call of the Wild personified, which some natures hear to their own destruction.'

'That's about it,' Hank said presently. 'An' there's no misunderstandin' when you hear it. It calls you by name right 'nough.'

Another pause followed. Then Dr Cathcart came back to the forbidden subject with a rush that made the others jump.

'The allegory *is* significant,' he remarked, looking about him into the darkness, 'for the Voice, they say, resembles all the minor sounds of the Bush—wind, falling water, cries of animals, and so forth. And, once the victim hears *that*—he's off for good, of course! His most vulnerable points, moreover, are said to be the feet and the eyes; the feet, you see, for the lust of wandering, and the eyes for the lust of beauty. The poor beggar goes at such a dreadful speed that he bleeds beneath the eyes, and his feet burn.'

Dr Cathcart, as he spoke, continued to peer uneasily into the surrounding gloom. His voice sank to a hushed tone.

'The Wendigo,' he added, 'is said to burn his feet—owing to the friction, apparently caused by its tremendous velocity—till they drop off, and new ones form exactly like its own.'

Simpson listened in horrified amazement; but it was the pallor on Hank's face that fascinated him most. He would willingly have stopped his ears and closed his eyes, had he dared.

'It don't always keep to the ground neither,' came in Hank's slow, heavy drawl, 'for it goes so high that he thinks the stars have set him all a-fire. An' it'll take great thumpin' jumps sometimes, an' run along the tops of the trees, carrying its partner with it, an' then droppin' him jest as a fish-hawk 'll drop a pickerel* to kill it before eatin'. An' its food, of all the muck in the whole Bush is—moss!' And he laughed a short, unnatural laugh. 'It's a moss-eater, is the Wendigo,' he added, looking up excitedly into the faces of his companions, 'moss-eater,' he repeated, with a string of the most outlandish oaths he could invent.

But Simpson now understood the true purpose of all this talk. What these two men, each strong and 'experienced' in his own way, dreaded more than anything else was—silence. They were talking against time. They were also talking against darkness, against the invasion of panic, against the admission reflection might bring that they were in an enemy's country—against anything, in fact, rather than allow their inmost thoughts to assume control. He himself, already initiated by the awful vigil with terror, was beyond both of them in this respect. He had reached the stage where he was immune. But these two, the scoffing, analytical doctor, and the honest, dogged backwoodsman, each sat trembling in the depths of his being.

Thus the hours passed; and thus, with lowered voices and a kind of taut inner resistance of spirit, this little group of humanity sat in the jaws of the wilderness and talked foolishly of the terrible and haunting legend. It was an unequal contest, all things considered, for the wilderness had already the advantage of first attack—and of a hostage. The fate of their comrade hung over them with a steadily increasing weight of oppression that finally became insupportable.

It was Hank, after a pause longer than the preceding ones that no one seemed able to break, who first let loose all this pent-up emotion in very unexpected fashion, by springing suddenly to his feet and letting out the most ear-shattering yell imaginable into the night. He could not contain himself any longer, it seemed. To make it carry even beyond an ordinary cry he interrupted its rhythm by shaking the palm of his hand before his mouth.

'That's for Défago,' he said, looking down at the other two with a queer, defiant laugh, 'for it's my belief'—the sandwiched oaths may be omitted—'that my ole partner's not far from us at this very minute.'

There was a vehemence and recklessness about his performance that made Simpson, too, start to his feet in amazement, and betrayed even the doctor into letting the pipe slip from between his lips. Hank's face was ghastly, but Cathcart's showed a sudden weakness— a loosening of all his faculties, as it were. Then a momentary anger blazed into his eyes, and he too, though with deliberation born of habitual self-control, got upon his feet and faced the excited guide. For this was unpermissible, foolish, dangerous, and he meant to stop it in the bud.

What might have happened in the next minute or two one may speculate about, yet never definitely know, for in the instant of profound silence that followed Hank's roaring voice, and as though in answer to it, something went past through the darkness of the sky overhead at terrific speed—something of necessity very large, for it displaced much air, while down between the trees there fell a faint and windy cry of a human voice, calling in tones of indescribable anguish and appeal—

'Oh, oh! this fiery height! Oh, oh! My feet of fire! My burning feet of fire!'

White to the very edge of his shirt, Hank looked stupidly about him like a child. Dr Cathcart uttered some kind of unintelligible cry, turning as he did so with an instinctive movement of blind terror towards the protection of the tent, then halting in the act as though frozen. Simpson, alone of the three, retained his presence of mind a little. His own horror was too deep to allow of any immediate reaction. He had heard that cry before.

Turning to his stricken companions, he said almost calmly—

'That's exactly the cry I heard—the very words he used!'

Then, lifting his face to the sky, he cried aloud, 'Défago, Défago! Come down here to us! Come down——!'

And before there was time for anybody to take definite action one way or another, there came the sound of something dropping heavily between the trees, striking the branches on the way down, and landing with a dreadful thud upon the frozen earth below. The crash and thunder of it was really terrific.

'That's him, s'help me the good Gawd!' came from Hank in a whispering cry half choked, his hand going automatically towards the hunting-knife in his belt. 'And he's coming! He's coming!' he added, with an irrational laugh of terror, as the sounds of heavy footsteps crunching over the snow became distinctly audible, approaching through the blackness towards the circle of light.

And while the steps, with their stumbling motion, moved nearer and nearer upon them, the three men stood round that fire, motionless and dumb. Dr Cathcart had the appearance as of a man suddenly withered; even his eyes did not move. Hank, suffering shockingly, seemed on the verge again of violent action; yet did nothing. He, too, was hewn of stone. Like stricken children they seemed. The picture was hideous. And, meanwhile, their owner still invisible, the footsteps came closer, crunching the frozen snow. It was endless—too prolonged to be quite real—this measured and pitiless approach. It was accursed.

VIII

THEN at length the darkness, having this laboriously conceived, brought forth—a figure. It drew forward into the zone of uncertain light where fire and shadows mingled, not ten feet away; then halted, staring at them fixedly. The same instant it started forward again with the spasmodic motion as of a thing moved by wires, and coming up closer to them, full into the glare of the fire, they perceived then that—it was a man; and apparently that this man was—Défago.

Something like a skin of horror almost perceptibly drew down in that moment over every face, and three pairs of eyes shone through it as though they saw across the frontiers of normal vision into the Unknown.

Défago advanced, his tread faltering and uncertain; he made his way straight up to them as a group first, then turned sharply and peered close into the face of Simpson. The sound of a voice issued from his lips—

'Here I am, Boss Simpson. I heered some one calling me.' It was a faint, dried-up voice, made wheezy and breathless as by immense exertion. 'I'm havin' a reg'lar hell-fire kind of a trip, I am.' And he laughed, thrusting his head forward into the other's face.

But that laugh started the machinery of the group of wax-work figures with the wax-white skins. Hank immediately sprang forward with a stream of oaths so far-fetched that Simpson did not recognize them as English at all, but thought he had lapsed into Indian or some other lingo. He only realized that Hank's presence, thrust thus between them, was welcome—uncommonly welcome. Dr Cathcart, though more calmly and leisurely, advanced behind him, heavily stumbling.

Simpson seems hazy as to what was actually said and done in those next few seconds, for the eyes of that detestable and blasted visage peering at such close quarters into his own utterly bewildered his senses at first. He merely stood still. He said nothing. He had not the trained will of the older men that forced them into action in defiance of all emotional stress. He watched them moving as behind a glass, that half destroyed their reality: it was dream-like, perverted. Yet, through the torrent of Hank's meaningless phrases, he remembers hearing his uncle's tone of authority—hard and forced—saying several things about food and warmth, blankets, whisky and the rest; . . . and, further, that whiffs of that penetrating, unaccustomed odour, vile, yet sweetly bewildering, assailed his nostrils during all that followed.

It was no less a person than himself, however—less experienced and adroit than the others though he was—who gave instinctive utterance to the sentence that brought a measure of relief into the ghastly situation by expressing the doubt and thought in each one's heart.

'It *is*—YOU, isn't it, Défago?' he asked under his breath, horror breaking his speech.

And at once Cathcart burst out with the loud answer before the other had time to move his lips. 'Of course it is! Of course it is! Only—can't you see—he's nearly dead with exhaustion, cold and terror? Isn't *that* enough to change a man beyond all recognition?' It was said in order to convince himself as much as to convince the others. The over-emphasis alone proved that. And continually, while he spoke and acted, he held a handkerchief to his nose. That odour pervaded the whole camp.

For the 'Défago' who sat huddled by the big fire, wrapped in blankets, drinking hot whisky and holding food in wasted hands, was no more like the guide they had last seen alive than the picture of a man of sixty is like the daguerreotype of his early youth in the costume of another generation. Nothing really can describe that ghastly caricature, that parody, masquerading there in the firelight as Défago. From the ruins of the dark and awful memories he still retains, Simpson declares that the face was more animal than human, the features drawn about into wrong proportions, the skin loose and hanging, as though he had been subjected to extraordinary pressures and tensions. It made him think vaguely of those bladder-faces blown up by the hawkers on Ludgate Hill, that change their expression as they swell, and as they collapse emit a faint and wailing imitation of a voice.

Both face and voice suggested some such abominable resemblance. But Cathcart long afterwards, seeking to describe the indescribable, asserts that thus might have looked a face and body that had been in air so rarified that, the weight of atmosphere being removed, the entire structure threatened to fly asunder and become—*incoherent.* . . .

It was Hank, though all distraught and shaking with a tearing volume of emotion he could neither handle nor understand, who brought things to a head without more ado. He went off to a little distance from the fire, apparently so that the light should not dazzle him too much, and shading his eyes for a moment with both hands, shouted in a loud voice that held anger and affection dreadfully mingled—

'You ain't Défaygo! You ain't Défaygo at all! I don't give a —— damn, but that ain't you, my ole pal of twenty years!' He glared upon the huddled figure as though he would destroy him with his eyes. 'An' if it is I'll swab the floor of hell with a wad of cotton-wool on a toothpick, s'help me the good Gawd!' he added, with a violent fling of horror and disgust.

It was impossible to silence him. He stood there shouting like one possessed, horrible to see, horrible to hear—*because it was the truth.* He repeated himself in fifty different ways, each more outlandish than the last. The woods rang with echoes. At one time it looked as if he meant to fling himself upon 'the intruder,' for his hand continually jerked towards the long hunting-knife in his belt.

But in the end he did nothing, and the whole tempest completed itself very nearly with tears. Hank's voice suddenly broke, he collapsed on the ground, and Cathcart somehow or other persuaded him at last to go into the tent and lie quiet. The remainder of the affair, indeed, was witnessed by him from behind the canvas, his white and terrified face peeping through the crack of the tent door-flap.

Then Dr Cathcart, closely followed by his nephew who so far had kept his courage better than all of them, went up with a determined air and stood opposite to the figure of Défago huddled over the fire. He looked him squarely in the face and spoke. At first his voice was firm.

'Défago, tell us what's happened—just a little, so that we can know how best to help you?' he asked in a tone of authority, almost of command. And at that point, it *was* command. At once afterwards, however, it changed in quality, for the figure turned up to him a face so piteous, so terrible and so little like humanity, that the doctor shrank back from him as from something spiritually unclean. Simpson, watching close behind him, says he got the impression of a mask that was on the verge of dropping off, and that underneath they would discover something black and diabolical, revealed in utter nakedness. 'Out with it, man, out with it!' Cathcart cried, terror running neck and neck with entreaty. 'None of us can stand this much longer . . . !' It was the cry of instinct over reason.

And then 'Défago,' smiling *whitely*, answered in that thin and fading voice that already seemed passing over into a sound of quite another character—

'I seen that great Wendigo thing,' he whispered, sniffing the air about him exactly like an animal. 'I been with it too——'

Whether the poor devil would have said more, or whether Dr Cathcart would have continued the impossible cross-examination cannot be known, for at that moment the voice of Hank was heard yelling at the top of his shout from behind the canvas that concealed all but his terrified eyes. Such a howling was never heard.

'His feet! Oh, Gawd, his feet! Look at his great changed—feet!'

Défago, shuffling where he sat, had moved in such a way that for the first time his legs were in full light and his feet were visible. Yet Simpson had no time, himself, to see properly what Hank had seen. And Hank has never seen fit to tell. That same instant, with a leap like that of a frightened tiger, Cathcart was upon him, bundling the folds of blanket about his legs with such speed that the young student caught little more than a passing glimpse of something dark and oddly massed where moccasined feet ought to have been, and saw even that but with uncertain vision.

Then, before the doctor had time to do more, or Simpson time to even think a question, much less ask it, Défago was standing upright in front of them, balancing with pain and difficulty, and upon his shapeless and twisted visage an expression so dark and so malicious that it was, in the true sense, monstrous.

'Now *you* seen it too,' he wheezed, 'you seen my fiery, burning feet! And now—that is, unless you kin save me an' prevent—it's 'bout time for——'

His piteous and beseeching voice was interrupted by a sound that was like the roar of wind coming across the lake. The trees overhead shook their tangled branches. The blazing fire bent its flames as before a blast. And something swept with a terrific, rushing noise about the little camp and seemed to surround it entirely in a single moment of time. Défago shook the clinging blankets from his body, turned towards the woods behind, and with the same stumbling motion that had brought him—was gone: gone, before any one could move muscle to prevent him, gone with an amazing, blundering swiftness that left no time to act. The darkness positively swallowed him; and less than a dozen seconds later, above the roar of the swaying trees and the shout of the sudden wind, all three men, watching and listening with stricken hearts, heard a cry that seemed to drop down upon them from a great height of sky and distance—

'Oh, oh! This fiery height! Oh, oh! My feet of fire! My burning feet of fire . . . !' then died away, into untold space and silence.

Dr Cathcart—suddenly master of himself, and therefore of the others—was just able to seize Hank violently by the arm as he tried to dash headlong into the Bush.

'But I want ter know, —— you!' shrieked the guide. 'I want ter see! That ain't him at all, but some —— devil that's shunted into his place . . . !'

Somehow or other—he admits he never quite knew how he accomplished it—he managed to keep him in the tent and pacify him. The doctor, apparently, had reached the stage where reaction had set in and allowed his own innate force to conquer. Certainly he 'managed' Hank admirably. It was his nephew, however, hitherto so wonderfully controlled, who gave him most cause for anxiety, for the cumulative strain had now produced a condition of lachrymose hysteria which made it necessary to isolate him upon a bed of boughs and blankets as far removed from Hank as was possible under the circumstances.

And there he lay, as the watches of that haunted night passed over the lonely camp, crying startled sentences, and fragments of sentences, into the folds of his blankets. A quantity of gibberish about speed and height and fire mingled oddly with biblical memories of the class-room. 'People with broken faces all on fire are coming at a most awful, awful, pace towards the camp!' he would moan one minute; and the next would sit up and stare into the woods, intently listening, and whisper, 'How terrible in the wilderness are—are the feet of them that——' until his uncle came across to change the direction of his thoughts and comfort him.

The hysteria, fortunately, proved but temporary. Sleep cured him, just as it cured Hank.

Till the first signs of daylight came, soon after five o'clock, Dr Cathcart kept his vigil. His face was the colour of chalk, and there were strange flushes beneath the eyes. An appalling terror of the soul battled with his will all through those silent hours. These were some of the outer signs. . . .

At dawn he lit the fire himself, made breakfast, and woke the others, and by seven they were well on their way back to the home camp—three perplexed and afflicted men, but each in his own way having reduced his inner turmoil to a condition of more or less systematized order again.

IX

THEY talked little, and then only of the most wholesome and common things, for their minds were charged with painful thoughts that clamoured for explanation, though no one dared refer to them. Hank, being nearest to primitive conditions, was the first to find himself, for he was also less complex. In Dr Cathcart 'civilization' championed his forces against an attack singular enough. To this day, perhaps, he is not *quite* sure of certain things. Anyhow, he took longer to 'find himself.'

Simpson, the student of divinity, it was who arranged his conclusions probably with the best, though not most scientific, appearance of order. Out there, in the heart of unreclaimed wilderness, they had surely witnessed something crudely and essentially primitive. Something that had survived somehow the advance of humanity had emerged terrifically, betraying a scale of life still monstrous and immature. He envisaged it rather as a glimpse into prehistoric ages, when superstitions, gigantic and uncouth, still oppressed the hearts of men; when the forces of nature were still untamed, the Powers that may have haunted a primeval universe not yet withdrawn. To this day he thinks of what he termed years later in a sermon 'savage and formidable Potencies lurking behind the souls of men, not evil perhaps in themselves, yet instinctively hostile to humanity as it exists.'

With his uncle he never discussed the matter in detail, for the barrier between the two types of mind made it difficult. Only once, years later, something led them to the frontier of the subject—of a single detail of the subject, rather—

'Can't you even tell me what—*they* were like?' he asked; and the reply, though conceived in wisdom, was not encouraging, 'It is far better you should not try to know, or to find out.'

'Well—that odour . . . ?' persisted the nephew. 'What do you make of that?'

Dr Cathcart looked at him and raised his eyebrows.

'Odours,' he replied, 'are not so easy as sounds and sights of tele-pathic communication. I make as much, or as little, probably, as you do yourself.'

He was not quite so glib as usual with his explanations. That was all.

At the fall of day, cold, exhausted, famished, the party came to the end of the long portage and dragged themselves into a camp that at first glimpse seemed empty. Fire there was none, and no Punk came forward to welcome them. The emotional capacity of all three was too over-spent to recognize either surprise or annoyance; but the cry of spontaneous affection that burst from the lips of Hank, as he rushed ahead of them towards the fire-place, came probably as a warning that the end of the amazing affair was not quite yet. And both Cathcart and his nephew confessed afterwards that when they saw him kneel down in his excitement and embrace something that reclined, gently moving, beside the extinguished ashes, they felt in their very bones that this 'something' would prove to be Défago—the true Défago, returned.

And so, indeed, it was.

It is soon told. Exhausted to the point of emaciation, the French Canadian—what was left of him, that is—fumbled among the ashes, trying to make a fire. His body crouched there, the weak fingers obey-ing feebly the instinctive habit of a lifetime with twigs and matches. But there was no longer any mind to direct the simple operation. The mind had fled beyond recall. And with it, too, had fled memory. Not only recent events, but all previous life was a blank.

This time it was the real man, though incredibly and horribly shrunken. On his face was no expression of any kind whatever—fear, welcome, or recognition. He did not seem to know who it was that embraced him, or who it was that fed, warmed and spoke to him the words of comfort and relief. Forlorn and broken beyond all reach of human aid, the little man did meekly as he was bidden. The 'some-thing' that had constituted him 'individual' had vanished for ever.

In some ways it was more terribly moving than anything they had yet seen—that idiot smile as he drew wads of coarse moss from his swollen cheeks and told them that he was 'a damned moss eater'; the continued vomiting of even the simplest food; and, worst of all, the piteous and childish voice of complaint in which he told them that his feet pained him—'burn like fire'—which was natural enough when Dr Cathcart examined them and found that both were dreadfully frozen. Beneath the eyes there were faint indications of recent bleeding.

The details of how he survived the prolonged exposure, of where he had been, or of how he covered the great distance from one camp to the other, including an immense detour of the lake on foot since he had no canoe—all this remains unknown. His memory had vanished completely. And before the end of the winter whose beginning witnessed this strange occurrence, Défago, bereft of mind, memory and soul, had gone with it. He lingered only a few weeks.

And what Punk was able to contribute to the story throws no further light upon it. He was cleaning fish by the lake shore about five o'clock in the evening—an hour, that is, before the search party returned—when he saw this shadow of the guide picking its way weakly into camp. In advance of him, he declares, came the faint whiff of a certain singular odour.

That same instant old Punk started for home. He covered the entire journey of three days as only Indian blood could have covered it. The terror of a whole race drove him. He knew what it all meant. Défago had 'seen the Wendigo.'*

W. F. HARVEY

August Heat

❧❧

PENISTONE ROAD, CLAPHAM.*

August 20th, 190—.

I HAVE had what I believe to be the most remarkable day in my life, and while the events are still fresh in my mind, I wish to put them down on paper as clearly as possible.

Let me say at the outset that my name is James Clarence Withencroft.

I am forty years old, in perfect health, never having known a day's illness.

By profession I am an artist, not a very successful one, but I earn enough money by my black-and-white work to satisfy my necessary wants.

My only near relative, a sister, died five years ago, so that I am independent.

I breakfasted this morning at nine, and after glancing through the morning paper I lighted my pipe and proceeded to let my mind wander in the hope that I might chance upon some subject for my pencil.

The room, though door and windows were open, was oppressively hot, and I had just made up my mind that the coolest and most comfortable place in the neighbourhood would be the deep end of the public swimming bath, when the idea came.

I began to draw. So intent was I on my work that I left my lunch untouched, only stopping work when the clock of St Jude's* struck four.

The final result, for a hurried sketch, was, I felt sure, the best thing I had done.

It showed a criminal in the dock immediately after the judge had pronounced sentence. The man was fat—enormously fat. The flesh hung in rolls about his chin; it creased his huge, stumpy neck. He was clean shaven (perhaps I should say a few days before he must have been clean shaven) and almost bald. He stood in the dock, his short, clumsy fingers clasping the rail, looking straight in front of him. The feeling that his expression conveyed was not so much one of horror as of utter, absolute collapse.

There seemed nothing in the man strong enough to sustain that mountain of flesh.

I rolled up the sketch, and without quite knowing why, placed it in my pocket. Then with the rare sense of happiness which the know-ledge of a good thing well done gives, I left the house.

I believe that I set out with the idea of calling upon Trenton, for I remember walking along Lytton Street and turning to the right along Gilchrist Road* at the bottom of the hill where the men were at work on the new tram lines.

From there onwards I have only the vaguest recollection of where I went. The one thing of which I was fully conscious was the awful heat, that came up from the dusty asphalt pavement as an almost palpable wave. I longed for the thunder promised by the great banks of copper-coloured cloud that hung low over the western sky.

I must have walked five or six miles, when a small boy roused me from my reverie by asking the time.

It was twenty minutes to seven.

When he left me I began to take stock of my bearings. I found myself standing before a gate that led into a yard bordered by a strip of thirsty earth, where there were flowers, purple stock and scarlet geranium. Above the entrance was a board with the inscription—

CHS. ATKINSON.   MONUMENTAL MASON.
WORKER IN ENGLISH AND ITALIAN MARBLES.

From the yard itself came a cheery whistle, the noise of hammer blows, and the cold sound of steel meeting stone.

A sudden impulse made me enter.

A man was sitting with his back towards me, busy at work on a slab of curiously veined marble. He turned round as he heard my steps and I stopped short.

It was the man I had been drawing, whose portrait lay in my pocket.

He sat there, huge and elephantine, the sweat pouring from his scalp, which he wiped with a red silk handkerchief. But though the face was the same, the expression was absolutely different.

He greeted me smiling, as if we were old friends, and shook my hand.

I apologised for my intrusion.

'Everything is hot and glary outside,' I said. 'This seems an oasis in the wilderness.'

'I don't know about the oasis,' he replied, 'but it certainly is hot, as hot as hell. Take a seat, sir!'

He pointed to the end of the gravestone on which he was at work, and I sat down.

'That's a beautiful piece of stone you've got hold of,' I said.

He shook his head. 'In a way it is,' he answered; 'the surface here is as fine as anything you could wish, but there's a big flaw at the back, though I don't expect you'd ever notice it. I could never make really a good job of a bit of marble like that. It would be all right in a summer like this; it wouldn't mind the blasted heat. But wait till the winter comes. There's nothing quite like frost to find out the weak points in stone.'

'Then what's it for?' I asked.

The man burst out laughing.

'You'd hardly believe me if I was to tell you it's for an exhibition, but it's the truth. Artists have exhibitions: so do grocers and butchers; we have them too. All the latest little things in headstones, you know.'

He went on to talk of marbles, which sort best withstood wind and rain, and which were easiest to work; then of his garden and a new sort of carnation he had bought. At the end of every other minute he would drop his tools, wipe his shining head, and curse the heat.

I said little, for I felt uneasy. There was something unnatural, uncanny, in meeting this man.

I tried at first to persuade myself that I had seen him before, that his face, unknown to me, had found a place in some out-of-the-way corner of my memory, but I knew that I was practising little more than a plausible piece of self-deception.

Mr Atkinson finished his work, spat on the ground, and got up with a sigh of relief.

'There! what do you think of that?' he said, with an air of evident pride.

The inscription which I read for the first time was this—

SACRED TO THE MEMORY
OF
JAMES CLARENCE WITHENCROFT.
BORN JAN. 18TH, 1860.
HE PASSED AWAY VERY SUDDENLY
ON AUGUST 20TH, 190—

'In the midst of life we are in death.'

For some time I sat in silence. Then a cold shudder ran down my spine. I asked him where he had seen the name.

'Oh, I didn't see it anywhere,' replied Mr Atkinson. 'I wanted some name, and I put down the first that came into my head. Why do you want to know?'

'It's a strange coincidence, but it happens to be mine.'

He gave a long, low whistle.

'And the dates?'

'I can only answer for one of them, and that's correct.'

'It's a rum go!' he said.

But he knew less than I did. I told him of my morning's work. I took the sketch from my pocket and showed it to him. As he looked, the expression of his face altered until it became more and more like that of the man I had drawn.

'And it was only the day before yesterday,' he said, 'that I told Maria there were no such things as ghosts!'

Neither of us had seen a ghost, but I knew what he meant.

'You probably heard my name,' I said.

'And you must have seen me somewhere and have forgotten it! Were you at Clacton-on-Sea* last July?'

I had never been to Clacton in my life. We were silent for some time. We were both looking at the same thing, the two dates on the gravestone, and one was right.

'Come inside and have some supper,' said Mr Atkinson.

His wife is a cheerful little woman, with the flaky red cheeks of the country-bred. Her husband introduced me as a friend of his who was an artist. The result was unfortunate, for after the sardines and watercress had been removed, she brought out a Doré Bible,* and I had to sit and express my admiration for nearly half an hour.

I went outside, and found Atkinson sitting on the gravestone smoking.

We resumed the conversation at the point we had left off.

'You must excuse my asking,' I said, 'but do you know of anything you've done for which you could be put on trial?'

He shook his head.

'I'm not a bankrupt, the business is prosperous enough. Three years ago I gave turkeys to some of the guardians* at Christmas, but that's all I can think of. And they were small ones, too,' he added as an afterthought.

He got up, fetched a can from the porch, and began to water the flowers. 'Twice a day regular in the hot weather,' he said, 'and then the heat sometimes gets the better of the delicate ones. And ferns, good Lord! they could never stand it. Where do you live?'

I told him my address. It would take an hour's quick walk to get back home.

'It's like this,' he said. 'We'll look at the matter straight. If you go back home to-night, you take your chance of accidents. A cart may run over you, and there's always banana skins and orange peel, to say nothing of falling ladders.'

He spoke of the improbable with an intense seriousness that would have been laughable six hours before. But I did not laugh.

'The best thing we can do,' he continued, 'is for you to stay here till twelve o'clock. We'll go upstairs and smoke; it may be cooler inside.'

To my surprise I agreed.

* * *

We are sitting now in a long, low room beneath the eaves. Atkinson has sent his wife to bed. He himself is busy sharpening some tools at a little oilstone, smoking one of my cigars the while.

The air seems charged with thunder. I am writing this at a shaky table before the open window. The leg is cracked, and Atkinson, who seems a handy man with his tools, is going to mend it as soon as he has finished putting an edge on his chisel.

It is after eleven now. I shall be gone in less than an hour.

But the heat is stifling.

It is enough to send a man mad.

E. F. BENSON

The Room in the Tower

❖

It is probable that everybody who is at all a constant dreamer has had at least one experience of an event or a sequence of circumstances which have come to his mind in sleep being subsequently realised in the material world. But, in my opinion, so far from this being a strange thing, it would be odder yet if this fulfilment did not occasionally happen, since our dreams are, as a rule, concerned with people whom we know and places with which we are familiar, such as might very naturally occur in the awake and daylit world. True, these dreams are often broken into by some absurd and fantastic incident which puts them out of court in regard to their subsequent fulfilment, but on the mere calculation of chances it does not appear in the least unlikely that a dream imagined by anyone who dreams constantly should occasionally come true. Not long ago, for instance, I experienced such a fulfilment of a dream which seems to me in no way remarkable, and to have no kind of psychical significance. The manner of it was as follows.

A CERTAIN friend of mine, living abroad, is amiable enough to write to me about once in a fortnight. Thus, when fourteen days or thereabouts have elapsed since I last heard from him, my mind, probably, either consciously or subconsciously, is expectant of a letter from him. One night last week I dreamed that as I was going upstairs to dress for dinner I heard, as I often heard, the sound of the postman's knock on my front door, and diverted my direction downstairs instead. There, among other correspondence, was a letter from him. Thereafter the fantastic entered, for on opening it I found inside the ace of diamonds, and scribbled across it in his well-known handwriting: 'I am sending you this for safe custody, as you know it is running an unreasonable risk to keep aces in Italy.' The next evening I was just preparing to go upstairs to dress when I heard the postman's knock, and did precisely as I had done in my dream. There, among other letters, was one from my friend. Only it did not contain the ace of diamonds. Had it done so, I should have attached more weight to the matter, which, as it stands, seems to me a perfectly ordinary coincidence. No doubt I consciously or subconsciously expected a letter from him, and this suggested to me my dream. Similarly, the fact that my friend had not written to me for a fortnight suggested to him that he should do so. But occasionally it is not so easy to find such an explanation, and for the following story I can find no explanation at all. It came out of the dark, and into the dark it has gone again.

All my life I have been a habitual dreamer: the nights are few, that is to say, when I do not find on awakening in the morning that some mental experience has been mine, and sometimes all night long, apparently, a series of the most dazzling adventures befall me. Almost without exception these adventures are pleasant, though often merely trivial. It is of an exception that I am going to speak.

It was when I was about sixteen that a certain dream first came to me, and this is how it befell. It opened with my being set down at the door of a big red-brick house where, I understood, I was going to stay. The servant who opened the door told me that tea was going on in the garden, and led me through a low dark-panelled hall with a large open fireplace on to a cheerful green lawn set round with flower beds. There were grouped about the tea-table a small party of people, but they were all strangers to me except one, who was a school-fellow called Jack Stone, clearly the son of the house, and he introduced me to his mother and father and a couple of sisters. I was, I remember, somewhat astonished to find myself here, for the boy in question was scarcely known to me, and I rather disliked what I knew of him; moreover, he had left school nearly a year before. The afternoon was very hot, and an intolerable oppression reigned. On the far side of the lawn ran a red-brick wall, with an iron gate in its centre, outside which stood a walnut tree. We sat in the shadow of the house opposite a row of ball windows, inside which I could see a table with cloth laid, glimmering with glass and silver. This garden-front of the house was very long, and at one end of it stood a tower of three stories, which looked to me much older than the rest of the building.

Before long Mrs Stone, who, like the rest of the party, had sat in absolute silence, said to me, 'Jack will show you your room: I have given you the room in the tower.'

Quite inexplicably my heart sank at her words. I felt as if I had known that I should have the room in the tower, and that it contained something dreadful and significant. Jack instantly got up, and I understood that I had to follow him. In silence we passed through the hall, and mounted a great oak staircase with many corners, and arrived at a small landing with two doors set in it. He pushed one of these open for me to enter, and, without coming in himself, closed it behind me. Then I knew that my conjecture had been right: there was something awful in the room, and, with the panic of nightmare growing swiftly and enveloping me, I awoke in a spasm of terror.

Now that dream, or variations on it, occurred to me intermittently for fifteen years. Most often it came in exactly this form, the arrival, the tea laid out on the lawn, the deadly silence succeeded by that one deadly sentence, the mounting with Jack Stone up to the room in the tower where horror dwelt, and it always came to a close in the nightmare of terror at that which was in the room, though I never saw what it was. At other times I experienced variations on this same theme. Occasionally, for instance, we would be sitting at dinner in the dining-room into the windows of which I had looked on the first night when the dream of this house visited me; but wherever we were there was the same silence, the same sense of dreadful oppression and foreboding. And the silence I knew would always be broken by Mrs Stone saying to me, 'Jack will show you your room: I have given you the room in the tower.' Upon which (this was invariable) I had to follow him up the oak-staircase with many corners, and enter the place that I dreaded more and more each time that I visited it in sleep. Or, again, I would find myself playing cards, still in silence, in a drawing-room lit with immense chandeliers that gave a blinding illumination. What the game was I have no idea; what I remember, with a sense of miserable anticipation, was that soon Mrs Stone would get up and say to me, 'Jack will show you your room: I have given you the room in the tower.' This drawing-room where we played cards was next to the dining-room, and, as I have said, was always brilliantly illuminated, whereas the rest of the house was full of dusk and shadows. And yet how often, in spite of those bouquets of lights, have I not pored over the cards that were dealt me, scarcely able for some reason to see them. Their designs, too, were strange: there were no red suits, but all were black, and among them there were certain cards which were black all over. I hated and dreaded those.

As this dream continued to recur, I got to know the greater part of the house. There was a smoking-room beyond the drawing-room at the end of a passage with a green baize door. It was always very dark there, and as often as I went there I passed somebody whom I could not see in the doorway coming out. Curious developments, too, took place in the characters that peopled the dream as might happen to living people. Mrs Stone, for instance, who, when I first saw her had been black-haired, became grey, and instead of rising briskly, as she had done at first when she said, 'Jack will show you your room: I have given you the room in the tower,' got up very feebly, as if the strength was leaving her limbs. Jack also grew up, and became a rather ill-looking young man with a brown moustache, while one of the sisters ceased to appear, and I understood she was married.

Then it so happened that I was not visited by this dream for six months or more, and I began to hope, in such inexplicable dread did I hold it, that it had passed away for good. But one night after this interval I again found myself being shown out on to the lawn for tea, and Mrs Stone was not there; while the others were all dressed in black. At once I guessed the reason, and my heart leaped at the thought that perhaps this time I should not have to sleep in the room in the tower; and though we usually all sat in silence, on this occasion the sense of relief made me talk and laugh as I had never yet done. But even then matters were not altogether comfortable, for no one else spoke, but they all looked secretly at each other. And soon the foolish stream of my talk ran dry, and gradually an apprehension, worse than anything I had previously known gained on me as the light slowly faded.

Suddenly a voice which I knew well broke the stillness, the voice of Mrs Stone saying, 'Jack will show you your room: I have given you the room in the tower.' It seemed to come from near the gate in the red-brick wall that bounded the lawn, and, looking up, I saw that the grass there was sown thick with gravestones. A curious greyish light shone from them, and I could read the lettering on the grave nearest me, and it was 'In evil memory of Julia Stone.' Then, as usual, Jack got up and again I followed him through the hall and up the staircase with many corners. On this occasion it was darker than usual, and when I passed into the room in the tower I could only just see the furniture, the position of which was already familiar to me. Also there was a dreadful odour of decay in the room, and I woke screaming.

The dream, with such variations and developments as I have mentioned, went on at intervals for fifteen years. Sometimes I would dream it two or three nights in succession; once, as I have said, there was an intermission of six months, but taking a reasonable average I should say that I dreamed it quite as often as once in a month. It had, as is plain, something of nightmare about it, since it always ended in the same appalling terror, which, so far from getting less, seemed to me to gather fresh fear every time that I experienced it. There was, too, a strange and dreadful consistency about it. The characters in it, as I have mentioned, got regularly older; death and marriage visited this silent family, and I never in the dream, after Mrs Stone had died, set eyes on her again. But it was always her voice that told me that the room in the tower was prepared for me; and whether we had tea out on the lawn, or the scene was laid in one of the rooms overlooking it, I could always see her gravestone standing just outside the iron gate. It was the same, too, with the married daughter: usually she was not present, but once or twice she returned again in company with a man, whom I took to be her husband. He, too, like the rest of them, was always silent. But, owing to the constant repetition of the dream, I had ceased to attach, in my waking hours, any significance to it. I never met Jack Stone again during all those years, nor did I ever see a house that resembled this dark house of my dream. And then something happened.

I had been in London in this year up till the end of July, and during the first week in August went down to stay with a friend in a house he had taken for the summer months in the Ashdown Forest district of Sussex. I left London early, for John Clinton was to meet me at Forest Row* station, and we were going to spend the day golfing and go to his house in the evening. He had his motor with him, and we set off, about five of the afternoon, after a thoroughly delightful day, for the drive, the distance being some ten miles. As it was still so early we did not have tea at the club house, but waited till we should get home. As we drove, the weather, which up till then had been, though hot, deliciously fresh, seemed to me to alter in quality, and become very stagnant and oppressive, and I felt that indefinable sense of ominous apprehension that I am accustomed to before thunder. John, however, did not share my views, attributing my loss of lightness to the fact that I had lost both my matches. Events proved however, that I was right, though I do not think that the thunder-storm that broke that night was the sole cause of my depression.

Our way lay through deep high-banked lanes, and before we had gone very far I fell asleep, and was only awakened by the stopping of the motor. And with a sudden thrill, partly of fear, but chiefly of curiosity, I found myself standing in the doorway of my house of dream. We went, I half wondering whether or not I was dreaming still, through a low oak-panelled hall and out on to the lawn, where tea was laid in the shadow of the house. It was set in flower-beds, a red-brick wall with a gate in it bounded one side, and out beyond that was a space of rough grass with a walnut tree. The façade of the house was very long, and at one end stood a three-storied tower, markedly older than the rest.

Here for the moment all resemblance to the repeated dream ceased. There was no silent and somehow terrible family, but a large assembly of exceedingly cheerful persons, all of whom were known to me. And in spite of the horror with which the dream itself had always filled me, I felt nothing of it now that the scene was thus reproduced before me. But I felt the intensest curiosity as to what was going to happen.

Tea pursued its cheerful course, and before long Mrs Clinton got up. And at that moment I think I knew what she was going to say. She spoke to me, and what she said was:

'Jack will show you your room: I have given you the room in the tower.'

At that for half a second the horror of the dream took hold of me again. But it quickly passed, and again I felt nothing more than the most intense curiosity. It was not very long before it was amply satisfied.

John turned to me.

'Right up at the top of the house,' he said, 'but I think you'll be comfortable. We're absolutely full up. Would you like to go and see it now? By Jove, I believe that you are right, and that we are going to have a thunderstorm. How dark it has become.'

I got up and followed him. We passed through the hall, and up the perfectly familiar staircase. Then he opened the door, and I went in. And at that moment sheer unreasoning terror again possessed me. I did not know for certain what I feared—I simply feared. Then, like a sudden recollection when one remembers a name which has long escaped the memory, I knew what I feared. I feared Mrs Stone, whose grave, with the sinister inscription, 'In evil memory,' I had so often seen in my dream just beyond the lawn which lay below my window. And then once more the fear passed, so completely that I wondered what there was to fear, and I found myself sober and quiet and sane in the room in the tower, the name of which I had so often heard in my dream, and the scene of which was so familiar.

I looked round it with a certain sense of proprietorship, and found that nothing had been changed from the dreaming nights in which I knew it so well. Just to the left of the door was the bed, lengthways along the wall, with the head of it in the angle. In a line with it was the fireplace and a small bookcase, opposite the door the outer wall was pierced by two lattice-paned windows between which stood the dressing table, while ranged along the fourth wall was the washing-stand and a big cupboard. My luggage had already been unpacked, for the furniture of dressing and undressing lay orderly on the washstand and toilet table, while my dinner clothes were spread out on the coverlet of the bed. And then, with a sudden start of inexplicable dismay, I saw that there were two rather conspicuous objects which I had not seen before in my dreams: one, a life-sized oil painting of Mrs Stone; the other, a black and white sketch of Jack Stone, representing him as he had appeared to me only a week before in the last of the series of these repeated dreams a rather secret and evil-looking man of about thirty. His picture hung between the windows, looking straight across the room to the other portrait which hung at the side of the bed. At that I looked next, and as I looked I felt once more the horror of nightmare seize me.

It represented Mrs Stone as I had seen her last in my dreams—old and withered and white-haired. But in spite of the evident feebleness of body a dreadful exuberance and vitality shone through the frail envelope of flesh, an exuberance wholly malign, a vitality that foamed and frothed with unimaginable evil. Evil beamed from the narrow leering eyes, it laughed in the demon-like mouth. The whole face was instinct with some secret and appalling mirth: the hands clasped together on the knee seemed shaking with suppressed and nameless glee. Then I saw also that it was signed in the left-hand bottom corner, and, wondering who the artist could be, I looked more closely, and read the inscription: 'Julia Stone, by Julia Stone.'

There came a tap at the door, and John Clinton entered.

'Got everything you want?' he asked.

'Rather more than I want,' said I, pointing to the picture.

He laughed.

'Hard-featured old lady,' he said. 'By herself, too. I remember. Anyhow, she can't have flattered herself much.'

'But don't you see?' said I. 'It's scarcely a human face at all. It's the face of some witch, of some devil.'

He looked at it more closely.

'Yes: it isn't very pleasant,' he said, 'Scarcely a bedside manner, eh? Yes; I can imagine getting the nightmare if I went to sleep with that close by my bed. I'll have it taken down if you like.'

'I really wish you would,' I said.

He rang the bell, and with the help of a servant we detached the picture and carried it out on to the landing, and put it with its face to the wall.

'By Jove, the old lady is a weight,' said John mopping his forehead. 'I wonder if she had something on her mind.'

The extraordinary weight of the picture had struck me, too. I was about to reply when I caught sight of my own hand. There was blood on it, in considerable quantities, covering the whole palm.

'I've cut myself somehow,' said I. John gave a little startled exclamation.

'Why, I have, too,' he said.

Simultaneously the footman took out his handkerchief and wiped his hand with it. I saw that there was blood also on his handkerchief.

John and I went back into the tower room and washed the blood off. But neither on his hand nor on mine was there the slightest trace of a scratch or cut. It seemed to me that having ascertained this, we both, by a sort of tacit consent, did not allude to it again. Something, in my case, had dimly occurred to me that I did not wish to think about. It was but a conjecture, but I fancied that I knew the same thing had occurred to him.

The heat and oppression of the air, for the storm we had expected was still undischarged, increased very much after dinner, and for some time most of the party, among whom was John Clinton and myself, sat outside on the path bounding the lawn where we had had tea. The night was absolutely dark, and no twinkle of star or moon-ray could penetrate the pall of cloud that overset the sky. By degrees our assembly thinned—the women went up to bed, men dispersed to the smoking or billiard room, and not long after eleven my host and I were the only two left. All the evening I thought that he had something on his mind, and as soon as we were alone he spoke.

'The man who helped us with the picture had blood on his hand, too, did you notice?' he said. 'I asked him just now if he had cut himself, and he said he supposed he had, but that he could find no mark of it. Now where did that blood come from?'

By dint of telling myself that I was not going to think about it, I had succeeded in not doing so, and I did not want, especially just at bedtime, to be reminded of it.

'I don't know,' said I, 'and I don't really care, so long as the picture of Mrs Julia Stone is not by my bed.'

He got up.

'But it's odd,' he said. 'Ha! Now you'll see another odd thing.'

A dog of his, an Irish terrier by breed, had come out of the house as we talked. The door behind us into the hall was open, and a bright oblong of light shone across the lawn to the iron gate which led on to the rough grass outside where the walnut-tree stood. I saw that the dog had all his hackles up, bristling with rage and fright; his lips were curled back from his teeth as if he was ready to spring at something, and he was growling to himself. He took not the slightest notice of his master or me, but stiffly and tensely walked across the grass to the iron gate. There he stood for a moment, looking through the bars and still growling. Then of a sudden his courage seemed to desert him; he gave one long howl, and scuttled back to the house with a curious crouching sort of movement.

'He does that half-a-dozen times a day,' said John. 'He sees something which he both hates and fears.'

I walked to the gate and looked over it. Something was moving on the grass outside, and soon a sound which I could not instantly identify came to my ears. Then I remembered what it was; it was the purring of a cat. I lit a match and saw the purrer, a big blue Persian, walking round and round in a little circle just outside the gate, stepping high and ecstatically, with tail carried aloft like a banner. Its eyes were bright and shining, and every now and then it put its head down and sniffed at the grass.

I laughed.

'The end of that mystery, I am afraid,' I said. 'Here's a large cat having Walpurgis night* all alone.'

'Yes, that's Darius,' said John. He spends half the day and all night there. But that's not the end of the dog mystery, for Toby and he are the best of friends, but the beginning of the cat mystery. What's the cat doing there? And why is Darius pleased, while Toby is terror-stricken?'

At that moment I remembered the rather horrible detail of my dreams when I saw through the gate, just where the cat was now, the white tombstone with the sinister inscription. But before I could answer the rain began, as suddenly and heavily as if a tap had been turned on, and simultaneously the big cat squeezed through the bars of the gate, and came leaping across the lawn to the house for shelter. Then it sat in the doorway, looking out eagerly into the dark. It spat and struck at John with its paw, as he pushed it in, in order to close the door.

Somehow, with the portrait of Julia Stone in the passage outside, the room in the tower had absolutely no alarm for me, and as I went to bed, feeling very sleepy and heavy, I had nothing more than interest for the curious incident about our bleeding hands, and the conduct of the cat and dog. The last thing I looked at before I put out my light was the square empty space by my bed, where the portrait had been. Here the paper was of its original full tint of dark red; over the rest of the walls it had faded. Then I blew out my candle and instantly fell asleep.

My awaking was equally instantaneous, and I sat bolt upright in bed, under the impression that some bright light had been flashed in my face, though it was now absolutely pitch dark. I knew exactly where I was, in the room which I had dreaded in dreams; but no horror that I ever felt when asleep approached the fear that now invaded and froze my brain. Immediately after, a peal of thunder crackled just above the house, but the probability that it was only a flash of lightning which awoke me gave no reassurance to my galloping heart. Something, I knew was in the room with me, and instinctively I put out my right hand which was nearest the wall to keep it away. And my hand touched the edge of a picture frame hanging close to me.

I sprang out of bed, upsetting the small table that stood by it, and I heard my watch, candle, and matches clatter on to the floor. But for the moment there was no need of light, for a blinding flash leaped out of the clouds, and showed me that by my bed again hung the picture of Mrs Stone. And instantly the room went into blackness again. But in that flash I saw another thing also—namely, a figure that leaned over the end of my bed, watching me. It was dressed in some close-clinging white garment, spotted and stained with mould, and the face was that of the portrait.

Overhead the thunder cracked and roared, and when it ceased and the deathly stillness succeeded, I heard the rustle of movement coming nearer me, and, more horrible yet, perceived an odour of corruption and decay. And then a hand was laid on the side of my neck, and close beside my ear I heard quick-taken eager breathing. Yet I knew that this thing, though it could be perceived by touch, by smell, by eye, and by ear, was still not of this earth, but something that had passed out of the body and had power to make itself manifest. Then a voice, already familiar to me, spoke.

'I knew you would come to the room in the tower,' it said. 'I have been long waiting for you. At last you have come. To-night I shall feast; before long we will feast together.'

And the quick breathing came closer to me; I could feel it on my neck.

At that the terror, which I think had paralysed me for the moment, gave way to the wild instinct of self-preservation. I hit wildly with both arms, kicking out at the same moment, and heard a little animal-like squeal, and something soft dropped with a thud beside me. I took a couple of steps forward, nearly tripping up over whatever it was that lay there, and by the merest good luck found the handle of the door. In another second I ran out on the landing, and had banged the door behind me. Almost at the same moment I heard a door open somewhere below, and John Clinton, candle in hand, came running upstairs.

'What is it?' he said. 'I sleep just below you, and heard a noise, as if—Good heavens, there's blood on your shoulder.'

I stood there, so he told me afterwards, swaying from side to side, white as a sheet, with the mark on my shoulder as if a hand covered with blood had been laid there.

'It's in there,' I said pointing. 'She—you know. The portrait is in there, too, hanging up on the place we took it from.'

At that he laughed.

'My dear fellow; this is mere nightmare,' he said.

He pushed by me and opened the door, I standing there simply inert with terror, unable to stop him, unable to move.

'Phew! What an awful smell,' he said.

Then there was silence; he had passed out of my sight behind the open door. Next moment he came out again, as white as myself, and instantly shut it.

'Yes, the portrait's there,' he said, 'and on the floor is a thing—

a thing spotted with earth, like what they bury people in. Come away, quick, come away.'

How I got downstairs I hardly know. An awful shuddering and nausea of the spirit rather than of the flesh had seized me, and more than once he had to place my feet upon the steps, while every now and then he cast glances of terror and apprehension up the stairs. But in time we came to his dressing-room on the floor below, and there I told him what I have here described.

* * *

The sequel can be made short, indeed some of my readers have perhaps already guessed what it was, if they remember that inexplicable affair of the churchyard at West Fawley* some eight years ago, where an attempt was made three times to bury the body of a certain woman who had committed suicide. On each occasion the coffin was found in the course of a few days again protruding from the ground. After the third attempt, in order that the thing should not be talked about, the body was buried elsewhere in unconsecrated ground. Where it was buried was just outside the iron gate of the garden belonging to the house where this woman had lived. She had committed suicide in a room at the top of the tower in that house. Her name was Julia Stone.

Subsequently the body was again secretly dug up, and the coffin was found to be full of blood.

WILLIAM HOPE HODGSON

The Derelict

⛌

'IT'S the *Material*,' said the old ship's doctor. . . . 'The *Material*, plus the Conditions; and, maybe,' he added slowly, 'a third factor—yes, a third factor; but there, there. . . .' He broke off his half-meditative sentence, and began to charge his pipe.

'Go on, Doctor,' we said, encouragingly, and with more than a little expectancy. We were in the smoke-room of the *Sand-a-lea*, running across the North Atlantic; and the Doctor was a character. He concluded the charging of his pipe, and lit it; then settled himself, and began to express himself more fully:—

'The *Material*,' he said, with conviction, 'is inevitably the medium of expression of the Life-Force—the fulcrum, as it were; lacking which, it is unable to exert itself, or, indeed, to express itself in any form or fashion that would be intelligible or evident to us.

'So potent is the share of the *Material* in the production of that thing which we name Life, and so eager the Life-Force to express itself, that I am convinced it would, if given the right Conditions, make itself manifest even through so hopeless-seeming a medium as a simple block of sawn wood; for I tell you, gentlemen, the Life-Force is both as fiercely urgent and as indiscriminate as Fire—the Destructor; yet which some are now growing to consider the very essence of Life rampant. . . . There is a quaint seeming paradox there,' he concluded, nodding his old grey head.

'Yes, Doctor,' I said. 'In brief, your argument is that Life is a thing, state, fact, or element, call-it-what-you-like, which requires the *Material* through which to manifest itself, and that given the *Material*, plus the Conditions, the result is Life. In other words, that Life is an evolved product, manifested through Matter and bred of Conditions—eh?'

'As we understand the word,' said the old Doctor. 'Though, mind you, there *may* be a third factor. But, in my heart, I believe that it is a matter of chemistry; Conditions and a suitable medium; but given the Conditions, the Brute is so almighty that it will seize upon anything through which to manifest itself. It is a Force generated by Conditions; but nevertheless this does not bring us one iota nearer to its *explanation,* any more than to the explanation of Electricity or Fire. They are, all three, of the Outer Forces—Monsters of the Void. Nothing we can do will *create* any one of them; our power is merely to be able, by providing the Conditions, to make each one of them manifest to our physical senses. Am I clear?'

'Yes, Doctor, in a way you are,' I said. 'But I don't agree with you; though I think I understand you. Electricity and Fire are both what I might call natural things; but Life is an abstract something—a kind of all-permeating Wakefulness. Oh, I can't explain it; who could! But it's spiritual; not just a thing bred out of a Condition, like Fire, as you say, or Electricity. It's a horrible thought of yours. Life's a kind of spiritual mystery. . . .'

'Easy, my boy!' said the old Doctor, laughing gently to himself; 'or else I may be asking you to demonstrate the spiritual mystery of life of the limpet, or the crab, shall we say.'

He grinned at me, with ineffable perverseness. 'Anyway,' he continued, 'as I suppose you've all guessed, I've a yarn to tell you in support of my impression that Life is no more a mystery or a miracle than Fire or Electricity. But, please to remember, gentlemen, that because we've succeeded in naming and making good use of these two Forces, they're just as much mysteries, fundamentally, as ever. And, anyway, the thing I'm going to tell you, won't explain the mystery of Life; but only give you one of my pegs on which I hang my feeling that Life is, as I have said, a Force made manifest through Conditions (that is to say, natural Chemistry), and that it can take for its purpose and Need, the most incredible and unlikely Matter; for without Matter, it cannot come into existence—it cannot become manifest. . . .'

'I don't agree with you, Doctor,' I interrupted. 'Your theory would destroy all belief in life after death. It would. . . .'

'Hush, sonny,' said the old man, with a quiet little smile of comprehension. 'Hark to what I've to say first; and, anyway, what objection have you to material life, after death; and if you object to a material framework, I would still have you remember that I am speaking of Life, as we understand the word in this our life. Now do be a quiet lad, or I'll never be done:—

'It was when I was a young man, and that is a good many years ago, gentlemen. I had passed my examinations; but was so run down with overwork, that it was decided that I had better take a trip to sea. I was by no means well off, and very glad, in the end, to secure a nominal post as Doctor in a sailing passenger-clipper, running out to China.

'The name of the ship was the *Bheotpte,** and soon after I had got all my gear aboard, she cast off, and we dropped down the Thames, and next day were well away out in the Channel.

'The Captain's name was Gannington, a very decent man; though quite illiterate. The First Mate, Mr Berlies, was a quiet, sternish, reserved man, very well-read. The Second Mate, Mr Selvern, was, perhaps, by birth and upbringing, the most socially cultured of the three; but he lacked the stamina and indomitable pluck of the two others. He was more of a sensitive; and emotionally and even mentally, the most alert man of the three.

'On our way out, we called at Madagascar, where we landed some of our passengers; then we ran Eastward, meaning to call at North West Cape;* but about a hundred degrees East, we encountered very dreadful weather, which carried away all our sails and sprung the jib-boom and fore t'gallant mast.*

'The storm carried us Northward for several hundred miles, and when it dropped us finally, we found ourselves in a very bad state. The ship had been strained, and had taken some three feet of water through her seams; the main top-mast had been sprung, in addition to the jibboom and fore t'gallant mast; two of our boats had gone, as also one of the pigsties (with three fine pigs), this latter having been washed overboard but some half hour before the wind began to ease, which it did quickly; though a very ugly sea ran for some hours after.

'The wind left us just before dark, and when morning came, it brought splendid weather; a calm, mildly undulating sea, and a brilliant sun, with no wind. It showed us also that we were not alone; for about two miles away to the Westward, was another vessel, which Mr Selvern, the Second Mate, pointed out to me.

'"That's a pretty rum looking packet,* Doctor," he said, and handed me his glass. I looked through it, at the other vessel, and saw what he meant; at least, I thought I did.

'"Yes, Mr Selvern," I said, "she's got a pretty old-fashioned look about her."

'He laughed at me, in his pleasant way.

' "It's easy to see you're not a sailor, Doctor," he remarked. "There's a dozen rum things about her. She's a derelict, and has been floating round, by the look of her, for many a score of years. Look at the shape of her counter, and the bows and cut-water.* She's as old as the hills, as you might say, and ought to have gone down to Davy Jones* a long time ago. Look at the growths on her, and the thickness of her standing rigging; that's all salt encrustations, I fancy, if you notice the white colour. She's been a small barque; but don't you see she's not a yard left aloft. They've all dropped out of the slings;* everything rotted away; wonder the standing rigging hasn't gone too. I wish the Old Man would let us take the boat, and have a look at her; she'd be well worth it."

'There seemed little chance, however, of this; for all hands were turned-to and kept hard at it all day long, repairing the damage to the masts and gear, and this took a long while, as you may think. Part of the time, I gave a hand, heaving on one of the deck-capstans; for the exercise was good for my liver. Old Captain Gannington approved, and I persuaded him to come along and try some of the same medicine, which he did; and we grew very chummy over the job.

'We got talking about the derelict, and he remarked how lucky we were not to have run full tilt on to her, in the darkness; for she lay right away to leeward of us, according to the way that we had been drifting in the storm. He also was of the opinion that she had a strange look about her, and that she was pretty old; but on this latter point, he plainly had far less knowledge than the Second Mate; for he was, as I have said, an illiterate man, and knew nothing of sea-craft, beyond what experience had taught him. He lacked the book-knowledge which the Second Mate had, of vessels previous to his day, which it appeared the derelict was.

' "She's an old 'un, Doctor," was the extent of his observations in this direction.

'Yet, when I mentioned to him that it would be interesting to go aboard, and give her a bit of an overhaul, he nodded his head, as if the idea had been already in his mind, and accorded with his own inclinations.

' "When the work's over, Doctor," he said. "Can't spare the men now, ye know. Got to get all ship-shape an' ready as smart as we can. But we'll take my gig, an' go off in the Second Dog Watch.* The glass is steady, an' it'll be a bit of gam for us."

'That evening, after tea, the captain gave orders to clear the gig and get her overboard. The Second Mate was to come with us, and the Skipper gave him word to see that two or three lamps were put into the boat, as it would soon fall dark. A little later, we were pulling across the calmness of the sea, with a crew of six at the oars, and making very good speed of it.

'Now, gentlemen, I have detailed to you with great exactness, all the facts, both big and little, so that you can follow step by step each incident in this extraordinary affair; and I want you now to pay the closest attention.

'I was sitting in the stern-sheets, with the Second Mate, and the Captain, who was steering; and as we drew nearer and nearer to the stranger, I studied her with an ever growing attention, as, indeed, did Captain Gannington and the Second Mate. She was, as you know, to the Westward of us, and the sunset was making a great flame of red light to the back of her, so that she showed a little blurred and indistinct, by reason of the halation of the light, which almost defeated the eye in any attempt to see her rotting spars and standing-rigging, submerged as they were in the fiery glory of the sunset.

'It was because of this effect of the sunset, that we had come quite close, comparatively, to the derelict, before we saw that she was all surrounded by a sort of curious scum, the colour of which was difficult to decide upon, by reason of the red light that was in the atmosphere; but which afterwards we discovered to be brown. This scum spread all about the old vessel for many hundreds of yards, in a huge, irregular patch, a great stretch of which reached out to the Eastward, upon our starboard side, some score, or so, fathoms away.

' "Queer stuff," said Captain Gannington, leaning to the side, and looking over. "Something in the cargo as 'as gone rotten an' worked out through 'er seams."

' "Look at her bows and stern," said the Second Mate; "just look at the growth on her."

'There were, as he said, great clumpings of strange-looking sea-fungi under the bows and the short counter astern. From the stump of her jibboom and her cutwater, great beards of rime and marine-growths hung downward into the scum that held her in. Her blank starboard side was presented to us, all a dead, dirtyish white, streaked and mottled vaguely with dull masses of heavier colour.

' "There's a steam or haze rising off her," said the Second Mate, speaking again; "you can see it against the light. It keeps coming and going. Look!"

'I saw then what he meant—a faint haze or steam, either suspended above the old vessel, or rising from her; and Captain Gannington saw it also:—

'"Spontaneous combustion!" he exclaimed. "We'll 'ave to watch w'en we lift the 'atches; 'nless it's some poor devil that's got aboard of 'er; but that ain't likely."

'We were now within a couple of hundred yards of the old derelict, and had entered into the brown scum. As it poured off the lifted oars, I heard one of the men mutter to himself:—"dam treacle!" and, indeed, it was something like it. As the boat continued to forge nearer and nearer to the old ship, the scum grew thicker and thicker; so that, at last, it perceptibly slowed us.

'"Give way, lads! Put some beef to it!" sung out Captain Gannington; and thereafter there was no sound, except the panting of the men, and the faint, reiterated suck, suck, of the sullen brown scum upon the oars, as the boat was forced ahead. As we went, I was conscious of a peculiar smell in the evening air, and whilst I had no doubt that the puddling of the scum, by the oars, made it rise, I felt that in some way, it was vaguely familiar; yet I could give it no name.

'We were now very close to the old vessel, and presently she was high above us, against the dying light. The Captain called out then to:—"in with the bow oars, and stand-by with the boat-hook," which was done.

'"Aboard there! Ahoy! Aboard there! Ahoy!" shouted Captain Gannington; but there came no answer, only the flat sound of his voice going lost into the open sea, each time he sung out.

'"Ahoy! Aboard there! Ahoy!" he shouted, time after time; but there was only the weary silence of the old hulk that answered us; and, somehow as he shouted, the while that I stared up half expectantly at her, a queer little sense of oppression, that amounted almost to nervousness, came upon me. It passed; but I remember how I was suddenly aware that it was growing dark. Darkness comes fairly rapidly in the tropics; though not so quickly as many fiction-writers seem to think; but it was not that the coming dusk had perceptibly deepened in that brief time, of only a few moments, but rather that my nerves had made me suddenly a little hypersensitive. I mention my state particularly; for I am not a nervy man, normally; and my abrupt touch of nerves is significant, in the light of what happened.

'"There's no one aboard there!" said Captain Gannington. "Give way, men!" For the boat's crew had instinctively rested on their oars, as the Captain hailed the old craft. The men gave way again; and then the Second Mate called out excitedly:—"Why, look there, there's our pigsty! See, it's got *Bheotpte* painted on the end. It's drifted down here, and the scum's caught it. What a blessed wonder!"

'It was, as he had said, our pigsty that had been washed overboard in the storm; and most extraordinary to come across it there.

'"We'll tow it off with us, when we go," remarked the Captain, and shouted to the crew to get-down to their oars; for they were hardly moving the boat, because the scum was so thick, close in around the old ship, that it literally clogged the boat from going ahead. I remember that it struck me, in a half-conscious sort of way, as curious that the pigsty, containing our three dead pigs, had managed to drift in so far, unaided, whilst we could scarcely manage to *force* the boat in, now that we had come right into the scum. But the thought passed from my mind; for so many things happened within the next few minutes.

'The men managed to bring the boat in alongside, within a couple of feet of the derelict, and the man with the boat-hook, hooked on.

'"'Ave ye got 'old there, forrard?" asked Captain Gannington.

'"Yessir!" said the bow-man; and as he spoke, there came a queer noise of tearing.

'"What's that?" asked the Captain.

'"It's tore, Sir. Tore clean away!" said the man; and his tone showed that he had received something of a shock.

'"Get a hold again then!" said Captain Gannington, irritably. "You don't s'pose this packet was built yesterday! Shove the hook into the main chains." The man did so, gingerly, as you might say; for it seemed to me, in the growing dusk, that he put no strain on to the hook; though, of course, there was no need; you see, the boat could not go very far, of herself, in the stuff in which she was embedded. I remember thinking this, also, as I looked up at the bulging side of the old vessel. Then I heard Captain Gannington's voice:—

'"Lord! but she's old! An' what a colour, Doctor! She don't half want paint, do she! . . . Now then, somebody, one of them oars."

'An oar was passed to him, and he leant it up against the ancient, bulging side; then he paused, and called to the Second Mate to light a couple of the lamps, and stand-by to pass them up; for darkness had settled down now upon the sea.

'The Second Mate lit two of the lamps, and told one of the men to light a third, and keep it handy in the boat; then he stepped across, with a lamp in each hand, to where Captain Gannington stood by the oar against the side of the ship.

'"Now, my lad," said the Captain, to the man who had pulled stroke, "up with you, an' we'll pass ye up the lamps."

'The man jumped to obey; caught the oar, and put his weight upon it, and as he did so, something seemed to give a little.

'"Look!" cried out the Second Mate, and pointed, lamp in hand . . . "It's sunk in!"

'This was true. The oar had made quite an indentation into the bulging, somewhat slimy side of the old vessel.

'"Mould, I reckon," said Captain Gannington, bending towards the derelict, to look. Then, to the man:—

'"Up you go, my lad, and be smart. . . . Don't stand there waitin'!"

'At that, the man, who had paused a moment as he felt the oar give beneath his weight, began to shin up, and in a few seconds he was aboard, and leant out over the rail for the lamps. These were passed up to him, and the Captain called to him to steady the oar. Then Captain Gannington went, calling to me to follow, and after me the Second Mate.

'As the Captain put his face over the rail, he gave a cry of astonishment:—

'"Mould, by gum! Mould. . . . Tons of it! . . . Good Lord!"

'As I heard him shout that, I scrambled the more eagerly after him, and in a moment or two, I was able to see what he meant—— Everywhere that the light from the two lamps struck, there was nothing but smooth great masses and surfaces of a dirty-white mould.

'I climbed over the rail, with the Second Mate close behind, and stood upon the mould-covered decks. There might have been no planking beneath the mould, for all that our feet could feel. It gave under our tread, with a spongy, puddingy feel. It covered the deck-furniture of the old ship, so that the shape of each article and fitment was often no more than suggested through it.

'Captain Gannington snatched a lamp from the man, and the Second Mate reached for the other. They held the lamps high, and we all stared. It was most extraordinary, and, somehow, most abominable. I can think of no other word, gentlemen, that so much describes the predominant feeling that affected me at the moment.

'"Good Lord!" said Captain Gannington, several times. "Good Lord!" But neither the Second Mate nor the man said anything, and for my part I just stared, and at the same time began to smell a little at the air; for there was again a vague odour of something half familiar, that somehow brought to me a sense of half-known fright.

'I turned this way and that, staring, as I have said. Here and there, the mould was so heavy as to entirely disguise what lay beneath; converting the deck-fittings into indistinguishable mounds of mould, all dirty-white, and blotched and veined with irregular, dull purplish markings.

'There was a strange thing about the mould, which Captain Gannington drew attention to—it was that our feet did not crush into it and break the surface, as might have been expected; but merely indented it.

'"Never seen nothin' like it before! . . . Never!" said the Captain, after having stooped with his lamp to examine the mould under our feet. He stamped with his heel, and the stuff gave out a dull, puddingy sound. He stooped again, with a quick movement, and stared, holding the lamp close to the deck. "Blest, if it ain't a reg'lar skin to it!" he said.

'The Second Mate and the man and I all stooped, and looked at it. The Second Mate progged* it with his forefinger, and I remember I rapped it several times with my knuckles, listening to the dead sound it gave out, and noticing the close, firm texture of the mould.

'"Dough!" said the Second Mate. "It's just like blessed dough! . . . Pouf!" He stood up with a quick movement. "I could fancy it stinks a bit," he said.

'As he said this, I knew suddenly what the familiar thing was, in the vague odour that hung about us—It was that the smell had something animal-like in it; something of the same smell, only *heavier,* that you will smell in any place that is infested with mice. I began to look about with a sudden very real uneasiness. . . . There might be vast numbers of hungry rats aboard. . . . They might prove exceedingly dangerous, if in a starving condition; yet, as you will understand, somehow I hesitated to put forward my idea as a reason for caution; it was too fanciful.

'Captain Gannington had begun to go aft, along the mould-covered maindeck, with the Second Mate; each of them holding his lamp high up, so as to cast a good light about the vessel. I turned quickly and followed them, the man with me keeping close to my heels, and plainly uneasy. As we went, I became aware that there was a feeling of moisture in the air, and I remembered the slight mist, or smoke, above the hulk, which had made Captain Gannington suggest spontaneous combustion, in explanation.

'And always, as we went, there was that vague, animal smell; and, suddenly, I found myself wishing we were well away from the old vessel.

'Abruptly, after a few paces, the Captain stopped and pointed at a row of mould-hidden shapes on either side of the maindeck . . . "Guns," he said. "Been a privateer in the old days, I guess; maybe worse! We'll 'ave a look below, Doctor; there may be something worth touchin'. She's older than I thought. Mr Selvern thinks she's about three hundred year old; but I scarce think it."

'We continued our way aft, and I remember that I found myself walking as lightly and gingerly as possible; as if I were subconsciously afraid of treading through the rotten, mould-hid decks. I think the others had a touch of the same feeling, from the way that they walked. Occasionally, the soft mould would grip our heels, releasing them with a little, sullen suck.

'The Captain forged somewhat ahead of the Second Mate; and I know that the suggestion he had made himself, that perhaps there might be something below, worth the carrying away, had stimulated his imagination. The Second Mate was, however, beginning to feel somewhat the same way that I did; at least, I have that impression. I think, if it had not been for what I might truly describe as Captain Gannington's sturdy courage, we should all of us have just gone back over the side very soon; for there was most certainly an unwholesome feeling abroad, that made one feel queerly lacking in pluck; and you will soon perceive that this feeling was justified.

'Just as the Captain reached the few, mould-covered steps, leading up on to the short half-poop, I was suddenly aware that the feeling of moisture in the air had grown very much more definite. It was perceptible now, intermittently, as a sort of thin, moist, fog-like vapour, that came and went oddly, and seemed to make the decks a little indistinct to the view, this time and that. Once, an odd puff of it beat up suddenly from somewhere, and caught me in the face, carrying a queer, sickly, heavy odour with it, that somehow frightened me strangely, with a suggestion of a waiting and half-comprehended danger.

'We had followed Captain Gannington up the three, mould-covered steps, and now went slowly aft along the raised after-deck.

'By the mizzen-mast,* Captain Gannington paused, and held his lantern near to it. . . .

'"My word, Mister," he said to the Second Mate, "it's fair thickened up with the mould; why, I'll g'antee it's close on four foot thick." He shone the light down to where it met the deck. "Good Lord!" he said, "look at the sea-lice on it!" I stepped up; and it was as he had said; the sea-lice were thick upon it, some of them huge; not less than the size of large beetles, and all a clear, colourless shade, like water, except where there were little spots of grey in them, evidently their internal organisms.

'"I've never seen the like of them, 'cept on a live cod!" said Captain Gannington, in an extremely puzzled voice. "My word! but they're whoppers!" Then he passed on; but a few paces farther aft, he stopped again, and held his lamp near to the mould-hidden deck.

'"Lord bless me, Doctor!" he called out, in a low voice, "did ye ever see the like of that? Why, it's a foot long, if it's a hinch!"

'I stooped over his shoulder, and saw what he meant; it was a clear, colourless creature, about a foot long, and about eight inches high, with a curved back that was extraordinarily narrow. As we stared, all in a group, it gave a queer little flick, and was gone.

'"Jumped!" said the Captain. "Well, if that ain't a giant of all the sea-lice that ever I've seen! I guess it's jumped twenty-foot clear." He straightened his back, and scratched his head a moment, swinging the lantern this way and that with the other hand, and staring about us. "Wot are *they* doin' aboard 'ere!" he said. "You'll see 'em (little things) on fat cod, an' such-like. . . . I'm blowed, Doctor, if I understand."

'He held his lamp towards a big mound of the mould, that occupied part of the after portion of the low poop-deck, a little foreside of where there came a two-foot high "break" to a kind of second and loftier poop, that ran away aft to the taffrail. The mound was pretty big, several feet across, and more than a yard high. Captain Gannington walked up to it:—

'"I reck'n this 's the scuttle," he remarked, and gave it a heavy kick. The only result was a deep indentation into the huge, whitish hump of mould, as if he had driven his foot into a mass of some doughy substance. Yet, I am not altogether correct in saying that this was the only result; for a certain other thing happened—— From a place made by the Captain's foot, there came a little gush of a purplish fluid, accompanied by a peculiar smell, that was, and was not, half-familiar. Some of the mould-like substance had stuck to the toe of the Captain's boot, and from this, likewise, there issued a sweat, as it were, of the same colour.

'"Well!" said Captain Gannington, in surprise; and drew back his foot to make another kick at the hump of mould; but he paused, at an exclamation from the Second Mate:—

'"Don't, Sir!" said the Second Mate.

'I glanced at him, and the light from Captain Gannington's lamp showed me that his face had a bewildered, half-frightened look, as if he were suddenly and unexpectedly half-afraid of something, and as if his tongue had given away his sudden fright, without any intention on his part to speak.

'The Captain also turned and stared at him:—

'"Why, Mister?" he asked, in a somewhat puzzled voice, through which there sounded just the vaguest hint of annoyance. "We've got to shift this muck, if we're to get below."

'I looked at the Second Mate, and it seemed to me that, curiously enough, he was listening less to the Captain, than to some other sound.

'Suddenly, he said in a queer voice:—"Listen, everybody!"

'Yet, we heard nothing, beyond the faint murmur of the men talking together in the boat alongside.

'"I don't hear nothin'," said Captain Gannington, after a short pause. "Do you, Doctor?"

'"No," I said.

'"Wot was it you thought you heard?" asked the Captain, turning again to the Second Mate. But the Second Mate shook his head, in a curious, almost irritable way; as if the Captain's question interrupted his listening. Captain Gannington stared a moment at him; then held his lantern up, and glanced about him, almost uneasily. I know I felt a queer sense of strain. But the light showed nothing, beyond the greyish dirty-white of the mould in all directions.

'"Mister Selvern," said the Captain at last, looking at him, "don't get fancying things. Get hold of your bloomin' self. Ye know ye heard nothin'?"

'"I'm quite sure I heard something, Sir!" said the Second Mate.

"I seemed to hear——" He broke off sharply, and appeared to listen, with an almost painful intensity.

'"What did it sound like?" I asked.

'"It's all right, Doctor," said Captain Gannington, laughing gently. "Ye can give him a tonic when we get back. I'm goin' to shift this stuff."

'He drew back, and kicked for the second time at the ugly mass, which he took to hide the companionway.* The result of his kick was startling; for the whole thing wobbled sloppily, like a mound of unhealthy-looking jelly.

'He drew his foot out of it, quickly, and took a step backward, staring, and holding his lamp towards it:——

'"By gum!" he said; and it was plain that he was genuinely startled, "the blessed thing's gone soft!"

'The man had run back several steps from the suddenly flaccid mound, and looked horribly frightened. Though, of what, I am sure he had not the least idea. The Second Mate stood where he was, and stared. For my part, I know I had a most hideous uneasiness upon me. The Captain continued to hold his light towards the wobbling mound, and stare:——

'"It's gone squashy all through!" he said. "There's no scuttle there. There's no bally woodwork inside that lot! Phoo! what a rum smell!"

'He walked round to the after-side of the strange mound, to see whether there might be some signs of an opening into the hull at the back of the great heap of mould-stuff. And then:——

'"LISTEN!" said the Second Mate, again, in the strangest sort of voice.

'Captain Gannington straightened himself upright, and there succeeded a pause of the most intense quietness, in which there was not even the hum of talk from the men alongside in the boat. We all heard it—a kind of dull, soft Thud! Thud! Thud! Thud! somewhere in the hull under us; yet so vague that I might have been half doubtful I heard it, only that the others did so, too.

'Captain Gannington turned suddenly to where the man stood:——

'"Tell them——" he began. But the fellow cried out something, and pointed. There had come a strange intensity into his somewhat unemotional face; so that the Captain's glance followed his action instantly. I stared, also, as you may think. It was the great mound, at which the man was pointing. I saw what he meant.

'From the two gapes made in the mould-like stuff by Captain Gannington's boot, the purple fluid was jetting out in a queerly regular fashion, almost as if it were being forced out by a pump. My word! but I stared! And even as I stared, a larger jet squirted out, and splashed as far as the man, spattering his boots and trouser-legs.

'The fellow had been pretty nervous before, in a stolid, ignorant sort of way; and his funk had been growing steadily; but, at this, he simply let out a yell, and turned about to run. He paused an instant, as if a sudden fear of the darkness that held the decks, between him and the boat, had taken him. He snatched at the Second Mate's lantern; tore it out of his hand, and plunged heavily away over the vile stretch of mould.

'Mr Selvern, the Second Mate, said not a word; he was just standing, staring at the strange-smelling twin streams of dull purple, that were jetting out from the wobbling mound. Captain Gannington, however, roared an order to the man to come back; but the man plunged on and on across the mould, his feet seeming to be clogged by the stuff, as if it had grown suddenly soft. He zigzagged, as he ran, the lantern swaying in wild circles, as he wrenched his feet free, with a constant plop, plop; and I could hear his frightened gasps, even from where I stood.

' "Come back with that lamp!" roared the Captain again; but still the man took no notice, and Captain Gannington was silent an instant, his lips working in a queer, inarticulate fashion; as if he were stunned momentarily by the very violence of his anger at the man's insubordination. And in the silence, I heard the sounds again:— Thud! Thud! Thud! Thud! Quite distinctly now, beating, it seemed suddenly to me, right down under my feet, but deep.

'I stared down at the mould on which I was standing, with a quick, disgusting sense of the terrible all about me; then I looked at the Captain, and tried to say something, without appearing frightened. I saw that he had turned again to the mound, and all the anger had gone out of his face. He had his lamp out towards the mound, and was listening. There was a further moment of absolute silence; at least, I know that I was not conscious of any sound at all, in all the world, except that extraordinary Thud! Thud! Thud! Thud! down somewhere in the huge bulk under us.

'The Captain shifted his feet, with a sudden, nervous movement; and as he lifted them, the mould went plop! plop! He looked quickly at me, trying to smile, as if he were not thinking anything very much about it:—"What do you make of it, Doctor?" he said.

'"I think——" I began. But the Second Mate interrupted with a single word; his voice pitched a little high, in a tone that made us both stare instantly at him:—

'"Look!" he said, and pointed at the mound. The thing was all of a slow quiver. A strange ripple ran outward from it, along the deck, like you will see a ripple run inshore out of a calm sea. It reached a mound a little fore-side of us, which I had supposed to be the cabin-skylight; and in a moment, the second mound sank nearly level with the surrounding decks, quivering floppily in a most extraordinary fashion. A sudden, quick tremor took the mould, right under the Second Mate, and he gave out a hoarse little cry, and held his arms out on each side of him, to keep his balance. The tremor in the mould, spread, and Captain Gannington swayed, and spread his feet, with a sudden curse of fright. The Second Mate jumped across to him, and caught him by the wrist:—

'"The boat, Sir!" he said, saying the very thing that I had lacked the pluck to say. "For God's sake——"

'But he never finished; for a tremendous, hoarse scream cut off his words. They hove themselves round, and looked. I could see without turning. The man who had run from us, was standing in the waist of the ship, about a fathom from the star-board bulwarks.* He was swaying from side to side, and screaming in a dreadful fashion. He appeared to be trying to lift his feet, and the light from his swaying lantern showed an almost incredible sight. All about him the mould was in active movement. His feet had sunk out of sight. The stuff appeared to be *lapping* at his legs; and abruptly his bare flesh showed. The hideous stuff had rent his trouser-legs away, as if they were paper. He gave out a simply sickening scream, and, with a vast effort, wrenched one leg free. It was partly destroyed. The next instant he pitched face downward, and the stuff heaped itself upon him, as if it were actually alive, with a dreadful savage life. It was simply infernal. The man had gone from sight. Where he had fallen was now a writhing, elongated mound, in constant and horrible increase, as the mould appeared to move towards it in strange ripples from all sides.

'Captain Gannington and the Second Mate were stone silent, in amazed and incredulous horror; but I had begun to reach towards a grotesque and terrific conclusion, both helped and hindered by my professional training.

'From the men in the boat alongside, there was a loud shouting, and I saw two of their faces appear suddenly above the rail. They showed clearly, a moment, in the light from the lamp which the man has snatched from Mr Selvern; for, strangely enough, this lamp was standing upright and unharmed on the deck, a little way fore-side of that dreadful, elongated, growing mound, that still swayed and writhed with an incredible horror. The lamp rose and fell on the passing ripples of the mould, just—for all the world—as you will see a boat rise and fall on little swells. It is of some interest to me now, psychologically, to remember how that rising and falling lantern brought home to me, more than anything, the incomprehensible, dreadful strangeness of it all.

'The men's faces disappeared, with sudden yells, as if they had slipped, or been suddenly hurt; and there was a fresh uproar of shouting from the boat. The men were calling to us to come away; to come away. In the same instant, I felt my left boot drawn suddenly and forcibly downward, with a horrible, painful gripe. I wrenched it free, with a yell of angry fear. Forrard of us, I saw that the vile surface was all a-move; and abruptly I found myself shouting in a queer frightened voice:—

'"The boat, Captain! The boat, Captain!"

'Captain Gannington stared round at me, over his right shoulder, in a peculiar, dull way, that told me he was utterly dazed with bewilderment and the incomprehensibleness of it all. I took a quick, clogged, nervous step towards him, and gripped his arm and shook it fiercely.

'"The boat!" I shouted at him. "The boat! For God's sake, tell the men to bring the boat aft!"

'Then the mould must have drawn his feet down; for, abruptly, he bellowed fiercely with terror, his momentary apathy giving place to furious energy. His thick-set, vastly muscular body doubled and writhed with his enormous effort, and he struck out madly, dropping the lantern. He tore his feet free, something ripping as he did so. The *reality* and necessity of the situation had come upon him, brutishly real, and he was roaring to the men in the boat:—

'"Bring the boat aft! Bring 'er aft! Bring 'er aft!"

'The Second Mate and I were shouting the same thing, madly.

' "For God's sake be smart, lads!" roared the Captain, and stooped quickly for his lamp, which still burned. His feet were gripped again, and he hove them out, blaspheming breathlessly, and leaping a yard high with his effort. Then he made a run for the side, wrenching his feet free at each step. In the same instant, the Second Mate cried out something, and grabbed at the Captain:—

' "It's got hold of my feet! It's got hold of my feet!" he screamed. His feet had disappeared up to his boot-tops; and Captain Gannington caught him round the waist with his powerful left arm, gave a mighty heave, and the next instant had him free; but both his boot-soles had almost gone.

'For my part, I jumped madly from foot to foot, to avoid the plucking of the mould; and suddenly I made a run for the ship's side. But before I could get there, a queer gape came in the mould, between us and the side, at least a couple of feet wide, and how deep I don't know. It closed up in an instant, and all the mould, where the gape had been, went into a sort of flurry of horrible ripplings, so that I ran back from it; for I did not dare to put my foot upon it. Then the Captain was shouting at me:—

' "Aft, Doctor! Aft, Doctor! This way, Doctor! Run!" I saw then that he had passed me, and was up on the after, raised portion of the poop. He had the Second Mate thrown like a sack, all loose and quiet, over his left shoulder; for Mr Selvern had fainted, and his long legs flogged, limp and helpless, against the Captain's massive knees as the Captain ran. I saw, with a queer, unconscious noting of minor details, how the torn soles of the Second Mate's boots flapped and jigged, as the Captain staggered aft.

' "Boat ahoy! Boat ahoy! Boat ahoy!" shouted the Captain; and then I was beside him, shouting also. The men were answering with loud yells of encouragement, and it was plain they were working desperately to force the boat aft, through the thick scum about the ship.

'We reached the ancient, mould-hid taffrail, and slewed about, breathlessly, in the half-darkness, to see what was happening. Captain Gannington had left his lantern by the big mound, when he picked up the Second Mate; and as we stood, gasping, we discovered suddenly that all the mould between us and the light was full of movement. Yet; the part on which we stood, for about six or eight feet forrard of us, was still firm.

'Every couple of seconds, we shouted to the men to hasten, and they kept on calling to us that they would be with us in an instant. And all the time, we watched the deck of that dreadful hulk, feeling, for my part, literally sick with mad suspense, and ready to jump overboard into that filthy scum all about us.

'Down somewhere in the huge bulk of the ship, there was all the time that extraordinary, dull, ponderous Thud! Thud! Thud! Thud! growing ever louder. I seemed to feel the whole hull of the derelict beginning to quiver and thrill with each dull beat. And to me, with the grotesque and monstrous suspicion of what made that noise, it was, at once, the most dreadful and incredible sound I have ever heard.

'As we waited desperately for the boat, I scanned incessantly so much of the grey-white bulk as the lamp showed. The whole of the decks seemed to be in strange movement. Forrard of the lamp, I could see, indistinctly, the moundings of the mould swaying and nodding hideously, beyond the circle of the brightest rays. Nearer, and full in the glow of the lamp, the mound which should have indicated the skylight, was swelling steadily. There were ugly, purple veinings on it, and as it swelled, it seemed to me that the veinings and mottlings on it, were becoming plainer—rising, as though embossed upon it, like you will see the veins stand out on the body of a powerful, full-blooded horse. It was most extraordinary. The mound that we had supposed to cover the companion-way, had sunk flat with the surrounding mould, and I could not see that it jetted out any more of the purplish fluid.

'A quaking movement of the mould began, away forrard of the lamp, and came flurrying away aft towards us; and at the sight of that, I climbed up on to the spongy-feeling taffrail, and yelled afresh for the boat. The men answered with a shout, which told me they were nearer; but the beastly scum was so thick that it was evidently a fight to move the boat at all. Beside me, Captain Gannington was shaking the Second Mate furiously, and the man stirred and began to moan. The Captain shook him again.

'"Wake up! Wake up, Mister!" he shouted.

'The Second Mate staggered out of the Captain's arms, and collapsed suddenly, shrieking:—"My feet! Oh, God! My feet!" The Captain and I lugged him up off the mould, and got him into a sitting position upon the taffrail, where he kept up a continual moaning.

'"Hold 'im, Doctor," said the Captain, and whilst I did so, he ran forrard a few yards, and peered down over the starboard quarter rail.

"For God's sake, be smart, lads! Be smart! Be smart!" he shouted down to the men; and they answered him, breathless, from close at hand; yet still too far away for the boat to be any use to us on the instant.

'I was holding the moaning, half-unconscious officer, and staring forrard along the poop decks. The flurrying of the mould was coming aft, slowly and noiselessly. And then, suddenly, I saw something closer:—

'"Look out, Captain!" I shouted; and even as I shouted, the mould near to him gave a sudden peculiar slobber. I had seen a ripple stealing towards him through the horrible stuff. He gave an enormous, clumsy leap, and landed near to us on the sound part of the mould; but the movement followed him. He turned and faced it, swearing fiercely. All about his feet there came abruptly little gapings, which made horrid sucking noises.

'"Come *back*, Captain!" I yelled. "Come back, *quick!*"

'As I shouted, a ripple came at his feet—lipping at them; and he stamped insanely at it, and leaped back, his boot torn half off his foot. He swore madly with pain and anger, and jumped swiftly for the taffrail.

'"Come on, Doctor! Over we go!" he called. Then he remembered the filthy scum, and hesitated; roaring out desperately to the men to hurry. I stared down, also.

'"The Second Mate?" I said.

'"I'll take charge, Doctor," said Captain Gannington, and caught hold of Mr Selvern. As he spoke, I thought I saw something beneath us, outlined against the scum. I leaned out over the stern, and peered. There was something under the port quarter.

'"There's something down there, Captain!" I called, and pointed in the darkness.

'He stooped far over, and stared.

'"A boat, by gum! A BOAT!" he yelled, and began to wriggle swiftly along the taffrail, dragging the Second Mate after him. I followed.

'"A boat it is, sure!" he exclaimed, a few moments later; and, picking up the Second Mate clear of the rail, he hove him down into the boat, where he fell with a crash into the bottom.

'"Over ye go, Doctor!" he yelled at me, and pulled me bodily off the rail, and dropped me after the officer. As he did so, I felt the whole of the ancient, spongy rail give a peculiar, sickening quiver, and begin to wobble. I fell on to the Second Mate, and the Captain came after, almost in the same instant; but fortunately, he landed clear of us, on to the fore thwart, which broke under his weight, with a loud crack and splintering of wood.

' "Thank God!" I heard him mutter. "Thank God! . . . I guess that was a mighty near thing to goin' to hell." '

'He struck a match, just as I got to my feet, and between us we got the Second Mate straightened out on one of the after thwarts. We shouted to the men in the boat, telling them where we were, and saw the light of their lantern shining round the starboard counter of the derelict. They called back to us, to tell us they were doing their best; and then, whilst we waited, Captain Gannington struck another match, and began to overhaul the boat we had dropped into. She was a modern, two-bowed boat, and on the stern, there was painted "Cyclone Glasgow." She was in pretty fair condition, and had evidently drifted into the scum and been held by it.

'Captain Gannington struck several matches, and went forrard towards the derelict. Suddenly he called to me, and I jumped over the thwarts to him.

' "Look, Doctor," he said; and I saw what he meant—a mass of bones, up in the bows of the boat. I stooped over them, and looked. There were the bones of at least three people, all mixed together, in an extraordinary fashion, and quite clean and dry. I had a sudden thought concerning the bones; but I said nothing; for my thought was vague, in some ways, and concerned the grotesque and incredible suggestion that had come to me, as to the cause of that ponderous, dull Thud! Thud! Thud! Thud! that beat on so infernally within the hull, and was plain to hear even now that we had got off the vessel herself. And all the while, you know, I had a sick, horrible, mental-picture of that frightful wriggling mound aboard the hulk.

'As Captain Gannington struck a final match, I saw something that sickened me, and the Captain saw it in the same instant. The match went out, and he fumbled clumsily for another, and struck it. We saw the thing again. We had not been mistaken. . . . A great lip of grey-white was protruding in over the edge of the boat—a great lappet of the mould was coming stealthily towards us; a live mass of *the very hull itself*. And suddenly Captain Gannington yelled out, in so many words, the grotesque and incredible thing I was thinking:—

' "She's Alive!"

'I never heard such a sound of *comprehension* and terror in a man's voice. The very horrified assurance of it, made actual to me the thing that, before, had only lurked in my subconscious mind. I knew he was right; I knew that the explanation, my reason and my training, both repelled and reached towards, was the true one. . . . . . . I wonder whether anyone can possibly understand our feelings in that moment. . . . The unmitigable horror of it, and the *incredibleness*.

'As the light of the match burned up fully, I saw that the mass of living matter, coming towards us, was streaked and veined with purple, the veins standing out, enormously distended. The whole thing quivered continuously to each ponderous Thud! Thud! Thud! Thud! of that gargantuan organ that pulsed within the huge grey-white bulk. The flame of the match reached the Captain's fingers, and there came to me a little sickly whiff of burned flesh; but he seemed unconscious of any pain. Then the flame went out, in a brief sizzle; yet at the last moment, I had seen an extraordinary raw look, become visible upon the end of that monstrous, protruding lappet. It had become dewed with a hideous, purplish sweat. And with the darkness, there came a sudden charnel-like stench.

'I heard the match-box split in Captain Gannington's hands, as he wrenched it open. Then he swore, in a queer frightened voice; for he had come to the end of his matches. He turned clumsily in the darkness, and tumbled over the nearest thwart, in his eagerness to get to the stern of the boat; and I after him; for we knew that thing was coming towards us through the darkness; reaching over that piteous mingled heap of human bones, all jumbled together in the bows. We shouted madly to the men, and for answer saw the bows of the boat emerge dimly into view, round the starboard counter of the derelict.

' "Thank God!" I gasped out; but Captain Gannington yelled to them to show a light. Yet this they could not do; for the lamp had just been stepped on, in their desperate efforts to force the boat round to us.

' "Quick! Quick!" I shouted.

' "For God's sake be smart, men!" roared the Captain; and both of us faced the darkness under the port counter, out of which we knew (but could not see) the thing was coming towards us.

' "An oar! Smart now; pass me an oar!" shouted the Captain; and reached out his hands through the gloom towards the oncoming boat. I saw a figure stand up in the bows, and hold something out to us, across the intervening yards of scum. Captain Gannington swept his hands through the darkness, and encountered it.

'"I've got it. Let go there!" he said, in a quick, tense voice.

'In the same instant, the boat we were in, was pressed over suddenly to starboard by some tremendous weight. Then I heard the Captain shout:—"Duck y'r head, Doctor;" and directly afterwards he swung the heavy, fourteen-foot ash oar round his head, and struck into the darkness. There came a sudden squelch, and he struck again, with a savage grunt of fierce energy. At the second blow, the boat righted, with a slow movement, and directly afterwards the other boat bumped gently into ours.

'Captain Gannington dropped the oar, and springing across to the Second Mate, hove him up off the thwart, and pitched him with knee and arms clear in over the bows among the men; then he shouted to me to follow, which I did, and he came after me, bringing the oar with him. We carried the Second Mate aft, and the Captain shouted to the men to back the boat a little; then they got her bows clear of the boat we had just left, and so headed out through the scum for the open sea.

'"Where's Tom 'Arrison?" gasped one of the men, in the midst of his exertions. He happened to be Tom Harrison's particular chum; and Captain Gannington answered him briefly enough:—

'"Dead! Pull! Don't talk!"

'Now, difficult as it had been to force the boat through the scum to our rescue, the difficulty to get clear seemed tenfold. After some five minutes pulling, the boat seemed hardly to have moved a fathom, if so much; and a quite dreadful fear took me afresh; which one of the panting men put suddenly into words:—

'"It's got us!" he gasped out; "same as poor Tom!" It was the man who had inquired where Harrison was.

'"Shut y'r mouth an' *pull!*" roared the Captain. And so another few minutes passed. Abruptly, it seemed to me that the dull, ponderous Thud! Thud! Thud! Thud! came more plainly through the dark, and I stared intently over the stern. I sickened a little; for I could almost swear that the dark mass of the monster was actually *nearer* . . . that it was coming nearer to us through the darkness. Captain Gannington must have had the same thought; for after a brief look into the darkness, he made one jump to the stroke-oar, and began to double-bank it.*

'"Get forrid under the thwarts, Doctor!" he said to me, rather breathlessly. "Get in the bows, an' see if you can't free the stuff a bit round the bows."

'I did as he told me, and a minute later I was in the bows of the boat, puddling the scum from side to side with the boat-hook, and trying to break up the viscid, clinging muck. A heavy, almost animal-like odour rose off it, and all the air seemed full of the deadening smell. I shall never find words to tell any one the whole horror of it all—the threat that seemed to hang in the very air around us; and, but a little astern, that incredible thing, coming, as I firmly believe, nearer, and the scum holding us like half melted glue.

'The minutes passed in a deadly, eternal fashion, and I kept staring back astern into the darkness; but never ceasing to puddle that filthy scum, striking at it and switching it from side to side, until I sweated.

'Abruptly, Captain Gannington sang out:—

'"We're gaining, lads. Pull!" And I felt the boat forge ahead perceptibly, as they gave way, with renewed hope and energy. There was soon no doubt of it; for presently that hideous Thud! Thud! Thud! Thud! had grown quite dim and vague somewhere astern, and I could no longer see the derelict; for the night had come down tremendously dark, and all the sky was thick overset with heavy clouds. As we drew nearer and nearer to the edge of the scum, the boat moved more and more freely, until suddenly we emerged with a clean, sweet, fresh sound, into the open sea.

'"Thank God!" I said aloud, and drew in the boat-hook, and made my way aft again to where Captain Gannington now sat once more at the tiller. I saw him looking anxiously up at the sky, and across to where the lights of our vessel burned, and again he would seem to listen intently; so that I found myself listening also.

'"What's that, Captain?" I said sharply; for it seemed to me that I heard a sound far astern, something between a queer whine and a low whistling. "What's that?"

'"It's wind, Doctor," he said, in a low voice. "I wish to God we were aboard."

'Then, to the men:—"Pull! Put y'r backs into it, or ye'll never put y'r teeth through good bread again!"

'The men obeyed nobly, and we reached the vessel safely, and had the boat safely stowed, before the storm came, which it did in a furious white smother out of the West. I could see it for some minutes beforehand, tearing the sea, in the gloom, into a wall of phosphorescent foam; and as it came nearer, that peculiar whining, piping sound, grew louder and louder, until it was like a vast steam whistle, rushing towards us across the sea.

'And when it did come, we got it very heavy indeed; so that the morning showed us nothing but a welter of white seas; and that grim derelict was many a score of miles away in the smother, lost as utterly as our hearts could wish to lose her.

'When I came to examine the Second Mate's feet, I found them in a very extraordinary condition. The soles of them had the appearance of having been partly digested. I know of no other word that so exactly describes their condition; and the agony the man suffered, must have been dreadful.

'Now,' concluded the Doctor, 'that is what I call a case in point. If we could know exactly what that old vessel had originally been loaded with, and the juxtaposition of the various articles of her cargo, plus the heat and time she had endured, plus one or two other only guessable quantities, we should have solved the chemistry of the Life-Force, gentlemen. Not necessarily the *origin,* mind you; but, at least, we should have taken a big step on the way. I've often regretted that gale, you know—in a way, that is, in a way! It was a most amazing discovery; but, at the time, I had nothing but thankfulness to be rid of it. . . . A most amazing chance. I often think of the way the monster woke out of its torpor. . . . And that scum. . . . The dead pigs caught in it. . . . I fancy that was a grim kind of net, gentlemen. . . . It caught many things. . . . It . . .'

The old Doctor sighed and nodded.

'If I could have had her bill of lading,'* he said, his eyes full of regret. 'If—— It might have told me something to help. But, anyway. . . .' He began to fill his pipe again. . . . 'I suppose,' he ended, looking round at us gravely, 'I s'pose we humans are an ungrateful lot of beggars, at the best! . . . But . . . but what a chance! What a chance—eh?'

EXPLANATORY NOTES

THESE notes have occasionally benefited from the work of previous editors of the individual authors. Quotations from the Bible are from the King James Version. *OED* is the *Oxford English Dictionary*.

E. T. A. HOFFMANN, *The Sandman*

Ernst Theodor Wilhelm Hoffmann (1776–1822), who wrote under the name Ernst Theodor Amadeus Hoffmann, was an enormously influential German Romantic writer, composer, and artist, whose works have been adapted and interpreted across a number of media, from ballet to psychoanalysis to graphic novels. Hoffmann is best known for his short fiction, collected in *Phantasiestücke in Callots Manner* (*Fantasy Pieces in Callot's Manner*, 4 vols., 1814–15), *Nachtstücke* (*Night Pieces*, 2 vols., 1817), and *Die Serapionsbrüder* (*The Serapion Brethren*, 4 vols., 1819–21). Hoffmann also wrote two novels, *Die Elixiere des Teufels* (*The Devil's Elixir*, 1815–16) and the musical satire *Lebens-Ansichten des Katers Murr* (*The Life and Opinions of Katers [Tomcat] Murr*, 1820–2).

'The Sandman' ('Der Sandmann') was written in 1815–16, and published as the opening story in volume i of *Night Pieces*. It is one of the most influential of all horror stories, not least because of the heavy use Freud makes of it in his essay on 'The Uncanny' (1919), the seminal psychoanalytic work on horror. This translation is by Ritchie Robertson, and was originally published in *The Golden Pot and Other Tales* (Oxford and New York: Oxford University Press, 1992).

4 *as Franz Moor begged Daniel*: in Friedrich Schiller's (1759–1805) first play, *Die Räuber* (*The Robbers*, 1781), the rationalist villain Franz Moor has a terrifying dream about the Last Judgement, and begs his servant Daniel to mock him for it.

The Sandman: in northern European folklore, the Sandman is a benign figure who ensures good dreams by sprinkling sand in children's eyes. See, for example, Hans Christian Andersen's 'Ole Lukøje' ('Ole the Eye-Closer', 1841). *Brewer's Dictionary of Phrase and Fable*, 18th edn. (London: Brewer's 2009), 1169, records 'The Sandman is here' as 'A playful remark addressed to children who are tired and "sleepy-eyed"'. Hoffmann's Sandman is a nightmare inversion of this figure.

5 *terror, indeed horror*: the distinction between 'terror' and 'horror' has been an important one in the aesthetics of the Gothic. 'Terror' is generally taken to be a sensation of dread or suspense, while 'horror' is one of disgust and revulsion. See the Introduction, p. xvi for an analysis of this distinction.

6 *Coppelius*: the character first appears as Coppelius and then as 'Coppola' (see note to p. 10).

10 *Piedmontese*: from Piedmont, a region of north-west Italy, bordering on France.

   Coppola: in Italian, a *coppola* is a peaked cap with a *visiera* (visor), but *coppo* is an archaic term for eye socket. The word is used in both linked senses (visor and eye socket) by Dante in the *Inferno*, canto 33: 'because the earliest tears a cluster form, | and, in the manner of a crystal visor | fill all the cup beneath the eyebrow full'.

13 *Spalanzani, like the famous naturalist*: Lazzaro Spalanzani (1729–99), Italian physiologist and naturalist, who did groundbreaking work on spermatozoa and the science of reproduction.

   Cagliostro: Giuseppe Balsamo (1743–95), or Count Alessandro di Cagliostro, celebrated Italian charlatan and impostor. He claimed to be a magician, healer, and alchemist, and travelled around Europe selling elixirs and love potions, and conducting high-society seances. Sentenced to death by the Inquisition, Cagliostro died in the fortress prison of San Leo in the Appenines.

   Chodowiecki: Daniel Chodowiecki (1726–1801), German artist and engraver, famous for his depictions of middle-class life.

15 *medias in res*: in medias res, 'in the midst things'. In his *Ars Poetica*, the Latin poet Horace (65–8 BC) recommends beginning epic narrative *in medias res* rather than *ab ovo* ('from the egg', from the beginning).

16 *Battoni's Mary Magdalen*: Pompeo Girolamo Batoni (1708–87), Italian neoclassical painter, famed for his historical and mythological studies. Batoni's *Mary Magdalene* was destroyed in the bombing of Dresden in 1945.

   Ruysdael: either Salomon van Ruysdael (1600–70) or his nephew Jacob (1628/9–82), both Dutch landscape artists.

22 *lorgnettes*: eyeglasses held in the hand, by a long handle.

23 '*Tre zecchini—three ducat!*': originating in Sicily, the ducat (*zecchino*) was a gold coin formerly in use throughout Europe. By the eighteenth century, 'ducat' had become a generic word for 'coin'.

24 *roulades*: 'a quick succession of notes, prop[erly] as sung to one syllable' (*OED*).

25 *cadenza*: 'a flourish given to a solo voice or instrument at the close, or between the divisions, of a movement' (*OED*).

26 *the legend of the dead bride*: in Goethe's poem 'Die Braut von Korinth' ('The Bride of Corinth', 1797), a vampire-bride returns to her lover from the dead.

28 *canzoni*: plural of *canzone*, 'a song resembling a madrigal, but less strict in style' (*OED*).

31 *Sapienti sat!*: 'enough for the wise', or 'a word to the wise is enough'.

WILLIAM MAGINN, *The Man in the Bell*

William Maginn (1794–1842), Irish writer and journalist. Born in Cork, Maginn entered Trinity College Dublin at the age of 11, where he had a distinguished academic career. Maginn was a regular contributor to the British periodical press in the early decades of the nineteenth century, and was particularly closely associated with *Blackwood's Edinburgh Magazine* and with *Fraser's Magazine*. His tendency towards scurrilous journalism resulted in several libel cases.

'The Man in the Bell' was first published anonymously in *Blackwood's Edinburgh Magazine*, 10/57 (Nov. 1821), 373–5. This is the version used here.

35 *chancel*: the eastern part of a church, where the clergyman officiates.

36 *a roc of the Arabian story-tellers*: the roc was a gigantic bird in Middle Eastern mythology. In the Fifth Voyage of Sinbad the Sailor, collected in *The Thousand and One Nights*, Sinbad's shipmates eat a roc egg, and his ship is attacked by these giant birds.

 Santon Barsisa: 'The History of Santon Barsisa' appeared in Richard Steele's journal *The Guardian*, 2/148 (Monday, 31 August 1713), 242–4, and tells of a holy man tempted into lust and murder by the Devil, to whom he forfeits his soul. The story was a major source for Matthew Lewis's Gothic classic *The Monk* (1796).

37 *The ancients have doomed . . . in their Tartarus . . . to annihilate him*: in one version of the Tantalus myth, recorded in Pindar's first *Olympian Ode* and elsewhere, Tantalus was punished by the gods by having a gigantic rock suspended above his head. Tartarus was the lowest part of Hades, the Greek underworld, where the gods imprisoned those who had displeased them.

 chimeras: in Greek myth, Bellerophon killed the chimera, a fire-breathing monster with a lion's head, a goat's body, and a serpent's tail. The word later came to mean 'A mere fancy, an unfounded conception' (*OED*): this is the sense in which it is used here.

38 *electric jar*: a Leyden jar—an electrical instrument probably first created in the University of Leiden by the physicist Pieter van Musschenbroek in 1746. The Leyden jar was used to store static electricity, which could then be used to deliver an electric shock.

39 *Alexander Selkirk, in Cowper's poem*: Alexander Selkirk (1676–1721), the Scottish sailor marooned for six years (1703–9) on Más a Tierra in the Juan Fernández islands in the Pacific Ocean, and a major source for Daniel Defoe's *Robinson Crusoe* (1719). William Cowper's (1731–1800) 'Verses Supposed to be Written by Alexander Selkirk, During his Solitary Abode in the Island of Juan Fernandez' (1782) opens with the line 'I am monarch of all I survey'. The reference here is to ll. 29–30: 'But the sound of the church-going bell | These vallies and rocks never heard.'

 Commander of the Faithful . . . Muezzin: 'Commander of the Faithful'

('Amīr al-Muʾminīn') is the title accorded an Islamic caliph. The muez-zin calls the faithful to prayer with his 'sonorous voice', rather than a bell.

JAMES HOGG, *George Dobson's Expedition to Hell*

James Hogg (*c*.1770–1835), Scottish novelist, poet, and short-story writer, sometimes known as 'The Ettrick Shepherd'. After befriending Sir Walter Scott, Hogg found fame as a poet and balladeer. He is now best known for the Gothic classic *The Private Memoirs and Confessions of a Justified Sinner* (1824). He was a regular contributor to *Blackwood's Edinburgh Magazine*, in which he published numerous stories of horror, folklore, and the supernatural.

'George Dobson's Expedition to Hell' (sometimes anthologized as 'The Expedition to Hell') was first published in *Blackwood's Edinburgh Magazine*, 12 (May 1827), 549–54, under the full title 'THE SHEPHERD'S CALENDAR.— BY THE ETTRICK SHEPHERD. DREAMS AND APPARITIONS. *Containing George Dobson's Expedition to Hell, and the Souters of Selkirk.*' Reprinted in *The Shepherd's Calendar* (Edinburgh: William Blackwood, and London: T. Cadell, 1829), 131–47. This is the text used here.

40 *no philosopher that ever wrote*: many philosophers have speculated about the provenance and meaning of dreams. Aristotle's (384–322 BC) treatise 'On Dreams' (one of the *Parva Naturalia* (*Short Treatises on Nature*)) may be the first recorded attempt at a materialist (rather than a proph-etic or supernatural) interpretation of dreams, which he believed to be sensory impressions filtered through sleep. It seems most likely here that Hogg is alluding to the ideas of René Descartes (1596–1650), whose 'Dream Argument' argued against trusting sensory perceptions as true judges of reality (since dreams often seem completely 'real').

He does not know what mind is: another likely allusion to Descartes, whose treatise *La Description du corps humain* (*Description of the Human Body*, 1647) famously argued for a dualism of material body and non-material mind: see also the observation on p. 41: 'there is no division between mat-ter and mind, but they are mingled together in a sort of chaos'.

whosoever can read his Bible, and solve a dream: there are many dream stor-ies in the Bible, invariably prophetic. The most famous biblical dreamer is probably Joseph, whose various dreams and interpretations of dreams are recorded in Genesis 40–1.

41 *When I was a shepherd*: Hogg worked as a shepherd and farm labourer after his father's bankruptcy *c*.1776.

42 *dickie*: driver's seat.

regular ticket: a ticket given on entry to a toll road; payment is made on presenting the ticket when leaving the road.

43 *ell*: a measure of length or distance. In England, an ell was 45 inches; in Scotland, 37.2 inches.

the Pleasance: a street in the Old Town of Edinburgh.

44 *his Majesty's license*: hackney licences were first granted in 1662, following the passing of 'An Ordinance for the Regulation of Hackney-coachmen in London and the places adjacent' by Parliament in 1654.

Roslin: or Rosslyn, 7 miles south of Edinburgh.

46 *bring in the Lord President to the Parliament House*: the Lord President of the Court of Session is the Chief Justice of Scotland. The Parliament House is near the Royal Mile in the Old Town of Edinburgh. Its oldest parts dating from 1639, it was home to the Scottish Parliament prior to the Act of Union of 1707.

maunna: must not (Scots).

47 *wha kens*: who knows? (Scots).

St Mary's Wynd: now St Mary's Street; turns south off High Street in Edinburgh Old Town, and turns into Pleasance.

48 *Wearmouth*: Sunderland, in the north-east of England. Wearmouth was the site of a landmark iron bridge, first constructed in 1796.

HONORÉ DE BALZAC, *La Grande Bretêche*

Honoré de Balzac (1799–1850), French novelist, dramatist, and short-story writer. *Les Chouans* (*The Chouans*, 1829) was the first novel in Balzac's enormous collection *La Comédie humaine* (*The Human Comedy*), a series comprised of ninety-one extant works, plus many more proposed or unfinished pieces. Balzac is now recognized as one of the greatest of European novelists, and a pioneering figure in literary realism. He died in Paris, possibly of exhaustion brought on by overwork.

'La Grande Bretêche' first appeared as one of *La Comédie humaine*'s 'Scènes de la vie privée' ('Scenes from private life') in 1832, later forming one of a series of stories and fragments collected together as *Autre étude de femme* (*Another Study of Woman*, 1842). The translation used here is by W. P. Trent, from *The Works of Honoré de Balzac*, v. *Eugénie Grandet* (New York: Thomas Y. Crowell, 1900).

49 *Chamfort . . . the Duc de Fronsac*: Chamfort was the pseudonym of the French writer and epigrammatist Sébastien-Roch Nicolas (1741–94). The duc de Fronsac was a title created in 1608, and revived in 1634 for Cardinal Richelieu. The last duc de Fronsac was Armand Emmanuel de Vignerot du Plessis (1766–1822).

Vendôme, on the banks of the Loir: Vendôme is a city in north-central France, in the Loir-et-Cher department. The River Loir runs through Vendôme on its way to joining the River Sarthe, which in turn feeds into the (much larger) River Loire. Balzac was educated at the Collège des Oratoriens at Vendôme from the ages of 8 to 14.

espaliers: frames for training ornamental shrubs or trees.

49 *purslane*: salad vegetable or herb with small flowers, often yellow.

50 *"Ultimam cogita."*: 'Consider the end', or 'Think on the last hour'; a common motto on sundials.

held in fief: held by the male line only.

51 *Atridæ*: in Greek mythology, the collective name for Agamemnon and Menelaus, the sons of Atreus.

the Commendatore's hand on Don Giovanni's neck: in Act II of Mozart's opera *Don Giovanni* (1787), the gigantic statue of the Commendatore (Knight Commander) comes to life, and drags Don Giovanni down to hell.

52 *Il bondo cani*: a cryptic reference, though Balzac's source here seems to be François-Adrien Boieldieu's opera *Le Calife de Bagdad* (*The Caliph of Baghdad*, 1800), an adaptation of 'Albondukani', one of the tales from *The Thousand and One Nights*, in which the Caliph takes a beggar-woman for his wife.

testatrix: a woman who dies leaving a will.

the number of doors and windows to assess the taxes: a window tax operated in France from 1798 to 1926.

Restoration: in this context, a reference to the restoration of the French Bourbon monarchy in 1814, after the fall of Napoleon, though also with overtones of 'Reinstatement in the favour of God, or to a prelapsarian state of innocence; salvation, redemption' (*OED*).

53 *Sterne's charming passion . . . his hobby-horse*: in Laurence Sterne's great anti-novel *Tristram Shandy* (1759–67), Uncle Toby's hobby horse (obsession) is restaging battles and military campaigns on his bowling green, with the aid of his servant, Corporal Trim.

licensed by the Keeper of the Seals: licensed to practise law. In France, 'Keeper of the Seals' is a title given to the Minister of Justice.

54 *the Sacrament*: the Last Rites, given to a dying Catholic.

Argand lamp: an oil lamp for domestic use, invented in 1780 by Aimé Argand.

tester: a canopy over a bed.

'Imitation of Christ': influential devotional book by (or attributed to) Thomas à Kempis (*c.*1380–1471), emphasizing the importance of spiritual over material life.

56 *codicil*: a supplement to a will.

57 *Radcliffe*: Ann Radcliffe (1764–1823), influential English Gothic novelist, best known for *The Mysteries of Udolpho* (1794).

Fleming: a native of Flanders, the Dutch-speaking northern part of Belgium.

Teniers: there are three Flemish artists called David Teniers (father, son, and grandson), but this reference is probably to David Teniers the Younger (1610–90), celebrated for his scenes of peasant life.

Picardy: a region of northern France.

58 *chatter-mags*: chatterboxes; compulsive talkers.

when the Emperor sent the Spaniards here, prisoners of war and others: a reference to the Franco-Spanish Peninsular War of 1807–14, part of the Napoleonic Wars, in which the French battled against the British, Spanish, and Portuguese for control of the Iberian Peninsula.

59 *breviary*: 'in the Roman Catholic Church, the book containing the "Divine Office" for the day, which those who are in orders are bound to recite' (*OED*).

doubloons: double-sided gold Spanish coins.

62 *the invasion of France*: in the summer of 1813, Wellington's British forces invaded Napoleonic France, culminating in heavy French defeats in the Battle of the Pyrenees (25–8 July).

EDGAR ALLAN POE, *Berenice—A Tale*

Edgar Allan Poe (1809–49), America's greatest Gothic writer, and a pioneering figure in the history of detective fiction and science fiction. Poe specialized in short fiction, a form in which his influence has been enormous, but also wrote poetry, literary essays, and one novel, *The Narrative of Arthur Gordon Pym of Nantucket* (1838). He died under mysterious circumstances on 7 October 1849 in his adopted city of Baltimore, Maryland.

The publication history of 'Berenice' is very complex. The story was first published as 'Berenice—A Tale' in the *Southern Literary Messenger*, 1/7 (Mar. 1835). Reprinted, with some material removed, in the first edition of *Tales of the Grotesque and Arabesque* (Philadelphia: Lean and Blanchard, 1840), ii. 167–81. Reprinted again, with a further four paragraphs removed, in the *Broadway Journal* (5 Apr. 1845), i. 217–19; and again, with an added epigraph (see notes below) and some further amendments, in *The Works of the Late Edgar Allan Poe*, ed. Rufus Wilmot Griswold, 4 vols. (New York: J. S. Redfield, 1850–6), i. 437–45. Poe agreed to change the story after complaints about its gruesomeness to the *Southern Literary Messenger*, writing to its editor, T. W. White, on 30 April 1835: 'The subject is far too horrible. . . . The Tale originated in a bet that I could produce nothing effective on a subject so singular, provided I treated it seriously. . . . I allow that it approaches the very verge of bad-taste—but I will not sin so egregiously again' (*The Collected Works of Edgar Allan Poe*, ii. *Tales and Sketches*, ed. Thomas Ollive Mabbott (Cambridge, Mass., and London: The Belknap Press of Harvard University Press, 1978), 207). Mabbott, Poe's most authoritative editor, agrees with this judgement: 'Yet even in its present form, from which four unpleasant paragraphs of the earlier versions were wisely omitted by the author, many readers find the tale too repulsive by far' (*Collected Works of Poe*, ed. Mabbott, ii. 207). The bet on the 'subject so singular' seems likely to have originated from a story in the *Baltimore Saturday Visiter* (23 Feb. 1833), about the 'robbing of graves for the sake of obtaining human teeth': see Lucille King, 'Notes on Poe's Sources', *University of Texas Studies in English*, 10 (1930), 128–34. (Poe's first published story, 'MS Found in a Bottle', appeared in the *Baltimore Saturday Visiter* (19 Oct. 1833).) This edition reproduces the full text of Poe's 1835 original in all its gruesome, 'bad-taste' glory.

67 *I have a tale to tell . . . feelings than of facts*: this sentence does not appear in editions from 1845 onwards.

Egæus: Egeus is the name of Hermia's father in *A Midsummer Night's Dream*. Mabbott suggests the name was chosen because Shakespeare's Egeus 'failed to understand love' (*Collected Works of Poe*, ed. Mabbott, ii. 208).

68 *Berenice*: the name is Greek for 'bearer of victory'. There have been a number of notable Berenices, including several of the wives of the Ptolemaic pharaohs of Egypt (3rd–1st century BC), and a number of Herodian queens of Judaea (1st century AD). St Veronica, or Berenice, gave her veil to Christ to wipe his forehead as he carried his cross: the image of his face became imprinted on the veil, which subsequently became an important part of Roman Catholic iconography (known as the 'Vernicle'). Pierre Corneille's tragedy *Tite et Bérénice* (1670) and Jean Racine's tragedy *Bérénice* (also 1670) both recount the doomed love of the Roman Emperor Titus for the Judaean Princess Berenice of Cilicia, daughter of Herod Agrippa (10 BC–AD 44). Handel's opera *Berenice, Queen of Egypt* was written in 1709 and first performed in 1737. The Harvard edition of Poe's *Collected Works* renders the name as 'Berenicë', which may point to Poe's intended pronunciation: 'In Poe's day Berenice was pronounced as four syllables, and rhyming with "very spicy"' (*Collected Works of Poe*, ed. Mabbott, ii. 208).

Sylph . . . Arnheim . . . Naiad: a sylph is a spirit of the air, a naiad is a water-nymph. Poe found the name 'Arnheim' in Sir Walter Scott's *Anne of Geierstein* (1829)—it is the name of the Swiss estate of the counts of Geierstein. Poe also wrote a short story entitled 'The Domain of Arnheim' (1847). See John Robert Moore, 'Poe's Reading of *Anne of Geierstein*', *American Literature*, 22 (Jan. 1951), 493–6.

Simoom: a scorching, suffocating Saharan sand-wind; from the Arabic 'to poison'. Later editions of the story have the variant spelling 'simoon'.

69 *monomaniac*: one who is fixated to the point of insanity on a single subject; monomania was a favourite theme of Poe's.

70 *incitamentum*: the incentive or stimulus.

Cælius Secundus Curio 'de . . . Dei': Caelius Secundus Curio (1503–69), Italian Protestant nobleman and thinker, author of *De amplitudine beati regni Dei* (*On the Great Extent of God's Blessed Kingdom*, 1554). Influenced by the Swiss Reformation theologian Ulrich Zwingli, Curio believed that virtuous heathens could be granted access to the kingdom of heaven, and that therefore the saved would outnumber the damned. Poe seems to have got this from Isaac D'Israeli's essay 'Hell': 'Cælius Secundus Curio, a noble Italian, published a treatise *De Amplitudine beati Regni Dei*, to prove that *Heaven* has more inhabitants than *Hell*,—or in his own phrase, that "the *elect* are more numerous than the *reprobate*"'. *The Works of Isaac Disraeli* (London: Routledge, 1858), i. 205.

St Austin . . . 'City of God': The City of God (*De civitate Dei*), AD 413–26, by St Augustine of Hippo (AD 354–430), Church Father and enormously influential theologian.

Tertullian . . . 'Mortuus . . . impossibile est': Tertullian was a Church Father and theologian (AD 160–225). The 'unintelligible' (that is, paradoxical) Latin quotation translates as 'The Son of God has died, it is to be believed because it is incredible; and, buried, He is risen, it is sure because it is impossible', from *De Carne Christi* (*On the Flesh of Christ*, AD 202–8). Mabbott (*Collected Works of Poe*, ii. 220) believes that Poe may have read this in 'Marginalia' 151, *Graham's Magazine* (Mar. 1846), 117.

Ptolemy Hephestion . . . Asphodel: Ptolemaeus Chennus (1st–2nd century AD), Greek grammarian, author of several lost works, whose writings only survive in the account given of them by the Byzantine Patriarch Photius (AD *c*.810–*c*.893), who criticizes Ptolemy for his credulity and error. The relevant passage is from *Bibliotheca*, codex 190: 'He speaks of the Palladium which Diomedes and Odysseus went together to steal, of the reed which repeated that Midas had the ears of an ass, of the acestalian birds which were sought in Stesichorus, of the raft of Gigo which is at the edge of the Ocean, which can only be moved with an asphodel and remains immovable by force.' Ptolemy Hephestion is also mentioned near the beginning of Poe's scientific fantasia *Eureka* (1848): 'let me beg the reader's attention to an extract or two from a somewhat remarkable letter, which appears to have been found corked in a bottle and floating on the Mare Tenebrarum—an ocean well described by the Nubian geographer, Ptolemy Hephestion' (*The Science Fiction of Edgar Allan Poe*, ed. Harold Beaver (London and Harmondsworth: Penguin, 1976), 212). *Asphodel* was the flower of the dead, which according to Homer covered the meadow of the dead in the underworld. Poe may have encountered this story in Jacob Bryant's *A New System; or, An Analysis of Antient Mythology*, 3rd edn. (London: J. Walker, 1807), v. 204: 'Ptolemy Hephæstion mentions a large stone upon the borders of the ocean, probably near Gades in Bœtica, which he calls Petra Gignina: and says, that it could be moved with a blade of grass.' If so, he went back to Photius' original, or also read another version, as Bryant's account omits the reference to asphodel.

71 *Halcyon*: the Halcyon Days are, according to Greek mythology, the seven days in winter during which storms never occur. These days are named for Alcyone, daughter of Aeolus, who, according to Ovid's *Metamorphoses*,

threw herself from a boat to escape Zeus' wrath, and was transformed into a kingfisher. During the Halcyon Days, kingfishers were reputed to lay their eggs.

71 *Simonides*: Greek poet (7th century AD) whose work survives only in fragments excerpted by other writers. Poe took this quotation directly from Robert Bland's *Translations Chiefly from the Greek Anthology, with Tales and Miscellaneous Poems* (London: Richard Phillips, 1806), 117, and also used it in an early version of his story 'Morella'.

72 *spectrum*: Smith's *Latin–English Dictionary* (1855) defines *spectrum* as 'A visible form; an image of something seen, continuing after the eyes are closed, covered or turned away. This is called an ocular spectrum.'

Mad'selle Sallé: Marie Sallé (1707–56), French dancer and choreographer. '*Que tous ses pas etoient des sentiments*': 'That her every step was a sentiment.' Mabbott (*Collected Works of Poe*, ii. 221) traces the quotation to Louis Fuzelier's 'Prologue' to the ballet *Les Festes grecques et romaines* (*Greek and Roman Festivals*, 1723), published in *Reçueil general des opéras* (*General Anthology of Operas*, 1734), vol. xiii. Poe picked up the quotation from Baron Jakob Friedrich Bielfeld's *Les Premiers Traits de l'erudition universelle* (*The Most Important Characteristics of Universal Wisdom*, Leiden: Chés Sam and Jean Luchtmans, 1776), 300. (Bielfeld's work also provides the epigraph to his story 'Bon-Bon'.)

que tous ses dents etoient des idées: 'that all her teeth were ideas'. Versions from 1845 follow this with the sentences '*Des idées!*—ah, here was the idiotic thought that destroyed me! *Des idées!*—ah, *therefore* it was that I coveted them so madly! I felt that their possession could alone ever restore me to peace, in giving me back to reason.'

73 *phantasma*: an illusion, apparition, or spectre.

Berenice was—no more: the beautiful dead woman is Poe's favourite subject, recurring in 'Morella', 'The Fall of the House of Usher', 'The Raven', 'Ligeia', 'Annabel Lee', and elsewhere. In his essay 'The Philosophy of Composition', Poe made it the cornerstone of his aesthetics: 'the death, then, of a beautiful woman is, unquestionably, the most poetical topic in the world' (Poe, *Selected Writings*, ed. G. R. Thompson (New York and London: W. W. Norton, 2004), 680).

74 *With a heart full of grief . . . mystery, and death*: these four 'bad-taste' paragraphs were removed from the 1845 and subsequent versions.

Ebn Zaiat: Mabbott (*Collected Works*, ii. 219) identifies Ebn Zaiat, or Ben Zaiat, as the Baghdad grammarian and poet Abou Giafar Mohammed ben Abdalmalek ben Abban (d. *c.*AD 208), and suggests that Poe got the reference from Barthélemy d'Herbelot's *Bibliothèque orientale* (1697). In later versions, Poe uses this quotation as the epigraph to the story.

75 *still alive!*: premature burial due to narcolepsy is another of Poe's favourite subjects: see, for example, 'The Fall of the House of Usher' and 'The Premature Burial'.

J. SHERIDAN LE FANU, *Strange Event in the Life of Schalken the Painter*

Joseph Sheridan Le Fanu (1814–73), Irish writer and journalist. Born in Dublin, Le Fanu attended Trinity College, where he became involved in the *Dublin University Magazine*, of which he later became proprietor, and which published many of his stories. A major figure in the Victorian Gothic tradition, Le Fanu is best known for the sensation novel *Uncle Silas* (1864), and for *In a Glass Darkly* (1872), a collection of interlinked stories which includes the influential lesbian vampire tale 'Carmilla' and the frequently anthologized 'Green Tea'. Le Fanu's *Dublin University Magazine* stories were posthumously published in three volumes as the *Purcell Papers* (1880).

'Strange Event in the Life of Schalken the Painter' was first published in the *Dublin University Magazine* (May 1839). Substantially rewritten for publication in *Ghost Stories and Tales of Mystery* (Dublin: James McGlashan, 1851), where it was simply entitled 'Schalken the Painter'. The version used here is from volume ii of the *Purcell Papers* (London: Richard Bentley, 1880), which returns to the original *Dublin University Magazine* text. There are good reasons for preferring the *Purcell Papers* text. Its opening, in particular, is sharper and more concise. Furthermore, W. J. McCormack, Le Fanu's most authoritative critic, has argued that, taken as a whole, the *Purcell Papers* gain a contextual political meaning. McCormack suggests that 'Schalken', like all of the *Purcell Papers*, and many of Le Fanu's other works, reflects its author's unease, as a member of the Anglo-Irish Protestant Ascendancy class, with the implications of political Catholicism in Ireland. See McCormack, *Sheridan Le Fanu and Victorian Ireland* (Oxford: Clarendon Press, 1980), 76–8. Apart from the opening paragraph, I do not here discuss the textual differences between the 1851 and 1880 versions. They are so different that doing this would mean, in effect, reproducing both texts in parallel.

76 [*Title*]: Godfried Schalcken (1643–1706), Dutch painter celebrated for his portraits and their atmospheric use of light, and particularly candlelight. It is probable that Le Fanu consulted Michael Bryan's *Dictionary of Painters and Engravers* (1812–16) for information about Schalken. Bryan writes: 'His small portraits were very popular, and he had painted the principal families at Dordrecht, when he was encouraged, by the extraordinary success of [Godfrey] Kneller, to visit England. Here, however, his success was small. There was no room for him. His manners, too, were against him, and many stories of his boorishness are told by the old writers. On his return to Holland, he settled at the Hague, where he continued to practise his art with success until his death in 1706. The chief merit of Schalken consists in the neatness of his finishing, and the perfect intelligence of his chiaro-scuro' (*Bryan's Dictionary of Painters and Engravers*, v (New York: Macmillan, 1905), 32).

the late Francis Purcell, P.P. of Drumcoolagh: the *Purcell Papers* take the form of a collection of tales gathered together by an antiquarian Catholic Priest. The opening to 'The Ghost and the Bone-Setter', the first story, introduces Purcell: 'In looking over the papers of my late valued and respected friend, Francis Purcell, who for nearly fifty years discharged the arduous duties of a parish priest in the south of Ireland, I met with the following document. It is one of many such; for he was a curious and industrious collector of old local traditions—a community in which the quarter where he resided mightily abounded. The collection and arrangement of such legends was, as long as I can remember him, his hobby; but I had never learned that his love of the marvellous and whimsical had carried him so far as to prompt him to commit the results of his inquiries to writing, until, in the character of residuary legatee, his will put me in possession of all his manuscript papers. To such as may think the composing of such productions as these inconsistent with the character and habits of a country priest, it is necessary to observe, that there did exist a race of priests—those of the old school, a race now nearly extinct—whose education abroad tended to produce in them tastes more literary than have yet been evinced by the *alumni* of Maynooth' (*Purcell Papers*, i. 1-2). The Royal College of St Patrick, the Catholic seminary at Maynooth, County Kildare, was founded in 1795. Prior to that, Irish priests tended to be trained at the English Jesuit College at Saint-Omer in northern France. Purcell's cosmopolitanism reflects Le Fanu's anxiety regarding Irish Catholicism, as by the time of first writing in 1839, the majority of Irish priests studied at Maynooth. P.P. is a Parish Priest; Drumcoolagh is a fictitious Irish parish.

76 *You will no doubt . . . the following narrative*: the 1851 text opens with the following paragraph, which is indicative of the difference between the two versions: 'There exists, at this moment, in good preservation, a remarkable work of Schalken's. The curious management of its light constitutes, as usual in his pieces, the chief apparent merit of the picture. I say *apparent*, for in its subject and not its handling, however exquisite, consists its real value. The picture represents the interior of what might be a chamber in some antique religious building; and its foreground is occupied by a female figure, in a species of white robe, part of which is arranged so as to form a veil. The dress however is not that of any religious order. In her hand she bears a lamp, by which alone her figure and face are illuminated; and her features wear such an arch smile as well becomes a pretty woman when practising some prankish roguery; in the back ground, and, excepting where the dim red light of an expiring fire serves to define the form, in total shadow, stands the figure of a man dressed in the old Flemish fashion, in an attitude of alarm, his hand being placed on the hilt of his sword, which he appears to be in the act of drawing.'

King William . . . Irish campaigns: King William III (William of Orange) overthrew the Catholic King James II in the 'Glorious Revolution' of 1688, and was crowned in 1689. With the assistance of the French, James consolidated his forces in Ireland, leading to the Williamite War of 1689–91, sparked off by the besieging of Derry by the Jacobite (Catholic) army in December 1688. Jacobite forces suffered a serious defeat at the Battle of the Boyne (July 1690) and a decisive one at the Battle of Aughrim (July 1691), finally surrendering after the Siege of Limerick, which ended in October 1691.

77 *doublet*: 'a close-fitting body-garment, with or without sleeves, worn by men from the 14th to the 18th centuries' (*OED*).

Gerard Douw: Gerrit Dou (1633–75), Dutch painter who studied under Rembrandt, celebrated for his use of candlelight and *chiaroscuro* (the artistic technique of strong contrasts between light and dark). As the story suggests, Godfried Schalcken was one of his pupils. *Bryan's Dictionary of Painters and Engravers*, Le Fanu's probable source, says of Dou: 'That he was a prosperous man is to be inferred from the large sums for which he sold his paintings. The wealthy connoisseur Van Spiring gave Dou an annual donation of a thousand florins merely to be allowed to have the first choice of the pictures that the artist had completed at the close of every year. Besides this annual grant, Van Spiring paid the ordinary price like any other purchaser for the pictures which he chose' (ii. 84–5). There seems to be some foundation, then, for Le Fanu's portrayal of Dou's cupidity.

78 *mien*: facial expression.

79 *St Anthony*: St Anthony of Egypt (*c*.AD 251–356), monk and desert hermit, whose asceticism and piety were challenged by the Devil in a long series of temptations and torments, including a theological debate with a satyr and a centaur. The temptation of St Anthony has been a popular subject for artistic representation, from Hieronymus Bosch to Salvador Dalí.

80 *beaver*: hat made of beaver fur.

Mynher: Mynheer, Dutch for 'My lord', a title conveying respectability. Often used as a generic term for 'Dutchman'.

82 *Stadhouse*: stadhuis, Dutch for town hall.

horologe: timepiece.

burgomaster: mayor or other town official.

Leyden: or Leiden; city in the southern Netherlands.

stadholder: Stadhouder, 'lieutenant', or 'steward' in administrative charge of a Dutch province.

Rhenish: wine from the Rhinelands, in modern Germany, Belgium, and Netherlands.

84 *rix-dollars*: generic English term for European silver currency.

church of St Lawrence: Grote of Sint-Laurenskerk, a landmark medieval church in Rotterdam, built from 1449.

90 *Boom-quay*: Le Fanu's source here may be the 'Journal of a Visit to Holland', *Edinburgh Magazine*, 84 (1819), 218: 'On reaching Rotterdam,

we proceed to the Bath, an English house upon the Boom Quay. This Boom Quay forms a most beautiful walk on the banks of the river, about a mile in length; the houses being shaded by a row of stupendous elm trees.'

90 *levity*: in this context, fickleness or inconstancy.

94 *polemic*: an aggressive religious controversialist.

NATHANIEL HAWTHORNE, *The Birth-Mark*

Nathaniel Hawthorne (1804–64), major American novelist and short-story writer, best known for *The Scarlet Letter* (1850). Many of Hawthorne's best works, such as *The Scarlet Letter* or 'Young Goodman Brown', deal with America's Puritan legacy, often using the medium of allegory or fable. 'The Birth-Mark' is one of several Hawthorne stories (others include 'Rappaccini's Daughter' and 'Dr Heidegger's Experiment') which are nightmare fantasies of scientific experimentation.

'The Birth-Mark' was first published in *The Pioneer* (March 1843). Reprinted in Hawthorne's collection *Mosses from an Old Manse* (1846). This is the text used here.

99 *the comparatively recent discovery of electricity*: researches into electricity date back to classical antiquity, though much pioneering modern work on electricity was done across the eighteenth century, by figures such as Benjamin Franklin (1706–90), Luigi Galvani (1737–98), and Alessandro Volta (1745–1827).

100 *Eve of Powers*: Hiram Powers (1805–73), American sculptor resident in Florence, best known for *The Greek Slave* (1843), exhibited to much acclaim in the Great Exhibition of 1851. *Eve Tempted* (1842), the statue to which Hawthorne refers here, now stands in the Smithsonian Museum, Washington DC, as does *Eve Disconsolate* (1855–61). Hawthorne met Powers when he visited Florence in June 1858.

101 *ineludible*: that which cannot be escaped.

bass relief: bas-relief, 'Sculpture or carved work in which the figures project less than one half of their true proportions from the background' (*OED*).

102 *Aminadab*: Brian Harding suggests that 'Aminadab' is 'an anagram for bad-in-man, or bad anima' (Hawthorne, *Young Goodman Brown and Other Tales*, ed. Brian Harding (Oxford and New York: Oxford University Press, 1987), 364).

103 *Pygmalion*: in Ovid's *Metamorphoses* (AD 8), King Pygmalion carves an ivory statue which he names Galatea, and with which he falls in love. The goddess Venus brings the statue to life. Famously, the subject of a 1913 play by George Bernard Shaw (1856–1950).

from the dark bosom of the earth: Aylmer was originally a geologist. Following the theories and discoveries of James Hutton (1726–97),

John Playfair (1748–1819), Georges Cuvier (1769–1832), and most particularly Charles Lyell's (1797–1875) *Principles of Geology* (1830–3), whose formulation of geological 'deep time' laid some of the theoretical groundwork for Darwin's theory of natural selection, geology was *the* cutting-edge scientific endeavour of the first half of the nineteenth century.

104 *pastil*: pastille, a small roll of aromatic paste, burned as a deodorizer or disinfectant.

105 *magic circle*: here and elsewhere in the second half of the story, Aylmer is represented more as a magician or alchemist than as a scientist (though historically these categories tended to overlap). Alfred S. Reid has persuasively suggested that Aylmer is closely modelled on the Renaissance courtier, philosopher, and magician-scientist (and cookery writer) Sir Kenelm Digby (1603–65), author of *Of the Nature of Bodies* and *Of the Nature of Mans Soule* (both 1644). Like Aylmer, Digby allegedly killed his wife (with a draught of 'viper-wine') when conducting experiments upon her to perfect her beauty. See Reid, 'Hawthorne's Humanism: "The Birthmark" and Sir Kenelm Digby', *American Literature*, 38/3 (1966), 337–51. Digby's posthumous recipe-book, *The Closet of the Eminently Learned Sir Kenelme Digbie Kt. Opened* (1669), contains a recipe for *aqua mirabilis*, which 'conserveth Youth, & procureth a good Colour: If this be given to one dying, a spoonful of it reviveth him', and for a 'beautifying Water . . . [which] smooths, whitens, beautifies & preserves the Complexion of Ladies' (Reid, 'Hawthorne's Humanism', 338).

106 *effected by rays of light striking upon a polished plate of metal*: Aylmer seems here to have pre-empted the invention of daguerreotype photography, a process actually invented in the 1830s by Louis-Jacques-Mandé Daguerre and Nicéphore Niépce.

elixir vitæ: elixir of life, which conveyed immortality. Discovering the *elixir vitæ* was one of the great goals of alchemy.

nostrum: a medical potion prepared by the person who recommends it; often taken to mean quack medicine.

108 *Albertus Magnus . . . Brazen Head*: all these figures are medieval and Renaissance alchemists and magi. Albertus Magnus (*c.*1200–80) was a German theologian, natural scientist, and teacher of Thomas Aquinas. According to popular legend, Albertus was an alchemist who discovered the philosopher's stone, the means of transforming base metal into gold. Cornelius Agrippa (Heinrich Cornelius Agrippa von Nettesheim, 1486–1535), physician, philosopher, and occultist, author of *De occulta philosophia* (*Occult Philosophy*, 3 vols., 1531–3). Cornelius Agrippa is a major source for the Faust legend—the scientist who sells his soul to the Devil for forbidden knowledge. Paracelsus (Philippus Aureolus Theophrastus Bombastus von Hohenheim, 1493–1541), German-Swiss physician, metallurgist, and alchemist. The 'famous friar who created the prophetic Brazen Head' is Roger Bacon (*c.*1220–92), English philosopher

and scientist, who did important work on optics. According to legend, Bacon constructed a giant brass head which was endowed with the gift of prophecy. Left in the care of Bacon's assistant, the head uttered the phrases 'Time is', 'Time was', and 'Time is passed', before falling on the floor and breaking to pieces.

108 *Transactions of the Royal Society*: the *Philosophical Transactions of the Royal Society* is a major scientific journal founded by the Royal Society of London in 1665. Reid ('Hawthorne's Humanism', 339) notes that Kenelm Digby was one of the charter fellows of the Royal Society.

109 *electrical machine*: a machine for producing electricity, an electrostatic generator. These were pioneered across the eighteenth century, with the invention of Johann Carl Wilcke's electrophorus ('electricity bearer', 1762) and Abraham Bennet's electroscope (1787). Cinematic representations have made the electrical machine a central component of the mad scientist's laboratory, with a panoply of colourful devices including the Wimshurst Machine (1880–3), the Tesla Coil (1891), and the Van de Graaff Generator (1929).

110 *thou man of clay*: see Isaiah 45: 9: 'Woe unto him that striveth with his Maker! Let the potsherd *strive* with the potsherds of the earth. Shall the clay say unto him that fashioneth it, What makest thou? or thy work, He hath no hands?' This is a reference to human mortality, then, and the vanity of usurping the creative power of God. 'Man of clay' may also refer here to the Jewish legend of the Golem, a clay figure infused with the spark of life, most famously in the story of Rabbi Judah Löw ben Bezulel's (*c*.1520–1609) creation of a golem to defend the Jews of the Prague Ghetto.

112 *geranium*: Reid ('Hawthorne's Humanism', 339–40) notes that one of Kenelm Digby's experiments was 'an attempt to restore to "living ver-dure" a dying geranium'.

HERMAN MELVILLE, *The Tartarus of Maids*

Herman Melville (1819–91), one of the greatest American novelists, born in New York to a family who had played notable roles in the American Revolution. Melville signed up on board the whaling ship *Acushnet* in 1841, and his experiences as a whaler and seaman from 1841 to 1844 were to inform many of his most important works, including *Typee* (1846), *Omoo* (1847), his masterpiece *Moby-Dick* (1851), and the posthumously published *Billy Budd* (1924).

'The Tartarus of Maids' was first published in *Harper's New Monthly Magazine* (April 1855), along with a companion piece, 'The Paradise of Bachelors', set amongst the lawyers of Temple Bar in London (and referred to several times in 'Tartarus'). Reprinted in *The Apple-Tree Table and Other Sketches*, ed. Henry Chapin (Princeton: Princeton University Press, 1922). This is the text used here.

115 [*Title*]: For 'Tartarus', see note to p. 37.

Woedolor Mountain: like all the place names in the opening part of the story, this is fictitious and obviously allegorical.

Gulf Stream: the North Atlantic Ocean current, discovered by Juan Ponce de Léon (1460–1521), the Spanish explorer who went in search of the Fountain of Youth, and later mapped by Benjamin Franklin.

hopper-shaped: a hopper is the cone into which grain is poured to be ground in a mill.

Plutonian: belonging to the underworld. Pluto is the Roman form of Hades, god of the underworld.

116 *Thurmberg*: Maus Castle, a fourteenth-century castle on the banks of the Rhine, Germany.

pung: 'a one-horse sleigh or sledge used in New England' (*OED*).

petrification: or petrifaction–a fossil, or something turned to stone.

118 *the ancient arch of Wren*: Temple Bar Gate, London, constructed 1669–72, and now standing at the entrance to Paternoster Square near St Paul's Cathedral.

Temple Church: twelfth-century church near Fleet Street, London, built for the Knights Templar, and now used by the Inns of Court.

119 *breeching*: a leather strap around the thighs of a carthorse, enabling it to push backwards.

dread-naught: a thick winter coat.

120 *tippet*: a fur or woollen neck or shoulder garment.

Actæon: Greek hunter who accidentally saw the goddess Artemis bathing, and was turned into a stag and torn to pieces by his own hounds.

Cupid: Roman version of Eros, the god of love; son of Mercury and Venus. Often depicted as a boy carrying a bow and arrow.

121 *East India-man*: 'East Indiaman' was a name given to merchant ships operating under licence from the East India Company, carrying cargo and passengers, roughly from the seventeenth to the nineteenth centuries.

pale chee—paper, I mean: the pale cheeks here reflect the paper and the snow, as a symbol for dehumanizing mechanical labour. Melville's overarching concern with the symbolic significance of whiteness reached its zenith in the chapter 'The Whiteness of the Whale', in *Moby-Dick*: 'This elusive quality it is, which causes the thought of whiteness, when divorced from more kindly associations, and coupled with any object terrible in itself, to heighten that terror to the furthest bounds' (Melville, *Redburn, White-Jacket, Moby-Dick*, ed. G. Thomas Tanselle (New York: Library of America, 1983), 994).

snath: the shaft of a scythe.

Leghorn: Livorno, port city on the coast of Tuscany, Italy.

122 *Bachelor's Buttons*: cornflowers; in folklore, worn by young men in love.

123 *albuminous part of an egg*: the white of an egg.

    germinous: capable of germination, of putting out shoots—this links to the narrator's profession as a seed-merchant.

124 *foolscap*: standard-sized writing paper, 17 × 13.5 inches, so called because of the jester's cap formerly used as a watermark on such paper.

125 *John Locke*: English utilitarian philosopher (1632–1704). Locke's *Essay Concerning Human Understanding* (1690) maintained that there were no innate or inherent ideas—rather, human beings were born as a *tabula rasa*, a blank slate or sheet, upon which the experience of life wrote itself, thus forming our characters.

    Behemoth: a gigantic creature. See Job 40: 15-18: 'Behold now behemoth, which I made with thee. He eateth grass as an ox. | Lo now, his strength *is* in his loins, and his force *is* in the navel of his belly. | He moveth his tail like a cedar: the sinews of his stones are wrapped together. | His bones *are as* strong as pieces of brass; his bones *are* like bars of iron.'

126 *Saint Veronica*: see note to p. 68.

FITZ-JAMES O'BRIEN, *What Was It?*

Fitz-James O'Brien (1828–62), Irish-American short-story writer, poet, and bohemian, dubbed 'the Celtic Poe'. Born in Cork, O'Brien squandered his inheritance in London, then emigrated to New York, where he befriended Walt Whitman and began to publish regularly in the periodical press. He enlisted as a Union soldier in the American Civil War, and died of his wounds during active service.

    'What Was It?' was first published as 'What Was It?: A Mystery' (*Harper's New Monthly Magazine*, 18/106 (Mar. 1859), 504–9). Reprinted in *The Poems and Stories of Fitz-James O'Brien*, ed. William Winter (Boston: James R. Osgood and Company, 1881), 390–407. This is the text used here.

128 *Twenty-sixth Street, in New York*: the house's location on 26th Street, between 7th and 8th Avenues, places it in what is today the fashionable Chelsea district of downtown Manhattan. The original *Harper's Monthly* text has 'in this city' rather than 'in New York'.

129 *balusters*: 'the uprights which support the handrail of a staircase' (*OED*).

    Bleecker Street: runs through Greenwich Village, Manhattan, south of Chelsea.

    the Hudson: river marking the western boundary of Manhattan Island.

    Weehawken: on the west bank of the Hudson River, in New Jersey; now connected to Manhattan by the Lincoln Tunnel.

    Mrs Crowe's 'Night Side of Nature': Catherine Crowe (1790–1872), English writer, noted for her novels and ghost stories. *The Night Side of Nature; or, Ghosts and Ghost Seers*, 2 vols. (London: T. C. Newby, 1848) was an extremely influential compendium of supernatural tales and folk-lore, with a long chapter on 'Haunted Houses' (ii. 64–146).

130 *had once written a story . . . ghost*: the original *Harper's Monthly* text identifies the story as 'The Pot of Tulips', an actual O'Brien story, first published in *Harper's New Monthly Magazine*, 11/66 (Nov. 1855), 8087–8114. Like 'What Was It?', 'The Pot of Tulips' is a haunted-house story set in New York.

asseverated: declared solemnly or emphatically.

potations: drinks; specifically, in this context, alcoholic drinks.

the drug of paradise: the veiled allusion here is to Samuel Taylor Coleridge's (1772–1834) opium-induced masterpiece 'Kubla Khan': 'For he on honeydew hath fed, | And drunk the milk of paradise.'

131 *'Tempest,' . . . Ariel . . . Caliban*: the *Harper's* original mistakenly has the spirit Ariel and the monstrous Caliban as characters from Shakespeare's *A Midsummer Night's Dream*.

Guebers: in the *Harper's* original, 'Gebers'. There are two Gebers, both scientists and, importantly, alchemists: the Persian chemist and natural philosopher Abū Mūsā Jābir ibn Hayyān (*c*.721–*c*.815), and the 13th–14th-century Spanish chemist known as Geber (named in honour of Jābir ibn Hayyān), one of the founding figures of European alchemy, who has been identified as a Franciscan monk, Paul of Taranto.

rana arborea: the tree frog, a native of South rather than North America.

meerschaums: pipes made of the white mineral sepiolite, often elaborately carved; frequently Turkish in origin.

like the nut in the fairy tale: a reference to E. T. A. Hoffmann's story 'The Nutcracker' (1816), famously turned into a ballet by Tchaikovsky in 1892. In the story, Princess Pirlipat is cursed with ugliness by the Queen of the Mice, and the only cure is to find a magic nut.

Haroun: the Caliph Hārūn al-Rashīd (*c*.776–809), opulent ruler of Baghdad celebrated in *The Thousand and One Nights*. Jābir ibn Hayyān (see above) was an alchemist in his court.

Black afreets . . . the copper vessel: an afreet (or efreet) is a jinn (genie). The reference here is to the story of 'The Fisherman and the Jinni' in *The Thousand and One Nights*: a poor fisherman finds a copper jar carrying the seal of Solomon in his net; Solomon himself has imprisoned a jinn in the jar. The jinn leads the fisherman to a pool of magical fish, which he gives to the Sultan, and makes his fortune.

132 *Brockden Brown's novel of "Wieland" . . . Bulwer's "Zanoni"*: in Charles Brockden Brown's novel *Wieland* (1798), Theodore Wieland goes insane after hearing voices which tell him to kill his family. In Edward Bulwer-Lytton's Rosicrucian novel *Zanoni* (1842), the 'Dweller of the Threshold', a 'grisly and appalling' creature, guards the boundary to the world of occult or forbidden knowledge.

132 *Hoffmanesque*: like E. T. A. Hoffmann; see headnote to 'The Sandman', p. 463. The story has already made a veiled allusion to Hoffmann's 'The Nutcracker'.

133 *Goudon's 'History of Monsters'*: fictitious.

137 *"spirit circles"*: seances. As part of a general spiritualist movement, very common in the second half of the 19th century.

138 *chloroform*: trichloromethane, a liquid once widely used as an anaesthetic.

139 *Gustave Doré, or Callot, or Tony Johannot . . . Un Voyage où il vous plaira*: Gustave Doré (1832–83), French illustrator, best known for his grotesque and fantastic illustrations of Dante and the Bible; Jacques Callot (1592–1635), French artist, celebrated for his grotesque caricatures; Tony Johannot (1803–52), French illustrator. Johannot illustrated Alfred de Musset and P.-J. Stahl's *Voyage où il vous plaira* (*Travel Where You Like*, Paris: J. Hetzel, 1843).

CHARLES DICKENS, *No. 1 Branch Line: The Signal-Man*

Charles Dickens (1812–70), one of the greatest English novelists and a successful and industrious magazine editor and proprietor. Dickens also produced a considerable body of short fiction, originally appearing in periodical form.

'No. 1 Branch-Line: The Signal-Man' is a Christmas ghost story, a subgenre Dickens pioneered with the publication of *A Christmas Carol* in 1843. The story was first published as part of *Mugby Junction*, a series of interconnected narratives (by Dickens and others) in the Christmas 1866 edition of Dickens's periodical *All the Year Round*, 20–5. This is the text used here.

The story's narrator is identified at the beginning of *Mugby Junction* as Young Jackson, the newly retired manager of a debt-collecting firm in the City of London. He is usually referred to by the name of his company, Barbox Brothers, as this is written on his luggage.

151 *perspective-glass*: a generic term applied to a variety of optical instruments. In this case, most likely a telescope.

ÉMILE ZOLA, *The Death of Olivier Bécaille*

Émile Zola (1840–1902), French novelist and political activist. His first novel, *La Confession de Claude* (*Claude's Confession*), was published in 1865; his monumental twenty-volume *Rougon-Macquart* saga of interconnected novels began with *La Fortune des Rougons* (*The Fortune of the Rougons*) in 1871, continuing through to *Le Docteur Pascal* (*Doctor Pascal*) in 1893. The series confirmed Zola's reputation as one of France's greatest novelists, and a pioneering figure in literary Naturalism.

'The Death of Olivier Bécaille' was first published in *Vestnik Evropy* (March 1879). This translation, by Elizabeth McNally, first appeared in *The Penguin Book of Horror Stories*, ed. J. A. Cuddon (London and Harmondsworth: Penguin, 1984).

152 *rue Dauphine*: a street in the Saint-Germain-des-Prés district, in the 6th arrondissement of Paris.

154 *Guérande, on the Piriac road*: Guérande is a coastal town in the Loire-Atlantique region of Brittany, western France. Piriac-sur-Mer is a few miles up the coast from Guérande.

Nantes: large city on the River Loire in western France, not far from Guérande and Piriac-sur-Mer.

156 *forty sous*: a sou is a French coin of low value.

159 *catalepsy*: a condition characterized by trance and bodily rigidity, in which the body does not respond to external stimuli. Since the signs of catalepsy can resemble those of death, it was a favourite subject for nineteenth-century horror, as a potential cause of premature burial: see, for example, Edgar Allan Poe's stories 'The Fall of the House of Usher', 'Berenice', and 'The Premature Burial'.

169 *private five-year plot*: it is likely that Bécaille is buried in Montparnasse, first opened in 1824, and one of Paris's four great nineteenth-century municipal cemeteries (the others are Père Lachaise, Montmartre, and Passy). Outside the direct control of the Church, the nineteenth-century municipal cemeteries of Paris, London, and other cities were generally funded by private or joint-stock companies.

173 *Boulevard Montparnasse*: major thoroughfare running through the Montparnasse district of central Paris.

175 *Jardins du Luxembourg*: the Jardin du Luxembourg is a large public park in the 6th arrondissement of Paris, its origins dating back to the seventeenth century.

RONALD ROSS, *The Vivisector Vivisected*

Sir Ronald Ross (1857–1932), Anglo-Scots physician, born and raised in India, where his father was an officer in the 66th Gurkha Regiment. He studied medicine at St Bartholomew's Hospital, London, and served for many years as an army medical officer in India and elsewhere. He was awarded the Nobel Prize for Medicine in 1902 for his work on malaria. The Ross Institute and Hospital for Tropical Diseases (now incorporated into the London School of Hygiene and Tropical Medicine) was founded in his honour in 1926 in Putney, south London. Ross wrote numerous books on malaria, but also verse, drama, fiction, and autobiography; his *Memoirs* was awarded the James Tait Black Memorial Prize for Biography in 1923.

'The Vivisector Vivisected' was first published in the horror anthology *Strange Assembly*, ed. John Gawsworth (London: Unicorn, 1932), 53–78. According to Ross's *Memoirs*, he wrote the story around 1881–2, while stationed 'at a little place called Vizanagram, about sixteen miles inland from Vizagatapam, on the east coast of the Indian peninsula some distance north of Madras' (Ross, *Memoirs, With a Full Account of the Great Malaria Problem*

Explanatory Notes

and Its Solution (London: John Murray, 1923), 47, 49). The poet and editor John Gawsworth discovered the story 'Hoarded, safe in the Ross archives at Putney' (*Strange Assembly*, 16), and published it, fifty years after it was written. Reprinted under the title 'The Vivisector' in Peter Haining (ed.), *The Frankenstein Omnibus* (London: Orion, 1994), 69–82. The text used here is from *Strange Assembly*.

176 [*Title*]: vivisection—medical experimentation upon live animals—was a highly controversial scientific practice in the last decades of the nineteenth century. The high-profile National Anti-Vivisection Society was founded by the Anglo-Irish feminist and activist Frances Power Cobbe in 1875. A number of sensational novels of the period dealt in a variety of ways with the subject of vivisection, both animal and human, for example, Wilkie Collins, *Heart and Science* (1883), Edward Berdoe, *St Bernard's: The Romance of a Medical Student* (1887), Sarah Grand, *The Beth Book* (1897), Barry Pain, *The Octave of Claudius* (1898), and most famously H. G. Wells, *The Island of Doctor Moreau* (1896).

the best medicine is water, taken internally: the narrator practises homeopathic medicine, a field established by the German physician Samuel Hahnemann (1755–1843), involving drinking supposed curative substances diluted almost to vanishing point. Homeopathy was particularly popular in nineteenth-century America, though it was and is widely regarded by the medical establishment as quackery.

El Dorados: El Dorado was a mythical City of Gold supposedly located somewhere in Central America. In the sixteenth and seventeenth centuries, the Spanish conquistadors and other European explorers launched a number of expeditions in search of El Dorado.

Snogginsville: fictitious American municipality.

encephalon: the brain; literally, 'that which is within the skull'.

gold produces effects . . . contraction of the flexors . . . extensors: that is, politicians' hands grab at gold, but not at copper. Flexors and extensors are paired muscles producing opposite effects: the former produce bending or curvature (here, the closed fist), the latter straightening or opening (the open palm).

177 *U.Sc.Phil.*: a non-existent academic qualification, perhaps implying that either Silcutt is a quack (we have seen the narrator recommending homeopathy) or that qualifications from Snogginsville Infirmary are worthless.

178 *ewer*: a pitcher or water jug, specifically used for washing the hands.

Maculligan was an Irish immigrant: throughout, the Maculligan brothers speak in Ross's attempt at rendering Hiberno-English; they are versions of the 'stage Irishman' common in late Victorian cultural discourse. Given that the Maculligans are from a wealthy and highly-educated Anglo-Irish family (they are upper-class Protestants), it is highly unlikely that their speech would be very heavily inflected with Hiberno-English in the way Ross renders it. There is so much dialect in the story that to translate it all would be effectively to paraphrase the whole story, and since a good deal of it is strictly meaningless, I have let it stand without comment.

179 *attrite*: 'worn or ground down by friction' (*OED*).

   100°: slightly above the average normal human body temperature of 98.6 °F (37 °C).

182 *Merion Square*: Merrion Square: then and now a very affluent and fashionable Georgian square in south Dublin.

183 *fistula*: 'a long, narrow, suppurating canal of morbid origin in some part of the body; a long, sinuous, pipe-like ulcer with a narrow orifice' (*OED*).

   mesentery: a folded section of the peritoneum, which covers the intestines.

184 *scalpels, directors, retractors, bone-forceps, aneurism needles*: all surgical implements; an aneurysm is a 'morbid dilation of an artery' (*OED*).

   vice-royess: from 1171 to 1922, the government of Ireland was overseen by the Lord Lieutenant, or viceroy, based in Dublin Castle. The viceroy's consort was technically called the vicereine. At the time of writing, the office-holder was either Francis Thomas de Grey Cowper, 7th Earl Cowper (viceroy 1880–2, married to Lady Catherine Compton), or John Poyntz Spencer, 5th Earl Spencer (viceroy 1882–5, married to Charlotte Seymour).

   a pay in its fourth ventricle, and a pin in its curvickle ganglion: the fourth ventricle is a cavity within the brain, filled with cerebrospinal fluid; the cervical ganglion is a nerve of the spinal cord. A 'pay' in this context is likely to refer to a substance or device for covering seams and making them watertight.

   Royal Society: initially the Royal Society for Improving Natural Knowledge; a learned society founded in 1660, and now the world's oldest scientific academy in continuous existence. Currently based in Carlton House Terrace, London SW1.

185 *Maculligan Castle, County Lietrim*: Maculligan Castle is fictitious; County Leitrim is in the north-west of Ireland. This home, together with the practice in Merrion Square (see note to p. 182), makes it highly unlikely that the Maculligan brothers would speak with the kind of stage-Irish dialect Ross uses throughout.

187 *breathing stertorously*: loud or snoring breathing, usually accompanying unconsciousness.

188 *Club for the Total Abolition of Vivisection*: probably a fictional version of the National Anti-Vivisection Society: see note to p. 176.

189 *pigeon battue*: a pigeon-shoot, in which the birds are driven or beaten from cover.

ROBERT LOUIS STEVENSON, *The Body-Snatcher*

Robert Louis Stevenson (1850–94), Scottish writer, born in Edinburgh and educated at Edinburgh University. Best known for the Victorian classics

Treasure Island (1881), *Kidnapped* (1886), and *Strange Case of Dr Jekyll and Mr Hyde* (1886), and the volume of poetry *A Child's Garden of Verses* (1885). Stevenson suffered throughout his short life from severe respiratory problems, diagnosed as tuberculosis, exacerbated by his chain-smoking. A very widely travelled writer, Stevenson spent many of the last years of his life in the South Seas, settling in Samoa from 1890 until his death. He is buried there, on the summit of Mount Vaea.

'The Body-Snatcher' was written in June 1881, as the first of a projected series of tales of terror. First published in the *Pall Mall Gazette Christmas Extra*, 13 (December 1884), reprinted in two parts in the *Pall Mall Gazette* (31 January 1895 and 1 February 1885). 'A Key to Mr Stevenson's "Body-Snatcher"', published anonymously in the *Pall Mall Gazette* (3 February 1885), asserts that Stevenson's story is 'strictly founded on fact'. The text used here is from the Manhattan edition of *The Works of Robert Louis Stevenson*, ed. Charles Curtis Bigelow and Temple Scott (New York: Charles C. Bigelow, 1906), iii. 247–76.

190 *Debenham*: village in Suffolk, East Anglia.

Fettes: the Fetteses are a wealthy Edinburgh merchant family; Stevenson's Dr Fettes has come seriously down in the world. Fettes College, the distinguished Edinburgh public school founded on a bequest from Sir William Fettes in 1870, is the alma mater of both James Bond and Tony Blair.

camlet: the name given to a variety of fine fabrics, usually made of a combination of wool, hair, and silk.

crapulous: debauched.

191 *Voltaire*: François-Marie Arouet (1694–1778), French Enlightenment philosopher, freethinker, and deist.

192 *broadcloth*: fine-quality black cloth, used to make gentlemen's garments.

auld lang syne: literally, 'old long since' (Scots), or 'long long ago'. 'For auld lang syne' translates as 'For the sake of old times'. A popular title of refrain for a number of Scots songs and ballads, most notably that written (or adapted) by Robert Burns ('Should auld acquaintance be forgot . . .').

194 *whom I shall here designate by the letter K*: Robert Knox (1791–1862), Edinburgh surgeon and anatomist. Though a brilliant teacher and pioneering anatomist, Knox's name has become inextricably linked with the 'bodysnatchers' Burke and Hare (see note below), who provided Knox with twelve murdered bodies for his classes. Knox's reputation never recovered from the Burke and Hare scandal: he was damned by Sir Walter Scott as the 'learned carcass-butcher'.

Burke: William Burke (1792/3–1829) and William Hare (born either 1792 or 1804, date of death unknown), Irish-born mass murderers. Though popularly known as bodysnatchers, all but one of the seventeen corpses Burke and Hare provided for Robert Knox's anatomy school and other surgeons were in fact murdered. After their arrest, Hare turned King's

Evidence on Burke, and was granted immunity from prosecution. Burke was hanged on 28 January 1829, and his corpse was publicly dissected in Edinburgh University Medical School, where his skeleton is still on display, along with his death mask, and the life mask of Hare. A pocketbook made from Burke's skin is now on display in the Edinburgh Surgeon's Hall Museum. The Burke and Hare case led directly to the passing of the Anatomy Act of 1832, which legalized the medical dissection of donated corpses.

bon vivant: lover of the good life.

195 *wynd*: a narrow street or alleyway (Scots).

'*quid pro quo*': 'this for that' (Latin); an equal exchange of goods or services.

197 *Castle Rock*: the site of Edinburgh Castle, towering over the city at the head of the Royal Mile.

198 *Great Bashaw*: 'bashaw' is an antiquated spelling of 'pasha', a Turkish lord or military commander. Colloquially, as here, a 'haughty or imperious person' (*OED*).

200 *cras tibi*: from the Latin 'Hodie mihi, cras tibi' (what is mine today is yours tomorrow). Often used as an epitaph on gravestones.

202 *Glencorse*: a parish church near Penikuik, Midlothian, Scotland. Stevenson knew Glencorse and Penikuik well; they provide some of the settings for *Kidnapped*.

cross road: according to tradition, the bodies of suicides, murderers, and the otherwise damned were buried at crossroads.

203 *precentor*: 'one who leads or directs the singing of a choir or congregation' (*OED*).

Resurrection Man: bodysnatcher.

mattock: 'an agricultural tool used for loosening hard ground' (*OED*).

Penicuik: Penikuik, see note to p. 202.

204 *Peebles*: town in the Scottish Borders, on the banks of the River Tweed.

206 *ululations*: howls of lament.

Auchenclinny: all published texts of 'The Body-Snatcher' follow the *Pall Mall Gazette* in this spelling, though it is a clear mistranscription of 'Auchendinny', a village near Penikuik.

RUDYARD KIPLING, *The Mark of the Beast*

Joseph Rudyard Kipling (1865–1936), English short-story writer, novelist, and poet. Winner of the Nobel Prize for Literature, 1907. The greatest of all writers of the British Empire, Kipling's best work, such as the volume of verse *Barrack-Room Ballads* (1892), the novel *Kim* (1901), and the short-story collections *The Jungle Books* (2 vols., 1894, 1895) and *Just So Stories* (1902), all deal with the British imperial experience in India.

'The Mark of the Beast' was first published in *The Pioneer* (12–14 July 1890). Reprinted in *Life's Handicap: Being Stories of Mine Own People* (London: Macmillan, 1891). This is the text used here.

208 [*Title*]: see Revelation 13: 16–18: 'And he causeth all, both small and great, rich and poor, free and bond, to receive a mark in their right hand, or in their foreheads: | And that no man might buy or sell, save he that had the mark, or the name of the beast, or the number of his name. | Here is wisdom. Let him that hath understanding count the number of the beast: for it is the number of a man; and his number *is* Six hundred threescore *and* six.'

Suez: the Suez Canal, Egypt, constructed under the supervision of Ferdinand de Lesseps (1805–94) and running from Port Said in the north to Suez in the south, provided a water route from the Persian Gulf to the Mediterranean Sea. As perhaps the main artery of imperial trade in the late nineteenth century, it was a strategically-vital and hotly-contested site, and became a focus for Egyptian nationalism. As Kipling suggests, the Suez Canal became a powerful symbol of, and location for, the divide between East and West.

Strickland . . . Dumoise . . . elsewhere described: Strickland also appears in 'The Return of Imray', the next story in *Life's Handicap*. Dumoise also appears in 'By Word of Mouth' (1888), where he is stricken by grief at the death by typhoid of his wife, and believes her to have returned from the grave. The story closes with his leaving for what is implied will be his own death.

Dharmsala: Dharamsala, or Dharamshala, a city in Himachal Pradesh, northern India, and the base of the 1st Gurkha Rifles regiment from 1860. Since 1960, Dharamsala has been the home of the Dalai Lama and the Tibetan Government-in-Exile.

Catch'em-Alive-O's: 'catch-em-alive-o' was a slang term for sticky fly-paper, whose first recorded use was in Charles Dickens's *Little Dorrit* (1857), ch. 16: 'Sticky old Saints, with . . . such coats of varnish that every holy personage served for a fly-trap, and became what is now in the vulgar tongue called a Catch-em-Alive-O.' It seems to have become a generic hawker's cry across the second half of the nineteenth century, and a refrain in popular ballads. Partridge's *Dictionary of Slang* defines the term thus: 'A catch phrase of circa 1850–1880. Originally a fisherman's phrase, but by 1865, if not a year or two earlier, it had a tremendous vogue. Its intent was to raise a smile, its meaning almost null.' Kipling seems to be using the term to describe Gurkha officers charged with hunting down insurgents.

Khyberee: the Khyber Pass runs through the Himalayas between Kabul and Peshawar in modern-day Afghanistan and Pakistan, and, as a crucial strategic location for control of the region, has long been a site of battles and skirmishes. The Khyber Pass came under British control after the Treaty of Gandamak, following the Second Afghan War of 1879.

209 *talking 'horse'*: boasting, an expression with its origins in horse-racing circles.

'Auld Lang Syne': see note to p. 192.

annexed Burma: Burma (Myanmar) in South East Asia was progressively annexed as a British colony across a series of three Anglo-Burmese Wars (1824–6, 1852–3, 1885–6). After complete annexation, Burma was made into a province of India in 1886.

Soudan . . . Fuzzies . . . Suakim: the Sudan was crucial to British imperial interests in the late nineteenth century, particularly because of its proximity to Egypt and the Suez Canal. Across the 1880s, the religious leader Muhammad Ahmad ibn al-Sayyid Abd Allah, known as al-Mahdī (1844–85), gathered a vast army to conduct a military-religious campaign which culminated in the capture of Khartoum in 1885, and the killing of General Charles George Gordon, the Sudanese governor-general. Mahdist warriors of the Sudanese Beja people were popularly known amongst the British as 'fuzzy-wuzzies', because of their elaborate hair-styles. 'Fuzzy-Wuzzy' is also the title of one of Kipling's *Barrack-Room Ballads*. Written in the voice of an ordinary British soldier, the poem praises the ferocity and bravery of the Sudanese warriors: 'So 'ere's to you, Fuzzy-Wuzzy, at your 'ome in the Soudan; | You're a pore benighted 'eathen but a first-class fightin' man.' Suakim, properly Suakin, or Sawakin, was an important Sudanese seaport. General Francis Grenfell's Hussars defeated a Mahdist army at the Battle of Suakin, 20 December 1888.

Benedictine: French liqueur, supposedly derived from a recipe developed by Benedictine monks in the Abbey of Fécamp, Normandy.

Hanuman: Hindu deity, a monkey-god and commander of the monkey army.

210 *'a leper as white as snow'*: the curse of the prophet Elisha upon his false servant Gehazi: 'The leprosy therefore of Namaan shall cleave unto thee, and unto thy seed for ever. And he went out from his presence a leper *as white* as snow' (2 Kings 6: 27). Also God's curse upon Miriam: 'And the cloud departed from off the tabernacle; and behold, Miriam *became* leprous, *white* as snow' (Numbers 13: 10). Leprosy, or Hansen's Disease, affects the skin, causing terrible disfigurement due to tissue degeneration and nerve loss. In reality, it is very difficult to catch leprosy; 95 per cent of people are immune to the bacterium, and the majority of those who are not immune recover in a matter of weeks. It is impossible that Kipling's 'Silver Man' could transmit leprosy, as sufferers are only contagious in the very earliest stages of the disease.

211 *Indian Penal Code*: chapter 15 of the Indian Penal Code of 1860 deals with 'Offences relating to Religion'. Fleete is in violation of sections 295 and 295A of the Penal Code: 'Injuring or defiling place of worship, with intent to insult the religion of any class', and 'Deliberate and malicious

acts intended to outrage religious feelings of any class by insulting its religion or religious beliefs'.

212 *blister-flies*: actually a species of beetle, able to secrete a blistering agent, cantharidin.

214 *a December evening*: actually a January evening, as this is New Year's Day.

215 *boot-jack*: 'a contrivance for pulling off boots' (*OED*).

'*Hydrophobia*': rabies. Fear of water (hydrophobia) is one of the symptoms of rabies, because paralysis of the throat muscles makes drinking impossible. The effect of rabies on the salivary glands also produces foaming of the mouth.

punkah-rope: a rope which operates a punkah, a large, swinging cloth fan.

curing a wolf's pelt: skinning a wolf alive to tan its hide for furs.

Pinafore . . . it was the cat: Act II of W. S. Gilbert and Arthur Sullivan's comic opera *HMS Pinafore* (1878) contains the song 'Carefully on Tip-Toe Stealing', which features the repeated refrain 'It was the cat!'

216 *mahseer-fishing*: a mahseer is a variety of Asian carp, traditionally caught with a rod and line.

217 *strychnine*: a highly poisonous alkaloid, commonly used in rat poison, which causes muscular convulsions.

219 '*There are more things . . .*': William Shakespeare, *Hamlet*, I. v. 166–7: 'There are more things in heaven and earth, Horatio, | Than are dreamt of in your philosophy.'

AMBROSE BIERCE, *Chickamauga*

Ambrose Bierce (1842–*c*.1914): American journalist, writer, and soldier, known for his sardonic wit and style, as exemplified by *The Devil's Dictionary* (1906). He enlisted as a Union officer at the outbreak of the American Civil War in 1861, and saw active service in a number of battles. His short stories, often nihilistic, appeared in the collections *Tales of Soldiers and Civilians* (1892) (later published as *In the Midst of Life*, the title by which the collection is generally known) and *Can Such Things Be?* (1893). A lifelong newspaperman, Bierce went to Mexico in 1913, probably to cover the Pancho Villa revolution. He was never heard from again.

'Chickamauga' was first published in the *San Francisco Examiner* (20 Jan. 1889); reprinted in *Soldiers and Civilians* and *In the Midst of Life*. The present text is taken from the first edition of *Tales of Soldiers and Civilians* (New York: Lovell, Coryell and Company, 1891) [actually published in 1892].

220 [*Title*]: the Battle of Chickamauga, fought on the Tennessee–Georgia border on 19–20 September 1863, was one of the bloodiest battles of the American Civil War. The battle resulted in a Confederate victory, though with massive casualties on both sides (and with the Confederate dead well outnumbering the Union dead). As the story suggests, the battle

was largely fought in a forest. Bierce himself fought at the Battle of Chickamauga.

the capital of a civilized race to the far South: the boy's father fought at the Battle of Mexico City, 8–15 September 1847, part of the Mexican–American War of 1846–8.

221 *curb the lust for war . . . loftiest star*: Byron, *Childe Harold's Pilgrimage* (1812–18), iii. 341–2. The reference here is to Napoleon Bonaparte.

acclivity: an ascending slope.

223 *freaked and maculated*: both words in this context are synonyms for 'stained'.

224 *'spoor'*: the trail of a wild animal, followed by a hunter.

'the thunder of the captains and the shouting': a description of a warhorse from Job 39: 25: 'He saith among the trumpets, Ha ha; and he smelleth the battle afar off, the thunder of the captains, and the shouting.'

a pillar of fire to this strange exodus: Exodus 13: 21: 'And the LORD went before them [the Children of Israel] by day in a pillar of cloud, to lead them the way; and by night in a pillar of fire, to give them light; to go by day and night'.

CHARLOTTE PERKINS GILMAN, *The Yellow Wall Paper*

Charlotte Perkins Gilman (1860–1935), American feminist, activist, and writer, born Charlotte Anna Perkins in Hartford, Connecticut. Author of numerous works of feminist sociology, including *Women and Economics* (1898) and *The Man-Made World; or, Our Androcentric Culture* (1911), as well as the seminal work of utopian fiction *Herland* (1915), set in an isolated all-female society. 'The Yellow Wall Paper', her most celebrated work, was written in the wake of an extended bout of post-partum depression following the birth of her daughter Katherine in 1884, and the 'rest cure' prescribed to treat it. In 1913, Gilman explained the genesis of the story in an article entitled 'Why I Wrote "The Yellow Wall Paper"' (*The Forerunner*, October 1913).

'The Yellow Wall Paper' was first published in the *New England Magazine* (January 1892). Reprinted in book form under her name by her first marriage: Charlotte Perkins Stetson, *The Yellow Wall Paper* (Boston: Small, Maynard and Company, 1899). This is the text used here.

226 *a slight hysterical tendency*: hysteria was a condition traditionally associated with women, and particularly with childbirth, due to its imagined connection with the womb (the word derives from the Greek *hystera*: uterus). Diagnoses of hysteria were particularly prevalent in the late nineteenth century. See Elaine Showalter, *The Female Malady: Women, Madness and English Culture, 1830–1980* (1985), and *Hystories: Hysterical Epidemics and Modern Media* (1997).

phosphates or phosphites: phosphates are salts of phosphoric acid (H_3PO_4); phosphites are salts of phosphorous acid (H_3PO_3). The narrator has probably been prescribed phosphates, used to treat rickets and particularly as a laxative.

230 *sticketh closer than a brother*: Proverbs 18: 24: 'A man *that hath* friends must shew himself friendly; and there is a friend *that* sticketh closer than a brother.'

231 *Weir Mitchell*: Dr Silas Weir Mitchell (1829–1914), American physician, author of *The Treatment of Certain Forms of Neurasthenia and Hysteria* (1887). Mitchell is 'the noted specialist in nervous diseases' ('Why I Wrote "The Yellow Wall Paper"') who treated Gilman's own post-partum depression.

232 *the principles of design*: the most influential Victorian design-manual was *The Grammar of Ornament* (1856) by the Welsh architect Owen Jones, whose floral and patterned designs for wallpaper, fabrics, and carpets, often with symmetrical or repeating devices and incorporating Arabic or oriental influences, were very important for the Arts and Crafts movement.

'debased Romanesque' with delirium tremens: Romanesque art and architecture flourished in the Middle Ages, and incorporated both European (Roman) and Byzantine influences. Romanesque architecture was revived, particularly in America, in the nineteenth century, where it was characterized by a heavy use of semicircular arches. *Delirium tremens* (Latin for 'shaking frenzy') is a form of acute delirium, including hallucinations, brought about by alcohol withdrawal.

frieze: 'a band of painted or sculptured decoration' (*OED*).

233 *rare meat*: sanguinary medicine; eating bloody meat to improve health and strength. Joseph Ferdinand Gueldry's painting *The Blood Drinkers* (1898) depicts middle-class women in an abattoir drinking the blood of a freshly slaughtered ox as a health tonic.

235 *arabesque*: a design incorporating flowing, intertwining branches, leaves, and flowers. Following the publication of Poe's *Tales of the Grotesque and Arabesque* (1840), the term took on a secondary meaning of 'strangely mixed, fantastic' (*OED*).

236 *smooches*: dirty smudges or smears.

238 *so many heads*: a reference to the floral design of the wallpaper, but also to the Hydra, the many-headed monster killed by Hercules as one of his twelve labours.

ARTHUR CONAN DOYLE, *The Case of Lady Sannox*

Sir Arthur Conan Doyle (1859–1930), British writer, best known for the Sherlock Holmes novels and stories, which began with *A Study in Scarlet* in *Beeton's Christmas Annual* 1887, and then appeared most famously in the *Strand Magazine* from July 1891. Born in Edinburgh of Scottish and Irish parents, Doyle studied in Edinburgh Medical School from 1876, and was a practising physician before becoming a full-time writer. One of the most significant of all genre writers, Doyle's large *oeuvre* includes the Professor Challenger books, the Brigadier Gerard books, and very many short stories. In later life, Doyle became a high-profile champion of the spiritualist movement.

'The Case of Lady Sannox' was first published in *The Idler* (November 1893). Republished in *Round the Red Lamp: Being Facts and Fancies of Medical Life* (London: Methuen, 1894). This is the text used here.

242 *confrères*: colleagues.

> *Marylebone Road . . . Oxford Street*: central London. Baker Street, where Sherlock Holmes lived, runs between these two streets.

243 *spud*: a narrow-bladed gardening implement, or fork, for digging or weeding.

244 *malachite*: hydrous carbonate of copper; a green mineral, used for decorative purposes to make vases or tables.

> *beeswing*: a translucent crust which forms on vintage bottles of port and other wines.

> *Smyrna*: Izmir, a large port city on the Anatolian coast of Turkey. The major trading port of the Ottoman Empire.

245 *Asia Minor*: the Anatolian Peninsula, covering the majority of modern Turkey. The westernmost point of the Asian land mass.

> *Almohades*: the Almohad Empire was an Islamic empire covering North Africa and Spain, 1130–1262.

246 *kismet*: from the Arabic for fate, or destiny.

> *bistouries*: scalpels.

247 *Mussulman*: Muslim.

> *chloroform*: see note to p. 138.

> *Caryatid*: a sculptured female form, used as an architectural column.

> *Euston Road*: north-central London; Euston Road opened in 1756, as the city's first traffic bypass.

> *repeater*: chiming pocket watch.

251 *Hotel di Roma, Venice*: presumably in the Piazzale Roma, the major point of entry to Venice.

BRAM STOKER, *The Squaw*

Bram (Abraham) Stoker (1847–1912), Irish writer and theatre manager. Stoker began his career working in the Irish Civil Service, and in 1878 he went to work with the great Victorian actor-manager Henry Irving at the Lyceum Theatre in London. The pair worked together until Irving's death in 1905. Although Stoker wrote twelve novels and many short stories, his reputation will be forever associated with the greatest of all works of Victorian Gothic, *Dracula* (1897). Other novels include *The Snake's Pass* (1890), *The Jewel of*

Seven Stars (1903), and *The Lair of the White Worm* (1911). Stoker died in 1912, possibly as the result of syphilis.

'The Squaw' was first published in *Holly Leaves: The Christmas Number of the Illustrated Sporting and Dramatic News* (2 December 1893). Reprinted in *Dracula's Guest and Other Weird Stories* (London: Routledge, 1914). This is the text used here.

252 *Nurnberg*: Nuremberg, a medieval city in Bavaria, Germany.

Irving had not been playing Faust: Goethe's *Faust* was one of Henry Irving's signature roles. Irving travelled to Nuremberg with members of the Lyceum company to perform *Faust* in 1885, though there is no evidence that Stoker was amongst the party, nor that he ever visited Nuremberg.

Isthmian City, Bleeding Gulch, Maple Tree County, Neb.: a fictional Nebraska township.

Frankfort: Frankfurt am Main, Germany.

Methusaleh of a town in Yurrup: 'the oldest town in Europe'.

the Burg: the twelfth-century Nuremberg Castle (Nürnberger Burg), set on a rock overlooking the city.

253 *Claude Lorraine*: Claude Gellée (1600–82), known as Claude Lorrain. Neoclassical French painter, famous for his idealized landscapes.

Torture Tower . . . Iron Virgin: Nuremberg Castle does contain a notorious torture chamber, the centrepiece of which was the Nuremberg Iron Maiden device (it was destroyed in Allied bombing in 1944). It is likely, however, that this was a modern device: it was first displayed in Nuremberg in 1802. There is, in fact, no evidence that any medieval torture chamber contained an Iron Maiden, which seems to have been an invention of the eighteenth-century Gothic imagination. 'The Squaw' gives an accurate depiction of the Nuremberg Iron Maiden, which Irving and company would have visited on their 1885 trip.

bastion and counterscarp: both parts of a fortification. The bastion is the name given to the projecting walls; the counterscarp is the outer wall surrounding the ditch.

as tender as a Maine cherry-tree: this simile, like much of Hutcheson's colourful American dialect, seems to have been Stoker's invention, though Maine is indeed celebrated for its cherry trees.

pooty: pretty.

254 *papoose*: archaic (and now offensive) term for an American Indian child, generally young enough to be carried in a sling of the same name.

255 *slipper-handed*: slippery-handed, clumsy.

256 *heeled*: armed with a weapon.

257 *the Gothic restorers of forty years ago*: like many European towns and cities, Nuremberg was restored as a result of the neo-Gothic vogue of the

second half of the nineteenth century. Many architectural commentators (including M. R. James) found this kind of restoration controversial, if not downright destructive.

the Pantheistic souls of Philo or Spinoza: Philo Judaeus, or Philo of Alexandria (*c.*15 BC–*c.*AD 50), Hellenistic Jewish philosopher and mystic, and an important precursor for Christian theology; Baruch (or Benedict) Spinoza, Dutch-Jewish Enlightenment philosopher, best known for his *Ethics* (1675). Pantheism is the belief that God encompasses the whole of the created universe, which often amounts to nature-worship. While Philo was not technically a pantheist, his philosophy did attempt to account for the all-encompassing essence of God. Spinoza argued that, as God is infinite, he must be identical with the entirety of creation, all of which (including humanity) is an aspect of God.

258 *headsmen's swords*: executioners' swords.

rondeur: roundness, or plumpness.

259 *rude*: unformed or shapeless.

exordium: the introductory part of a discourse.

260 *buffler*: buffalo.

Billy Broncho gold mine in New Mexico . . . Buffalo Bridge: both fictional New Mexico locations. It is very unlikely that the 'Billy Broncho gold mine' has anything to do with the cowboy star Broncho Billy Anderson (1880–1971).

261 *Eve was made out of the rib of a dwarf!*: the creation of Eve from Adam's rib is in Genesis 2: 21–2: 'And the rib, which the LORD God had taken from man, made he a woman'.

Wapping: in the nineteenth century, Wapping, on the north bank of the Thames in east London, was most famous for its docks.

dod-rotted: 'god-rotted', godforsaken.

262 *I'm euchered!*: euchre is a card game, very popular in the US in the nineteenth century. The meaning here is 'I'm trumped!', or 'I'm done for!'.

ROBERT W. CHAMBERS, *The Repairer of Reputations*

Robert William Chambers (1865–1933), American writer and artist, born Brooklyn, New York, brother of the celebrated New York architect Walter B. Chambers. Chambers studied art at the École des Beaux-Arts and the Académie Julian in Paris, and returned to New York to become an illustrator for *Life* and *Vogue* magazines. Author of many novels and short-story collections, beginning with *In the Quarter* (1894).

'The Repairer of Reputations' is the opening story of *The King in Yellow* (1895), the collection for which Chambers is best known, and which is dedicated to his brother. *The King in Yellow* is a volume of interconnected short stories, mostly featuring the eponymous verse drama, a work of decadent literature which brings madness and death to those who read it. The text here is taken from the first edition of *The King in Yellow* (New York: F. Tennyson Neely, 1895).

264 *Carcosa*: Chambers took the name from Ambrose Bierce's story 'An Inhabitant of Carcosa' (in the collection *Can Such Things Be?*), in which a disorientated and possibly delusional narrator stumbles upon 'the ruins of the ancient and famous city of Carcosa', the city where he was born (Bierce, *The Devil's Dictionary, Tales, and Memoirs* (New York: Library of America, 2011), 372). Since Bierce and Chambers, the city of Carcosa has appeared regularly in works of fantastic literature.

Hyades: a star cluster in the constellation Taurus, some sixty-five light years from Earth, containing the red giant star Aldebaran. Again, this is taken from Bierce's 'An Inhabitant of Carcosa': 'Looking upwards, I saw through a sudden rift in the clouds Aldebaran and the Hyades!' (Bierce, *The Devil's Dictionary, Tales, and Memoirs*, 372).

'Ne raillons . . . la différence': 'Let us not mock the insane; their madness lasts longer than ours. . . . That is the only difference.' This epigraph is Chambers's own.

The war with Germany: following the publication of General Sir George Tompkyns Chesney's *The Battle of Dorking* (1871), imagined wars with Germany were a staple of future fictions in the last decades of the nineteenth century; see I. F. Clarke (ed.), *The Great War with Germany, 1890–1914* (Liverpool: Liverpool University Press, 1997).

Samoan Islands: in the South Pacific. America established a naval base in Pago Pago, Samoa, in 1878. Germany and the US were in fact vying for control of Samoa in the 1890s. A treaty of 1899 divided Samoa in two, with Germany controlling the western islands and the US the eastern (a territory still affiliated to the US as American Samoa).

Norfolk: a port city in Virginia, still home to a large US naval base.

265 *coaling station*: a fuelling station for warships.

Prussian system: a military system with a general central command (general staff), and a separate staff for each division and corps, formally established in Prussian military academies in 1806. The US military remains unusual amongst large armed forces in not having adopted the Prussian system of command.

second great fire: the Great Fire of Chicago burned from 8 to 10 October 1871, killing hundreds and destroying large sections of the city. It led directly to the rebuilding of modern Chicago, complete with landmark skyscrapers (from the 1880s onwards).

foreign-born Jews: this remark about anti-Semitism makes 'The Repairer of Reputations' a characteristic work of the mid-1890s, following the Dreyfus Affair of 1894, in which a French-Jewish military officer was convicted of treason, on no grounds other than anti-Semitism, for allegedly selling military secrets to Germany. Zola played a significant role in Dreyfus's exoneration. The notorious and influential *Protocols of the Learned Elders of Zion*, a forged document purporting to reveal the plans for a Jewish takeover of the world, first appeared in Russia in 1903.

Suanee: the Suwanee Valley, marking the border between Georgia and Florida. Suwanee carried heavy racial overtones in America following the composition of Stephen Foster's 'The Old Folks at Home' ('Way down upon de Swanee ribber') in 1851, for the 'blackface' Christy Minstrels, and containing the lines 'Still longing for de old plantation, | And for de old folks at home. . . . Oh! darkeys how my heart grows weary, | Far from de old folks at home.' (It is now the state song of Florida.)

266 *Elevated Railroads*: New York's elevated railway was built from the 1860s, and is still very much in use.

the Dodge Statue: William Earl Dodge (1805–83), American mine-owner and one of the founders of the Young Men's Christian Association (YMCA). John Quincy Adams Ward's statue of Dodge, unveiled in 1885, originally stood in Herald Square, but was moved to Bryant Park in 1941.

Washington Square: a major urban square and park at the south end of Fifth Avenue, Manhattan.

267 *Wooster Street*: now in SoHo, Manhattan.

268 *Ionic columns*: classical columns crowned with volutes (scrolls or spirals).

Boris Yvain: 'The Mask', the second story in *The King in Yellow*, takes up the story of the sculptor Boris Yvain, born in America to French and Russian parents.

269 *Bleecker Street*: Greenwich Village, Manhattan.

Hawberk: the armourer has adopted a name from his trade: a hauberk is a piece of armour protecting the neck and shoulders.

greaves: armour protecting the leg below the knee.

270 *Metropolitan Museum*: the Metropolitan Museum of Art, founded 1870, is on the eastern edge of Central Park, Manhattan.

Quai d'Orsay: on the left bank of the Seine, Paris. Famous as a gathering place for artists.

271 *Westchester County*: immediately north of New York City, and tradition-ally home to some of New York's most prosperous families.

Mr Wilde: 'The King in Yellow' has clear connections with Lord Henry Wootton's depraved 'yellow book', which Dorian reads in Oscar Wilde's *The Picture of Dorian Gray* (1891). Though Wilde does not name it, it seems likely that Lord Henry's 'poisonous French novel' is J.-K. Huysman's decadent classic *A rebours* (*Against Nature*, 1884).

tassets and cuissards: tassets are skirts of armour to protect the thighs; cuissards, or cuisses, are plates of armour for the thighs.

Pell Street: a small street in what is now Chinatown, Manhattan.

273 *a welcher*: one who defaults on paying debts.

Fairbeach, New Jersey . . . the Bowery: Fairbeach is fictitious. The Bowery is a street and district of downtown Manhattan, notorious in the nineteenth century for its brothels and saloons, and for its violent gangs. The implication is that the 'Minister of the Gospel' has been paying for sex with prostitutes.

Dieppe: port town in Normandy.

274 *the 'Fancy and the Talent'*: those who bet on sports. 'The Fancy' specifically applied to followers of boxing, and 'The Talent' to horse racing.

275 *Hastur*: another borrowing from Bierce's *Can Such Things Be?*: 'He rose with the sun and went forth to pray at the shrine of Hastur, the god of shepherds' ('Haïta the Shepherd', in Bierce, *The Devil's Dictionary, Tales, and Memoirs*, 364). Bierce was a great admirer of Chambers; H. P. Lovecraft in turn borrowed the name Hastur for his story 'The Whisperer in Darkness', where it is associated with 'the Yellow Sign' (Lovecraft, *Tales* (New York: Library of America, 2005)).

276 *Mount St Vincent*: in the Riverdale district of the Bronx, in northern New York City.

English seat: an equestrian discipline, where the rider sits far back in the saddle, and the horse trots with very high steps.

the Herald and the Meteor: the *New York Herald* was a major New York newspaper founded by James Gordon Bennett, Sr in 1835, which ran until 1924. The *Meteor* appears to be fictitious.

277 *Memorial Church . . . marble arch*: the Judson Memorial Church (1891), a Baptist church on Washington Square South. The Washington Arch (1892) is in Washington Square Park. Both the church and the arch were designed by the great New York architect Stanford White (1853–1906).

Peter Stuyvesant: one of the founders of New York City (c.1612–72), Director-General of the Dutch Colony of New Netherland from 1647 to 1664. He was responsible for building large parts of what is now downtown Manhattan, then known as New Amsterdam.

Garibaldi: Guiseppe Garibaldi (1807–82), Italian nationalist leader, and a central figure in the nineteenth-century unification of Italy. Giovanni Turini's statue of Garibaldi (1888) stands in Washington Square Park.

278 *Delmonico's*: originally dating from 1827, and by the 1890s New York's smartest and most famous restaurant. There were several branches of Delmonico's, but the most celebrated was in South William Street, downtown Manhattan.

279 *Brunswick cocktail*: 2 shots of rye whiskey, ¾ shot freshly squeezed lemon juice, ¾ shot claret, ½ shot cane sugar syrup. Reputedly invented at the Old Hotel Brunswick, Madison Square, Manhattan.

North River: the southernmost section of the Hudson River, between Manhattan and New Jersey.

Spring Street: runs from the Bowery through SoHo to the Hudson River.

from the battery to 190th Street: the entire length of Manhattan Island. Battery Park is its southernmost tip; 190th Street is in far northern Manhattan.

General Sheridan: Philip H. Sheridan (1831–88), Union general in the American Civil War. In 1895, there was no statue of Sheridan in New York, though Sheridan Square in what is now the West Village, Manhattan, was named in his honour in 1896. Joseph Pollia's statue of Sheridan was unveiled in nearby Christopher Park in 1936.

Staten Island: the least-populated of New York's five boroughs; lies off the southern point of Manhattan.

280 *de-classé tramp steamers*: a tramp steamer is a cargo ship with no fixed schedule or destination, available for hire or charter; *de-classé* (déclassé) means it has come down in the world.

Governor's Island: see note to p. 282.

"Tarpon" . . . *"Osceola"*: a tarpon is a large seafish; Princeton, NJ, is an Ivy League college town; Champlain is a large lake on the Vermont–New York border, and reaching up into Quebec, Canada; Erie is one of the Great Lakes, on the US–Canadian border. Admiral David Farragut (1801–70) was a US military commander who saw active service across a number of nineteenth-century wars, from the US–British War of 1812 to the American Civil War, in which he fought on the Union side. Monitors were a class of small, heavily-armed ironclad warships. There were a number of navy ships called the *Osceola* in service from 1863 to 1973; all were named after the Seminole chief and warrior Osceola (1814–38).

281 *the Rangelys*: while there is a Rangely in Colorado, this most likely refers to Rangeley, Maine, the name given to a local lake, river, and town.

282 *Castle William*: Castle Williams, a circular sandstone fort on Governor's Island in New York Harbour, built 1807–11; this is 'the old Red Fort on Governor's Island' referred to on p. 280.

285 *Presidio*: a military base on the northern tip of the San Francisco Peninsula, California; originally established by the Spanish in 1776. It became a National Park in 1994.

286 *collodion*: a gelatinous solution of cellulose, used in the treatment of wounds.

287 *Sing Sing*: a maximum security prison in Ossining, New York State, first opened in 1828.

Sheepshead Bay: Brooklyn, New York.

289 *sallyport*: the secured entrance to a prison or fortress.

290 *St Francis Xavier*: Roman Catholic church on West 16th Street in Chelsea, Manhattan; the current church dates from 1882.

ARTHUR MACHEN, *Novel of the White Powder*

Arthur Llewelyn Jones Machen (1863–1947), Welsh writer, occultist, actor, and journalist. Though he spent his adult life in London, Machen was born in Caerleon, Monmouthshire, a town with its origins as a Romano-British fort, Isca Augusta, whose ruins are still prominent. This Welsh background provides the setting for many of Machen's most important works, including the *fin-de-siècle* classic *The Great God Pan* (1894) and the semi-autobiographical *The Hill of Dreams* (1907). Machen was a member of the occult society the Hermetic Order of the Golden Dawn, along with W. B. Yeats, Aleister Crowley, Algernon Blackwood, and others.

'Novel of the White Powder' is one of the series of interconnecting stories that form the portmanteau novel *The Three Impostors* (London: John Lane, 1895). The text here is taken from the Caerleon Edition of *The Works of Arthur Machen*, vol. ii (London: Martin Secker, 1928).

294 *My name is Leicester*: an alias. The narrator is one of the 'Three Impostors' of the novel's title, agents of a sinister secret society who are searching London for 'the man with the spectacles', a member of the society who has betrayed them and absconded with a valuable Roman coin, 'The Gold Tiberius'. Also going under the alias of Lally, she is 'incomparably the most subtle and the most deadly' of the Impostors (*Works of Machen*, ii. 213).

   feudal tenures: the duties of a tenant to a feudal landlord.

295 *Lord Chancellor*: the Lord High Chancellor of Great Britain, historically the most senior member of the British judiciary and a member of the Cabinet. As chair of the Judicial Committee of the House of Lords, the Lord Chancellor was also the presiding judge of the Supreme Court of England and Wales. The duties of the Lord Chancellor were redefined (and reduced) by the Constitutional Reform Act of 2005.

   Bibliothèque Nationale: the National Library of France, in Paris.

296 *malacca cane*: a walking stick made from a palm stem, named after the Malacca district in Malaysia.

299 *glamour*: enchantment.

300 *quinine*: crystalline alkaloid from the bark of the cinchona tree, used as an anti-malarial treatment.

301 *earthly tabernacle*: St Paul describes the human body as an 'earthly tabernacle' (temple) in 2 Corinthians 5: 1: 'For we know that if our earthly house of *this* tabernacle were dissolved, we have a building of God, an house not made with hands, eternal in the heavens.'

304 *adze*: 'a tool, like an axe with the blade set at right-angles to the handle and curving inwards towards it; used for chipping or slicing away at the surface of wood' (*OED*).

306 *theosophies*: theosophy is esoteric philosophy or investigation, very popular in the late nineteenth century. The Theosophical Society was founded in 1875 by Madame Helena Blavatsky and others.

nothing less than transcendental: the limits of scientific materialism were widely discussed in the late Victorian period, particularly by those with an interest in the spiritualist movement. The high-profile Society for Psychical Research was founded in 1882 to investigate paranormal and supernatural phenomena.

Omnia exeunt in mysterium: 'All things pass into mystery.' It is likely that Machen got this from Coleridge's *Aids to Reflection* (1825): '*Omnia exeunt in mysterium*, says a schoolman: that is, there is nothing, the absolute grounds of which is not a mystery. The contrary is indeed a contradiction in terms: for how can that, which is to explain all things, be susceptible of an explanation?'

a peak in Darien: the closing words of John Keats's sonnet 'On First Looking into Chapman's Homer': 'Or like stout Cortez, when with eagle eyes | He stared at the Pacific—and all his men | Look'd at each other with a wild surmise— | Silent, upon a peak in Darien.' Darién is a region of Panama, Central America.

307 *theory of telepathy*: telepathy, the transference of thoughts, is a term coined in 1882 by Frederic W. H. Myers, one of the founders of the Society for Psychical Research. The SPR were greatly interested in this phenomenon for its potential to contradict traditional materialist interpretations of science. See Roger Luckhurst, *The Invention of Telepathy* (Oxford and New York: Oxford University Press, 2002).

Vinum Sabbati: witches' wine, or literally Sabbath wine. This seems to be Machen's own invention.

308 *Payne Knight's monograph*: Richard Payne Knight (1751–1824), British art historian and classical scholar, author of *An Account of the Remains of the Worship of Priapus* (London: T. Spilsbury, 1786), a work which drew clear connections between pagan rites and Christian sacraments. This is the passage to which Machen alludes: 'The ineffable name [of God] also, which, according to the Massorethic punctuation, is pronounced *Jehovah*, was anciently pronounced *Jaho* . . . which was a title of BACCHUS, the nocturnal sun; as was also *Sabazius*, or *Sabadius*, which is the same word as *Sabaoth*, one of the scriptural titles of the true God, only adapted to the pronunciation of a more polished language' (p. 194).

Aryan: for nineteenth-century philologists and ethnologists, the Aryans (from the Sanskrit *arya*, 'noble' or 'distinguished') were the putative speakers of the first Indo-European language, and were believed to have been a light-skinned race from Persia and northern India. Following the work of the Comte de Gobineau (1816–82), the term Aryan entered modern racial theory, to designate a 'superior' white race.

graal: grail.

sumentes calicem principis inferorum: 'taking from the chalice of the prince of the shades below' (or literally 'the prince of the bottom-dwellers').

The 'old author' here seems to be Machen himself, who has invented this quotation.

308 *nuptiæ Sabbati*: Sabbath nuptials.

RICHARD MARSH, *The Adventure of Lady Wishaw's Hand*

Richard Marsh (1857–1915), British author, born Richard Bernard Heldmann. Best known for the *fin-de-siècle* schlock classic *The Beetle* (1897), Marsh wrote over eighty novels and collections of short stories.

'The Adventure of Lady Wishaw's Hand' was first published in *Curios: Some Strange Adventures of Two Bachelors* (London: J. Long, 1898). This is the text used here. *Curios* is a collection of short stories featuring the unscrupulous collectors Mr Pugh and Mr Tress.

311 *gewgaw*: a gaudy trifle or trinket.

313 *ormolu . . . Chippendale*: ormolu is gilded bronze, used to make clocks or tables, particularly popular in the eighteenth and nineteenth centuries. Thomas Chippendale (1718–79) was the celebrated English cabinetmaker and furniture designer, whose distinctive Rococo style lent its name to much eighteenth-century British furniture.

314 *the society*: the Society for Psychical Research. See note to p. 306.

315 *petit faux pas*: little error.

cumber the ground: from the Parable of the Vineyard, Luke 13: 7: 'Then he said unto the dresser of his vineyard, Behold, these three years I come seeking fruit on this fig tree, and find none: cut it down; why cumbereth it the ground?'

317 *"A Horrible Tale"*: probably a generic work of nineteenth-century periodical horror, such as those published in *Blackwood's Edinburgh Magazine*.

320 *teetotum*: a small spinning top, spun with the fingers.

323 *As the scriptural writers have it, my heart melted within me*: Psalm 22: 14: 'I am poured out like water, and all my bones are out of joint: my heart is like wax; it is melted in the midst of my bowels.'

W. W. JACOBS, *The Monkey's Paw*

William Wymark Jacobs (1863–1943), English short-story writer, novelist, and humorist. Working as a minor Civil Service clerk, Jacobs came to prominence in the 1890s, writing short stories for the London periodical press, including the *Strand Magazine* and Jerome K. Jerome's magazines *The Idler* and *To-Day*. Jacobs also wrote seven novels, though is by far best known for a small number of classic short stories, most particularly 'The Monkey's Paw'.

'The Monkey's Paw' was first published in *Harper's Monthly Magazine* (September 1902). Reprinted almost immediately in *The Lady of the Barge* (London and New York: Harper Brothers, 1902). This is the text used here. 'The Monkey's Paw' is one of the most influential and frequently anthologized of all horror stories. It was adapted for the theatre in 1903, the adaptation subsequently published as *The Monkey's Paw: A Story in Three Scenes*, dramatized by Louis N. Parker (London and New York: Samuel French, 1910). Adaptations of and allusions to the story pop up regularly across a variety of different media, including popular music and television (as well as a number of straight adaptations, the story has featured in episodes of both *The Monkees* and *The Simpsons*). Stephen King's novel *Pet Sematary* (1983) is heavily influenced by 'The Monkey's Paw', as are a number of stories by H. P. Lovecraft (see note to p. 327).

327 *Laburnam Villa*: the story is set in what is presumably an outer suburb of London, a frequent setting for horror stories of the period; see, for example, Arthur Machen's *The Three Impostors* (1895), Richard Marsh's *The Beetle* (1897), and parts of Bram Stoker's *Dracula* (1897). This suburb, with its unfinished roads and underpopulated streets, is brand new, as is 'the huge new cemetery, two miles distant' (one of a number of municipal cemeteries built in London across the nineteenth century). Readers of 1902 would have recognized 'Laburnam Villa' as a wholly typical name for a suburban residence.

Herbert White: 'The Monkey's Paw' was influential for some of the work of the great American horror writer H. P. Lovecraft (1890–1937). The name of the protagonist of his story 'Herbert West, Reanimator' seems to carry clear overtones of Jacobs's Herbert White, while 'The Thing on the Doorstep' revisits the climax of 'The Monkey's Paw' in Grand Guignol style.

328 *rubicund*: red-faced.

fakirs: Indian mystics and holy men.

330 *Arabian Nights*: *The Thousand and One Nights*, the most important collection of Arabic folk tales and legends, compiled gradually and approximately between the eighth and twelfth centuries. The framing narrative tells of Scheherazade, wife of the Indian King Shahryar, forced to tell a different story each night in order to prevent her execution. *The Thousand and One Nights* was famously translated in the Victorian period by the orientalist Sir Richard Burton (16 vols., 1885–8).

332 *"Maw and Meggins"*: the manufacturing firm for which Herbert works is well named. Maw means mouth, but also stomach, and carries overtones of rapacity or unquenchable appetite.

337 *fusillade*: 'a simultaneous discharge of firearms' (*OED*).

MARY E. WILKINS FREEMAN, *Luella Miller*

Mary Eleanor Wilkins Freeman (1852–1930), American short-story writer and novelist. She was born in Randolph, Massachusetts, where she spent much of her life. The majority of Freeman's stories deal with New England life. Best known for the collections *A Humble Romance and Other Stories* (1887) and

A New England Nun and Other Stories (1891), and the novel *Pembroke* (1894). In 1926 Freeman was the first recipient of the American Academy of Arts and Letters' William Dean Howells Medal for Distinction in Arts and Letters.

'Luella Miller' was first published in *Everybody's Magazine* (December 1902). Reprinted in Mary E. Wilkins, *The Wind in the Rose-Bush and Other Stories of the Supernatural* (New York: Doubleday, Page & Company, 1903). This is the text used here.

343 *valerian . . . catnip*: valerian is a herb used for medicinal purposes, as a sedative or antispasmodic; catnip is a herb used in herbal teas as a stress-reliever and relaxant, named after its peculiar attractiveness to cats.

347 *the days of witchcraft*: a reference to the Salem Witch Trials of 1692–3, the culmination of a witch-hunting craze (an episode of mass hysteria), in which 19 women were hanged and imprisoned (of whom at least 5 died in prison). At least 12 other women were hanged for witchcraft in New England in the years leading up to the Salem Witch Trials. Salem (now Danvers), Massachusetts, is some 25 miles from Freeman's home town of Randolph.

M. R. JAMES, *Count Magnus*

Montague Rhodes James (1862–1936), British manuscript scholar, antiquarian, and the foremost ghost-story writer in English. Educated at Eton College and King's College, Cambridge, James was one of the most distinguished of all manuscript scholars, and was variously dean and provost of King's College, vice-chancellor of Cambridge University, and (in semi-retirement) provost of Eton. Many of James's ghost stories were written and first read as Christmas entertainments for his colleagues and students in Cambridge and Eton. James published four slim volumes of ghost stories: *Ghost Stories of an Antiquary* (London: Edward Arnold, 1904); *More Ghost Stories of an Antiquary* (London: Edward Arnold, 1911); *A Thin Ghost and Others* (London: Edward Arnold, 1919); and *A Warning to the Curious* (London: Edward Arnold, 1925).

'Count Magnus' was written in 1901 or 1902; first published in *Ghost Stories of an Antiquary*. The text here is taken from M. R. James, *Ghost Stories of an Antiquary* (London: Arnold, 1904).

351 *Horace Marryat's Journal . . . Isles*: Horace Marryat, *Journal of a Residence in Jutland, the Danish Isles, and Copenhagen* (2 vols., 1860). Marryat also wrote *One Year in Sweden: Including a Visit to the Isle of Gotland* (2 vols., 1862).

Pantechnicon fire: the Pantechnicon was an enormous (2-acre) warehouse for storing furniture in Motcombe Street, Belgravia, London; it was destroyed by fire on 14 February 1874. 'Pantechnicon' (Greek for 'all the crafts') is now used to refer to any large furniture-removal van.

352 *Brasenose*: college of the University of Oxford, founded 1509; originally 'Brazen Nose', after the bronze door-knocker, shaped like a nose, that hangs above high table in the main hall.

Vestergothland: Västergötland, a province of southern Sweden.

Råbäck: James visited Råbäck on a trip to Sweden with his friend James McBryde, August 1901.

Dahlenberg's Suecia antiqua et moderna: Erik Jönsson, Count Dahlbergh, *Suecia Antiqua et Hodierna* (*Sweden Ancient and Modern*), 3 vols. (1660–1716). A celebrated collection of engravings of Swedish architecture and landscape, compiled by Dahlbergh, in part aimed to display Sweden as a modern world power.

De la Gardie: a prominent Swedish noble family. Magnus Gabriel de la Gardie (1622–86) was variously Lord High Treasurer, Lord High Chancellor, and Lord High Steward of Sweden.

353 *mausoleum*: James visited the De la Gardie mausoleum at the Cistercian abbey of Varnhem in August 1901.

355 *Black Pilgrimage*: the 'Black Pilgrimage' to Chorazin may have been James's invention, but it has subsequently been taken up by a number of writers and occultists.

Skara: small cathedral city in southern Sweden, which James visited in 1901.

The book of the Phœnix . . . and so forth: *The Book of the Phoenix* is a fictitious work of alchemical writing. The *Book of the Thirty Words* is also fictitious. The *Book of the Toad* is likely to be Trinity MS 1399, *Bufo Gradiens* ('Toad Passant'). Miriam, the sister of Moses, was, according to Jewish tradition, an alchemist; see Raphael Patai, *The Jewish Alchemists: A History and Source Book* (Princeton: Princeton University Press, 1994), chs. 5 and 6. The *Turba Philosophorum* (*Assembly of the Philosophers*) is a Latin alchemical text reputedly dating to the twelfth century, but first published in 1572; translated into English by Arthur Edward Waite in 1896 as *The Turba Philosophorum, or Assembly of the Sages*.

'Liber nigræ peregrinationis': 'Book of the Black Pilgrimage'.

356 *Chorazin*: a city in Galilee rebuked by Christ for its faithlessness; see Matthew 11: 20–2. Because of this condemnation, Chorazin became identified as the birthplace of the Antichrist, a tradition which seems to have its origin in the seventh-century *Apocalypse of Pseudo-Methodius*, a significant text for medieval eschatology—as James, author of numerous studies of Latin apocalypses, certainly knew; he had written the entry on 'Man of Sin and Antichrist' for Hastings's *Dictionary of the Bible* (1898–1902), iii. 226–8, which makes reference to Pseudo-Methodius.

'of the air': the 'Prince of the Air' is Satan; see Ephesians 2: 2: 'Wherein in time past ye walked according to the course of this world, according to the prince of the power of the air, the spirit that now worketh in the children of disobedience'. For an analysis of Satan as ruler of the air (hence his iconographic wings), see Jeffrey Burton Russell, *The Devil: Perceptions of Evil from Antiquity to Primitive Christianity* (Ithaca, NY, and London: Cornell University Press, 1977), 246.

359 *devil-fish*: generic term for 'various large and formidable fishes'; it usually refers to angler fish, but in this context is most likely 'the octopus, cuttle-fish or other cephalopod' (*OED*).

361 *Skåne . . . Trollhättan*: Skåne is the southernmost province of Sweden. Trollhättan is a city in southern Sweden, near Skara; its name, which means 'Trolls' hoods', is clearly significant in the context of the story's hooded demon.

362 *Harwich*: major port in Essex, on the south-east coast of England.

Belchamp St Paul: a village in north Essex, very near the Suffolk border.

FRANCIS MARION CRAWFORD, *For the Blood is the Life*

Francis Marion Crawford (1854–1909), American novelist and short-story writer. Born in Bagni di Lucca, Italy, and educated at Cambridge, Heidelberg, Rome, and Harvard, Crawford studied Sanskrit in India. He wrote many novels, often historical works set in Italy, where he lived permanently from 1883. He died in Sorrento, Italy.

'For the Blood is the Life' was first published in *Collier's Magazine* (December 1905). Reprinted in *Wandering Ghosts* (New York: Macmillan, 1911). This is the text used here.

363 [*Title*]: Leviticus 17: 10–14: 'And whatsoever man *there be* of the house of Israel, or of the strangers that sojourn among you, that eateth any manner of blood; I will set my face against that soul that eateth blood, and will cut him off from among his people. | For the life of the flesh *is* in the blood: and I have given it to you upon the altar to make an atone-ment for your souls: for it *is* the blood that maketh an atonement for the soul. | Therefore I say unto the children of Israel, No soul of you shall eat blood, neither shall any stranger that sojourneth among you eat blood. | And whatsoever man *there be* of the children of Israel, or of the strangers that sojourn among you, which hunteth and catcheth any beast or fowl that may be eaten; he shall even pour out the blood thereof, and cover it with dust. | For *it is* the life of all flesh; the blood of it *is* for the life thereof: therefore I said unto the children of Israel, Ye shall eat the blood of no manner of flesh: for the life of all flesh *is* the blood thereof: whosoever eateth it shall be cut off.'

Calabria . . . Charles V . . . Barbary pirates . . . Francis I: Calabria is the 'toe' of Italy, the region south of Naples. Charles V (1519–56) was Holy Roman Emperor and King of Spain; he conducted the Franco-Italian War of 1521–6 against his great rival Francis I (1494–1547), King of France. Francis I forged an alliance against Charles V with the Ottoman Emperor Suleiman the Magnificent (1494–1566). The Barbary pirates were Ottoman corsairs operating out of North Africa (the 'Barbary Coast', now Morocco, Tunisia, Algeria, and Libya).

Cape Scalea: Calabria, Italy. For the Judas Iscariot legend, see also Crawford's *The Children of the King* (1885): 'Past Scalea, then, where tradition says that Judas Iscariot was born and bred and did his first murder.' Crawford, *The Children of the King: A Tale of Southern Italy* (New York: Macmillan, 1893).

366 *Paola*: a town in Calabria.

367 *Maratea*: a coastal town in northern Calabria.

368 *San Domenico*: the church of San Domenico (founded 1448), Cosenza, Calabria.

369 *carabineers*: *carabinieri*, Italian military police.

374 *Salerno*: city in the Campania region of Italy, north of Calabria.

375 *neither quick nor dead*: quick means living. The phrase 'the quick and the dead' occurs three times in the New Testament, most famously in 1 Peter 4: 5: 'Who shall give account to him that is ready to judge the quick and the dead.'

stole: a strip of silk or linen worn over the shoulders of a priest.

377 *tallow*: candle-grease, made from animal fat.

ALGERNON BLACKWOOD, *The Wendigo*

Algernon Blackwood (1869–1951), English writer of supernatural fiction. Blackwood studied at Edinburgh University, though he did not graduate. While still at school, he discovered theosophy and Esoteric Buddhism (he remained a Buddhist throughout his life), and later became a member of the Hermetic Order of the Golden Dawn. In 1889 he moved to Canada, where he worked variously (and unsuccessfully) as a journalist, a farmer, and a hotelier. He moved to New York, before returning to England in 1899, where he began to make a living as a writer of fiction. He wrote numerous novels and short-story collections, achieving his greatest success with the psychic detective collection *John Silence: Physician Extraordinary* (1908). Later in life Blackwood became famous as a broadcaster on radio and television: he appeared on Britain's first television programme, *Picture Page*, in 1936. He was awarded the CBE in 1949.

'The Wendigo' was first published in *The Lost Valley and Other Stories* (London: Nash, 1910). This is the text used here. The meaning of 'Wendigo', as Blackwood uses it, becomes apparent in the story, and the word is glossed at the end of these notes: see note to p. 421.

378 *Nimrods*: hunters; from Genesis 10: 9: 'He was a mighty hunter before the LORD: wherefore it is said, Even as Nimrod the mighty hunter before the LORD.'

'Wee Kirk': the Free Church of Scotland, sometimes known as the 'Wee Frees', a Calvinistic Protestant order which remained outside the merger of the original Free Church of Scotland and the United Presbyterian Church of Scotland to form the United Free Church of Scotland in 1900.

'Canuck': Canadian.

378 *Rat Portage . . . Canadian Pacific Railway*: Rat Portage, understandably renamed Kenora in 1905, is a small city on the northern shore of the Lake of the Woods in western Ontario, Canada. The Canadian Pacific Railway, running across the US–Canadian border, was built between 1881 and 1885.

380 *Garden Lake*: a small lake near the city of Sault Ste Marie, Ontario.

   Fifty Island Water: fictitious.

385 *.303 rifle*: the Lee-Enfield Rifle, the standard British military rifle from 1895 to 1957, which used a .303-inch cartridge.

   'blaze': 'to mark (trees) with white by chipping off bark' (*OED*).

386 *balsam*: an aromatic resin, though Blackwood here seems to be using it in the sense of soft wood, as in 'balsa wood'.

387 *brulé*: burnt.

390 *covey*: a brood of partridges—but here used metaphorically to refer to a branch of leaves.

   tenderfoot: newcomer; inexperienced person.

412 *pickerel*: young pike.

421 *Wendigo*: the wendigo, or windigo, is a supernatural spirit occurring in the legends of the Algonquin peoples of Canada and the northern United States. Wendigo legends take a variety of forms, but are generally associated with cannibalism: it was believed that any person who practised cannibalism would transform into a wendigo. 'Wendigo psychosis' is a term sometimes given to an insatiable desire amongst Native Americans to consume human flesh, though the reality of this disorder is questioned.

W. F. HARVEY, *August Heat*

William Fryer Harvey (1885–1937), English short-story writer, best known for 'The Beast with Five Fingers' (1928). Born in York to a Quaker family, Harvey studied at the universities of Oxford and Leeds, qualifying as a doctor. He volunteered as an ambulance man during the First World War, before serving as a surgeon-lieutenant in the Royal Navy. In 1920, he became warden of Fircroft Working Men's College, Birmingham, but retired in 1925 due to ill health, and moved to Switzerland.

   'August Heat' was first published in *Midnight House and Other Stories* (London: Dent, 1910). This is the text used here.

422 *PENISTONE ROAD, CLAPHAM*: Clapham is a suburban district of south London, most famous for its common and its large railway junction. There is a Penistone Road near Clapham, in the Borough of Lambeth, London SW16.

   St Jude's: a church in Dulwich, not far from Clapham Common.

423 *Lytton Street . . . Gilchrist Road*: both fictitious, though they may be

named for two noted writers of supernatural fiction, Edward Bulwer-
Lytton (1803–73) and Robert Murray Gilchrist (1867–1917).

425 *Clacton-on-Sea*: a seaside resort in Essex, a popular holiday destination
from its foundation in 1871.

Doré Bible: popular Victorian edition of the Bible, first produced in 1866,
with fantastic illustrations by the artist Gustave Doré (1832–83).

426 *guardians*: 'guardians' were created following the 1834 Poor Law
Amendment Act. Parishes were grouped together in unions, and in each
of these an elected Board of Guardians became responsible for adminis-
tering poor relief and maintaining workhouses.

E. F. BENSON, *The Room in the Tower*

Edward Frederic Benson (1867–1940), English novelist, short-story writer,
and classicist. He was educated at Marlborough College and at King's College,
Cambridge, where he was an outstanding student of Classics. Benson was the
son of E. W. Benson, headmaster of Wellington College and Archbishop of
Canterbury from 1883 to 1896, and the brother of the writers and scholars
A. C. Benson and R. H. Benson, both of whom also wrote supernatural tales.
A highly prolific writer, Benson published over sixty novels, plus numerous
collections of short stories and non-fiction books. He is best known today for
the six comic-satiric 'Mapp and Lucia' novels (1920–39) and for a handful of
supernatural tales, of which 'The Room in the Tower' is the most celebrated.

'The Room in the Tower' was first published in the *Pall Mall Magazine*
(January 1912), and reprinted in *The Room in the Tower and Other Stories*
(London: Mills and Boon, 1912). The text used here is the *Pall Mall Magazine*
version.

431 *Ashdown Forest . . . Forest Row*: Ashdown Forest is an area of heathland
and woodland in East Sussex; Forest Row is a village in Sussex, near
Ashdown Forest.

435 *Walpurgis night*: Walpurgisnacht, a European spring festival, celebrated on
31 April or 1 May, is often associated with the supernatural or the spirit
world, and sometimes identified as the date of the Witches' Sabbath.

438 *West Fawley*: there are a number of Fawleys in England, but none in
Sussex.

WILLIAM HOPE HODGSON, *The Derelict*

William Hope Hodgson (1877–1918), English author, sailor, and bodybuilder.
The son of an Anglican clergyman, Hodgson ran away to sea at the age of 13.
Many of his stories and novels deal with aspects of maritime life, including
a number of works of horror set around the Sargasso Sea (*The Boats of the
Glen Carrig*, 'From the Tideless Sea', and others). Hodgson is now best known
as the creator of the psychic detective Carnacki, and for his work of spiritualist terror *The House on the Borderland* (1908) and his apocalyptic fantasy *The*

Night Land (1912). He was also a high-profile advocate of the Physical Culture (bodybuilding) movement. Hodgson enlisted as an officer in the Royal Field Artillery at the outbreak of the First World War, and was killed by a shell in Ypres on 19 April 1918.

'The Derelict' was first published in the *Red Magazine* (1 December 1912), and reprinted in *Men of the Deep Waters* (London: Holden & Hardingham, 1914). This is the text used here.

441 *Bheotpte*: meaning unknown. This seems to be Hodgson's own coinage, though it may derive from the name of his wife, Bessie.

   North West Cape: a peninsula in north-western Australia. Sailing from Madagascar to Western Australia, the *Bheotpte* is lost somewhere in the Indian Ocean. Although the Sargasso is in the Atlantic, the adventures recounted in 'The Derelict' clearly link this story to Hodgson's Sargasso cycle.

   jib-boom . . . fore t'gallant mast: jib-boom: 'A spar run out of from the end of the bowsprit [the spar at the front of a ship], to which the tack of the jib [the triangular sail at the front of a ship] is lashed' (*OED*). The topgallant mast (pronounced 't'gallant mast') is the tallest mast on a sailing ship.

   packet: a boat sailing on a regular schedule between two destinations, shipping mail, goods, and passengers.

442 *cut-water*: cutwater, the forward edge of the prow of a ship.

   Davy Jones: Davy Jones's Locker, a nautical term for the bottom of the sea.

   slings: a sling is 'a device for securing or grasping bulky or heavy articles while being hoisted or lowered, usually a belt, rope, or chain formed into a loop and fitted with hooks and tackle' (*OED*).

   Second Dog Watch: on board ship, the dog-watches were two two-hour watches, from 4 to 6 p.m. and from 6 to 8 p.m.

447 *progged*: probed or poked.

449 *mizzen-mast*: the rearmost mast of a three-masted ship.

451 *companionway*: 'the staircase, porch or berthing of the ladder-way to the cabin' (*OED*). The companion ladder led from the ship's deck to its cabin or quarterdeck.

453 *star-board bulwarks*: raised woodwork along the starboard (left) side of a ship.

460 *to double-bank it*: to row with two rowers for each oar.

462 *bill of lading*: 'an official detailed receipt given by the master of a merchant vessel to the person consigning the goods, by which he makes himself responsible for their safe delivery to the consignee' (*OED*).

American Literature

British and Irish Literature

Children's Literature

Classics and Ancient Literature

Colonial Literature

Eastern Literature

European Literature

Gothic Literature

History

Medieval Literature

Oxford English Drama

Philosophy

Poetry

Politics

Religion

The Oxford Shakespeare

A complete list of Oxford World's Classics, including Authors in Context, Oxford English Drama, and the Oxford Shakespeare, is available in the UK from the Marketing Services Department, Oxford University Press, Great Clarendon Street, Oxford OX2 6DP, or visit the website at www.oup.com/uk/worldsclassics.

In the USA, visit www.oup.com/us/owc for a complete title list.

Oxford World's Classics are available from all good bookshops. In case of difficulty, customers in the UK should contact Oxford University Press Bookshop, 116 High Street, Oxford OX1 4BR.

CHARLES DICKENS	The Old Curiosity Shop
	Our Mutual Friend
	The Pickwick Papers
GEORGE DU MAURIER	Trilby
MARIA EDGEWORTH	Castle Rackrent
GEORGE ELIOT	Daniel Deronda
	The Lifted Veil and Brother Jacob
	Middlemarch
	The Mill on the Floss
	Silas Marner
EDWARD FITZGERALD	The Rubáiyát of Omar Khayyám
ELIZABETH GASKELL	Cranford
	The Life of Charlotte Brontë
	Mary Barton
	North and South
	Wives and Daughters
GEORGE GISSING	New Grub Street
	The Nether World
	The Odd Women
EDMUND GOSSE	Father and Son
THOMAS HARDY	Far from the Madding Crowd
	Jude the Obscure
	The Mayor of Casterbridge
	The Return of the Native
	Tess of the d'Urbervilles
	The Woodlanders
JAMES HOGG	The Private Memoirs and Confessions of a Justified Sinner
JOHN KEATS	The Major Works
	Selected Letters
CHARLES MATURIN	Melmoth the Wanderer
HENRY MAYHEW	London Labour and the London Poor

Anthony Trollope

The American Senator
An Autobiography
Barchester Towers
Can You Forgive Her?
Cousin Henry
Doctor Thorne
The Duke's Children
The Eustace Diamonds
Framley Parsonage
He Knew He Was Right
Lady Anna
The Last Chronicle of Barset
Orley Farm
Phineas Finn
Phineas Redux
The Prime Minister
Rachel Ray
The Small House at Allington
The Warden
The Way We Live Now